If There Be Thorns

Seeds of Yesterday

By V.C. Andrews ®

SIMON PULSE

New York   London   Toronto   Sydney

SIMON PULSE

An imprint of Simon & Schuster Children's Publishing Division
1230 Avenue of the Americas, New York, NY 10020
First Simon Pulse paperback edition June 2010
If There Be Thorns copyright © 1981 by the Vanda General Partnership
Seeds of Yesterday copyright © 1984 by the Vanda General Partnership
All rights reserved, including the right of reproduction in whole or in part in any form.
SIMON PULSE and colophon are registered trademarks of Simon & Schuster, Inc.
V.C. Andrews® and Virginia Andrews® are registered trademarks of the Vanda General Partnership.
For information about special discounts for bulk purchases, please contact Simon & Schuster Special Sales at 1-866-506-1949 or business@simonandschuster.com.
Designed by Paul Weil
The text of this book was set in Aldine 721.
Manufactured in the United States of America
6 8 10 9 7 5
Library of Congress Control Number 2010924978
ISBN 978-1-4424-0656-8
These books were originally published individually by Pocket Books.

If There Be Thorns

For Mary,
For Joan

Prologue

In the late evening when the shadows were long, I sat quiet and unmoving near one of Paul's marble statues. I heard the statues whispering to me of the past I could never forget; hinting slyly of the future I was trying to ignore. Flickering ghostly in the pale light of the rising moon were the will-o'-the-wisp regrets that told me daily I could and should have done differently. But I am what I have always been, a person ruled by instincts. It seems I can never change.

I found a strand of silver in my hair today, reminding me that soon I might be a grandmother, and I shuddered. What kind of grandmother would I make? What kind of mother was I? In the sweetness of twilight I waited for Chris to come and join me and tell me with the true blue of his eyes that I'm not fading; I'm not just a paper flower but one that's real.

He put his arm about my shoulder and I rested my head where it seemed to fit best, both of us knowing our story is almost over and Bart and Jory will give to both of us, either the best or the worst of what is yet to be.

It is their story now, Jory's and Bart's, and they will tell it as they knew it.

PART ONE

Jory

Whenever Dad didn't drive me home from school, a yellow school bus would let me off at an isolated spot where I would recover my bike from the nearest ravine, hidden there each morning before I stepped onto the bus.

To reach my home I had to travel a winding narrow road without any houses until I came to the huge deserted mansion that invariably drew my eyes, making me wonder who had lived there; why had they deserted it? When I saw that house I automatically slowed, knowing soon I'd be home.

An acre from that house was our home, sitting isolated and lonely on a road that had more twists and turns than a puzzle maze that leads the mouse to the cheese. We lived in Fairfax, Marin County, about twenty miles north of San Francisco. There was a redwood forest on the other side of the mountains, and the ocean too. Ours was a cold place, sometimes dreary. The fog would roll in great billowing waves and often shrouded the landscape all day, turning everything cold and eerie. The fog was spooky, but it was also romantic and mysterious.

As much as I loved my home, I had vague, disturbing memories of a southern garden full of giant magnolia trees dripping with Spanish moss. I remembered a tall man with dark hair turning gray; a man who called me his son. I didn't remember his face nearly as well as I remembered the nice warm and safe feeling he gave me. I guess one of the saddest things about growing bigger, and older, was that no one was large enough, or strong enough, to pick you up and hold you close and make you feel that safe again.

Chris was my mother's third husband. My own father died before I was born; his name was Julian Marquet, and everyone in the ballet world knew about him. Hardly anyone outside of Clairmont, South Carolina, knew about Dr. Paul Scott Sheffield, who had been my mother's second husband. In that same southern state, in the town of Greenglenna, lived my paternal grandmother, Madame Marisha.

She was the one who wrote me a letter each week, and once a summer we visited her. It seemed she wanted almost as much as I did, for me to become the most famous dancer the world had ever known. And thus I would prove to her, and to everyone, that my father had not lived and died in vain.

By no means was my grandmother an ordinary little old lady going on seventy-four. Once she'd been very famous, and not for one second did she let anyone forget this. It was a rule I was never to call her Grandmother when others could over-hear and possibly guess her age. She'd whispered to me once that it would be all right if I called her *Mother*, but that didn't seem right when I already had a mother whom I loved very much. So I called her Madame Marisha, or Madame M., just as everyone else did.

Our yearly visit to South Carolina was long anticipated during the winters, and quickly forgotten once we were back and safely snuggled in our little valley where our long redwood house nestled. "Safe in the valley where the wind doesn't blow," my mother said often. Too often, really—as if the wind blowing greatly distressed her.

I reached our curving drive, parked my bike, and went inside the house. No sign of Bart or Mom. Heck! I raced into the kitchen where Emma was preparing dinner. She spent most of her time in the kitchen, and that accounted for her "pleasingly plump" figure. She had a long, dour face unless she was smiling; fortunately, she smiled most of the time. She could order you to do this, do that, and with her smile take the pain from the ordeal of doing for yourself, which was something my brother Bart refused to do. I suspected Emma waited on Bart more than me because he spilled when he tried to pour his own milk. He dropped when he carried a glass of water. There wasn't anything he could hold on to, and nothing he could keep from bumping into. Tables fell, lamps toppled. If an extension wire was anywhere in the house Bart would be sure to snag his sneaker toes underneath and down he'd go—or the blender, the mixer, or the radio, would crash to the floor.

"Where's Bart?" I asked Emma, who was peeling potatoes to put in with the roast beef she had in the oven.

"I tell you, Jory, I'll be glad when that boy stays in school just as long as you do. I hate to see him come in the kitchen. I have to stop what I'm doing and look around and anticipate just what he might knock off or bump into. Thank God he's got that wall to sit on. What is it you boys do up on that wall, anyway?"

"Nothing," I said. I didn't want to tell her how often we stole over to the deserted mansion beyond the wall and played there. The estate was off-limits to us, but parents weren't supposed to see and know everything. Next I asked "Where's Mom?" Emma said she'd come home early after canceling her ballet class, which I already knew. "Half her class has colds," I explained. "But where is she now?"

"Jory, I can't keep my eye on everybody and still know what *I'm* doing. A few minutes ago she said something about going up to the attic for old pictures. Why don't you join her up there and help her search?"

That was Emma's nice way of saying I was in her way. I headed for the attic stairs, which were hidden in the far end of our large walk-in linen closet in the back hall. Just as I was passing through the family room I heard the front door open and close. To my surprise I saw my dad standing stock-still in the foyer, a strange look of reflection in his blue eyes, making me reluctant to call out and break into his thoughts. I paused, undecided.

He headed for his bedroom after he put down his black doctor's bag. He had to pass the linen closet with its door slightly ajar. He stopped, listening as I was to the faint sound of ballet music drifting down the stairs. Why was my mother up there? Dancing there again? Whenever I asked why she danced in such a dusty place, she explained she was "compelled" to dance up there, despite the heat and dust. "Don't you tell your father about this," she'd warned me several times. After I questioned her, she'd stopped going up there— and now she was doing it again.

This time I was going up. This time I was going to listen to the excuses she gave *him*. For Dad would catch her!

On tiptoe I trailed him up the steep, narrow stairs. He paused directly under the bare electric bulb that hung down from the apex of the attic. He riveted his eyes upon my mom, who kept right on dancing as if she didn't see him there. She held a dustmop in one hand and playfully swiped at this or that, miming Cinderella and certainly not Princess Aurora from *The Sleeping Beauty*, which was the music she had on the ancient record player.

Gosh. My stepfather's heart seemed to jump right up into his eyes. He looked scared, and I sensed she was hurting him just by dancing in the attic. How odd. I didn't understand what went on between them. I was fourteen, Bart was nine, and we were both a long, long way from being adults.

The love they had for each other seemed to me very different from the love I saw between the parents of the few friends I had. Their love seemed more intense, more tumultuous, more passionate. Whenever they thought no one was watching they locked eyes, and they had to reach out and touch whenever they passed one another.

Now that I was an adolescent, I was beginning to take more notice of what went on between the most meaningful models I had. I wondered often about the different facets my parents had. One for the public to view; another for Bart and me; and the third, most fervent side, which they showed only to each other. (How could they know their two sons were not always discreet enough to turn away and leave like they should?)

Maybe that was the way all adults were, especially parents.

Dad kept staring as Mom whirled in the *pirouettes* that fanned her long blonde hair out in a half circle. Her leotards were white, her *pointes* white too, and I was enthralled as she danced, wielding that dustmop like a sword to stab at old furniture that Bart and I had outgrown. Scattered on the floor and shelves were broken toys, kiddy-cars and scooters, dishes she or Emma had broken that she meant to glue back together one day. With each swipe of her dustmop she brought zillions of golden dustmotes into play. Frenzied and crazy they struggled to settle down before she attacked again and once more drove them into flight.

"Depart!" she cried, as a queen to her slaves. "Go and stay away! Torment me no more!"—and round and round she spun, so fast I had to turn to follow her with my eyes or end up dizzy just from watching. She whipped her head, her leg, doing *fouettes* with more expertise than I'd seen on stage. Wild and possessed she spun faster! faster! keeping time to the music, using the mop as part of her action, making housework so dramatic I wanted to kick off my shoes and jump in and join her and be the partner my real father had once been. But I could only stand in the dim purplish shadows and watch something I sensed I shouldn't be watching.

My dad swallowed over the lump which must have risen in his throat. Mom looked so beautiful, so young and soft. She was thirty-seven, so old in years but so young in appearance, and so easily she could be wounded by an unkind word. Just as easily as any sixteen-year-old dancer in her classes.

"Cathy!" cried Dad, jerking the needle from the record so the music screeched to a halt. "STOP! What are you doing?"

She heard and fluttered her slim pale arms in mock fright, flittering toward him, using the tiny, even steps called *bourrées*. For a second or so only, before she was again spinning in a series of *pirouettes* around him, encircling him—and swiping at him with her dustmop! "STOP IT!" he yelled, seizing hold of her mop and hurling it away. He grabbed her waist, pinioning her arms to her sides as a deep blush rose to stain her cheeks. He released his hold enough to allow her arms to flutter like broken bird wings so her hands could cover her throat. Above those crossed pale hands her blue eyes grew larger and very dark. Her full lips began to quiver, and slowly, slowly, with awful reluctance she was forced to look where Dad's finger pointed.

I looked too and was surprised to see two twin beds set up in the portion of the attic that was soon to be under construction. Dad had promised her we'd have a recreation room up here. But twin beds in all this junk? Why?

Mom spoke then, her voice husky and scared. "Chris? You're home? You don't usually come home this early . . ."

He'd caught her and I was relieved. Now he could straighten her out, tell her not to dance up here again in the dry, dusty air that could make her faint. Even I could see she was having trouble coming up with some excuse.

"Cathy, I know I brought those bedsteads up, but how did you manage to put them together?" Dad shot out. "How did you manage the mattresses?" Then he jolted for a second time, spying the picnic hamper between the beds. "Cathy!" he roared, glaring at her. "Does history have to repeat itself?

Can't we learn and benefit from the mistakes of others? *Do we have to do it all over again?*"

Again? What was he talking about?

"Catherine," Dad went on in the same cold, hard voice, "don't stand there and try to look innocent, like some wicked child caught stealing. Why are those beds here, all made up with clean sheets and new blankets? Why the picnic hamper? Haven't we seen enough of that type of basket to last us our whole lives through?"

And here I was thinking she'd put the beds together so she and I could have a place to fall down and rest after we danced, as we had a few times. And a picnic hamper was, after all, just another basket.

I drifted closer, then hid behind a strut that rose to the rafters. Something sad and painful was between them; something young, fresh, like a raw wound that refused to heal. My mother looked ashamed and suddenly awkward. The man I called Dad stood bewildered; I could tell he wanted to take her in his arms and forgive her. "Cathy, Cathy," he pleaded with anguish, "don't be like *her* in every way!"

Mom jerked her head high, threw back her shoulders, and, with arrogant pride, glared him down. She flipped her long hair back from her face and smiled to charm him. Was she doing all of that just to make him stop asking questions she didn't want to answer?

I felt strangely cold in the musty gloom of the attic. A chilling shiver raced down my spine, making me want to run and hide. Making me ashamed, too, for spying—that was Bart's way, not mine.

How could I escape without attracting their attention? I *had* to stay in my hidden place.

"Look at me, Cathy. You're not the sweet young *ingenue* anymore, and this is not a game. There is no reason for those beds to be there. And the picnic basket only compounds my fears. *What the hell are you planning?*"

Her arms spread wide as if to hug him, but he pushed her away and spoke again: "Don't try to appeal to me when I feel sick to my stomach. I ask myself each day how I can come home and not be tired of you, and still feel as I do after so many years, and after all that has happened. Yet I go on year after year loving you, needing and trusting you. Don't take my love and make it into something ugly!"

Bewilderment clouded her expression. I'm sure it clouded mine, too. Didn't he truly love her? Was that what he meant? Mom was staring at the beds again, as if surprised to see them there.

"Chris, help me!" she choked, stepping closer and opening her arms again. He put her off, shaking his head. She implored, "Please don't shake your head and act like you don't understand. I don't remember buying the basket, really I don't! I had a dream the other night above coming up here and putting the beds together, but when I came up today and saw them, I thought you must have put them there."

"Cathy! I DID *NOT* PUT THE BEDS THERE!"

"Move out of the shadows. I can't see you where you are." She lifted her small pale hands, seeming to wipe away invisible cobwebs. Then she was staring at her hands as if they'd betrayed her—or was she really seeing spiderwebs tying her fingers together?

Just as my dad did, I looked around again. Never had the attic been so clean before. The floor had been scrubbed, cartons of old junk were stacked neatly. She had tried to make the attic look homey by hanging pretty pictures of flowers on the walls.

Dad was eyeing Mom as if she were crazy. I wondered what he was thinking, and why he couldn't tell what bothered her when he was the best doctor ever. Was he trying to decide if she was only pretending to forget? Did that dazed, troubled look in her terrified eyes tell him differently? Must have, for he said softly, kindly, "Cathy, you don't have to look scared.

You're *not* swimming in a sea of deceit anymore, or helplessly caught in an undertow. You are *not* drowning. *Not* going under. *Not* having a nightmare. You don't have to clutch at straws when you have me." Then he drew her into his arms as she fell toward him, grasping as if to keep from drowning. "You're all right, darling," he whispered, stroking her back, touching her cheeks, drying the tears that began to flow. Tenderly he tilted her chin up before his lips slowly lowered to hers. The kiss lasted and lasted, making me hold my breath.

"The grandmother is dead. Foxworth Hall has been burned to the ground."

Foxworth Hall? What was that?

"No, it hasn't, Chris. I heard her climbing the stairs a short while ago, and you know she's afraid of small, confined places—how could she climb the stairs?"

"Were you sleeping when you heard her?"

I shivered. What the devil where they talking about? Which grandmother?

"Yes," she murmured, her lips moving over his face. "I guess I did drift into nightmares after I finished my bath and lay out on the bedroom patio. I don't even remember climbing the stairs up here. I don't know why I come, or why I dance, unless I am losing my mind. I feel I am *her* sometimes, and then I hate myself!"

"No, you're not her, and Momma is miles and miles away where she can never hurt us again. Virginia is three thousand miles from here, and yesterday has come and gone. Ask yourself one question whenever you are in doubt—if we could survive the worst, doesn't it stand to reason we should be able to bear the best?"

I wanted to run, wanted to stay. I felt I, too, was drowning in their sea of deceit even when I didn't understand what they were talking about. I saw two people, my parents, as strangers I didn't know—younger, less strong, less dependable.

"Kiss me," Mom murmured. "Wake me up and chase

away the ghosts. Say you love me and always will, no matter what I do."

Eagerly enough he did all of that. When he had her convinced, she wanted him to dance with her. She replaced the needle on the record and again the music soared.

Shriveled up tight and small, I watched him try to do the difficult ballet steps that would have been so easy for me. He didn't have enough skill or grace to partner someone as skilled as my mom. It was embarrassing to even see him try. Soon enough she put on another record where he could lead.

Dancing in the dark,
Till the tune ends, we're dancing in the dark . . .

Now Dad was confident, holding her close, his cheek pressed to hers as they went gliding around the floor.

"I miss the paper flowers that used to flutter in our wake," she said softly.

"And down the stairs the twins were quietly watching the small black-and-white TV set in the corner." His eyes were closed, his voice soft and dreamy. "You were only fourteen, and I loved you even then, much to my shame."

Shame? Why?

He hadn't even known her when she was fourteen. I frowned, trying to think back to when and where they'd first met. Mom and her younger sister, Carrie, had run away from home soon after Mom's parents were killed in an auto accident. They'd gone south on a bus and a kind black woman named Henny had taken them to her employer Dr. Paul Sheffield, who had generously taken them in and given them a good home. My mom had started ballet classes again and there she had met Julian Marquet—the man who was my father. I was born shortly after he was killed. Then Mom married Daddy Paul.

And Daddy Paul was Bart's father. It had been a long, long time before she met Chris, who was Daddy Paul's younger brother. So how could he have loved her when she was *fourteen?* Had they told us lies? Oh gosh, oh gosh . . .

But now that the dance was over, the argument began again: "Okay, you're feeling better, yourself again," Dad said. "I want you to solemnly promise that if anything ever happens to me, be it tomorrow, or years from now, you swear that you will never, so help you God, hide Bart and Jory in the attic so you can go unencumbered into another marriage!"

Stunned, I watched my mom jerk her head upward before she gasped: "Is that what you think of me? *Damn you for thinking I am so much like her!* Maybe I did put the beds together. Maybe I did bring the basket up here. But never once did it cross my mind to . . . to . . . Chris, you know I wouldn't do that!"

Do what, what?

He made her swear. Really forced her to speak the words while her blue eyes glared hot and angry at him all the while.

Sweating now, hurting too, I felt angry and terribly disillusioned in my dad, who should know better. Mom wouldn't do that. She couldn't! She loved me. She loved Bart, too. Even if she did look at him sometimes with shadows in her eyes, still she would never, never hide us away in this attic.

My dad left her standing in the middle of the attic as he strode forward to seize the picnic hamper. Next he unlatched, then pushed open the screen and hurled the basket out the open window. He watched it fall to the ground before once more turning to confront my mom angrily:

"Perhaps we are compounding the sins of our parents by living together as we are. Perhaps in the end both Jory and Bart will be hurt—so don't whisper to me tonight when we're in bed about adopting another child. We cannot afford to involve another child in the mess we've made! Don't you realize, Cathy, that when you put those beds up here you were unconsciously planning what to do in case our secret is exposed?"

"No," she objected, spreading her hands helplessly. "I wouldn't. I couldn't do that . . ."

"You have to mean that!" he snapped. "No matter what happens, we will not, or *you* will not, put your children in this attic to save yourself, or me."

"I hate you for thinking I would!"

"I am trying to be patient. I am trying to believe in you. I know you still have nightmares. I know you are still tormented by all that happened when we were young and innocent. But you have to grow up enough to look at yourself honestly. Haven't you learned yet that the subconscious often leads the way to reality?"

He strode back to cuddle her close, to soothe and kiss her, to soften his voice as she clung to him desperately. (Why did she have to feel so desperate?)

"Cathy, my heart, put away those fears instilled by the cruel grandmother. She wanted us to believe in hell and its everlasting torments of revenge. There is no hell but that which we make for ourselves. There is no heaven but that which we build between us. Don't chip away at my belief, my love, with your 'unconscious' deeds. I have no life without you."

"Then don't go to see *your* mother this summer."

He raised his head and stared over hers, pain in his eyes. I slid silently on the floor to sit and stare at them. What was going on? Why was I suddenly so afraid?

Bart

"And on the seventh day God rested," read Jory as I finished patting the earth nice and firm over the pansy seeds that were meant to honor my aunt Carrie's and uncle Cory's birthday on May fifth. Little aunt and uncle I'd never seen. Both been dead a long, long time. Dead before I was born. People died easy in our family. (Wonder why they liked pansies so much? Silly little nothing flowers with pudding faces.) Wish Momma didn't think honoring dead people's birthdays was so darn important.

"You know what else?" asked Jory, like nine was a dumb age, and he was a big adult. "In the beginning, when God created Adam and Eve, they lived in the Garden of Eden without wearing any clothes at all. Then one day an evil talking snake told them it was sinful to walk around naked, so Adam put on a fig leaf."

Gosh . . . naked people who didn't know naked was wicked. "What did Eve put on?" I asked as I looked around, hoping to see a fig leaf. He went on reading in a singsong way that took me to olden times when God was looking out for everyone—even naked people who could talk to snakes. Jory said he could put Biblical stories into "mind" music, and that made me mad and scared—him dancing to "mind" music *I* couldn't hear! Made me feel stupid, invisible, dumber than crazy. "Jory, where d'ya find fig leaves?"

"Why?"

"If I had one, I'd take off all my clothes and wear it."

Jory laughed. "Good golly, Bart, there's only one way for a boy to wear a fig leaf—and you'd be embarrassed."

"I would not!"

"You would too!"

"I'm never embarrassed!"

"Then how do you know what it's like? Besides, have you ever seen Dad wear a fig leaf?"

"No . . ." But I figured since I'd never seen a fig leaf, how could I know whether or not I had? I said this to Jory.

"Boy, you'd know!" he answered, with another laugh to mock me.

Then he was grinning, jumping up to leap up all the marble steps in one long bound that I couldn't help but admire. Me, I had to trail along behind. Wish I was graceful like him. Wish I could dance and charm everybody into likin me. Jory was bigger, older, smarter—but wait a minute. Maybe I would make myself smarter if not bigger. My head was big. Had to have a big brain inside. I'd grow taller by and by, catch up with Jory, bypass him. Why, I'd grow taller than Daddy; taller than the giant in "Jack and the Beanstalk"—and that giant was taller than anybody!

Nine years old . . . wish I was fourteen.

There was Jory sitting on the top step, waitin for me to catch up. Insultin. Hateful. God sure hadn't been kind to me when he passed out coordination. Remembered five years ago when I was four and Emma gave each of us a baby chick, all soft yellow fuzz, making chirps and cheeps. Never felt nothin so good before in my whole livelong life. There I was lovin it, holdin it, sniffin its baby smell before I put it kindly on the ground—and darn if that chick didn't fall over dead.

"You squeezed," said Daddy, who knew about stuff like that. "I warned you not to hold it too tight. Baby chicks are fragile and you have to handle them with care. Their hearts are very near the surface—so next time, gentle hands, okay?"

Thought God might strike me dead then and there, even though most of it was His fault anyway. Wasn't my fault he didn't make my nerve endings go all the way to the surface of my skin. Wasn't my fault I couldn't feel pain like everybody else—was His! Then I'd shivered, fearful He might do something. But when He was forgivin I went an hour later to the little pen where Jory's live chick had been walkin around lonesome. I picked him up and told him he had a friend. Boy, we had a good time with me chasin him and him chasin me, when all of a sudden, after only two hours of havin fun—that chick keeled over dead too!

Hated stiff cold things. Why'd it give up so easily? *"What's the matter with you?"* I shouted. *"I didn't squeeze!* My hands didn't hold you! I was careful—so stop playin dead and get up or my daddy will think I killed you on purpose!" Once I'd seen my daddy haul a man out of the water and save his life by pumpin out the water and blowing in air, so I did the same things to the chick. It stayed dead. Next I massaged its heart, then I prayed, and still it stayed dead.

I was no good. No good for nothin. Couldn't stay clean. Emma said clean clothes on me were a waste of her good time. Couldn't hold on to a dish when I dried it. New toys fell apart soon after they came my way. New shoes looked old in ten minutes after knowin my feet. Weren't my fault if they scuffed up easily. People just didn't know how to make good, unscuffable shoes. Never saw a day when my knees weren't scabby or covered with bandaids. When I played ball I tripped and fell between bases. My hands didn't know how to catch right, so my fingers bent backward and twice I'd had fingers broken.

Three times I'd fallen from trees. Once I broke my right arm, once my left arm. Third time I only got bruises. Jory never broke anything.

Was no wonder my mom kept telling me and him not to go next door to that big ole house with so many staircases, 'cause sooner or later she knew I'd fall down steps and break all my bones!

"What a pity you don't have much coordination," mumbled Jory. Then he stood up and yelled, "Bart, stop running like a girl! Lean forward, use your legs like pumps. Put your heart in it and let go! Forget about falling. You won't if you don't expect to. And if you catch me I'll give you my superspeed ball!"

Boy, wasn't nothin I wanted in this whole wide world more than I wanted that ball of his. Jory could throw it with a curve. When he pitched at tin cans setting on the wall, he'd hit 'em one after another. I never hit anything I aimed for—but I did hit a lot I didn't even see, like windows and people.

"Don't want yer ole speedball!" I gasped, though I did want it. It was a better ball than mine; they were always givin him better than me.

He looked at me with sympathy, making me want to cry. Hated pity! "You can have it even if you don't win the race and you can give me yours. I'm not trying to hurt your feelings. I just want you to stop being afraid of doing everything wrong, and then maybe you won't—sometimes getting mad enough helps you win." He smiled, and I guess if my momma had been around she would have thought his flash of white teeth was charmin. My face was born for scowlin. "Don't want yer ole ball," I repeated, refusing to be won over to someone handsome, graceful, and fourteenth in a long line of Russian ballet dancers who'd married ballerinas. What was so great about dancers? *Nothin', nothin'!* God had smiled on Jory's legs and made them pretty, while mine looked like knobby sticks that wanted to bleed.

"You hate me, don't you? You want me to die, don't you?"

He gave me a funny, long look. "Naw, I don't hate you and I don't want you to die. I kinda like you for my brother even if you are clumsy and a squealer."

"Thanks heaps."

"Yeah . . . think nothing of it. Let's go look at the house."

Every day after school we went to the high white wall and sat up there, and some days we went inside the house. Soon school would be over and we'd have nothing to do all day but play. It was nice to know the house was there, waitin for us. Spooky ole house with lots of rooms, jagged halls, trunks full of hidden treasures, high ceilings, odd-shaped rooms with small rooms joinin, sometimes a row of little rooms hidin one behind the other.

Spiders lived there and spun webs on the fancy chandeliers. Mice ran everywhere, havin hundreds of babies to put droppins all over. Garden insects moved inside and climbed the walls and crept on the wood floors. Birds came down the chimneys and fluttered about madly as they tried to find a way out. Sometimes they banged against walls, windows, and we'd come in and find 'em dead and pitiful. Sometimes Jory and I would arrive in the nick of time and throw open windows and doors so they could escape.

Jory figured someone must have abandoned the ole house quickly. Half the furniture was there, settin dusty and moldin, givin off smelly odors that made Jory wrinkle his nose. I sniffed it and tried to know what it was sayin. I could stand real still and almost hear the ghosts talking, and if we sat still on a dusty ole velvet couch and didn't talk, up from the cellar would come faint rustling like the ghosts wanted to whisper secrets in our ears.

"Don't you ever tell anybody ghosts talk to you, or they'll think you're crazy," Jory had warned. We already had one crazy person in our family—our daddy's mother, who was in a nuthouse way back in Virginia. Once a summer we went East to visit her and ole graves. Momma wouldn't go in the long brick building where people in pretty clothes strolled over green lawns, and nobody would have guessed they were crazy if attendants in white suits hadn't been there too.

Every summer Momma would ask, when Daddy came back from seein his mother, "Well, is she better?" And Daddy would look sad before he'd say, "No, not really much progress . . . but there would be if you would forgive her."

That always shook Momma up. She acted like she wanted that grandmother to stay locked up forever.

"You listen to me, Christopher Doll," my momma had snapped, "it's the other way around, remember! She's the one who should go down on her knees and plead—she should ask for *our* forgiveness!"

Last summer we hadn't gone East to visit anybody. I hated ole graves, ole Madame Marisha with her black rusty clothes, her big bun of white and black hair—and I didn't care even now if two ole ladies back East never had a visit from us again. And as for them down in those graves—let 'em stay there without flowers! Too many dead people in our lives, messin it up.

"C'mon, Bart!" called Jory. He had already scaled the tree on our side of the wall, and he was sittin up there waitin for me. I managed the climb, then settled down next to Jory, who insisted I sit against the tree trunk—just in case. "You know what?" said Jory wistfully. "Someday I'm gonna buy Mom a house just as big. Every once in a while I overhear her and Dad talking about big houses, so I guess she wants one larger than the one we've already got."

"Yeah, they sure do talk a lot about big houses."

"I like our house better," said Jory, while I set about drummin my heels against the wall, which had bricks under the crumblin white stucco. Momma had mentioned once she thought the bricks showin through added "interesting texture contrast." I did what I could to make the wall more interestin'.

But it was sure true that in a big house like that one over there you could get lost in the dark and ramble on and on for days on end. None of the bathrooms worked. No water. Crazy sinks with no water and stupid fruit cellar with no fruit, and wine cellar with no wine.

"Gee, wouldn't it be nice if a big family moved in over there?" Jory said, wishin like me we could have lots and lots of nearby friends to play with. We didn't have anybody but each other once we came home from school.

"And if they had two boys and two girls it would be just perfect," went on Jory dreamily. "Sure would be neat to have *all* girls living next door."

Neat, sure. I'll bet he was wishin Melodie Richarme would move in over there. Then he could see her every day and hug and kiss her like I'd seen him do a few times. Girls. Made me sick. "Hate girls!—want all boys!" I grouched. Jory laughed, saying I was only nine and soon enough I'd like girls more than boys.

"What makes Melodie's arms rich?"

"Do you realize how dumb that makes you sound? That's her last name and doesn't mean anything."

Just when I wanted to say he was the dumb one because all names had to mean somethin, or else why have them?— two trucks pulled up in the long driveway of the mansion. Wow! Nobody ever went over there but us.

We sat on and watched the workmen runnin around doin this and that. Some went up on the orange roof Momma said was called "pantile" and began to check it over. Others went inside the house with ladders and cans that looked like they held paint. Some had huge rolls of wallpaper under their arms. Others checked over the windows, and some looked at the shrubs and trees.

"Hey!" said Jory, very upset lookin. "Somebody must have bought that place. I'll bet they'll move in after it's fixed up."

Didn't want no neighbors who would disturb Momma

and Daddy's *privacy*. All the time they were talking about how nice it was not to have close neighbors to "disturb their privacy."

We sat on until it grew dark, then went into our house and didn't say a word to our parents—for when you said something out loud, that meant it was really true. Thoughts didn't count.

Next day it was Sunday and we went on a picnic at Stinson Beach. Then came Monday afternoon and Jory and I were back up on the wall, starin over at all that activity. Was foggy and cold, but we could see just well enough to be bothered. We couldn't go over there and have a place of our own anymore. Where would we play now?

"Hey, you kids!" called a burly man on another day when we were only watchin. "Whadaya doin' up there?"

"Nothing!" yelled Jory. (I never talked to strangers. Jory was always teasin me for not talking to anybody much but myself.)

"Don't you kids tell me you're not doin' nothin' when I see you over here! This house is private property—so stay off these grounds or you'll hear from me!"

He was real mean, and fierce lookin; his workclothes were old and dirty. When he came closer I saw the biggest feet in my life, and the dirtiest boots. I was glad the wall was ten feet high and we had the advantage over him.

"Sure we play over there a little," said Jory, who wasn't scared of anybody, "but we don't hurt anything. We leave it like we found it."

"Well, from now on stay off altogether!" he snapped, glarin first at Jory, then at me. "Some rich dame has bought this place and she won't want kids hangin around. And don't you think you can get by with anything because she's an old lady livin alone. She's bringin servants with her."

Servants. Wow!

"Rich people can have everything their own way," muttered

the giant on the ground as he moved off. "Do this, do that, and have it done yesterday. Money—God, what I wouldn't do to have my share."

We had only Emma, so we weren't really rich. Jory said Emma was like a maiden aunt, not really a relative *or* a servant. To me she was just somebody I'd known all my life, somebody who didn't like me nearly as much as she liked Jory. I didn't like her either, so I didn't care.

Weeks passed. School ended. Still those workmen were over there. By this time Momma and Daddy had noticed, and they weren't too happy about neighbors they didn't intend to visit and make welcome. Both me and Jory wondered why they didn't want friends comin to our house.

"It's love," whispered Jory. "They're still like honeymooners. Remember, Chris is our mom's third husband, and the bloom hasn't worn off."

What bloom? Didn't see any flowers.

Jory had passed on to the junior year of high school with flyin colors. I sneaked into the fifth grade by the skin of my teeth. Hated school. Hated that ole mansion that looked like new now. Gone were all the spooky, eerie times when we'd had lots of fun over there.

"We'll just bide our time until we can sneak over there and see that old lady," Jory said, whispering so all those gardeners trimming the shrubs and snippin at the trees wouldn't hear.

She owned acres of land, twenty or more. That made for lots of cleanup jobs, since the workmen on the roof were lettin everythin fall. Her yard was littered with papers, spills of nails, bits of lumber left over from repair jobs, plus trash that blew through the iron fence in front of the driveway that was near what Jory called "lover's lane."

That hateful construction boss was pickin up beer cans as he headed our way, scowlin just to see us when we weren't doin a thing bad. "How many times do I have to tell you boys?" he bellowed. "Now, don't force me to say it again!" He put his huge fists on his hips and glared up at us. "I've warned you before to stay off that wall—now *Scat!*"

Jory was unwillin to move from the wall when it wasn't any harm to just sit and look.

"Are the two of you deaf?" he yelled again.

In a flash Jory's face turned from handsome to mean. "No, we are *not* deaf! We live here. This wall is on the property line, and just as much *ours* as it is *hers*. Our dad says so. So we will sit up here and watch just as long as we like. And don't you dare yell and tell us to 'scat' again!"

"Sassy kid, aren't yah?" and off he wandered without even lookin at me, who was just as sassy—inside.

Introductions

It was breakfast time. Mom was telling Dad about one of her ballerinas. Bart sat across the table from me, poking at his cold cereal and scowling. He didn't like to eat much of anything but snack foods, which Dad said were bad for him.

"Chris, I don't think Nicole is going to pull out of this," Mom was saying with a worried frown. "It's awful that cars hurt so many people, and she's got a little girl only two years old. I saw her a few weeks ago. Honestly, she reminded me so much of Carrie when she was two."

Dad nodded absently, his gaze still fixed on the morning newspaper. The scene between them in the attic still haunted me, especially at night when I couldn't sleep. Sometimes I'd just sit alone in my room and try and remember what was hidden way back in the dark recesses of my mind. Something important I was sure, but I couldn't remember what it was.

Even as I sat and listened to them talk about Nicole and her daughter, I kept thinking of that attic scene, wondering what it meant, and just who was the grandmother they were afraid of. And how could they have known each other when Mom was only fourteen?

"Chris," implored Mom, her tone trying to force him to put down the sports page. "You don't listen when I talk. Nicole has no family at all—did you hear that? Not even an uncle or an aunt to care for Cindy if she dies. And you know she has never been married to that boy she loved."

"Hmmm," he answered before biting into his toast. "Don't forget to water our garden today."

She frowned, really annoyed. He wasn't listening as I was. "I think it was a huge mistake to sell Paul's home and move here. His statues just don't look right in this kind of setting."

That got his attention.

"Cathy, we have vowed never to have regrets about anything. And there are more important things in life than having a tropical garden where everything grows rampant."

"Rampant? Paul had the most manicured garden I've ever seen!"

"You know what I mean."

Silent for a second, she spoke again about Nicole and the two-year-old girl who would go into an orphanage if her mother died. Dad said someone was sure to adopt her quickly if she did. He stood up to pull on his sports jacket. "Stop looking on the darkest side. Nicole may recover. She's young, strong, basically healthy. But if you're so worried, I'll stop by and have a talk with her doctors."

"Daddy," piped up Bart, who'd scowled darkly all morning. "Nobody here can make me go East this summer! I won't go and can't nobody make me!"

"True," said Dad, chucking Bart under the chin and playfully rumpling his already unruly dark hair. "Nobody can make you go—I'm just hoping you'd rather go than stay home alone." He leaned to kiss Mom good-bye.

"Drive carefully." Mom had to say this every day just as he was leaving. He smiled and said he would, and their eyes met and said things I understood, in a way.

"There was an ole lady who lived in a shoe," chanted Bart. "She had so many children she didn't know what to do."

"Bart, do you have to sit there and make a mess? If you aren't going to finish your meal, excuse yourself and leave the table."

"Peter, Peter, Pumpkin Eater, had a wife and couldn't keep her; put her in a pumpkin shell, and there he kept her very well." He grinned at her, got up, and left the table—that was his way of excusing himself.

Great golly, almost ten and he was still chanting nursery rhymes. He picked up his favorite old sweater, tossed it over his shoulder, and, in so doing, he knocked over a carton of milk. The milk puddled to the floor, where Clover was soon lapping it up like a cat. Mom was so enthralled with a snapshot of Nicole's little girl that she didn't notice the milk.

It was Emma who wiped up the milk and glared at Bart, who stuck out his tongue and sauntered away. "Excuse me, Mom," I said, jumping up to follow Bart outside.

Again on the top of the wall, we sat and stared over, both of us wishing the lady would hurry and move in. Who knows, maybe she'd have grandchildren.

"Missin that ole house already," complained Bart. "Hate people who move in our place."

We both fiddled away the day, planting more seeds, pulling up more weeds, and soon I was wondering how we were going to pass a whole summer without going next door even once.

At dinner Bart was grouchy because he too missed the house. He glared down at his full plate. "Eat heartily, Bart," said Dad, "or else you may not have enough strength to enjoy yourself in Disneyland."

Bart's mouth fell open. "Disneyland?" His dark eyes widened in delight. "We're goin there really? Not goin East to visit ole graves?"

"Disneyland is part of your birthday gift," explained Dad.

"You'll have your party there, and then we'll fly to South Carolina. Now don't complain. Other people's needs have to be considered as well as yours. Jory's grandmother likes to see him at least once a year, and since we skipped last summer, she's doubly anticipating our visit. Then there's my mother, who needs a family too."

I found myself staring at Mom. She seemed to be smoldering. Every year she was like this when the time came to visit "his" mother. I thought it a pity she didn't understand why mothers were so very important. She's been an orphan so long maybe she'd forgotten—or maybe she was jealous.

"Boy, I'd rather have Disneyland than heaven!" said Bart. "Can never, never get enough of Disneyland."

"I know," said Dad in a dry way.

But no sooner did it sink in that Bart was getting his "heart's delight" than he was complaining again about not wanting to go East. "Momma, Daddy, I am not goin! Two weeks is too long for visitin ole graves and ole grandmothers!"

"Bart," said Mom sharply, "you show such disrespect for the dead. Your own father is one of those dead people whose grave you don't want to visit. Your aunt Carrie is there too. And you are going to visit their graves, and Madame Marisha too, whether you want to or not. And if you open your mouth again, there will be no trip to Disneyland!"

"Momma," now a subdued Bart wanted to make up. "Why did your daddy who's dead in Gladstone, Pa. . . ."

"Say Pennsylvania, not Pa."

"How come the picture of him looks so much like the daddy we have now?"

Pain flashed in her eyes. I spoke up, hating the way Bart had of grilling everyone. "Gee, Dollanganger is sure some whopper of a name. Bet you were glad to get rid of it."

She turned to stare at a large photograph of Dr. Paul Sheffield, then quietly said, "Yes, it was a wonderful day when I became Mrs. Sheffield."

Then Dad was looking upset. I sank deeper into the cut-velvet plush of a dining chair. All about me in the air, creeping on the floor, hiding in the shadows, were pieces of the past that they remembered and I didn't. Fourteen years old, and still I didn't know what life was all about. Or what my parents were about either.

Finally the day came when the mansion was completed. Then came the cleaning ladies to work on the windows and scrub the floors. Yard men came to rake, mow, trim again, and we were there all the time, peeking into windows, then running swiftly back to the wall and skimming up a tree, hoping not to get caught. On the top of the wall we quietly sat as if we'd never disobey any rule made by our parents. "She's a'comin!" whispered Bart, very excited, "Any moment, that ole lady, she's a'comin!"

The house was fixed up so grand we expected to see a fancy movie actress, a president's wife, somebody important. One day when Dad was at work and Mom was shopping, and Emma was still in the kitchen like always, we saw a huge long black limousine turn slowly into the long drive next door. An older car followed, but still, it was a snazzy-looking car. Two weeks ago that driveway had been cracked and buckled concrete, and now it was smooth black asphalt. I nudged Bart to calm his excitement. All about us the leaves made a fine concealing canopy, and still we could see everything.

Slowly, slowly, the chauffeur pulled the long, luxurious car to a stop; then he got out and circled the car to let out the passengers. We watched breathlessly. Soon we'd see her—that rich, rich woman who could afford anything!

The chauffeur was young and had a jaunty air. Even from a distance we could tell he was handsome, but the old man who stepped from the limo wasn't handsome at all. He took me by surprise. Hadn't that workman told us a lady and servants? "Look," I whispered to Bart, "that must be the butler. I never knew butlers rode in the same car as their employer."

"Hate people who move in our house!" grumbled Bart.

The feeble old butler stretched out his hand to help an old woman out of the backseat. She ignored him and took the arm of the chauffeur instead. Oh, gosh! She wore all black, from head to toe covered over like an Arab woman. A black veil was over her head and face. Was she a widow? A Moslem? She looked so mysterious.

"Hate black dresses that drag on the ground. Hate ole ladies who want black veils over their heads. Hate spooks."

All I could do was watch, fascinated, thinking that the woman moved rather gracefully beneath the black robe. Even from our hidden place, I could tell she felt nothing but scorn for the feeble old butler. Gee—intrigue.

She looked around at everything. For the longest time she stared our way, at the white wall, at the roof of our house. I knew she couldn't see very much. Many a time I'd stood where she was, looking homeward, and I'd seen only the peak of our roof and the chimney. Only when she was inside on her second floor could she see into some of our rooms. I'd better tell Mom to plant some more big trees near the white wall.

It occurred to me then why two workmen might have chopped down a number of her large eucalyptus trees. Maybe she wanted to look over at our house and be nosy. But it was more likely she didn't want those trees growing so near her house.

Now the second car drew up behind the first. Out of this one stepped a maid in a black uniform with a fancy white apron and cap. Following her came two servants dressed in gray uniforms. It was the servants who rushed about, carrying in many suitcases, hatboxes, live plants and such, all while the lady in black stood stock-still and looked at our chimney. I wonder what she was seeing?

A huge yellow moving van drew up and began to unload elegant furniture, and still that lady stayed outside and let the maids decide where to put each piece. Finally, when one of the maids kept running to her and asking questions, she turned away and disappeared into the mansion. All the servants vanished with her.

"Bart, would you look at that sofa those men are carrying in! Have you ever seen such a fancy sofa?"

Long ago he'd lost interest in the movers. He was now staring intently at the yellow and black caterpillar undulating along a thin branch not far below his dirty sneakers. Pretty birds were singing all around. The deep blue sky was full of fluffy white clouds. The air felt fresh, cool, fragrant with pine and eucalyptus—and Bart was staring at the one ugly thing in view. A blessed horny caterpillar!

"Hate ugly things that creep with horns on their heads," he mumbled to himself. I knew he always had a desire to know what was inside. "Betcha got icky-sticky green goo under all that pretty-colored fuzz. You mean little dragon on the branch, stop comin my way. Get too close and yer dead."

"Quit that silly talk. Look at that table those men are taking in now. Boy, I'll bet that chair came from a castle in Europe."

"Jus' one more inch and something ugly is gonna get it!"

"You know what? I'll bet that lady who's moving in is kinda nice. Anybody who has such good taste in furniture must be real quality."

"One more inch . . . and yer dead!" Bart told the caterpillar.

As the sun set, the sky turned rosy, and wide streaks of violet came to make the early evening even more beautiful.

"Bart, look at the sunset. Have you ever seen more glorious colors? Colors are like music to me. I can hear them singing. I'll bet if God struck me deaf and blind this very moment I'd go right on hearing the music of colors, and seeing them behind my eyes. And in darkness I'd dance and never know it wasn't light."

"Crazy talk," mumbled my brother, his eyes still on the fuzzy worm coming closer and closer to that deadly sneaker held above him. "Blind means black as pitch. No colors. No music. No nothin. Dead is silence."

"Deaf . . . d-e-a-f—not *dead*."

Just then Bart smashed down his sneaker on the caterpillar. Then he jumped from the tree to the ground, and there he wiped the sticky green goo on the lady's new lawn.

"That was a mean thing you did, Bart Winslow! Caterpillars go through a stage called metamorphosis. The kind you just killed makes the most beautiful butterfly of all. So you didn't kill a dragon but a fairy king or queen—the sweetest lover of roses."

"Stupid ballet talk," was his opinion, though he did manage to look slightly scared. "I can make up for it," he said uneasily, looking around nervously. "I'll set a trap, catch a caterpillar alive. Keep it for a pet, and wait until it turns into a fairy king, and then I'll let it go."

"Hey, I was just joking, but from now on, don't kill any insect that isn't on the roses."

"If I find some on the roses can I kill 'em all?"

Puzzling the way Bart needed to kill all insects. Once I'd caught him pulling off a spider's legs one by one before he squashed it between his thumb and forefinger. Then the black blood held his interest. "Do bugs feel pain?"

"Yeah," I said, "but don't let it worry you. Sooner or later you'll feel pain too. So don't cry. It was only a fuzzy worm, not a fairy king or queen. Let's go home now." I was feeling sorry for him because I knew he was sensitive about not being able to feel pain like I did, though gosh knows he should be glad.

"NO! Don't wanna go home! Want to see inside that house next door."

Just then Emma came out to ring her dinner bell, making us scamper home quickly.

~   ~   ~

Next day we were right back on the wall. The movers had finished up after we'd gone to bed. No more trucks coming and going. I'd spent most of my morning and early afternoon in Mom's ballet class, while Bart stayed home and played alone. And summer days were long. He smiled, happy to have me with him again. "Ready?" I asked.

"Ready!" he agreed. Having decided on our course of action earlier, we slipped over the wall and down to the other side by climbing down a sapling tree. It was ground we'd been forbidden to step on, but rightly or wrongly it was ground we considered ours, for it had belonged to us first. Like two shadows freed, we slithered along. Bart looked at the shrubs that had been trimmed into shapes of animals! How weird. A strutting rooster beside a fat hen on a nest. Neat, really neat. Who would have guessed that old Mexican man was so clever with those snippers?

"Don't like shrubs that look like animals," complained Bart. "Don't like green eyes. Green eyes are mean eyes. Jory—they're watchin us!"

"Shhh, don't whisper. Watch where you put your feet. Step only where I step." I glanced over my shoulder to see that the sky had changed to a dark plum color streaked with crimson that looked like freshly spilled blood. Soon night would descend, and the moon wasn't always a friendly face.

"Jory," came Bart's whisper as he tugged on my shirttail, "didn't Momma tell us to be home by dark?"

"It's not dark yet." But almost. The creamy white of the mansion in daylight was bluish white in the dusk and scary-looking.

"Don't like bony-lookin ole house made to look like new."

Bart and his ideas.

"Sure must be time to be gettin home now."

I resisted his tugs. Since we'd come this far we might as

well go all the way. I put my finger to my lips, whispered "Stay where you are," and by myself stole to the only window that was bright in a huge house of many windows.

Instead of staying where I'd told him to, Bart followed at my heels. Again I cautioned him, then I climbed a small oak tree just strong enough to bear my weight. I climbed high enough to peek into the house. At first I couldn't see anything but a huge dim room cluttered with cartons as yet unpacked. A tall and fat lamp blocked my view, and I had to lean away from the tree to see around it. Fuzzily I could make out a black-robed figure seated in a hard wooden rocker that looked very uncomfortable, after the soft, luxurious couches and chairs I'd seen carried inside. Was that a woman under the black veil?—the same one I'd seen outside?

Arab men wore dresses, so that could be the feeble butler, but then I saw a pale, slim hand with many sparkling rings and I knew it was the mistress of this manor. Shifting my weight, I sought a better viewing position, and, as I did, the branch supporting my weight cracked. The woman inside lifted her head and stared my way.

Her eyes were wide and frightened-looking. I told myself that people in a bright room couldn't look out into darkness and see. My heart throbbed in triple time as I held my breath. Little winged night insects buzzed around my head and began to nibble on my skin.

Below me Bart was growing impatient. He shook my frail tree. I tried to hang on and at the same time signal to Bart to stop. Fortunately, at that moment a maid opened the door and came in with a large silver tray laden with many covered dishes.

"Hurry up!" grouched scaredy-cat. "I want to go home!"

What was he afraid of? *I* was the one about to fall from the tree. The clatter of the dishes and silverware being taken from the tray and placed on a small table covered the noise Bart was making. No sooner was that maid out of the room than the veiled woman lifted her hands to take off the veil.

She began to eat. All alone, she picked at her food. Just when I felt sure she hadn't heard any noise to warn her someone was spying—the weak branch of my tree made a splitting sound.

She turned her head. Now was my chance to see her without the black veil. I saw her. Really saw her! But I didn't really see her nose, her lips, her eyes; I saw only the jagged rows of scars on each side of her face. Had a cat scratched her and made those scars? I felt suddenly sorry for an old woman who had to sit alone at a table without enough appetite to enjoy anything. It didn't seem fair to live such a lonely, unloved life. Not fair either for fate to show me how age could steal the beauty of someone who might have been just as lovely as my mother—once.

"Jory . . . ?"

"Shhh . . ."

She kept on staring, then quickly lowered the veil over her face. "Who's out there?" she called. "Go away, whoever you are! If you don't, I'll call the police!"

That did it. I jumped to the ground, seized Bart by his hand and took off. He stumbled and fell, holding me back as usual. I jerked him upright and ran on, forcing him to run faster than he could have without my help. He gasped, "Jory! Not so fast! What did you see? Quick, tell me—was it a ghost?"

Worse than that. I'd seen how my mother might look thirty years from now, if she lived long enough to be ravaged by time.

"Where've you two been?" Mom blocked our way as we tried to slip into the bathroom to wash up before she had a chance to notice our disheveled clothes.

"We came from the garden in back," I answered, feeling

guilty. Immediately she saw my guilt and grew suspicious. "Where were you really?"

"Just out back . . ."

"Jory, are you going to grow evasive like Bart?"

I threw my arms about her and pressed my face against the softness of her breast. I was too old to do this, but I had the sudden need to feel safe and comforted.

"Jory darling, what's wrong?"

Nothing was wrong. I didn't know what bothered me, not really. I'd seen old age before, my own grandmother Marisha, but she'd always been old.

That night Momma came in my dreams and was a lovely angel who put an enchanted spell over all the world to stop people from growing older. I saw two-hundred-year-old ladies as young and pretty as when they'd been twenty—all but one old woman in black, all alone, rocking in her chair.

Toward morning Bart slipped into my bed and cuddled up behind my back, watching with me the gray fog that obliterated the trees, erased the golden grass, smothered all signs of life, and made the world out there seem dead.

Bart rattled on to himself. "Earth is full of dead people. Dead animals and plants too. Makes all that stuff Daddy calls mulch."

Death. My half brother Bart was obsessed by death, and I pitied him. I felt him cuddle closer as we both stared out at the fog that was so much a part of our lives.

"Jory, nobody ever likes me," he complained.

"Yes, they do."

"No, they don't. They like you better."

"That's because you don't like them and it shows."

"Why do you like everybody?"

"I don't. But I can put on a smile and pretend even when I don't. Perhaps you'd better learn to put on a false face sometimes."

"Why? It's not Halloween."

He troubled me. Like those beds in the attic troubled me. Like that strange thing between my parents that rose up every so often, reminding me that they knew something that I didn't.

I closed my eyes and decided everything always worked out for the best.

Gone Hunting

❧

They looked at me, but they didn't see me. They didn't know who I was. To them I was just a thing to sit at their table and try to swallow the stuff they put on my plate. My thoughts were all around, but they didn't read my mind, couldn't figure me out at all. I was goin next door to the mansion to where I'd been invited. And when I went I'd remember to pronounce my "ings"—always they were telling me to say the G's. I'd do it right, everything, for the old lady next door.

Gonna go alone and not tell Jory. Jory didn't need new friends anyway. He had his ole ballet classes, with pretty girls all around and that was enough. With Melodie, more than enough. Me—I didn't have nobody but parents who didn't understand. Soon as I was excused from breakfast I'd make it quickly to our garden while Jory was still inside eatin his stack of pancakes with melted maple sugar poured all over. Pig, that's what he was . . . a darn hog!

Day was hot. Sun was too bright. Shadows long on the ground. White wall rose up so dratted high—had that wall known in advance I was comin, and I'd be clumsy, and "they" wanted to make it difficult? Tree I climbed wasn't so bad.

Yard was so big it tired my short legs. Wish I had long pretty legs like Jory. Always fallin, always hurtin myself, but never felt no pain. Daddy had been amazed when he first found that out. "Bart, because your nerve endings don't reach your skin, you will have to be doubly careful of infections. You could seriously hurt yourself and not even know it. So always wash all your cuts and scratches with soap and water, then tell your mother and me so we can put on disinfectant."

Washing with soap kept away germs. Wonder where they went?—up to heaven, down to hell? Wonder what a germ looked like? Monsters, Jory had said, ugly itty-bitty monsters. A billion of them could sit on the point of a pin. Wish I had eyes like a microscope.

I gave her yard another long-long look, then jumped, closed my eyes so I couldn't see the ground smack me. Landed square in a clump of her rose bushes. More cuts and scratches to add to my collection. More germs too. Didn't care. Crouched down low, squinted my eyes against the sun, and tried to spot all the dangerous wild animals that lurked in dark, mysterious places—like this.

Look over there. Behind that big bush—a tiger! I raised my rifle and took careful aim. It swished its long tail and sparked its yellow eyes, then licked its chops, thinking soon it would have me for lunch. I squeezed hard on the trigger. BANG! BANG! BANG! Got yah! Dead as a doornail!

Slingin my rifle over my shoulder, I wended a careful way along all the dangerous jungle paths. Ignorin an orange and white kitten that mewed "plaintively." (Plaintively was one of the new words I had to use. One new word each day, and Daddy gave a list of seven words to both Jory and me, insistin we use today's word at least five times in our conversation. Didn't need a bigger vocabulary. Knew how to talk good enough already.)

A tune popped into my head. Came from a movie I saw last night on TV about West Point. That song was right:

There was somethin about a soldier . . .
that is fine, fine, fine . . .

Marchin to the tune in my head, I carried my rifle smartly on my shoulder, my chest out, my chin in. Straight up to her front door I marched. Then I banged hard, usin the brass knocker that was a lion's head with a loose jaw.

My perfect military bearin was so admirable I just knew that ole lady would be impressed. Doctors weren't so special. Dancers either. But a five-star general—that was impressive! Nobody had a name longer than mine: General Bartholomew Scott Winslow Sheffield. Even Jory Janus Marquet Sheffield was not so long, not so good soundin. Just wait until the enemy knew who was in charge of the war.

Should have been that creepy ole butler who opened the door, but it was the ole lady herself. I'd seen her a few times in her yard. She held the door open a slot and stingily allowed a long wedge of sunlight to shine on her floor. "Bart . . . ?" she whispered, her voice surprised and happy. Was she really so glad to see me? Gee, and she didn't even know me yet.

"Bart, how wonderful! I was hoping you'd come."

"Step aside, Madame!" I commanded. "My men got you surrounded." Made my voice deep and gruff to scare the living lights out of her. "No use resistin. Better to give up and raise yer white flag. The odds are all against you."

"Oh, Bart," she said with silly giggles. "It's so sweet of you to accept my invitation. Sit down and talk to me. Tell me about yourself, your life. Tell me if you're happy; if your brother is happy, if you like where you live, and love your parents. I want to know everything!"

Forcefully I kicked the door to behind me, as all good generals did. BANG! To see her blue eyes smiling while her lips were covered by that dratted black veil was very weird. My tough military composure vanished. Why'd she have to wear that scary veil? "Lady," I said weakly, feeling young and timid again, "you did call over the wall yesterday. You said you wanted me to come over when I was lonely. I sneaked over . . ."

"Sneaked?" she asked in an odd voice. "Do you have to slip away from your parents? Do they punish you often?"

"Naw," I said. "Wouldn't do them no good. Couldn't hurt me with spankins; couldn't starve me for I don't like food anyway." I hung my head and whispered, "Momma and Daddy tole me not to pester rich ole ladies who live in big spooky houses next door."

"Oh!" she said with a sigh. "Do you have a great many big spooky houses next door with rich old ladies inside?"

"Heck no, ma'am," I drawled, then sauntered over to a wall in a pretty parlor where I could look out and see who was comin, who was goin. I slouched against the wall and took the makins for a good smoke from my pocket and rolled my own as she sat down in a rocker to watch. She kept watchin me blow smoke rings in her air, faintly smiling as they wreathed around her head. Stupid veil puffed in and out as she breathed. Wonder if she slept with that thing over her head and face.

"Bart, often I hear you and your brother talking in your yard. I use a stepladder sometimes to look over the wall—I hope you don't mind." Wouldn't answer. Blew smoke rings right in her face. "Please talk, Bart . . . sit down and relax, feel comfortable, feel at home. I want my house to feel like your home, open to you and Jory. My own life is so lonely, all I have is myself and John Amos, my butler. To have a real family living next door is so comforting. You can say anything you want to me, anything at all."

Wasn't nothin to say—but here was an adult who wanted

to listen. What could we talk about? "People shouldn't spy on me and my brother."

"I wasn't spying," she said in hurry, "just taking care of my roses that climb the wall and need pruning—and I can't help if I overhear, can I?"

Spy. That's what she was. Ground out the butt of my cigarette with my dusty boot heel. Sun was getting in my eyes again, makin me tilt the brim of my hat. Ole Devil sun makin me thirsty. "Ma'am, ya'll done asked me over and here ah is . . . so get t' the point."

"Bart, if you take a chair, we'll have refreshments soon. See that bell-pull? My maid will bring in ice cream and cake. It is a long time until lunch, so your appetite shouldn't be spoiled."

Might as well stay a bit longer. Fell into a soft chair and fixed my eyes on her feet, which could barely be seen. Was she wearing high heels?—fancy sandals?—painted toenails? Then in the door came a pretty Mexican maid with a tray full of goodies. Wow-wow! The maid smiled at me, nodded to the lady, then disappeared. I politely accepted what she gave me—not enough of anything—and set to. Didn't like food that was good for me; it tasted so bad. I stood up to go as soon as I polished off my treats.

"Thank you, ma'am, for takin kindly to an ole cowpoke who just ain't used to yer kind of hospitality. I've got to be ambling on now. . . ."

"All right, if you have to go," she said sadly, and I felt sorry for her livin with servants only, no kids like me. "Come back tomorrow if you want, and bring Jory with you. I'll have whatever you want. . . ."

"Don't want to bring Jory!"

"Why not?"

"You're *my* secret! He gets to do everything. I never get to do nothin! Nobody ever likes me."

"I like you."

Gee, she made me feel good. I peeked at her face, but couldn't see anything but her blue eyes. "Why do you like me?" I asked with so much wonder—nobody else did.

"I don't just like you, Bart Winslow," she said queerly, "I love you."

"Why?" I didn't believe her. Ladies fell at first sight for Jory, never for me.

"Once I had two sons, now I don't," she said with her eyes cast down and her voice sad and tight. "Then I wanted to have another son by my second husband, and I couldn't." She looked up and met my eyes. "So I want *you* to take the place of the third son I couldn't have. I'm very rich, Bart. I can give you anything you want."

"My heart's desire—my real heart's desire?"

"Yes, anything that can be bought with money, I can give you."

"Can't everything be bought?"

"Sadly, it can't. I used to think it could, but now I know money can't buy the most important things. Things I used to take for granted and treated lightly—oh, if I had my life to live over, how different I would be! I've made so many mistakes, Bart. I want to do everything right for you, with you . . . and if you have to keep me as your secret, perhaps one day . . . well, let's save that for later. You will come again?"

She sounded so pitiful and made me feel so uneasy. I shuffled my feet about and decided I'd better get away quick before she tried to kiss me. "Ma'am, gotta get back to camp. My men will be wonderin if I'm wounded or dead. But remember this—I got you surrounded and you cannot win this war!"

"I know," she said, her voice so sad sounding. "I've never won any game I've tried to play. I've always gone down in defeat even when I thought I held the winning cards."

Just like me! Made me feel sorry for her. "Lady, you play your cards right and I'll come over every day and pay you a visit—or even two or three."

"Thank you, Bart. You just tell me what cards to play and I'll have them on the table waiting for you."

Had me an idea then. Lots and lots of things I wanted and never got. Didn't want books, games, toys, or other ordinary stuff. One thing I had to have, and hopefully I stared at her . . . maybe she'd be the one to give it to me. "What's your name?"

"Come again and I'll tell you."

I'd be comin again. Darn if I could stay away now.

Went home and nobody even noticed I was there. Momma went right on talking about that baby girl she had to have if her favorite student Nicole died. *God, don't let Nicole die,* I silently prayed.

"Jory, let's play ball."

"Can't. Mom's driving me to afternoon class. Melodie's parents are taking me to dinner tonight, then to a movie."

Nobody ever took me anywhere—except my parents. No friends. No pet of my own. Dratted Clover liked Jory better, squealin like he was hurt when I stepped on his tail by accident, or stumbled over him, and he was always underfoot.

A few days later I again headed for the back door. "Where are you going?" asked Momma, who had been starin at a picture of that little girl she wanted for her own. Weren't enough she had two boys—had to have a daughter too. Sissy-silly girl.

"Bart, answer me. Where are you going?"

"Nowhere."

"Every time I ask you what you do, and where you go, you say you haven't been anywhere and haven't done anything. Now I want to hear the truth."

Jory laughed and hugged her. "Gee, Mom, you oughta know him by this time. When Bart steps out the back door he's *everywhere*. You never saw a kid so crazy about pretending. He's this, he's that, and the only thing he never is . . . is himself."

The power I poured into my mean, piercing eyes should have shut Jory up—but he went right on. "He prefers fantasy to reality, Mom, that's all."

Weren't so. Was bored, that's all. Didn't get enough of what I wanted in real life, and in my pretend games I did everything right—and got everything I wanted. Then he and Momma were laughing, and I was shut out again. Mad. They were makin me mad.

Drat everybody who made fun of me! But hatin everybody made me feel bad, and pretendin made me happy. What did I have to lose if I went over to *her* place? Nothin, nothin at all.

Riskin my life in the darkest of dangerous jungles, I fought my way over to her place. Bravely I struggled onward, facin death over and over just to get to her . . . climbin that slippery tree that wanted me to fall. Scalin that high wall to get to her. Through the wind and snow, through the sleet and rain, freezin my feet, blindin my eyes, I struggled onward to her.

I stumbled to her house for the fifth time in three days. And there she was, smilin beneath her veil, lovin me as no one else did. I felt happy and warm all over as she called and opened her arms wide. I went flyin into them, huggin her, eager to sit on her lap and be petted and pampered. She needed me. She wanted to love me like her own. Her lap didn't burn me as I was afraid it would. It didn't feel so awful to be kissed on my cheeks—but it did feel dry. Drat that veil!

Because she loved me, and I loved her now, she'd given me a room of my own to hold all the things she gave me. Two miniature electric trains with all the accessories, toy cars, trucks, and games. All this stuff for me to play with—in her house, not mine.

Time went by. I was gettin to love her more and more each day. Then one Tuesday I found that creepy ole butler John Amos in her favorite room, messin around with her things, mutterin to himself about a fool and her money bein soon parted. Didn't like him touchin her things. Didn't like him talking mean about her behind her back.

"You get out of here!" I said in my big man voice. "You tell my lady I'm here, and tell your chef I want chocolate ice cream today with Oreo cookies, not brownies."

He was an awful sight. "You can trust a few some of the time, and most none of the time. Feel lucky if you have even one to trust *all* of the time."

What was that supposed to mean? I scowled and tried to draw away. Didn't like his false teeth that kept slippin so he had to push them back, and they clacked too, as if they didn't fit his mouth.

"You like her, don't you?" he asked, slyly smilin, noddin his head up and down, from side to side, so I could be confused if I wanted. "When you want the full truth about who you are—and who she is—come to me." The lady's steps on the stairs sent him scurryin off.

Creepy. He made me feel creepy and scared. I knew who I was—most of the time.

All alone now. Nothin to do. I sat down and crossed my legs like my daddy did, then leaned back to light up an expensive cigar, which Daddy never did. (Momma didn't like men who smoked.) Nothin wrong with smokin as far as I could tell, I thought, as I blew four perfect smoke rings into the air . . . and away they sailed toward the Pacific. They'd end up in Japan over Mt. Fugi.

"Good morning, Bart darling. I'm so glad to see you." She came in and sat in the rocker.

"You got my pony yet?"

Her voice sounded worried. "Sweetheart, I know I promised you a pony as your heart's desire, but I did that without knowing how much trouble a pony can be."

"You promised!" I cried. Was I puttin my trust in the wrong person? One who failed to deliver what she promised.

"Sweetheart, a pony needs a stall, and ponies make you smell bad. When you went home your parents and Jory would guess you had a pet over here."

Instead of answerin, I began to cry. "All my life I been wantin a pony," I sobbed. "All my livelong life, and now I've got to grow old without havin one . . ." Sobbed some more, then hung my head and headed for home, never to return.

"Bart . . . there is a beautiful big dog that won't smell and betray your secrets. A St. Bernard—a dog so big you can ride it like a pony. If you keep him clean and fluffy he won't betray you with his odors . . ."

Slowly I turned to glare at her. "Ain't no dog as big as a pony!"

"Isn't there?"

"NO! You're tryin to make fun of me. I don't like you anymore! I'm goin home and never comin back—not until you have a pony I can name Apple."

"Darling, you can call your puppy Apple—but he won't eat them—and just think how jealous Jory would be if you have a dog more marvelous than his."

Turned to the door. Disgusted.

"Only the super rich can afford to feed a St. Bernard, Bart!"

Like I was a pin and she was the magnet, I turned back to her unwillingly. She lifted me up on her lap and cuddled me there, and it wasn't so awful after all. "You can call me Grandmother."

"Grandmother." Felt good to have a grandmother at last. I snuggled closer and waited for her to call me Baby, but she just went right on rockin and singin a lullaby. I put my thumb in my mouth. Nice to be hugged and kissed and made to feel helpless and loved. And she didn't smell like mothballs after all.

"Are you ugly under that veil?" I asked, always curious about what she looked like. The veil was almost transparent, but not enough.

"I guess you would think so, but once I was very beautiful—like your mother."

"You know my mother?" I asked.

The door opened and my favorite pretty maid came in with a dish of ice cream and hot brownies fresh from the oven. "Now only eat one brownie, and let this little bit of ice cream be enough so you can come over after lunch." She went on to tell me not to shove in such huge mouthfuls because it was not good manners, and was also a shock to my digestive system.

I had good manners. My momma taught me all the time. For some reason I was angry enough to jump down from her lap, wonderin just what it was John Amos had to tell me. As I stumbled toward the door, all of a sudden John Amos was there in the hall, smiling at me spooky-like. He bowed a little and put a small red-leather book in my hands. "I sense you're not very confident about yourself," he whispered, making lots of hissin sounds like a snake. "It's time you knew just who you really are. That lady who told you to call her grandmother *is really your true grandmother.*"

Oh, good golly! I didn't know I had my own true grandmother. I thought my grandmothers were either dead or in the looney bin.

"Yes, Bart, she's your grandmother, and not only that, once she was married to your father. Your *real* father."

Didn't know what to think, except I was awful happy havin a genuine true grandmother of my very own, just like Jory had his own. And she wasn't dead, or crazy.

"Now you listen to me, boy, and you will never feel weak and ineffective again. You read a little of this book every day and it will teach you to be like your great-grandfather, Malcolm Neal Foxworth. Never on this earth did there live a man who was smarter than your own great-grandfather—the father of your grandmother who sits in that rocker and wears that ugly black veil."

"She's pretty underneath," I said. I didn't like what he

was sayin and the way he was lookin. "Never have seen her face, but I can tell from her voice that she's pretty—prettier than you!"

He sneered, then quickly changed his expression to smilin.

"All right, have it your way. But after you read this book written by your own dear great-grandfather, you will understand that women are not to be trusted, especially pretty women. They have ways, cunning ways, of making men do what they want. You'll find that out soon enough when you become a man. A man as handsome as your own father was, and she took him and made him her slave, made him her lap dog like she's making you."

Wasn't no lap dog, wasn't!

"He was her second husband, Bartholomew Winslow, and eight years younger than her, and he didn't know any better. He thought he could use her—but she used him. I want to save you from her so you won't end up like your father did—dead."

Dead. Almost everybody was dead in our family. Wasn't really surprised by nothin he said, except I hadn't known women were that bad. Always suspected they were, but never really knew. I should warn Jory.

"Now, if you want to save your everlasting soul from the fires of eternal hell, you will read this book and grow strong and powerful like your great-grandfather. The women will never rule you again. You will rule them."

I looked up into his long gaunt face, seein his skinny mustache and his yellowish teeth through which he not only hissed but sometimes whistled. He was uglier than anyone I'd seen before. But I'd heard Emma say more than once that pretty was as pretty did. So I guessed I might as well give my powerful great-grandfather a try, and read his little red-leather book with its sprawly handwritin.

Didn't take much to readin. Wasn't my kind of thing to do at all. But when I was in the barn near the stall that would soon be a home for my pony, I snuggled down in the hay. Wanted that pony so bad it hurt. Didn't really care if it smelled bad and was lots of trouble. I opened the book, which looked mighty old.

I am beginning this journal with the most bitter day of my life, the day my beloved mother ran away and left me for another man. She left my father, too. I remember how I felt when he told me what she'd done, how much I cried, how lost I felt without her. How lonely to go to bed and have no mother to kiss me good night and hear my prayers. I was five years old. And until she left, she'd always said I was the most important person in her life. How could she have left me, her only son? What evil thing possessed her so she could turn her back on a loving son?

I was so innocent then, so unknowing. When I read the words of the Lord, I began to realize that ever since Eve women have betrayed men in one way or another, even mothers. Corrine, Corrine, how I began to hate that name.

Funny. Felt strange as I lifted my eyes from that red journal with its small, cramped handwriting that sometimes sprawled larger at the bottom of the page, as if he had to use every bit of space.

I too had always been scared my momma might up and go for no reason except she didn't want to be near me anymore. And I'd be left alone with a stepfather who couldn't possibly love me as much as if I'd been his own true son. Jory would be all right, for he had his dancin and that was all that really mattered to him.

"You like that book?" asked John Amos, who had sneaked into the barn and was standing still in the shadows and watchin me with small, glittery eyes.

"Sure, it's a good book," I managed to say, though it made me feel bad inside, and so afraid Momma might run away too with some man who wasn't a doctor. All the time she was wishin Daddy wasn't a doctor and could stay home more.

"Now, you keep reading that book each day," advised John Amos, who might really like me, even though his face was mean, "and you will learn all about women and how to control them." I could listen better when I couldn't see him very good. "And not only will you learn how to control women, but also all people. That small red book in your hands will save you from making the mistakes so many men make. You remember that when you grow tired of reading. You remember it is the god-given duty of men to dominate women who are basically weak and stupid."

Gee, I hadn't guessed Momma was weak and stupid. I thought she was strong and wonderful. Just like my grandmother was generous and kind . . . and in some ways, much better than my own mother, who always seemed too busy to bother with me.

"Malcolm was the kind of man other people looked up to, Bart. The kind of man everyone respected and feared. When you can inspire that kind of awe it makes you revered—like a god. You don't have to tell your grandmother about this book. It would be better if you didn't, and just went on pretending to love her as much as before. Never let women know what you're thinking. Keep your honest thoughts to yourself."

Maybe he was right. Maybe if I read this book to the very end I'd end up smarter than Jory, and the whole world would look up to me.

I smiled that night in my bed, hugging the journal of Malcolm close to my heart. Here I had the tool to use to make me the richest man in the world—just like Malcolm Neal Foxworth, who used to live in a faraway place called Foxworth Hall.

I had two friends now. My lady grandmother in black and John Amos, who talked to me more than my daddy ever did. Boy, sure was funny how strangers came into my life and started givin me more than my parents.

Sugar and Spice

Mom had purchased a ballet school that still bore the name of the original owner. She adopted that name, *Marie DuBois School of Ballet*, and led her students to think she was Marie DuBois. She explained to me and Bart later that it was easier than changing the name of the school and more profitable, too. Dad seemed to agree.

Her school was located on the top floor of a two-story building in San Rafael, not far from where Dad had his medical office. Often they ate lunch together or spent the night in San Francisco so they could see a ballet or go to movies and not have to drive back and forth. Emma was with us, so we didn't really mind too much, except sometimes I felt left out to see them come home so happy and glowing. It made me think we weren't as important to them as we liked to believe.

One night when I was restless and couldn't sleep, I silently stole out of my bedroom with the idea of a midnight snack on my mind, nothing else. The second my feet hit the hall near the living room I could hear the sound of my parents' voices.

Loud. They were arguing, and they seldom even spoke crossly to one another.

I didn't know what to do, to stay or to return to my room. Then I remembered that scene in the attic, and for my protection and Bart's, too, I felt I had to know what this was all about.

Mom still wore the pretty blue dress she'd worn out to dinner with Dad. "I don't know why you keep objecting!" she stormed, as she paced back and forth, throwing Dad furious looks. "You know as well as I do that Nicole isn't going to get well. And if we wait until she's buried, then the state will have custody of Cindy, and we'll have a devil of a time getting her away from them! Let's move now. Possession is nine-tenths of the law, and that landlady doesn't want to be bothered any longer. Chris, *please make up your mind!*"

"No," he said coldly. "We have two children and that's enough. There are other young couples who will be delighted to adopt Cindy. Couples who don't have as much to lose as we do when the adoption agency starts to investigate . . ."

Mom threw her hands wide. "That's what I'm saying! If we have Cindy before Nicole dies, the agency won't have any reason to investigate. I'll go tonight and tell Nicole what I plan. I'm sure she'll agree and sign whatever legal papers are needed."

"Catherine," said my stepfather in a firm voice, "you can't have everything the way you want it. Nicole may very well recover in a few weeks, and even if she is permanently crippled, she'll still want her child."

"But what kind of mother will she make?"

"That's not for us to decide."

"She can't recover! You know it, and I know it—and what's more, Christopher Doll, I have already gone to the hospital and talked to Nicole, and she *wants* me to have her daughter. She signed the papers I took, and I had Simon Daughtry with me. He's an attorney, and had his secretary along—so what can you do now to stop me?"

Appearing shocked, my stepdad put his hands to his face, while my mother railed on and on:

"Christopher, stop cringing behind your hands. Show your face, and recognize what you made me do. You were there the night Bart was born—there with your pleading eyes telling me Paul wouldn't be enough, and it would be you in the end who won. If you hadn't been there, pleading with those damned blue eyes, I wouldn't have let the doctors talk me into signing those papers and allowing the sterilization! I would have borne another child even if it did kill me. But you were there, and I gave in—for your sake, damn it! *For your sake!*"

Sobbing, she fell to the floor and lay curled up on her side, her fingers working in the deep shag of the carpet. Her long blonde hair spread like a golden fan on the carpet and cushioned her cheek as she cried on and on, berating him and herself for what they were doing.

What were they doing?

She rolled onto her back, spreading her arms wide. Dad uncovered his face and stared at her, looking deeply wounded.

"You're right, Christopher! You are always right! There's only been one time when I was right, but that single time might have saved Cory's life." Sobbing, she jerked her head away from Dad, who knelt beside her and tried to pull her into his embrace. She hit at him, making me gasp.

"You were right again when you told me not to marry Julian! I'll bet you gloated when our marriage turned out to be a miserable failure. I'll bet you were delighted when Julian sat back and allowed Yolanda Lange to destroy everything we owned. Everything happened just the way you predicted, making you so happy. Then Bart suffocated in the fire that burned Foxworth Hall to the ground. Were you laughing inside then too?—glad to be rid of him? Did you think I'd run straight into your arms and forget about all I owed Paul? Did you doubt I loved Paul?" Her voice rose to a shrill shriek. "When Paul and I were lovers I never thought of him as too old, until you kept harping on his age. Perhaps I wouldn't have paid any attention to Amanda and what she said if you hadn't bugged me so much about marrying a man twenty-five years older."

I shrank into a tighter ball. Ashamed to stay and listen; afraid to get up and go now that I'd overheard so much. Mom was wound up, as if she'd saved this for a long time, ready to throw it into his face at the right opportunity—and here it was. He recoiled from the viciousness of her attack.

"Remember the afternoon I married Paul?" she yelled. "Remember? Think of the moment when you handed me the ring he put on my finger. You hesitated so long the minister had to urge you with a whisper. And all the time you were pleading with your eyes. I resisted you then, as I should have resisted you after he died. Did you wish for him to die soon so that you'd have YOUR chance? A self-fulfilling wish, Christopher Doll! YOU WIN! YOU ALWAYS WIN! YOU SIT BACK AND WAIT WHILE YOU DO WHAT YOU CAN TO MESS UP MY LIFE! WELL, HERE I AM! RIGHT WHERE YOU WANTED ME!—in your bed, acting as your wife. Are you enjoying yourself? ARE YOU?" She sobbed, then slapped his face hard.

He reeled backward but didn't say a word. She hadn't finished with him even then. "Don't you realize I would never have gone to Bart in the first place if you hadn't always been hanging around, coming between Paul and me; making me ashamed of what Momma had done to you, to me? I had to take Bart away from her then—it was the only way I could punish her for what she did to us. And now, after all Paul did for us, you won't even have the decent generosity to take in a poor little girl who will soon be an orphan. Even when I have paved the way legally so there won't be any investigation by the authorities. Still you want me for yourself, thinking two sons are enough to get in the way of our privacy, and another child might bring down our house of cheating cards."

"Cathy, please . . . ," he moaned.

She hit at him with small, balled fists, then yelled again, "Perhaps you even told me it was all right for Paul to have sex just so he would have another heart attack!"

The she sank back, panting, tears streaking her face while her watery blue eyes stared up at Dad, but he only stayed still, hunkered down on his heels as if frozen by all she'd said.

I wanted to cry, for him, for her, for Bart and for me. Though I didn't understand nearly enough.

My dad began to shiver uncontrollably, as if winter had come unexpectedly into our living room. Had Mom told the truth? Was he the one who was behind all the deaths in our lives? I was scared too, for I loved him.

"Great God, Catherine," he said at last, rising to his feet and heading toward their bedroom. "I'll pack my bags and move out before the hour is over, if that's what you want. And I hope you're satisfied. This time, you win!"

In one single graceful bound, she was on her feet and running after him. She caught hold of his arm and spun him around before she flung her arms about his waist and clung. "Chris!" she cried out, "I'm sorry! So sorry. I didn't mean a word I said. It was cruel, and I know it. I love you; I've always loved you; I lie, I cheat, I say anything I want to get my way. I'll put the blame on anyone. I can't bear it as my own. Don't look so hurt, so betrayed. You're right to deny me Nicole's daughter, for I do end up hurting everyone I love. I do destroy what I care about most. If I'd been the right kind of person I would have found the right words to say to Carrie, but I didn't say anything right to her then, and nothing right to Julian either."

She still clung to him while he stood like a tall stick of wood in her embrace, doing nothing to return all the passion she lavished with her words, her kisses, her embraces. She took one of his limp hands and tried to slap her face with it, and failing, she slapped her own face with her free hand.

"Why don't you hit me, Chris? God knows I've given you

reason enough tonight. And I don't have to have Cindy, not when I have you, and my sons . . ."

I could tell my stepdad felt impotent against all the anguish she displayed. Her histrionics had driven him into a corner and he wanted to stay there long enough to reason out his position. But she was at him, demanding of him, until she was yelling out again: "What's the matter now, Christopher Doll? There you stand, wooden, saying nothing, trying to judge me by your own ethics. Recognize the truth—*that I don't have any ethics!* You want to believe I am only an actress playing a role, like our mother played hers. Even now, after all these years, you can't tell when I'm acting and when I'm not. Do you know why?" Now her voice became nasty, cynical. "Since you have never bothered to analyze my pathetic case, I'll do it for you. Christopher, you are afraid to look at me honestly. You don't want to know what I am really like. If I'm not acting, and this side I'm showing you now is the real me—then you can't face up to being a fool. You would discover then you have based your great unselfish love on a woman who is ruthless, demanding, and utterly selfish. Go on, see the truth! I'm not a divine goddess and never was, never will be! Chris, you've been a fool all your adult life, trying to make me into something I'm not—so that makes you a liar too. Doesn't it?" She laughed as he paled.

"Look at me, Christopher. Who do I remind you of?" She pulled back and looked at him in silence for a long time as she waited. When he refused to answer she said, "Come on, say it—I'm like her, right? This is the way she was that last night in Foxworth Hall when the guests were there swarming about the Christmas tree in the ballroom, and in the library she was screaming as I'm screaming now!—yelling out how her father beat her and made her do what she did. What a pity you weren't there. So yell at me, Chris! Strike out and hit me! Scream as I'm screaming and show you're human!"

Slowly, slowly he was losing his temper. I was so afraid of what might happen next. I wanted to rush in and stop what was going on, for if he did raise his hand to strike her, I'd run to her defense. I'd never let him hit my mother.

Did she hear my silent pleas? She let go of him and slid down to the floor again. I was so confused to see them fighting, really going at it. And why was the name Foxworth Hall stirring up hidden fears I didn't want to come out into the light? And who was this *her* Mom kept screaming about? And where had Daddy Paul been at this time?—at this too distant time when Mom had not yet met his younger brother?—or so they'd told me. Did parents tell lies?

Foxworth Hall, why did that have such a familiar ring?

Once more he went down on his knees beside her, and this time with great tenderness he took her in his arms and she didn't fight him off. His quick kisses rained on her pale face, his lips trying to smother her words which kept coming anyway. "Chris, how can you keep on loving me when I'm such a bitch? How can you keep on understanding why I'm ugly so often? I know I'm as much a bitch as *she* is, only I would give my life to undo the harm she's done us."

Without a word he locked eyes with her until their breathing began to come in short pants. Between them that passion that was always just below the surface ignited, caught fire, and something electric tingled my skin too.

Lest I see too much, I silently crawled back to my room with the embarrassing vision of them rolling about on the floor still on my mind. Over and over again, turning, clutching at each other, both wild—and the last thing I heard was a zipper being pulled. His or hers, I didn't know. Though I wondered about it. Did a woman ever pull down a man's fly zipper of her own free will—even a wife?

I ran into the garden. In the dark, near the great white wall, near a pale, nude statue of marble, I fell down on the ground and cried. Rodin's statue "The Kiss" was the first thing I saw when I looked up. Just a copy, but it told me a whole lot about adults and their feelings.

I'd been a child believing my parents' integrity was flaw-less, their love a brilliant, smooth ribbon of unbroken satin. Now it was tattered, stained, and no longer shining. Had they argued many times and I just hadn't heard? I tried to remem-ber. It seemed to me that they'd never had such a terrible argument before, only brief conflicts that had been resolved.

Too old to cry, I told myself. Though fourteen was almost a man's age. Already I was sprouting a few hairs above my lips and other places. Sniffling, choking my sobs back, I ran to the white wall and climbed the oak tree. Once there on the wall I sat in my favorite place and stared off at the huge white man-sion, which looked ghostly in the moonlight. I thought and I thought about Bart and who was his father. Why hadn't he been named after Daddy Paul? Surely a son should have his father's name. Why Bart instead of Paul?

As I watched, as I wondered, fog from the sea began to roll in, curling back upon itself, enfolding the mansion until I couldn't see it. All about me spread the thick gray mist. Eerie, frightening, mysterious.

From the grounds next door came strange muffled noises. Was that someone crying over there? Great wracking sobs that were punctuated by moans and short prayers that asked for forgiveness.

Oh, God! Was that pitiful old woman crying just like my mother had cried? What had *she* done? Did everyone have some shameful past to conceal? Would I be like them when I grew up?

"Christopher," I heard her sob. Startled, I jerked and tried to find where she was. How did she know my dad's name? Or did she have a Christopher of her own?

I knew one thing. Something dark and threatening had come into our lives. Bart was acting stranger than usual. Something or someone had to be influencing him in subtle ways I couldn't quite put my finger on. Whatever was chang-ing Bart didn't have anything to do with Mom and Dad. If I couldn't understand them, Bart wouldn't have a chance. But whatever it was between my parents, and whatever was going on with Bart, I felt I had the weight of the world on my shoulders, and they weren't that strong yet.

One afternoon I deliberately hurried home from ballet class early. I wanted to find out what Bart did with himself when I was away. He wasn't in his room, he wasn't in the garden, so that left only one place he could possibly be. Next door.

I found him easily. Much to my surprise, he was inside the house and sitting on the lap of the old woman who never wore any clothes that weren't black.

I sucked in my breath. The little rascal cuddled up cozily on her black lap. I stole closer to the window of the parlor she seemed to favor above the others. She was singing softly to him as he gazed up into her veil-shrouded face. His huge dark eyes were full of innocence before his expression suddenly changed to that of someone sly and old. "You don't really love me, do you?" he asked in the strangest voice.

"Oh, yes I do," she said softly. "I love you more than I have ever loved anyone before."

"More than you could love Jory?"

Why the Devil should she love me?

She hesitated, glanced away, answered, "Yes . . . you are very, very special to me."

"You will always love me best of all?"

"Always, always . . . "

"You will give me everything I want, no matter what?"

"Always, always . . . Bart, my dear love, the next time you come over you will find waiting for you—your heart's desire."

"You'd better have it here!" said Bart in a hard way that surprised me. All of a sudden he sounded years older. But he was always changing his way of talking, walking. Playacting, always pretending.

I'd go home and tell Mom and Dad. Bart really needed friends his own age, not an old lady. It wasn't healthy for a boy not to have peers to play with. Then again, I wondered why my parents never asked any of their friends to our home the way other parents had their friends over occasionally. We lived all to ourselves, isolated from neighbors—until this Moslem woman, or whatever she was, came to win my brother's affections. I should be glad for him; instead, I was uneasy.

Finally Bart got up and said, "Good-bye, Grandmother." Just his ordinary little boy voice—but what the heck did he mean by *grandmother*?

I waited patiently until I was sure Bart was in our yard before I circled the huge old house and banged hard on her front door. I expected to see that old butler come shambling down the long hall to the foyer, but it was the old lady herself who put an eye to the peekhole and asked who it was.

"Jory Marquet Sheffield," I said proudly, just as my dad would.

"Jory," she whispered. In another moment she had flung open the door. "Come in," she invited happily, stepping aside to admit me. Way back in the shadows I thought I glimpsed someone who quickly dodged out of sight. "I'm so happy to have you visit. Your brother was here and had depleted our supply of ice cream, but I can offer you a cola drink and cake or cookies."

No wonder Bart wasn't eating Emma's good cooking. This woman was feeding him junk food. "Who are you?" I asked angrily. "You have no right to feed my brother anything."

She stepped back, appearing hurt and humble. "I try to tell him he should wait until after his meals, but he insists. And please don't judge me harshly without giving me a chance to explain." Her gesture invited me to take a chair in one of her fancy parlors. Though I wanted to decline, my curiosity was aroused. I followed her into what must have been the grandest room outside of a French palace! There was a concert grand piano, love seats, brocade chairs, a desk, and a long marble fireplace. Then I turned to look her over good. "Do you have a name?"

Floundering, she managed a small voice. "Bart calls me ... Grandmother."

"You're not his grandmother," I said. "When you tell him you are, you confuse him, and Lord knows, lady, if there is one thing my brother doesn't need, it is more confusion."

A slow redness colored her forehead. "I have no grand-children of my own. I'm lonely, I need someone ... and Bart seems to like me ..."

Pity for her overwhelmed me, so I could hardly say what I'd planned beforehand, but I managed nevertheless. "I don't think coming over here is good for Bart, ma'am. If I were you I would try to discourage him. He needs friends his own age ..." and here my voice dwindled away, for how could I tell her she was too old? And two grandmothers, one in a nut house, and the other a ballet nut, were more than enough.

The very next day Bart and I were told that Nicole had died in the night, and from now on her daughter, Cindy, would be our sister. My eyes met Bart's. Dad had his eyes on his plate, but he wasn't eating. I looked around, startled, when I heard a young child crying. "That's Cindy," said Dad. "Your mother and I were at Nicole's side when she died. Her last words were a request for us to take care of her child. When I thought about you two boys being left alone like Cindy, I knew I could die feeling more at peace knowing my children had a good home ... so I let your mother say what she's been wanting to say ever since Nicole's accident."

Mom came into the kitchen. In her arms she carried a small girl with blonde ringlets and large blue eyes almost the same color as hers. "Isn't she adorable, Jory, Bart?" She kissed a round rosy cheek while the big blue eyes looked from one to the other of us. "Cindy is exactly two years and two months and five days old. Nicole's landlady was delighted to be rid of what she thought a heavy burden." She gave us a happy smile. "Remember when you asked for a sister, Jory? I told you then I couldn't have more children. Well, as you can see, sometimes God works in mysterious ways. I'm crying inside for Nicole, who should have lived to be eighty. But her spine was broken and she had multiple internal injuries—"

She left the rest unsaid. I knew it was terribly sad for someone as young and pretty as nineteen-year-old Nicole Nickols to die just so we could have the sister I'd only mentioned casually a long time ago.

"Was Nicole your patient?" I asked Dad.

"No, son, she wasn't. But since she was a friend, and your mother's student, we were notified of her failure to respond to medical treatment. We rushed to the hospital to be with her. I suppose neither of you heard the phone ring about four this morning."

I stared at my new sister. She was very pretty in her pink pajamas with feet. Her soft curls fluffed out around her face. She clung to my mother and stared at strangers before she ducked her head and hid from our eyes. "Bart," said Mom with a sweet smile, "you used to do that. If you hid your face, you thought we couldn't see you just because you couldn't see us."

"Get her out of here!" he yelled, his face a red mask of anger. "Take her away! Put her in the grave with her mother! Don't want no sister! I hate her, hate her!"

Silence. No one could speak after this outburst.

Then, while Mom stood on looking too shocked even to breathe, Dad reached to control Bart, who jumped up to hit Cindy! Then Cindy was crying, and Emma was glaring at my brother.

"Bart, I have never heard anything so ugly and cruel," said Dad as he lifted Bart up and sat him on his knee. Bart wiggled and squirmed and tried to get away, but he couldn't escape. "Go to your room and stay there until you can learn to have some compassion for others. You would feel very lucky in Cindy's place."

Grumbling under his breath, Bart stomped to his room and slammed his door.

Turning, Dad picked up his black bag and prepared to leave. He gave my mother a chastising look. "Now do you see why I objected to adopting Cindy? You know as well as I that Bart has always had a very jealous streak. A child as lovely and young as Cindy wouldn't have been two days in an orphanage before some lucky couple seized her up."

"Yes, Chris, you are right, as always. If Cindy had been taken into legal custody she would have been adopted by others—and you and I would have gone daughterless all our lives. As it is I have a little girl who seems so much like Carrie to me."

My father grimaced as if from sharp pain. Mom was left sitting at the table with Cindy on her lap, and for the first time since I could remember, he didn't kiss her good-bye. And she didn't call out, "Be careful."

In no time at all Cindy had me enchanted. She toddled from here to there, wanting to touch everything and then have a taste. A nice warm feeling rushed over me to see the little girl so well cared for, so loved and pampered. The two of them together looked like mother and daughter. Both dressed in pink, with ribbons in their hair, only Cindy had on white socks with lace.

"Jory will teach you to dance when you're old enough." I smiled at Mom as I passed her on my way to ballet class. Quickly Mom got up to hand Cindy over to Emma, then she joined me in her car that was still parked in our wide garage. "Jory, I think Bart will soon learn to like Cindy a little more, don't you?"

I wanted to say, no he wouldn't, but I nodded, not letting

her know how worried I was about my brother. *Trouble, trouble, boil and double . . .*

"Jory, what was that you just mumbled?"

Gee, I didn't know I said it aloud. "Nothing, Mom. Just repeating something I overheard Bart saying to himself last night. He cries in his sleep, Mom. He calls for you, screaming because you've run away with your lover." I grinned and tried to look lighthearted. "And I didn't even know you play around."

She ignored my facetious remark. "Jory, why didn't you tell me before that Bart has nightmares?"

How could I tell her the truth?—that she was much too taken up with Cindy to pay attention to anyone else. And never, never should she give anyone more attention than Bart. Even me.

"Momma, Momma!" I heard Bart cry out in his sleep that night. "Where are you? Don't leave me alone! Momma, please don't leave me. I'm not bad, really not bad . . . just can't help what I do sometimes. Momma Momma . . . !"

Only crazy people couldn't help what they did. One crazy person in our family was enough. We didn't need another living under our roof.

So . . . it was up to me to save Bart from himself. Up to me to straighten out something crooked that had begun a long time ago. And way back in the shadow recesses of my brain, there were vague, unsettling memories of something that had troubled me years ago when I was too young to understand. Too young to put the jigsaw pieces together.

Trouble was, I'd been doing so much thinking about the past, that now it was waking up, and I could remember a man with dark hair, a man different from Daddy Paul. A man Mom used to call Bart Winslow—and those were my half brother's first and second names.

My Heart's Desire

Wicked little girl, that Cindy. Didn't care who saw her naked. Didn't care who saw her sit on the potty. Didn't care about being decent or clean. Took my toy cars and chewed on them.

Summer wasn't so good no more. Nothin t'do. No where t'go but next door. Ole lady kept promising that pony and never did it show up. Leading me on, teasing me. I'd show her. Make her sit over there all alone, wouldn't visit. Punish her. Last night I heard Momma telling Daddy how she saw that ole lady in black standing on a ladder propped against the wall. "And she was staring at me. Chris. Really staring!"

Daddy laughed. "Really, Cathy. What harm can her stares do? She's a stranger in a strange land. Wouldn't it have been friendly of you to wave and say hello—perhaps introduce yourself?" I snickered to myself. Grandmother wouldn't have answered. She was shy around all strangers but me. I was the only one she trusted.

Another day of being mean to Cindy had caused everywhere to be named off-limits to me. But I was clever and stole outside and snuck quickly away, to next door, to where people liked me.

"Where's my pony?" I screeched when I saw the barn still empty. "You promised me a pony—so if you don't give me one I'll tell Momma and Daddy you are trying to steal me away!"

She seemed to shrink inside her ugly black robe while those pale, thin hands of hers fluttered to the neckline so she could tug out a heavy rope of pearls she usually kept hidden.

"Tomorrow, Bart. Tomorrow you get your heart's desire."

Met John Amos on the way home. He led me into his secret cubbyhole and whispered of "man-doings." "Women like her are born rich and they never need brains," said John Amos, his watery eyes hard and slitlike. "You listen to me, boy, and never fall in love with a stupid woman. And *all* women are stupid. When you deal with women you have to let them know who is boss right from the start—and never let them forget it. Now, your lesson for today. Who is Malcolm Neal Foxworth?"

"My great-grandfather who is dead and gone but powerful even so," I said, not really understanding even as I said it.

"What else was Malcolm Neal Foxworth?"

"A saint. A saint deserving of a lordly place in heaven."

"Correct. But tell it all, leave nothing out."

"Never was there a man born smarter than Malcolm Neal Foxworth."

"That's not all I've taught you. You should know more about him from reading his journal. Are you reading it daily? He wrote in that book faithfully all his life. I've read it a dozen or more times. To read is to learn and to grow. So never stop reading your great-grandfather's journal until you are just as clever and smart as he is."

"Is clever the same as being smart?"

"No, of course not! Clever is not letting people suspect just how smart you are."

"Why didn't Malcolm like his momma?" I asked, though I knew she'd run away, but would that make me hate my momma?

"Like his mother? Lord God above, boy, Malcolm was wild about his mother until she ran off with her lover and left Malcolm with his father, who was too busy to pay him any attention. If you read on, boy, you'll find out soon just what turned Malcolm against all women. Read on and increase your knowledge. Malcolm's wisdom will become yours. He will teach you to never trust a woman to be there when you need her."

"But my momma is a good momma," I defended weakly, not so sure anymore that it was true. Life was so "devious." (New word for today, devious.)

"Now, Bart," Daddy had said early this morning when he carefully printed the word and explained to me exactly what it meant, "I want you and Jory to find a way to fit *devious* into your conversation today at least five times. It means departing from the shortest way; crooked and unfair—D-E-V-I-O-U-S."

Spelled it for me, Golly day, I sure hated living in a "devious world." Dratted new vocabulary words were teaching me how *devious* everyone could be.

"Now I'm going to leave you alone so you can read more of Malcolm's words," said John Amos before he shuffled off, bent slightly forward and to the side.

I opened the book to the page where the leather bookmark was.

Today I just wanted to try a little of my father's tobacco, so I filled his pipe with what I found in his office, then stole outside and smoked behind the garage.

I don't know how he found out unless one of the servants told on me, but he knew. Fire came in his hard eyes and he ordered me to strip down to naked. Cringing, I cried when he whipped me, and then he put me in the attic until I could learn the ways of the Lord and redeem my sins. While I was up there I found old photographs of my mother when she was a just a girl. How beautiful she was, so innocent and sweet-looking. I hated her! I wanted her to die that very moment wherever she was in the world. I wanted her to be suffering as I was, with cuts bleeding down my back, while I nearly suffocated in that airless hot attic.

I found things in that attic, corsets with laces so a woman swelled out in front, deceiving men into believing she has more than what came naturally. I knew I would never be deceived by any woman, no matter how beautiful. For it was beauty that put me in the attic, and beauty that used the whip on my back, and it wasn't really my father's fault what he did. He was hurting too, like I was.

Now I knew what he'd said all the time was true: No woman could be trusted. And most especially those with beautiful faces and seductive bodies.

Lifting my eyes I stared into space, seeing not the barn and all the hay, but the sweet and beautiful face of my mother. Was *she* devious? Would she one day run away with her "lover" and leave me to fend for myself with a stepfather who didn't love me nearly as much as he loved Jory and Cindy?

What would I do then? Would my grandmother take me in?

I asked her later on. "Yes, my love, I will take you in. I will care for you, fight for you, do what I can for you, for you are the true son of my second husband, Bart Winslow. Haven't I told you that before? Trust me, believe in me, and stay away from John Amos. He is not the kind of friend you should have."

Son of her second husband. Did that mean my momma had been married to him too? All the time marryin somebody! I closed my eyes and thought about Malcolm, who was long gone in his grave. Rock, rock, rock went her chair. Thud, thud, thud went the dirt on my grave. Dark now. Smothery. Cramped and cold. Heaven . . . where was Heaven?

"Bart, your eyes are glassy."

"Tired, Grandmother, so tired."

"Soon you will have your heart's desire."

Money, wanted money, piles and piles of greenbacks. At that moment someone banged on the front door. I jumped off her lap and quickly hid.

Jory ran in ahead of John Amos, who had admitted him. "Where is my brother?" he asked, looking around the room. "I don't like what's happening to him and I think it has something to do with coming over here—"

"Jory," said my grandmother, putting out her hand with all the sparkling, jeweled fingers. "Don't glare at me. I don't harm him. I only give him a little ice cream after his meals. Sit down and talk for a while. I'll send for refreshments."

Ignoring her, with the nose of a bloodhound Jory raced straight to me and yanked me out from behind the potted palms. "No thank you, lady," he said coldly. "My mom gives me all I need to eat—and what you're doing over here is changing him, so please don't let him come again."

Her barely visible lips clamped together and I saw tears in her eyes as I was pulled away. Jory shook me in our backyard. "Don't you ever go back there again, Bart Sheffield! She is not your grandmother! You look at her as if you like her more than Mom!"

There were some who said Bart Winslow Scott Sheffield was not as tall as other boys at nine. But I knew as soon as I hit ten I'd shoot up like a weed in the summertime. Soon as I was in Disneyland again, I'd be inspired enough to grow as tall as a giant.

"Why are you looking so solemn, darling?" asked Grandmother when I was snuggled on her lap again the next day. The pony still hadn't come.

"Not coming to see you no more," I said grumpily. "Daddy will give me a pony for my birthday when I tell him again I want one. Won't need yours."

"Bart, you haven't told your parents about me, have you?"

"No, ma'am."

"If you lie God will punish you."

Sure, why not? Everybody else did. "Never tell nobody nothing," I mumbled. "Momma and Daddy don't like me noway. They got Jory. Now they got Cindy, too. That's enough for them."

She took a quick glance around, paying special attention to the pocket doors that were closed and latched tight. She whispered. "Bart, I've seen you talking to John, I've asked you to stay away from him. He's an evil old man who can be very cruel. Keep that in mind."

Gee, who could I trust? He said the same thing about her. Once I'd thought everyone in my family could be trusted. Now I was learning people weren't always what they seemed to be on the surface. Weren't loving, never cared enough, especially when it came to me. Maybe it was only Grandmother who really cared—and John Amos. Then I was bewildered again. Was John Amos my true friend? If he was, then my grandmother couldn't be. Had to choose. Which to choose? How did I make big decisions like that? Then, when Grandmother had her arms about me, my face held to her soft breast, I knew, she was the one who loved me best. She was my own true-for-a-fact grandmother.

But . . . what if she wasn't?

I'd seen my grandmother a dozen or more times. John Amos had been my friend only for a few days. Maybe if he waited for me seven times in a row that would tell me he was lucky and good for me. Seven times of anything meant good luck. Five times of talking to me in his spooky place had taught me already that women were sneaky and devious.

"Bart, my darling," whispered my granny, putting her dry lips on my cheek near my ear. "Don't look so afraid, just leave John Amos alone, and don't believe anything he tells you." She stroked my face, then I felt her smile. "Now, if you run down to the barn and take a look inside, you will find something any boy would love to have, and those who don't will envy you."

She started to say something else, but I jumped from her lap and raced from her room and ran all the way to the barn. Oh gosh, oh gee, every day I carried an apple in my pocket, just hoping. Every day I carried lumps of Momma's sugar, just hoping. Prayed every night for that pony I just had to have. This pony was going to love me more than anybody! I ran to the barn and didn't fall once. Then I pulled up short and stared. THAT wasn't a pony!

It was only a dog. A big hairy dog who stood with his tail waggin, and his eyes lookin at me adoringly already, and I hadn't done one thing to win his love. I wanted to cry. It was leashed and tied by a rope to a stump in the barn dirt floor. The dog wiggled all over, as if happy to see me—and I hated that dog.

Behind me she came runnin up, all breathless and pantin. "Bart, darling, don't be disappointed. I really wanted to give you a pony, but as I told you, if I did, you would go home reeking of horses, and Jory and your parents would find out, and never let you come back to visit me."

I sank down on my knees and bowed my head. I wanted to die. I'd eaten all that ice cream, suffered through all those kisses and hugs . . . and still she hadn't given me a pony. "You lied to me." I choked, with tears in my eyes. "You've made me waste all my days visitin you when I could have done somethin better." And there I went, dropping my G's again. Not so grown up after all.

"Bart, darling, you don't understand about St. Bernards at all!" she said, gathering me up in her arms. "This dog is still just a puppy, and see how big he is. He will grow up to be as big as a pony. You can saddle him and ride him around. And did you know in the mountains they use this breed of dog to rescue people who have been lost in the snow? A keg of brandy is tied around the dog's neck, and all by himself, a dog like this can find a lost man and save his life. A St. Bernard is the world's most heroic dog."

I didn't believe her. Still, I had to stare at the puppy with more interest—that was a puppy? He strained at his leash, trying to get at me, and I liked him a little more for doing that. "Will he really grow up to be as big as a pony?"

"Bart, he's only six months old, and already he's almost as big as some ponies!" She laughed and caught my hand and pulled me inside the barn. "See," she said, pointing to a red saddle with bit and bridle, and then to a little two-wheeled red cart. "You can ride him, or hitch him to the cart—and have an all-purpose dog or pony, whatever you want. All you have to do is use your imagination."

"Will he bite me?"

"No, of course not. Darling, look at him, how happy he is to see a boy. Put out your hand and let him sniff your palm. Treat him kindly, feed him well, and keep his hair free of briars and tangles, and you will not only have the most beautiful dog in the world, but the best friend of your life."

Fearfully I inched my hand away from my body—and the puppy licked it like ice cream. Slurpy kisses. I laughed because it tickled. "Go way, Grandmother," I ordered.

She backed way reluctantly while I knelt in front of the pony so I could tell it what it was. "Now you look here," I said firmly, "and you remember what I say. You *are not* a dog but a pony. You are not meant to carry brandy in kegs to people who are lost and snowed in—you are meant for carrying me only. You are my pony, and mine alone!"

He looked at me as if bewildered, cocking his big shaggy head to one side as he sat on his haunches. "Don't you sit like that!" I yelled. "Ponies don't sit, only dogs."

"Bart," came my grandmother's soft voice, "be kind, remember."

I ignored her. Women didn't count in man-doings like

this. John Amos had told me that. Men ruled the world, and women had to sit back and keep quiet.

I had to cast a spell and make a puppy over into a pony. Mean witches on stage knew how to do that. I thought and thought about every stage witch I'd seen in ballets and finally I thought I knew just how it was done.

Needed a long hooked nose and a jutting long chin, and hollowed-out eyes and bony long fingers with black nails two inches long. Only thing I had right was mean, black, piercing eyes—maybe that would do the trick. Knew how to make mean eyes real good.

I flung my arms overhead, curled my fingers into claws, hunched my back, and cast my spell: "I chrisss-en thee Apple! With this magic potion I give, and with this spell I put upon thee, I make you into a pony." I gave him the magic potion which was an apple. "Now you are mine, all mine! Never will you eat or drink if I am not the one to give you the food and water. Never will you love anyone but me. You will run to me and die when I do. MINE, APPLE, MINE! NOW AND FOR-EVERMORE . . . MINE!"

The power of my magic spell had Apple sniffing at the fruit I offered. He whimpered unhappily and turned his nose away, showing more interest in the sugar I was saving for later. "Now, don't you whinny and try to eat everything," I scolded, biting into the apple myself to show him how it was done. Again I held the apple out for my pony to eat. Again he turned away his giant white and golden head. Some of his fur was reddish gold and sorta pretty. I bit into the apple again and chewed, showing him what good food he was missing.

"Bart," called Grandmother with a choke in her voice, "perhaps I made a mistake. I'll take the puppy back to the pet shop and buy you that pony you wanted."

I looked from her to my new pet, then toward my home, considering. They'd be sure to smell a horse, if ponies smelled horsey. And doggy smells would seem natural; they'd be convinced Clover had finally learned to trust me—when he never would let me near him. "Grandmother, I'm going to keep this here puppy-pony. I'll teach him all about how to play horse. If he doesn't learn before I go to Disneyland you can take him back—and never can I come to visit you again."

Laughing and happy then, I fell onto the hay and frolicked with my puppy-pony, the only puppy-pony in the whole wide world. And his big warm body felt good in my arms, real good.

I looked at her, then, and I knew John Amos was wrong. Women were not evil and devious, and I was so relieved to have found out at last that it was John Amos who was devious, and Momma and my grandmother were the best things in my whole life—next to Apple.

"Grandmother, are you truly my real grandmother, and my real daddy was your second husband?"

"Yes, it's true," she said with her head bowed. "But it's a secret. Just between us. You must promise not to tell anyone." She seemed to droop, looking sad, but I was so happy inside I wanted to burst. A puppy-pony and a real grandmother who had been married to my real father. Gosh, I was getting lucky at last.

And there I was saying my "ings." That's what loving Apple and my grandmother did for me, taught me how to pronounce the "ings" with a G. In only one day they had succeeded, when Momma and Daddy had been trying for years and years.

Soon I found out that eating had lots to do with loving. The more food I gave Apple, the more he loved me. And without the help of more spells, he was mine, all mine. When I came in the mornings he raced to me, jumping up and spinning in circles, wagging his tail, licking my face. When I hitched him to the new pony cart he bucked just like a real horse. Tried his best to rid himself of the small saddle I put on his back too. Boy, just wait until Jory got a load of the kind of magic I could work.

"Gonna be eleven soon," I said to Grandmother one

day, in hopes of giving her a few ideas. "Ten," she corrected. "You will be ten on your next birthday."

"Eleven!" I shouted, insisting. "All year I've been going on ten. I have to be eleven by now."

"Bart, don't start wishing your life away. Time goes by quickly enough. Hold on to your youth, stay as you are."

I went on stroking Apple's head. "Granny, tell me about your little boys."

She looked sad again, not from her face I couldn't see, but from the way her shoulders drooped. "One went to heaven," she whispered hoarsely, "the other ran away."

"Where did the other go?" I asked, thinking maybe I'd go there too.

"South," she said simply, drooping more.

"I'm going south too. Hate that place!—full of ole graves and full of ole grandmothers. One is locked up in a looney bin. The other is a mean-faced ole witch. You're my best grandmother," for by now I knew she couldn't be Daddy's crazy mother, but the mother of my real daddy. And women changed names when they changed husbands, so that's . . . and then I knew I didn't even know her last or first name. "Corrine Winslow," she said when I asked, her head still bowed. I could see a little of her face where her nose lifted the black veil from her cheeks. A bit of her hair showed too. Gray hair with streaks of gleaming gold, soft hair. I pitied her. She was really going to suffer when I was gone.

"Going to Disneyland, Grandmother. Gonna stay there one week and have a party with more gifts from Momma and Daddy and Jory and Emma, and then we'll all fly East and spend two rotten weeks just visiting—"

"I know," she interrupted with a smile in her voice, "two weeks wasted by visiting ole graves and ole grandmothers. But you have a good time anyway." She leaned to kiss and hug me tight. "And while you're gone I'll take good care of Apple."

"NO!" I screamed, terrified Apple would love her more

than me when I came back. "You leave my pet alone. He's mine. Don't you go feedin him and makin him more yours than mine."

She agreed to do what I wanted. I told her next I was gonna find a way to go to Disneyland, then sneak back to take care of Apple. How I was gonna do this wasn't really clear in my mind—and from the way she looked, it wasn't clear in hers either.

Later I was in the barn with Apple. John Amos stood tall and skinny above, as I sprawled on the hay. He lectured again on how evil women were, and how they made men "sin."

"Nobody does anything for nothing," he said. "Don't you think for one second she doesn't have wicked plans for you, Bart Winslow."

"Why'd you call me that?"

"It's your name, isn't it?"

I grinned, really proud to tell him I had the longest name ever.

"That's not important," he said with no patience. "Be attentive, boy. You asked me yesterday about sin and I wanted to tell you exactly, but I had to plan the wording. Sin is what men and women do together when they close their bedroom door."

"What's so bad about sin?"

He scowled, showing his teeth, and I shrank back into the hay, wishing he'd go away and leave me and Apple alone.

"Sin is what women use to make a man weak. You've got to face up to certain facts. Inside of every man there is a weak, spineless streak, and women know how to find it by taking off their clothes and using earthly pleasures to sap a man's strength by desire. Watch your own mother, see how she smiles at your father, how she paints her face and nails and wears skimpy clothes, and see your stepfather's eyes light up—both are on their way to sinning when you see that."

I swallowed, kinda hurting inside. Didn't want my parents to do bad things to make God punish them.

"Now hear the words of Malcolm again. 'I cried and cried for five years after my mother went away and left me with my father, who hated me for being hers. He told me all the time she was married to him she was unfaithful, deceiving him with many lovers. And then he couldn't love me. Couldn't stand for me to be near him, and it grew so lonely shut up in that big house with no one who cared. Time and again Father told me he'd never be able to remarry because of me. None of his paramours liked me. But they did fear me. You can bet I let them know what I thought. I knew they'd burn in the eternal fires of hell.'"

"What's a paramour?" I asked, bored sometimes with Malcolm.

"A derelict soul on its way to hell." His eyes burned into me. "And don't you think you can go away on a vacation and leave the care of Apple to another. When you accept the love of an animal, that animal is your responsibility for its entire life. You feed him, water him, groom and exercise him—or God will see that you suffer!"

I shivered and looked at my puppy-pony, who was chasing his tail.

"There is power in your dark eyes, Bart. The same kind of power Malcolm had. God has sent you to carry out an unfinished duty. Malcolm will never rest easy in his grave until all the Devil's spawn are sent down to roast over the fires of hell!"

"Fires of hell," I repeated dully.

"Two are there already . . . three more to go."

"Three more to go."

"Evil seeds reproduce and multiply over and over."

"Over and over."

"And when you have done your duty, Malcolm will rest easy in his grave."

"Rest easy in my grave."

"What's that you said?"

I was confused. Sometimes I pretended *I* was Malcolm. John Amos smiled for some reason and seemed pleased. I was allowed to go home then.

Jory came on the run to question me. "Where've you been? What do you do over there? I see you talking to that old butler. What does he tell you?"

He made me feel like a mouse facing up to a lion. Then I remembered Malcolm's book and how he handled situations like this. I put a cold mask on my face. "John Amos and I have secrets that are none of your damn business."

Jory stared. I strode off.

Under a huge spreading tree Momma was pushing Cindy in her baby-swing. Sissy girls had to be strapped in to keep from falling out. "Bart," she called, "where have you been?"

"Nowhere!" I snapped.

"Bart, I don't like smart answers."

I stopped and decided I'd do like Malcolm and wither her small with my mean glare—instead I saw to my amazement she wore a skimpy blue halter-top that didn't meet the top of her white shorts, showing her belly button. She was showing bare skin! Sin was connected to bare skin. In the Bible the Lord had commanded Adam and Eve to put on clothes and cover their wicked flesh. Was my momma just as sinful as that wicked Corrine who had run off with her "paramour"?

"Bart, don't stare like you don't know who I am."

Into my mind popped one of the lines from the Bible John Amos was always quoting. Bit by bit I was learning what God expected from the people he created. "Be warned, Momma, the Lord will see when I do not, and He will punish."

Momma almost jumped. Then she swallowed and in a dry voice asked, "Why did you say that?"

Look at her tremble, I thought. I turned my head to glare at all the naked statues in this evil garden of sin. Wicked naked people made Malcolm rest uneasy in his grave.

But I loved her; she was my mother; sometimes she came

and kissed me good night and stayed to hear my prayers. Before Cindy came she was better and spent more time with me. And she didn't appear to be in love with a "paramour."

Didn't know what to do. "Sleepy, Momma," I said and then drifted away, feeling at odds with myself and the rest of the world. What if what Malcolm wrote, and John Amos quoted, was true? Was she evil and sinful, luring men to be like animals? Was it bad to be like animals? Apple wasn't bad, or sinful. Not even Clover was, and he didn't like me.

Inside Jory's room I paused before his thirty-gallon aquarium. The air made a steady stream of tiny bubbles that burbled to the surface like the champagne Momma had let me sip once.

Pretty fish wouldn't live in my tank. Fish in Jory's tank never died. My empty tank held nothing but water, and a toy pirate ship spilled out fake jewels on the fake ocean floor. Jory's tank grew seaweed that snaked in and out of a small castle. His fish darted in and out of coral reefs.

Jory did everything better than me. I didn't like being Bart anymore. Bart had to stay home and forget about Disneyland now that he had responsibilities.

A pet could be a heavy, heavy burden.

I fell on my bed and stared up at the ceiling. Malcolm didn't need his power and strength anymore, or his clever brain that was smart too. He was dead and his talents were wasted. Nobody ever made Malcolm do anything he didn't want to after he grew up. Didn't want to be a boy anymore. Wanted to be a man, like Malcolm the powerful, the financial wizard.

Was gonna make people jump when I spoke. Tremble when I looked. Cower when I moved. The day was coming. Felt it.

Shadows

Jory," said Mom as we picked up our totes and headed for her car, "I can't understand what's happening to Bart this summer. He's not the same child. What do you think he does outside alone all the time?"

I felt uncomfortable. I wanted to protect Bart and let him have the old lady next door for this friend, and I couldn't tell Mom that woman was saying she was Bart's grandmother. "Don't you worry about Bart, Mom," I assured her. "You just keep on having fun with Cindy. She's sure a cute kid, like you must have been."

She smiled and kissed my cheek. "If my eyes aren't deceiving me, there's another cute kid you admire too."

I felt a blush heat up my cheeks. I couldn't help but look at Melodie Richarme. She was so darn pretty, with hair that was a deeper shade of blonde than Mom's, but blue eyes that were just as soft and shining. I thought I'd never love any girl who didn't have blue eyes. Just then Melodie showed up, running to her father's car, making me stare at the way she was turning into a woman. Gosh, it was miraculous the way flat-chested little girls showed up one day with bosoms, tiny waists, and swelling hips, and suddenly they were ten times more interesting.

The minute we hit home Mom had me hunting up Bart. "If he's over in that other yard, you tell me. I don't want you children bothering an old recluse, though I wish to heaven she'd stop climbing that ladder and staring at me over the wall."

Climbing, jumping, calling, I searched until I found Bart in the old barn that had once been what was called in olden times "a carriage house." Now it had empty stalls where horses used to live, and Bart was in one, using a rake to pull out the dirty hay. I stared, disbelieving my eyes. With him was a St. Bernard puppy. The dog was almost as big as he was. It was easy enough to tell it was only a puppy, for it had kiddish ways, frolicking and making puppy noises.

Bart threw down his rake and scolded the dog. "You stop jumping around like that, Apple! Ponies don't jump anything but hurdles—now you eat that hay or I won't give you clean hay tomorrow."

"Bart . . . ," I called softly, leaning against the barn wall and smiling to see *him* jump. "Dogs don't eat hay."

His face flamed. "You go 'way! You get out of here! You don't belong!"

"Neither do you."

"You get out of here," he sobbed, hurling down his rake and pulling the huge puppy into his arms. "This is my dog; he was supposed to have been a pony—so I'm making him both a puppy and a pony. Don't you laugh and think I'm crazy."

"I don't think you're crazy," I said, a lump in my throat to see him so upset. It really was a shame I had more affinity for animals than he did. They seemed to know he'd step on their tails or trip over them. In fact, even I wasn't too comfortable lying on the floor when Bart was around.

"Who gave you the puppy?"

"My grandmother," Bart said, with so much pride in his eyes. "She loves me, Jory, really loves me more than Momma does. And she loves me more than your ole Madame Marisha loves you!"

That was the trouble with Bart. No sooner did I feel close to him than he slapped me in my face, making me regret I'd ever let him under my skin.

I didn't pat the beautiful puppy on his head, though he was making up to me. I let Bart have his way; maybe this time he'd make a friend after all.

He smiled at me happily as we headed for home. "You're not mad at me?" he asked. Of course I wasn't. "You won't tell on me, Jory? It's important not to tell Momma or Daddy."

I didn't like to keep secrets from my parents, but Bart was insistent, and what would it hurt anyway if a kind lady gave Bart a few gifts and a new puppy? She was making him feel loved and happy.

In the kitchen Emma was spooning cereal into Cindy's open mouth. Cindy had been dressed by Mom in new baby-blue coveralls with a white blouse embroidered with pink rabbits. Mom had done that embroidery work herself. Cindy's hair had been brushed until it gleamed like silvery gold; a blue satin ribbon held her ponytail high on the back of her head. She was so clean and fresh I wanted to hug her, but I only smiled. I knew better than to be demonstrative when Bart was around to get jealous. Strangely, it was Bart who fascinated Cindy far more than me. Perhaps because he wasn't so much larger than she was.

My brother hurled himself down into a kitchen chair that almost toppled over backward from the force. Emma looked his way and frowned. "Go wash your hands and face, Bart Winslow, if you expect to eat at my table."

"Not your table," he grouched as he headed for the bathroom. He pulled his dirty hands along the walls to leave long smudges.

"Bart! Take your filthy hands off the walls!" called Emma sternly.

"Not her walls," he mumbled. It took him forever to wash his hands, and when he was back only his palms were clean. He stared with disgust at the soup and sandwiches Emma had prepared.

"Eat up, Bart, or you'll fade away to nothing," said Emma. Already I was on my second sandwich, my second bowl of homemade vegetable soup, and ready for dessert while Bart still nibbled on half of his sandwich, his soup as yet untouched.

"What do you think of your new sister?" asked Emma, wiping Cindy's messy mouth, taking off the soiled bib. "Isn't she a living doll?"

"Yeah, she's sure cute," I agreed.

"Cindy's not our sister!" flared Bart. "She's just another messy little baby that nobody but our mother would want!"

"Bartholomew Winslow . . . don't you ever let me hear you talk like that again." Emma gave him a long, chastising look. "Cindy is a lovely child who resembles your mother so much she could be her own daughter."

Bart continued to scowl at Cindy, at me, at Emma, even at the wall. "Hate blonde hair and red lips that are wet all the time," he mumbled under his breath before he stuck out his tongue at Cindy, who laughed and patty-caked. "If Momma didn't fuss around her so much, curling her hair and buying her new clothes, she'd be ugly."

"Cindy will never be ugly," denied Emma, looking at the little girl with admiration. Then she leaned to kiss the child's pretty small face.

That kiss drew another of Bart's darkest frowns.

I sat there, uptight, frightened. Each morning I woke up knowing I'd have to face a brother who was growing more and more strange. And I loved him; I loved my parents, and darn if I wasn't beginning to love Cindy too. Somehow I knew I had to protect everyone—but from what I didn't know and couldn't even guess.

Changeling Child

Drat Jory and Emma, I was thinking as I slipped through the hot Arizona desert. Good thing I had Apple to love me as well as my grandmother, or I'd be in a sorry state. There stood my lady in black with her arms wide open to welcome me and I was kissed and hugged much more than Cindy ever was.

She served me a bowl of soup. It was so good, with cheese on top. "Why can't I tell my parents how much I like you, and how much you love me? That would be so neat." I didn't tell her I thought she wasn't really my own true grandmother, but only said that to please her. In a way that made her love better, for families had to love each other. Strangers didn't.

Square in the middle of one of her tables she put a large dump truck before she answered my question. Odd she seemed so sad, and in a way scared, when a moment ago she'd seemed happy enough.

"Your parents hate me now, Bart," she whispered thinly. "Please don't tell them anything about me. Keep me your secret."

My eyes widened. "Did you know them once?"

"Yes, a long, long time ago, when they were very young."

Gee. "What did you do to make them hate you?" Everyone hated me, almost, so I wasn't surprised someone might hate her.

Her hand reached for mine. "Bart, sometimes even adults make mistakes. I made a terrible mistake that I'm paying for dearly. Every night I pray for God to forgive me; I pray for my children to forgive me. I find no peace when I look in the mirror, so I hide my face from myself, from others, and sit in uncomfortable rockers so I'll never forget for one second all the harm I did to those I loved most."

"Where did your children go?"

"Have you forgotten?" she sobbed, tears in her eyes now. "They ran away from me. Bart, that hurts so much. Don't you ever run away from your parents."

Gosh, hadn't intended to run. World out there was too big. Too scary. Safe, had to stay where it was safe. I ran to embrace her, then turned to play with my truck—and that's when John Amos limped into the room, his watery eyes angry. "Madame! You do not develop strength in young children by indulging their every whim. You should know that by now."

"John," she said haughtily, "don't you ever come in this room again without knocking—stay in your place."

Tough. My grandmother was tough. I smiled at John Amos, who backed away, mumbling under his breath about how she wasn't giving him *any* place, or not the place he deserved. I forgot him the moment he was out of sight as I fell under the spell of my enchanting new dump truck and why it worked like it did. Soon I'd find out—and maybe my curiosity was the same thing as being mean, for everything given to me ended up broken within an hour.

My grandmother sighed and looked unhappy as my truck came apart.

~ ~ ~

Long summer days passed slowly, with John Amos teaching me lots of important things about being powerful and fearsome like Malcolm, who knew all about being sneaky and clever. In his own kind of way John Amos was fascinating, with his queer shuffling walk, his skinny legs more knobby than mine, his whistling breath, his hissing words, his stringy mustache and bald head where one white hair grew. One day I was gonna pull it out. Wonder why my grandmother didn't like him. She was the boss, she could fire him, and yet she didn't. Something hard and mean was between them.

I was happy living between them, blessed on one side by my grandmother, with all her nice gifts, her hugs and kisses, and on the other side by John Amos, who was teaching me how to be a powerful man who could make women do his bidding. And now that I had someone who loved me for myself, no matter how mean or clumsy I was, I began to feel that special kind of magic that Momma and Jory shared. I thought I, too, could hear the music of sunset colors. I thought the lemon tree made little harp chords sound. I had Apple, my puppy-pony. And, best of all, Disneyland was waiting for me and my birthday was coming up soon.

Now that I was getting brilliant like Malcolm, I tried to figure out a way to keep Apple's love while I went away for three weeks. It woke me up at night. Worried me all day. Who would feed Apple and steal his love while I was gone? Who?

I went back to the wall and checked on a peach pit that hadn't sprouted any roots as yet. It was supposed to be growing—and it wasn't. Next I checked my sweetpea seeds. Dumb things were just lying there, not doing anything.

Cursed. I was cursed. I glared at the part of the garden Jory cared for. All his flowers were in full bloom. Wasn't fair how even flowers wouldn't grow for me. I crawled to where Jory's hollyhocks grew. My knees crushed petunias, squashed portulaca. What would Malcolm do if he was me? He'd rip up all of Jory's flowers, dig holes with his thumbs in his own garden, and stick in the blossoms.

One by one I filled my thumb holes with Jory's hollyhocks. They refused to stand up straight, but I arranged them so they could lean against one another and now I had blooming flowers in my garden too. Clever. Devious and sneaky—smart too.

Glanced down at my filthy knees and saw I'd ripped my new pants on the doghouse I'd started building for Clover. It was my way of asking forgiveness for tripping over him so often. Right now he was up on that "veranda" keeping a keen eye on me, afraid to sleep while I was in sight. I didn't need him now. Once I had, but now I had a better pet.

Bugs were biting my face. I rubbed at my eyes, not caring if my hands were covered with grease from fooling around in my dad's garage workshop. Emma wouldn't like seeing my new white tank top that had grease all over, and even Momma couldn't repair the rip from neck to shirttail. I chewed on my lip.

Saturdays were for having fun and I wasn't having any. Nothing special to do like Jory. Wasn't born to dance, only to get dirty and have scratches. Momma had Cindy. Daddy had patients. Emma had cooking and cleaning. Nobody cared if I was bored. I threw Clover a hateful look. "I gotta dog better than you!" I yelled. Clover backed up closer to the house, then hid under a chair. "You're just a miniature French poodle!" I screamed. "You don't know how to save people lost in the snow! You don't know how to wear a red saddle or eat hay either!" Every day I was giving Apple a little more hay that I mixed up in his dogfood just so he'd get to like hay better than meat.

Clover looked ashamed. He inched himself under the chair more and gave me another of his sad looks that got on my nerves. Apple never did that.

I sighed, got up, brushed off my knees, my hands. Time to visit Apple. On my way over I got distracted by the white wall, which needed more texture. Picking up a stone, I began to pound on the wall in order to chip off more of the white stucco. Gosh, what if this wall went on forever? It might even end up in China, keeping out the Mongol hordes. Wonder what Mongols were? Apes? Yeah, sounded like apes—mean kind of big apes that ate people who were in the *throes* of something. Would be nice to be as huge as King Kong so I could step on things I hated.

I'd step on teachers first, schools next—and step over churches. Malcolm respected God, and I didn't want to make God mad with me. I'd pluck the stars from the sky and stick them on my fingers for diamond rings, like my grandmother's. I'd wear the moon for my cap. I'd leave the sun alone because it might burn my hand—but if I picked up the Empire State Building I could use it as a bat and swat that sun right out of our universe! Then everything would go black as tar. There'd be no daytime and only forever night. Black was like being blind, or dead.

"Bart," came a soft voice, making me jump.

"Go 'way!" I ordered. I was having fun all by myself. And what was she doing up on that ladder again? Spying on me? I sat on the ground again and poked at it with a stick.

"Bart," she called again. "Apple is waiting for you to feed him, and he needs fresh water. You promised to be a good master. Once you make an animal love and trust you, you are obligated to it."

Today her eyes weren't covered over; the veil only covered from her nose downward. "I want cowboy boots, a new genuine cowboy saddle of real leather, not fake, and a hat, buckskins, chaps, spurs, and beans to cook over campfires."

"What is that you just dug up?" She poked her head up higher to see better. She looked funny, like a head on the wall with no body underneath.

Gosh . . . look what was buried in the dirt. Dead bones. Where had the fur gone? And the soft white ears?

I began to tremble, very scared as I tried to explain. "Tiger.

There I was the other night, helpless, wearing only my pajamas, when out of the dark came this man-eating tiger with the green eyes. He snarled, then jumped me. He meant to eat me. But I grabbed up my rifle in the nick of time and shot him through his eye!"

Silence. Silence meant she didn't believe me. Pity was in her voice when she spoke. "Bart, that's not the skeleton of a tiger. I see a bit of the fur. Is that the kitten I used to have? The stray one I took in and cared for? Bart, why did you kill my kitten?"

"NOOO!" I yelled. "Wouldn't kill a kitty! Wouldn't ever do that! I like kitties. This is a tiger, a not so big one. Old bones been here a mighty long time, way before I was born." Yet, they looked like kitty bones, they did. I rubbed at my eyes so she wouldn't see the tears.

Malcolm wouldn't cry like this. He'd be tough. Didn't know what to do. Ole John Amos over there kept telling me to be like Malcolm, and hate all women. I decided it was better to act like Malcolm than like me who was a sorry thing. Wasn't no good trying to be King Kong, Tarzan, or even Superman; being Malcolm was better, for I had his book of instructions of how to do it right.

"Bart, it's growing very late. Apple is hungry and waiting for you."

Tired, so tired. "I'm coming," I said wearily. Gee, pretending to be an old man was tiring. Bad to act so old, better to be a boy again. Old meant no time off from work and trying to make money with no fun at all. Took all my time getting there now that I made my legs walk slow. Foggy all around. Summer wasn't so hot when you were old. *Momma, Momma, where are you? Why don't you come when I need you? When I call, why don't you answer? Don't you love me anymore, Momma? Momma, why aren't you helping me?*

I stumbled on, trying to think. Then I found the answer. Nobody *could* like me, for I didn't belong here, and I didn't belong there. I didn't belong anywhere.

PART TWO

Tales of Evil

I gobbled down my bacon, scrambled eggs with sour cream and chives, and a third slice of toast as Bart nibbled on and on as if he didn't have any teeth at all. His toast grew cold—waiting for Bart to sip orange juice as if it were poison. An old man on his deathbed could have had more appetite.

He shot a hostile glance my way before he fixed his eyes on Mom. I was jolted. I knew he loved her—how could he look like that?

Something weird was going on in Bart's head. Where was the shy, introverted little brother I used to have? Gradually he was changing into an aggressive, suspicious, cruel boy. Now he was staring at Dad as if he'd done something wrong—but it was Mom who drew most of his scathing looks.

Didn't he know we had the best mother alive? I wanted to shout this out, make him go back to the way he used to be, mumbling to himself as he stumbled around hunting big game, fighting wars, riding herd on cattle. Where had all his love and admiration for Mom gone? Soon as I had the chance I backed Bart up against the garden wall. "What the heck is wrong with you, Bart? Why do you look at Mom so mean?"

"Don't like her no more." He crouched over, put out his arms horizontally and turned himself into a human airplane. That was normal—for Bart. "Clear the way!" he ordered. "Make way for the jet taking off for faraway places!—it's kangaroo shootin time in Australia!"

"Bart Sheffield, why do you always want to kill something?"

His wings fluttered; his plane stalled; his engine died and he was staring at me in confusion. The sweet child he'd been at the beginning of summer came fleeting to his dark brown eyes. "Not gonna kill real kangaroos. Just gonna capture one of those itty-bitty ones and put it in my pocket and wait for it to grow big."

Dumb. Dumb! "First of all, you don't have a pocket with a nipple for the baby to suck." I sat him down hard on a bench. "Bart, it's time you and I had a man-to-man talk. What's troubling you, fella?"

"In a big bright house setting on a high-high hill, while the night was on and the snow came down, the flames of red and yellow shot up higher, higher! Snowflakes turned pink. And in that big old house was an old-old lady who couldn't walk and couldn't talk and my real daddy who was an attorney ran to save her. He couldn't!—and he burned!—burned!—burned!"

Spooky. Crazy. I pitied him. "Bart," I began carefully, "you know that isn't the way Daddy Paul died." Why had I put it like that? Bart had been born only a few years before Daddy Paul died. How many years? Almost I could remember my thoughts back then. I could ask Momma, but somehow I didn't want to trouble her more, so I led Bart toward our house. "Bart, your real daddy died while he was sitting on his front veranda reading the newspaper. He didn't die in a fire. He had heart trouble that led to a coronary thrombosis. Dad told us all that, remember?"

I watched his brown eyes grow darker, his pupils dilate, before he raged with a terrible temper. "Don't mean *that* daddy! Talking about my *real* daddy! A big strong lawyer daddy who never had a bad heart!"

"Bart, who told you that lie?"

"Burning!" he screamed, whirling around like a man blinded by smoke as he tried to find his way outside. "John Amos told me how it was. All the world was on fire, one Christmas night when the tree burned up. People screamed, ran, stepped on the ones who fell down!—and the biggest, grandest house of them all snared my true father so he died, died, died!"

Boy, I'd heard enough. I was going straight into the house and tell my parents. "Bart, you hear this. Unless you stop going next door and listening to lies and crazy stories, I'm telling Mom and Dad about you—and them next door."

He had his eyes squinted shut, as if trying to see some scene scorched on his brain. He seemed to be looking inward as he described it in more detail to me. Then his dark eyes flew wide open. His look was wild and crazy. "Mind your own damn business, Jory Marquet, if you don't want yours." He swooped to pick up a discarded baseball bat, then took a wild swing that might have splattered my brains if I hadn't ducked. "You tell on me and Grandmother and I'll kill you while you sleep." He said it loud, cold and flat, his eyes challenging mine.

Swallowing, I felt fear raise the hair on my neck. Was I scared of him? No. I couldn't be. As I watched, he suddenly lost his bravado and began to gasp and clutch at his heart. I smiled, knowing his secret—his way of backing out of a real fighting encounter. "All right, Bart," I said coldly. "Now I'm going to let you have it. I'm going next door and I am going to speak to those old people who fill your head with garbage."

His old-man act was quickly abandoned. His lips gaped apart. He stared at me pleadingly, but I whirled on my heel and strode off, never thinking he'd do anything. Wham! Down flat on my face I fell with a weight on my back. Bart had tackled me. Before I could congratulate him for being fast and accurate for a change, he began to pummel my face with his fists.

"You won't look so pretty when I finish." I warded him off as best I could before I noticed he was delivering his blows with his eyes squeezed shut, punching blindly, childishly, sobbing as he did. And I swear, as much as I wanted to I couldn't punch out my kid brother.

"Got yah scared, huh?" He pulled back his upper lip and snarled, looking pleased with himself. "Guess yah know now who's boss, huh? Ain't got nearly the guts you thought you had, do yah?"

I shoved him hard. He fell backward, but darn if I could fight a baby like him, who was strong only when he was angry. "You need a good spanking, Bart Sheffield, and I might be just the one to give it to you. The next time you pull any stunt on me think twice—or *you* might be the one left without guts."

"Yer not my brother," he sobbed, all the fight gone out of him. "You're only a half brother, and that's as good as none." He choked on his own emotions and ground his fists into his eyes as he wailed louder.

"You see! That old woman is putting nutty ideas in your head, and one thing you don't need is more nuts in the belfry. She's turning you against your own family—and I'm going to tell her exactly that."

"Don't you dare!" He shrieked, his tears gone, his rage back. "I'll do something terrible. *I will! I swear I will! If you go you'll be sorry!*"

My smile was wry. "You and who else is gonna make me sorry?"

"I know what you want," he said, all child again. "You want my puppy-pony. But he won't like you, he won't! You want my grandmother to love you more, but she won't! You want to take everything from me—but you can't!"

I felt sorry for him, but I'd neglected my duty long enough. "Aw, go suck your baby bottle!" and with that I was off. He screamed behind me, yelling out how he'd make me sorry by hurting something that couldn't fight back. "And you'll cry, Jory!" he warned. "You'll cry more than you ever have before!"

The road was dappled with sunlight and shadows, and soon enough Bart and his temper were far behind me. The sun burned down hot on top of my head, and behind me little feet came running. I turned to see Clover racing to catch up. Waiting, I knelt to catch him as he leaped into my arms, licking my face with the same devoted adoration he'd given me since I was three.

Three years old. I remembered where Mom and I had lived then, in the Blue Ridge Mountains of Virginia, in a little cottage nestled down near the mountains. I remembered a tall man with dark eyes had given me not only Clover but also a cat named Calico, and a parakeet we called Buttercup. Calico had roamed off in the night and never came back. And Buttercup had died when I was seven. "Would you like to be my son?" I heard the man's voice in my memory. That man who was called . . . What was his name? Bart? Bart Winslow? Oh, golly, was I just beginning to understand something that had slipped over my head until now? Was my half brother Bart the son of that man, and not Daddy Paul? Why would Mom name her baby for a man not her husband?

"You gotta go back home now, Clover," I said, and he seemed to understand. "You're eleven years old and not up to frisking around in the noonday sun. Go back and find your favorite cool place and wait for me, okay?"

Wagging his tail, he turned obediently and headed home, looking back often to see if I'd turn away and he could follow again. I watched until he was out of sight around the bend in the road. Then I headed once more for the huge old mansion. In my head the distant past beat like muffled drums, reminding me of events I'd forgotten. The ballet on Christmas Eve, and the handsome man who gave me my first electric train. I shut off memories, wanting to keep my mother sacred, my love for Daddy Paul intact, my respect for Chris intact too. No, I wasn't going to let myself remember too much.

Lovers came and went in everyone's life, I told myself, if ballets were just true stories exaggerated a bit. And like my dad would, I strode boldly up to the iron fence and demanded into the box to be let in. The iron gates swung silently open, like jail bars to beckon me forward. I almost ran up the curving drive until I was before the double front doors, and there I jabbed at the doorbell, then banged the brass knocker as loud as I could.

Impatiently I waited for that crotchety old butler to show up. Behind me the iron gates had closed. I felt like I was walking into a trap. Gee, just like Bart and his imagination that gave him fun, I used my ballet background to write this script. I felt like some wretched, unwanted prince who didn't possess the magic password. Only Bart knew that.

Confusion and regrets brewed and unsettled my determination. This didn't seem the castle of some wicked fairy queen, only the big, outdated home of a lonely old woman who needed Bart just as much as he needed her. But she couldn't be his grandmother, she just couldn't be. That grandmother was way back in Virginia, locked up for something terrible she'd done once.

Quiet was all around me, smothering me, making me feel old. My home was full of noises from the kitchen, music, Clover barking, Cindy squealing, Bart shouting, and Emma bossing. Not even a squeak came from this house. Nervously I shuffled my feet about, thinking I might give up my idea of confronting her. Then I glimpsed a dark shadow behind one of the windows draped with sheer curtains. I shivered. Almost left. But just then the door opened a crack, enough to allow the butler to put a squinty watery eye to the slit. "You can enter," he said inhospitably, "but don't you stay too long. Our lady is frail and tires easily."

I asked her name, tired of calling and thinking of her as old woman, or woman in black. My request was ignored. The butler intrigued me with his shuffling gait, his suggestion of a limp, his bald pate that was pink and shiny. His thin white mustache hung in long strands on either side of his grim lips. But as old as he was, and as weak as he appeared, he still managed to convey a scary, sinister air.

He beckoned me onward, but I hesitated. Then he smiled cynically, showing his too large, too even, and too yellow teeth. I squared my shoulders and followed him bravely, thinking I could set everything straight and our lives would be as happy as they'd been before they came to live in this house that used to be ours alone.

I didn't know suspicions were in my head. I thought it was only curiosity.

The room she always used surprised me again, though I couldn't say exactly why. Maybe it was because she kept her drapes drawn together on such a beautiful summer day. Behind the drapes the window shutters were closed, making bars of light on the window coverings. The shutters and the drapes held the heat outside at bay, making her parlor unexpectedly chill. There was no real need for air-conditioning in our area. The nearby Pacific kept our weather cool, making sweaters in the evenings a real necessity, even in the middle of summer. But this house was unnaturally cold.

Again she was in that wooden rocker staring at me. Her thin hand made some welcoming gesture to draw me closer. I knew instinctively she was a threat to my parents, to my own security, and most of all to Bart's mental health.

"You don't have to be afraid of me, Jory," she said in a sweet voice. "My home belongs to you as much as to Bart. I will always welcome you here. Sit down and chat for a while. Will you share a cup of tea with me, and a slice of cake?"

Beguiled, our word yesterday to add to our growing vocabulary Daddy insisted upon. "The world belongs to those who know how to speak well, and fortunes are made by those who write well," he'd said.

I admit, she beguiled me, that woman in her hard rocker, sitting so old and yet so proud. "Why don't you open your shutters, pull your drapes, and let in some light and air?" I asked.

Her nervous gestures brought into play the sparkling rays of the many gems she wore. Rubies, emeralds, and diamonds on her fingers, each color spectrum. Her jewels seemed so out of place when she had to wear that plain black chiffon—but today her eyes were revealed, her blue, blue eyes. Such familiar blue eyes.

"Too much light hurts my eyes," she explained in a faint husky whisper when I kept staring.

"Why?"

"Why does the light hurt my eyes?"

"Yes."

Her sigh was small. "For a long time I lived locked away from the world, shut up in a small room, but even worse than that, locked up within myself. When you are forced to encounter yourself for the first time in your life, you draw back from the shock. I recoiled when first I looked deep within myself, staring in a mirror they had in my room, and I was frightened. So now I live in rooms full of mirrors, but I cover my face so I can't see too much. I keep my rooms dim as I no longer admire the face I used to adore."

"Then take down the mirrors."

"How easy you make it. But you are young. The young always think everything is easy. I don't want to take down the mirrors. I want them there to remind me constantly of what I've done. The closed windows, the stuffy atmosphere are my punishments, not yours. If you want, Jory," she went on as I sat silently, "open the windows, spread the shutters; let in the sunlight and I will take off my veils and let you look at the face I hide from—but you won't find it pleasant. My beauty is gone, but it is a small loss compared to everything else that has come and gone, all the things I should have held on to valiantly."

"Valiantly?" I asked. That was a word not too familiar to me in any meaningful way, just a word suggesting bravery.

"Yes, Jory, valiantly I should have protected what was mine. I was all they had, and I let them down. I thought I was right, they were wrong. I convinced myself each day I was right. I resisted their pitiful pleas, and even worse, at the time I didn't even think they were pitiful. I told myself I was doing all I could because I brought them everything. They grew to distrust me, dislike me, and that hurt, hurt more than any pain I've ever felt. I hate myself for being weak, so cowardly, so foolishly intimidated when I should have stood my ground and fought back. I should have thought only of them and forgotten what I wanted for myself. My only excuse is that I was young then, and the young are selfish, even when it comes to their own children. I thought my needs were greater than theirs. I thought their time would come and then they could have their way. I felt it was my last chance at happiness. I had to grab for it quick, before middle age made me unattractive, and there was a younger man I loved. I couldn't tell him about them."

Them? Who was she talking about?

"Who?" I asked weakly, for some reason wishing she wouldn't tell me anything—or at least not too much.

"My children, Jory. My four children, fathered by my first husband, whom I married when I was only eighteen. He was forbidden to me, and yet I wanted him. I thought I never would find a man more wonderful . . . and yet I did find one just as wonderful."

I didn't want to hear her story. But she pleaded for me to stay. I sat on the edge of one of her fine chairs.

"So," she continued, "I put my fear out in front, allowed my love for a man to blind me to their needs, and I ignored what they wanted—their freedom—and now, as the result, I cry myself to sleep every night."

What could I say? I didn't understand what she was talking about. I reasoned she must be crazy, and no wonder Bart was acting just as nutty. She leaned forward to peer at me more closely.

"You are an exceptionally handsome boy. I suppose you know that already."

I nodded. All my life I'd heard remarks about my good looks, my talent, my charm. But talent was what counted, not looks. In my opinion looks without talent were useless. I knew, too, that beauty faded with the passing years, but still I loved beauty.

Looking around, I saw this woman loved beauty as much as I did, and yet . . . "What a pity she sits in the dark and refuses to enjoy all that's been done to make this place beautiful," I murmured without thought.

She heard and replied tonelessly, "The better to punish myself."

I didn't reply, only sat on in the chair while she rambled on and on about her life as a poor little rich girl who made the mistake of falling in love with her half uncle, who was three years older, and for this she was disinherited. Why was she telling me her life history? I didn't care. What did her past have to do with Bart? He was my reason for being here.

"I married for a second time. My four children hated me for doing that." She stared down at her hands folded on her lap, then began to twist the sparkling gems one by one. "Children always think adults have it so easy. That's not always true. Children think a widowed mother doesn't need anyone but them." She sighed. "They think they can give her enough love, because they don't understand there are all kinds of love, and it's hard for a woman to live without a man once she's been married."

Then, almost as if she'd forgotten me, she jolted to see me there. "Oh! I've been a poor hostess. Jory, what would you like to eat and drink?"

"Nothing, thank you. I came only to tell you that you must not encourage Bart to come over here anymore. I don't know what you tell him, or what he does here, but he comes home with weird ideas, acting very disoriented."

"Disoriented? You use large words for a boy so young."

"My father insists we learn one new word each day."

Those nervous hands of hers flitted up to her throat to play with her string of large pearls with a diamond butterfly clasp. "Jory, if I ask you a hypothetical question, would you give me an answer—a truthful answer?"

I got up to go. "I'd really rather not answer questions . . ."

"If your mother or your father ever disappointed you, failed you in some way, even a major one—could you find it in your heart to forgive them?"

Sure, sure, I thought quickly enough, though I couldn't imagine them ever failing me, Bart, or Cindy. I backed to the door that would allow me to leave while she was waiting for my answer. "Yes, Madame, I think I could forgive them anything."

"Murder?" she asked quickly, standing too. "Could you forgive them for that? Not premeditated murder, but accidental?"

She was crazy, just like her butler. I wanted to get out of there, and fast! I cautioned her one more time to send my brother home. "If you want Bart to stay sane, leave him alone!"

Her eyes teared before she nodded and inclined her head. I'd hurt her, I knew that. I had to harden my heart not to say I was sorry. Then, just as I was leaving, a deliveryman was banging on the door, and I opened to allow him to carry in a huge oblong crate. It took two men to rip off the nailed cover.

"Don't go, Jory," she begged. "Stay! I'd like you to see what's inside this crate."

What difference did it make? But I stayed, having the same curiosity as most people about the contents of a closed box.

The old butler came tapping down the hall, but she shooed him away. "John! I didn't ring for you. Please stay in your part of the house until you're sent for."

He gave her a smoldering look of resentment and hobbled into his hole, wherever that was.

By this time the crate was open, and the two men were pulling out packing straw. Then they lifted a huge thing wrapped in a gray quilt from its nest in the crate.

It was like waiting for a ship to be launched. I grew sort of breathless in anticipation, even more so because she had such a look on her face . . . as if she couldn't wait for me to see the contents. Was she giving me a gift, like she gave Bart anything he wanted? He was the greediest little boy ever born, needing double the amount of affection most people required.

I gasped then and stepped backward.

It was an oil painting the men unwrapped.

There stood my beautiful mother in a formal white gown, pausing on the next to the bottom step with her slender hand resting on a magnificent newel post. Trailing behind her lay yards and yards of the shimmering white fabric. The curving stairs behind her rose gracefully and faded into swirling mists through which the artist had cleverly managed to give the impression of gold and glittering jewels, hinting at a palace-like mansion.

"Do you know whose portrait that is?" she asked when the men had hung it in place in one of the parlors she didn't seem to use often. I nodded, dumbfounded and speechless.

What was she doing with my mother's portrait?

She waited for the two men to go. They smiled, thrilled with the tip she gave them. I was panting, hearing my heavy breathing and wondering why I felt sort of numb. "Jory," she said softly, turning again to me, "that's a portrait of *me* that my second husband commissioned shortly after we were married. I was thirty-seven when I posed for that."

In the portrait the woman looked just like my mother

looked today. I swallowed and wanted to run, suddenly needing the bathroom badly, but still I wanted to stay. I wanted to hear her explain, even though I was paralyzed with the fear of what she might tell me.

"My second husband, who was younger, was named Bartholomew Winslow, Jory," she said quickly, as if to make sure I heard before I got up and ran. "Later on, when my daughter was old enough, she seduced him, stole his love away from me, just so she could hurt me with the child she gave him. The child I couldn't have. Can you guess who that child is, can you?"

I jumped up and backed away. Holding out my hands to ward off any more information I didn't want to hear.

"Jory, Jory, Jory," she chanted, "don't you remember me at all? Think back to when you lived in the mountains of Virginia. Think of that little post office, and the rich lady in the fur coat. You were about three then. You saw me, and smiling, you came to stroke my coat, and you told me I was pretty—remember?"

"No!" I cried more stoutly than I felt. "I have never seen you before in my life, not until you moved here! And all blondes with blue eyes look somewhat alike!"

"Yes," she said brokenly, "I suppose you're right. I just thought it would be amusing to see your expression. I shouldn't have played a trick on you. I'm sorry, Jory. Forgive me."

I couldn't look at those blue, blue eyes. I had to get away.

I felt miserable as I slowly trudged home. If only I hadn't stayed. If only the portrait hadn't been delivered while I was there. Why did I have to sense that that woman was more a threat to my mother than my stepfather? What had I accomplished? *Was it you, Mom, who stole her second husband's love?* Was it? Didn't it make good sense when Bart had the same name as him? Everything she'd said confirmed the suspicions that had been sleeping in my mind for so many years. Doors were opening, letting in fresh memories that almost seemed like enemies.

I climbed the stairs of the veranda Mom jokingly called "Paul's kind of southern veranda." Certainly it wasn't the customary California patio.

There was something different about the patio today.

If I had been less troubled, perhaps I would have spotted immediately what was missing. As it was, it took me minutes to realize Clover wasn't there. I looked around, distressed, calling him.

"For heaven's sake, Jory," called Emma from the kitchen window, "don't yell so loud. I just put Cindy down for a nap and you'll wake her up. I saw Clover a few minutes ago heading into the garden, chasing a butterfly."

Of course, I felt relieved. If one thing brought out the puppy in my old poodle, it was a fluttery yellow butterfly. I joined Emma in the kitchen and asked, "Emma, I've been wanting to ask for a long time, what year did Mom marry Dr. Paul?"

She was leaning over, checking inside the refrigerator, grumbling to herself. "I could swear there was some fried chicken in here, left over from last night. Since we're having liver and onions tonight I saved what was left of the chicken for Bart. I thought your finicky brother could eat the leftover thighs."

"Don't you remember the year they were married?"

"You were just a little one then," she said, still rummaging through covered dishes.

Emma was always vague about dates. She couldn't remember her own birthday. Maybe deliberately. "Tell me again how my mother met Dr. Paul's younger brother . . . you know, the stepfather we have now."

"Yes, I remember Chris, he was so handsome, tall and tan. But not one whit better-looking than Dr. Paul was in his own way . . . a wonderful man, your stepfather Paul. So kind, so soft-spoken."

"It's funny Mom didn't fall for a younger brother instead of an older one—don't you think it's odd?"

She straightened and put a hand to her back, which she said hurt all the time. Next she wiped her hands on her spotless white apron. "I sure hope your parents aren't late tonight. Now you run and hunt up Bart before it's too late for him to take a bath. I hate for your mother to see him so filthy."

"Emma, you haven't answered my questions."

Turning her back she began to chop green bell peppers. "Jory, when you need answers, you go to your parents and ask. Don't come to me. You may think of me as a family member but I know my place is that of a friend. So run along and let me finish dinner."

"Please, Emma, not just for my sake, but Bart's too. I've got to do something to straighten out Bart, and how can I when I don't have all the facts?"

"Jory," she said, giving me a warm smile, "just be happy you have two such wonderful parents. You and Bart are very lucky boys. I hope Cindy grows up to realize how blessed she was the day your mother decided she had to have a daughter."

Outside the day was growing old. Search as I would I couldn't find Clover. I sat on the back steps and stared unhappily at the sky turning rosy with bright streaks of orange and violet. I felt overwhelmingly sad and burdened, wishing all this mystery and confusion would go away. Clover, where was Clover? I never knew until this moment how very much he added to my life, how much I'd miss him if he was gone for good. Please don't let him be gone for good, God, please.

One more time I looked around our yard, then decided I'd better go in the house and call the newspapers. I'd offer a reward for a missing dog—such a big reward somebody would bring Clover back. "Clover!" I yelled, "chow time!"

My call brought Bart stumbling out of the hedges, his clothes torn and filthy. His dark eyes were strangely haunted. "Why yah yellin?"

"I can't find Clover," I answered, "and you know he never goes anywhere. He's a home dog. I read the other day about people who steal dogs and sell them to science labs for experimentation. Bart, I'd want to die if somebody did something so awful to Clover."

He stared at me, stricken-looking. "They wouldn't do that... would they?"

"Bart, I've got to find Clover. If he doesn't come back soon, I'll feel sick, really sick enough to die. Suppose he's been run over?"

I watched my brother swallow, then begin to tremble. "What's wrong?"

"Shot me a wolf back there, I did. Shot me a big bad wolf right through his mean red eye. He came at me lickin his chops, but I was smarter and moved quick and shot him dead."

"Oh, come off it, Bart!" I said impatiently, really getting irritated with somebody who could never tell the truth. "There aren't any wolves in this area, and you know it."

Until midnight I searched all around our neighborhood, calling for Clover. Tears kept clogging my voice, my eyes. I had the strongest premonition that Clover would never come home again.

"Jory," said Dad, who'd been helping me hunt, "let's hit the sack and look again in the morning if he doesn't come home by himself. And don't you lie in your bed and worry. Clover may be an old dog, but even the elderly can feel romantic on a moonlit night."

Aw, heck. That didn't make much sense. Clover had stopped chasing female dogs a long time ago. Now all he wanted was a place to lie where Bart wasn't likely to stumble over him or step on his tail.

"You go to bed, Dad, and let me look. I don't have to be in ballet class until ten, so I don't need my sleep as much as you do."

He briefly embraced me, wished me luck, and headed for

his room. An hour later, I decided it was fruitless effort. Clover was dead. That's the only thing that would keep him away.

I decided I had to tell my parents what I suspected.

I stood beside their bed looking down at them. Moonlight streamed through the windows and fell over their bodies. Mom was half-turned on her side so she could cuddle up close to Dad, who was on his back. Her head was on his bare chest, while his left arm encircled her so his hand lay on her hip. The covers were pulled up just high enough to shield their nudity, which made me back away, feeling very guilty. I shouldn't be here, sleep made them look vulnerable, younger, moving me but giving me a deep sense of shame too. I wondered why I felt ashamed. Dad had taught me the facts of life a long time ago, so I knew what men and women did together to make babies—or just for fun.

I sobbed and turned to go.

"Chris, is that you?" asked my mother, half-asleep and rolling over on her back.

"I'm here, darling. Go back to sleep," he mumbled sleepily. "The grandmother can't get us now."

I froze, startled. They both sounded like children. And again that grandmother.

"I'm scared, Chris, so afraid. If they ever find out, what will we say? How can we explain?'

"Shhh," came his whisper, "life will be good to us from now on. Hold fast to your faith in God. We have both been punished enough; He won't punish us more."

Run, run, had to run fast to my room and hurl myself down. I felt hollow inside, emptiness all around instead of the confidence and love I used to feel here. Clover was gone. My dear little harmless poodle who had never done even one bad thing. And Bart had shot a wolf.

What would Bart do next? Did he know what I did? Was that why he was behaving so strangely? Turning his mean glare on Mom like he wanted to hurt her. Tears rose in my eyes again, for memory couldn't be denied forever. I knew now that Bart was not the son of Dr. Paul. Bart was the son of that old lady's second husband with the same name as my half brother—that tall, lean man who sometimes haunted my dreams along with Dr. Paul and my own real father, whom I'd seen only in photographs.

Our parents had lied to both of us. Why hadn't they told us the truth? Was the truth so ugly they couldn't tell us? Did they have such little faith in our love for them?

Oh, God, their secret must be something so dreadful we could never forgive them!

And Bart, he could be dangerous. I knew he could be. Day by day it was beginning to show more and more. In the morning I wanted to run up to Mom or to Dad and tell them. But when morning came I couldn't say anything. Now I knew why Dad insisted that we learn one new word each day. It took special words to put across subtle ideas, and as yet I wasn't as educated as I needed to be to express my troubled thoughts that wanted to reassure them. And how could I reassure them when Bart was before me, his dark eyes hard and mean?

Oh, God, if you're up there somewhere looking down, hear my prayer. Let my parents have the peace they need so they don't have to dream of evil grandmothers at night. Right or wrong, whatever they've done, I know they've done the best they could.

Why did I put it like that?

Safe was a word that no longer had substance. Like dead people who were only shadows in my memory, nothing as concrete as Bart's hate, which was growing larger day by day.

Lessons

July. My month. "Conceived in fire, born in heat," said John Amos when I told him it would soon be my tenth birthday. Didn't know what he meant and didn't care either. Disneyland would see me in a few days. Hip-hip-hooray! Drat Jory for not looking happy, spoiling my fun with his long, sad face just because some silly little ole dog wouldn't come home when he called.

I was making plans that would see Apple through until I could steal back to him after seeing Disneyland. John Amos grabbed me when I went over and hauled me up to his room over the garage. I looked around, thinking it smelled sour, old, like medicine.

"Bart, you sit down in that chair and read aloud to me from Malcolm's journal. For the Lord will punish you if you say you're reading his book when you are not."

I didn't need John Amos as much as I used to, so I looked at him with scorn. With the kind of scorn Malcolm would show for a bent and lame old man who couldn't speak without hissing, whistling, or spitting. But I sat and I read from Malcolm's red-leather journal.

My youth had been squandered in earthly pleasures, and as I approached thirty I realized what was missing in my life was a purpose other than money. Religion. I needed religion, and redemption for all my sins, for despite the vows of my childhood, I had regressed into desiring women, and the more wicked they were, the more they seemed to please me. There was no sight more pleasurable to me than to see some haughty beautiful woman, humbled and made to do obscene things that went against the rules of decency. I took pleasure in beating them, putting red welts on their fair unbroken skins. I saw blood, their blood, and it made me excited. That's when I knew I needed God. I had to save my everlasting soul from hell.

I looked up, tired of trying to figure out all those long words that didn't mean much to me.

"Do you see what Malcolm is telling you, boy? He's telling you no matter how much you hate women, still there is pleasure to be had from them—*but at a cost, boy,* at a dear, dear cost. Unfortunately God built into mankind sensual desires—you must try to smother yours as you approach manhood. Plant it in your mind so deep it can never be removed: Women will be your destruction in the end. I know. They have destroyed me and kept me a servant when I could have been far more."

I got up and walked away, sick of John Amos. I was going to my grandmother, who loved me more than God ever would. More than anyone ever would. She loved me for myself. She loved me so much she even made up lies, like me, to tell me she was my own true grandmother when I knew that just couldn't be so.

Saturday was the best day of the week. My stepfather stayed home and made Momma happy. She hired some dumb assistant to help out on Saturday in her ballet class now that she had to spend so much time dolling up Cindy—like anybody cared how she looked. Jory had to go to ballet class on Saturdays too so he could see his stupid girlfriend. By noon he'd be home to mess up all my plans. Had lots of plans to fill my time. Take care of Apple. Sit on my grandmother's lap and let her sing to me. Why, mornings could pass quicker than a wink with all I had to do.

John Amos gave me more lessons on how to be like Malcolm, and darn if it wasn't working. I was feeling his power growing bigger and stronger.

That afternoon Cindy was in a brand-new plastic swimming pool. The old one wasn't good enough for *her*. Bratty kid has to have everything new, even a bathing suit with red and white stripes and little red straps that tied over her shoulders to keep the thing up. Little bows she was trying to undo!

Jory jumped up and rushed into the house for his camera, then ran back to take Cindy's picture. Snap, snap, snap. He tossed the camera to Momma, who caught it. "Take my picture with Cindy," he said.

Sure, she was happy to take *his* picture with Cindy. Didn't bother to ask about me. Maybe once too often I'd made a face, ducked my head, or stuck out my tongue. Everyone was always saying Bart sure did know how to ruin a perfectly good shot.

Dratted bushes were all around me, scratching my legs, arms. Bugs crawled on me. Hated bugs! Slapped at them as I narrowed my eyes to see that sissy girl splashing in the water, having more fun than I ever had in a pool.

When they tried to take me East from Disneyland, I'd sneak away and catch a ride and come home and take care of Apple—that's what Malcolm would do. Dead people wouldn't miss me. They wouldn't care if I wasn't there to put flowers on their graves. Jory's nasty grandmother would be glad I wasn't there.

Ran to where I could climb the tree, the wall, and on to the barn to visit with Apple, who was growing huge. I shoved a doggy biscuit in Apple's mouth. It vanished in a second. He jumped and made me fall down. "Now you eat this carrot—it will be like a toothbrush to clean your teeth!" Apple sniffed at the carrot. Wagged his tail. Jumped and then swiped at the carrot with his paw. Apple still didn't know how to play pony games at all.

Soon I had Apple hitched up to my new pony cart and we flew all over the place. "Gitty-up!" I yelled. "Catch those rustlers over yonder! Run faster, you gol-durn horse, if yer gonna get me home before chow is served!" I saw a movement in the hills. Twisted round and spied Indians comin lickity-split—scalpin Indians! Indians gave us a mad chase until we lost them in the hills that soon became desert. Tired and thirsty, my mount and I looked for an oasis. Saw a mirage.

There she was, the woman of the oasis mirage. Wearin her flutterin black rags, her bare feet sandy, glad to welcome us both back to the land of the livin . . .

"Water," I gasped. "Need cold, clear water." I sprawled in a fancy chair and spread out my long, thin legs that ended in dusty, worn boots. I reached to flick sand from my chaps. "Make it a beer," I said to the saloon girl. She brought me beer, all foamy and brown, and cold, too cold. Hit my stomach like a rattler, makin me hunch over and give her the eye. "What's a nice girl like you doin in a rotten place like this?"

"I'm the local schoolmarm. Snapping Sam, don't you remember?" Behind her veil she cast down her eyelids and fluttered her lashes. "But when hard times come, a lady must do what she can to survive." She was playin my game. Nobody ever played my games with me. It felt so good to have a playmate.

I smiled, real friendly like. "Took good care of Apple. He's so clean he can't die."

"Darling, you play too hard. And it's not healthy to think so much about dying. Come sit on my lap and let me sing you a song."

Nice. Liked being treated like a baby. Cozy on her soft

lap, with my face on her breast, and her singing in my ears. Each rock of the chair put me more and more in a trance. I looked up and tried to see through her veils. Was I getting to love her more than Momma? I saw then that her veils were attached to little combs she caught in her hair, for today she had left her hair uncovered. Most of it was silver-colored with streaks of gold.

Didn't want Momma to grow old and have gray hair. Already she was leaving me each day she cared for Cindy; leaving me for others to take over. Why did Cindy have to come and spoil my life?

"More, please," I whispered when she stopped rocking. "Do you love me more than Madame M. loves Jory?" I asked. If she said yes, much, much more, I might move in.

"Does Jory's grandmother love him a great deal?" Was that envy in her voice? I felt mad, mean—and she saw this and began to cover my face with kisses, dry kisses on account of that veil.

"Granny, got to tell you somethin."

"Fine . . . but remember to sound your G's. Tell me anything, I've got the rest of my life to listen." She stroked my hair back from my face and tried to make it neat. Couldn't.

"Two days before my birthday we're heading for Disneyland. A week there and we fly to where the graves are. Gotta visit cemeteries, buy flowers, put the flowers in the sun where they can die. Hate graves. Hate Jory's grandmother, who don't like me 'cause I can't dance."

Again she kissed me. "Bart . . . tell your parents there have been too many graves in your life. Tell them again how unhappy it makes you feel."

"Won't listen," I said dully. "They don't ask what I want like you do. They just tell me I have to do."

"I'm sure they'll listen if you tell them about your dreams of being dead. They'll know then they have taken you too many times into cemeteries. Just tell them the truth."

"But . . . but . . . ," I sputtered unhappily. "I want Disney-land!"

"You tell them like I said, and I'll take care of Apple."

Felt frantic. Once I turned the care of Apple over to any-one, he'd never be all mine again. I sobbed because life was so impossible. And my plan to escape had to work, it would, had to . . .

We rocked on and on, and she said we were on a sailing ship riding choppy waters to a beautiful island called peace. I lost my land legs, so when I reached there I couldn't stand or find my balance. She disappeared. Alone, all alone. Like on Mars—and way back on Earth Apple was waiting for me to show up. Poor Apple. In the end he'd have to die.

I woke up, I think—where was I? Why was everyone so old? Momma . . . why have you got your face covered with black?

"Wake up, sweetheart. I think you'd better hurry home before your parents become alarmed. You've had a nice nap, so you must feel better."

Next morning I was in the yard trying to finish up that dog-house I was building for Clover. Poor Clover should have had his own house all along, and then he wouldn't have run away looking for one. From Daddy's toolshed I took a hammer, nails, saw, wood, and lugged it out into the yard. I set to. Drat-ted saw didn't know how to cut straight. Gonna have a crooked house. If Clover complained I'd give him a kick. I picked up my jaggedly sliced board and put it on the roof. Dratted nail! Didn't stand still, made the hammer hit my thumb. Stupid hammer didn't see my fingers! I went right on hammering. Good thing I couldn't feel little pains or I'd be crying. Then I smashed my thumb good and it hurt. Gosh, I was feeling pain like any normal boy.

Jory dashed out of the house yelling at me: "Why are you

building a house for Clover when he's been gone two weeks? Nobody has answered our ads. He's no doubt dead by now, and if he does come home he will sleep on the foot of my bed, remember?" Dumb. Dumb, that's what he meant, and Clover might come back. Poor Clover.

I sneaked a glance and saw Jory swipe at the tears in his eyes. "Day after tomorrow we're leaving for Disneyland, and that should make you happy," he said hoarsely. Did it make me happy? My swollen thumb began to ache a little. Apple was gonna die from loneliness.

Then I had an idea. John Amos had told me that prayers brought about miracles, and God was up there in his heaven looking out for dumb animals down here and people too. Momma and Daddy had always told me not to ask for things in my prayers, only blessings for other people, not myself. So, as soon as Jory was gone I threw down my hammer and raced to where I could kneel and pray for my puppy-pony and for Clover. Next I went to Apple, rolling with him on the golden grass, me laughing, him trying to whinny-bark. His tongue slurped my face with wet kisses. I kissed him back. When he lifted his leg and aimed at the roses—I took off my pants and let go too. We did everything together.

It came to me then just what to do. "Don't you worry none, Apple. I'll only spend one week in Disneyland before I come back to you. I'll hide your puppy-pony biscuits under the hay and leave the water tap dripping in your pail. But don't you dare eat or drink anything John Amos gives you, or my grandmother either. Don't you let anybody bribe you with goodies."

He wagged his tail, telling me he'd be good and obey my orders. He'd made a big pile of do-do. I picked it up and squashed it through my fingers, letting him know I was a part of him now and he was really mine. I wiped my hands on the grass and saw ants come running and flies going to work. No wonder nothing lasted, no wonder.

"Time for your lessons, Bart," called John Amos from the

barn, his bald head gleaming in the sunlight. I felt captured as I lay on the hay and stared at him towering over me. He smelled old and stale.

"Are you reading Malcolm's journal faithfully?" he asked.

"Yes, sir."

"Are you teaching yourself the ways of the Lord and saying your prayers dutifully?"

"Yes, sir."

"Those who follow in his footsteps will be judged accordingly, as will those who don't. Let me give you an example. Once there was a beautiful young girl who was born with a silver spoon in her mouth, and she had everything money could buy—but did she appreciate all she had? *No, she didn't!* When she grew older she began to tempt men with her beauty. She'd flaunt her half-nakedness before their eyes. She was high and mighty, but the Lord saw and He punished her, though it took Him some time. The Lord, through Malcolm, made her crawl and cry and pray for release, and Malcolm bested her in the end. Malcolm always bested everyone in the end—*and so must you.*"

Boy, he sure could tell boring stories. We had naked people in our garden and I wasn't tempted. I sighed, wishing he had more subjects to talk about than God and Malcolm . . . and some darn beautiful girl.

"Beware of beauty in women, Bart. Beware of the woman who shows you her body without clothes. Beware of all those women who lie in wait to do you in and be like Malcolm, *clever!*"

Finally he let me go. I was glad to be done with pretending I was like Malcolm. All I had to do to feel really good was to crawl sneakily on the ground, listening to the jungle noises in the dense foliage where wild animals lurked. Dangerous animals ready to gobble me down. I jerked. Bolted upright. *No!* That couldn't be what I thought it was. Just wasn't fair for God to send a dinosaur. Taller than a skyscraper. Longer than a train. I had to jump up and run off to find Jory and tell him what we had hangin around our backyard.

A noise in the jungle ahead! I stopped short, gasping for breath.

Voices. Talking snakes?

"Chris, I don't care what you say. It is not necessary for you to visit her again this summer. Enough is enough. You've done what you can to help her and you can't. So forget her and concentrate on us, your family."

I peeked around a bush. Both my parents were in the prettiest part of the garden, where the larger trees grew. Momma was on her knees, mulching the ground around the roses. Green thumb she had, and he did too.

"Cathy, must you stay a child forever?" he asked. "Can't you ever learn to forgive and forget? Perhaps you can pretend she doesn't exist, but I can't. I keep thinking we are the only family she has left." He pulled her to her feet, then put his hand over her mouth when it opened to interrupt. "All right, hold on to your hatred, but I'm a doctor sworn to do what I can for those in distress. Mental illnesses can be more devastating than physical ailments. I want to see her recover. I want her to leave that place—so don't glare at me and tell me again that she was never insane, that she was only pretending. She'd have to be crazy to do what she did. And for all we know the twins might never have grown tall anyway. Like Bart. He's not of normal height for a boy his age."

Oh, wasn't I?

"Cathy, how can I feel good about myself, or anything, if I neglect my own mother?"

"All right!" stormed Momma. "Go on and visit her! Jory, Bart, Cindy, and I will stay on with Madame Marisha. Or we could fly on to New York so I can visit with some old friends until you're ready to join us again." She gave him a crooked smile. "That is, if you still want to join us."

"Where else would I go but to you? Who cares if I live or die but you and our children? Cathy, think about this—the day I turn my back on my mother will also be the day I turn my back on all women, including you."

She fell into his arms then and did all that mushy loving stuff I hated to see. I backed away, still on my hands and knees, wondering about what Momma had said, and why she hated his mother so much. I felt a little sick in my stomach. What if my grandmother next door really was my stepfather's mother, truly crazy, loving me only because she had to. What if John Amos was telling the truth?

It was so hard to figure out. Was Corrine Malcolm's real daughter like John Amos had told me?—was she the one who had "tempted" John Amos? Or was that Malcolm who hated someone pretty and half-naked. Sometimes I got confused after reading Malcolm's book; he'd skip back to his childhood and write about his memories even after he was grown up, like his childhood was more important than his adult life. How odd. I couldn't wait to grow up.

I heard them again, coming at me. Quickly I crawled under the nearest hedges.

"I love you, Chris, as much as you love me. Sometimes I think we both love too much. I wake up at night if you're not there. I want you to not be a doctor, but a man who stays home every night. I want my sons to grow up, but each day brings them nearer to learning our secret, and I'm so afraid they'll hate us and won't understand."

"They'll understand," he said. How could he know I would understand when I wasn't good at understanding even simple things, much less something so bad it woke Momma up at night.

"Cathy, have we been bad parents? Haven't we done the best we could? After living with us from their childhood, how can they help but understand? We'll tell them how it was, give them all the facts, so they will see it as we lived it. In so doing, they'll wonder, as I often wonder, how we survived without losing our minds."

John Amos was right. They had to be sinning or they wouldn't be so afraid we wouldn't understand. And what secret? Whatever were they hiding?

I stayed under the hedges long after my parents went into the house. I had favorite caves I'd made deep in the hedges, and when I was inside them I felt like some small woody animal, scared of everything human that would kill me if possible.

Malcolm was on my mind, him and his brain that was so wise and cunning. I thought of John Amos, who was teaching me about God, the Bible, and sinning. It wasn't until I thought of Apple and my grandmother that I felt good. Not real good, only a little good.

Fell on the ground and began to sniff around, trying to find something I'd buried last week, or a month ago. Looked in the little fishpond Daddy wanted us to have so we could watch how baby fish were born. I'd seen itty-bitty fish come out of eggs, and the parents swam like crazy to gobble down their children!

"Jory! Bart!" called Momma from the open kitchen door. "Dinnertime!"

I peered into the water. There was my face, all funny-looking, with jagged edges, hair up in points, not curly and pretty like Jory's. Something dark red was on my face—ugly face that didn't belong in a pretty garden where the little birds came to bathe in a fancy bath. I was bleeding tears. I dipped my hands in the fish water and washed my face. Then sat back to think. That's when I saw the blood on my leg—lots of blood that was drying in a big dark clot on my knee. Didn't really matter because it didn't hurt too much.

Wonder how it got there? I retraced my crawl with my eyes. That board with the rusty nail—had I driven that in my knee? I crawled over to the board and felt the blood sticky on its end. Daddy called nail holes in skin "punctures," and I guess I had one. "Now, it's very important that a puncture bleeds freely," he explained. Mine wasn't bleeding freely.

I put my finger in the puncture and stirred up the blood so it would run. Freaky people like me could do awful things like that, while sissy people like Momma would look sick. Blood in my wound felt hot and thick, just like that pudding stuff Apple had made and I had squeezed through my fingers because it not only made him more mine, but it felt good too.

Maybe I wasn't so freaky after all, for all of a sudden I was beginning to feel real pain. Mean pain.

"BART!" bellowed Daddy from the back veranda. "You get in this house instantly! Unless you want a spanking!"

When they were in the dining room they couldn't see me sneak in the family room sliding door, and that's just what I did. In the bathroom I washed my hands, put on my pj's to hide my bad knee, and, quiet and meek, joined my family at the table.

"Well, it's about time," said Momma, who looked pretty.

"Bart, why do you insist on causing trouble every time we sit down to eat?" asked Daddy. I hung my head, not feeling sorry, just not feeling well. Knee was really throbbing with pain, and what John Amos said about God punishing those who disobeyed must be right. I was being judged, and a knee puncture was my own hellfire.

Next day I was back in the garden, hiding in one of my special places. All day I sat there and enjoyed my pain, which meant I was normal, not a freak. I was being punished like all other sinners who'd always felt pain. Wanted to miss dinner. Had to go and see Apple. Couldn't remember if I'd been over there or not. Drank a little from the fishpond. Lap, lap, lap, like a cat.

Momma had been packing all day, smiling even early this morning when she put my clothes in a suitcase first. "Bart, try to be a good boy today for a change. Come to your meals on time and then Daddy won't have to spank you before bed-time. He doesn't like punishing you, but he does have to have a way to discipline you. And do try to eat more. You won't enjoy Disneyland if you feel sick."

Sunset changed the blue sky to pretty colors. Jory ran outdoors to watch the colors he said were like music. Jory could also "feel" colors; they made him glad, sad, lonely, and "mystical." Momma was another one who could "feel" colors. Now that I was getting the knack of feeling pain, maybe soon I'd learn to feel colors too.

Real night started coming. Darkness could bring out the ghosts. Emma tinkled her little crystal bell to call me in to dinner. Wanted so badly to go, but couldn't do it.

Something rotting was in the hollow tree behind me. I turned and crawled out of my cave and peeked into the dark hole in the tree. Rotten eggs inside! Phew! I put my hand in slowly, feeling around for what I couldn't see. Something stiff and cold and covered with fur! Dead thing had a collar around its neck with points that cut my hand—was that barbed wire? Was that rotten dead thing Clover?

I sobbed, wild with fear.

They'd think I did it.

They were always thinking I did everything that was bad. And I'd loved Clover, I had. Always wanted him to like me more than Jory. Now poor Clover would never live in that wonderful doghouse I'd finish someday.

Jory came down the main garden path, calling and searching for me. "Come out from where you are, Bart! Don't make waves now that we're all ready to leave."

Found me a new place he didn't know about and lay flat on my stomach.

Jory left. Next came my mother. "Bart," she called, "if you don't come inside . . . Please, Bart. I'm sorry I slapped you this morning." I sniffed away my tears of self-pity. I had only accidentally dumped a whole box of detergent in the dishwasher thinking I could help. How was I to know one small box could make a whole ocean of suds? Foamy suds that filled the kitchen. This time it was Daddy. "Bart," he called in a normal voice, "come in and eat your dinner. No need to sulk. We know what you did was an accident. You are forgiven. We realize you were trying to help Emma, so come in."

On and on I sat, feeling guilty for making them suffer more. Panic had been in Momma's voice, as if she really did love me, and how could she when I never did anything right? Wasn't fit for her to love.

The pain in my knee was much worse. Maybe I had lockjaw. Kids at school had told me all about how it made your jaws lock together so you couldn't eat, making doctors knock out your front teeth so they could put a tube in your mouth and you could suck in soup. Soon the ambulance would come screaming down our street, and, with me inside it, would sound its siren all the way to Daddy's hospital. They'd rush me to the emergency room and a masked surgeon would shout: "Off with his rotten, stinking leg!" They'd hack it off short, and I'd be left with a stump full of poison that would put me in my coffin.

Then they'd put me in that cemetery in Clairmont, South Carolina. Aunt Carrie would be at my side, and at last she'd have someone small like her to keep her company. But I wouldn't be Cory. I was me, the black sheep of the family—so John Amos had called me once when he was mad about me playing with his "choppers."

On my back, with my arms crossed over my chest, I lay just like Malcolm Neal Foxworth, staring upward as I waited for winter to come and go and summer to bring Momma, Daddy, Jory, Cindy, and Emma to my grave. Bet they wouldn't bring *me* pretty flowers. Down in my grave I'd stiffly smile, not letting them know I liked the killer Spanish moss much better than I liked the smelly roses with prickly thorns.

My family would leave. I'd be trapped in the ground, in the dark, forever and ever. When at last I was in the cold-cold ground, and the snow lay all around, I wouldn't have to pretend to be like Malcolm Neal Foxworth. I pictured Malcolm when he was old. Frail, with thin hair and a limp like John Amos, and only a little better-looking than John Amos, who was very ugly.

Just in the nick of time, I was solving all of Momma's problems and Cindy could live on and on in peace.

Now that I was dead.

Wounds of War

Dinnertime came and went. Bedtime was drawing nearer and still Bart didn't show up. We had all searched, but I was the one who kept it up longest. I was the one who knew him best. "Jory," said Mom, "if you don't find him in ten more minutes I'm calling the police."

"I'll find him," I said, not nearly as confident as I tried to sound. I didn't like what Bart was doing to our parents. They were trying to do the best they could for us. They weren't getting any big kick out of visiting Disneyland for the fourth time. That was Bart's treat, and he was too dumb to understand.

He was bad, too. Dad and Mom should punish him severely, not indulge him like they did. He'd know, at least, that they cared enough to punish him for his wicked ways.

Yet when I'd mentioned this to them once or twice, both had explained they'd learned in the worst way about parents who were strict and cruel. I'd thought it odd at the time that both of them had come from the same kind of heartless parents, but my teacher often said that likes were attracted to one another more than opposites. All I had to do was look at them to know this was true. Both had the same shade of blonde hair, the same color blue eyes, and the same dark eyebrows and long, black, curling lashes—though Momma used mascara, which made Daddy tease her, for he didn't think she needed any.

No, they wouldn't punish Bart severely even when he was wicked, for they had found out firsthand what harm it could do.

Boy did Bart love to talk about wickedness and sin. A new kind of talk, like he'd been reading the Bible and taking from it the kind of ideas that some preachers screamed out behind the pulpits. He could even quote passages from the Bible— something from the song of Solomon, and a brother's love for his sister whose breasts were like . . .

Gee, I didn't even like to think about that kind of thing. Made me feel so uneasy, even more uneasy than when Bart spoke of how he hated graves, ole ladies, cemeteries, and almost everything else. Hate was an emotion he felt often, poor kid.

I checked his little cave in the shrubs and saw a bit of cloth torn from this shirt. But he wasn't there now. I picked up a board meant for the top of the doghouse Bart was building, and stared at the rusty, bloody end of the nail.

Had he hurt himself with his nail and crawled off somewhere to die? Dying was all he talked about lately, excluding talk of those already dead. He was always crawling around, sniffing the ground like a dog, even relieving himself like a dog. Boy, he was a mixed-up little kid.

"Bart, it's Jory. If you want to stay out all night, I'll let you, and won't tell our parents . . . just make some noise so I can know you're alive."

Nothing.

Our yard was big, full of shrubs and trees and blooming bushes Mom and Dad had planted. I circled a camellia bush. Oh, golly—was that Bart's bare foot?

There he was, half under the hedge, with only his legs stretched out. I'd overlooked him before because this was not his usual place to hide. It was really dark now, the fog making it even more difficult to see.

Gently I eased him out from the shrubs, wondering why he didn't complain. I stared down at his flushed hot face, his murky eyes staring dully at me. "Don't touch me," he moaned. "Almost dead now . . . almost there."

I picked him up and ran with him in my arms. He was crying, telling me his leg hurt . . . "Jory, I really don't want to die, I don't."

By the time Dad picked him up and put him in his car, he was unconscious. "I don't believe this," said Dad. "That leg of his is swollen three times larger than it should be. I only pray he doesn't have gas gangrene."

I knew about gangrene—it could kill people!

In the hospital Bart was put to bed immediately, and other doctors came to check over his leg. They tried to force Dad to leave the room, since it was professional ethics for doctors not to treat someone in their own family. Too emotionally involved, I guessed.

"No!" stormed Dad, "he's my son, and I'm staying to see what's done for him!" Mom cried all the time, kneeling and holding on to Bart's slack hand. I was sick inside too, thinking I hadn't done nearly enough to help Bart.

"Apple, Apple," whimpered Bart whenever his eyes opened. "Gotta have Apple."

"Chris," said Mom, "can't he have an apple?"

"No. He can't eat in his condition."

What a terrible state he was in. Sweat beaded on his forehead and his small, thin body soaked the sheets. Mom began to really sob. "Take your mother out of this room," ordered Dad. "I don't want her to watch all of this."

As Mom cried in the waiting room down the hall, I stole back inside Bart's private room and watched Dad shoot penicillin into Bart's arm. I held my breath. "Is he allergic to penicillin?" asked another doctor. "I don't know," said Dad in a calm way. "He's never had a serious infection before. At this point there isn't much else we can do but take a chance. Get everything ready in case he reacts." He turned to see me crouched in the corner, trying to stay out of the way. "Son, go to your mother. There's nothing you can do to help here."

I couldn't move. For some reason, perhaps guilt for neglecting my brother, I had to stay and see him through. Soon enough Bart was in worse trouble. Dad frowned, signaled a nurse, and two more doctors came. One of them inserted a tube in Bart's nostril. Next something so dreadful happened I couldn't believe my eyes. All over his body, Bart was breaking out in huge, swollen welts. Red as fire, and they itched, too, because his hand kept moving from one patch of fire to another. Then Dad was lifting Bart and putting him on a stretcher so orderlies could wheel him away.

"Dad!" I cried, "where is that stretcher going? They're not going to take off his leg, are they?"

"No, son," he said calmly. "Your brother is having a severe allergic reaction. We have to move fast and perform a tracheotomy before his throat tissues become inflamed and cut off his air passage."

"Chris," called the doctor pushing one side of the stretcher, "it's okay. Tom has cleared an air passage—no trache necessary."

A day passed and still Bart was no better. It seemed likely Bart would scratch himself raw and die from another kind of infection. With fascinated horror I stayed very late watching his stubby, swollen fingers work convulsively in useless efforts to relieve the torment of his itching body. His entire body was scarlet. I could tell his condition was serious from Dad's face and from the attitudes of the other professionals all around his bed. Then Bart's hands were bandaged so he couldn't scratch. Next his eyes puffed up so much they looked like two huge, red goose eggs. His lips swelled and protruded three inches beyond normal.

I couldn't believe all this could happen just on count of an allergic reaction.

"Oh!" cried out Mom, clinging tightly to Dad, her tired eyes glued on Bart. He'd been sick forever, or so it seemed. Two days passed and still Bart was no better. He'd spent his tenth birthday on a hospital bed, delirious and raving, his fourth trip to Disneyland canceled, our trip back to South Carolina put off for another year.

"Look," said Dad, pointing with a glow of hope on his tired face. "The hives are diminishing."

The second hurdle cleared. I thought now Bart would get well fast. Wasn't so. His leg grew ever larger—and soon he proved allergic to every antibiotic they had. "What are we going to do now?" cried Mom with so much anxiety I feared for *her* health.

"We're doing everything we can," was all Dad would say.

"Oh, Lord, why hast thou forsaken me?" mumbled Bart in his delirium. Tears streamed down my face and fell on my shirt like rain.

"The Lord has not forsaken you," said Dad. He knelt by Bart's bed and prayed, holding fast to his small hand while Mom slept on a cot put in the room for her to use. She didn't know the pills Dad had given her were tranquilizers, not aspirin for her headache. She'd been too upset to even notice the color.

Dad touched my head. "Go home and sleep, son. There's only so much you can do, and you've done that." Slowly I got up, stiff from sitting for so long, and headed for the door. When I gave Bart one more long last glance, I saw him tossing restlessly as my father fitted himself on the cot behind my mother.

The next day Mom had to rush to the hospital from ballet class, leaving me to warm up to piano music. "Life goes on, Jory. Forget your brother's problems for a while, if you can, and join us later on." No sooner was she out of sight than something dawned on me. Apple! Of course! Bart didn't want *an apple* . . . he wanted his dog. His puppy-pony!

In ten minutes I was out of my leotards and in a telephone booth calling my father. "How's Bart?" I asked.

"Not very good. Jory, I don't know how to tell your mother, but the specialist working on Bart wants to amputate his leg before the infection has a chance to weaken him more. I can't let him do that—and yet, we don't want to lose Bart."

"Don't you let them amputate!" I almost screamed. "You tell Bart—and make him hear—that I'm going home to take care of Apple. Please let Bart keep both his legs." God knows, Bart would feel even more inferior if he lost one.

"Jory, your brother lies on his bed and refuses to cooperate. He isn't trying to recover. It seems he wants to die. We can't give him any kind of antibiotic and his temperature is steadily rising. But I'm with you. There must be something we can do to bring down that fever."

For the first time in my life I hitched a ride home. A nice lady let me off at the bottom of the hill and I raced the rest of the way. Once Bart knew Apple was okay he'd get well. He was punishing himself, just the way he beat his fists against the rough bark of a tree when he broke something. I sobbed with the realization my kid brother was more important to me than I'd known before. Nutty little kid who didn't like himself very much. Hiding in his pretend games, telling tall tales so everyone would be impressed. Dad had told me a long time ago, ". . . indulge him in his pretense, Jory." But maybe we'd indulged him too much.

I gasped when I saw Apple in the barn of the mansion. He was chained to a stake driven into the ground of the floor. A dish of moist dog food was placed just beyond his reach.

His thick shaggy fur told the story of his hunger. He was

ragged, panting, looking at me with huge pleading eyes. Who had done this? He'd clawed the ground in his futile efforts to dig free, and now, still only an overgrown puppy, he lay and panted in the barn, which had been closed and shuttered cruelly.

"It's all right, boy," I soothed, as I set about getting him fresh water. He lapped it up so thirstily I had to take it away. I knew a little about doctoring. Dogs, like people, had to drink sparingly after a long thirst. Next I set him free and went to his shelf of supplies and took what looked best to me from a long row of cans. Apple was starving in the midst of plenty. I could feel his ribs when I ran my hands over his pitiful shabby coat that had been so beautiful.

When he'd eaten and had his fill of water, I curry-combed his thick mat of hair. Then I sat on the dirt floor and held his huge head on my lap. "Bart's coming home to you, Apple. He'll have two good legs too, I promise. I don't know who did this to you and why, but you can bet I'll find out." What worried me most was the awful suspicion that the very person who loved Apple most might be the very one who'd starved and punished his pet. Bart had such an odd way of reasoning. To his way of thinking, if Apple really suffered when he was gone, Apple would be ten times more grateful to see him.

Could Bart be that heartlessly cruel?

Outside, the July day was mildly hot. As I approached the great mansion I heard the low voices of two people. That old woman in black and the creepy old butler, both of them seated on a cool patio lush with colorful potted palms, and ferns planted in huge stone urns.

"John, I feel I should go down again and check on Bart's puppy. He was so happy to see me this morning, I couldn't understand why he was so hungry. Really, do you have to keep him chained up like that? It seems so cruel on a beautiful day like this."

"Madame, it is not a beautiful day," said the mean-looking

butler, as he sipped a beer and sprawled in one of her chaise longues. "When you insist on wearing black, naturally you feel hotter than anyone else."

"I don't want your opinion on how I dress. I want to know why you keep Apple chained."

"Because the dog might run off to look for his young master," said John sarcastically. "I guess you didn't think of that."

"You could lock the barn door. I'm going down to look at him again. He seemed so thin, so desperate."

"Madame, if you have to concern yourself, make it worthy of the bother. Be concerned for your grandson, who is about to lose his leg!"

She'd half risen from her chair, but at this announcement she sank back on the pillows. "Oh. He's worse? Did Emma and Marta talk again this morning?"

I sighed, knowing Emma liked to gossip and she shouldn't. Though I honestly didn't think she'd say anything important. She never told me any secrets. And Mom never had time to listen.

"Of course they did," grouched the butler. "Did you ever hear of a woman who didn't? Those two use stepladders every day to gab away. Though to hear Emma talk, the doctor and his wife are perfect."

"John, what did Marta find out about Bart? Tell me!"

"Well, Madame, it seems that kid has managed to drive a rusty nail into his knee and now he has gas gangrene—the kind of gangrene that demands amputation of the limb or the patient dies."

I stared from my hidden place at the two who sat and talked, the one very upset, the other totally unconcerned, almost amused at the reaction of his mistress.

"You're lying!" screamed the woman, jumping to her feet. "John, you tell me lies just to torture me more. I know Bart will be fine. His father will know what to do to help him recover. I know he will. He has to . . ." And then she broke into tears. She took off the veil then and wiped at her tears, and I glimpsed her face, not noticing the scars so much this time, only her look of suffering. Did she really care so much for Bart? Why should she care? Could she really be Bart's grandmother?—naw, she couldn't be. His grandmother was in a mental institution in Virginia.

I stepped forward then to let my presence be known. She appeared surprised to see me, remembered her bare face, and hastily put on her veil again.

"Good morning," I said addressing myself to the lady and ignoring the old man I couldn't help but detest. "I heard what your butler said, ma'am, and he's right only to a certain extent. My brother is very ill, but he does not have gas gangrene. And he will not lose his leg. My father is much too good a doctor to let that happen."

"Jory, are you sure Bart will be all right?" she asked with so much concern. "He's very dear to me . . . I can't tell you how much." She choked and bowed her head, working her thin, ringed hands convulsively.

"Yes, ma'am," I said. "If Bart wasn't allergic to most of the drugs the doctors have given him, they would have destroyed the infection—but that won't matter in the long run, for my dad will know what to do to help him. My father always knows just what to do." I turned then toward the butler and tried to put on adult authority. "As for Apple, he does not need to be kept chained in a hot barn with all the windows shuttered over. And he doesn't need to have his food and water placed just out of his reach. I don't know what's going on in this place, and why you want to make a nice dog like that suffer—but you'd better take good care of him if you don't want me to report you to the humane society." I whipped about and started toward home.

"Jory!" called the lady in black. "Stay! Don't leave yet. I want to know more about Bart."

Again I turned to look at her. "If you want to help my

brother, there's only one thing you can do—leave him alone! When he comes back, you tell him some nice reason why you can't be bothered—but don't you hurt his feelings."

She spoke again, pleading for me to stay and talk, but I strode on, thinking I'd done something to protect Bart. To protect him from what, I didn't know.

That very night Bart's fever raged higher. His doctors ordered him to be wrapped in a thermal blanket that worked like a refrigerator. I watched my father, I watched my mother, I saw them look at each other, touch each other, giving each other strength. Strangely, both turned to pick up cubes of ice that they rubbed on Bart's arms and legs, then his chest. Like one person with no need to speak. I choked up and bowed my head, feeling moved by their kind of love and understanding. I wanted then to speak up and tell them about the woman next door, but I'd promised Bart not to tell. He had the first friend in his life, the first pet that could tolerate him; yet the longer I withheld what I knew, the more my parents might be hurt in the long run. Why did I have to think that? How could that old lady hurt my parents?

Somehow I knew she could. Someday I knew she would. I wished I were a man, with the ability to make right decisions.

As I grew sleepier, I remembered the expression Dad used so often: "God works in mysterious ways his wonders to perform."

Next thing I knew Dad was shaking me awake. "Bart's better!" he cried. "Bart's going to keep his leg and recover!"

Slowly, day by day, that hideous swollen leg diminished in size. Gradually it turned a normal color, though Bart seemed listless and uncaring as he stared blankly ahead, not saying anything to anybody.

We were at the breakfast table one morning when Dad rubbed his tired eyes and informed us of something incredible.

"Cathy, you're not going to believe this, but the lab technicians found something odd in the culture they took from Bart's wound. We suspected rust; they found rust, which caused the tetanus, but they also found the very kind of staphylococcus often associated with fresh animal feces. It's truly a miracle Bart still had both of his legs."

Looking pale and tired enough to be sick herself, Mom nodded before her head bowed weakly to his shoulder. "If Clover were still around, I'd easily understand how he might—"

"You know how our Bart is. If anything filthy is within a mile he'll be the one to step on it, crawl in it, or pick it up and check it over. You know, when he kept on raving last night about apples I gave him one I'd bought and he let it fall to the floor, showing no interest." Mom closed her eyes while he went on stroking her back and talking. "When I told him we weren't flying East I could tell he was pleased." He looked my way. "I hope you're not too disappointed, Jory. We'll have to wait until next summer to visit your grandmother, or maybe this Christmas I can get away."

I was thinking mean thoughts. Bart always got what he wanted. He'd figured out a sure way to avoid visiting "ole" graves and "ole" grandmothers. He'd even given up Disneyland. And it wasn't like Bart to give up anything.

That evening I was with Bart alone, and Mom and Dad were in the hospital corridor talking to friends. I told Bart about the conversation I'd overheard between the old lady and her butler. "There they were, Bart, both of them on her terrace. She was so worried about you."

"She loves me," he whispered proudly, his voice very faint. "She loves me more than anybody," and here he looked thoughtful, "except perhaps, Apple."

Bart, I thought, don't think like that. But I couldn't speak and steal his pride in having found love outside his family.

With mixed emotions I watched his expressive face, my own emotions a tumble of uncertainty. What kind of kid brother did I have? Surely he had to know his parents would love him more than anyone else.

"Grandmother is afraid of that ole butler," he said, "but I can handle him good. I've got hidden powers real powerful."

"Bart, why do you keep going over there?"

He shrugged and stared at the wall. "Don't know. Jus' wanna go there."

"You know that Dad would give you a dog, any kind you want. All you have to do is ask, and he'll give you a puppy just like Apple."

His fierce, angry eyes drilled a hole in me. "There ain't no other dog like my puppy-pony. Apple is special."

I changed the subject. "How do you know that woman is scared of her butler? Did she tell you?"

"She don't have to tell me. I can jus' tell. He looks at her mean. She looks at him scared."

Scared, the same way I was beginning to look at just about everything.

Homecoming

Nice the way Momma kept fussing over me. Wouldn't last. She'd change as soon as I got well. Two long long weeks in this stinking hospital that wanted to take my leg and burn it in their furnace. Made me happy to look down and see my leg still there. Boy, just wait until I went back to school and I told them how I nearly had an "amputated" leg. They'd be impressed. Was made of good stuff that refused to rot and die. And I hadn't cried. Was brave too.

I remembered how Daddy hovered over me, looking sad and worried. Maybe he really did love me even if I wasn't his own true son. "Daddy!" I cried when I saw him. "You got good news, I can tell."

"It's nice to see you bright and happy-looking." He sat on the side of my bed and pulled me into his arms before he gave me a big kiss. Embarrassing. "Bart, I have great news. Your temperature is normal. Your knee is healing nicely. But being a doctor's son has a few advantages. I'm signing you out today. If I don't I fear you'll fade away to nothing. Once you're home I know Emma's delicious food will soon put some meat on those bones."

He looked at me in a kind way, like I really mattered just as much as Jory; it made me want to cry. "Where's Momma?" I asked.

"I had to get away early, so she stayed home to arrange a special homecoming party for you—so you really can't mind, can you?"

Could so! Wanted her here! Bet she didn't come 'cause she had to fiddle around with that lil ole Cindy, putting ribbons in her hair. I kept my silence and allowed Daddy to carry me out to his car. Felt good to be out in the sun, going home.

In the foyer Daddy stood me on my wobbling legs. I stared at Momma, who went first to Daddy and kissed him on the cheek—when I was there, wanting to be kissed first. I knew why she'd done that. She was afraid of me now. She saw my skinny body, my ugly, bony face. She was forcing herself to smile when she looked my way. I cringed when she finally came my way to do her duty to her son who hadn't died. Look at her fake happiness. I knew she didn't love me, didn't really want me anymore. And there was Jory, too, smiling and pretending he was happy for me to be home again when I knew all of them would have been glad to see me dead. I felt like Malcolm when he'd been a little boy, unwanted and unneeded, and so darn miserable.

"Bart, my darling!" said Momma. "Why do you look unhappy? Aren't you glad to be home?" She gathered me in her arms and tried to kiss me, but I yanked away. Saw her hurt face but that didn't count. She was only pretending, like I had to pretend all the time.

"It's so wonderful to have you here again, sweetheart," she went on with her lies. "Emma and I have been busy all morning planning just what we can do to make you happy. Since you complained so much about the awful hospital food, we've made all your favorite dishes." She smiled again and reached once more to hug me, but I wasn't gonna let her get under my skin with her "feminine wiles" John Amos had told me about. Good food and smiles and kisses were all parts of "feminine wiles."

"Bart, don't look so skeptical. Emma and I did fix *every one* of your favorite dishes." I stared at her. She turned red, then said with an effort, "You know, the ones you like best."

She went on forcing herself to be nice as Daddy came up and gave me a short cane. "Bear most of your weight on that until your knee is stronger."

Kinda fun hobbling around like an old man, like Malcolm Foxworth. Liked having them fuss over me, worried when I wouldn't eat. None of the presents they had for me were as good as what my grandmother next door would give. "Good gosh, Bart," whispered Jory during dinner, "do you have to act so ungrateful? Everybody went to an awful lot of trouble to please you."

"Hate apple pie."

"You said before apple pie was your favorite kind."

"Never said that! Hate chicken, too, and mashed potatoes, green salads—hate everything!"

"I believe it," said a disgusted brother who turned his back and ignored someone as picky as me. Then he reached to take a chicken leg from my plate. "Well . . . as long as you don't want it, it shouldn't go to waste." He ate every last piece of the chicken. Now I couldn't sneak into the kitchen late at night and stuff myself when they weren't watching. Let 'em all worry about me fading away to skin and bones, ending up in a damp, cold grave. Let 'em find out how much they missed me.

"Bart, please try and eat a little something," pleaded Momma. "What's wrong with the pie?"

I scowled, then slapped Jory's hand when he reached to take my slice of pie. "Can't eat pie without ice cream on top."

She smiled at me brilliantly, then called, "Emma, bring in the ice cream."

I shoved my plate away and slouched in my chair. "Don't feel so good. Need to be alone. Don't like people making such a fuss over me. Spoils my appetite."

Daddy looked as if he were losing patience with me. He didn't scold Jory for taking my pie either. That's all it took—one hour and they were tired of me and wishing I had died.

"Cathy," said Daddy, "don't plead with Bart anymore. If he doesn't want to eat he can excuse himself. He'll eat when he's hungry enough."

Stomach was rumbling right now. I couldn't eat that stuff in front of me now that Jory had taken away what I wanted most. There I sat, starving, while everyone forgot me and began to talk, laugh, and act like I was still in the hospital. I got up and hobbled toward my room. Daddy called, "Bart, I don't want you playing outside until that leg has time to heal thoroughly. Take a nap with your leg propped up. Later on you can watch television."

TV. What kind of homecoming treat was that? Appearing obedient, I entered my bedroom and stood near the doorway so I could shout to those in the dining room, "Don't nobody disturb my rest!"

Kept me two weeks in that hospital, and now I was home they were gonna keep me locked inside some more. I'd show 'em! Nobody was gonna keep me inside for another rotten week! But somebody kept an eye on me night and day before finally I could escape through the window after six whole days of being kept a prisoner. Already I'd missed too much of summer, and my Disneyland trip. Wasn't gonna miss anything else.

The big ole tree by the wall was not friendly, making it harder for me to climb. By the time I was next door my leg would ache. Pain wasn't nearly as good as I'd thought it would be. Being "normal" wasn't so hot. Jory sprained his ankle once and went right on dancing, ignoring the pain. I could ignore pain too.

When I was on top of the wall I looked behind to see who might be following. Nobody. Nobody cared what I did to hurt myself. Began to sniff—what was that rotten stinking smell coming from out of the hollow oak tree? Ah, I could just remember. Something dead in the hollow tree. What was it? Couldn't remember good anymore. Mind was fuzzy, full of mists that rolled like the fog.

Apple, better to think of Apple. Forget the stiff and aching knee by pretending it belonged to some frail ole man like Malcolm grew up to be. My young leg wanted to run, but my old one controlled all of me, taking over my mind, forcing me to lean heavily on my cane.

Ohh! What a pitiful sight it would be to see poor Apple lying dead in the barn. A pitiful bag of fur, skin, and bones. I'd cry, scream, hate those who'd tried to force me to fly East and abandon the very best friend I had. Animals were the only ones who knew how to really love with devotion.

A hundred years had come and gone since last I came this way before. More years passed, it seemed, while I limped to its doors. Get a grip on yourself, I thought. Steel your spine, like Malcolm steeled his. Prepare your eyes for a grisly sight, for Apple loved you too much, and now he had to pay the price by dying. Never, never again would I find such a true friend as the puppy-pony who'd been my Apple.

My balance, never good, swayed me right to left, from front to back, and made me feel hazy and crazy. I sensed something was behind me. I peeked over my shoulder and saw no one there. Nothing but those frightening animal shapes that were only green shrubs. Stupid gardeners should have something better to do than waste their time snipping at bushes when real money was out there waiting for real brains to pick it up. Thinking now just like Malcolm; John Amos would be pleased. Had to hunt up John Amos so he could smarten up my brains some more.

Suspecting the worst, I approached the place that Apple liked most. Now I couldn't see. Gone blind! My cane tapped the ground ahead of me. Dark. Why was it so dark? I inched along, peering this way and that. All the barn shutters were closed. Poor Apple, left in the dark to starve. A lump rose in my throat while I cried inside for a pet who'd loved me more than life itself.

I had to force myself to take another step forward. To see Apple dead would scar my soul, my eternal soul which John Amos said had to stay clean and pure if I was to get to heaven's pearly gates where Malcolm had gone.

One step more. I stopped. There was my Apple—and he wasn't dead! He was in a stall with the window open and he was chasing a red ball, swatting it with his huge pawlike hoofs—and there was plenty of food in his dish. Clean water in his bowl too. I stood there shaking all over as Apple ignored me and went on playing like I wasn't even there. *Why, he hadn't missed me at all!*

"YOU! YOU!" I screamed. "You've been eating and drinking, and having a good time! And all the time I was at death's door and you didn't care. And I thought you loved me. I thought you'd miss me a whole lot. And now you don't even bark-whinny to tell me you're glad I'm back! I HATE YOU, APPLE! HATE YOU FOR NOT CARING ENOUGH!"

Apple saw me then and ran to me, leaping to put his huge paw-hoofs on my shoulders as he slurped my face. His tail wagged furiously, but he wasn't fooling me. He'd found someone else to take care of him better—darn if *I'd* made his coat look so pretty. "Why didn't you die from loneliness?" I shrieked. I glared hatred at him, wanting him to wither away and disappear. He sensed my anger and dropped to all fours and stood with his tail between his legs and his head hanging down, his eyes rolled slantwise.

"YOU GET AWAY FROM ME! YOU NEED TO SUF-FER AS I SUFFERED! THEN YOU'LL BE GLAD TO HAVE ME BACK!" I took all his food, his water, and threw them in a wooden barrel. I picked up his red ball and hurled that so far he'd never find it. All the time Apple stood there, watching, not wagging his tail. He wanted me back, but now it was too late.

"You'll miss me now," I sobbed, stumbling away, locking him in the barn with all the windows closed and the shutters too. "Stay in darkness and die of hunger! I'll never come back, never!"

No sooner was I in the sunlight than I thought of the nice soft hay he had inside to lie on. I went into the barn again, seized up a pitchfork and raked all the hay away. He was whimpering now, trying to nuzzle up to me. Wouldn't let him. "You lie on the cold, hard floor! It will make all your bones ache, but I don't care, for I don't love you now!" Angry, I wiped the tears away and scratched my face.

In all my life I'd made only three friends. Apple, my grandmother, and John Amos. Apple had killed my love, and one of the other two had betrayed me by feeding him and stealing his love. John Amos wouldn't bother—had to be Grandmother.

Drifted home in a daze. That night my leg ached so badly Daddy came in and gave me a pill. He sat on the side of my bed and held me in his arms, making me feel safe as he spoke softly about falling into sweet dreams.

Fell into ugliness. Dead ones everywhere. Blood gushing out in great rivers, taking pieces of human beings down into the oceans of fire. Dead. I was dead. Funeral flowers on the altar. People sent me flowers who didn't know me, telling me they were glad to see me dead. Heard the sea of fire play devil music, making me hate music and dancing even more than I had.

The sun came in my window and fell on my face, stealing me from the devil's grasp. When I opened my eyes, terrified of what I might see, I saw only Jory at the foot of my bed, looking at me with pity. Didn't need pity. "Bart, you cried last night. I'm sorry your leg still hurts."

"Leg don't hurt at all!" I yelled.

Got up to go limping into the kitchen where Momma was feeding Cindy. Blasted Cindy. Emma was frying bacon for my breakfast. "Coffee and toast only," I yelled. "That's all I want to eat."

Momma winced, then looked up with her face strangely pale. "Bart, please don't yell. And you don't drink coffee. Why would you ask for coffee?"

"Time I started acting my age!" I barked. Carefully I eased myself down into Daddy's chair with arms. Daddy came in and saw me in his chair, but he didn't order me out. He just used my armless chair, then poured coffee into a cup until it was half full. He filled the cup to an inch of the brim with cream and then gave it to me.

"Hate cream in my coffee!"

"How can you be so sure when you haven't tried it?"

"Just know." I refused to drink the coffee he'd spoiled. (Malcolm like his coffee black—and so would I from now on.) Now all I had before me was dry toast—and if I had to be like Malcolm and grow smart brains, I couldn't spread butter and strawberry jam on my toast. Indigestion. Like Malcolm, had to worry about indigestion.

"Daddy, what's indigestion?"

"Something you don't need to have."

Sure was hard trying to be like Malcolm all the time. Seconds later Daddy was down on his knees, checking over my bad leg. "It looks worse today than it did yesterday," he said as he lifted his head, met my eyes, and scowled suspiciously. "Bart, you haven't been crawling on this bad knee, have you?"

"No!" I yelled, "I'm not crazy! The covers rubbed off some of my skin. Rough sheets. Hate cotton sheets. Like silk ones best." (Malcolm wouldn't sleep on anything but silk.)

"How would you know?" asked Daddy. "You've never had silk sheets." He continued to care for my knee, washing it first and then sprinkling on some white powder before covering my wound with a gauze pad held on with sticky tape. "Now, I'm serious, Bart. I warn you to stay off that knee. You stay in the house, out of the garden, or sit on the back veranda—no crawling in the dirt."

"It's a patio." I scowled to let him know he didn't know everything.

"All right, a patio—does that make you feel happy?"

No. Never was happy. Then I gave it more thought. Yes, I was happy sometimes—when I was pretending to be Malcolm, the all-powerful, the richest, the smartest. Playing the role of Malcolm was easy and better than anything or anyone else. Somehow I knew if I kept it up I'd end up just like Malcolm—rich, powerful, loved.

Longest kind of dull day dragged on endlessly with everybody keeping a close eye on me. Twilight came, and Momma got busy making herself prettier for Daddy who was due home any minute. Emma was fixing dinner. Jory was in his ballet class, and I slipped off the patio unseen. Down into the garden I hurried before anybody stopped me.

Evening time was spooky, with long, mean shadows. All the little humming, buzzing creatures of night came out and swarmed about my head. I fanned them away. I was going to John Amos. He was sitting alone in his room, reading some magazine that he hid as quickly as I entered without knocking. "You shouldn't do that," he said sourly, not even smiling to say he was glad I was alive, with two legs.

It was easy to put on Malcolm's glum look and scare him. "Did you give Apple water and food while I was sick?"

"Of course not," he said eagerly. "It was your grandmother who fed him and cared for him. I told you women can never be trusted to keep their word. Corrine Foxworth is no better than any other women with their wiles to trick men into being slaves."

"Corrine Foxworth—is that her name?"

"Of course, I've told you that before. She is Malcolm's daughter. He named her after his mother so he'd always be reminded of how false women are, how even a daughter could betray him—though he loved her well, too well, in my opinion."

I was growing bored of tales of women and their "wiles."

"Why don't you get your teeth fixed?" I asked. I didn't like the way he hissed and whistled through teeth too loose.

"Good! You said that just like Malcolm. You're learning. Being sick has been good for your soul—as it was for his. Now, listen carefully, Bart. Corrine is your real grandmother and was once married to your real father. She was Malcolm's most beloved child and she betrayed him by doing something so sinful she has to be punished."

"Has to be punished?"

"Yes, punished severely, but you are not to let her know your feelings for her have changed. Pretend you still love her, still admire her. And in that way she will be made vulnerable."

Knew what vulnerable meant. Another of those words I had to learn. Weak, bad to be weak. John Amos went for his Bible and put my hand on its worn black cover, all cracked and peeling. "Malcolm's own Bible," he said. "He left it to me in his will . . . though he could have left me more . . ."

I realized that John Amos was the one person in the world who had not yet disappointed me. Here was the true friend I needed. Old—but I could be old too when I wanted. Though I couldn't take my teeth from my mouth and put them in an ivory-colored cup.

I stared at the Bible, wanting to pull my hand away but afraid of what might happen if I did. "Swear on this Bible that you will do as Malcolm would have wanted his great-grandson to do—wreak vengeance against those who harmed him most."

How could I promise what he wanted, when a little of me still loved her? Maybe John Amos was lying. Maybe Jory had fed Apple.

"Bart, why do you hesitate? Are you a weakling? Have you no spine? Look again at your mother, at how she uses her body, her pretty face, her soft kisses and hugs to make your father do anything she wants. Take notice of how late he works at night, how tired he is when he comes home. Ask yourself why. Does he do it for himself—or for her, so he can buy her new clothes, fur coats, jewelry, and a big fine house to live in. That's how women use men, making them work while they play."

I swallowed. Momma had a job. She taught ballet dancing. But that was more fun than work, wasn't it? Did she ever buy anything with her money? Couldn't remember.

"Now, you go in to see your grandmother, and be like you were before, and soon you will find out who betrayed you. It wasn't me. You go in and pretend you are Malcolm. Call her Corrine—watch the guilt and shame flood her face, watch her eyes show fear, and you will know which one of us is loyal and trustworthy."

I had sworn hurt on those who had betrayed Malcolm, but I wasn't happy with myself as I limped on to the front parlor she liked best of all. I stood in the doorway and stared at her, my heart pounding, for I wanted so much to run to her arms and sit on her lap. Was it right for me to pretend to be Malcolm when I hadn't given her a chance to explain?

"Corrine," I said in a gruff voice. Oh, the game was so good, I couldn't be just Bart and feel secure. When I was Malcolm I felt so strong, so right.

"Bart," she cried happily, rising to extend her arms. "You've finally come to see me! I'm so glad to see you well and strong again." Then she hesitated. "Who told you my name?"

"John Amos told me," I said, frowning at her. "He told me you fed Apple and gave him water while I was away. Is that true?"

"Yes, darling, of course I did what I could for Apple. He missed you so much I pitied him. Surely you aren't angry."

"You stole him from me," I cried like a baby. "He was the best friend I ever had; the only one who really loved me, and you stole him away so now he likes you better."

"No, he doesn't. Bart, he likes me, but he loves you."

Now she wasn't smiling and pleased-looking. Just like John Amos had said, she knew I was on to her wiles. She was gonna tell me more lies. "Don't speak to me so gruffly," she begged. "It doesn't become a boy of ten years. Darling, you've been gone so long, and I've missed you so much. Can't you even show me a little affection?"

Suddenly, despite my promise, I was running into her arms and throwing my arms about her. "Grandmother! I really did hurt my knee bad! I was sweating so much my bed was wet. They wrapped me in a cold blanket and Momma and Daddy rubbed me down with ice. There was a man doctor who wanted to cut off my leg, but Daddy wouldn't let him. That doctor said he was glad I wasn't his son." I paused to take a breath. I forgot all about Malcolm. "Grandmother, I found out my daddy loves me after all—or else he would have been glad for that doctor to cut off my leg."

She seemed shocked. "Bart, for heaven's sake! How can you have the slightest doubt that he loves you? Of course he does. He'd have to love you, and Christopher was always a kind, loving boy . . ."

How did she know my daddy's name was Christopher? I narrowed my eyes. She was holding her hands over her mouth like she'd given away some secret. Then she was crying.

Tears. One of the ways women had to work men.

I turned away. Hated tears. Hated people who were weak. I put my hand on my shirtfront and felt the hard cover of Malcolm's book against my bare chest. That book was giving me his strength, transferring it from the pages to my blood. What if I did wear a child's weak, imperfect body? What difference did it make when soon she'd know just who was her master?

Home, had to get home before they missed me.

"Good night, Corrine."

I left her crying, still wondering how she knew my daddy's name.

In my garden I checked my peach pit again. No roots yet. I dug up my sweetpeas again. Still not sprouting. I didn't have luck with flowers, with peach pits, with nothing. With nothing but playing Malcolm the powerful. At that I was getting better and better. Smiling and happy, I went to bed.

The Horns of Dilemma

Never was Bart in our yard where he should be. I climbed the tree and sat on the wall, and then I saw Bart over in that lady's yard, down on his knees crawling. Sniffing the ground like a dog. "Bart!" I yelled, "Clover's gone, and you can't take his place."

I knew what he was doing—burying a bone and then sniffing around until he found it. He looked up, his eyes glazed and disoriented—and then he began to bark.

I yelled to set him straight, but he went on playing the frolicking puppy before he suddenly became an old man who dragged his leg. And it wasn't even the leg he'd hurt. What a nut he was. "Bart, straighten up! You're ten, not a hundred. If you keep walking crooked you'll grow that way."

"Crooked days make crooked ways."

"You don't make good sense."

"And the Lord said: 'do unto others as they have done unto you.'"

"Wrong. The correct quotation is: 'Do unto others *as you would have done unto you.*'" I reached to assist what seemed to be an old man. Bart scowled, panted, grabbed at his chest, then cried out about his bad heart that shouldn't have to endure tree-climbing.

"Bart, I'm fed up with you. All you do is make trouble. Have some sympathy for Mom and Dad—and me. It's going to be embarrassing having you for my brother when we go back to school."

He limped along behind me as I headed toward home, still panting, muttering between moans about how already he was a master of finances. "Never was born a brain more clever than mine," he mumbled.

He has really gone bananas, was all I could think as I listened to him. When he'd scrubbed his filthy hands with a brush as if he really wanted to get them clean, I gasped. That wasn't like Bart at all. He was still pretending to be someone else. Soon he had his teeth clean and was in bed. I ran fast to where I could eavesdrop on my parents, who were in the living room dancing to slow music.

As always, something sweet, soft, and romantic stole over me to see them like that. The tender way she looked at him; the gentle way he touched her. I cleared my throat before they did anything too intimate. Without changing their positions, both looked at me questioningly. "Yes, Jory," said Mom, her blue eyes dreamy.

"I want to talk to you about Bart," I said. "I think there are a few things you should know."

Dad looked relieved. Mom seemed to shrink into herself as she quietly sat beside Dad on the sofa. "We've been hoping you would come to us with Bart's secret."

None of it was easy to say. "Well," I began slowly, hoping to find the right words, "first, you should know Bart has lots of nightmares in which he wakes up crying. He pretends too much, such as hunting big game and normal kid stuff like that, but when I catch him crawling around sniffing the ground, then digging up a nasty old bone and carrying it between his teeth to bury it somewhere else, that's going too far." I paused and waited for them to say something. Mom had her head turned as if she were listening to hear the wind. Dad leaned forward, watching me intensely.

"Go on, Jory," he urged. "Don't stop now. We're not blind. We see how Bart is changing."

Dreading to tell more, I hung my head and spoke very low. "I've tried several times to tell you before. I was afraid then too. You've both been so worried about Bart that I couldn't speak."

"Please don't hold anything back," Dad said.

I looked only at my father, unable to meet my mother's fearful gaze. "The lady next door gives Bart all sorts of expensive gifts. She's given him a St. Bernard puppy he calls Apple, two miniature electric trains along with a small village and mountain settings—the complete works. She's had one huge room of hers turned into a playroom just for him. She would give me gifts too, but Bart won't let her."

Stunned, they turned to one another. Finally Dad said, "What else?"

I swallowed and heard my odd, husky voice. This was the worst part, the part that really hurt. "Yesterday I was in the backyard near the wall . . . you know, where that hollow tree is. I had the hedge clippers and was pruning like you showed me, Dad, when I smelled something putrid. It seemed to come from that hole in the tree. When I checked . . . I found . . ." Again I had to swallow before I could say it. "*I found Clover. He was dead and decaying. I dug a grave for him.*" Hastily I turned my back to wipe away tears, then I told them the rest. "I found a wire twisted around his neck. Somebody deliberately murdered my dog!"

They just sat on the sofa looking shocked and scared. Mom blinked back her tears; she too had loved Clover. Her hands trembled when she reached for a handkerchief. Next she locked her nervous hands together and kept them on her lap. Neither she nor Dad asked who had killed Clover. I figured they thought the same as I did.

Before he went to bed, Dad came into my room and talked to me for an hour, asking all sorts of questions about Bart, what he did with his time, where he went, and about the woman next door, and that butler too. I felt better now that I'd warned them. Now they could plan what to do with Bart. And I cried that night for the last time over Clover, who had been my first and only pet. I was going on fifteen, almost a man's age, and tears were only for little boys—not for someone almost six feet tall.

"You leave me alone!" yelled Bart when I asked him not to go next door. "You stop telling tales on me or you'll be sorry."

Each day took us closer to September and school days. As far as I could see, Bart wasn't responding to the tender loving care my parents gave him. They were too understanding in my opinion. "You listen to me, Bart, and stop pretending you're an old man named Malcolm Neal Foxworth, whoever he is!" But Bart couldn't let go of his pretend limp, his fake bad heart that made him gasp and pant. "Nobody is waiting for you to die to inherit your fortune. Dear little brother, you don't have any fortune!"

"Got twenty billion, ten million, fifty-five thousand, and six hundred and forty-two cents!" He used his fingers to tally up. "But I can't remember how much I have in stocks and bonds, so I guess you could triple that figure. A man isn't rich if he can name what he owns."

I hadn't known he could even name a figure like that. Just when I would say something sarcastic, Bart let out a yelp and doubled over. He fell to the floor and gasped. "Quick . . . my pills. I'm dying! My left arm is going numb! Save me, send for my doctors!"

That's when I left the house and went outdoors. I sat on

a lawn chair and pulled out a paperback novel to read. Bart was getting to me, really getting to me. It was like living with Jekyll and Hyde. If he had to act, why the heck didn't he choose some role better than a lame old guy with a bad heart?

"Jory, don't you care if I die?" Bart came out and asked me.

"Nope."

"You've never liked me!"

"I liked you better when you acted your own age."

"Would you believe Malcolm Neal Foxworth is the father of that lady next door, and she is my real grandmother, truly my own grandmother?"

"She told you that?"

"No. John Amos told me some, she told me more. John Amos tells me lots of stuff. He told me Daddy Paul and Daddy Chris were not brothers, that my momma only said that so we wouldn't find out her sin. He says a man named Bartholomew Winslow was my real daddy and he died in a fire. Our mother seduced him."

Seduced? I gave him a long searching look. "Do you know what that word means?"

"Nope—but I know it's bad, *real* bad!"

"Do you love our mother?"

Worry tormented his dark eyes. He sat heavily on the ground and contemplated his sneakers. He should have answered quickly, spontaneously. "Bart, do me a big favor and yourself too—go into the house and tell Mom and Dad what's bothering you. They'll understand anything. I know you think Mom loves me best, but it's not so. She has room in her heart for ten children."

"Ten?" he screamed. "You mean Momma is gonna adopt more?" He jumped up and ran then, haltingly, as if pretending to be old had made him lose what little agility he had. That hospital stay had robbed him of a great many things, in my opinion.

It was sneaky of me and not quite honorable, but I had

to hear what Bart told our mother when they were alone. She was on the back veranda. Cindy was on her lap, dozing as Mom read a book. When Bart ran up she quickly put the book down, then shifted Cindy onto a nearby chair as Bart stood staring at her, mutely pleading with his eyes.

Then, of all things, he asked, "What's your name?"

"You know my name," she said.

"Does it begin with a C?"

"Yes, of course it does." Now she looked disturbed.

"But—but—" he stumbled, "I know someone who cries after you go away. Someone little like me who is locked in closets and other scary places by his father, who doesn't like him anymore. Once the father put him in the attic for punishment. Big, dark, scary attic with mice and spooky shadows and spiders everywhere."

She seemed to freeze. "Who told you all of that?"

"His stepmother had dark red hair until he found out she was only his father's paramour."

Even from where I hid I could hear Momma breathing hard and fast, as if that small boy she lifted on her lap had suddenly turned dangerous. "Darling, you don't know what a paramour is, do you?"

He stared ahead into space. "There was a lady slender and fair who had red in her dark-dark hair. And she wasn't even married to his father who didn't care what he did, how he cried, or even if he died."

Her lips trembled, but she forced a smile. "Bart, I believe you have some poet in you. All that has a cadence, and it rhymes, too."

He scowled, turning dark burning eyes on her. "I despise poets, artists, musicians, dancers!"

She shivered, and I can't say I blamed her. He scared me, too. "Bart, I have to ask you this, and you must give me a truthful answer. Remember, no matter what you say you won't be punished. Did you hurt Clover?"

"Clover done gone away. Won't come back to live in my doghouse now."

She pushed him away then and quickly got up to leave the patio. Then she remembered Cindy and rushed back to pick her up. None of what she did made me feel better as I watched Bart's eyes.

As always, soon after one of his mean "attacks," Bart grew tired and sleepy and went to bed without his dinner. My mother smiled, laughed, and dressed to attend a formal celebration in honor of my father, who had been voted chief-of-staff of his hospital. I stood at the window and watched Dad lead her proudly to his car.

Late, way after two, I heard them come in. I had yet to fall asleep, and I could hear their conversation in the living room.

"Chris, I don't understand Bart at all, the way he talks, the way he moves, or even how he looks. I feel afraid of my own son, and that's sick."

"Come now, darling," he said with his arm about her shoulders, "I think you exaggerate. Bart will grow up to be a great actor if he keeps this up."

"Chris, I know sometimes high fevers leave a child with brain damage. Did the fever destroy part of his brain?"

"Look, Cathy, Bart tested out just fine. Don't go getting notions just because we gave him that test. All high fever patients have to undergo such examinations."

"But did you find anything unusual?" she persisted.

"No," Dad said firmly, "he's just an ordinary little boy with lots of emotional problems, and we, if anyone can, should understand what he's going through."

What did that mean?

"But Bart has everything! He isn't growing up as we did. He should be happy. Don't we do everything we can?"

"Yes, but sometimes even that isn't enough. Each child is

different, each has different needs. Obviously we are not giving Bart what he needs."

Mom was given to hot quick answers. Yet she sat on, silent and still, as I waited for more information. Dad wanted her to go to bed immediately, which was easy enough to see from the way he kissed her neck. But she was deep in thought. Her eyes were fixed on her silver sandals as she spoke of how Clover had died.

"It couldn't have been Bart," she said slowly, as if to convince herself as well as Dad. "It had to be some sadist who tortures animals—you know how we read that the animals in the zoo were being crippled? One of them must have seen Clover," and her voice died away, for so seldom did we ever see a stranger on our road.

"Chris," she added, while that horrible look of fright was still on her face, "today Bart took me completely by surprise. He told me about a little boy who was locked in closets and in the attic. Later on he told me that little boy's name was Malcolm. Could he know about him? Who could have told him that name? Chris, do you think somehow Bart has found out about us?"

I jerked. What was there to know about them that I didn't already know? I knew they had some terrible secret. I crawled away, then raced to my room and threw myself on my bed. Something awful was wrong with our lives. I felt it in my bones—and Bart must have sensed it in his, too.

The Snake

Sun and fog were playing games, keeping each other company. I had to sit alone in our garden. For fun I stared down at the thick scabs on my knee. I'd been warned by Daddy not to pick them off or they'd leave scars—but who cared about scars? I began to carefully lift the edges of the crust just to see what was underneath. I didn't see a darn thing but red, tender-looking flesh, ready to bleed again.

Sun won the game in the sky and shone hot on my head. Almost heard my brains frying. Didn't want fried brains. I moved to the shade.

Now my head was aching. I bit down on my lower lip hard enough to draw blood. Didn't hurt but later it would swell up so big Momma would have to feel worried. That would be good. She should be worried about what was happening to me.

Used to be Momma's little boy who got lots of attention until that dratted little girl came to take my place. Soon Momma and Jory would return from ballet class. That's all they cared about—dancing and Cindy. I knew about the important things in life, what really counted most—money.

Having lots of it, then you didn't have to think about needing it or how to get it. John Amos and Malcolm's book had taught me that.

"Bart," said Emma, who'd stolen up behind me. "I'm so sorry you missed your birthday trip to Disneyland. To make up for that I've made you a little birthday cake of your very own." She held in her hands a tiny cake with one candle in the middle of the chocolate. Was not just one year old! I struck that cake from her hands so it fell to the ground. She cried out, looking hurt enough to cry as she backed off. "That wasn't very grateful, or very kind," she said in a choked way. "Bart, why do you have to act so ugly? We all try to do our best."

I stuck out my tongue. She sighed and left me alone.

Later Emma came out again with that bratty girl in her arms. Wasn't my sister. Didn't want any sister. I hid behind a tree and peeked around. Emma put Cindy in the plastic swimming pool. She began to kick and splash the shallow water. Dumb, dumb, dumb . . . couldn't even swim. See how Emma laughed and enjoyed all her baby-doings when I could stand on my head. If I sat in that pool and splashed with my hands and feet she wouldn't think it was cute.

I waited for Emma to go away, but she pulled up a chair, sat down, and began to shell peas. Plop, plop, plop went the green peas into the blue bowl. "That's it, dearie," Emma encouraged Cindy. "Splash the water, kick your pretty legs, flap your sweet arms, and make your limbs strong so soon you'll be swimming."

I watched and waited, each pea she shelled telling me that soon Emma would have to get up and go into the kitchen. Cindy would be left alone. All alone. And she couldn't swim. Cats crouched down low like me when they wanted to catch a bird. Wish I had a tail to swish.

The last green pea fell. Emma rose to leave. I tensed my muscles. Just then Momma drove up in her bright red car and pulled to a stop by the garage. Emma waited to say hello. First it was Jory bounding over the lawn. "Hi, Emma!" he called. "What's for dinner?"

"You'll like my dinner no matter what," answered Emma, all grins for him, her handsome darling. *Not like she treated me—the brat!* "As for Bart," she went on, "I know he'll hate the peas, the vegetable casserole, the lamp chops, and the dessert. Lord knows that boy is hard to please."

Momma stopped to talk to Emma like she wasn't a servant, then she ran to play with Cindy, kissing and hugging her as if she hadn't seen the dummy in ten years. "Mom," sang out Jory, "why don't we both put on swimsuits and join Cindy in her pool?"

"I'll race you to the house, Jory!" agreed Momma, and off they ran like little kids.

"Now, you be a good little girl and keep on playing with your rubber ducky and boat," said Emma to Cindy. "Emma will be right back."

My head lifted before I began to wiggle on my belly on the ground. The brat in the pool stood up and took off her bathing suit. Stark naked and bold she hurled her wet suit at me, then teased and laughed and tormented me with her bare flesh. Then, as if bored with my reaction, she sat again in the shallow water and stared down at herself with a secret little smile. Wicked! Shameless! Imagine her showing her private parts to me.

Mothers should teach their daughters how to act decent, proper, modest. My mother was just like Corrine, whom John Amos had said was weak and never punished her children enough. "Yes, Bart, your grandmother ruined her children, and now they live in sin and flaunt God and his moral rules!"

I guess it was up to me to teach Cindy a lesson about modesty and shame. Forward I wiggled. *Now* I had her attention. Her blue eyes opened wide. Her rosy full lips parted. At first she seemed happy that finally I was gonna play kiddy games with her. Then, something wise put fright in her eyes. She froze and made me think of a timid rabbit scared by a vicious snake. Snake. Much better to be a snake than a cat. Snake in The Garden of Eden doing unto Eve what should have been done in the beginning. *Lo, said the Lord when he spied Eve in her nakedness, go forth from Eden and let the world hurl their stones.*

Hissing and flicking my tongue in and out, I edged closer. Was the Lord who spoke and I who obeyed. Wicked mother who refused to punish had made me what I was, an evil snake willing to do the Lord's bidding, even if it wasn't my own way.

I tried to flatten my head with willpower and make it small, flat, and reptilelike. Tears came to Cindy's huge, scared eyes, and she began to bawl as she tried to wiggle over the rounded rim of the wading pool. The water wasn't deep enough for a little girl to drown in, or else Emma wouldn't have left her alone.

But . . . if a boa constrictor from Brazil was on the loose— what chance did a two-year-old have?

I wiggled over the side and squirmed in the water. She screamed, "Barr-tie! Go'way, Barr-tie!"

"Hsss . . . ssss," I went. My S's longer than John Amos's. I coiled my body around her small naked one and hooked my legs under her neck, dragging her down into the water. Couldn't really drown, but the Lord above had to warn those who sinned. I'd seen jungle snakes unhinge their jaws on TV. I tried to unhinge mine. Then I could swallow Cindy whole.

All of a sudden another snake had me! I yelped and released my grip on Cindy to keep from drowning . . . or being eaten alive! *Lord, why hast thou forsaken me?*

"What the Devil do you think you're doing?" yelled Jory, red with rage as he shook me until my head rolled. "I watched you wiggle your way along to see what you had in mind. Bart—did you try to drown Cindy?"

"No!" I gasped. "Just punishing her a little, not much."

"Yeah," he sneered, "like you punished Clover a little."

"Never did nothing to Clover. I take good care of Apple. I am not a bad boy . . . I'm not, not, not."

"Why are you crying if you are so innocent? You killed him! I see it in your eyes!"

I glared hard at Jory, fury washing over me. "You hate me! I know you do!" I lunged forward and tried to hit him. Couldn't. I lowered my head, backed up, and ran forward to butt him squarely in the stomach. Down he went, all doubled over, crying out from the pain. Before he could kill me, I kicked him but didn't know it would end up where it did. My aim was never good. Gee . . . that must hurt a lot.

"Unfair to kick in the groin," he groaned, his face so pale he seemed on the edge of a faint. "That's dirty fighting, Bart. Gross, too."

Meanwhile Cindy had recovered enough to scramble from the pool, and she tottered off naked toward the house, howling at the top of her lungs.

"Wicked sinful girl!" I screamed. "All this is her fault! Her fault!"

From the back door Emma came on the run, her white apron fluttering, her hands covered with flour. She was closely followed by Momma, who had put on a skimpy blue bikini. "Bart, what have you done?" screamed Momma. She swept Cindy up in her arms, then swooped to pick up a towel Emma had dropped.

"Mommy," sobbed Cindy. "Big snake came . . . big snake!"

Why, imagine that. She'd known what I was. Not so dumb after all. Momma wrapped the towel about Cindy and stood her on the ground. She glared at me just as I had my foot raised to kick Jory, who was panting with pain. "Bart . . . if you dare to kick Jory again, you will regret it!"

Emma glared at me with hatred. I looked from one to the other. Everybody hated me, would be glad to see me in my grave.

Sore and full of pain, Jory tried to rise, not so graceful now. Just as awkward as me. He wasn't so handsome now. Still he could shout: "You're crazy, Bart! Crazy as a loon!"

"Bart, don't you dare throw that stone at your brother!" cried Momma when she saw me swoop to pick up one.

"You dreadful boy! Don't you throw that!" screamed Emma.

I whipped around and ran to pound on Emma with my fists. "You stop calling me names!" I yelled. "I'm not dreadful! I'm not bad!"

Momma raced toward me and grabbed me and threw me down. "Don't you ever throw another stone as long as you live, or use your fists on another woman!" Momma shouted as she pinned my shoulders to the ground.

Red rage entered my mind, making me see her as all women with "beguiling" curves and wiles. Malcolm knew about them all, told everything about how he'd wanted to pound all their breasts flat. I filled my eyes with Malcolm's malicious hatred, and it worked. Momma trembled as she held me down. "Bart, what's wrong with you? You don't know what you're saying or doing. You don't even look like yourself."

I bared my teeth as if to bite her—then I tried to. She slapped me, hard, repeatedly, until I began to cry.

"You go up into the attic and stay there, Bart Sheffield, until I come up and see what has to be done to set you straight!"

Scary in the attic. I sat on the edge of one of those little beds and waited for her to come in. She'd never spanked me. A few slaps besides the ones on my face today were all the punishment I'd had up until now . . . and now she was doing to me just what had been done to Malcolm. I was just like Malcolm.

The door into the attic opened and I heard her climbing the steep, narrow stairs. Her mouth was set in a grim line as she towered above me, staring downward, as if forcing herself to look at me. I never thought she could look so mean.

"Pull down your pants, Bart."

"No!"

"Do as I say or your punishment will be much worse."

"No! You can't hurt me. You lay one hand on me and I'll wait until you're in your ole ballet class and then I'll get Cindy—and Emma won't be able to stop me! I can be in a thousand places before she can move to one—and the police won't put me in jail because I'm a minor!"

"Bart, I'm losing patience with you."

"That won't be all you'll lose if you hit me!" I bellowed.

She paused three feet from where I sat on the bed. Her small pale hands rose to her throat and she said quietly, "Oh, God . . ." and it was just a hoarse whisper. "I should have known a child conceived under such circumstances would turn out like this. Bart, I'm so sorry your son is a monster."

A monster? Was I a monster?

No—she was the monster! She was doing to me just what Malcolm's mother had done, the cause of him being put in the attic and punished. I hated her then, just as much as I'd loved her before.

I screamed it out: "I hate you, Momma! I hope you drop dead!"

That's when she backed away, tears in her eyes. Then she turned and ran. But before she went down the stairs she locked the door to keep me up in that miserable dry attic that I hated and feared. She was gonna make me strong like Malcolm, and mean too. Someday she'd pay. I'd make her pay for doing this to me, when I wanted to be good, and wanted her to love me just a little more than Cindy or Jory. I began to cry. Nothing ever worked out the way I wanted it to.

It was Daddy who spanked my bare bottom after he came home and heard all they had to tell him about me. I admired him for ignoring the way I pleaded and apologized.

"Did you feel any of that?" he asked when he was finished, and I pulled up my pants.

I smiled. "No. To hurt me you gotta break my bones, and then the police would throw you in jail for child abuse."

He studied me with those stern blue eyes. "You think you

have the best of us, don't you?" he asked in his calm, rational way. "You think because you are a minor there is no law that can touch you, but you are wrong, Bart. We live in a civilized society where people are expected to conform to the rules. No one is ever beyond the control of the law, even the President. And one of the worst punishments for a child to endure is being locked away so he cannot come and go at his own free will." He looked sad then. "That can be a very traumatic experience."

I didn't say anything. He spoke again. "Your mother and I have decided we can no longer tolerate your behavior. So as soon as I can arrange it, you will go once a day to a psychiatrist. If we have to, if you persist in defying us, we will leave you in the care of doctors who can help you to learn how to behave normally."

"You can't make me," I gasped, terrified some shrink would have me locked away behind bars forever. "If you try and force me, I'll kill myself!"

He looked at me sternly. "Bart, you won't kill yourself. So don't you sit there and think you can outwit your mother or me. Your mother and I have faced up to bigger and better than a ten-year-old boy—remember that."

Later that evening when I was in my bed, I heard Momma and Daddy really yelling at each other, yelling like I'd never heard them before.

"Why did you send Bart into the attic, Catherine? Did you have to do that? Couldn't you just have ordered him to stay in his room and wait until I came home?"

"No! He likes being in his room. He has everything in there to make it a pleasant place to be—and as you know well, the attic is not pleasant. I did what I had to."

"What you had to? Cathy—do you realize who you sound like?"

"Well," she said with ice in her voice, "haven't I been telling you all along that's what I am—a bitch who cares only about herself?"

~   ~   ~

They took me to a shrink the very next day, shoved me down
in a chair and told me to stay there. They sat beside me until
a door opened and we were called inside. A woman doctor was
behind a big desk. At least they could have chosen a man. I
hated her because her hair was slick and black like Madame
Marisha's hair when she was young and posing for pictures.
Her white blouse bulged in front so I had to turn my eyes
away.

"Dr. Sheffield, you and your wife can wait outside, we will
talk later." I watched my parents go out the door. Never had I
felt so all alone as when that woman turned to me and looked
me over with her kind eyes that were hiding mean thoughts.
"You don't want to be here, do you?" she asked. I wouldn't give
her the satisfaction of letting her know I heard. "My name is
Dr. Mary Oberman."

So what?

"There are toys over on that table . . . help yourself."

Toys . . . I wasn't a baby. I glared at her. She turned her
head and I knew she was uncomfortable, though trying not to
let it show. "Your parents have told me you like to play pretend
games. Is that because you don't have enough playmates?"

Didn't have any. But darn if that idiot woman was
gonna know. I'd be a fool to tell her John Amos was the best
friend I had. Once it had been my grandmother, but she had
betrayed me.

"Bart, you can sit there and be silent, but you only suc-
ceed in hurting those who love you most, and *you* are hurt
more than anyone else. Your parents want to help you. That's
why they brought you here. You have to cooperate and try. Tell
me if you're happy. Tell me if you feel frustrated, and if you
like the way your life is going."

Wouldn't say yes, wouldn't say no. Wouldn't say anything
and she couldn't make me. Then she talked about people who
kept themselves locked up, and how that could ruin them

emotionally. All her words were like rain on the windowpane I made myself into.

"Do you hate your mother and father?"

Wouldn't answer.

"Your brother Jory, do you like him?"

Jory was okay. He'd be better if he was more clumsy than me, and ugly too.

"Your adopted sister Cindy . . . what do you think of her?"

Maybe my eyes told her something, for she scribbled away on her notepad. "Bart," she began when she put her pen aside, her face trying to look motherly and kind, "if you refuse to cooperate, we will have no choice but to put you in a hospital where many doctors can try to help you regain control of your emotions. You won't be mistreated, but it won't be as nice as being at home. You won't have your own room, your own things, your own parents except once a week for an hour. So don't you think it would be much nicer to try and help yourself before this goes any further? What is it that changed you from the boy you were last summer?"

Didn't want to be locked in some crazy house with lots of nuts who might be bigger and meaner than me, and I wouldn't be able to visit John Amos and Apple.

What could I do? I remembered words from Malcolm's book, and how he made people think he was "giving in," all the time going his own way.

I'd cry, I'd say how sorry I was, and when I did this, even I thought I was sincere. I said, "It's Momma . . . she loves Jory more than me. She loves Cindy better too. I don't have anybody. I hate not having anybody."

It went on and on. Even after I really blabbed, she told my parents I'd have to continue seeing her for a year or more. "He's a very confused little boy." She smiled and touched my mother's shoulder. "Don't blame yourself. Bart seems programmed for self-loathing, and though he might seem to hate you for not loving him enough, he doesn't like himself.

Therefore he believes anyone who does love him is a big fool. It's a sickness all right. As real as any physical disease, and worse in many ways, for Bart cannot find himself."

I was hiding, eavesdropping, surprised to hear her say what she did.

"He loves you, Mrs. Sheffield, with a love almost religious. Therefore he expects you to be perfect, at the same time knowing he is unworthy of your attention; and still, paradoxically, he wants you to see him and acknowledge him as the best son you have."

"But I don't understand," said Momma, leaning her head on Daddy's shoulder. "How can he love me and want to hurt me so much?"

"Human nature is very complex. Your son is very complex. The good and the bad are fighting to dominate his personality. He is unconsciously aware of this battle and has found a very intriguing solution. He identifies the evil side of himself as an old man he's named Malcolm. Just another of the many characters who enable him to like himself better."

Both my parents sat very still with wide eyes, looking sort of helpless.

Hours later, before I said my bedtime prayers, I crept down the long hall and listened outside my parents' bedroom. Momma was saying, "It's as if we will always be in the attic and never, never set free."

What did the attic have to do with Malcolm and me? Was it only because both of us had been sent up there for punishment?

On my hands and knees I stole away down the hall, crept into my bed, and lay there quietly, scared of myself and my "subconscious."

Beneath my pillow was Malcolm's journal, which I was absorbing day by day, night by night. Growing stronger, and smarter.

Gathering Darkness

In the living room the next evening. Mom and Dad settled down before the fire I'd kindled. Forgotten by them because I said so little, I crouched down on the floor near the doorway, hoping they wouldn't see me there, and they'd think I'd gone away as I should have. I didn't feel good about deliberately deceiving them, but sometimes it was better to know for certain than to keep on guessing.

At first Mom didn't say anything much, then she brought up the visit to Dr. Oberman. "Bart hates me, Chris. He hates you too, and Jory, and Cindy. I think he's got Emma on his list too, but more than anyone, it's me he despises. He resents me for not loving him exclusively." He pulled her closer to his chest and held her there as on and on they talked. When they mentioned slipping into Bart's bedroom and seeing if he was there, I quickly scurried into a nearby closet and waited for them to pass on to Bart's room.

"Has he eaten dinner?" asked Dad.

"No." She said this like she wanted him to stay asleep so she could avoid the problem he was when awake. But just them being there, staring down at him, brought Bart out of his nap, and without a word in response to their affectionate greetings, he followed them into the dining room. Meals had to be eaten, even when a ten-year-old boy sat silent and scowling, refusing to meet anyone's eyes.

It was a terribly awkward meal, with no one comfortable. Appetites were small, and even Cindy was cross. Emma didn't speak either, only performed her duties silently. Even the wind that blew incessantly died down and the trees stood still, their leaves hanging as if frozen. All of a sudden it felt so cold, making me think of the graves Bart was always talking about.

I sat wondering how Mom and Dad could force Bart to go to Dr. Oberman's sessions. How could anyone force him to talk when he could be so darn stubborn? And Dad was busy enough without taking time from his patients—that alone should show Bart who cared enough.

"Going to bed now," said Bart coldly, standing without asking permission to leave the table. He left the dining room. We sat on, caught in some kind of spell Bart had cast.

Dad broke the silence. "Bart isn't himself. Obviously something is bothering him so much he can't even eat. We have to find out what it is."

"Mom," I said, "I think if you went in and sat on Bart's bed first tonight, and stayed a long time with him, and didn't come in to my room or Cindy's, that might make up for a lot."

She gave me a strange, long look, as if not believing it could be that simple. Dad agreed with me, saying it wouldn't do any harm.

Bart was faking sleep, it was easy to see that. I backed away and stood near Dad in the hallway, in the shadows where Bart couldn't see us. I was ready to spring forward and save Mom if Bart turned mean. Dad kept a restraining hand on my shoulder, and whispered softly, "He's just a boy, Jory, a very troubled little boy. A bit smaller than most ten-year-old boys, a bit thinner too, and maybe that's part of the problem.

Bart is having more trouble growing up than most boys do."

Tensing, I waited for him to say more. "It's amazing how he could be born with so little grace, when his mother has so much."

I looked to where Mom stood gazing down on Bart, who looked darkly sullen in sleep—if he was asleep. Then she came running from his room, throwing Dad a wild, distraught look. "Chris, I'm afraid of him! You go in. If he wakes up and yells at me as he did before, I'll slap him. I'll feel like putting him in the closet, or up in the attic." Both her hands rose to clamp over her mouth. "I didn't mean that," she whispered weakly.

"Of course you didn't. I hope he didn't hear you. Cathy, I think you'd better take two aspirins and go to bed, and I'll tuck Bart and Jory into bed." He gave me a big joking smile as I grinned back. Our nighttime talks were the kind of tucking in he gave me . . . advice on how to handle difficult situations. Man-to-man stuff a woman didn't have to know about.

It was Dad who had the nerve to approach Bart, and he perched with ease on the side of his bed. I knew Bart always slept lightly, and when Dad sat down, the depression he made rolled Bart's slight figure onto his side. That would awaken even someone like me, who *used* to sleep deeply and soundly.

Cautiously I stole closer, wanting to see for myself if Bart was faking. Behind his closed lids his eyeballs were jerking spasmodically, as if he watched a tennis game or something much more terrifying.

"Bart . . . wake up."

As if Dad had fired the words from a giant cannon put near his ears, Bart jolted wide awake. He bolted upright, his dark eyes bulging and terrified. He stared at Dad.

"Son, it's not eight o'clock yet. Emma has made a lemon pie for dessert that she had to leave in the fridge to set. Don't tell me you don't want a slice. It's a beautiful evening. I used to think, when I was your age, that twilight was the best time of all to play outside. Hide-and-seek, or red light, green light . . ."

Bart stared at Dad as if he spoke in a foreign tongue.

"Come, Bart, don't sulk alone. I love you, and your mother loves you. It doesn't matter if sometimes you move less than gracefully. There are other things that count more, such as honor and respect. Stop trying to be what you aren't. You don't have to be anyone super-special; in our eyes, you already are super-special."

Bart just sat on his bed and stared at Dad with hostility. Why couldn't Dad see him as I did? Could a man as smart as Dad be blind when it came to seeing his son honestly? Had Bart opened his eyes when Mom was in the room, and had she seen the hatred there? She could always see more than Dad, even if he was a doctor.

"Summer's almost gone, Bart. Lemon pies get eaten by others. What you don't take today may not be there tomorrow."

Why was he being so nice to that boy who looked at him with daggers that could kill?

Obediently, when Dad turned to leave the room, Bart tagged along behind him. I was Bart's unseen shadow. Suddenly Bart ran ahead of Dad, who was on the back porch now, and skipped backward until he nearly tumbled down the steps. "You aren't my father," he growled, "and you can't fool me. You hate me and want me dead!"

Heavily Dad sat in a chair close to the one where Mom was sitting with Cindy on her lap. Bart went to the swings to sit, not pushing with his feet, just sitting and holding fast to the ropes, as if he might fall off the wooden slat.

We all ate a slice of Emma's delicious lemon pie, all but Bart, who just sat where he was and refused to budge. Then Dad was getting up and saying he had to check on a patient in the hospital. He threw Bart a worried glance and spoke softly to Mom. "Take it easy, darling. Stop looking so troubled. I'll be home soon. Maybe Mary Oberman isn't the best psychiatrist for Bart. He seems to have a great deal of hostility toward women. I'll find another psychiatrist, a man." He leaned to kiss her upturned face. I heard the soft moist sound of their lips meeting. Then they stared deep into each other's eyes and I wondered what they saw. "I love you, Cathy. Please stop worrying. Everything will work out fine. We will all survive."

"Yes," she said dully, throwing Bart a doubtful look, "but I can't help worrying about Bart . . . he seems so confused."

Straightening, Dad cast Bart a long, hard, observant look. "Yes," he said without doubt. "Bart's a survivor too. See how fast he clings to the ropes, and he's less than two feet from the ground. He just doesn't trust or believe in himself. I think he seeks strength in pretending to be older and wiser; security is in something other than himself. As a ten-year-old boy, he is lost. So it's up to us to find the right person to help him, even though it seems we cannot."

"Drive carefully," she said, as she always did watching him depart with her heart in her eyes.

Very determined to stay up and protect Mom and Cindy, I still found myself growing sleepy. Every time I checked I saw Bart still on the swing, his dark eyes staring blankly into space, as very gently he moved the swing an inch or so, no more than the wind could blow his weight.

"I'm going to put Cindy to bed now, Jory," Mom said to me, then called to Bart, "Bedtime . . . I'll be in to see you in a few minutes. Clean your teeth and wash your hands and face. We saved you a slice of lemon pie to eat before you brush your teeth."

No replay from the swing, but he did get up awkwardly, pausing to glance at his bare feet, stopping to stare at his hands, to finger his pajamas, to glance up at the sky, at the distant hills.

Inside the house Bart wandered aimlessly from object to object, picking one up, turning it over, and staring at the bottom before he set it down. A small Venetian glass sailboat held his attention for a moment, and then he seemed to freeze as his eyes found a lovely porcelain ballerina in arabesque position. It was a figurine my mom had given to Dr. Paul after she married my father; in many ways the dancer was like Mom must have looked when she was very young.

Gingerly he picked up the delicate figure with its fluffy frozen froth of lace tutu and frail, pale arms and legs. He turned it over, stared at the information printed on the bottom. *Limoges*, it said, for I'd read it too. Next he touched the golden hair, parted in the middle and drawn softly back in waves and held in place with pink china roses.

Then deliberately he let it slip from his hands.

It fell to the bare floor and broke into several large pieces. I dashed forward, thinking I could glue them back together and maybe Mom wouldn't notice—but Bart put his foot on the ballerina's head and ground it fiercely with his bare foot.

"Bart!" I cried out, "that was a hateful thing to do! You know mother prizes that more than anything else. You shouldn't have."

"Don't tell me what I shouldn't and should do! You leave me alone and say nothing about what you just saw. It was an accident, *boy*, an accident."

Whose voice was that? Not Bart's. He was pretending to be that old man again.

I ran for a broom and a dustpan to clean up the shards of what had been a lovely ballerina, hoping Mom wouldn't notice she was missing from the shelf.

When I remembered Bart again, I hurried to find him slyly watching Mom as she held Cindy on her lap, brushing her hair.

Mom glanced up and happened to catch Bart watching. I saw her blanch and try to smile, but something she saw made her smile fade before it even shone.

In a flashing streak Bart ran forward and shoved Cindy from Mom's lap. Cindy squealed as she fell on the floor—then jumped up to howl. She raced to Mom, who picked her up again, then rose to tower over Bart. "Bart, why did you do that?"

He spread his legs and stared up into her face scornfully. Then he left the room without looking back.

"Mom," I said, as she calmed Cindy down and put her into bed, "Bart's very sick in his head. You let Dad take him to any shrink he wants, but make him stay there until he's well."

I heard her sob, but it wasn't until later that she broke and cried.

This time it was me who held her; my arms that gave her comfort. I felt so adult and responsible.

"Jory, Jory," she sobbed, clinging fast to me, "why does Bart hate me? What have I done?"

What could I say? I didn't know any of the answers.

"Maybe you should try to figure out why Bart is so different from me, for I would die rather than make you unhappy."

She held me, then stared into space. "Jory, my life has been a series of obstacles. I feel if one more horrible thing happens, I may break . . . and I can't allow that to happen. People are so complicated, Jory, especially adults. When I was ten, I used to think that adults had it so easy, with all the power and rights to do as they wanted. I never guessed being a parent was so difficult. But not you, darling, not you . . ."

I knew her life had been full of sadness, losing her parents, then Cory, Carrie, my father, and then her second husband.

"The child of my revenge," she whispered as if to herself. "All the while I carried Bart I suffered from the guilt I felt. I loved his father so much . . . and in a way I helped kill him."

"Mom," I said with sudden insight, "maybe Bart senses your guilt when you look at him—do you think?"

PART THREE

Malcolm's Rage

Sunlight fell on my face and woke me up. When I was dressed, suddenly I didn't feel so old like Malcolm, and in a way I was glad. In another way I was sad, for Malcolm was so dependable.

Why didn't I have friends my own age, like other boys? Why was it only old people liked me? It didn't matter now that my grandmother had said she loved me, now that she'd stolen Apple. I had to face up to the fact that only John Amos was my true friend.

Went outside and crawled around before breakfast, sniffed at the ground, smelled the wild things that were scared of me in daylight. Little rabbit ran like crazy and I wouldn't hurt it, wouldn't.

They kept watching me at the breakfast table like they expected me to do something awful. I noticed that Daddy didn't ask Jory how he was today, only asked me. I scowled down at my cold cereal. Hated raisins! Looked like little dead bugs.

"Bart, I just asked you a question."

Knew that already. "I'm okay," I said without looking at Daddy, who always woke up in a good mood and never looked glum like me—and Momma. "I just wish you'd hire a really good cook. Or better if Momma would stay home and cook our meals like other mothers. Emma's stuff ain't fit for man nor beast to eat."

Jory stared at me hard and kicked my leg under the table like he was trying to warn me to keep my mouth shut.

"Emma didn't cook your cold cereal, Bart," said Daddy. "It comes that way in a box. And until this morning you always liked plenty of raisins. You used to want Jory's. But if raisins offend you in some way this morning, don't eat them. And why is your lower lip bleeding?"

Was it? Doctors were always seeing blood 'cause they were always cutting up people.

Jory took it on himself to answer. "He was playing wolf this morning, Dad, that's all. I guess when he jumped at the rabbit and tried to bite off its head, he bit himself." He grinned at me as if pleased with my stupidity.

Something was up. Could tell because nobody asked why I would play wolf. They just looked at me as if they expected me to act crazy.

Heard Momma and Daddy whispering beyond the pantry— talking about me. Heard doctors mentioned, new head shrinks. Wouldn't go! Couldn't make me!

Then Mom was back in the kitchen talking to Jory as Daddy went on to the garage and started his car.

"Mom, are we really going through with the performance tonight?"

She threw me a troubled glance, then forced a smile and said, "Of course. I can't disappoint my students, their parents, and the other guests who have already bought their tickets."

Fools and their money were soon parted.

Jory said, "I think I'll call Melodie. Yesterday I told her the show might be canceled."

"Jory, why would you tell her that?"

He looked at me, as if I were to blame for everything, even shows that weren't canceled—and I wouldn't go. Not even if they remembered to ask me. Didn't want to see sissy-silly ballet where everybody danced and said nothing. They weren't even going to dance *Swan Lake,* but the dumbest, dullest ballet of all—*Coppelia.*

Daddy came back in the house then, having forgotten something as usual. "I guess you'll be the prince," he said to Jory, who turned on him with scorn.

"Gosh, Dad, don't you ever learn? There isn't a prince in *Coppelia!* Most of the time I'm only in the *corps,* but Mom will be terrific in her role. She's choreographed it herself."

"What are you saying?" roared Daddy, turning to glare at Momma. "Cathy, you know you're not supposed to dance on your trick knee! You promised me you would never dance professionally again. At any moment that knee could give way, and down you'd go. One more fall and you may end up crippled for life."

"Just one more time," she pleaded, as if her whole life depended on dancing again. "I'm going to be only the mechanical doll, sitting in a chair—don't get so worked up over nothing."

"No!" he stormed again. "If you go on tonight and don't fall, then you'll think your knee is fine. You'll want to repeat your success, and one more time might see your knee permanently damaged. Just one serious fall and you could break your leg, your pelvis, your back . . . it's happened before, you know that!"

"Name every bone in my body!" she shrilled back at him, and I was thinking, thinking: If she broke her bones and couldn't dance again, then she'd have to stay home with me all the time.

"Honestly. Chris, sometimes you act like I'm your slave! Look at me. I'm thirty-seven years old, and soon I'll be too old to dance at all. Let me feel useful, as you feel useful. I have to dance—*just one more time.*"

"No," he repeated, but less firmly. "If I give in it won't be the last time. You'll want to do it again . . ."

"Chris, I'm not going to plead. There is not a student I have capable of playing the role—and I am going on whether or not you like it!" She threw me a glance, as if she worried more about what I thought than what he thought. I was happy, very happy . . . for she *was* going to fall! Deep inside of me I knew I could make her fall with my wishes. I'd sit in the audience and give her the evil eye; then she'd be my playmate. I'd teach her how to crawl around and sniff the ground like a dog or an Indian, and she'd be surprised at all that could be found out from sniffing.

"I am not talking of a trifling injury, Catherine," said that hateful husband. "All your life you have given your joints a great deal of stress and disregarded the pain. It's time you started realizing that the good health of your family depends on your well-being."

I scowled at Dad, sorry he'd forgotten something and had to come back and hear too much. Momma didn't even seem surprised he'd forgotten his wallet again, and he was a doctor who was supposed to have a good memory. She gave him his wallet, which had been left beside his breakfast plate, and smiled at him crookedly. "You do this every day. You go out to the garage, start your car, and then remember you don't have your wallet."

His smile was just as crooked as hers. "Yes, of course I do. It gives me the opportunity to come back and hear all the things you don't tell me." He stuffed the wallet in his hip pocket.

"Chris, I don't like to go against your wishes, but I can't allow a second-rate performance, and it's Jory's big chance to show off in his solo . . ."

"For once in your life, Catherine, listen to what I say. That knee has been x-rayed, you know the cartilage is broken, and you still complain of chronic pain. You haven't danced on stage for years. Chronic pain is one thing—acute pain another. Is that what you want?"

"Oh, you doctors!" she scoffed. "All of you have such dreary notions of how frail the human body is. My knee hurts, so what? All my dancers complain of aches and pains. When I was in South Carolina, the dancers complained, in New York they complained, in London . . . so what is pain to a dancer? Nothing, doctor, absolutely nothing I can't put up with."

"Cathy!"

"My knee has not hurt seriously in more than two full years. Have you heard me gripe about pain? No, you haven't!"

With that, Dad strode from the kitchen, through the utility room, and on into the garage.

In a flash she was running after him, and I was running after her—hoping to hear more of this argument—and hoping she'd win. Then I'd have her for my very own.

"Chris," she cried, throwing open the passenger door and slipping inside his car, where she threw her arms about his neck. "Don't go away angry. I love you, respect you, and vow on my word of honor that this will be the very last time I perform. I swear I will never, never dance on stage again. I know why I should stay home . . . I know . . ."

They kissed. Never saw people who liked to kiss so much. Then she was pulling away and looking softly into his eyes, stroking his cheek as she murmured, "This is my first chance to dance professionally with Julian's son, darling. Look at Jory, how much he resembles Julian. I've choreographed a special *pas de deux* in which I'm the mechanical doll and Jory is a mechanical soldier. It's the best thing I've ever done. I want you out in the audience watching, feeling proud of your wife and son. I don't want you sitting there worrying about my knee. Honestly, I've rehearsed, and it does not hurt!"

She stroked him and kissed him some more, and I could see he loved her more than anything, more than us, even more than himself. Fool! Damned fool to love any woman that much!

"All right," he said. "But this must be the last time. Your knee cannot take years and years of practice. Even in teaching you use that knee too much, so much so that other joints could become impaired."

I watched her turn from him and leave the car, her voice so sad when she spoke. "Years ago Madame Marisha told me there would be no life for me without dancing, and I denied this was so. Now I'm going to have the chance to find out."

Good!

Just the words he needed to hear to make him come up with a new idea. He leaned and called to her: "Cathy, what about that book you said you were going to write? This is a good time to start . . ." He gave me a long look, and I felt like a clear windowpane. "Bart, remember you are very loved. If you feel resentment about anyone, or anything, all you have to do is tell me, or tell your mother. We are willing to listen and do what we can to make you happy."

Happy? I'd be happy only when he was gone from her life. Happy only when I had her all to myself—and then I remembered that old man . . . two old men. Neither one of them wanted her to stay alive . . . neither one. I wanted to be like them, especially like Malcolm, so I pretended *he* was in the garage, waiting for Daddy to drive away, and I'd be alone. *He* liked it when I was alone, when I felt sad, lonely, mean, angry . . . and right now *he* was smiling.

No sooner had Momma and Jory driven away, shortly after Daddy left, than Emma was at me again, pestering me, hating me.

"Bart, can't you wipe that blood from your lip? Do you have to keep on biting down? Most people refrain from deliberately hurting themselves."

What did she know about being me? I didn't feel pain when I chewed on my lip. Liked to taste the blood.

"I'll tell you one thing, Bartholomew Scott Winslow Sheffield, if you were my little boy you'd feel the sting of my hand on your bottom. I believe you like to torment people and do every mean thing you can just to gain their attention. It doesn't take any psychiatrist with ten diplomas to know that!"

"SHUT UP!" I yelled.

"Don't you dare yell and tell me to shut up. I've had all I am going to take from you! You are responsible for all the terrible things going on in this house. You broke that expensive figurine your mother prized. I found it in the trashcan, wrapped in newspaper. You may sit there and scowl at me with your black ugly eyes, but I'm not afraid. You are the one who wrapped that wire around Clover and killed your brother's pet. You should be ashamed! You're a mean, hateful little boy, Bart Sheffield, and it's no wonder you don't have any friends, no wonder at all! And I'm going to save your parents thousands of dollars when I turn you over my knee and paddle your bottom until it's black and blue. You won't sit comfortably for two weeks!"

She towered over me, making me feel small and helpless too. I wanted to be anybody but me, anybody who was *strong*.

"You touch me and I'll kill you!" I said in a cold voice. I rose stiffly, planted my feet wide apart, put my hands on the table to steady my balance. Inside I was boiling with rage. I knew now how to turn into Malcolm and be ruthless enough to get what I wanted, when I wanted.

Look at her, afraid now. Now *her* eyes were big and scared. I curled my upper lip and showed my teeth, then allowed both lips to curl into a sneer. *"Woman, get the hell away from me before I lose control of myself!"*

Silently, Emma backed away, and then she was running into the dining room, heading for the hall so she could protect Cindy.

~   ~   ~

All day I waited. Emma thought I was hiding in my hole in the shrubs, so she left Cindy alone in her sandbox under the shade of a huge old oak tree. Had a pretty little canopy too. Nothing too good for Cindy and she was only adopted.

She tittered when she saw me limping up, as if I looked funny and was only pretending to be an old man. Look at her smile and try to charm me. Sitting there half naked, nothing on but little green and white shorts. She'd grow up, become more beautiful and be like all women, sinfully enticing men to be their worst. And she'd betray the man who loved her, betray her children, too. But . . . but . . . if she were ugly, what man would want her then? Wouldn't make babies if she was ugly. Wouldn't be able to charm men then. I'd save all her children from what she'd do later on. Save the children, that was important.

"Barr-tee," she said, smiling at me, sitting crosslegged so I could see her lacy panties beneath her play shorts. "Play, Barr-tee? Play with Cindy . . . ?"

Plump little hands reached for me. She was trying to "seduce" me! Only two years old and a few months and already she knew all the wicked ways of women.

"Cindy," called Emma from the kitchen, but I was down low and she couldn't see me behind the bushes, "are you all right?"

"Cindy's playing sand castle!" answered little nobody, as if to protect me. Then she picked up her favorite red sand pail and offered it to me—and the red and yellow shovel too.

In my hand I gripped the handle of my pocket knife tighter. "Pretty Cindy," I crooned softly as I crawled closer, putting a sweet smile on my face that made her giggle. "Pretty Cindy wants to play beauty parlor . . ."

She clapped her hands "Ohhh," she trilled. "Nice."

The blonde hair in my hand felt silky and clean. She laughed when I tugged at her hair and took the ribbon from the ponytail. "I'm not going to hurt you," I said, showing her my pearl-handled knife. "So don't you scream . . . just sit quietly in the beauty parlor until I've finished."

In my room I had my list of new words. Had to pronounce them, practice spelling them, and use them at least five times in that same day—and from then on. Had to know big words in order to impress people, make them know I was smarter.

Intimidating. Got that—meant to make people scared of you.

Ultimately—had that down too. Meant sooner or later my time would come.

Sensuous—bad word. Meant thrills you got from touching girls. Had to do away with sensuous things.

Grew tired after a short while of big words I had to learn in order to gain respect. Grew tired of pretending to be Malcolm. But the trouble was, I was losing the real me. Now I wasn't Bart all the way through. And now that he was slipping away, suddenly Bart didn't seem nearly as stupid and pitiful as he once had.

I reread a certain page in Malcolm's book when he was the very same age I was. He'd hated pretty blonde hair like his mother's, like his daughter's—but he didn't know about his little "Corrine" when he wrote:

Her name was Violet Blue, and her hair reminded me of my mother's hair. I hated her hair. We attended the same Sunday school class, and I'd sit in back of her and stare at that hair that would beguile some man someday and make him want her, as that lover had wanted my mother.

She smiled at me one day, expecting a compliment, but I fooled her. I said her hair was ugly. To my surprise she laughed. "But it's the same color hair you have."

I shaved off all my hair that day—and the next day I caught

Violet Blue and threw her down. When she went home crying, she was as bald as I was.

All that pretty blonde hair that used to be Cindy's was blowing on the wind. She was crying in the kitchen. Not because I'd scared her, or hurt her. It was Emma's shriek that told her something had gone wrong. Now Cindy's hair looked like mine. Stubby, short, and ugly.

The Last Dance

Jory," called Mom in relief when she saw me come in, "thank God you're back. Did you enjoy your lunch?"

Sure, I said, fine lunch, and she didn't pay much attention if I didn't elaborate, for she was much too busy with last-minute details. This was the way it went on performance days: class in the morning, rehearsal in the afternoon, and the performance at night. Rush, rush, rush, all the while making yourself believe the world would stop turning if you didn't dance your role to the best of your ability. When the world wouldn't stop . . .

"You know, Jory," gushed Mom happily in the dressing room we were sharing—she was behind a screen, and we really couldn't see one another—"all my life the ballet has thrilled me. But this night will be the grandest of them all because I will be dancing with my own son! I know you and I have danced many times together, but this night is special. Now you're good enough to dance solo. Please, please, do your best so Julian in heaven can be proud of his only son."

Sure, I'd do my best, always did. The foots went on, the

overture ended; the curtain lifted. There was a moment of silence before the first-act music began. Mom's kind of music and mine—taking us both to that happy never-never land where anything could happen, even happy endings.

"Mom, you look wonderful—prettier than any of the other dancers!" She did too. She laughed joyfully and told me I certainly knew how to please a woman, and if I kept it up I'd be the Don Juan of the century. "Now listen carefully to the music, Jory. Don't get so absorbed in counting that you forget the music—that's the best way to catch the magic, by feeling the music!"

I was so keyed up and tense I'd likely burst in another second or two. "Mom, I hope the father I love best will be sitting front row center."

That's when she ran to where she could peek out and see the audience. In certain places the foots didn't blind my eyes. "He's not there," she said dismally, "nor Bart either . . ."

No time for me to answer. I heard my musical cue and danced out with the other members of the *corps*. Everything went just fine, with Mom up on the balcony as the beautiful doll Coppelia, lifelike enough to inspire love from afar.

But when the first act was over she was left gasping and panting for breath. She hadn't told Dad she was also dancing the role of the village girl, Swanhilda, who loved Franze even as he fell foolishly in love with a mechanical doll. Two roles for Mom—difficult roles too, as she had choreographed them. Dad certainly would have forbidden her to dance if he had known the full truth about her last dance. Had I been wrong to help her deceive him?

"Mom, how's your knee feeling?" I asked when I saw her grimace once or twice between acts.

"Jory, my knee is fine!" she said sharply, once more trying to see Dad and Bart in their seats. "Why aren't they out there? If Chris doesn't show up to see me dance for the last time, I'll never forgive him!"

I saw Dad and Bart just before the second act started. They sat in the second row, and I could tell Bart had been brought along forcibly. His lower lip pouted sullenly as he glared at the curtain that would lift and display beauty and grace—and he'd frown more. Beauty and grace did not light up Bart's life as they did mine.

Third act time. Mom and I danced together, dolls wound up by huge keys attached to our backs. Woodenly we began, limbering up our squeaky joints. The huge room where Dr. Coppelius kept his inventions was mysteriously dim, and made more dramatic by blue lights. I could tell Mom was having trouble, but she didn't miss a step as we both kept time to the music and turned on all the other mechanical toys that came alive to dance with us. "Mom, are you okay?" I asked in a whisper when we were close enough. "Sure," she said, still smiling, never doing anything but smiling, for it was supposed to be painted on.

I felt scared for her even as I admired her courage. I knew out in the audience Bart was looking at us, thinking us stupid fools and feeling jealous of our grace.

Suddenly I could tell from Mom's tight smile that she was in terrible pain. I tried to dance closer, but one of the down dolls kept getting in my way. It was going to happen. I knew it would—just what Dad feared.

Next came a series of whirling pirouettes which would take her in a circle around the stage. To do these she had to know precisely where everyone else was located, and all the props too. When she spun near me I reached out to keep her on balance before she whirled on by. Oh, golly, I couldn't stand to watch. Then I saw she was going to make it; pain or not, she'd dance without falling. Joyfully now, I bounded into the air and landed on one knee as I playfully proposed marriage to the doll of my dreams. Then my heart jumped. One of the ribbons of her points had come undone!

"Your ribbons, Mom, watch out for your left shoe ribbon!"

I called above the music, but she didn't hear. The dragging ribbon was stepped on by another dancer. Mom was thrown off balance. She put out her arms to steady herself and might have succeeded in doing this—but I saw her painted-on smile turn into a silent shriek of pain as her knee gave way and down she went. Right in the center of the stage.

People in the audience screamed. Some stood up to see better. We on the stage went right on dancing as the manager came out and carried Mom backstage. Her back-up whirled onto the stage, and the ballet went on.

At last the curtain descended. I didn't wait to take any bows. I couldn't get to Mom fast enough. Terribly afraid, I raced up to where Dad held her in his arms while ambulance men in white suits were feeling her legs to find out if one or both might be broken.

"Chris, did I do all right?" she was asking, though pain had made her face very pale. "I didn't really louse up the show, did I? You did see Jory and I in our *pas de deux?*"

"Yes, yes," he said, kissing her face all over and looking so tender as he helped lift her onto a stretcher. "You and Jory were magnificent. I've never seen you dance better—and Jory was brilliant."

"And this time I didn't have to bleed on my feet," she whispered before she closed her eyes wearily, "I only had to break a leg."

What she said didn't make much sense. I turned my thoughts to the look on Bart's face as he stared at her. He seemed to be glad, almost gloating. Was I being unfair to him? Or was it guilt I saw in his eyes?

I sobbed as Mom was lifted onto a stretcher and put in an ambulance that would drive her and Dad to the nearest hospital. Melodie's father promised he'd drop me off at the hospital, then drive Bart home safely. "Though I'm sure Melodie wishes it was Jory who'd go home, and Bart who'd insist on staying with his mother in the hospital."

~   ~   ~

Much later Mom awakened from the sedatives given her to stare at the flowers filling her room. "Why, it looks like a garden," she breathed. She smiled weakly at Dad, stretching out her arms to embrace him and then me. "I know you're going to say I told you so, Chris. But until I fell, I did dance well, didn't I?"

"It was your slipper ribbon," I said, anxious to protect her from his anger. "If it hadn't loosened you wouldn't have fallen."

"My leg isn't broken, is it?" she asked Dad.

"No, darling, just torn ligaments and some broken cartilage that was repaired during the operation." Then he sat on the edge of her bed and gravely told her every detail of her injury, which wasn't as minor as she wanted to believe.

Mom reflected aloud: "I really can't understand how that ribbon could come loose. I always carefully sew on the ribbons myself, not trusting anyone else . . ." She paused, staring into space.

"Where are you hurting now?"

"Nowhere," she flared as if annoyed. "Where's Bart? Why didn't he come with you?"

"You know how Bart is. He hates hospitals and sick people, just as much as he hates everything else. Emma's taking good care of him and Cindy. But we want you home soon, so do what your doctor and nurses tell you—and don't be so damned stubborn you won't listen or obey."

"What's wrong with me?" she asked, alerted as I was. I sat up straighter, feeling something was about to slam down on all of us.

"Your knee is in bad shape, Cathy. Without going into specifics, you are going to have to sit in a wheelchair until some torn ligaments heal."

"A *wheelchair?*" Stunned-looking, she said that like it was an electric chair! "What's really wrong? You're not telling me everything. You're trying to protect me!"

"When your doctors are sure, you will know. But one thing is certain, you can never dance again. And they have told me, too, that you cannot even demonstrate to your pupils. No dancing whatsoever, not even waltzing." He said it so firmly, but compassion and pain were in his eyes.

She looked stunned, not believing that such a small fall could have done so much harm. "No dancing . . . ? None at all?"

"None at all," he repeated. "I'm sorry, Cathy, but I warned you. Think back and count the times you have fallen and hurt that knee. How much damage do you think it can take? Even walking won't be as effortless as it used to be. So cry your heart out now. Get it out of your system."

She cried in his arms, and I sat in a chair and sobbed inwardly, feeling as bereft as if it had been me who had lost the use of my legs for dancing.

"It's all right, Jory," she said when she had dried her tears and put on a faltering smile. "If I can't dance, I'll find something better to do—though Lord knows what it will be."

Another Grandmother

In a few days Mom was feeling much better, and that's when Dad brought to the hospital a portable typewriter, a thick stack of yellow legal pads, and other writing utensils. He stacked everything on the table that rolled over Mom's bed and gave her one of his big, charming smiles. "This is a fine time to finish that book you began so long ago," he said. "Look at your old journals, and let it all loose—and be damned to those you might hurt! Hurt them as you've been hurt, as I've been hurt. Stab a few times for Cory and Carrie too. And while you're at it, throw in a few blows for me, Jory, and Bart, for they too are affected."

They looked at each other for long moments, then unhappily she took an old memorandum book from his hands and opened it so I could see her large girlish handwriting. "I don't know if I should," she murmured with a strange look in her eyes. "It would be like living it all over again. All the pain would come back."

Dad shook his head. "Cathy, do what you think you must. There must have been a good reason for you to have started those books in the first place. Who knows, perhaps you'll be on your way to a new career more satisfying than the last."

It didn't seem possible to me that writing could ever replace dancing, but when I visited her in the hospital the next day, she was scribbling away like crazy. On her face I saw a strange intense look, and in a way, I felt envious.

"How much longer?" she asked Dad, who had driven me to see her.

We were all there waiting, Emma with Cindy in her arms, and me holding fast to Bart's hand. Dad lifted Mom out of the front seat and put her in the folding chair he'd rented. Bart stared at that rolling chair with repulsion, while Cindy called out "Mommy, Mommy!" She didn't care how Mom came home, as long as she did, but Bart hung back and eyed Mom up and down, as if he were looking at a stranger he didn't like.

Next Bart turned and headed for the house. He hadn't even said hello. An expression of hurt passed over Mom's face before she called, "Bart! Don't go away before I've had a chance to say hello to you. Aren't you glad to see me? You just don't know how much I've missed you. I know you don't like hospitals, but I wish you had come just the same. I know, too, that you don't like this chair, but I won't be using it forever. A lady in the physical therapy class showed me how much can be done while sitting in this kind of chair . . ." She faltered because his dark, ugly look didn't encourage her to go on.

"You look funny sitting in that chair," he said with his brows knitted together. "Don't like you in that chair!"

Nervously Mom laughed. "Well, to be honest, it's not my favorite throne either, but remember it's not a permanent part of my life, only until my knee heals. Come, Bart, be friendly to your mother. I forgive you for not visiting me in the hospital, but I won't forgive you if you can't show me a little affection."

Still frowning, he backed away as she wheeled forward. "No! Don't touch me!" he cried out in a loud voice. "You didn't have to dance and fall! You fell because you didn't want to come home and see me again! You hate me now for cutting off Cindy's hair! And now you want to punish me by sitting in that chair when you don't need to!"

Wheeling around, he raced for the backyard, using the stepping stones. He'd covered two when he tripped and fell. Picking himself up, he ran on again, bumping into a tree and crying out. I could see his nose was bleeding. Boy, talk about awkward!

Dad made light of Bart's rebellion as he pushed Mom into the house, with Cindy delighted to ride on her lap. "Don't worry about Bart . . . he'll come back and be contrite . . . he's missed you very much, Cathy. I've heard him crying in the night. And his new psychiatrist, Dr. Hermes, thinks he's getting better, working out some of this hostility."

She didn't say anything, just kept running her hand over the smooth cap of Cindy's short-short hair. She looked more like a boy in her coveralls, though Emma had tried to tie a ribbon in a short tuft of her hair. I guessed Dad had told Mom what Bart had done to Cindy, for she didn't ask questions.

Later on in the evening when Bart was in bed, I ran for a book I'd left in the family room and heard Mom's voice coming from "her" room. "Chris, what am I going to do about Bart? I tried to show love and affection for him, and he rejected me. Look what he did to Cindy, a helpless child who trusts that no one will hurt her. Did you spank him? Did you do anything to punish him? Does he show respect to any of us? A few weeks in the attic might teach him a thing or two about obedience."

Hearing Mom talk like this made me feel depressed. So sad I had to hurry away and hurl myself onto my bed and stare at the walls with the posters of Julian Marquet dancing with Catherine Dahl. This wasn't the first time I'd wondered what my real father had been like. Had he loved my mother very much? Had she loved him? Would my life have been happier if he hadn't died before I was born?

Then there was Daddy Paul, who came after that tall man with the dark hair and eyes. Was Bart really Dr. Paul's son— or was he . . . ? I couldn't even finish the question, it made me feel so disloyal for doubting.

I closed my eyes, feeling in the air around me a dreadful tension, as if an invisible sword were held, ready to hack all of us down.

Early the next evening, I cornered Dad in his study and burst out with all I'd held back until now.

"Dad, you've just got to do something about Bart. He frightens me. I don't see how we can go on living with him in the house, when it seems he is going mad—if he isn't already there."

My dad bowed his head into his hands. "Jory, I don't know what to do. It would kill your mother if we had to send Bart away. You don't know all she's been through. I don't think she can take too much more . . . another child gone would destroy her."

"We'll save her!" I cried passionately. "But we have to prevent Bart from going to visit those people next door who tell him lies. He goes over there all the time, Dad, and that old lady holds him on her lap and tells him stories that make him come home acting queer, like he's old, like he hates women. It's all her fault, Dad, that old woman in black. When she leaves Bart alone he'll go back to where he was before she came."

He stared at me in the strangest way, as if something I'd said had triggered thoughts in his head. As always he had places to go and patients to see, but this time he called his hospital and told them he had an emergency at home. And he did, you bet he did!

I often looked at my mother's third husband and wished he were my own blood father, but at that moment when he canceled his appointments to save Bart—and Mom—I knew in all the ways that counted that he was my true father.

That evening, shortly after dinner, Mom went to her room to work on her book. Cindy was in bed and Bart was out in the yard when Dad and I donned warm sweaters and slipped out the front door.

It was murky with fog, cold with damp as we strode side by side toward the huge shadowy mansion with its impressive black iron gates. "Dr. Christopher Sheffield," said Dad into the black box attached to the side of the gates. "I want to see the lady of the house." As the gates swung silently open, he asked why I'd never learned the woman's name. I shrugged, as if she didn't have a name, and as far as I was concerned, didn't need one. Bart had never called her anything but Grandmother.

At the front door Dad banged the brass knocker. Finally we heard shuffling noises in the hall, and John Amos Jackson admitted us.

"Our lady tires easily," said John Amos Jackson, his thin, long face hollow-cheeked, gaunt-eyed, his hands trembling, his narrow back bent. "Don't say anything to upset her."

I stared at the way Dad looked at him, frowning and perplexed as the bald-headed man shuffled away, leaving us to enter a room whose door he'd opened.

The lady in black was seated in her rocking chair.

"I'm sorry to interrupt," said Dad, staring at her intensely. "My name is Dr. Christopher Sheffield and I live next door. This is my eldest son, Jory, whom you have met before."

She seemed excited and nervous as she gestured us in and indicated the chairs we were to use. We perched tentatively, not intending to stay very long. Seconds stretched by that seemed like hours before Dad leaned forward to speak: "You have a lovely home." He glanced around again at all the elaborate chairs and other fine furnishings, and he stared at the paintings, too. "I have the strangest sense of *déjà vu*," he murmured almost to himself.

Her black-veiled head bowed low. Her hands spread expansively, supplicating, it seemed, for his understanding for her lack of words. I knew she spoke English perfectly well. Why was she faking?

Except for those aristocratic hands with all the glittering rings she sat so still, but her hands fluttered, knotted the pearls I knew she wore beneath her black dress. His eyes shot her way, and quickly she sat on her hands.

"You don't speak English?" Dad asked in a tight voice.

Vigorously she nodded, indicating she could *understand* English. His brows knitted. Puzzled-looking again. "Well, to get to the point of our visit, my son Jory has told me you and my youngest son Bart are very familiar. Jory says you give Bart expensive gifts and feed him sweets between meals. I'm sorry, Mrs. . . . Mrs. . . . ? He paused, waiting for her to give her name. When she didn't he went on: "When Bart comes again I want you to send him home unrewarded. He's done a number of ugly things that deserve punishment. His mother and I cannot have a stranger coming between Bart and our authority. When you indulge him here we face the consequences." All this time he was doing his darnedest to see her hands—as she did her best to keep them hidden.

What was this all about? Why did Dad want to see her hands? Was it all those fabulous rings that held his fascination? I'd never guessed he liked things like that, since Mom had an aversion for jewelry of any kind but earrings.

And then, when Dad seemed to be looking toward another of her original oil paintings, her hands came into view and fluttered up near her throat to the magnet of her hidden pearls.

His head jerked around. Dad spoke then out of context, startling me, startling her. "Those rings you wear—I've seen those very rings before!"

When she too obviously shoved her hands inside her full sleeves, Dad jumped to his feet as if thunderstruck. He stared at her, spun around once more to survey the sumptuous room, and once more nailed her with his eyes. She cringed.

"The . . . best . . . that . . . money . . . can . . . buy," Dad said slowly, separating each word. I caught his bitterness, though I didn't understand. It seemed lately I never understood anything.

"Nothing too good for the elegant and aristocratic Mrs. Bartholomew Winslow," he said. "Those rings, Mrs. Winslow—why didn't you have the good sense to hide them away? Then your disguise might have worked, though I doubt it. I know your voice, and your gestures too well. You wear black rags but your fingers sparkle with your status symbols. Do you forget what those symbols did to us? Do you think I've forgotten those endless days of suffering from the cold or heat, from the loneliness—all our pain symbolized by a string of pearls and those rings on your fingers?"

I was shocked and bewildered. Never before had I seen Dad so upset. He wasn't easily provoked—and who was this woman he knew and I didn't? Why had he called her Mrs. Bartholomew Winslow—the very name of my half brother? Could it be true she really was Bart's grandmother—and Bart might not be the son of Daddy Paul?

Dad railed on. "*Why*, Mrs. Winslow, *why*? Did you think you could hide here and we wouldn't find out? How can you fool anyone when even the way you sit and hold your head betrays your true identity? Haven't you done enough to hurt me and Cathy? Do you have to return to do more? I should have guessed that you were behind Bart's confusion—behind his weird behavior. What have you been doing to our son?"

"Our son?" she asked. "Don't you mean, more correctly, *her* son?"

"Mother!" he raged before he looked at me guiltily. Looking from one to the other of them, I thought, how wonderful and how strange. At last his mother was free from the loony bin and she really was Bart's grandmother after all. But why

did he call her Mrs. Winslow? If she was his mother and Dr.
Paul's mother, then she'd have to be Mrs. Sheffield—wouldn't
she?

I was thinking all of this even as she said, "Sir, my rings
are not that exceptional. Bart has told me you're not his real
father, so please leave my home. I didn't come to harm him—
or anyone." It seemed she gave my father a warning look. I
guessed she was giving him a road out on account of me.

"My dear mother, the game is up." She sobbed, then
covered her veiled face with her hands. He shot out with no
regard for her tears, "When did your doctors release you?"

"Last summer," she whispered. Her hands lowered so she
could use her voice better for pleading. "Even before I moved
here I had my lawyers do what they could to help you and
Cathy buy whatever piece of land you selected. I ordered them
to keep me anonymous, knowing you wouldn't want my help."

Dad fell into a chair, bent over to rest his elbows heavily
on his knees.

Why wasn't he happy to see his mother free from that
place? She was living nearby, and he'd always wanted to visit
her. Didn't he love his own mother? Or was he afraid she might
go crazy any moment? Did he think Bart might have inherited
her madness?—or her insanity might infect Bart like a physical disease? And why didn't my mother like her? I looked from
one to the other, wanting answers to my unspoken questions,
and so afraid I might learn Paul wasn't Bart's father at all.

When Dad lifted his head I could see his drawn face, the
deep lines that etched from his nose to his mouth. Lines I'd
never seen before.

"I cannot in good conscience call you Mother again," he
said dully. "If you helped buy the land my home sits on, I
thank you. Tomorrow I'll see that a *For Sale* sign is put up, and
we'll move far away if you refuse to move first. I will not allow
you to turn my sons away from their parents."

"Their parent," she corrected.

"The only parents they have," he said in return. "I should have known you'd come here. I've called your doctor and he told me you'd been released, but he didn't say when, or where you went."

"Where else do I have to go?" she cried pitifully, wringing her bejeweled hands like pale limp rags. It was as if she reached out and touched him then, even as she restrained herself from reaching for him. Each word she said, each look she gave him, said she loved him—even I could tell.

"Christopher," she pleaded, "I have no friends, no family, no home—and nowhere to go but to you and yours. All I have left is you and Cathy and the sons she bore—my grandsons. Would you take them from me too? Each night I pray on my knees that you and Cathy will forgive me and take me back and love me as you once did."

He seemed made of steel, so unreachable, but I was on the verge of crying.

"My son, my beloved son, take me back and say you love me again. And if you cannot do that, then just let me live where I can see my grandsons now and then."

She paused then, waiting for him to respond. When he refused, she went on: "I hoped you could be lenient if I stayed over here and never let her know who I was. But I've seen her, heard her voice; heard yours, too. I hide behind the wall and listen. My heart throbs. My chest aches with longing. Tears fill my eyes from holding back my voice that wants to cry out and let you know I'm sorry! So terribly sorry!"

Still he didn't say anything. He wore his detached, professional look.

"Christopher, I would gladly give ten years of my life to undo the wrong I've done! I'd give another ten years just to sit at your table and feel welcomed by my own grandchildren!"

Tears were in her eyes, in mine too. My heart cried for my father's mother even as I wondered why he and Mom hated her.

"Christopher, Christopher, don't you understand why I

wear these rags? I cover my face, my hair, my figure, so she won't know! But all the time I keep hoping, praying that sooner or later both of you can forgive me enough to let me become a member of your family again! Please, please, accept me as your mother again! If you do, perhaps then she can too!"

How could he sit here and not feel the same pity for her that I did? Why wasn't he crying like I was?

"Cathy will never forgive you," he said tonelessly.

Strangely, she cried out happily, "Then you will? Please say it—you forgive me!"

I trembled as I waited for him to speak.

"Mother, how can I say I forgive you? By saying that I would betray Cathy, and I can never betray her. Together we stand and together we will fall, still believing we did right, while you stand guilty and alone. Nothing you say or do can undo death. And every day that you stay here sees Bart more and more deranged. Do you realize he is threatening our adopted daughter Cindy?"

"No!" she cried, shaking her head so the veils swung violently. "Bart would not hurt his sister."

"Wouldn't he? He hacked off her hair with a knife, Mrs. Winslow. And he's threatened his mother as well."

"NO!" she yelled more passionately than before. "Bart loves his mother! I give Bart treats because you are too busy with your professional life to give him all the attention he needs. Just as his mother is too busy with her life to care if he has enough love. But I cater to his needs. I try to take the place of the peers he doesn't have. I do everything I can to make him happy. And if feeding him treats and giving him gifts makes him feel better, what harm can I do? Besides, once a child has all the sweets he can eat, soon he loses the taste for them. I know. Once I was like Bart, loving ice cream, candy, cookies, and other sweets . . . and now I cannot tolerate them at all."

Dad got up and motioned to me. I stood and moved to his side as he looked at his mother with pity. "It's a terrible shame you came too late to try to redeem your actions. Once I would have been touched by any sweet word you said. Now your very presence shows how little you care if we are deeply hurt again, as we will be if you stay."

"Please, Christopher," she begged. "I have no other family, and no others who care if I live or die. Don't deny me your love when to do so will kill the very best part of you, the part that makes you what you are. You've never been like Cathy. Always you could hold on to some of your love—hold fast to it now, Christopher. Hold so fast and so true, you can eventually help Cathy to find a little love for me too!" She sobbed and weakened. "Or if not love, help her find forgiveness, for I admit that I could have served my children better."

Now Dad was touched, but not for long. "I have to think of Bart's welfare first. He's never had much confidence in himself. Your tales have disturbed him so much he has nightmares. Leave him alone. Leave us alone! Go away, stay away, we don't belong to you anymore. Years ago we gave you chance after chance to prove you loved us. Even when we ran you could have answered the judge's summons and spared us the pain of knowing we weren't loved enough for you to even appear and show some interest in our futures.

"So get out of our lives! Make another life for yourself with the riches you sacrificed us to get. Let Cathy and me live the lives we've worked so hard to achieve."

I was baffled—what was he talking about? What had his mother done to her two sons, Christopher and Paul—and what did my mother have to do in their youthful lives?

She rose too, standing tall and straight. Then, slowly, slowly, she removed the veil that covered her head and face. I gasped. My dad gasped. Never before had I seen a woman who could look so ugly and so beautiful at the same time. Her scars looked as if a cat had scratched her face. Her jowls sagged with age; her pretty blonde hair was streaked with gray. I'd been terribly curious to see up close what she hid under her veil—now I wished I hadn't.

Dad bowed his head. "Did you have to do that?"

"Yes," she said. "I wanted you to see what I did so I would no longer look like Cathy." She gestured to her wooden rocker. "See that chair? I have one in every room in this house." She indicated all the comfortable chairs with fluffy soft cushions. "I sit in hard wooden chairs to punish myself. I wear the same black rags every day. I keep mirrors on the walls so I can see how ugly and old I am now. I want to suffer for the sins I committed against my children. I despise this veil, but I wear it. I can't see well through the veil, but I deserve that too. I do what I can to make the same kind of hell for myself as I made for my own flesh and blood, and I keep on believing that there will come a time when you and Cathy will recognize how I am trying to atone for my sins so that you can forgive me and return to me, and we can be a whole family again. And when you and Cathy can do that, I can go peacefully into my grave. When I meet your father again, perhaps he won't judge me too harshly."

"Oh," I cried out spontaneously, "I forgive you for whatever you did! I'm sorry you have to wear black all the time, with that veil over your face!" I turned to Dad and tugged on his arm. "Say you forgive her, Dad. Please don't make her suffer more! She *is* your mother, and I could always forgive my mother, no matter what she did."

He spoke to my grandmother as if he hadn't even heard me. "You were always good at persuading us to do what you wanted." I'd never heard him speak so coolly. "But I'm not a boy anymore," he went on. "Now I know how to resist your appeal, for I have a woman who has never let me down in any important way. She has taught me not to be as gullible as I once was. You want Bart because you think he should have been yours. But you cannot have Bart. Bart belongs to us. I used to think Cathy did wrong when she sought revenge and stole Bart Winslow from you. But she didn't do wrong—she did what she had to do. And so we have two sons instead of one."

"Christopher," she cried, looking desperate, "you don't want the world to know of your indiscretion, surely you don't."

"Yours too," he responded coldly. "If you expose us, you expose yourself as well. And remember, we were only children. Who do you think a judge and jury would favor—you or us?"

"For your own sakes!" she called as we stepped from her parlor and headed toward the double front doors (he had to push me ahead of him, for I was holding back, pitying her), "love me again, Christopher! Let me redeem myself, please!"

Dad whirled about, furious and red-faced. "I cannot forgive you! You think only of yourself. As you have always thought only of yourself. I don't know you, Mrs. Winslow. I wish to God I had never known you!"

Oh, Dad, I thought, you're going to be sorry. Forgive her, please.

"Christopher," she called once more, her voice so weak and thin it sounded old and brittle, "when you and Cathy can love me again, you'll find better lives for yourselves and for your children. There is so much I could do to help if only you would let me."

"Money?" he asked with scorn. "Are going to use black-mail? We have enough money. We have enough happiness. We have managed to survive, and managed to love, and we have not killed anyone to achieve what we have."

Killed? Had she killed?

Dad pulled me by my hand as he stalked to the door. I said to him on the way home from her mansion, "Dad, it seemed I could smell Bart in that room. He might have been hiding and listening. He was there, I'm sure of it."

"All right," he answered in a tired way. "You go back and look for him."

"Dad, why don't you forgive her? I believe she's truly sorry for whatever she did to make you hate her—and she is your mother." I smiled and tugged on his arm, wanting him to go back with me and say he loved her. "Wouldn't it be nice to have both my grandmothers here for Christmas?"

He shook his head and strode away leaving me to race back to the big house. He'd taken only a few steps before he turned. "Jory, promise not to tell your mother anything about tonight."

I promised, but I was unhappy about it, unhappy about everything I'd heard. I didn't know if I had heard the full truth about my dad and his mother, or only part of a long, secret story never told to me. I wanted to run after Dad and ask why he hated his mother so much, but I knew from his expression what he wouldn't tell me. In some odd way, I was glad not to know more.

"If Bart is over there, you bring him home and sneak him into his room, Jory. Please, for God's sake, don't mention anything to your mother about the woman next door again. I'll take care of her. She'll go away, and it will be just as it was before she came."

Being what I was, I believed, though I felt sorry for his mother, I didn't owe her the loyalty I owed him, but I couldn't keep the most important question from my tongue. "Dad, what did your mother do that makes you hate her so much? And if you hate her, why did you always insist upon going to visit her, when Mom wouldn't?"

He stared off into space, and, as if from a far distance, his voice came to me, "Jory, I fear you will know all of the truth soon enough. Give me time to find the right words, the true explanation that will satisfy your need to know. But believe this: your mother and I always intended to tell you. We were only waiting for you and Bart to grow up enough, and when you hear our story, I think you will understand how I can both love and hate my mother. It's sad to say, but there are many children who feel ambiguous about their mothers or fathers."

I hugged him, even if it was unmanly. I loved him, and if

that was unmanly too, then darn if being manly was so great. "Don't you worry about Bart, Dad," I said. "I'll bring him home safely."

I managed to squeeze between the gates just in the nick of time. Softly they clanked behind me. Then . . . silence. If there was a more silent place in the world than those spacious grounds, I've never been there.

I jumped and quickly dodged behind a tree. John Amos Jackson had Bart by the hand, and he was leading him away from the house.

"Now you know what you have to do, don't you?"

"Yes, sir," intoned Bart, as if in a stupor.

"You know what will happen if you don't do as I say, don't you?"

"Yes, sir. Bad things will happen to everyone, even me."

"Yessss, bad thingsss, thingssss you will regret."

"Bad things I will regret," he repeated flatly.

"From woman man is born into sin . . ."

"From woman man is born into sin . . ."

"And those who originate the sin . . ."

"Must suffer."

"And how must they suffer?"

"In all ways, by any ways, by death they will be redeemed."

I froze where I crouched, not believing my ears. What was that man doing to Bart?

They drifted beyond my hearing, and I peeked just in time to see Bart disappearing over the wall, going home. I waited until John Amos Jackson shuffled into the house and turned out all the lights.

Then suddenly I realized I hadn't heard Apple bark. Wasn't a dog as old and big as Apple supposed to bark and warn those in the house that a prowler was on the grounds? I sneaked into the barn and called Apple by name. He didn't come running to lick my face and wag his tail. "Apple," I called again, louder. I hit a kerosene lamp that hung near the door and I shone it into the horse stall where Apple had his home.

I sucked in my breath! Oh, no! NO!

Who would be so cruel as to starve a dog like that? Who could then drive a pitchfork into that poor bag of bones covered by beautiful fur . . . and now he was all bloody. Dark with old blood that had dried to the color of black rust. I ran outside and threw up. An hour later Dad and I were digging a grave and burying a huge dog that never had a chance to reach maturity. Both of us knew "they" would lock Bart up forever if ever this got out.

"He may not have done it," said Dad when we were home. "I can't believe he did it." By now I could believe anything.

There was an old woman who lived next door.
Who wore black rags and black covered her hair.
She was twice Mom's mother-in-law, twice hated,
  and much more.

And all I could do was wonder, wonder what she had done to my mom and my dad. Dad hadn't yet explained it all to me as he'd promised. Though I had found a glimmer of a fuzzy solution—I'd let my emotions run away with me, and for a moment I'd thought she was my grandmother too, for Chris was so much my real father in my heart.

But in reality, it was Bart who was Paul's son, and I knew why his grandmother wanted him so badly and not me. I belonged to Madame Marisha as Bart belonged to her. It was the blood relationship that made them love each other. And I sighed to be only a stepgrandson to such a mysterious and touching woman who felt she had to suffer to redeem her mistakes. I thought I should take better care of Bart—protect him, guide him, keep him straight.

Right away I had to get up and look at Bart, who was

curled on his side in his bed with his thumb in his mouth. He looked like a baby—just a little boy who'd always stood in my shadow, always trying to live up to what I'd done at his age, and never achieving the goals I'd already set. He hadn't walked sooner, talked at a younger age, or smiled until he was almost a year old. It was as if he'd known from birth that he'd always be number two, never number one. Now he'd found that one person in the world who would let him come first. I was happy Bart had his very own grandmother. Even if she did wear nothing but black, I could tell she'd once been very beautiful. More beautiful than my Grandmother Marisha could ever have hoped to be when she was young.

Yet . . . yet . . . some pieces in the puzzle were missing,

John Amos Jackson—just where did he fit into the picture? Why would a loving grandmother and mother who wanted to be reunited with her son and his wife and her grandson . . . why would she bring that hateful old man along with her?

Honor Thy Mother

He never bothered to look around. He thought I was safely asleep, in that little bed where they liked to keep me. But I saw Daddy leave the house. Was he going to see my grandmother? Wish everybody'd leave her alone, so I could have her back like she used to be, all mine.

Apple was gone. Gone to where puppies and ponies went. "That great big pasture in the sky," said John Amos with his glittery pale eyes watching me carefully, like he thought I was the one who stabbed the pitchfork in. "You saw Apple dead? You really saw him dead?"

"Deader than a doornail."

I sneaked along the winding jungle paths that were taking me straight into hell. Down, down, down. Caves and canyons and deep pits, and sooner or later we'd find the door. Red. The door to hell would be red—maybe black.

Black gates. Magic gates swung wide to let Daddy through. She wanted him. Fine son he was, putting his mother into the loony bin, and next he'd put me in one of those funny farms where they laced you up in straitjackets (wonder what they were?). Terrible anyway, whatever it was.

The gates clanked together. Knew Mom was back in her room typing away those pages like she really thought it was just as important as dancing. She didn't seem to mind sitting in that wheelchair, didn't seem to mind at all unless she heard Jory playing that dance music. Then her head would lift; she'd stare into space; her feet would begin to keep time.

"What's intricate mean, Momma?" I'd asked when she said Jory had the concentration to learn *intricate* dances quickly.

"Complicated," she'd answered, just like a dictionary. She had dictionaries all over the place, little ones, middle-sized ones, a huge fat one that had its own stand that swiveled around.

Had to make my feet do *intricate* things. I tried as I slipped along behind Daddy, who never glanced backward. I was always looking over my shoulder, staring to the left or to the right, wondering, always wondering. Dratted shoelace—ouch! Down I was—again. If he heard me cry out, he didn't look back. Good . . . had to do all this secret stuff like a good spy. Or a thief, a jewel thief. Rich ladies had lots and lots of jewels. Ought to get in some practice while she was gabbing with her doctor son, crying and constantly asking him to forgive her, have mercy, take her back and love her again. Boring. Didn't like Daddy so much now, was back to how I used to feel before he saved my leg from being "amputated." Dratted man was trying to drive away the one grandmother I had. What other kid had a grandmother so rich she could give him everything?

"Where you going, Bart?"

John Amos appeared out of nowhere, his eyes glowing in the dark. "None of your damn business!" I snapped like Malcolm would have done. Had Malcolm's journal flat against my chest, under my shirt. The red leather was sticking to my skin. I was learning how to make money out of rage.

"Your father is in that house, talking with your grandmother.

Now you get in there and do your job, and report back to me
every word they say. You hear?"

Hear? Was him who needed a hearing aid, not me. Else
he would do his own spying through the keyhole. But all he
could do was peek, couldn't hear very good. Couldn't bend
over much better, and couldn't pick up anything he dropped.

"Bart . . . did you hear me? What the devil are you doing
heading for the back stairs?"

Turned to stare at him. On the fifth step I was taller. "How
old are you, John Amos?"

He shrugged and scowled. "Why do you want to know?"

"Never saw anybody older, that's all."

"The Lord has ways of punishing those who show disrespect to their elders." He gritted his teeth. They made the
sound of dishes clinking in the sink.

"I'm taller than you are now."

"I'm six feet tall—or I used to be. Boy, that's a height you
will never reach unless you always stand on stairs."

I narrowed my eyes and made them mean like Malcolm
would. "There will come a day, John Amos, when I'll stand
head and shoulders taller than you. And on your knees you
will come begging to me, pleading, pleading; sir, sir, you'll
say, please let me get rid of those attic mice. And I will say to
you, How do I know you are worthy of my trust, and you will
say to me, In your footsteps I will follow, even when you lie in
your grave."

What I said made him slyly smile.

"Bart, you are learning to be as clever as your great-
grandfather, Malcolm. Now, put off whatever you plan to do.
Go back to your father, who is with your grandmother this
very second. Remember every word you hear, and report back
to me."

Like a spy, I crawled through the dumbwaiter, which was
hidden behind a pretty Oriental screen. From there I could
sneak my way to a hidden place behind the potted palms.

There they were, the two of them, doing the same old thing. Grandmother pleading, Daddy rejecting. Sat down and made myself comfortable before I pulled out my pack of roll-my-owns. Cigarettes helped when life got boring, like now. Nothing to do but listen. Spies never got to say anything, and it was action I needed.

Daddy looked nice in his pale gray suit, like I wanted to look when I grew up—but I wouldn't—I didn't have his kind of good looks. I sighed, wishing I was his real son.

"Mrs. Winslow, you promised to move, but I look around and see you haven't even packed one box. For the sake of Bart's mental health, for the sake of Jory whom you say you love well too, and most of all for Cathy, go away. Move to San Francisco. That's not too far away. I swear I'll visit you when I can. I'll be able to find opportunities to see you and Cathy will never suspect."

Boring. Why couldn't he say something different? Why did he care so much what my momma said about his mother? If ever I was so unlucky as to have a wife, I'd tell her she'd better accept my mother or get out. Get the hell out, as Malcolm would put it.

"Oh, Christopher," she sobbed, pulling out another of those lacy handkerchiefs to wipe at her tears. "I want Cathy to forgive me so I can have a small place in your lives. I stay on because I'm hoping eventually she'll realize I'm not here to harm any of you . . . I'm here only to give what I can."

Daddy smiled bitterly. "I suppose you are talking again about material things, but that's not what a child needs. Cathy and I have done all we can to make Bart feel needed, loved, and wanted—but he can't seem to understand his relationship to me. He isn't secure in what he is, who he is, or where he's going. He doesn't have a dance career like Jory to guide him into the future. Now he's grasping, trying to find himself, and you aren't helping. He keeps his innermost self very private, locked up. He adores his mother, he distrusts his mother. He suspects she loves Jory more than she loves him. He knows that Jory is handsome, talented, and most of all, adroit. Bart is not adroit at anything but pretending. If he would confide in us, or his psychiatrist, he could be helped—but he doesn't confide."

I had to wipe a tear from my eye. So hard to hear about myself, and what I was, and worse, what I wasn't—like they knew me inside out, and they didn't. They couldn't.

"Did you hear any of what I just said, Mrs. Winslow?" Daddy shouted. "Bart does not like his image that reflects only weakness—no skills, no grace, and no authority. So he borrows from all the books he's read, from all the TV shows he's watched, and sometimes he even borrows from animals, pretending he's a wolf, a dog, a cat."

"Why, why?" she moaned. He was telling all my secrets. And a secret told had no value, none at all.

"Can't you guess why? Jory has thousands of photographs of his father, Bart has none. Not even one."

That made her bolt straight up. She flared with anger. "And why should he have his father's pictures? Is it my fault my second husband didn't give his mistress his photograph?"

I felt stunned. *What was this?* Sure, John Amos had told me crazy stories, but I'd thought he made them up, just as I made up stories to chase away boredom. Was it all true that my own momma had been the bad woman who had seduced my own grandmother's second husband? Was I really the son of that lawyer-man named Bartholomew Winslow? Oh, Momma, how can I ever stop hating you now?

Daddy was wearing that funny smile again. "Perhaps your beloved Bart thought he didn't need to give her his photograph when she'd have the living man in her own home and in her bed as her lawful husband. She told him before he died that she was expecting his child, and he would have divorced you to be the father of his child, and have Cathy—I don't doubt that in the least."

I was in a tight ball, agonized by all I'd heard. My poor, poor daddy, who died in the fire at Foxworth Hall. John Amos *was* a true friend, the only one who treated me like an adult and told me the truth. And Daddy Paul, whose picture set in my bedroom on the night table, had been only another stepfather, like Christopher. Was crying inside from losing yet another daddy. My eyes rolled from Daddy to her, trying so hard to know what to feel about him and her—and Momma. It wasn't right for parents to mess up the lives of little babies who weren't even born, mess it up so much I'd never really know who I was.

Hopefully I stared at my grandmother, who seemed to be very hurt by what her son had said. Her white hands fluttered up to her forehead, which was glistening with beads of sweat, touching it as if her head ached. Oh, how easily she could feel pain, why couldn't I?

"All right, Christopher," she said when I thought she might never find the words, "you've had your say, now let me have mine. When it came down to an ultimatum, Cathy and her unborn child, or me and my fortune—Bart would have stayed with me, his wife. He might have kept her on as his mistress until he tired of her, but then he would have figured out some legal way to take possession of his child—and then my husband would have bowed out of Cathy's life, holding fast to his son. I know he would have stayed on with me, even as he looked around for the next pretty face and younger body."

My own daddy. My own blood father wouldn't have wanted my momma after all. Tears stuck to my lashes. My throat hurt, proving I was human after all, not the freak I'd believed. I could feel a different kind of pain. But still I couldn't feel happy; why couln't I feel happy and real? Then I remembered some of her words . . . my real daddy would have found some "legal way" to take possession of me. Did that mean he would have stolen me away from my own mother? That thought didn't make me happy either.

Grandmother sat on, unmoving. I shriveled even smaller, scared, so scared of what I might hear next. *Daddy, don't let out any more bad secrets and make me take action.* John Amos would force me to take action. I glanced behind me, suspecting he might be listening with a glass held to the wall so he could hear better.

"Well," said my father, wound up now. "Bart's psychiatrist shows an incredible interest in you, whom he believes to be my mother only. I wonder why time and again he keeps harping back to you. He seems to think you are the clue to Bart's secret inner life. He thinks you lived a secret inner life too—did you, Mother? When your father made you feel less than human, did you sit alone and plot how to have your own kind of revenge, and make him suffer?"

What was this?

"Don't," she pleaded, "please don't. Have mercy on me, Christopher. I did the best I could under the circumstances. I swear I did my best!"

"Your best?" He laughed and sounded like Momma when she poked mean fun. "When your father's younger half brother walked into Foxworth Hall at age seventeen, did you immediately seize hold on an inspiration?—the supreme way to punish your father for making you dislike yourself? Did you set out to make our father fall in love with you? Did you? Did you hate him in a way too, because he looked like Malcolm? I think you did. I think you schemed and plotted to wound your father in the one way that would shatter his ego most, so it might never recover. And I think you succeeded! You eloped and married the younger half brother he despised, and you thought you'd won in two ways. You had stung him where it hurt most. Now you had power to gain his tremendous fortune through our father!—but it didn't work, did it? I haven't forgotten those days when we lived in Gladstone, when I overheard you pleading with my father to sue, to get what was rightfully his. But our father refused to cooperate. He loved you and married you for what he thought you were, and not for the money you couldn't keep from dreaming about."

Stunned again, I stared at my grandmother. She was crying, her frail body shaking; even her rocking chair seemed to quiver. I was quivering too, crying too—inside.

"You're wrong, so wrong, Christopher!" she sobbed, her chest heaving. "I loved your father! You know I loved him! I gave him four children and the best years of my life—the best I had in me to give to anyone."

"Your best is so poor, Mrs. Winslow, so very, very poor."

"Christopher!" she cried out, getting to her feet painfully. She spread her hands in a helpless way, stepping closer to look up into his face. The black shroud she wore fluttered as she shook. She threw a fearful glance around the room, forcing me to shrink smaller into the dim shadowy corner. Her voice lowered.

"All right, we've said enough about the past. Live with Cathy, but accept me into your lives. Let me have Bart as my own son. You have Jory and that little girl you adopted. Let me take Bart and go away, so far away you'll never see or hear from me again. I swear I'll never let anyone know about you and Cathy. I'll do what I can to protect your secret—but let me have Bart for my own, please, please!"

She fell to her knees and clutched at his hands, and when he quickly moved them out of reach, she pulled on his jacket.

"Don't embarrass me further, Mother," he said uneasily, but I could tell he was touched. "Cathy and I don't give away our children. He is not our pride and joy at this moment, but we love him, we need him, and we will do what is necessary to see that he is mentally healthy again."

"Tell me what to do, and I'll do it," she pleaded, tears streaking her cheeks as at last she caught hold of his evasive hands and she crushed them to her breasts. "Tell me what to do—anything but leave. I need to see him and watch and admire as he pretends. He's wonderfully gifted." She began to kiss his hands as he tried to pull them away, but he must not have tried too hard, for she was able to retain them both with her fragile strength.

"Mother, please . . . ," he begged, looking away before he sat down and hid his face.

"He needs me, Christopher, more than any of my own children have ever needed me. He loves me too . . . I know he does. He sits on my lap and I rock him, and I see a look of contentment on his face. He's so young, so vulnerable, so bewildered by things he can't understand. And I can help. I know I can help him.

"Something inside of me says I won't be here too much longer," she whispered, and I had to strain my ears to hear. "Let me have him until then . . . please, as one last gift to the mother you used to love very much . . . the mother of your youth, Christopher . . . the mother who cared for you when you had the measles, the chicken pox, all those colds from staying out in the snow too long. Remember? I remember. Without my memories of the good times, I could never have lived through the bad . . ."

She was getting to him. He was staring down at her, his eyes soft.

"You said a while ago I seduced your father and deliberately schemed to hurt my father by marrying him. You are wrong. I loved your father from the first moment I laid eyes on him. I could no more have held back from loving him than you held back from loving Cathy. Chris, I have nothing left of my past. I've lost everything. John's the only one from my past," she murmured low, like she was scared. "He's the only one I have left from the days at Foxworth Hall."

"He must know who I am then! And who Bart is!"

Leaning forward, she stretched to put her pale hand with all the rings on his trousered knee—I saw him shudder at her touch. "I don't know what John knows. He thinks all my children ran off and were lost somewhere in the world. As far as

I know, he doesn't know Bart's middle name is Winslow . . . but then again, he's so sly, he may know everything." She trembled and withdrew her hand as if she knew it offended him. "All this land around here belonged to my father. So he thinks it's only natural I would come out here and settle down on an estate that's been in our family for years and years."

He shook his head. "And you did arrange for me to buy my land cheaper?"

"Christopher, my father owned land everywhere. Now I own all of it. But I would give it all away just to have you and Cathy back as my family. No one knows about you and Cathy but me, and I'll never tell anyone who you are. I promise not to shame and hurt you—just let me stay! Let me be your mother again!"

"Get rid of John!"

First she sighed, then bowed her head. "I wish to God I could."

"What do you mean?"

"Can't you guess?" she asked, her graying head lifted so her eyes could search his.

"Blackmail?"

"Yes. He doesn't have any family either. He pretends not to know about you and Cathy, but I can't be sure. He's sworn to help me keep my whereabouts a mystery, for there are news reporters who would be hot on my heels if they knew where I was. So I give him a good home and plenty of money to keep me safe."

"Bart is not safe. Jory has seen John Amos whispering to him. I think he knows who we are."

"But he won't do anything," she cried. "I'll talk to him, make him understand. He won't tell . . . I'll pay him off."

Daddy stood up to leave. For a moment his hand rested lightly on her head. Then, looking guilty, he quickly withdrew it. "All right. You speak to John, order him to leave Bart alone. Don't let Bart know you are his natural grandmother—let him keep on believing you are only a kind-hearted woman who needs him for a friend. Can you do this one small thing for me?"

"Yes, of course," she agreed weakly.

"And please start wearing that veil over your head again. Jory knows you are my mother . . . but, well, you know. And who knows when Cathy might decide to be friendly and visit her new neighbor? She was busy with her dance classes before. Now that she's not so occupied, she'll need to see people. That was one of the hardest things for her to bear when she was young . . . to be kept locked up for what seemed to her centuries, and only her mother and grandmother . . . That made her need even greater."

Again her head drooped. "I know. I've sinned and I regret it. I pray to turn back the clock, but I wake up to another lonely day—and I have only Bart to give me hope."

Oh, gosh, they'd known so much before I came along.

"I have to ask something," she said in a faint whisper. "Do you love her as a man loves . . . a wife?"

He turned so she could see only his back. "That is none of your business."

"But I'd understand. I question Bart but he doesn't know what I mean. But he's told me you share one bedroom."

Angry, he flared, glaring at her: "And one bed. Now, are you satisfied?" Once more he spun on his heel, and this time he left.

Puzzling, gosh darn puzzling. Why did Momma hate his momma? And why did my grandmother ask about bedrooms and bed?

Ran home next. Didn't stop to report to John Amos. Momma was at that dratted barre, trying to pull herself out of that ugly wheelchair. I hid and watched. Strange to see her awkward—like me. Clumsy like me, but she managed to pull herself to her feet and then she stood shaking all over. Her face in the mirror was pale, her hair a frame of gold.

Molten gold, hot as hell, burning as running lava.

"Bart, is that you?" she called. "Why do you stare at me so strangely? I won't fall, if you're thinking that. Each day I feel better, stronger. Come sit with me and talk to me. Tell me what you do all the time when I can't see you. Where do you go? Teach me to play your pretend games. When I was your age I liked to pretend too. Why, I used to dream about being the world's most famous prima ballerina, and I made that the most important thing in my whole life. Now I know it was never that important. Now I know it's making the ones you love happy that matters most. Bart, I want to make you happy . . ."

I hated her for "seducing" my real father and taking him from my poor lonely grandmother, who was her own mother-in-law. And she must have been married then to Dr. Paul Sheffield, who was Chris's brother but not my real father at all. Look at her, trying to make up to me for her neglect! Too late! I wanted to run and shove her down. Hear her bones break, all of them. She was unfaithful to all husbands! But I couldn't say any of this. My legs went rubbery and weak and made me sink to the floor as all the silent screams bounced in my head. Wicked sinful evil woman! Sooner or later she'd run away with some lover—like Malcolm's mother did. Like all mothers did.

And why hadn't my grandmother come right out and told me who she was? Why was she keeping it a secret? Didn't she know I needed a real grandmother? She even lied to me about who my daddy was! Only John Amos told me the truth.

"Bart—what's wrong?"

Alarm on her face. Should be alarmed. Never, never did she tell me anything but lies. There was no one I could trust but John Amos. All the while he shuffled along, looking weird and old, he was honest, doing his best to set the world straight.

"Bart, what's the matter? Can't you tell me, your own mother?"

Stared at her. Saw all that mass of hair as golden snares to ruin men. Took all men and made them suffer. Her fault. All her fault. Took my real daddy from my grandmother and "seduced" him.

"Bart, don't crawl on the floor. Stand up and use your legs. You're not an animal."

I threw back my head and howled. Howled all the rage and hate I felt. It wasn't fair for God to give me her for a mother. Wasn't fair when he burned my real daddy to death. Gotta do something. Make it all right.

"Bart, please tell me what's wrong!"

I could barely see her. She tried to take a few steps away from the barre and her hands reached for me, as if she wanted me in her arms.

I'd never let her touch me again. Never, never, never!

"I hate you!" I screamed, jumping to my feet and backing away. "I hope you never walk again. I hope you fall down and die. I hope your house burns up and you and Cindy too!"

Ran—ran and ran until my sides hurt and my mind was empty.

In Apple's stall I fell down to rest. I kept Malcolm's journal there, hidden under the old hay and I fished it out to read more. Boy, he sure did hate women, especially when they were pretty. Didn't seem to notice the ugly ones. I lifted my head and stared into space. Alicia. Nice name—wonder what made him love Alicia more than Olivia? Just because she was only sixteen when she married his old, old father of fifty-five?

Alicia slapped his face when he tried to kiss her. Maybe Malcolm wasn't as good at kissing as his father.

The more I read the more I learned how Malcolm succeeded in everything he did, except in making women love him. Proving to me I'd better leave all women alone since I was so much like Malcolm. Over and over I was reading his words so I could turn into him, all powerful.

C names. Wonder why women like C names so much?

Catherine, Corrine, Carrie, and Cindy—whole wide world full of C names. Wish I liked my grandmother like I used to. Now that I knew she was my real grandmother it wasn't as good. She should have told me. She was just another lying, sneaking, cunning female. Just as John Amos had warned me.

I could smell Apple faintly. My ears heard him munching his food; I felt his cold nose nuzzling my hand—and I was crying. Crying so hard I wanted to die and join him. But Apple should have missed me more. He made me do it. He was supposed to suffer when I did—and he didn't. He was mine and he let Grandmother feed him, give him water—so it was his own fault. And there was Clover, dead too. Strangled and stuffed in the hollow oak.

Boy, I was bad.

Thinking about my badness made me sleepy. Dreamed of Apple, who loved me. I woke up and it was almost dark. John Amos was grinning down at me, smirking too. "Hello, Bart. Do you feel lonely in Apple's stall?"

Towering above me, John Amos didn't notice the hay that fell from the loft above and caught on his stringy mustache and made him look gruesome.

"How did Malcolm make all his money, John Amos?" I asked just to see if the hay fell off his mustache when he spoke.

"By being more clever than those who would stop him."

"Stop him from what?" The hay didn't fall off.

"From getting what he wanted."

"What did he want?"

"Everything. Everything that wasn't his he wanted—and to get everything that belongs to others you have to be ruthless and determined."

"What's ruthless?"

"Doing what you have to to get what you want."

"Doing anything?"

"Anything," he repeated. Stiffly he bent over to peer into my eyes. "And don't hesitate to step on those who get in your way—including members of your own family. For they would do the same to you if you stood in their way." He smiled thinly. "You know, of course, that sooner or later that doctor who is dissecting your personality bit by bit will lock you in an institution. That's what your parents are doing—getting ready to remove from their lives a little boy who is proving to be too much of a problem."

Baby tears got in my eyes.

John Amos scowled. "Don't show weakness with tears that belong to women. Be hard, like your great-grandfather Malcolm was." He paused to eye me up and down. "Yes, you have inherited many of his genes. Someday, if you keep going as you are, you will be just as powerful as Malcolm."

"Where've you been, Bart?" snapped Emma, who looked at me all the time like she was disgusted, even when I was clean. "Never in my life have I seen a boy who could get dirtier more quickly than you. Look at your shirt, your pants, your face and hands! Filthy, that's what. What do you do, make mud puddles and wallow in them?"

Didn't answer. Headed for the bathroom down the hall.

Momma looked up from her desk in her bedroom. "Bart, I've been wondering where you were. You've been gone for hours."

Was my own business, none of hers.

"Bart . . . answer me."

"Was outside."

"I know that. Where outside?"

"Near the wall."

"What were you doing there?"

"Digging."

"Digging for what?"

"For worms."

"Why do you need worms?"

"Goin' fishin."

She sighed. "It's too late to go fishing, and you know I don't like you to go off by yourself. Ask your father if he will take you fishing this Saturday."

"He won't."

"How can you be so sure?"

"He never has time."

"He'll take time."

"No, he won't. Never has, never will."

Again she sighed. "Bart, try to be understanding. He's a doctor, and he has many very sick patients. You wouldn't want his patients to go unattended, would you?"

Wouldn't care. Rather go fishing. Too many people in the world anyway . . . especially women. I ran to bury my face in her lap. "Momma, please get well quick. YOU take me fishin! Now you don't have to dance, you can do all the things Daddy never has time for. You can spend all the time with me you used to spend with Jory dancing. Momma, Momma, I'm sorry about what I said," I sobbed, "I don't really hate you! I don't want you to fall down and die. I just feel mean sometimes and I can't stop. Momma, please don't hate me for what I said."

Her hands were soft and comforting in my hair as she tried to smooth it down and make it stay neat. Hairbrushes and hairspray never worked, so how could her hands? I buried my face deeper in her lap, thinking of how John Amos would scold me if he knew, though I'd already told him what I'd said to her, and he'd smiled, so pleased I was talking like Malcolm. "You shouldn't have done that, Bart," he said to confuse me. "You have to be clever, make her think she's having her way. If you let her know how you feel she'll find a way to defeat our purpose. And we do have to save her from the Devil, don't we?"

I raised my head to stare up into her pretty face, making tears streak my face for the living lie she had to be. Been married three times, John Amos had told me. I didn't really care if she was good or evil. I'd make her good. I'd teach her to leave all men alone—but me.

To win I had to play my cards just right, and deal out the aces one by one, like John Amos had told me. Fool her, fool Daddy, make them think I wasn't crazy. But I got mixed up. I wasn't crazy, only pretending to be Malcolm.

"What are you thinking, Bart?" she asked, still stroking my hair.

"Got no playmates. Got none but what I make up. Got nothing but bad genes from inbreeding—and as for my environ—well, that's no good either. You and Daddy don't deserve any children. You don't deserve anything but the hell you have already made for yourself!"

Left her sitting stunned. Glad to make her unhappy, like she was always making me. But why didn't happiness come and make me laugh? Why did I run to my room and throw myself down on my bed and cry?

Then I remembered the one person who didn't need anyone—Malcolm. He knew he was strong. Malcolm never hesitated in making decisions, even wrong ones, for he knew how to twist them about and make them right. So I scowled, hunched my shoulders, stood up, and shuffled down the hall, wanting what Malcolm wanted. I saw Jory dancing with Melodie and went in Momma's room to report to her. "Stop what you're doing!" I yelled. "Sinning is going on between Jory and Melodie—they're kissing—making a baby."

Her flying fingers paused over the typewriter keys. She smiled. "Bart, it takes more than hugging and kissing to make a baby. Jory is a gentleman and won't take advantage of an innocent young girl who is decent and wise enough to know when to say stop."

She didn't care. All she cared about was that damn book she was writing. I didn't have any more chance with her now than I'd had when she was a dancer. Always, always she found something better to do than play with me.

I clenched my fists and hit at the doorframe. There'd come a time when I was her boss, and she'd listen then. She'd know who she'd better play with. She'd been a better mother when she taught ballet classes. At least she had a free moment once in awhile. Now all she did was write, WRITE. Mountains and mountains of white paper.

Again she stopped paying attention to me, and reloaded her typewriter as if she had a shotgun to kill the world. She didn't even notice when I took a box she'd filled and put aside as she began to fill another with her words on paper.

John Amos would be interested in what she'd written. But before he read a sheet, I'd read them first. Even if I had to use a dictionary every minute I struggled to understand some of the longer words she used. Appropriate . . . knew what that meant. I think.

"Good night, Momma."

She didn't hear me. Just went right on as if I weren't there.

Nobody ever ignored Malcolm. When he spoke people jumped to do his bidding. I was gonna make myself over into Malcolm.

A week later I was spying on Mom and Jory. They were before the long mirror in the "rec" room and Jory was helping Momma use her bad leg. "Now, don't think of falling. I'm right in back and I'll catch you if your knee gives way. Just take it easy, Mom, and soon you will be walking just fine."

She didn't walk just fine. Every step she took seemed to hurt. Jory kept his hands on her waist to keep her from even tottering, and somehow she made it to the end of the barre without falling. Weakly she waited for him to push up her chair so she could sit down again. He turned the footrests into position as she held up her legs. "Mom, you're stronger each day."

"But it's taking so long."

"You sit and write too long at a time. Remember, your doctor said to get up more often, and sit less . . ."

She nodded, looking exhausted. "Who was that long distance call from? Why didn't they want to speak to me?"

His face breaking into a smile, Jory explained: "It was my grandmother Marisha. I wrote and told her about your fall, and now she's flying west so she can replace you in your school. Isn't that great, Mom?"

She didn't look happy even a little bit. As for me, I hated that ole witch!

"Jory, you should have told me before."

"But, Mom, she wanted it to be a surprise. I wouldn't have told you today, but I think it's not very polite for people to drop in out of the blue. I knew you'd want to get ready, look pretty, tidy up the house . . ."

Funny kind of look she gave him. "In other words, I don't look my best now, and my house is messy?"

Jory smiled with all that charm I hated. "Mom, you're always pretty, you know that, but too skinny, and too pale. You've got to eat more and get outside a little more each day. After all, great novels aren't written in a few weeks."

Later on that same day I followed Jory out into the yard, then I hid in my special hideaway place to spy on Momma and Jory as both took turns pushing hateful Cindy in her baby swing. Never let me swing Cindy. Nobody trusted me. Head shrink wasn't getting anywhere, so why couldn't everybody give up and leave me alone?

"Jory, it's sometimes a torment to hear your ballet music and not be able to dance and express all the emotions I feel. Now when I hear an overture begin, I tighten up and cringe inside. I yearn to dance, and the more I yearn, the harder I have to write. Writing saves me, but it seems Bart resents my writing as much as he used to resent my dancing. It seems I am never going to have the ability to please my younger son."

"Aw, heck, Mom," said Jory with his dark blue eyes sad and worried too, "he's only a little boy who doesn't know what he wants. I know something weird is going on in his mind."

I wasn't weird. They were the weird ones, thinking dancing and stupid fairy tales mattered, when all others with sense knew money was king, queen, and God almighty.

"Jory, I give as much of myself to Bart as I can. I try to show affection and he pulls away. Then he's running away from me, or to me, and putting his face in my lap and crying. His psychiatrist says he's torn between hating me and loving me. And I'll tell you this in confidence: His behavior isn't helping me recover from my accident."

Left then. Heard enough. Good time to sneak into her bedroom and steal some more of her book pages. Stuffed in my shirt drawer I had the ones John Amos had read and returned, so I put those back and took some new ones.

In my little green cave made of hedges I sat down to read. Stupid Cindy was laughing and squealing while her two adoring slaves pushed her into the air. Boy, wish I had the chance to swing her. I'd push so hard she'd sail right over the white wall and end up in the swimming pool next door. The pool that never had any water.

Reading Momma's book was very interesting. "The Road to Riches," read the title of one of her chapters. Was that girl really my own mother? Were she and her two brothers and one sister really going to be locked up in one bedroom?

Read on until the day grew old and the fog came in and smothered me.

Got up and went inside the house, thinking about another title in her book. "The Attic." What a wonderful place to hide things. I stared at Momma, who was kissing Daddy's lips, teasing him, asking him about his pretty nurses, and had he found someone to replace her yet. "A beautiful young blonde of twenty or so?"

He appeared hurt. "I wish you wouldn't make a joke out of my devotion. Cathy, don't provoke me with silly remarks like that. I give all I can to you because I love you with a passion I recognize as idiotic."

"Idiotic?" she asked.

"Yes, it is, when you don't respond as passionately as I do! I need you, Cathy. Don't let this writing come between us."

"I don't understand."

"You *do* understand! Our past is coming alive. You're living it again as you write. I peek in and see your face, watch the tears streak your face and fall on the paper. I hear you laugh and say aloud the words that Cory said, or Carrie. You're not just writing, Cathy . . . you are reliving."

Her head bowed down and her loose hair fell and covered her face. "Yes, what you say is true. I sit at the desk and relive it all again. I see again the attic gloom, the dusty, immense space; I hear the silence more terrifying than thunder. Loneliness that knew me well then comes and burdens my shoulders, so I look up startled to see where I am, wondering why the windows aren't heavily covered over and when the grandmother will come in and catch us with windows not covered. Sometimes I'm startled to look up and catch Bart standing in the doorway staring at me. First I think he's Cory, then I can't account for his dark hair and his brown eyes. I look at Cindy and think she should be larger, as old as Cory with the dark hair, and I'm confused, not knowing the past from the present."

"Cathy." His voice was worried. "You've got to give this up."

Yes, yes, Daddy . . . make her give it up!

She sobbed as she fell into his arms, and tightly he cradled her to his heart, murmuring sweet love words in her ear that I couldn't hear. Rocking back and forth, like true wicked lovers. They look like the couples I spied on sometimes, the ones who "made out" on lover's lane, which wasn't so far from my grandmother's mansion.

"Will you put the book away, wait until the children are grown and safely married . . . ?"

"I can't!" Even I could hear the agony in her voice, as if she'd like to if she could. "That story is in my brain screaming to get out, to let others know how some mothers can be. Something intuitive and wise tells me that when I have it down, and it's sold to a publisher, and made into a book for everyone to read—only then will I be set free from all the hate I feel for Momma!"

Daddy couldn't speak. Just went on holding her, rocking, and his blue eyes, staring into space above the head that was pressed against his chest, seemed tormented.

Stole away to play alone in the garden. Jory's old witch grandmother was coming. Didn't want to ever see her again. Momma didn't like her either; I could tell from the way she grew tense and careful around her, as if afraid her quick tongue would betray her.

"Bart, my darling," called my own grandmother softly from her side of the thick white wall, "I've been waiting for you to come over all day. When you don't come I get worried, and then I'm unhappy. Darling, don't sit alone and pout. Remember I'm over here, willing to do anything I can to make you happy."

I ran. Fast as my legs could take me. I climbed the tree, and she had a stepladder waiting there for me so I could get to the ground safely. It was the same ladder she used to peer over at us.

"I'm going to leave the ladder there for you to use," she whispered, hugging me, covering my face with her kisses. Lucky for me she took off that dry veil first. "I don't want you to fall and hurt yourself. I love you so much, Bart. I look at you and think of how proud your father would be. Oh, if only he could see his son. His handsome, brilliant son!"

Handsome? Brilliant? Gee . . . didn't know I was either one. It felt good to be told I was wonderful. She made me believe I was every bit as good-looking as Jory, and every bit as talented, too. *This* was a grandmother. The kind I'd always wanted. One who loved me and no one else. Maybe John Amos was wrong about her after all.

Again I sat on her lap and let her spoon ice cream into my mouth. She fed me a cookie, a slice of chocolate cake, then held the glass of milk for me to drink. With a full stomach I snuggled more comfortably on her lap and rested my head on the softness of her full breasts that smelled of lavender. "Corrine used to use lavender," I mumbled sleepily with my thumb in my mouth. "Sing me a lullaby . . . nobody ever sang me to sleep like Momma sings to Cindy . . ."

"Lullaby and good night . . ."

Funny. As she sang softly, seemed I was only two years old, and a long, long time ago I'd sat just like this on my mother's lap, and heard her sing that very song.

"Wake up, darling," she said, tickling my face with the edge of her sleeve. "Time for you to go home now. Your parents will be worried—and they have suffered enough without having more anxiety about your whereabouts."

Oh! Over in the corner John Amos had overheard her speak. It was in his watery pale blue eyes that gleamed dangerously. He didn't like my grandmother or my parents or Jory or Cindy. He didn't like anyone but me and Malcolm Foxworth.

"Grandmother," I whispered, hiding my face so he couldn't see my lips move, "don't let John Amos hear you say you feel sorry for my parents. I heard him say yesterday they didn't deserve sympathy." I felt her shiver and try not to let him know she was aware he was there.

"What's sympathy mean exactly?"

Sighing, she held me tighter. "It's an emotion you feel when you understand the troubles of others. When you want to help, but there's nothing you can do."

"Then what good is sympathy?"

"Not much good in any meaningful way," she said with

her eyes looking sad. "Its only good is letting you know you are still human enough to have compassion. The best kind of sympathy moves one into action to solve problems."

John Amos whispered as I sneaked out into the evening shadows: "The Lord helps those who help themselves. Remember that, Bart." Gravely he returned the pages of my mother's manuscript I'd given him to read. "Put these back exactly as you found them. Don't get them soiled. And when she's written more, bring those—and you will be able then to solve all your own problems. Her book is telling you how. Don't you understand, that's why she's writing it."

Ever Since Eve

She was coming now, coming from Greenglenna, South Carolina, where the graves grew like weeds. Any day I could expect to look up and see her ugly mean face.

My own grandmother was a thousand times better. Sometimes lately she left her face unveiled. She'd wear a little makeup to please me—and it did. Sometimes she even put on a pretty dress—but never-never did she let John Amos see her in anything but that black robe and the veil over her face. Only for me was she pretty.

"Bart, please don't spend too much time with John."

He'd warned me many times she wouldn't approve. "No, ma'am. John Amos and me don't get along."

"I'm glad. He's an evil man, Bart—cold, cruel, and heartless."

"Yes, ma'am. He don't like women much."

"He told you that?"

"Yep. Tells me he gets lonely. Tells me you treat him like dirt and refuse to speak to him for days on end."

"Leave John alone. Avoid him all you can—but keep on

coming to see me. You're all I have now." She patted the soft sofa cushion, inviting me to sit beside her. I knew by now that she sat in comfortable chairs whenever John Amos had gone into the city.

"What does he do in San Francisco?" I asked. He went there often.

Frowning, she pulled me into her arms and held me close against the soft silk of her rose-colored dress. "John is an old man, but still he has many appetites that must be satisfied."

"What does he like to eat?" I asked, curious about an old man who had false teeth and great difficulty chewing even chicken, much less steak. Mush, jello, bread sopped in milk— that's what John Amos usually ate.

She chuckled and kissed the top of my hair.

"How's your mother? Is she walking well now?"

Changing the subject. Didn't want to tell me what he ate. I shifted away. "Bit by bit she's getting well, so she tells my daddy, but she's not so hot. When he's not home sometimes she gets a cane and uses that, but she doesn't want Daddy to know."

"Why not?"

"I don't know. All she wants to do now is play with Cindy, or write. That's all she does, honest Injun! Writing books is just as exciting to her as dancing . . . sometimes she gets all hot and bothered lookin.'"

"Oh," she murmured weakly, "I was hoping she'd give it up."

So was I. But it didn't seem likely. "Jory's grandmother is comin' soon, *real* soon. Think I might run away if she decides to stay in our house."

Again she said "oh" as if surprises were stealing her tongue. "It's all right, Granny," I said, "don't like her like I like you."

Went home around lunchtime, chock full of ice cream and cake. (Really was beginning to hate sweets.) Momma was at the barre, doing exercises before the long mirror, and I had to be careful she didn't spot me when I ducked behind a chair. I guess we had the only family room in the world with a barre at one end and a ten-foot-long mirror in back of it.

"Bart, is that you hiding behind the chair?"

"No, ma'am, it's Henry Lee Jones . . ."

"Really? I've been looking for Henry Lee for some time. I'm glad you've finally been found around the corner, around the bush . . . always looking for Henry Lee."

Made me giggle. It was the game we used to play when I was little, real little. "Momma, can you take me fishin today?"

"I'm sorry. I've got a full day planned. Perhaps tomorrow."

Tomorrow. It was always tomorrow.

In a dark corner I hid myself, crouched down so small I felt nobody could see me. Sometimes when I was following Momma in her chair, I tiptoed with my back hunched, making myself into the way John Amos said Malcolm looked when he was old and at his peak of power. I stared and stared at her, mornings, afternoons, nights, trying always to decide if she was as bad as John Amos said she was.

"Bart." Jory could always find me no matter how I hid. "Whatyah doing now?" he asked. "We used to have fun together. You used to talk to me. Now you don't talk to anyone."

Did so. Talked to my grandmother, to John Amos. I smiled crookedly, sneering my lips in the way John Amos curled his lips as I turned to watch Momma, who was walking just as clumsy as me now.

Jory went away and left me to amuse myself, when I didn't know how to anymore except by playing Malcolm. Was Momma really so sinful? How could I talk to Jory like I used to, when he wouldn't believe Momma told lies about who was my real father? Jory still thought it was Dr. Paul, and it wasn't, wasn't.

Later on at dinner, while Momma and Daddy were exchanging glances, and saying silly things that made them laugh, and Jory too, I sat and glared at the yellow tablecloth. Why did Daddy want Momma to use a yellow tablecloth at least once a week? Why did he keep saying she had to learn to forgive and forget?

Then Jory spoke up.

"Mom," Jory said, "Melodie and I have a date tonight. I'm taking her to a movie and then to a supperclub that doesn't serve hard liquor. Will it be all right if I kiss her good night?"

"Such a momentous question," she said with a laugh, while I sat in my corner. "Yes, kiss her good night, and tell her how much you enjoyed the evening . . . and that's all."

"Yes, Mother," he said mockingly, grinning. "I know your lesson by heart. Melodie is a sweet, nice, innocent girl who would be insulted if I took advantage of her, so I'll insult her by *not* taking advantage."

She made a face at him—he just smiled back. "How's the writing going?" Jory sang out before he returned to his room to moon over the picture of Melodie that he kept on his nightstand.

Stupid question. Already she'd told him writing absorbed her every wakeful moment, and new ideas woke her up at night, and Daddy was complaining she kept him awake with her light on. As for me, I couldn't wait to read what was going to happen next. Sometimes I thought she was making it all up, and it hadn't happened to her, it hadn't. She was pretending, the way I did.

"Jory," she asked, "have you been bothering my script? I can't find some of my chapters."

"Gosh, Mom, you know I wouldn't read what you write without your permission—do I have your permission?"

She laughed. "Some day when you are a man, I'm going to insist you read my book, or books. It keeps growing and growing, so it may end up two books."

"Where are you getting your ideas?"

Stooping, she picked up an old spiral-bound book. "From this book, and from my memory." She quickly flipped through the pages. "See how large I wrote when I was twelve? As I grew older my writing became more precise and much smaller."

Suddenly Jory snatched the spiral-bound book from her hands, then ran to a window where he could read a few lines before she had it back in her hands. "You misspelled a few words, Mom," he teased.

I hated their relationship; they were more like friends than mother and son. Hated the way she kept scribbling on lined paper before she typed those words up. Hated all her junk, her pencils, pens, erasers, and the new books she'd bought for her new project. Didn't have a mother anymore; didn't have a father. Never had a real father. Had nobody, not even a pet.

Summer was getting old now, like me. My bones felt old and brittle, my brain wise and cynical. And I thought, as Malcolm wrote in his journal, that nothing was as good as it used to be, and no toy gave me the pleasure I thought it would before I had it. Even my grandmother's mansion didn't look as huge as it had.

In Apple's stall, which was my special place for reading Malcolm's journal, I fell on the hay and tried to read the ten pages a day John Amos had assigned me. Sometimes I hid the book under the hay, sometimes I wore it next to my skin. As I began to read I chewed on a piece of the hay, finding my place marked with one of Momma's little leather bookmarks:

I remember so well the day when I was twenty-eight and came home to find my widowed father had finally remarried. I stared at his bride, whom I later found out was only sixteen. I knew immediately a girl so young and beautiful had married him only for his money.

My own wife, Olivia, had never been what anyone would call a beauty, but she'd had some appealing aspects when I married her, and her father was very wealthy. Suddenly I found out after she'd

*borne me two sons, she had no appeal for me whatsoever. She seemed
so grim compared to Alicia, my stepmother of sixteen . . .*

I'd read this mushy love-junk before. I'd lost my place,
gosh darn it. But I had a way of flipping through the book and
reading here and there, especially when boring stuff like kissing came into Malcolm's story. It seemed so odd, as much as
he hated women, that he'd want to kiss them.

Now, here it was, where I'd left off.

*Alicia was giving birth to her first child, whom I hoped desper-
ately would be a girl. But no, it had to be another son to compete
with me for my father's fortune. I remember standing and looking at
her, and the baby she snuggled at her side in the big swan bed, and I
hated them both.*

*I said to her when she smiled up at me innocently, and so proud
of her son, as if I'd welcome him as much as my father did, "My
dear stepmother, your son will never live long enough to inherit your
husband's fortune, for I am alive to prevent that."*

*She annoyed me then so much I could have slapped her beauti-
ful, cunning face. "I don't want your father's money, Malcolm. My
son won't want it either. MY SON will earn his way, not inherit
what money other men have made. I'll teach my son the true values
in life—the values YOU know nothing about."*

Wonder what she'd been talking about? What were values
anyway?—sale prices? I turned my attention to Malcolm's journal again. He had skipped fifteen years before he wrote again.

*My daughter, Corrine, grew more and more like the mother who
had abandoned me when I was only five.*

I saw her changing, beginning to develop into a woman, and I'd find myself staring at her young budding breasts that would soon entice some man. Once she saw me staring there and blushed. I liked that—at least she was modest. "Corrine, promise that you will never marry and leave your father when he's old and sick. Swear to me you won't leave me EVER."

Her face grew very pale, as if she feared I might send her back into the attic if she refused my simple request. "ALL my fortune, Corrine, if you promise—every cent I will leave to you if you never leave me."

"But, Father," she said, inclining her head and looking miserable, "I want to get married and have babies."

She swore she loved me, but in her eyes I could see she'd leave me at the first opportunity.

I'd see to it she had no boys or men in her life. She'd attend a school for girls only, a strict religious school that would allow no dating.

I closed the book and headed home. To my way of thinking Malcolm should never have married Olivia and had any children—but then, as I thought about it more, I would never have known my grandmother.

And even though she was a liar and had betrayed me, still I wanted to love and trust her again.

Another day I was in the barn reading about Malcolm when he was fifty. He wasn't so regular now about writing in his journal.

There's something sinful going on between that younger half brother of mine and my daughter. I've done what I can to catch them touching, or looking at each other in a suggestive way, but they are both very clever. Olivia tells me my fears are groundless, that Corrine could never feel anything for her half uncle, but then, Olivia is just

*another woman, true to her devious sex. Damn the day she talked
me into taking that boy into our home. It was a mistake, perhaps the
most grave mistake of my life.*

So, even Malcolm made a few mistakes, but only with
those people who were members of his family. Why was it he
couldn't stand for his sons to be musicians?—for his daughter to marry? If I'd been Malcolm, I'd have been glad to get
rid of her, just like I wished day after day that Cindy would
disappear.

I hurled Malcolm's journal to the floor and kicked hay
over it, then stomped toward the mansion, wanting Malcolm
to write about *power*, and how to get it, and *money*, and how
to earn it, and *influence*, and how to demand it. All he did
was write about how miserable his two sons, his wife, and his
daughter made him, to say nothing of that young half brother
who liked Corrine.

"Hello, darling!" cried my grandmother when I limped
into her parlor. "Where've you been? How's your mother's
knee?"

"Bad," I said. "Doctors say Momma will never dance
again."

"Oh," she sighed. "How dreadful. I'm so sorry."

"I'm glad she won't dance again," I assured her. "She and
Daddy can't even waltz anymore, and they used to do a lot of
that in the living room which they don't want us to use."

She looked so sad. Why should she look so sad? "Grandmother, my momma don't like you."

"You should watch your grammar, Bart," she choked as she
wiped away her tears. "You should say, she doesn't like you—
and how can you say that, when she doesn't know I'm here?"

"Sometimes you sound like her."

"I'm so sorry I'll never see her again on stage. She was so
wonderfully light and graceful she seemed a part of the music.

Your mother was born for dancing, Bart. I know she must feel lost and empty without it."

"No, she doesn't," I answered quickly. "Momma's got that typewriter and her book to work on all day and most of the night, and that's all she needs. She and Daddy lie in bed for hours and hours, especially when it rains, and they talk about some big old house in the mountains, and some big ole grandmother who wore gray dresses all the time, and I hide in the closet and think it's just like some dumb fairy tale."

She appeared shocked. "Do you spy on your parents? That's not very nice, Bart. Adults need privacy—everyone needs privacy."

I smiled and felt good to tell her I spied on everyone— ever her sometimes.

Her blue eyes grew wider and she stared at me for a long time before she smiled. "You're teasing me, aren't you? I'm sure your father has taught you better than that. Bart, if you want people to love you and respect you, you have to treat them as you would want to be treated. Would you like for me to spy on you?"

"NO!" I roared.

Another day, another trip to the office of that gray-haired old doctor who made me lie down and close my eyes so he could sit behind me and ask dumb questions.

"Are you Bart Sheffield today or Malcolm?"

Wouldn't say nothing.

"What is Malcolm's last name?"

Was none of his business.

"How do you feel about your mother now that she can't dance ballet anymore?"

"Glad."

Took him by surprise. He got busy scribbling down notes, getting real excited so his face was red when I opened my eyes and turned to take a peek. I thought I'd give him more to get excited about. "I wish Jory would fall and smash both his kneecaps. Then I could walk faster than him, and run faster than him, and do everything better too. Then when I come into the room everyone will look at me, not him."

He waited for more. When nothing else came he said gently, "I understand, Bart. You fear your mother and father don't love you as much as they do Jory."

Rage took me over. "Yes, she does! She loves me better! But I can't dance. It's the dancing that makes her laugh with Jory, and frown with me. I was gonna grow up and be a doctor— but now I don't want to. Cause my real daddy wasn't a doctor like they told me. He was an attorney."

"How do you know that?" he asked.

Wouldn't tell him. None of his business. John Amos told me. Heard Grandma telling Dad, too. Lawyers were smart, real smart. That would make me smart too. Dancers didn't have good brains, just good legs.

"Is there anything else you would like to tell me, Bart?"

"Yeah!" I snapped, jumping up from the couch and grabbing his letter opener. "Last night the moon was full. I looked out of the window and heard it calling to me. I wanted to howl. Then I needed to taste blood. I ran like crazy into the woods, and on into the hills, when out of the night appeared a woman who was beautiful, with long, long golden hair."

"And what did you do?" asked the doctor when I paused.

"I killed her, then ate her."

He scribbled away, and I picked up several of the lollipops he kept for his younger patients. Then I took about six more, thinking my grandmother might want one, at least.

When I was home I hurried over to Apple's stall and flipped backward through the pages of Malcolm's journal. I needed to find out something—and I'd skipped some mushy pages before. I wanted to know what drew him toward women whom he despised.

It was fall again, and all the trees wore brilliant autumn colors. I followed Alicia into the woods as she rode her horse with admirable skill. I had to spur my horse to make him gallop and give chase. She was so enchanted with the beauty of the season she didn't seem to hear the beat of my horse's hoofs. For a brief second I lost sight of her when she disappeared into a thicket. That's when I suspected she might be headed for the lake where I swam when I was a child. One last swim before summer was gone and winter turned the water icy.

Cherry-flavored lollipops were my favorites. I licked and licked until I could stick out my tongue and see it red as blood. Good to read and eat sweet stuff as I skimmed through the sickening glop that followed for pages on end. Gee, Malcolm must have started making money and gaining power when he was much older.

Just as I suspected, she was in the pool, her glorious body as flawless as I'd guessed it would be. And to think my father was enjoying all of that while I had to endure the frigid body of a woman who could only submit, never enjoy.

Dripping and shimmering she stepped from the lake to the grassy bank where her clothes lay waiting. My breath caught as I beheld her in sunlight. The spill of her glorious hair caught red, gold, with dark amber shadows, and the floss between her thighs curled wet and dark.

She saw me then and gasped. I hadn't realized I'd stepped out of the shadows.

Thank God she slapped him, and told him off. Now, now, he was getting to be like the Malcolm I knew him to be: mean, hard, ruthless, and rich.

"You'll pay for this, Alicia. Both you and your son will pay, and dearly pay. Nobody rejects me after leading me on, and letting me believe—"

Closed the book and yawned.

Madame M

Another letter had come from my grandmother Marisha to announce that she was on her way to take over my mother's ballet class. "And I'll have the chance to see my grandson more often, and give him the benefit of my experience."

Mom was none too happy, since she and Madame M. did not have a close or warm relationship, and this had always bothered me. I loved them both, and wanted them to love each other.

We were all waiting for Madame to show up, all starving because already she was an hour late. She'd telephoned to say she didn't want anyone to meet her, as she was independent and not accustomed to being waited on. Nevertheless, Mom had helped Emma prepare a gourmet meal, and now it was growing cold.

"Lord, but that woman can be inconsiderate," complained Dad after looking at his watch for the tenth time. "If she had allowed me to meet her at the airport, she'd be here by now."

"Isn't it strange," asked Mom with a mocking smile, "when she always insisted that her students be punctual."

Finally, an hour after Dad ate alone and hurried off to do his hospital rounds, Mom retired to her bedroom to work on her book until my grandmother arrived.

"Bart," I called, "come on and play some game with me. Checkers?"

"No!" he bellowed, keeping to his dark corner, his eyes black and mean as he crouched there, almost unblinking. "I'm wishing for that ole lady to fall from the sky."

"That's mean, Bart. Why do you always say such hateful things?"

He refused to answer, just sat on staring at me.

The doorbell rang. I jumped up and ran to open the door.

My grandmother stood there smiling and rather disheveled looking.

She was at least seventy-four, I knew that, crinkled, old, and gray. Sometimes her hair was jet black, and sometimes it had two inches of white near the roots. Bart said it made her look like a skunk or an old black seal. He thought her hair was so slick she kept it oiled. But I thought she looked wonderful when she threw her arms about me and hugged me close, tears streaking her rouged cheeks. She didn't even give Bart a glance.

"Jory, Jory, how handsome you are," she said. Her bun of hair was so huge I guessed it might be false.

"Can I call you Grandmother when we're not in class?"

"Sure, yah," she agreed, nodding like a bird. "But only when nobody else is around, you hear?"

"There's Bart," I said to remind her to be polite—which she seldom was. She didn't like Bart, and he didn't like her. She gave Bart a brief nod, then casually dismissed him as if he didn't exist.

"I'm so glad to have a few moments alone with you," Madame gushed, hugging me again. She pulled me to the family room sofa, and together we sat while Bart stayed in his dim corner. "I tell you, Jory, when you wrote and said you weren't coming again this summer, I felt ill, really ill. I made up my mind then and there that I'd had enough of this once-a-year grandson, and I was selling my own dance studio and coming out here to help your mother. Of course I knew she wouldn't want me, but so what? I cannot endure two long years of longing to see my only grandchild.

"The flight here was ghastly," she went on. "Turbulence all the way. They searched me too before I boarded, like some criminal. Then we had to circle round and round the airport, wait our turn to land. It made me sick enough to vomit. Finally, just before our plane ran out of fuel, we landed—bumpiest landing, I thought my neck would break. Great God in heaven, you should have heard what that man wanted for his rented car. He must have thought I was made of money. Since I've come to stay, I decided then and there I'd buy a car of my own. Not a new one, but a nice old one that Julian would have loved. Have I told you before your father loved to tinker around with old cars and fix them up so they'd run?"

Boy had she told me that before.

"So, I paid those crooks the exorbitant price of eight hundred dollars, and stepped into my new red car and took off for your place, reading a map as my car choked and chugged along. I felt so happy to be on my way to you, my beloved grandson, Georges's only heir. Why, it was just like it used to be when your father was an adolescent, and he'd rush home so proud to take me for a spin in his new car made out of old junk he salvaged from the city dump."

Her sparkling jet eyes seemed young, and she won me again with her affection, her praise. ". . . and like old ladies everywhere, you have to understand once I get started thinking backward all sorts of memories are triggered. Your grandfather felt so happy the day Julian was born. I held your father in my arms and stared up at my husband who was so handsome, like Julian, like you, and I could have burst with the pride I felt to give birth at my age for the first time with so little difficulty. And such a perfect baby your father was, so wonderful from his very beginning."

I wanted to dare and ask how old she was when my father was born—but I didn't have the nerve. Somehow the question must have shown in my eyes. "None of your damn business how old I am," she snapped, then leaned to kiss me again. "My, but you are even better-looking than your father was at your age, and I didn't think that possible. I always told Julian he would have looked better with a healthy suntan, but he'd do anything to defy me, *anything*—even keep himself unnaturally pale." Sadness clouded her eyes. To my surprise she glanced then at Bart, who was listening too—and another surprise, he seemed interested.

She still wore the same black dress that seemed stiff with age, and over that she wore a ratty old leopard-skin bolero that had seen better days. "No one really knew your father, Jory, just as no one really possessed him. That is, no one but your mother."

She sighed, then went on as if she had to say it all before my mother appeared. "So, I've determined I have to know my Julian's son better than I knew him. I've decided too you have to love me, because I was never sure Julian ever did. I keep telling myself that the son born of the union between my son and your mother would have to make the most wonderful dancer, with none of Julian's hang-ups. Your mother is very dear to me, Jory, very dear, though she refuses to believe that. I admit I used to be nasty to her sometimes. She took that as my true feeling, but I was only angry because she never seemed to appreciate my son."

Uncomfortable with this sort of talk, I shifted away from her; my first loyalty was to my mother, not to her. She noticed my attitude but went on regardless:

"I'm lonely, Jory, I need to be near you, near her too." Remorse like evening shadows came to darken her eyes, putting additional years on her face. "The worst thing about growing old is being lonely, feeling so alone, so purposeless, so used up."

"Oh, Grandmother!" I cried, throwing my arms about her. "You don't need to ever feel lonely or purposeless again. You have us." I hugged her tighter, kissed her again. "Isn't this the most beautiful house? You can live here with us. Have I told you before my mother designed it herself?"

Madame looked with great curiosity around the family room. "Yes, this is a lovely home, so like Catherine. Where is she?"

"She's in her room writing."

"Writing letters?" She looked hurt, as if Mom should be a better hostess and not attending to trivialities.

"Grandmother, Mom is writing a book."

"A book? Dancers can't write books!"

Grinning, I jumped up and did a few practice steps out of habit. "Madame Grandmother, dancers can do anything they set their minds to. After all, if we can endure the kind of pain we do, what else is there to fear?"

"Rejections," snapped Madame. "Dancers have sky-high egos. One rejection slip too many and Mommy will come crashing down."

I smiled, thinking that was a good one. She'd never come crashing down even if the mailman brought her a thousand rejection slips.

"Where's your father?" she asked next.

"Making his evening rounds at his hospitals. He said to give you his apologies. He wanted to be here and welcome you to our home, but you didn't show up on schedule."

She snorted, as if that were his fault somehow. "Well," she said, getting up and looking around the room somewhat more critically, "I guess it's time I went in and said hello to Catherine—though certainly she must have heard my voice."

Certainly she should have, it was shrill enough. "Mom

gets very engrossed, Grandmother. Sometimes she doesn't even hear her name spoken from a foot away."

"Har-rumph!" she snorted again. Then she followed me down the hall. I rapped softly on Mom's closed door, and cautiously opened it when she mumbled something like . . . "Yes? . . ."

"You've got company, Mom."

For a second it seemed I saw dismay in my mother's eyes before Madame stalked arrogantly into her bedroom. Grand-mother flung herself down, without an invitation to sit, on the velvet chaise longue.

"Madame M.!" cried Mom. "How wonderful to see you again. At last you've decided to come and see us instead of the other way around."

Why was she so nervous? Why did she keep glancing at the portraits on her nightstand? Same old portraits of Dad and Daddy Paul. Even my father was there, but in a small oval frame, not wide silver ones.

Madame glanced at the nightstand too—and frowned.

"I have many wonderfully framed portraits of Julian," Mom hastily explained, "but Jory likes to keep them in his room."

Again Madame snorted. "You're looking well, Catherine."

"I'm feeling well, thank you. You look well too." In her lap her hands worked nervously, just as her feet kept the swivel deskchair in constant motion.

"Your husband, how is he?"

"Fine, fine. He's making hospital rounds. He waited for you, but when you didn't show up . . ."

"I understand. I'm sorry I'm late, but people in this state are robbers. I had to pay eight hundred for a piece of junk, and it dripped oil all the way here."

Mom ducked her head. I know she was hiding a laugh. "What else can you expect for eight hundred?" Mom finally managed.

"Really, Catherine. Julian never paid much for any car he owned, you know that." Her strident voice grew reflective. "But then he knew what to do with the junk and I don't. I guess I let sentiment run away with my common sense. I should have bought the better one for a thousand, but I'm also thrifty." Next came her question about my mother's knee. Was it healed? How soon would she be dancing again?

"It's fine," said Mom testily. (She hated for people to question her about her knee.) "I only notice a little pain when it rains."

"And how is Paul? It's been so long since I saw him last. I remember after you married him I felt so angry I never wanted to see you again, and I gave up teaching for a few years." Again she glance at the portrait of Dad. "And does your brother still live with you?"

Silence came and burdened the air as Mom studied the smiling portrait of my stepfather Chris. What brother was she talking about? Mom didn't have a brother anymore. Why did Madame look at Dad when she asked about Cory?

"Yes, yes, of course," said Mom, making me puzzled as to what she meant. "Now tell me all about Greenglenna and Clairmont. I want to hear about everybody. How is Lorraine DuVal? Whom did she marry? Or did she go on to New York?"

"He never married, did he?" pursued Grandmother with her eyes narrowed.

"Who?"

"Your brother."

"No, he hasn't married yet," answered Mom, again testy. Then she was smiling. "Now, Madame, I have a big surprise for you. We have a daughter now and her name is Cindy."

"Hah!" snorted Madame, "I already know about Cindy." There was a strange gleam in her eyes. "But still I would like to see and hear more about this paragon of all little girls. Jory writes she may have some dancing abilities."

"Oh, she does, she does! I wish you could see her in her

little pink leotards trying to imitate Jory or me—I mean when I could dance."

"Your husband must be getting along in years by now," Madame said, disregarding photographs Mom tried to show her of Cindy, who was already in bed for the night.

"Did Jory tell you I'm writing a book? It's really fascinating. I didn't think it would be when I first started but after I mastered transitions I really surprised myself, and now writing is more fun than work. Just as satisfying as dancing." She smiled and fluttered her hands about, plucking at lint on her blue pants, tugging down her white sweater, fiddling with her hair, shuffling papers to tidy her desk. "My room is a mess. I apologize for that. I need a study, but in this house we don't have the room . . ."

"Is your brother making hospital rounds too?"

I sat there, not understanding who this brother was. Cory was dead. He'd been dead for years. Though nobody laid in his grave, nobody at all. Little headstone beside Aunt Carrie and nobody there. . . .

"You must be hungry. Let's go into the dining room and Emma can heat up the spaghetti. The second time around it's always better . . ."

"Spaghetti?" snapped Madame. "You mean you eat that kind of junk? You allow my grandson to eat starches? Years and years ago I warned you to stay away from pasta! Really, Catherine, don't you ever learn?"

Spaghetti was one of my favorite dishes—but we'd had leg of lamb tonight in Madame's honor, fixed the way Momma thought she liked it best. Why had she said spaghetti? I gave my mother a hard look and saw her flustered and breathless, looking as young as Melodie, as if she were terribly afraid something might go wrong—and what could?

Madame M. wouldn't eat at our house, wouldn't sleep there either, for she didn't want to "inconvenience" us. Already she'd found a room in town, close to Mom's dance school. "And though you haven't asked me, Catherine, I'll be delighted to stay on and replace you. I sold out my school the moment Jory wrote and told me of your accident."

Mom could only nod, looking queerly blank.

A few days later Madame looked around the office that had been Mom's. "She keeps everything so neat, not like me at all. Soon I'll have it looking like my own."

I loved her in an odd kind of way, the way you love winter when you're hot in summer. And then when winter was shivering your bones, I wished it would go away. She moved so young and looked so old. When she danced she could almost make you think she was eighteen. Her black hair came and went according to which day of the week it was. I'd learned by now she used some color rinse that was shampooed in and soon came out to darken the teeth of her white comb. I liked it best when it was white, silvery under the lights.

"You are everything my own Julian was!" she cried, smothering me with too much gushing affection. Already she'd dismissed the young teacher Mom had hired. "But what makes you so arrogant, huh? Your momma tell you that you are sensational? Always your momma thinks the music is what counts most in the dance, and is not, *is not*. It is the display of the beautiful body that is the essence of ballet. I come to save you. I come to teach you how to do everything perfect. When I am done with you, you will have flawless technique." Her shrill voice lowered an octave or two. "I come too because I am old and may soon die and I do not know my grandson at all. I come to do my duty by being not only your grandmother, but also your grandfather and your father too. Catherine was a big fool to dance when she knew her knee could fold any second—but your mother was always a big fool, so what's new?"

She made me furious. "Don't you talk like that about my mother. She's not a fool. She's never been a fool. She does what

she feels she must—so I'll tell you the truth and you let her be.
She danced that last time because I pleaded and pleaded for
her to dance at least one time with me professionally. She did
it for *me*, Grandmother, for *me,* not herself!"

Her small dark eyes turned shrewd. "Jory, take lesson
number one in my philosophy course: Nobody ever does anything for anyone else unless it gives them even more."

Madame swept all the little mementos Mom cherished
into the trashcan, like they were so much junk. Next she
hauled up a huge beat-up satchel, and in minutes had the
desk more cluttered with her junk than it had been before.

Immediately I knelt to take from the trashcan all the
things I knew my mother loved.

"You don't love me like you love her," complained
Madame in a gritty voice of self-pity that sounded weak and
old. Startled at the pain in her voice, I looked up and saw her
as I'd never seen her before—an old woman, lonely and pitiful, clinging desperately to the only meaningful link to life
she had—me.

Pity flooded me. "I'm glad you're here, Grandmother, and
of course I love you. Don't ask if I love you more than anyone
else, only be happy that I love you at all, as I'm happy you love
me for whatever reason." I kissed her wrinkled cheek. "We'll
get to know each other better. And I'll be the kind of son you
wanted my father to be—in some ways—so don't cry and feel
alone. My family is your family."

Nevertheless, tears were in her eyes, streaking her face,
making her lips quiver as she clutched at me desperately. Her
voice came cracked and old: "Never did Julian run to me like
you just did. He didn't like to touch or be touched. Thank you,
Jory, for loving me a little."

Until now she'd been just a summer event in my life, flat-
tering me with too much praise, making me feel special. Now
I was uncomfortable to know she'd be here always, shadowing
all our lives—perhaps.

Everything was going wrong in our lives. Maybe I could put all the blame on that old woman next door. Yet there was another old woman in black, ten times more trying than Bart's grandmother, more dominating, too. Bart was a kid who needed some control, but I was almost a man and didn't need more mothering. With some resentment I pulled away from her clutching, clawlike hands and asked, "Grandmother, why is it all grandmothers like to wear black?"

"Ridiculous!" she snapped. "Not all do!" Her jet eyes were like stones of black fire.

"But I've never seen you wear any color but black."

"You will never see me wear another color."

"I don't understand. I've heard my mother say you wore black before my grandfather died, before my father died. Are you in perpetual mourning?"

She sneered scornfully. "Ah, I see. You feel uncomfortable around black clothes, yah? Makes you feel sad, yah? Makes me feel glad. It makes me different. Anyone can wear pretty colors. Takes someone special to be pleased with only black clothes—and besides, it saves money."

I laughed and drew away farther. I was sure it was more the money she saved than anything else.

"What other grandmother you know who wears black?" she asked, her eyes very narrow and suspicious.

I smiled and backed away more; she frowned and drew closer. My face took on a broader smile as I neared the door. "It's great having you here, Grandmother Madame. Be especially nice to Melodie Richarme. I'm going to marry her someday."

"Jory!" she yelled. "You come back here! Do you think I flew halfway around the world just to replace your mother? I came for one reason only. I am here to see that Julian's son dances in New York, in every major city in the world, and achieves all the fame and glory that was due his father. Because of Catherine he was robbed, robbed!"

She made me angry, she made me want to hurt her as her words hurt me, when only a moment ago I'd loved her. "Will my fame and glory help a father who lies dead in his grave?" I shouted back. I wasn't putty for her to mold—I was already a great dancer and my mother had done that for me. I didn't need her to teach me more about dancing—I needed her to teach me more about learning to love someone hateful, old, and bitter. "I know how to dance already, Madame, my mother has taught me well."

Her look of contempt made me blanch, but she surprised me when she got up to drop to her knees and put her hands in prayer position beneath her chin. She tilted her thin face backward and seemed to stare God straight in his face.

"Julian!" she cried passionately, "if you are up there looking down, hear the arrogance of your fourteen-year-old son. I will make a pact with you today. Before I die I will see your son is the most acclaimed dancer in the world. I will make of him what you could have been if you hadn't cared so damned much for cars and women, to say nothing of your other vices. Your son, Julian—through him you will live to dance again!"

I stared as she fell exhausted into the swivel deskchair again, sprawling her powerful legs before her. "Damn Catherine for marrying a doctor years and years older. Where was her common sense?—where was his? Though to give credit where credit is due, he was handsome years ago and appealing enough, but she should have known he'd be old before she even reached her sexual maturity. She should have married a man nearer her own age."

I stood before her, baffled, trembling, beginning to feel closet doors in my mind opening—creakily opening, reluctantly. No, no, my mind kept saying, keep quiet Madame. I watched her jerk upright, her dark stabbing eyes riveting me to one spot so I was unable to leave when what I wanted most was to run, and run fast.

"Why do you tremble?" she asked. "Why do you look so strange?"

"Do I look strange?"

"Don't answer questions with questions," she barked. "Tell me about Paul, your stepfather, how he fares, what he does. He was twenty-five years older than your mother, and she's thirty-seven now. Doesn't that make him sixty-two?"

I swallowed over an aching lump that came to clog my throat. "Sixty-two is not so old," I said meekly, thinking she should know that; she was in her seventies.

"For a man it is old; for a woman life is only beginning to stretch out."

"That is cruel," I said, beginning to dislike her again.

"Life is cruel, Jory, very cruel. You snatch from life what you can while you are young, for if you wait for better times to come tomorrow, you wait in vain. I told Julian that time and again, to live his life and forget Catherine, who loved that older man, but he refused to believe any girl could prefer a middle-aged man to someone as handsome and vibrant as he was, and now he lies dead in his grave, as you just said. Dr. Paul Sheffield enjoys the love that rightly belonged to my son, to your father."

I was crying tears she couldn't see. Hot scalding tears of disbelief. Had my mother lied to Madame and made her believe Daddy Paul was still alive? Why would she lie? What was wrong about marrying Dr. Paul's younger brother Christopher?

"You look ill, Jory. Why?"

"I feel fine, Madame."

"Don't lie to me, Jory. I can smell a lie a mile away, see a lie from across three thousand miles. Why is it Paul Sheffield never accompanies his family to his own hometown? Why is it your mother always brings only her children and that brother, Christopher?"

My heart was pounding. Sweat glued my shirt to my

skin. "Madame, have you never met Daddy Paul's younger brother?"

"Younger brother? What's that you say?" She leaned forward and peered into my eyes. "Never heard of any brother even during that awful time when Paul's first wife drowned their son. That was spread all over the newspapers, and no younger brother was mentioned. Paul Sheffield had only one sister—no brother, younger or older."

I felt sick, ready to throw up. Ready to cry out and run and do something wild and painful to myself, like Bart did when he was hurt and disturbed. Bart—for the first time I was feeling what it was to be like Bart. I stood on unsteady ground, afraid everything might crumble if I dared to move.

Through my mind kept running the steady stream of age, years and years of age difference, and Dad wasn't that much older than Mom, only two years and a few months. She was born in April, he was born in November. And they were so much alike in coloring, in background, they spoke without even saying a word, just a glance and they understood.

Madame was sitting coiled, ready, so it seemed, to spring upon me—or Mom? Deeper lines etched around her narrowed eyes, her grim-thin lips. She pursed her lips and reached into some hidden pocket of her drab outfit for her pack of cigarettes. "Now," she said as if to herself, seemingly forgetting I was still there, "what was it Catherine gave as an excuse the last time Paul didn't come? Let's see, she called first, long distance, explaining Chris would come with her because Paul was too ill with his heart trouble to travel. She was leaving him in the care of his nurse. Thought that odd at the time, that she'd leave him when he needed a nurse, and travel with Chris." She bit down on her lower lip, chewed it unconsciously. "And last summer no visit because Bart hated ole graves and ole ladies—and I suspect, *me* in particular. Spoiled brat. This summer they don't come again because Bart has driven a rusty nail into his knee and develops blood-poisoning or something similar. Damn kid is more trouble than he's worth—serves her right too for playing around so soon after my son's death. And Paul has heart trouble, on and on he has heart trouble, yet he never has a fatal attack. Every summer she gives me that same worn excuse. Paul can't travel because of his heart—but Chris, he can always travel, heart or no heart."

Abruptly she stopped talking, for I had moved to leave. I tried to make my eyes blank and erase all the milling suspicions I didn't want her to see. Never had I felt more afraid than I did at that moment, just watching her scheming eyes, the wheels churning, planning something I knew.

At that moment she jumped to her feet with great agility. "Put on your coat. I'm going home with you to have a long chat with your mother."

The Terrible Truth

J ory," began Madame when we were in her ratty old car and driving homeward. "Your parents don't confide in you much about their past, do they?"

"They tell us enough," I said stiffly, resenting the way she kept prying, when it didn't matter, it didn't. "They are very good listeners, and everyone says they make the best kind of conversationalists."

She snorted. "Being a good listener is the perfect way to avoid answering questions you'd rather ignore."

"Now you look here, Grandmother. My parents like their privacy. They have asked both Bart and me not to talk about our home life to our friends, and after all, it does make good sense for a family to stick together."

"Really . . . ?"

"Yes!" I shouted, "I like my privacy too!"

"You are of an age to need privacy; they are not."

"Madame, my mother was a celebrity of sorts, and Dad is a doctor, and Mom has been married three times. I don't think she wants her former sister-in-law, Amanda, to know where we live."

"Why not?"

"My aunt Amanda is not a very nice person, that's all."

"Jory, do you trust me?"

"Yes," I said, but I didn't.

"Then tell me all you know about Paul. Tell me if he's as sick as she says, or if he is alive at all. Tell me why Christopher lives in your home, and is the one who acts like the father of you and Bart."

Oh, I didn't know what to say, and I was trying hard to be a good listener so she'd keep on talking and I'd be able to put the pieces of the puzzle together. Certainly I didn't want her to get the picture before I did.

A long silence grew, and finally she spoke. "You know, after Julian died, your mother lived with you in Paul's home, then she took you and her younger sister, Carrie, to the mountains of Virginia. Her mother lived there in a fine home. It seems Catherine was determined to ruin her mother's second marriage. The husband of your mother's mother was named Bartholomew Winslow."

That cursed darn lump came back in my throat and ached there. I wasn't going to tell her that Bart was the son of anyone but Daddy Paul, I wasn't!

"Grandmother, if you want me to keep on loving you, please do not tell me ugly things about my mother."

Her skinny hand reached to squeeze mine. "All right, I admire you for being so loyal. I just want you to know the facts." About that time she almost careened off the road into another ditch.

"Grandmother, I know how to drive. If you are tired and can't see the road signs very well, I can take over, and you could sit back and relax."

"Let a fourteen-year-old kid drive me around? Are you crazy? Are you saying you don't feel safe with me at the wheel? All my life I've been driven around, first in hay wagons, then carriages, then taxis or limousines, but three weeks before

I came here, soon after your letter came telling about your mother's accident, I took driver's lessons at the age of seventy-four . . . and you see now how well I learned."

Finally, after four near misses, we made the turn into our circular drive. And there out front was Bart stalking some invisible animal with his pocketknife held like a dagger, ready to thrust and kill.

Madame ignored him as she pulled to a stop. Briskly I jumped out and raced to open her door, but she was out before I got there, and just behind her Bart was stabbing into the air with his knife. "Death to the enemy! Death to all old ladies who wear black raggedy clothes! Death, death, death!"

Calmly, as if she didn't hear and didn't see, Madame strode on. I shoved Bart aside and whispered, "If you want to be locked up today, keep on with what you're doing."

"Black . . . hate black . . . gotta wipe out all dark black evil."

But he put the knife in his pocket after he carefully folded it and stroked the pearl handle he admired. He should. It had cost me seven bucks for that present.

Without waiting for a response to her impatient push on the doorchimes, Madame stalked into our house and tossed her purse on the love seat in the foyer. The clack of typewriter keys came to us faintly.

"Writing," she said, "I guess she goes at that just as passionately as she did dancing . . ."

I didn't say anything, but I did want to run ahead and warn Mom. She wouldn't let me. Mom looked up very startled to suddenly encounter Madame Marisha again in her bedroom.

"Catherine! Why didn't you tell me Dr. Paul Sheffield was dead."

Momma's face went red, then white. She bowed her head and put her hands up to cover her face. Regaining her composure almost immediately, she raised her head, flashed angry eyes at Madame, then began to shuffle her papers into a neat

pile. "How nice to see you, Madame Marisha. It would have
been nicer if you had called in advance. However, I'm sure
Emma can split the lamb chops unevenly and let you have
two . . ."

"Don't evade my question with silly talk of eating. Do you
think for one moment I would pollute my body with your stupid lamb chops? I eat health foods, and health foods only."

"Jory," said Mom, "in case Emma saw Madame, run tell
her not to set another place."

"What is all this idiotic chatter about lamb chops? I drove
here to ask an important question, and you talk about food.
Catherine, answer my question—is Paul Sheffield dead?"

Mom looked at me and gestured I was to disappear, but
I couldn't. I stood my ground and defied her. She paled more
and seemed appalled that I, her darling, would not obey.
Then, as if resigned, she muttered in an indistinct way: "You
never asked me about myself, about my husband, so I took it
you weren't interested in anyone but Jory."

"Catherine!"

"Jory, please leave this room immediately. Or do I have to
get up and shove you out?"

I backed out the door just before she reached to throw it
shut.

Barely could I make out what she said on the other side of
the door, but I pressed my ear against it and heard. "Madame,
you don't know how much I have needed someone to confide
in. But you were always so cold, so remote, I didn't think you
could understand."

Silence. A snort.

"Yes, Paul died, years ago. I try not to think of him as
dead but as still alive, though invisible. We brought his
marble statues and benches here and tried to make our garden grow like his. We failed. But still, when twilight comes
and I'm not in the garden it seems I can sense him near, still
loving me. We were married for such a short time. And he

was never really well . . . so when he died, I was left feeling unfulfilled, still yearning to give him the years of happy married life I owed him. I wanted somehow to make up for Julia, his first wife."

"Catherine," said Madame softly, "who is this man your children call Father?"

"Madame, what I do is none of your business." I could hear the anger building in Mom's voice. "This is not the same kind of world you grew up in. You have not lived my life, and been inside my mind. You have not known the kind of deprivations I suffered when I was young and needed love most. Don't you sit there and condemn me with your dark mean eyes, for you can't understand."

"Oh, Catherine, how little credit you give my intelligence. Do you think me dumb, blind, and insensitive? I know now very well who the man is my grandson calls Dad. And it's no wonder you could never love my Julian enough. I used to think it was Paul, but now I see it wasn't Paul you truly loved; it wasn't that Bartholomew Winslow either—it was Christopher, your brother. I don't give a damn what you and your brother do. If you sleep in his bed and you find the happiness you feel was stolen from you long ago, I can rationalize and say that much worse goes on every day than brother and sister who pretend to be husband and wife. But I must protect my grandson. He comes first. You have no right to make your children pay the price for your unlawful relationship."

Oh!—What was she saying?

Mom, do something, say something, make me feel good again! Make me feel safe and real again—make it all go away, this talk of your brother you've never mentioned.

I crouched down lower, bowing my head into my hands, not wanting to hear, not daring to leave.

Mom's voice came strained and very hoarse, as if she were having trouble keeping tears away. "I don't know how you found out. Please try to understand . . ."

"As I said before, I don't give a damn—and I think I do understand. You couldn't love my son, as you could never love any man more than you loved your brother. I'm bitter about that. I'm crying inside for Julian, who thought you an angel of perfection, *his* Catherine, *his* Clara, *his* sleeping beauty that he could never wake up. That's what you were to him, Catherine, the personification of all the dancing dolls of the ballet, virgin and pure, sweet and chaste, and in the end you are no better than the rest of us."

"Please!" cried Mom. "I tried to escape Chris. I tried to love Julian more. I did, I really did."

"No, you didn't try. If you had, you would have succeeded."

"You can't know!" came Mom's distressed cry.

"Catherine, you and I have traveled the same road for many a year, and you've let little bits and pieces of information drop along the way. And then there is Jory, who tries his best to shield you . . ."

"He doesn't know? Please say he doesn't know!"

"He doesn't know," Madame soothed in what was a soft voice—for her. "But he talks, and spills more than he knows. The young are like that; they think the old are so senile they can't put two and two together. They think the old can live to be seventy and still not know more than they do at fourteen. They think they have a monopoly on experience, because they see us not doing very much, while every moment of their lives are full, forgetting we too were young once. And we have turned all our mirrors into windows . . . and they are still behind the mirrors looking only at themselves."

"Madame, please don't speak so loud. Bart has a way of hiding and eavesdropping."

Her strident voice toned down, making it more difficult for me to hear. "All right, I'll have my say and go. I don't think your home is the proper place for a boy of Jory's sensitivities to grow up in. The atmosphere here is tense, as if a bomb might explode any moment. Your younger son is obviously in need of psychological help—why, he tried to stab me as I approached your home."

"Bart is always playing games . . . ," said Mom weakly.

"Hah! Some games he plays! His knife almost slit my coat. And this coat is almost new. It will be my last coat, the one I'll wear until I'm dead."

"Please, Madame, I'm not in the mood for talk of death."

"Did I ask for your pity? If you took it that way, then I reverse positions. I'll wear this coat as long as I live. And before I die I have to see Jory achieve the fame that should have been Julian's."

"I'm doing what I can," said Mom wearily, sounding so terribly tired.

"What you can? Hell and damnation! You live here with your brother, risking public humiliation, and sooner or later your fragile bubble will pop. Jory will suffer. His schoolmates will taunt him. The reporters will hound you, him, everyone in this house. The law will take your children from you."

"Please sit down, stop pacing."

"Damn you, Catherine, for not listening. I guessed a long time ago that in time you would succumb to your brother's adoration. I thought even when you married your Dr. Paul that you and your brother . . . well, never mind what I thought, but you married a man almost dead. Was it a guilty conscience?"

"I don't know. I used to think it was because I loved him and I owned him. I had a thousand reasons for marrying him, the most important being he wanted me, and that was enough."

"All right, you had reasons enough. But you hurt my son. You didn't give him what he needed, and I never understood how you could resist. He used to cry, saying you didn't love him enough. Always he said there was some mysterious man you loved more—and I didn't believe him then. Fool, wasn't I? Fool, wasn't he? But we were all fools when it came to you, Catherine. You were so beautiful, so young and innocent seeming. Were you born old and clever? How did you know so well, so early, all the ways of making a man love you beyond reason?"

"Love is sometimes not enough," she said dully, while I felt almost paralyzed with the dreadful information I was overhearing. Moment by moment, heartbeat by heartbeat, I was losing the mother I loved, I was also losing the only father I'd ever had long enough to love. "How did you find out about Chris and me?" Mom asked, making me quiver more.

"Does it matter?" shrieked Madame. I was pinning my hopes to her, hoping she too wouldn't betray me. "I'm not dumb, Catherine, as I said before. I asked a few questions. I listened to Jory's answers, and I added up the facts. It's been years since I saw Paul—but Chris was always there. Bart is on the brink of insanity from what Jory innocently lets out— never intentionally, only carelessly, for he loves you. Do you think I can stand quietly by and let you and your brother wreck my grandson's life too? I refuse to let you ruin his career, his mental health. You give me Jory to take back East with me, where he'll be safe and far removed from the bomb that will explode and splatter your lives onto the front pages of every newspaper in this country!"

I was sick. I'd opened the door a bit, enough to see my mother was paler than death. She began to tremble, as I was trembling—but she didn't have tears in her eyes as I had in mine. Momma, how could you live with your brother when the whole world knows that's wrong? How could you deceive Bart and me? How could Chris do that to us? And all this time I'd thought he was so perfect, so right for you, for us. Sin, sin. No wonder Bart went around chanting about sin and the torments of everlasting hell. Somehow Bart had found out before me.

I sank to my knees and leaned my head against the door, closing my eyes and trying to breathe deeply to stop my stomach rumbling and wanting to rise.

Mom spoke again. It was easy to tell she was trying hard to hold on to her temper.

"To lose Bart for even a few months in some institution is nearly driving me crazy. But to lose Jory as well *would* drive me crazy. I love my sons, Madame, both of them. Though you have never given me credit for having mercy on Julian, I did the best I could for him. He was not an easy man to live with. You and your husband made him what he was, not me. I didn't force him to dance when he would have played ball if given his way. I didn't punish him by making him practice every weekend, so he never had time for fun—you and Georges did that. But it was me who paid that price. He wanted to devour me alive, forbidding me any friends but him. Jealous of every man who looked my way, every man I looked at. Do you know what it is to live with a man who suspects you deceive him when you're out of his sight? And it wasn't me who did the betraying—it was him. I was faithful to Julian. I never let another man touch me, but he couldn't have said the same thing. He wanted every pretty girl he saw. He wanted to use them, discard them, then come back to me and have me hold him in my arms and tell him how wonderful he was . . . and I couldn't say he was wonderful when the stench of some other woman's perfume was all over him. Then he'd hit me, did you know that? He had to prove something to himself. I didn't know then what he had to prove, but now I do—he had to find the love you denied him."

I felt weaker, sicker, as I saw my grandmother blanch. Now I was losing my real father, whom I'd adored as a saint.

"You make your points very well, Catherine, and they hurt. But now let me make mine. Georges and I did make mistakes with Julian, I admit that, and you and our son paid the price. Are you going to punish Jory in the same way? Let me take him back to Greenglenna. Once we're there I'll arrange for an audition for him in New York. I have important connections. I did manage to turn out two brilliant dancers, one named Julian, the other named Catherine. I was not all bad, nor was Georges. Perhaps we let our own dreams blind us to what others wanted and we tried too hard to live through our child. That's all we wanted, Catherine, to live through Julian. Now Julian is dead and he has left behind one child, one only—your son. Without Jory I have no reason to stay alive. With Jory I have every reason to go on. For once in your life *give,* don't take."

NO, NO! I didn't want to go with Madame.

I watched Mom bow her head until her hair fell in two soft wings of pale gold. Her trembling hand fluttered to touch her brow, as if another of those terrible headaches was paining. I didn't want to leave her, sinner or not. This was my home, my world, and she was still my mother and Chris was still my stepdad, and there was Bart, Cindy, and Emma too. We were a family—rightly, wrongly, we were a family.

Finally Mom seemed to find a solution. Hope rose in my heart.

"Madame, I'm throwing myself on your mercy, and hoping to God you have some. I realize you could very well be right, but I cannot give up my firstborn son. Jory is the one good thing that came from my marriage to Julian. If you take him, you take part of me, a very important part of me I cannot surrender without dying. Jory loves me. He loves Chris as much as he could love his own father. Even if I have to risk his career, I cannot risk losing his love by letting him go away with you . . . so don't ask for the impossible, Madame, I cannot let Jory go."

Madame stared at her long and hard while my heart thumped so loudly I was sure they'd both hear. Then Grandmother stood up and prepared to leave. "Hah," she snorted. "I'm going to speak honestly now, Catherine, and perhaps for the first time I'll give you the full truth. I have, since the first day I met you, envied your youth, your beauty, and most of all your genius for the dance. I know you have passed on to Jory your extraordinary skill. You have been a superb teacher. I see so much of you in him, and so much of your brother in him too. The patience Jory has, the cheerful optimism, the drive and dedication—derived from your family, not from Julian. But there is some of Julian in him too. He looks like my son. He has the fire of my son, and the fleshy desires of my son for women. But if I must hurt you to save him, I will do so. I will not spare your brother, or your youngest son either. If you do not turn Jory over to me I will do what I can to bring down your house. The law will give me custody of Jory, and there will not be one thing you can do to stop me once I go to them with the facts. And if you force me to do it this way, which is not the way I would choose, I will take Jory East, and he will never see you again."

Mom rose to her feet and stood taller than my grandmother. I'd never seen her look taller, prouder, stronger. "Go on, do what you must. I will not give in one inch, and allow you to steal from me what is mine. Never will I give a child of mine away. Jory is mine. I gave birth to him after eighteen hours of striving. If I have to face up to the whole world and its condemnation, still I will stand with my head held high, and hold fast to my children. There is no force in this world, you, the law, anything, that can force me to give up my children."

Turning to go, Madame glanced around the room, allowing her eyes to linger longest on the thick stack of papers on Mom's small desk. "You'll see things my way," she said in a soft cat's purr. "I pity you Catherine, as I pity your brother. I pity Bart too, savage as the little monster is. I pity everyone in your household, for all will be hurt. But I won't let my compassion for you, and my understanding of what made you the way you are, hold back my hand. Jory will be safe with me, with my name, not yours."

"GET OUT!" screamed Mom, who had lost all control. She picked up a vase with flowers and hurled it at Madame's head! "YOU RUINED YOUR SON'S LIFE AND NOW YOU WANT TO RUIN JORY! YOU WANT HIM TO BELIEVE THERE IS NO LIFE BUT IN THE BALLET, DANCING,

DANCING—BUT I AM LIVING! I WAS A DANCER, AND STILL I AM SURVIVING!"

Madame looked around the room again, as if she too would like to hurl some object, and slowly she bent over to pick up the broken vase at her feet. "I gave you this. How ironic that you would hurl it at me." Something brittle and hard seemed to crack as she looked at Mom with softness, and she spoke with rare humility. "When Julian was a boy, I tried to do for him what was best, just as you try to do for yours what is best . . . and if my judgment was wrong, it was done with the best of intentions."

"Isn't everything?" said Mom with bitterness. "Always the intentions are so right, so reasonable—and in the end even the excuses ride the waves of indignation like that fabled straw everyone tries to grasp to keep from drowning. It seems all my life I've been grasping for straws that don't exist. I tell myself each night, before I climb into bed with my brother, that this is the reason I was born, and for every wrong I have done I have consoled myself by saying I have balanced the scales with the right decisions. I have finally given my brother the only woman he can love, the wife he so desperately needed. I have made him happy—and if that is wrong in your eyes, and in the eyes of the world, I don't give a damn. I don't give a damn what the world thinks!"

My grandmother just stood there, with conflicting emotions torturing her aged face. I could tell she, too, was hurting. I watched her thin, heavily veined hand reach to touch my mother's hair, but she drew it away and kept her eyes blank and her voice under control: "Again I say, I pity you, Catherine. I pity all of you, but most of all I pity Jory, for he is the one with the most to lose."

Quickly I backed away and hid as she hurled herself out of Mom's bedroom and strode down the back hall, bypassing Bart, who stabbed at her with his unsheathed knife.

"Witch, old black witch!" he snarled, pulling back his

upper lip in a frightful way. "I hope you never come back, never, never!"

I was miserable enough now to want a hole to crawl into and die. *My mother was living with her brother.* The woman I'd loved and respected all my life was worse than any mother I'd ever heard of. None of my friends would believe, but when they did, I'd be so shamed, ridiculed, I'd never be able to face them. Then it hit me. Dad was my real uncle. Not just Bart's but mine too. Oh, God, what did I do now? Where did I run? It was not a platonic brother-sister relationship, a fake marriage for appearances sake, it was incest. They were lovers. I knew! I'd seen!

Suddenly everything was too sordid, too ugly, too shocking. Why had they allowed their love to start? Why hadn't they stopped it from happening?

I wanted to get up and go and ask, but I couldn't bear to look at Mom, or Dad either when he came home. In my room I fell on my bed, with the locked door making me feel safer. When I was called to dinner I said I wasn't hungry. Me, who was always starving. Mom came to the closed door and pleaded: "Jory, did you overhear anything your grandmother said to me?"

"No, Mother," I answered stiffly. "I think I'm coming down with a cold, that's all. I'll feel fine in the morning, just fine." I had to say something to explain why my voice was husky.

Somewhere in all those tears I shed I lost the boy I was earlier today. Now I had to become a man. I felt old, cold, like nothing mattered very much anymore, and for the first time I knew why Bart was so confused and peculiar acting—he must know too.

I sneaked to watch Mom writing in her fine blue-leather journal, and when I had the chance, I stole into her room and read every word she'd written, as dishonest as that was. I was becoming just like Bart. But I had to know.

Madame Marisha visited today and brought with her all the night-mares that haunt my days. I have other nightmares for sleeping. When she was gone I felt panic throbbing so loud my heart sounded like a jungle drum beating out the rhythm of the last battle. I wanted to run and hide as we used to hide when we were locked away in Foxworth Hall. I ran to Chris when he came home, and clung, clung, unable to tell him anything. He didn't notice my desperation. He was tired from a long exhausting day.

Then he kissed me, and was off for his evening rounds, and I sat alone in my room, both of my sons silent and locked behind their bed-room doors. Do they know that soon our world is coming to an end?

Should I have let Madame take Jory and keep him safe from the scandal and humiliation? Was I selfish to want to hold fast to him? And Bart, what about Bart? And what would happen to Cindy if our secret were revealed?

Suddenly I felt I was back in Charlottesville, with Chris and Carrie, and again we were on our way to Sarasota. My memory seemed like a movie as that huge black woman struggled to board the slow bus with all her bags and bundles. Henrietta Beech. Dear, dear Henny. It's been so long since I last thought of her. Just to remember her broad beaming smile, her kind eyes, her gentle hands and a cer-tain peace steals over me, like she is taking me again to Paul, who would save us all.

But who will save us now?

Tears were in my eyes when I put her journal away. I stole into Bart's room and found him sitting on the floor, in the dark, hunched over like an old man. "Bart, go to bed," I said. But he didn't get up. He seemed not to hear me.

The Gates of Hell

Knew it, just knew it. Jory had to spy and check up on what deviltry I was up to. Pretended not to notice. Soon as his room was dark, I pulled out the last pages of Momma's story. Knew it was the end for she'd written her initials and address near the bottom of the page.

Didn't know why I was crying. Malcolm wouldn't feel pity for her and my daddy. Now I'd have to grow tough, mean, pretend nothing could hurt me nearly as much as it hurt others.

Morning came and I went into the kitchen where Momma was helping Emma do little housekeeping chores, making cookie dough, talking about cakes. The woman thought evil could go on unnoticed forever. Unpunished forever. She should know better.

I sat in my corner, hunched over on the floor, my knees pulled up under my chin, my shins wrapped with my arms. Bony arms. Getting skinnier by the day. I stared at Momma, at Daddy, hoping to look into their minds and find out what they really thought of me, of themselves and what they were doing. I closed my eyes. Behind my lids I saw Momma dancing like she used to before she hurt her knee. Last summer, not so long after I came home from the hospital and I had trouble falling asleep, I'd stumbled into the kitchen to rob the fridge while nobody could see. I wanted them all to worry and think about me starving to death. But before I could gobble down all the cold chicken legs, Momma had danced into the family room wearing a little white tutu with hardly any top, and Daddy had trailed along behind. He didn't even see me. Couldn't see anybody but her.

She'd looked pretty in that costume, whirling around, always smiling and flirting with the man who stood in the shadows watching her. She teased him by tugging at his tie, pulling him out into the center of the room, forcing him to turn around and around, and trying to make him dance that ballet stuff. But he'd grabbed her in his arms and pressed his lips down on hers. I'd heard the sound, wet and mushy. Then her arms tightened around his neck. I stared to see him unhooking all those little dark things that held her tutu on! It slipped and fell to the floor at her feet, and she was wearing nothing but white leotards that he soon tugged off. Naked. He made her naked. Next he lifted her in his arms, and while her lips were still pressed to his, he carried her off to their room— and all the time he'd been her brother.

Oh, no wonder John Amos said they had to be punished. No wonder. Whore! Bitch! Sinners with my own blood! They wouldn't get away with this. They'd have to *burn, burn*—burn like my daddy, like my real daddy named Bartholomew Winslow.

I read all her story. I know how ugly and mean some mothers could be. Hiding her four children, making them stay upstairs in one room, forcing them to play in a hot miserable attic that was freezing in the winters. All those years locked up, whipped too, and starved—and tar in my mother's beautiful golden hair. I hated Malcolm, who'd done so many wicked things to his own grandchildren. I hated that old lady next door who put arsenic on their sugared doughnuts. What kind of crazy nut was she? Had she put poison on my ice cream, my cake and cookies too? I shivered and felt queasy in my stomach. Why hadn't the police locked her up until they dragged her to the electric chair to burn, burn?

No, whispered a sly voice in my head, they don't let pretty ladies die in electric chairs when clever lawyers can call killers insane. They were locked in pretty palaces tucked away in green hills. That crazy woman was the same one my daddy had to visit each summer. The mother of my momma too. Oh, the sins of my momma and daddy piled clear up to the sky. Certainly God was gonna punish them now—and if he didn't, Malcolm would see that I did.

Went to bed that night and tried to sleep. But I kept thinking. Daddy was really Momma's brother—and that made him really my uncle, and Jory's uncle. Oh, Momma, you are not the saint or angel Jory thinks you are. You tell him not to do this, and not to do that with Melodie, and all the time you keep going into the bedroom with your brother and closing the door. Telling us never to enter when that door was shut without knocking first. Shame, shame! Privacy, always needing privacy to do what brother and sister should never do. Incest!

Wicked, both of them, just as wicked as I was sometimes. Just as wicked as Jory wanted to be with Melodie, with other girls—doing all the shameful things Eve did with Adam after she bit into the apple. Doing those horrible things the boys whispered about in the restrooms. Didn't want to live with them no more. Didn't want to love Momma or her brother.

Jory knew too. I knew Jory knew too—he was gonna go crazy like Momma thought I was. But I was finally gaining sense, good sense, like Malcolm's. The children of incestuous parents deserved to suffer as I was being made to suffer, as Jory was suffering. Cindy has to suffer too, even if she was too young and dumb to know big words like "incest."

Yet, yet, why did I keep praying for God not to let tomorrow come? What was I gonna do tomorrow? Why did I want
to die tonight, and save myself from doing even worse than
"incest"?

Another breakfast to eat. Hated food that tasted nasty.
Stared down at the tablecloth that would soon be soiled when I
accidently knocked something over. Jory looked as lost as I felt.

Days came, days went, and nobody was happy. Dad walked
about looking sick. I guessed he knew we knew, and Momma
knew too. Now neither one of them could meet our eyes or
answer Jory's questions. I never asked any. I heard Momma
one day rapping on Jory's locked bedroom door. "Jory, please
let me in. I know you overheard when Madame M. was here—
let me try to explain how it was. When you understand you
won't hate us."

Yes he would. I'd read that damn book. Wasn't fair for life
to cheat us by not giving us honorable parents.

Thanksgiving Day, and ole hateful ugly Madame M.
showed up when she should never have had the nerve to
accept any invitation. Momma shouldn't have given her one.
I thought she was gloating when she watched Dad carve the
turkey and not once did he smile, and then she was looking
at Momma, whose eyes were red and swollen. Crying, she'd
been crying. Served her right. Didn't like turkey anyway,
wasn't nearly as good as chicken. Daddy asked me what meat
I liked, dark or white. I scowled, not answering, thinking his
voice was so husky he must have a cold, but he didn't cough or
sneeze, and his eyes didn't look weak like mine when I had a
cold. And Daddy was never sick.

Only Emma was happy, and Cindy, hateful Cindy.

"Come, come," said Emma with a big cheerful smile that
wouldn't do any good, "it's time for rejoicing!—for giving
thanks for our many blessings, including having a new daughter to sit at our table."

Revolting to hear that.

Silently Dad picked up his carving knife and fork again, no smiles, and even I stared at him for forgetting to give me the thigh. I looked at Momma, who seemed upset though I could tell she was trying to pretend everything was still all right. She ate a bite or two of her meal, then jumped up and ran from the dining room. Down the back hall I heard her bedroom door slam. Daddy excused himself, saying he had to go and check on her.

"Good Lord, what's wrong with everybody?" asked Emma while ole Madame Marisha sat on silently, looking glum too. She was part of it all. I glared at her, hating her, hating my own grandmother even more—hating everybody and Cindy too, and all the time thinking maybe Emma had done some evil too by keeping her mouth shut and letting all this sinning go on under her long nose. Jory tried to laugh and smile, teasing Cindy to make her laugh and eat. But I knew he was bleeding deep down in his heart, just as I was bleeding, crying for my real daddy who died in that fire. And maybe Jory was crying for his real daddy, whom Momma hadn't loved nearly enough because all the time she had a brother who loved her too much.

I wished I hadn't found out. Why did Momma have to go and write that book? I wouldn't really have believed anything John Amos told me about her, for I'd thought he was a liar, a pretender, like me. Now I knew he was the only truthful person in the whole world, the only one who respected me enough to tell the truth.

Sobbing, I got up and left the table, glancing at Cindy, who was sitting on Jory's lap and laughing as she played with some little toy he'd given her. Never gave *me* anything. Nobody but a lying-black-witch-grandmother who didn't count gave me gifts . . . nobody.

Then, there came a Sunday when Momma didn't seem to feel so "wretched," maybe because she thought Madame M. was gonna leave us alone, and maybe even go back East where she belonged. I knew then Momma could pretend too, like me, like she and Daddy pretended in their marriage game.

I hid in the shadows near her open bedroom door and watched her go down on her knees in prayer. Silent prayers. Wondered if God ever listened.

Back in the family room I crouched in my corner and began to light matches one by one, holding the flames so close to my face I could feel the heat. How awful it was gonna be to be purified and redeemed by fire. How awful it had been when my real daddy's soul went up in black smoke. And I was just a tiny thing then, hiding in my momma's womb, called an "embryo" and not Bart, and maybe I'd even been a girl then too, worst of all.

Wish Daddy wouldn't tell me so much about things I didn't want to understand.

My head began to ache. Made my hand that held the match shake so much I dropped the match. Quickly I had to snuff it out before someone smelled the carpet burning. They'd blame me, like they always blamed me, not even knowing Jory was outside doing something perhaps just as bad.

What was it John Amos kept saying? "Your mother made all the bad things happen. Every one of the bad things was her fault—that's the way of women, especially beautiful women. Evil through and through, tricky, sinful beautiful women, out to steal from men."

Yeah, I thought, my momma, my grandmother, all tricky beautiful sinful women. Telling me lies, hiding from me who she really was, showing me her portrait when she was young and beautiful, seducing my real father when he was too young for her anyway. My head ached more. Darn dratted Momma had done the same thing to my real daddy.

I sighed, thinking I'd better get on with my own business of being the angel of the Lord, sent to act in Malcolm's stead. After all, I was his great-grandson, and getting almost as smart as him. Acted like Malcolm more and more, making my bones feel tired; making my muscles sore and aching, getting the true feel of being old like Malcolm had been when he was wisest. Though it did get painful to make my heart throb so fast. Disgusted with all women, all. Had to fix them all, everyone. Momma thought I didn't know, thought only Jory knew . . . but I'd been there too when old Madame Marisha shrilled out loud enough for everyone to hear and I'd read her book.

Head hurt worse. Didn't know who I was anymore. Malcolm? Bart? Yeah, was Malcolm now, bad heart, weak legs, thinning hair, but so damned clever and wise.

Stupid daughter, hiding her four children on the second floor and thinking I wouldn't find out sooner or later. Fool. She should have known John would tell me everything. She should have known so many things she ignored, or forgot. So, she thinks I'm going to die soon, and I'll never climb the stairs, but why should I when John will do that for me. Spy, I told John, spy on my daughter, see what she does when she's out of my sight. She thinks I'm going to die soon, John, and I'll change my will and write her back in, but I'll have the last laugh. She's not going to inherit all my hard-earned money. Jingle, jingle, jingle, hear the money in my pockets, like music, the best kind of music. Never too old to outsmart all of them, never too old—and I'll win as I always win in the end.

Shuffling my feet along, I headed for their bedroom which smelled of their evil acts of love. I paused just outside their closed door. Inside I felt like a little boy who was quietly sobbing, but I had to be Malcolm—the stronger, older, wiser part that was me. Where were the blue-misted mountains? This wasn't a great house sitting high on a hillside. Where were the servants, the grand ballroom, the winging staircases?

Confused, so confused. Head ached worse. Knee began to throb. Back pained, heart was going to have an attack.

"Straighten up there, Bart," said that man who was really my uncle. Scared me. Made me jump and grow more confused. "You're too young to be hobbling around like an old man, Bart. And your knee is just fine." He gave me a friendly pat on my head and opened the door to his bedroom, where I could see my mother was waiting for him in the bed, her eyes wide open and staring up at the ceiling. Was she crying? Had he just come home from those hateful hospitals with all their germs?

"I hate you!" I whispered fiercely, trying to stab him with the glare of my eyes. "You think you are safe, don't you? You think a doctor can't be punished—but God has sent the black angel of his wrath to see that you and your sister are punished for the evil you have done!"

He froze on the spot and stared at me as if he'd never seen me before. Defiantly I glared back. He closed the door to his bedroom and led me down the hall so *she* wouldn't hear. "Bart, you go to visit your grandmother every day, don't you?" His face looked troubled, but he kept his voice soft and kind. "You have to learn not to believe everything you hear. Sometimes people tell lies."

"Devil's spawn!" I hissed. "Seed planted in the wrong soil to create Devil's issue."

This time he grasped my arm so tightly it hurt, and he shook me. "Never let me hear you say that again! You are never to mention any of this to your mother. If you do, I'll burn your bottom so hard you may never sit down again. And the next time you see that woman next door, you remind her that it was she who planted all the seeds and started the flowers growing. Watch her face when you speak . . . and then guess who is the evil one."

I shrank back, didn't want to hear what he had to say. I ran off, bumping into a hall table, upsetting an expensive lamp that toppled to the floor.

In my room I fell on my bed, shaking all over, panting and gasping for breath. In my chest was that awful throbbing pain that made iron bands tighten about me, squeezing me, wanting to shut off my air.

Felt like toothpaste being squeezed from the bottom, then I was rolled up tight as a coil. Painfully I rolled over on my back and stared up at the ceiling as I started to cry. Huge fat tears slid off my face to wet my pillow. If I wet the bed for any other reason I'd get spanked for ten years old was too old for such baby-doings.

Did I want to be ten, or eighty? Who was making me be so old? God? Was it those children hiding in the attic, laughing, laughing, making the best out of the worst that was driving me to prove Malcolm was smarter and they'd never get away even after he was put in the ground.

Momma's gone and left me.
Left me for good this time.
Momma's gone and left me,
Now I don't know how to end what I've begun . . .

Fell asleep and tossed around. The little boy kept right on crying as the old man hurled him in the trashcan so soon I'd be dumped outside the city limits—fit only for burning.

For sinners of sinners, those born of incest, they had to be punished too, even me, even me who was dying in the trash-can.

Rage of the Righteous

The rain came down like bullets fired by God. I stood at the back windows and watched the rain batter the faces of those marble statues, punishing them for being naked and sinful. I waited for Jory to come home and look for me.

Bad. We were both bad from living with parents who weren't supposed to be parents.

Behind me Momma came in from a shopping spree, all rosy-cheeked and laughing, shaking the rain from her hair, greeting Emma like everything was okay. She dumped her parcels in a chair, took off her coat, and said she felt she might be catching a cold.

"I hate it when it rains, Emma. Hello, Bart—I didn't see you there until now. How've you been? Lonesome for me?"

Wouldn't answer. Didn't have to talk to her now. Didn't have to be polite, nice, or even clean. Could do anything I wanted. They did. God's rules didn't mean anything to them. Meant nothing now to me either.

"Bart, it's going to be so nice this Christmas," said Momma, not looking at me but at Cindy, who needed more new clothes. "This will be our first Christmas with Cindy. The best kind of families always have children of both sexes, and in that way boys can learn about girls, and vice versa." She hugged Cindy closer. "Cindy, you just don't know how lucky you are to have two wonderful older brothers who will absolutely adore you as you grow up into a real beauty—if they don't adore you already."

Boy, if she only knew. But like Malcolm had said, beautiful women were dumb. I looked into the kitchen at Emma, who was not beautiful and never could have been. Was she wiser? Did she see through me?

Emma's eyes lifted and met mine. I shivered. Yes, drab women were smarter. They knew the world wasn't beautiful just because they had hold of beauty for a while.

"Bart, you haven't told me what you want Santa Claus to bring you."

I stared hard at her. She knew what I wanted most. "A pony!" I said. I took out the pocketknife Jory had given me and began to pare my nails. That made Momma stare at me, then her eyes moved to Cindy's short hair that was just beginning to look pretty again.

"Bart, put that knife away. It makes me nervous. You might accidently cut yourself." She sneezed then, then sneezed again and again. Always her sneezes came in threes. She pulled tissues from her purse to wipe her nose, then blow it. Contaminating my nice clean air with her filthy cold germs.

Jory didn't come home until way after dark, soaked and miserable-looking as he stalked into his room and slammed his door. I grinned as I saw Momma frown. So, now her darling didn't love her either. That's what came of doing wrong.

Still the rain came down. She looked at me, her eyes large, her face pale, her hair a tangle all around her face, and I knew some men would think her beautiful. I yanked a hair from my head and held one end between my teeth as I pulled with one hand to stretch it taut. Easily my knife sliced it in two. "Good knife," I said, "sharp as a razor for shaving. Good for cutting off legs, arms, hair . . ." I grinned as she looked scared. Powerful. I felt so powerful. John Amos was right. Women were only timid, fearful imitations of men.

Rain came down harder. The wind blew it around the house and made howling noises. Cold outside, dark and cold. All night it rained, next morning it was still coming down. Emma drove away just because it was Thursday and she couldn't miss a visit with a friend. "You take it easy now, ma'am," she said to Momma in the garage. "You don't look well. Just because you don't have a fever doesn't mean you won't come down with something. Bart—you behave yourself and don't make trouble for your mother."

I left the garage and went into the kitchen, and somehow or other my arm that was really a plane wing knocked several breakfast dishes to the floor. I saw my bowl of cereal with raisins, little bugs on a creamy sea . . .

"Bart, you did that deliberately!"

"Yes, Momma, you always say I do everything on purpose. This time I let you see how right you are." I picked up my glass of milk, hardly touched, and hurled it at her face. It missed her by inches, for she was quick to dodge.

"Bart, how dare you do that. When your father comes home I'm going to tell him, and he'll punish you severely."

Yeah, already I knew what he'd do. He'd spank my behind, give me a lecture on obedience and having respect for my mother. And his spanking wouldn't hurt. His lecture wouldn't be heard. I could tune him out and Malcolm in.

"Why don't you spank me, Momma? Come on . . . let me see what *you* can do to hurt me." I held my knife in position, ready to jab it if she dared to move closer.

Was she going to faint? "Bart, how can you act so ugly when you know I don't feel well today. You promised your father you would behave. What have I done to make you dislike me so much?"

I grinned meaningfully.

"Where did you get that knife? That's not the knife Jory gave you."

"The old lady next door gave it to me. She gives me everything I ask for. If I told her I wanted a gun, a sword, she'd get them, for she's like you are—weak, so eager to please me, when there isn't a woman alive who will ever please me."

Real terror was in her eyes now. She moved closer to Cindy, who was still in her highchair, making a big mess with her graham cracker and her glass of milk, dipping in the cracker until it was mushy, then trying to rush it into her mouth before the mushy part fell off. And *she* wasn't scolded.

"Bart, go to your room this moment. Shut and lock the door from the inside, and I'll lock it from the outside. I don't want to see you until your father is home. And since you didn't think enough of your breakfast to eat it, then you don't deserve any lunch."

"You can't tell me what to do. If you dare, I'll tell the world what you and 'your husband' are doing. Brother and sister living together. Living in sin. Fornicating!" (A good "Malcolm" word.)

Staggering, she raised her hands to her face, wiped at her running nose again, stuffed the tissues in her pants pocket, then picked up Cindy.

"What yah gonna do, harlot? Use Cindy for a shield? It won't work, won't work, I'll get the both of you . . . And the police can't touch me. I'm only ten years old, only ten, only ten, only ten, only ten . . ." and on and on I kept saying that like I was a needle stuck in the same groove.

In my ears was John Amos's voice, telling me what to do. I spoke as in a dream: "Once long ago there was a man in London called Jack the Ripper, and he killed prostitutes. I kill strumpets too, and bad sisters who don't know right from wrong. Momma, I'm going to show you how God wants you to be punished for committing incest."

Trembling and looking weak as a white rabbit, too scared
to move, she stood with Cindy held in her arms, and waited as
I stalked her . . . closer, closer, jabbing with my knife.

"Bart," she said, her voice stronger, more under control, "I
don't know who has been telling you stories, but if you harm
me or Cindy, God will have his revenge on you—even if the
police don't lock you up, or put you in the electric chair."

Threats. Empty threats. John Amos had already told me
a boy my age could do anything he wanted and the police
couldn't do a thing to stop or punish him.

"Is that man you live with your brother? Is he?" I yelled.
"Tell me a lie and you'll both die."

"Bart, calm down. Don't you know it will soon be Christmas? You don't want to be put away and miss all the toys Santa
Claus will put under the tree for you."

"No Santa Claus!" I shrieked, even more furious—did she
think I believed in that nonsense?

"You used to love me. All your life you have held back telling me so in words, but I could see it in your eyes. Bart, what
has changed you? What have I done to make you hate me? Tell
me so I can change, so I can be better."

Look at that, trying to win me moments before her
death . . . and her redemption. God would feel pity for her
when she was butchered, humiliated in every way possible.

Squinted my eyes and raised my razor-sharp blade that
my grandmother had not given me—it had been a gift from
John Amos, given shortly after that old witch Marisha came.

"I am the dark angel of the Lord," I said in my quivering
old voice, "and I am here to deal out justice, for mankind has
not yet discovered your sins."

Swiftly she moved Cindy and turned her body so the
little girl wouldn't be injured when I thrust. Then, while I
was watching what she was doing, her right leg shot out and
caught my wrist with a hard kick. The knife went flying. I ran
to get it, but she moved quicker and kicked the knife under

the counter. I threw myself down to feel for it, and in that time she must have put Cindy on the floor, for suddenly she was on top of me, twisting my arm behind me. With a handful of my hair in her other hand, she made me stand up.

"Now we'll see who is boss, and who will be punished." She shoved and dragged me, and never released my arm or my hair, as she forced me into my room and threw me on the floor. Quicker than I could scramble to my feet, she slammed the door and I heard the key turn. I was locked in.

"You whore, let me out. You let me out or I'll set this house on fire. And we'll burn, all burn, burn."

I heard her raspy breathing as she panted, leaning on my closed bedroom door. I tried to find the stash of matches and candles I'd stored in my room. Gone. All my matches, all my candles, even the cigarette lighter I'd stolen from John Amos.

"Thief!" I roared. "Nothing in this house but thieves, cheats, whores, and liars! All of you after my money too! You think I'll die today, tomorrow, next week, or next month—but I'll live to see you dead, Momma! I'll live to see every last one of the attic mice dead!"

Down the hall she sped. I heard the clickity-clack of her satin mules. I'd scared myself; now I didn't know what to do. Hadn't John Amos told me to wait until Christmas night, so everything would coincide with the other fire in Foxworth Hall. Do it the same way, only differently.

"Momma," I whispered, down on my knees and crying, "I didn't mean none of that mean stuff. Momma, please don't go away and leave me alone. Don't like to be alone. Don't like what's happening to me, Momma. Why did you have to go and pretend you were married to your brother? Why couldn't you just have lived with him and us, and been decent?" I sobbed, afraid of what I could be when I felt mean.

She didn't need to lock the door when she had Cindy with her, did she? Never could she trust me to do the right thing.

But that must be because she couldn't help herself either, no more than me. She was born bad and beautiful, and only through death could God redeem her sinful soul. I sighed and got up to do what I could to save her from the mess she'd made of her life, and ours. "Momma!" I yelled, "unlock my door! I'll kill myself if you don't! I know all about you now, what you and your brother are doing—the people next door told me everything about your childhood. And your book told me the rest. Unlock my door, if you don't want to come in and see me dead."

She came to my door and unlocked it, staring down in my face, even as she wiped her nose and ran her hand through her hair. "What do you mean the people next door told you everything? Who are the people next door?"

"You'll find out when you see her," I said smugly, all of a sudden mean again. Drat that Cindy she had to hold on to all the time. Was me she gave birth to, not Cindy. "There's an old man over there too, he knows about you and your attic days. Just go over and talk to them, Momma, and you won't feel so happy to have a daughter anymore."

Her mouth gaped open as a wild look of horror came to her blue eyes and made them look dark, dark. "Bart, please don't tell me lies."

"Never tell lies, not like you do," I said, watching as she began to tremble so much she almost dropped Cindy. Pity she didn't. But it wouldn't hurt if she just fell to the carpeted floor.

"Now you stay here and wait for me," she said as she headed for the coat closet. "For once in your life do as I say. Sit down and watch TV—eat all the candy you want—but stay in this house and out of the rain."

She was going next door. I felt panicky inside, afraid she wouldn't come back. Afraid she wouldn't be saved, afraid maybe after all, this wasn't a game John Amos was playing, not a game after all. But I couldn't speak. For God was on the side of John Amos—he'd have to be since *he* wasn't sinning.

Dressed in her warmest white winter coat, wearing white boots, Momma picked up Cindy, who was dressed warmly too. "Be a good boy, Bart, and remember always I love you. I'll be back in less than ten minutes, though heaven only knows what that woman in black can know about me."

I flicked a quick shamed glance at her pale, worried face. Momma was gonna crack up when she met my grandmother, who was her own mother. Momma was gonna end up in a straightjacket and I'd never see her again.

Why wasn't I glad that already God was punishing her, beginning her redemption? My head ached again. My stomach felt queasy. Legs didn't want to obey, but had a leaden weight of their own that knew their mind. Pulling me along with them to the coat closet as Momma slammed the front door behind her.

Momma, my soul was crying, *don't go and leave me alone. Don't like to be alone. Nobody will love me but you, Momma, nobody will. Please don't go over there—don't let John Amos see you.* Shouldn't have said anything. Should have known you wouldn't stay here where it was safe. I pulled on my coat and raced to the front windows to watch her carrying Cindy into the wind and cold rain. Just as if she, a mere woman, could face up to God and his black wrath.

Soon as she was out of sight I slipped outside and began to follow her. Did this new coat mean she really did love me? No, said the wise old man in my brain, didn't mean anything. Gifts, toys, games, and clothes were easy things to give—things that all parents gave their children even when they were about to feed them arsenic on sugared doughnuts. Parents held back what was most important, security.

I sighed wearily, hoping someday, somewhere, I'd find the mother who would stay forever, the mother who was right for me—who would always understand I was doing the best I could.

Outside, the wind blew my slicker against my body and

drove the rain into my face. About ten yards ahead I could see Momma was having a rough time attempting to hold Cindy, who was trying to wiggle free and run back home as she screamed: "Don't like rain! Take me home! Momma, don't wanna go!"

Trying to comfort her while she kept her footing and at the same time trying to keep the hood over her hair, she finally gave up efforts to keep herself dry and settled for keeping Cindy as dry as possible. Soon her hair was pasted down flat to her head, as flat to her head, as flat as my hair was by now, for never never would I slip a hood over my head—made me scared to look in a mirror.

Momma slipped on the mud that was being washed down from the hills, and she almost lost her footing. But she caught herself and rebalanced. Cindy screamed and beat at her face with small fists. "HOME! I WANT HOME!"

Ran fast, for she wasn't looking backward. All her concentration was on the winding road ahead. "Stop fighting me, Cindy!"

High walls. Iron pickets. Strong gates. Magic boxes to speak into. Small voice coming back—and hear the wind blow. Privacy didn't mean nothing to God and the wind, not nothing at all.

Heard my momma's voice as she shouted to be heard above the shriek of the wind and rain: "This is Catherine Sheffield. I live next door and Bart is my son. I want to come in and talk to the lady of the house."

Silence, only the wind.

Then my momma was calling out again: "I want to see her, and if I have to climb this fence I'll do just that. I'm coming in, one way or another—so open the gates and save me the trouble."

I stood back and waited, gasping as if my heart truly did hurt. Slowly, slowly, the wide black iron gates swung open.

For a moment I wanted to shriek out, *NO! Don't walk*

into a trap, Momma! But I really didn't know if there was a trap at all. I was just afraid that, between John Amos and the Malcolm that was inside of me, nothing good would come of Momma's venture into my grandmother's house. Quickly I ducked inside the gates just before they clanged softly closed. Sounded like prison doors.

She trudged on ahead, all the while Cindy was screaming and crying. By the time they reached the door both seemed soaked to the skin, for I was, and I'd had two hands to hold my slicker together.

Up the stairs Momma stumbled, clasping Cindy, who was still trying to kick free. She lifted the loose jaw of the brass lion's head and banged loud.

John Amos had been expecting her, for he swung one side of the double doors open immediately and bowed very low, as if admitting a queen. Ran, ran then as fast as I could so I wouldn't miss a thing. Quickly into the side door, and down the corridor to the dumbwaiter—hoping that she'd be in that room, for behind the potted palms was not such a secure place. Jory had found me there once, and it could happen again.

I crawled into the dumbwaiter after I dropped my coat on the floor, then slid open the door just a slot. Momma was probably still in the foyer taking off her wet coat and muddy white boots.

Then she appeared in the doorway, minus her coat and boots. I hadn't even had the time to check and see if my grandmother was in her rocking chair—but she was there all right.

Stiffly she rose, facing my momma, hiding her trembling hands behind her back, the veil hiding most of her face as it hid all of her hair.

Something small, weak, and young inside of me wanted to cry as I saw Momma step into "her" room, still carrying Cindy, only Cindy's outer clothes had been taken off. She was completely dry, while Momma's hair stuck to her face and head like strings. Her flushed face looked so feverish I again wanted to cry. What if God struck her dead this second? What if death by hellfires was what He really wanted?

"I'm sorry to burst in on you like this," said my momma. I'd thought she'd pitch right into her. "But I must have a few answers to my questions. Who are you? What is it you tell my youngest son? He's told me terrible things he claims you told him. I don't know you, and you don't know me, so what can you tell him but lies?"

So far my grandmother hadn't said a word. She kept staring at Momma, then at Cindy.

My grandmother gestured toward a chair, then inclined her head as if to say she was sorry. Why didn't she speak?

"What a lovely room," said Momma, glancing around at all the fine furniture. There was a troubled look in her eyes, even her smile seemed forced. She put Cindy on her feet and tried to hold on to her hand, but Cindy wanted to explore and see all the pretty things.

"I'm not going to stay any longer than necessary," Momma went on, keeping an eye on Cindy, who had to touch everything. "I have a severe cold and want to be home in bed, but I must find out just what you have been telling my son so he comes home and says terrible things. And doesn't respect me as his mother. When you can explain, Cindy and I will leave."

Grandmother nodded, keeping her eyes lowered, like she truly was some Arab woman. I guessed from the odd way Momma kept looking at her she was thinking this was a foreigner of some kind who didn't understand our good English.

Momma sat down uninvited near the fire, as Cindy came to perch on the raised hearth near her legs.

"This is an isolated area, so when Bart comes home and tells me the lady next door has told him this and that, I knew it had to be you. Who are you? Why are you trying to turn my son against me? What have I ever done to you?" Her questions went on and on, for the woman in black wouldn't speak. Momma leaned forward to peer more closely at Grandmother.

Was Momma suspicious already? Was she so smart she could tell despite the disguise of the black veil, the long loose black dress? "Come now, I've given you my name. Be courteous enough to tell me yours."

No answer, just a shy nod of the black veiled head.

"Oh, I think I understand," said Momma with a perplexed frown. "You must not speak English."

The woman shook her head again. Momma's frown deepened. "I truly don't understand. You seem to understand what I say, yet you don't answer. You can't be mute or you wouldn't have been able to tell my son so many lies."

Time was ticking away loudly. Never heard the clock on the marble mantle tick so loud before. My granny just rocked on and on in her chair, like she'd never speak or raise her head.

Momma was beginning to be annoyed. Suddenly Cindy jumped up and raced to pick up a porcelain kitty. "Cindy, put that down."

Obeying reluctantly, Cindy carefully replaced the cat on the marble table. The minute the cat was out of her hands, Cindy looked around for something else to do. She spied the archway to the next room and ran that way. Jumping to her feet, Momma hurried to prevent Cindy from roaming. Cindy had a way, like me, of wanting to examine everything—though she didn't drop things as often as I did.

"Don't go in there!" cried out my grandmother, as she too stood up.

As if stunned, my mother slowly turned around, Cindy forgotten. Her blue eyes widened and the color drained from her face as she kept staring at the woman in black who couldn't keep her nervous hands from straying up to the neckline of her black dress. Soon she had the rope of pearls and was twisting them between her fingers.

"Your voice, I have heard it before."

Grandmother didn't speak.

"Those rings on your fingers, I've seen them before. Where did you get those rings?"

Helplessly my grandmother shrugged and quickly released the pearls, which dropped down out of sight under her black robe. "Pawn shop," she said in a strange, raspy, foreign way. "Bargain."

Momma's eyes narrowed as she continued to stare at the woman who wasn't a stranger. I sat breathless, wondering what would happen when she knew. Oh, Momma would find out. I knew my mother couldn't be so easily fooled.

As if her knees were suddenly weak, Momma sank down on the nearest chair, unmindful that her clothes were still wet, unmindful that Cindy had wandered into the other room.

"You do understand a little English, I see," she said in a quiet slow way. "The moment I walked into this room, it was as if the clock had been turned backward, and I was a child again. My mother had the same taste in furnishings, the same choice of colors. I look at your brocade chairs, your cut velvet ones, the clock on your mantelpiece, and all I can think of is how very much my mother would have approved of this room. Even those rings on your fingers look like the rings she used to wear. You found them in a pawn shop?"

"Many women like this type of room . . . and jewelry," said that lady in black.

"You have a strange voice . . . Mrs. . . . ?"

Another shrug from the black figure.

Momma got up again and went into the other room to fetch Cindy. I held my breath. The portrait was in there. She'd see it. But she must not have looked around, for in another second she was back, pulling Cindy and standing close to the fireplace, keeping a tight hold on Cindy's hand.

"What a remarkable home you have. If I closed my eyes I could swear I was looking at Foxworth Hall as I saw it from the balcony."

Dark, dark were the eyes of my grandmother.

"Are you wearing pearls? I thought I saw pearls when you were fiddling around your neck. Those rings are so beautiful. You show your rings, why not your pearls?"

Again another shrug from Grandmother.

Dragging Cindy along with her, Momma stepped closer to the woman I didn't want to think of as my grandmother anymore. "As I stand here all sorts of memories come flooding back," said Momma. "I remember a Christmas night when Foxworth Hall burned to the ground. The night was cold and snowy, yet it lit up like the Fourth of July. I yanked all the rings from my fingers and hurled the diamond and emerald jewelry into the deep snow. I thought no one would ever find it—but Madame, you are wearing the emerald ring I threw in the snow! Later Chris picked up all that jewelry because it belonged to *his* mother! *His precious mother!*"

"I am sick too. Go away," whispered that forlorn figure in black, standing in the middle of her room, avoiding the rocking chair that might trap her.

But she was already trapped.

"YOU!" cried my mother. "I should have known! There is no other rope necklace of pearls with a diamond butterfly clasp except yours.

"Of course you are sick!" screamed my mother. "What else could you be but sick! I know who you are. Now everything makes sense. How dare you come into my life again. After all you have done to us, you come back again to do more. I hate you. I hate you for everything you have done, but I've never had the chance to pay you back. Taking Bart from you wasn't enough. Now I have the chance to do more."

Releasing Cindy's hand, she lunged forward and caught hold of my grandmother, who tried to back away and fight her off. But my mother was stronger. Breathless and excited I watched the two women pull at one another.

My grandmother cringed away from the fierce attack. She didn't seem to know what to do. Then Cindy let out a howl of fear, and began to cry. "Mommy, let's go home."

The door opened and John Amos shambled inside the room. As my mother prepared another attack, he reached out to lay a large knobby hand on my grandmother's shoulder. I'd never seen him touch her before.

"Mrs. Sheffield," he began in his whiny-hissy voice, "you were graciously admitted into this house, and now you try to take advantage of my wife, who has not been well for several years. I am John Amos Jackson, and this is my wife, Mrs. Jackson."

Stunned, Momma could only stare.

"John Amos Jackson," repeated my mother slowly, savoring the name. "I've heard that name before. Why, just yesterday I was rereading my manuscript, and I had to think of a way to change that name slightly. You are the John Amos Jackson who once was a butler in Foxworth Hall! I remember your bald head and how it shone under the chandeliers." She swiveled about and reached for Cindy's hand, or so I thought. But instead she snatched the veil from my grandmother's face.

"Mother!" she screamed. "I should have known months ago it was you. From the moment I entered this house I sensed your presence, your perfume, the colors, the choice of furniture. You had sense enough to cover your face and body in black, but you were stupid enough to wear your jewelry. Dumb, always so damned dumb! Is it insanity, or is it stupidity that makes you think I could forget your perfume, your jewelry?" She laughed, wild and hysterically, spinning around and around so John Amos, who was trying to prevent what she might do, was stumbling, clumsily trying to grab hold of her before she could attack again.

Look at her—she was dancing! All around my grandmother she whirled, flicking out her hand to slap at her—and even as she whipped her legs around, she screamed: "I should have known it was you. Ever since you moved in Bart has been

acting crazy. You couldn't leave us alone, could you? You had
to come here and try and ruin what Chris and I have found
together—the first time we've been happy. And now you've
ruined it. You've managed to drive Bart insane so he'll have to
be put away like you were. Oh, how I hate you for that. How I
hate you for so many reasons. Cory, Carrie, and now Bart—is
there no end to what you can do to hurt us?" She kicked and
hooked her foot behind my grandmother's knee and threw her
off balance, and the moment my grandmother spilled to the
floor in a heap of black rags, my mother was on top of her,
ripping at that rope of pearls with its diamond butterfly clasp.

Using both her hands, she forced the knotted string to
part, and the pearls scattered all over the Oriental rug that
silently swallowed them up.

John Amos roughly seized hold of my momma, and pulled
her to her feet. He held her and shook her until Momma's
head rolled. "Pick up the pearls, Mrs. Sheffield," he ordered
in a hard, mean voice that was suddenly very strong. I was
surprised that he would handle my mother so cruelly. I knew
what Jory would do—he'd run to fight John Amos and save
Momma. But me, I didn't know if I should. God was up there
wanting Momma to suffer for her sins, and if I saved her, what
would God do to me? Besides, Jory was bigger. And Daddy
was always saying everything happened for the best—so this
was meant to be, despite the miserable way I felt.

But Momma didn't need my help after all. She threw back
her head and butted her skull squarely against his false teeth.
I heard them crack as she whirled free. Then he went after her
with more determination. He was gonna kill her, and be the
agent of God's wrath himself!

Quicker than I could move, Momma's knee came up
and caught him squarely in the groin. John Amos screamed,
doubled over, clutching at himself as he fell to the floor and
rolled about moaning: "Damn you to hell!"

"Damn *you* to hell, John Amos Jackson!" my momma

screamed back. "Don't you ever touch me again, or I will dig out your eyes."

By this time my grandmother had gained her feet, and she stood in the center of the room swaying unsteadily as she tried to fit the torn veil over her face again. That's when my mother's slap caught her cheek, so Grandmother fell backward into her rocker. "Damn you to hell too, Corrine Foxworth! I hoped never to see your face again. I hoped you'd die in that 'rest home' and spare me the agony of looking at you again, and hearing that voice that I used to love. But I've never been lucky. I should have known you wouldn't be considerate enough to die and leave me and Chris alone. You are like your father, clinging desperately to a life not worth living."

Oh, I hadn't known before my mother had such a terrible temper. She was just like me. I felt shocked, scared as I watched my mother tackle my old grandmother so her chair tipped over and both of them fell to the floor, rolling over and over as John Amos groaned, maybe never to recover. In a few moments Momma was sitting on top of my grandmother, ripping off all those glittering, expensive rings. Weakly my grandmother tried to defend herself and her jewelry.

"Please, Cathy, don't do this to me," she pleaded.

"*You!* How I've longed to see you on the floor, pleading with me as you are. I was wrong a moment ago—this is my lucky day. My chance to have my revenge again for all you've done. You watch and see what I do to your precious rings." She raised her arm, and with one wild gesture she hurled all those rings into the roaring fire. "There, there! It's done!" cried my momma. "What should have been done long ago on the night Bart died."

With a gloating expression she ran to pick up Cindy; ran to the foyer closet to yank on Cindy's coat, and then reached for her own coat and boots she'd pulled off.

John Amos had picked himself off the floor, muttering to himself about Devil's issue that should have died when she was caged and helpless. "Damned hellcat should have been slaughtered before she could create more Devil's issue!"

I heard.

Maybe Momma didn't.

I moved out of the dumbwaiter unseen by my grandmother, who was crying as she sat on the floor in a broken heap.

Momma had on her boots now, her white coat, though she was shivering as she came to the door and looked in on the woman still on the floor. "What did you say, John Amos Jackson? Did I hear you call me a hellcat, Devil's issue? Say that again to my face! Go on, say it to me now! Now that I'm an adult and not a frightened child anymore. Now that my legs and arms are strong and yours are weak. Don't think you can do away with me so easily now—for I'm not old, and I'm not weak, and I'm not scared anymore."

He headed her way, holding in his hand a poker he must have taken from the fireplace. She laughed, seeming to think he was a fool and an easy enemy. Quickly she dodged, then shot out her good leg and kicked his bottom hard so he fell prone upon his face, screaming out his rage as he fell.

I was screaming too. This was wrong! This was not the way John Amos and I had planned for God to have his revenge. He wasn't supposed to hurt her.

Momma saw me then. Her blue eyes widened, her face paled, and she seemed to crumple. "Bart."

I whispered, "John Amos told me all the things I had to do."

She whirled on my grandmother. "Look what you have done. You have turned my own son against me. And all the time you get by with everything, even murder. You poisoned Cory, poisoned Carrie's mind so she had to kill herself, killed Bart Winslow when you sent him back into the fire to save the life of a wretched old woman who didn't deserve to live—and now you poison the mind of my son against me. And you escaped justice by pleading insanity. You weren't insane when you set fire to Foxworth Hall. That was the first clever stunt you pulled in your life but this is my time for revenge." And with those words she raced to the fireplace, picked up the small shovel for ashes, pushed aside the fire-screen, and began to pull red hot coals from the fire onto the Oriental rug.

As the rug began to smoke, she called to me, "Bart, put on your coat, we're going home, and we'll move so far away she'll never find us, never!"

I screamed. My grandmother screamed. But my mother was so busy buttoning up Cindy's coat she didn't see that John Amos had the poker in his hand again. As I froze, my lips parted to scream a warning again—the poker came down on her head. She slumped quietly to the floor like a rag doll.

"You fool!" cried my grandmother. "You may have killed her!"

Things were happening too fast. Everything was going wrong. Momma wasn't supposed to be hurt. I wanted to say this, but the face of John Amos was twisted, his lips snarled as he advanced on my grandmother.

"Cathy, Cathy," she pleaded, down on her knees and cradling my mother's head, "please don't die. I love you. I've always loved you. I never meant for any of you to die. I nev—"

The whack was so hard she slumped over the body of my mother. Rage was in my head. Cindy was screaming. "John Amos!" I yelled. "That wasn't in God's plan!"

He turned, smiling and confident. "Yes, it was, Bart. God spoke to me last night and told me what to do. Didn't you hear your mother say she was going far-far away? She wouldn't take a bothersome boy like you with her, would she? Wouldn't she put you away first in some institution? Then she'd go, and never would you see her again, Bart. Just like your great-grandfather, you'd be abandoned forever. Just like your grandmother you'd be locked up, and you'd never see her again either! That's the cruel way life treats those who try to do their best. And it's me, only me who is trying to take care of you and see you escape confinement worse than prison."

Prison, prison, so much like poison.

"Bart, are you listening? Have you heard? Do you understand I'm doing what I can to save both of them for you?"

I stared at him; didn't really understand anything. "Yes, Bart, instead of one, you will have two souvenirs."

Didn't know what or who to believe. I stared down at the two women on the floor, my momma, my grandmother who had fallen crosswise over the slight body of my momma. It came over me in an overwhelming flood—I loved those two women. I loved them more than I'd known I had. Wouldn't want to stay alive if I lost one, much less two. Were they as evil as John Amos had said? Would God punish me if I kept them from being "redeemed" by fire?

And there he was in front of me, John Amos the only one who had been fully honest with me from the beginning, telling me from the start who my real daddy was, who my real grandmother was, who Malcolm the wise and clever was.

I looked into his small narrow eyes for instructions. God was behind John Amos or else he wouldn't have lived to be so old.

He smiled and chucked me under the chin, and I shivered. Didn't like people to touch me when I couldn't even feel the touch.

"Now listen to me carefully, Bart. First you are to take Cindy home. Then you make her swear not to tell anything or you will cut out her little pink tongue. Can you make her promise?"

Numbly I nodded. Had to make Cindy promise.

"You won't hurt my momma and my grandmomma?"

"Of course not, Bart. I'll just put them away where they'll be safe. You can see them whenever you want. But not one word to that man who calls himself your father. *Not one word.* Remember he, too, will take you away from your home and have you locked up. He thinks you're crazy too. Don't you know that's why they keep taking you to shrinks?"

I swallowed; my throat hurt. Didn't know what to do.

John Amos knew. "Now, you go home with Cindy, keep the brat quiet, lock yourself in your room, play dumb, know nothing. And remember . . . you threaten that kid sister so horribly she'll be scared to let out a squeak."

"She's not my kid sister," I whispered weakly.

"What's the difference?" he snarled irritably. "You just do as I say. Follow instructions, as God wants men to believe in him unquestioningly—and never let out to your brother or your father that you know his secret, or that you have any idea where your mother went. Play dumb. You should be good at that."

What did he mean? Was he making fun of me?

I knitted my brows and turned on my best glower, and imitated Malcolm. "You hear this, John Amos. The day you can outsmart me will be the day the earth sits on the head of a pin, and I swallow it. So don't you mock me, and think I'm dumb . . . for in the end, I'll win. I'll always win, dead or alive."

Power swelled up huge within me. Never felt so stuffed full of brains. I looked down at the two women I loved. Yes, God had planned for it to happen this way, give me two mothers to keep forever as my own . . . and I'd never be lonely again.

"Now, you keep your mouth shut, and don't tell Daddy or Jory one word or I'll cut out your tongue," I said to Cindy when we were home and in our kitchen together. "Do you want your tongue cut out?"

Her small face was wet with rain and tears, streaked with dirt too. Her lips gaped and her eyes bulged, and whimpering like a baby, she allowed me to put on her pajamas and put her in bed. I kept my eyes closed all the time so none of her girl's body would shame me into hating her more.

Where's Momma?

There was somebody I had to tell off. Somebody who seemed to have started a tornado that was going on forever and ruining our lives. Dad and I had talked about it a lot, but things were still very tense and I was so confused. Why did she have to come and start all this? Finally I could hold in my anger no longer, and as soon as ballet class was over, I raced to Madame's office.

"I hate you, Madame, for all the mean things you said to my mom. Everything's been terrible ever since that day. You leave her alone from now on, or I'll go and never come back to see you. Did you fly all the way here just to make her sick? She can't dance now, and that's bad enough. If you don't stop causing so much trouble, I'll quit dancing too. I'll run away and you'll never see me again. For in ruining my parents lives, you have managed to ruin not only theirs, but mine and Bart's too."

She paled and looked very old. "You sound so very much like your father. Julian used to blaze his dark eyes at me in the same way."

"I used to love you."

"Used to love me . . . ?"

"Yes, used to. When I thought you cared about me, about my parents, then I believed that dancing was the most wonderful thing in the world. Now I don't believe."

She looked stricken, as if I'd stabbed her in her heart. She reeled back against the wall and would have fallen if I hadn't stepped forward to support her. "Jory, please," she gasped, "don't ever run away. Don't stop dancing. If you do, then my life has been meaningless and Georges will have lived for nothing, and Julian too. Don't take everything from those I have loved and lost."

I couldn't speak, I was so confused. So I ran, ran like Bart always ran when things got too heavy.

Behind me Melodie called out: "Jory, where are you going in such a hurry? We were going to have a soda together."

I ran on. I didn't care anymore about anyone or anything. My life was all screwed up. My parents weren't married. How could they be? What minister or judge would marry a brother and his sister?

Once I hit the sidewalk I slowed down, then went on to a public park where I sat down on a green bench. On and on I sat, staring down at my feet. A dancer's feet. Strong, tough with calluses, ready for the professional stage. What would I do now when I grew up? I didn't really want to be a doctor, though I'd said that a few times just to please the man I loved as a father. What a joke. Why should I try and lie to myself—there was no life for me without dancing. When I punished Madame, my mother, my stepdad who was really only my uncle, I punished myself even worse.

I stood up and looked around at all the old people sitting lonely in the park, wondering if one day I'd be like them, and I thought, No. I'll know when to say I made a mistake. When to say I'm sorry.

~   ~   ~

Madame M. was in her office, her head bowed down into her thin hands when I opened the door quietly and stepped inside her office. I must have made some noise, for she looked up and I saw tears in her eyes. Joy flooded them when she saw me, but she didn't mention all that had happened half an hour ago.

"I have a gift for your mother," she said in her naturally shrill voice. She slid open a desk drawer and withdrew a gold box bound with red satin ribbon. "For Catherine," she said stiffly, not meeting my eyes. "You are right about everything. I was ready to take you from your mother and father because I felt I was doing the right thing for you. I see now I was doing what I wanted for myself, not for you. Sons belongs with their mothers, not their grandmothers." She smiled bitterly as she looked at the pretty gold box. "Lady Godiva candy. The kind your mother was nuts about when she lived in New York and was with Madame Zolta's company. Then she couldn't eat chocolates for fear of adding weight—though she was the kind of dancer who burned off more calories than most when she danced—still I allowed her only one piece of candy a week. Now that she won't dance again, she can indulge to her heart's desire."

That was Bart's phrase.

"Mom has an awful cold," I explained just as stiffly as she had. "Thank you for the candy and what you just said. I know Mom will feel better knowing you won't try and take me away from her." I grinned then and kissed her dry cheek. "Besides, don't you realize there is enough of me to share? If you aren't stingy, she won't be. Mom is wonderful. Not once has she ever told me you and she had any difficulties." I settled down in her single office chair and crossed my legs. "Madame, I'm scared. Things are going crazy in our house. Bart acts weirder each day. Mom is sick with that cold; Dad seems so unhappy. Clover is dead. Emma doesn't smile anymore. Christmas is coming and nothing is being done about it. If this keeps up, I think I'll crack up myself."

"Hah!" she snorted, back to her old self. "Life is always like that—twenty minutes of misery for every two seconds of joy. So, be everlastingly grateful for those rare two seconds and appreciate; appreciate what good you can find, no matter what the cost."

My smiles were false. Underneath I was truly depressed. Her cynical words didn't really help. "Does it have to be that way?" I asked.

"Jory," she said, thrusting her old pastry-dough face closer to mine, "think about this. If there were no shadows, how could we see the sunlight?"

I sat there in her gloomy office and allowed this kind of sour philosophy to give me some peace. "Okay, I get your meaning, Madame. And if you can't say you are sorry, then I can."

She whispered as if it hurt, "I'm sorry too."

I hugged her close, and we had come to some sort of compromise.

All the way home I held the gold box of chocolates on my lap, dying to open it. "Dad," I began falteringly, "Madame is sending Mom this candy as a reconciliation gift, I guess."

He threw me a glance and a smile. "That's nice."

"I think it's terribly strange Mom is staying sick with that cold for so long. She's never been sick more than a day or two. Don't you think she looks very tired?"

"It's that writing, that damned writing," he grouched, watching the heavy traffic, turning on the windshield wipers, leaning forward to peer more closely at the traffic signal to the right. "I wish it would stop raining. Rain always bothers her. Then she's up till four in the morning, next day up at dawn to scribble on legal pads, afraid to use the typewriter for fear of waking me. When the candle is burned at both ends something has to give—and that's her health. First that fall, now this cold." He gave me another sideways glance. "Then there's Bart and his problems, and you and yours. Jory, you know our secret now. Your mother and I have talked it over, and you and I have talked about it for hours and hours. Can you forgive us? Haven't I managed to help you understand?"

I bowed my head and felt ashamed. "I'm trying to understand."

"Trying? Is it that difficult? Haven't I told you how it was with us, up there, all four of us in one room, growing up, finding out in our adolescence that we had only each other . . ."

"But, Dad. When you ran away and found a new home with Dr. Paul, couldn't you have found someone else? Why did it have to be her?"

Sighing, he set his lips. "I thought I explained to you how I felt then about women. Your mother was there when I needed her. Our own mother had betrayed us. When you're young you fix very strong ideas in your mind. I'm sorry if you've been hurt by my inability to love anyone but her."

What was there for me to say? I couldn't understand. The world was full of beautiful young women, thousands, millions. Then I thought of Melodie. If she were to die could I go out and find another? I thought and thought about that as Dad turned silent and his lips stayed in that grim line, and the rain came down, down, driving hard. It was as if he could read my mind. For yes, if ever I was so unfortunate to lose Melodie, if she moved away and I never saw her again, I'd go on living, and eventually I'd find another to take her place. Anything was better than—

"Jory, I know what you're thinking. I've had years and years to think about why it had to be my sister and no one else. Perhaps it was because I'd lost faith in all women because of what our mother was doing to us and only my sister could give me comfort. She was the one who kept me from falling apart during those long years of deprivations. She was the one who made of that one room a whole house. She was a mother to

Cory and Carrie. She made that room seem a home, making the table pretty, making the beds, scrubbing clothes in the bathroom tub, hanging them in the attic to dry, but more than anything, it was the way she danced in the attic that made me love her, and put her in my heart forever. For it seemed as I stood in the shadows and watched her, she was dancing only for me. I thought she was making me the prince of her dreams, as I made her the princess of mine. I was romantic then, even more so than she. Your mother is made of different stuff than most women, Jory. She could live on hate and still flourish, I couldn't. I had to have love or die. When we escaped Foxworth Hall, she flirted with Paul, wanting him to take her from me. She married your father when Paul's sister, Amanda, told her a lie. She was a good wife to your father, but after he was killed she ran to the mountains of Virginia to complete her plans for revenge, which included stealing her mother's second husband. As you have found out, Bart is the son of my mother's husband, and not the son of Paul as we told you and told him. We had to tell lies then, to protect you. Then, after your mother married Paul, and he died, she came to me. During all those years I waited, I somehow knew eventually she'd be mine as long as I held fast to my faith, and kept the flame of my first love burning. It was so easy for her to love other men. It was impossible for me to find any woman who could compare. She took me for her own when I was about your age, Jory. Be careful whom you love first, for that is the girl you will never forget."

I let out a long withheld breath, thinking that life was not at all like fairy tale ballets or TV soap operas. Love did not come and go with the seasons as I'd kinda hoped it would.

The drive home seemed to take forever. Dad was forced to drive very slowly and carefully. From time to time he flicked his eyes to the dashboard clock. I stared out of the windows. Everywhere there were Christmas decorations. Through picture windows I saw gaily lit Christmas trees. Longingly I stared at the windows we passed, seeing everything in that smeary way that made scenes ten times more romantic in the rain. I wished it was last year. I wished we had the happiness that had seemed so permanent then. I wished that old woman next door had never come into our lives and messed up what I thought was perfect. I wished too that Madame M. had never flown here to snoop in their lives, and reveal all their secrets better left hidden. Worst of all, those two women had destroyed the pride I had for my parents. Try as I might, I still resented what they were doing, what they had done, risking scandal, risking ruining my life and Bart's, Cindy's too, and all because one man couldn't find another woman to love. And that one woman must have done something to keep him faithful and hoping.

"Jory," began Dad as he turned into our driveway, "from time to time I hear your mother complain about chapters she's misplaced. Your mother isn't the kind of woman to be careless in any important work project. I'm presuming you've been slipping her completed chapters out of her desk drawer and reading them . . ."

Should I tell him the truth?

Bart was the one who first stole pages from her script. And yet my sense of morality hadn't kept me from reading them too. Though as yet I hadn't read to the end. For some reason I couldn't force myself to read beyond the time when first a brother betrayed his sister by forcing himself upon her. That this man beside me could rape his own sister when she was only fifteen was beyond my comprehension, beyond my ability to sympathize no matter how desperate his need had been, or what the circumstances had been to drive him to commit such an unholy act. And certainly she shouldn't tell the whole world.

"Jory, have I lost you?"

I slowly turned my eyes his way, feeling sick and weak inside, wanting to hide from the torment I plainly saw on his face. Yet I couldn't say yes—or no.

"I guess you don't need to answer," said Dad in a tight way. "Your silence gives your answer, and I'm sorry. I love you as my own son, and I hoped you loved me enough to understand. We were going to tell you when we thought you were old enough to empathize with us. Cathy should have locked her first drafts in a drawer and not trusted two sons to remain uninterested."

"It's fiction, isn't it?" I asked hopefully. "Sure, I know it is. No mother could do that to her own children . . ." and I threw open the passenger door and was racing to the house before he could answer.

My lips parted to call out to Mom. Then I shut my mouth and said nothing. It was easier for me to avoid her.

Usually when I came home I dashed out into the garden and ran around, doing practice leaps and positions, and on rainy days like this, I spent more time at the barre. Today I threw myself in front of the television set in the family room, pushed the remote control button, and lost myself in a silly but entertaining soap opera.

"Cathy!" called Dad as he came in, "where are you?"

Why hadn't he sung out, "Come greet me with kisses if you love me?" Did he feel silly, guilty saying that now that he knew we knew where that line came from?

"Have you said hello to your mother?" he asked as he came in.

"Haven't seen her."

"Where's Bart?"

"Haven't looked for him."

He threw me a pleading look, then went on into the bedroom he shared with his "wife."

"Cathy, Cathy," I could hear him calling, "where are you?"

A few seconds later he was in the kitchen behind me, checking there—and not finding her. He began to race around from room to room, and finally banged on Bart's locked door. "Bart, are you in there?"

First a long silence, then came a reluctant, surly reply, "Yeah, I'm in here. Where else would I be with the door locked?"

"Then unlock it and come out."

"Momma locked me in from the outside so I *can't* come out."

I sat on, immersing myself in the show, keeping myself detached, wondering how I was going to survive and grow up normally when I felt so unhappy.

Dad was the type to have duplicate keys to everything, and soon Bart was out and undergoing a third degree. "What did you do to cause your mother to lock you up and then go away?"

"Didn't do nothin!"

"You must have done something that made her furious."

Bart grinned at him slyly, saying nothing. I looked their way feeling anxious and scared.

"Bart, if you have done anything to harm your mother, you won't get out of this lightly. I mean that."

"Wouldn't do nothing to hurt her," said Bart irritably. "She's the one always hurtin me. She don't love me, only Cindy."

"Cindy," said Dad, suddenly remembering the little girl, and away he strode to her pretty room. He showed up minutes later with her.

"Where is your mother, Bart?"

"How do I know? She locked me up."

Despite myself, I was losing my ability to stay uninvolved. "Dad, Mom left her car in the garage a few days ago, and Madame drove us home the rest of the way, so she couldn't have gone far."

"I know. She told me—something wrong with her brakes." He threw Bart a long scrutinizing look. "Bart, are you sure you don't know where your mother is?"

"Can't look through solid doors."

"Did she tell you where she was going?"

"Nobody ever tells me nothin."

Suddenly Cindy piped up: "Mommy went out in rain . . . rain got us all wet . . ."

Bart whirled around to stab her with his glare. She froze and began to tremble.

Smiling, Dad picked up Cindy again and sat down to hold her on his lap. "Cindy, you're a lifesaver. Now, think back carefully and tell me where Mommy went."

Trembling more, she sat staring at Bart and unable to speak.

"Please, Cindy, look at me, not Bart. I'm here, I'll take care of you. Bart can't hurt you when I'm here. Bart, stop scowling at your sister."

"Cindy ran out in the rain, Daddy, and Momma had to chase outside and catch her, and then she came in dripping water, and coughing, and I said something, and she got mad at me and shoved me in my room and slammed the door."

"Well, I guess that explains Cindy's tangled hair," said Dad. But he didn't look relieved. He put Cindy on her feet and began to make a series of phone calls to all Mom's friends, and Madame Marisha. My grandmother said she'd drive right over.

Then he was talking to Emma, who couldn't return until tomorrow because of the storm. I thought of my grandmother on the road, trying to drive here in the downpour. Even in perfect weather, she wasn't what I'd call a safe driver.

"Dad, let's check all the rooms, even the attic," I said, jumping up and running toward the linen closet. "She may have gone up there to dance like she does sometimes, and accidently locked herself in, or fallen asleep on one of those beds . . . or something." I concluded this lamely, thinking he was looking at me in an odd way.

When Dad started to follow me up the attic stairs, Cindy let out a loud wail of fright. Quickly he returned to the hall and picked her up as if to take her with us. Bart pulled out a new pocketknife and began to whittle on a long tree branch. It seemed he was going to skin off all the tree bark and make a smooth switch. Cindy couldn't take her eyes off of that knife or switch.

Dad, Cindy, and me looked all over our house, in the attic, in the closets, under the beds, everywhere. Mom was nowhere to be found. "It's just not like Cathy to do anything like this," Dad said worriedly. "Especially I know she wouldn't leave Cindy alone with Bart. Something is very wrong."

Yeah, I thought, if there was a fish in the house, it was watching us and whittling away on a limb that should be used on his bare bottom.

"Dad," I whispered as he stood in the middle of his bedroom again, looking around with bleak eyes, "why don't we presume Bart knows where she's gone? He's not the most honest kid ever born. You know how crazy he's been acting lately."

We set off together, Dad still carrying Cindy, and hunted now for Bart. Now we couldn't find *him*. He was gone.

Dad and I stared at each other. He shook his head.

I stared around, knowing Bart had to be hiding behind a chair, or was crouched down low in some corner that was dim, or perhaps out in the rain, acting like an animal.

But the storm was getting worse. His cave in the hedges wouldn't keep him dry. Even Bart had more sense than to stay out in the cold and wet.

My thoughts in a turmoil, I felt wild inside, like the storm. I hadn't done anything to deserve all this trouble—yet I was in the midst of it, suffering along with Dad, with Mom, with Cindy . . . and maybe Bart, too.

"Are you hating me now, Jory?" asked Dad, looking at me squarely. "Are wheels churning in your head saying your mother and I brought this all on ourselves and we deserve to pay the price? Are you thinking you shouldn't have to pay any price? If that's what you're thinking, I'm thinking the same thing. Maybe your mother's life would have turned out better, and yours and Bart's too, if I had gone away and left her to live in Paul's home until she found another man. But I still loved her. I love her now, tomorrow and forever. God help me for not being able to think about life without her."

Dully I turned away. So that was what everlasting burning love was like, destroying everything that got in its way.

On my bed I lay down and sobbed.

Finally, I sat I up and wondered again where Mom was. For the first time it really hit me—she might be in danger. She wouldn't leave Dad. Something terrible must have happened or she'd be here, setting the table as she did every Thursday when Emma had her day off. Thursdays were very special to them for reasons I was just beginning to understand.

Thursday, the day the maids of Foxworth Hall went into the city. Thursday, the day Mom and Dad could climb out the attic dormer window and lie on the roof and talk, and as they talked, as they looked at each other in their high and lonely place, they fell mindlessly, uncontrollably in love.

For now I knew why Mom had married one man after another. Trying always to escape the sinful love she felt too.

I got up. Decided. It was up to me to find Bart.

When I found Bart, I'd find my mother.

My Attic Souvenirs

In the huge kitchen of the mansion John Amos had everything under control. The maids and cook were scurrying about. "Madame had to leave early," he told them. "Now you are to pack up what clothes she'll need for her trip to Hawaii, and be quick about it. Lottie, I want you to drive her bags to the airport and put them on the plane. Don't just stand there and stare at me with your blank face looking so stupid. You understand English. Do as I say!"

Boy, he could act mean when he wanted to. They scattered like scared birds, one this way, one that, and then we were alone and he was grinning at me with his cracked teeth. "How did your end go?"

Just like the movies, him and me. I swallowed over some lump that stayed in my throat and wouldn't go away. "They don't know where Momma is. They're worried, and keep asking, where is she?"

"Never mind about them," he said in his funny old voice that made me wonder why God had chosen him for such a special job, "I'll take care of everything until God sends his signal that your mother and grandmother have been redeemed, and saved from hellfires. You just go home and keep quiet."

Fire in my mind, growing bigger, hotter. "You told me my momma would be my attic souvenir. And now you won't even tell me where you put her. I've looked in the attic and they're not up there. You tell me where they are, or I'll go home and tell my daddy what you've done."

"What I've done?" he asked with a curling sneer. "It's what you have done, Bart Winslow Sheffield. Do you think for one moment, with your violent psychiatric history that you can be believed and not blamed? The law will take you and find you guilty, and you will be locked away."

When he saw the red Malcolm anger in my eyes he tried to smile. "Come now, Bart, I was only testing you, trying to see if you'd break and lose your courage. But you're strong and full of the righteous power, the same as your great-grandfather, Malcolm. Every power he had you have. And now is your chance to use those powers. For now you'll be in charge of the adults—your mother and grandmother. You will control their lives, and feed them—if you will—or let them starve if you are so inclined. But you have to be careful. You must keep them a secret until . . . well, remember always your father and brother will be suspicious, and they may betray you if you give them the least hint of what you're up to."

People always suspected me. If something was broken it was always my fault. If the toilet stopped up and overflowed it was always because I'd thrown down too much paper. If Momma lost her jewelry, that was my fault too. Whatever bad thing happened in our house, they said it was my fault. I'd show 'em now how wrong it was for them not to love me.

"Bread and water," I said. "Bread and water is good enough for women who are unfaithful to husbands and sons."

"Fine, fine," mumbled John Amos.

Down, down the narrow cellar steps John Amos led me, carrying a small flashlight. Made eerie shadows on the walls, felt clammy. Long time ago when this house belonged to Jory and me we'd found every nook, every cranny. But this was where ghosts lived, where I'd never felt comfortable, so I stayed close at the heels of John Amos, terrified if he moved more than a yard ahead of me. "They'll look down here," I whispered, scared of waking up things that might be sleeping.

"No, they won't look where I have them hid," answered John Amos. He chortled. "Your father will be sure they are in the attic, and why not? That would be the perfect revenge. But they'll never-never find the snug little cage the workmen made when they put up a new brick wall to reinforce the wine cellar."

Wine cellar. Didn't sound nearly as good as the attic. Wasn't nearly as scary, but it was very cold and dark down here.

John Amos began brushing away spiderwebs, then he shoved old furniture aside, and finally came to a board door that was very hard to open. "Now you go in and peek through the little door at the bottom of that door over there," he said. "We used to have a stray kitten your grandmother took in, but it disappeared shortly after you started coming over here. She had me cut this little door in the larger one so the cat could come and go when it wanted to."

With the flashlight held beneath his chin he looked like something dead and dug up. Didn't trust him not to slam the door shut behind me, and I'd never be able to wiggle through that little kitty door.

"No. You go in the wine cellar first," I ordered like Malcolm would. For a moment he didn't move. Maybe he thought I might slam the door behind him. Then he gave me a long look before he went slowly into the wine cellar. He put the flashlight on one of the wine racks while he tugged and tugged at the back rack holding many bottles of dusty ole wine bottles.

Finally it creaked open. Smelled bad in there. I held my

nose and stared, and then stared some more. John Amos held his flashlight high so I could see the two women prisoners better.

Oh, oh. Momma, Grandmother—how pitiful my momma looked, lying on the damp concrete with her head held on my grandmother's lap. Both of them raised their hands to shield their eyes from the bright light come so suddenly into their dark evil cell. I could barely see, it was so dim.

"Who is it?" asked my momma weakly. "Chris, is that you? Have you found us?"

Was my momma blind now? How could she think John Amos was my daddy? If my momma went blind and crazy too, would God think that enough punishment?

My grandmother spoke up. "John, I know that's you. You let us out of here this minute. Do you hear me—let us out immediately."

John Amos laughed.

I didn't know what to do, but Malcolm came in my brain and told me. "You give me the key, John Amos," I ordered sternly. "You go up the stairs and let *me* give the prisoners their bread and water."

Wonder why he obeyed? Did he really think I was as strong as Malcolm? I watched until he was out of sight, then I ran to bolt another door so he couldn't sneak up behind me.

Feeling more like Malcolm than like Bart, I crept on my hands and knees, shoving along the silver tray with its half loaf of bread, and its silver pitcher of water. It didn't seem to me funny to be serving prison meals from a silver tray, for that's the way my grandmother always did things, elegantly.

Big door was shut now. It appeared only another of the wine shelves full of dusty old bottles. Flat on my stomach I reached under the lower shelf and opened the little door that would swing inward or outward—wonder why the kitten liked it back in the darkest part?

"Bread, water," I said in a hard gruff voice and quickly

shoved in the tray. I slammed the little door shut and picked up a brick to wedge it so they couldn't see me if they pushed.

I stayed to spy on them. I heard my mother moaning, and crying out for Chris. Then she surprised me. "Momma, where has Momma gone, Chris? It's been so long since she visited us, months, months, and the twins don't grow."

"Cathy, Cathy, my poor darling, stop thinking about the past," said my grandmother. "Please hold on, eat and drink to keep up your strength. Chris will come to save us both."

"Cory, stop playing that same tune over and over. I'm so tired of your lyrics. Why do you write such sad songs? The night will end, it will. Chris, tell Cory the day will begin soon."

I heard sobs then. From my grandmother?

"Oh, my God!" she cried. "Is this the way it's going to end? Can't I do anything right? This time I was so sure I could work it out. Please, God, don't let me fail all of them, please." I listened to her pray out loud. Praying for my mother to get well, for her son to come and find them before it was too late. Over and over she said the same words as my mother asked crazy questions.

I sat and listened for a long time. Legs got cramped and uncomfortable, got old and weary inside, like I was locked up in there with them, crazy too, hungry, hurting, dying.

"Goin now," I said in a whisper. "Don't like this place."

Nobody was home and it was dark. Now I could run to the refrigerator and steal the food. I was stuffing in another ham slice when Madame Marisha opened the door from the garage and stalked into the kitchen. "Good evening, Bart," she said, "Where's your father and Jory?"

I shrugged. Nobody told me nothin. Didn't know why Daddy and Jory would go off and leave Cindy alone with me. Then Emma was calling out from another room. "Hello, Madame Marisha. Dr. Sheffield told me you were due here any moment. I'm sorry you went to so much trouble. Once I knew Cathy had disappeared, I couldn't stay away. I have to know what's happened to her, and she was so sick, so feverish, I should have known better than to leave her." Then Emma saw me. "Bart! You wicked little boy. How dare you add to your father's worries by disappearing too. You are a bad boy, and I'll bet my life you know something about where your mother is!"

Both old women glared at me. Hating me with their mean-mean eyes. I ran. Ran from knowing soon I'd be crying and I couldn't let anybody see me cry—now that I had to act just like Malcolm—the heartless.

The Search

The night was not fit for man nor beast. It was raining like when Noah was building his ark. The wind howled and shrieked and was trying to tell us something, like wild music that would destroy your brain. I kept pace with Dad, though that wasn't easy since I'd yet to grow legs as long as his. His hands were balled into fists. I fisted mine too, ready to do battle beside him when the need arose.

"Jory," said Dad, striding on without pausing, "how often does Bart come over here?" We'd reached the black iron gates by this time, then he leaned to speak into the box which sent his voice into the house.

"I don't know," I said miserably. "Bart used to trust me, but now he doesn't tell me what he does anymore."

Slowly, slowly, the black gates swung open. They seemed like black skeleton hands welcoming us into our graves. I shivered, thinking I was getting as morbid as Bart. I had to run then to keep up with Dad. "I've got to say something," I yelled so I could be heard above the wind. "When I first found out you are Mom's brother and our own uncle, I thought I hated you and her, too. I thought I could never forgive either one of you for making me so ashamed, so disappointed. I thought I'd dry up inside and never love or trust anyone again. But now that Mom's gone I know I'll always love her and you. I can't hate either one of you, even if I want to."

In the hard driving rain, in the dark, he turned to clasp me against his chest, his hand pressing my head against his heart. I think I heard him sob. "Jory, you don't know how much I've longed to hear you say you don't hate me or your mother. I always hoped you'd understand when we told you—and we were going to tell you when you were older. We thought, perhaps foolishly, that we needed to wait a few more years, but now that you have found out on your own, and you can still love us, maybe later on you will come to understand."

I drew closer to Dad as we continued on our way to the shadowy mansion. I felt a new bond had developed between us that was stronger than what we'd had before. In a way he was more my father, because he had much of my own kind of blood. Blood of my blood, I thought, my own uncle and Bart's, though I'd always thought he was Bart's uncle, and that had made me a little jealous. Now I could lay claim to him too. But why hadn't they realized I was mature for my age, and I would have understood when they told me Mom had an affair with Bart's father . . . I would have . . . I think.

We reached the steps. Before Dad could bang on the door-knocker, the left side of the double doors swung open and there stood that butler, John Amos Jackson. "I'm packing," he said in way of greeting, scowled up and ugly-looking, "and my wife has gone to Hawaii. I have a million things to take care of here without entertaining the neighbors. I plan to join her as soon as I'm done here."

"Your wife?" bellowed Dad, his astonishment so clear it slapped me too.

Something smug came and went in the butler's watery

eyes. "Yes, Dr. Christopher Sheffield, Mrs. Winslow is now married to me."

I thought Dad would fall from shock. "I want to see her. And I don't believe you. She'd be out of her mind to marry you."

"I don't lie," said that grim, ugly butler. "And she *is* out of her mind. Some women can't live without a man to run their affairs, and that's what I am—someone to lean on."

"I don't believe you," stormed my dad. "Where is she? Where is my wife? Have you seen her?"

The butler smiled. "Your wife, sir? I have enough to do keeping up with my own wife without looking out for yours. Yesterday my wife railed about this terrible weather and took off with one of our maids. She told me to join her later, after I'd arranged to close up this house. And after all the trouble and expense she went to having this place redecorated and refurbished—now she wants to move."

Dad stood staring at John Amos Jackson. I thought we'd leave then, but Dad seemed rooted. "You know who I am, don't you, John? Don't deny it. I see it in your eyes. You are the butler who made love to the maid Livvie while I lay on the floor behind the sofa and heard you tell her about the arsenic on the sugared doughnuts meant to kill the attic mice."

"I don't know what you're talking about," denied the butler, while I looked from him back to Dad. Oh, I should have finished every page of Mom's manuscript. Things were even more complicated than I'd realized.

"John, perhaps you are married to my mother and perhaps you are lying. Regardless, I think you know what has happened to my wife, and now I'm concerned about my mother as well. So, get out of my way. I'm going to search this house from top to bottom."

The butler paled. "You can't come over here and tell me what to do," he muttered indistinctly, "I could call the police . . ."

"But you won't, and if you want to, go ahead, call them. I am going to search now, John. There's nothing you can do to stop me."

The old butler shuffled away, shrugging helplessly. "Go on then, have your way, but you won't find anything."

Together Dad and I searched. I knew the house much better than he did, all the closets, the secret places. Dad kept saying the attic was where they would be. But when we were up there and looking, there was nothing but junk and dusty clutter.

Again we returned to the parlor where the woman he called Mother had her hard wooden rocker which I sat in and found quite uncomfortable. Restlessly Dad prowled the room, then paused in the archway that led to the adjacent room, that parlor where the huge oil portrait hung. "If Cathy came over here she would have seen that, and she could have come if Bart told her something."

Rocking back and forth in the chair, I made it "walk" a little closer to the fire that was guttering out. Something crunched beneath one of the rockers. Dad heard the sound and bent to pick up an object. It was a pearl.

He tested it between his teeth and smiled bitterly. "My mother's string of pearls with a butterfly clasp. She always wore them, just as our grandmother always wore her diamond brooch. I don't believe my mother would go anywhere without those pearls."

Another hour of searching the house, and questioning the Mexican maid and cook who did not understand English very well, and both he and I were frustrated. "I'll be back, John Amos Jackson," said Dad as he opened the front door, "and the next time I'll have the police with me."

"Have it your way, Doctor," said the butler with a tight malicious smile.

"Dad, we can't notify the police—can we?"

"We will if we have to. But let's wait at least until tomorrow. He wouldn't dare harm Cathy or my mother, or he'd land up behind bars."

"Dad, I'll bet Bart knows what is going on. He and John Amos are very thick."

I explained then how Bart was always talking to himself whenever he believed he was alone. He talked in his sleep too, and when he stalked around playing pretend games. It seemed the most important part of Bart's life was spent alone, talking to himself.

"All right, Jory, I understand what you're saying. I have an idea I hope works. This may well be the most important part you've ever played, so pay attention. Tomorrow morning you are only to pretend to go to school. I'll let you out as soon as we turn the corner onto the highway. You run back home and make sure Bart doesn't see you. I'll try to find out if my mother really flew to Hawaii, and if she really married that horrible old man."

Whispering Voices

Questions, questions, all they did was ask me questions.

Didn't know nothing, nothing. Wasn't guilty, wasn't. Why ask me? Crazy kids didn't give straight answers. "Momma's gone 'cause she always hated me, even when I was a little baby."

That night whores, harlots, and strumpets came to dance in my head. Woke up. Heard the rain beating on the roof. Heard the wind blowing at my window.

Fell asleep again and dreamed I was like Aunt Carrie who didn't grow tall enough. Dreamed I prayed and prayed and one day God let me grow so tall my head touched the sky. Looked down and saw all the little people running around like ants, afraid of me. I laughed and stepped in the ocean, making tidal waves rise up and wash over the tall cities. More pipsqueak screams. All the people I didn't squash were drowned. Sat in the ocean then that came to my waist and cried. My tears were so huge they made the ocean rise up again—and all I could see all around me was my reflection, and how handsome I was now. Now that there wasn't a girl or woman left alive to love and admire me, I was handsome, tall, and strong.

I told John Amos about my dreams. He nodded his head and told me he used to dream when he was young about girls and how much he could love them, if only they wouldn't see how long his nose was. "I had other attributes I couldn't show them, but they never gave me a chance, never a chance."

Next morning Jory left with Daddy. Easy to slip away from Emma and Madame Marisha, for they had to fool around with Cindy so much. But it gave me the chance to steal into the mansion next door. I sneaked around to find John Amos. He was packing all the beautiful lamps, paintings, and other valuables in boxes. "The silver should be wrapped in tarnish-proof papers," he said to one of the maids, "and be careful with that china and crystal. When the movers show up, have them put in the best furniture first, for I may be busy elsewhere."

The prettiest maid was young, and she frowned. "Mr. Jackson, why we go? Thought Madame liked it here. She never say we moving."

"Your mistress is a woman of changing moods—it's that nutty boy next door. That little one who keeps coming over here. He's gotten to be a real nuisance. He killed the dog she gave him. I suppose none of you know that?"

I stared in the room and saw the maid's lips part in horror. "No . . . thought the dog went over to boy's home . . ."

"The brat is dangerous! That's why Madame has to move—he's threatened her life more than one time. He's under the care of a psychiatrist."

They looked from one to the other and made circles above their heads. Mad! Mad as hell at John Amos, telling lies about me.

Waited until he was alone, sitting at the fancy desk where my grandmother kept her checkbook. He jumped when I came in. "Bart, I wish you wouldn't sneak around like that.

Make some noise when you enter, clear your throat, cough . . .
do something to announce you are there."

"I heard what you told the maids. I'm not crazy!"

"Of course you're not," he said, his S's hissing as always.
"But I do have to tell them something, don't I? Otherwise they
might become suspicious. As it is, they think your grandmother has gone on a trip to Hawaii . . ."

I felt sick inside, standing there, toeing in my sneakers,
and staring down at them. "John Amos . . . can I give my
momma and granny sandwiches to eat today?"

"No. They can't be hungry already."

Knew he would say that.

He forgot me then. He was reading over her bankbooks,
her savings accounts, her receipts and giggling to himself. He
found a little key and opened a tiny drawer way back behind
another door. "Stupid woman, thought I didn't notice where
she hid her key . . ."

I left him having his fun with my granny's things, and I
stole down to where my caged mice were. Made me feel better
to think of them as only mice.

My momma was groaning, half crying from the cold as I
peeked inside and saw they had the little stub of candle lit. I'd
shoved in the candle along with some matches so I could see
what they were doing. Momma looked little and white, and
still my granny held her head in her lap, and wiped her face
with a rag she must have torn from her slip, for it had lace on
one ragged edge.

"Cathy my love, my only daughter left, please listen to me.
I have to speak now for I may never have another chance. Yes,
I made mistakes. Yes, I allowed my father to torment me until
I didn't know right from wrong, or which way to turn. Yes, I
put arsenic on your sugared doughnuts thinking each one of
you would get only a little sick, then I could slip you out one
by one. I didn't want one of you to die. I swear I loved you, all
four of you. I carried Cory out to my car where he breathed

his last breath just as I laid him on the backseat and covered
him with two blankets. I panicked. I didn't know what to do.
I couldn't go to the police, and I was so ashamed, so guilty."

She shook my mother, while I trembled too.

"Cathy, my daughter, please wake up and listen," she
pleaded. Momma had awakened and seemed to be trying to
focus her eyes. "Darling, I don't think Bart killed the dog I
gave him. He loved Apple. I think John did that hoping Bart
would be blamed and considered crazy and dangerous so the
police would put the blame on Bart when you and I disappeared. I think John strangled Jory's little pet poodle too, and
killed my kitten as well.

"Bart is a very lonely, confused little boy, Cathy, but he's
not dangerous. He likes to pretend he is, and in that way he
can feel like he's going to be a powerful man. But it's John
who is dangerous. He hates me. I didn't know until a few years
ago that if I hadn't returned to Foxworth Hall after your father
died, John would have inherited all the Foxworth fortune. My
father trusted John as he trusted no one else, perhaps because
they were so much alike. But when I came back, he forgot
John. He wrote John out of his will and put me back in as his
sole heir. Cathy, are you listening?"

"Momma, is that you, Momma?" asked my mother in a
small voice that sounded like a child in trouble. "Momma,
why don't you look at the twins when you come in to see us?
Why don't you notice that they don't grow as they should? Are
you deliberately *not* seeing?—just ignoring them so you won't
feel guilty and ashamed?"

"Oh, Cathy!" cried Grandmother, "if only you knew how
much it hurts to hear you say those things after all these years.
Did I hurt you so deeply you can never heal, you and Chris,
too? It's no wonder you and your brother—I'm sorry, so sorry
I could die." But in a moment or so she pulled herself together
and went on with what she called a "desperate urgency."

"Even if you are delirious and can't fully understand

now, I must speak, or I may not live to tell you everything. When John Amos was a young man, about twenty-five, he lusted after me, though I was only ten. He'd hide in corners and spy on me, then hurry to my father and make the worst of innocent deeds on my part. I couldn't tell my parents that John told lies for they never believed me—they believed him. They refused to recognize a young girl is often preyed upon by older men, even older relatives. John was third cousin to my mother, the only member of her family my father could stand. I think my father put it in his head after my older two brothers died, that if ever I fell out of his favor, John would benefit. That was my father's way of extracting the most out of everyone—dangling his sugar plums that would vanish when reached for. John wanted my mother's wealth too. They encouraged him to think he might inherit. They thought him a saint. He wore a pious look all the time, he acted godly, and all the while he was seducing every pretty young maid who ever came into Foxworth Hall. And my parents never suspected. They couldn't see any evil but what their children did. Can you understand now why John hates me? Why he hated my children, too? He would have been the beneficiary if I had stayed in Gladstone.

"One day I heard him in the back hall whispering to Bart, your son, that I used my 'feminine wiles' to cajole my father into disinheriting the only man who was his friend, his best confidant."

Grandmother began to cry then. I shriveled up tight, hurting deep inside from all I was finding out. Malcolm, were you evil too? Who was I to trust now? Was John Amos just as conniving with his "masculine wiles" as my granny was with her feminine ones? Was everybody just as wicked as my granny and momma? Was God on my side, on her side, or John's?

"Momma, are you still there, Momma?"

"Yes, darling, I'm still here. I'll stay and take care of you as I never took care of you before. This time I'll be the mother

I should have been before. This time I'll save you and Chris."

"Who are you?" demanded my mother, bolting up again and shoving my grandmother away. "Oh!" she screamed, "it's you! You weren't satisfied just to kill Cory and Carrie, now you've came back to kill me, too. Then you'll have Chris all to yourself, all yours, all yours," she broke then and cried; then she began to scream like she was crazy, shrieking out over and over again how much she hated her mother. "Why don't you die, Corrine Foxworth—why don't you die?"

Went away. Couldn't stand any more of that. They were both evil.

But why was this hurting so much?

Detective

Just as Dad and I had planned, early the next morning Dad drove me off toward school, then he let me out on the road that led to our house. "Now, take it easy, Jory. Don't do anything that will endanger your life, and don't let Bart or that butler know what you're up to—they could be dangerous, remember that." He hugged me close, as if afraid I might be foolhardy. "Listen carefully to me now. I'm going to see Bart's psychiatrist this morning so I can tell him what has happened. Then I'm checking the airports to see if my mother has flown anywhere, though God knows that's not likely. But for both women to disappear in the same day is just too much of a coincidence."

I had to say it. As much as I dreaded hearing the words come from my own lips, I had to speak. "Dad, have you considered that Bart might have . . . well, you know. Clover was strangled with wire. Apple was starved and then stabbed with a pitchfork. Who knows what he might do next?"

He patted my shoulder. "Yes, of course I've thought of that. But I can't picture Bart overcoming your mother. She's very strong even if she does have a cold. That's what worries me most, Jory. She had a temperature of one hundred, and fevers do make a person weaker. I should have stayed home to take care of her. A woman is a fool to marry a doctor," he concluded bitterly, as if he'd forgotten I was there. And all the while his motor was purring softly. He bowed his head down on his hands that held the steering wheel.

"Dad . . . you go on and do what you can to check the airlines. I'll handle everything here." And I added with a big burst of overconfidence, "And remember—Madame M. is here. And you know how she is. Bart won't pull anything with her around."

Smiling, as if I'd given him the assurance he needed, he waved good-bye, and drove off, leaving me standing there and wondering just what to do. The fierce rain of yesterday had dwindled to a slow drizzle that was miserable and cold, but not wild.

Home again, and I was hiding behind the shrubbery all wet and dripping, as Bart sat in the kitchen and refused to eat his breakfast. "Hate everything you cook," he said sullenly. It was surprising to hear his voice coming to me so clearly. Then I smiled, not feeling spooked as I had before. It was the inter-com system, left on. Often delivery men came to our back door rather than use the special drive that circled the front. Our breakfast nook wasn't too far from the panel on the wall with dozens of buttons. I remembered when our house was being constructed how Mom had wanted "music in every room—so housework won't seem such a bore." Then came Madame's strident voice. "Bart, what's wrong with your cereal?"

"Don't like cereal with raisins."

"Then don't eat the raisins."

"They get in the way."

"Nonsense. If you don't eat breakfast, then you won't eat lunch either. And if you don't eat lunch, there will be no dinner—and one ten-year-old boy is going to bed very hungry!"

"You can't starve me to death!" Bart shrieked. "This is my house! You don't belong here! You get out!"

"I will NOT get out. I am staying until your mother returns safely. And don't you dare raise your voice to me again or I might turn you over my knee and paddle your behind until you scream for mercy!"

"It won't hurt," he jeered—and it wouldn't. Spankings never bothered Bart who had skin with no surface nerve endings.

"Thank you for telling me," said Madame with great aplomb. "I will then think of a better punishment—such as keeping you indoors, locked in your room."

By this time I was peering in a window. There sat Bart with a secret smile on his face.

"Emma," ordered Madame, "take Bart's plate away, take his bowl, his orange juice too. Bart—go straight to your room and don't let me hear another word out of you until you can come to this table and eat your meals without complaints."

"Witch, old black witch come to live in our house," Bart chanted as he ambled away. But he didn't go to his room. He bolted out of the garage door when Madame wasn't looking, and from there he headed toward the garden wall, and the old oak tree he could climb to take him over the wall.

I ran as fast as I could, following him. But once I was inside the mansion I lost sight of him. Where had Bart gone? I stared right and left, looked behind me, turned around slowly. Had he disappeared up the stairs or down into the cellar? I hated this house with its maze of long corridors, with so many niches between the walls where Mom could be hidden. Usually a builder used the leftover spaces to make closets or put in shelves. But this one, I knew for a fact, had secret doors, only I'd already searched all the secret rooms. Useless to look in them again.

Suddenly I heard a footfall. Bart was right behind me. He looked right through me, his eyes glazed as he stared bleakly at nothing. I couldn't believe he didn't see me.

I followed silently, believing he'd take me to where Mom and her mother were hidden. Unfortunately, he headed for home. Sickened, disheartened, I trailed along behind, feeling I'd betrayed my father and failed him.

Lunchtime and Dad came home tired and distressed-looking. "Any luck, Jory?"

"No. How about you?"

"None. My mother did not fly to Hawaii. I checked with all the airlines. Jory, both Cathy and my mother must be inside that house next door."

I had an idea. "Dad, why don't you have a long talk with Bart? Don't jump on him, or condemn him, just say nice things. Praise him for being nice to Cindy, tell him how much you care about him. I know he's behind this for he keeps mumbling about the Lord and being His dark angel of revenge."

Dad couldn't find any words to say as he digested my information. Then silently, he set off to find Bart and do what he could to make an unwanted little boy feel needed—if it wasn't already too late.

The Last Supper

Later I went down to the cellar again with John Amos. "Corrine," John Amos called softly as he bent over stiffly. Clumsy like me, he got down on his knees and peered through the small kitty door he opened. "I want you and your daughter to know this is your last meal, so I made it a good one." He lifted the lid of the silver teapot and spat inside, then poured the steaming hot liquid into fine china cups. "One for you, one for your daughter," he said. He shoved one cup and saucer inside the kitty door, then the other set. Next he picked up a plate of sandwiches which looked stale and kinda dirty, then managed to drop the plate on the filthy cellar floor.

He picked up the little triangles and wiped them off against his trouser leg, shoved the meat that had fallen out back in, then put the plate of coal-dusted food in through the kitty door. "Here you are, Corrine Foxworth," snarled John Amos in his hissy voice. "I hope you find these dainty sandwiches to your liking, you bitch! I took your word when you married me, truly believing you'd be my wife—and though you have never been my wife in the way I'd hoped, still I will inherit what is rightfully mine. Finally I have managed to destroy you and yours—just as Malcolm wanted to kill all your Devil's issue."

Did he have to hate my granny so much? Maybe she wasn't to blame, like me who sometimes did bad things and couldn't help it. Why was everybody doing bad things to everybody else and calling the excuse "inheritance"?

"You flaunted your beauty before me!" screamed out an enraged old man, "tormenting me when you were a child—teasing me when you were an adolescent, thinking you could have your fun and I could never harm you. Then when you married your half uncle and came back to disinherit me, you treated me like I wasn't even there—just another piece of furniture to ignore. Well, are you arrogant now, Corrine Fox-worth? Do you feel haughty sitting in your own filth, holding your dying daughter's head on your filthy lap? I have made you crawl at last, haven't I? I have beaten you at our game, stolen Bart's affection from you, made him mistrust you and trust me. You can't use your charm and feminine wiles now. It's too late. I hate you now, Corrine Foxworth. For every woman I have fantasized was you, I have paid, but no longer. I have won, and though I am seventy-three now, I will live on at least another five or six years in luxury enough to make up for all the years I've suffered at your hands."

My grandmother was sobbing quietly. I was crying too, wondering again who was right, him or her?

John Amos was saying terrible things. Nasty evil bad words that little boys wrote on bathroom walls. Grown up old men shouldn't talk like that, and in front of my grandmother and my momma.

"John!" yelled Grandmother, "haven't you done enough? Let us out, and I'll be your wife in the way you want, but please do not punish my daughter more. She's very sick. She needs to be in a hospital. The police will call this murder if you let her die and me too."

John Amos just laughed and walked heavily back up the stairs.

I couldn't move. I was frozen, so confused I didn't know who was good and who was bad.

"Bart!" screamed my grandmother. "Run fast to your father and tell him where we are! *Run, run!*"

Bleary-eyed, I just stood there. Didn't know what to do. "Please, Bart," she begged. "Go tell your father where we are."

Malcolm—was that him over in the corner, his ghost face frowning at me? Passed my smutty hand over my blurry eyes. Dark, so dark. I pretended to leave, but I snuck back. I wanted to hear more of the truth.

Out of the darkness came my mother's thin voice screaming at that old woman who was her mother, my grandmother.

"Oh, yes, Mother. I understood everything you said. We didn't stand a chance no matter who died and who didn't die when you took us into Foxworth Hall and locked us away. Now, years later, we will die just because that crazy old butler didn't inherit the money he expected, promised to him years ago by a dead man—and if you believe any of that—you are just as crazy as he is."

"Cathy. Don't deny the truth because you hate me so much. I'm telling you the truth. Can't you see how John has used your son, the son of my Bart. Don't you see how perfect his revenge is?—to use the son of the man he hated, the man he felt took his place, when it could have been him who married me if my father could have forced me to do it. Oh, you don't know how Father tried to tell me I owed it to John to marry him, and allow him to have half of his fortune—he didn't guess, or maybe he did, that John wanted it all. And when you and I die, it won't be John who is found guilty—it will be Bart. It's John who killed Clover, then Apple. It's John who dreams of having Malcolm's power, Malcolm's wealth. It's not my imagination when I hear him mumbling to himself incessantly."

"Like Bart," mumbled Momma, so funny sounding. "Bart's always pretending he's old and feeble, but powerful and rich. Poor Bart. What about Jory—has he got Jory? Where is Jory?"

Why did she pity me and not Jory? Got up and left.

Was I crazy too—like him? Was I a killer at heart—like him? Didn't know nothing about myself. Was foggy-minded, hazy seeing, but I did manage to move my heavy legs and somehow I climbed up all those old stairs.

Waiting

He was the only father I could remember well, and I loved him even more in that relationship. He held out his hand and told me what we had to do, and I followed, as I would have followed blindly anywhere he led. For out of every terrible situation something good had to come, and I knew now how much he meant to me.

With Dad leading the way, we went once more to the house next door. We hadn't seen Bart all afternoon. How stupid of me to let him outsmart me, and sneak away when I had my head turned, watching some cute thing Cindy did as she tried to dance like me.

Mom had been missing a full twenty-four hours.

That old butler let us in, standing back to scowl at us.

"My mother has not flown to Hawaii," stated Dad, his blue eyes hard and cold.

"So? She is not an organized woman. She may have gone on to visit friends for the holidays. She has no friends here."

"You smoke expensive cigarettes," said my father dryly. "I remember that night when I was seventeen lying behind the sofa while you and Livvie the maid were there . . . and you smoked the same cigarettes—French?"

"Right," said John Amos Jackson with a sneering grin. "Old Malcolm Neal Foxworth's tastes gave me the habit . . ."

"You pattern yourself after my grandfather, don't you?"

"Do I?"

"Yes, I believe you do. When I checked this house the last time, I opened a closet full of expensive men's clothes—yours?"

"I am married to Corrine Foxworth. She is my wife."

"How did you blackmail her to marry you?"

Again the old man smiled. "Some women have to have a man in the house or they don't feel safe. She married me for a companion. As you can see, she treats me like a servant still."

"I think not," said my father with his narrowed eyes sweeping over the butler who was wearing a new suit. "I think you were thinking of your future when, or if, my mother should die."

"How interesting," replied John Amos Jackson, grinding out his stub of quickly smoked cigarette. "I've made my departure plans. I'm flying back to Virginia where I expect my wife will join me when she becomes tiresome to her hosts. Her daughter ruined her socially in Virginia years ago, which you must know, but still she will go there."

"Why?"

John Amos Jackson grinned widely. "She is having Foxworth Hall reconstructed, Dr. Sheffield. From out of the ashes, Foxworth Hall shall rise again—like the fabled Phoenix!"

Dad faltered, still staring at the cigarette. "Foxworth Hall," he said in a haunted voice, "how far along is it?"

"Almost finished," answered John Amos Jackson smugly. "Soon I shall reign as king where Malcolm ruled, and his arrogant beautiful daughter will reign at my side." He laughed crazily, seeming to enjoy my father's discomfort. "She'll have her facial scars reconstructed, her face lifted again. She'll color her hair and make it blonde again, and she'll sit at the foot of my dining table. Behind me will stand one of my own cousins, where I used to stand. It will all be as it was before, except this time I shall be the lord and master."

Wheels were churning in Dad's head. "You will never rule anywhere but in prison," he said before he turned and left.

"Dad," I said when we were home, "did you believe what that butler told us?"

"I don't know yet. I do know he's more clever than I thought. When I was a boy in Foxworth Hall looking down on his bald head, I never suspected he had any power. He seemed just another servant. However, I can see now he laid his plan a long time ago and is now fulfilling his schedule for revenge."

"For revenge?"

"Jory, can't you see that man is insane? You have told me that Bart imitates a man he calls Malcolm who has been dead for years. But the man Bart is really imitating is John Amos Jackson, who is himself imitating my grandfather. Malcolm Foxworth, dead and gone, but still influencing our lives."

"How do you know? Did you ever see your grandfather?"

"I saw him one time only, Jory," he said in a sad reflective way. "I was fourteen, your age. Your mother and I hid in a huge chest on the second floor and looked down in the ball-room, and Malcolm Foxworth was in a wheelchair. He was a far distance away, and I never heard his voice. But our mother used to come to us with descriptions of how he talked about sin and hell, quoting from the Bible, talking about Hell and Judgment Day."

Night came. We turned on all the lights hoping that would light Mom home and Bart too. Emma and Madame put Cindy to bed early. Emma went from Cindy's room back into the kitchen, but Madame came into the family room and slouched in a chair across from Dad. Just about that time Bart came in the door and crouched down in a corner. "Where have you been so long?" asked Dad, sitting up straighter and fixing

Bart with a strange long look. Madame M. riveted her dark ebony eyes on Bart too. Bart ignored them, and continued to make shadow pictures on the wall by holding his hands in contorted positions.

The TV set behind me was turned on though no one was watching. A choir of boys were singing Christmas carols. I felt exhausted from trying to follow Bart around all day. Exhausted more from worrying about Mom, to say nothing about what would happen to all of us . . .

I decided I had to escape by going to bed, and rose to say good night, but Madame put her finger before her lips and gestured to Dad so he too would pay attention to what Bart was muttering to himself as he made the eerie picture of an old man talking to a child.

"Bad things happen to those who defy the laws of God," he crooned in a hypnotizing way. "Bad people who don't go to church on Sundays, who don't take their children, who commit incestuous acts, will all go to hell and burn over the everlasting fires as demons torment their eternal souls. Bad people can be redeemed only by fire, saved from hell and the Devil and his pitchfork only by fire, fire."

Weird, really weird.

Dad could control his impatience and rage no longer.

"Bart! Who told you all that hocus-pocus?"

My brother jerked upright, his dark brown eyes went blank. "Speak when spoken to, said the wise man to the innocent child. The child says in return, unholy people who commit sins will come to a fiery end."

"Who told you that?"

"Old man from his grave. Old man likes me better than Jory, who does sinful dancing. Old man hates dancers. Old man says only I am fit to rule in his place."

Dad was listening intently. I was remembering what Bart's shrink had advised. "Play along with the boy; pretend to believe everything he says, no matter how ridiculous.

Remember he's only ten and at that age a child can believe in almost anything, so let him express himself in the only safe way he's found so far. When the 'old man' speaks, you are hearing your son speaking of what bothers him most."

"Bart," said Dad, "listen to me carefully. If your mother didn't know how to swim, and she was drowning, and I was there but looking the other way—would you tell me so I could jump in and save her?"

Any son should have said yes immediately, but Bart considered this heavily, frowning, weighing his answer when it should have come spontaneously.

Finally he answered. "You wouldn't have to do anything to save Momma from drowning, Daddy, if Momma was pure and without sin. God would save her."

Judgment Day

Nobody understood me and what I was trying to do. Wasn't no good trying to explain. Had to do it all on my own. I slipped away from Daddy, from Jory, from all those people who saw me as bad and unnecessary in their lives. I had come, and I could go, and it would make no difference to anyone. They didn't know I was trying to help right all the wrongs they'd done before I was even born, and all those done after I was born.

Sin. The world was full of sin and sinners.

Wasn't my fault if Momma had to be punished. Though it did worry me some why God didn't want Daddy included in the punishment.

John Amos had told me that men were meant for better things. Heroic things like going off to war and doing brave deeds. No matter if legs and arms were shot off—was a far-far better way to suffer than what God had in mind for women.

Got to thinking hard on the subject. What if the pearly gates of heaven didn't open to receive my momma's purified soul? "Go forth and sin no more" I'd say if I were God. I stamped my golden staff on heaven's golden floor and struck a huge boulder far below so it split wide open and I could write on it my twenty commandments. (Ten weren't enough.) Wonder how I could split open the Pacific and let all the righteous escape the heathens that were on their heels?

Gee, thinking like this made me feel bad in my head, in my legs, and it made my hands and feet cold. *Momma, why did you have to be so bad? Why did you have to go and live with your brother and put the burden of your death on me?*

Jory was outside my door. Spying on me. Knew it was him. Was always him sneaking around, trying to find out what I was up to. I'd ignore him and concentrate on my momma's last hours. She and Grandmother oughta have good food for their last meal. Every prisoner had her favorite meal before the end. Had to do right by my momma and grandmother. What did they like to eat most? I like sandwiches best, so maybe they did too. Sandwiches, pie and ice cream should be just fine. Just as soon as everyone was in bed, I'd slip their last meal over to them.

Black night came. All the lights were turned off. Soon everything was very, very quiet. What was that? Was it snoring I heard across the hall, in the guest room next to Jory's room? Old Madame Marisha snored. Disgusting.

I slapped turkey between slabs of Emma's homemade cheese bread. With two slices of cherry pie and a quart of ice cream in my sack, I made my way to the white whale of a house, moving as quiet as a mouse.

Down, down, down all the steep stairs into the cellar where rats, mice, and spiders roamed, and two women were moaning and groaning and calling for me. Made me feel important. I lifted the kitty door that was under the wine shelves and shoved in the sack with all the goodies.

The light from the candle stub I'd given them was very dim, flickering, showing forms that didn't seem solid at all. My grandmother was trying to calm my mother who raged on and on: "Take your hands off of me, Mrs. Winslow. For a while I felt like a child again, and I was glad you were with me in the dark, but now I remember. How much are you paying that butler to do this to me? Why are *you* here?"

"Cathy, Cathy, John hit me over the head, just like he did you. He hates me, too. Didn't you hear all I explained?"

"Yes, I heard. It was like a bad dream, all the same things Chris used to say to me, trying to explain why you acted as you did. Even though he pretends to hate you, underneath it all, I've always known he still loved you, despite all you did. He kept a little of his faith in you . . . but he's stupid in his loyalty to women. First you, now me."

I was glad I knew so many big words, so some day I could write in my own journal and tell everyone how I saved my momma from hellfires.

I could see straw in Momma's hair which wasn't so pretty now. Same old straw that once was in the barn where Apple stayed. They hadn't even thanked me for making their prison softer and warmer with that hay—had shoved it all in while they were both sleeping.

"Cathy, don't you really love your brother? Have you just used him?"

My momma seemed almost crazy as she struck out at my grandmother. "Yes, I love him! You made me love him. It was your fault and now we have to live ashamed and guilty. Afraid any day our children will find out. And now they have, because of you!"

"Because of John," whispered Grandmother. "I only came here to help, to be near you, to share, just a little in your lives. But stop feeling guilty, make it my shame and my guilt. I accept it as mine, all mine. You are right. You have always been right in your judgment of me, Cathy. I'm weak, foolish, and manage always to make the wrong decisions. I think they're right when I make them, but never do they prove anything but wrong."

Momma quieted down. She sank back on her heels and

stared at her mother. "Your face, why did you dig at your face?"

My grandmother bowed her head. She seemed to have aged ten years in one long-long day. "I wanted to die after Bart died. I wanted to destroy my beauty so no man would ever want me again. I didn't want to look in a mirror and see you staring back at me, for I hated you too for a long time. It was Chris who came each summer and talked to me about you, who made me see your side of your affair with my husband. He told me you really loved Bart, that you should have had Bart's child aborted for your own health, but you wouldn't have it done. You wanted to keep his baby. Cathy, thank you for doing that. Thank you for giving me another Bart, for he is mine as Jory will never be."

Oh, they both loved me! Momma had risked her health to give me life. Grandmother had stopped hating Momma on account of me. I wasn't nearly as bad as I thought.

"Cathy, please forgive me," pleaded my granny. "Say it, please say it at least once. I need so to hear you say it. It was Christopher who loved me, who defended me, but it was you who kept me awake at nights, tormenting me even on my honeymoon with Bart—it is your face, the faces of the twins that haunt me still. Christopher will always be mine—and yours, but give me back my daughter."

My mother screamed. Loud, shrill, crazy, she screamed over and over. She lunged at my grandmother and pounded her with her fists. "*No!* I can never say what you want!" She knocked the candle and it turned over and the hay caught on fire. Old newspaper they'd used to keep warm soon was ablaze, and my grandmother and mother were beating at the flames with their bare hands, trying to put it out.

"Bart!" screamed my grandmother, "if you're out there listening to us, run for help! Call the fire department! Tell your father! Do something quick, Bart, or your mother will die in this blaze—and God will never forgive you if you help John Amos kill us!"

What? Was I helping John Amos or God?

I ran like mad up the cellar stairs and out into the garage where John Amos was putting his bags in the last one of the black limousines. The other was gone, driving the maids to safety.

He slammed down the trunk of the car, turned to me with a wide grin, and said, "Well, tonight is the night. At twelve o'clock sharp—remember that. Trip slowly down the stairs and into their place and light the string."

"That smelly string?"

"Yes. It's soaked in gasoline."

"I didn't like the smell, so I threw it away. Didn't want their last meal to be eaten in a smelly place."

"What are you talking about? Have you been feeding them?" He whirled as if to hit me and then out of nowhere Jory sprang upon John Amos. The old man fell on his back, with Jory astride, and then Daddy raced into the garage.

"Bart . . . we watched you make sandwiches and slice the pie—and take the ice cream—now where are your mother and your grandmother?"

Didn't know what to do.

"Dad!" yelled Jory, "I smell smoke!"

"Where are they, Bart?"

John Amos yelled out at Daddy, "Take that crazy kid away from here—him and his matches! He's started a fire. Him and his crazy stunts, like killing that dear little puppy who loved him so much. It's no wonder Corrine panicked and ran without telling me where she was going." He cried real tears and wiped at his runny nose. "Oh, God . . . I wish to heaven we'd never come here to live. I told Corrine no good would come of this."

Lies! He was telling lies on me! Wasn't none of that true!

"You did it all! You are the crazy man, John Amos!" and like Malcolm would, I ran over to kick at him. "Die, John Amos! Die and be redeemed through death!"

My arms were caught and I was lifted away. Daddy had
me in his arms and was trying to calm me. "Your mother . . .
where is your mother? Where is the fire?"

A red haze was in my eyes, but I reached in my pants
pocket and gave my daddy the key. "In the wine cellar," I said
dully, "waiting for the fire to end them like they ended Foxworth Hall. Malcolm wanted it that way—all the little attic
mice to burn and stop reproducing contaminated seed."

Far away from my body I was standing, watching the
stunned terror in Daddy's eyes as he tried to delve into my
eyes . . . but I knew they were blank—for I wasn't there. Didn't
know where I was. Didn't care.

Redemption

Fire. The mansion was on fire.

I straddled John Amos, who fought me off—or tried to, but soon he knew who had the best of the battle. "You can't get away, old man. You've poisoned my brother's mind, made him think awful things. I hope to God you rot in some jail cell for the rest of your life for what you've done."

While John Amos and I had at it, Dad sped off to find Mom and his mother, with Bart at his heels screaming out how he could get to the wine cellar.

"Get off me, boy!" yelled John Amos Jackson. "That brother of yours is crazy—dangerous! He starved that poor puppy then stabbed him with a pitchfork. Is that the act of a sane child?"

"Why didn't you stop him if you saw him do all that?"

"Why, why . . . ," sputtered the old man, "he would have turned on me like a wild beast. The boy is insane like his grandmother. Why it was my own wife who saw him dig up the skeleton of her pet kitten. Ask her, go on, ask her."

Some of what he said was getting to me. Bart was irrational.

Yet, yet—was he a killer? "Bart talks in his sleep, old man. He repeats everything he hears during the day like a parrot. He quotes from the Bible and pronounces words he wouldn't be able to if someone like you wasn't coaching him."

"You fool boy! He doesn't know who he is! Can't you see that? He thinks he is his great-grandfather Malcolm Foxworth . . . and like Malcolm he's driven to kill every last living member of the Foxworth clan!"

At that moment I saw my father stumble into the garage carrying my mother in his arms, with his mother, dirty and in rags, following behind. I jumped up and ran. "Mom, oh Mom!" I cried, overjoyed to see she was still alive. But she looked dreadful, dirty, pale, and thin . . . but alive, thank God!

She was conscious. "Where's Bart?" she whispered.

With that question she lost consciousness and slumped in Dad's arms. While looking around for Bart, I noticed that John Amos Jackson was no longer to be seen. "Dad," I said to draw his attention, and just then out of the dim shadows of the garage, the butler appeared with a heavy shovel. He brought that shovel down hard on top of Dad's head. Silently, without a groan, Dad slumped to the floor with Mom still in his arms. Again that butler raised the shovel as if to kill Dad—and maybe Mom, too. I ran, and I kicked with my right leg as I'd never kicked before. The shovel went spinning away, and as John Amos Jackson whirled to face me, I let him have it with my left foot square in his stomach. He groaned and slumped over.

But Bart—where was Bart?

"Jory," called the mother of my parents, "get your parents out of this garage as quickly as you can! Pull them so far away they won't be hurt if the garage blows when the fire reaches the gasoline in here. *Hurry!*" I started to object, but she took care of that. "I'll find Bart. You just keep my son and daughter safe."

It was easy to pick up Mom and run with her to a safe

place and lay her down, but not so easy to drag Dad by his shoulders to lie beside her under a tree—still I managed. The house now smoked from several windows. My brother was in there—and my grandmother, too.

John Amos Jackson had recovered and he too rushed inside the burning house. In the kitchen I saw John Amos struggling with my grandmother. He was battering her face with slaps. I ran to rescue her though the smoke was in my eyes. "You'll never get away with this, John!" she yelled as he tried to choke her. I fell over a chair that had been turned over, and jumped to my feet just in time to see her bring down a heavy Venetian glass ashtray so it struck him on his temple. He slumped to the floor like a bird shot down from a rifle.

That's when I saw Bart. He was in the parlor trying to lug that huge portrait to safety. "Momma," he was sobbing, "gotta save Momma. Momma, I'm gonna get you out of here, don't you fear, 'cause I'm just as brave as Jory, just as brave . . . can't let you burn. John Amos was lying, he doesn't know what God wants, doesn't know . . ."

"Bart," crooned my grandmother. Her voice was so like my mom's. "I'm here. You can save me—not just the portrait." She stepped forward, limping badly, and I guessed she'd tripped and sprained her ankle, for at each step she grimaced. "Please, darling, you and I have to leave the house."

He shook his head. "Gotta save Momma! You're not my momma!"

"But *I* am," said another voice in another doorway. My eyes widened to see my mother standing there, clinging weakly to the doorframe as she pleaded with Bart. "Darling, let go of the portrait and all of us will leave this house." Bart looked from her to his grandmother, still clinging to the huge heavy portrait that he could never have the strength to drag from the house. "Gonna save my momma, even if she hates me," muttered Bart to himself as he tugged at the huge heavy portrait. "Don't care no more if she loves Jory and Cindy better. Gotta do one good thing and then everybody will know I'm not bad, and not crazy."

Mom ran to him and covered his small dirty face with kisses, as all around us the room filled with smoke.

"Jory!" called my grandmother, "call the fire department! Take Bart out of here, and I'll lead your mother out."

But Mom didn't want to go; she seemed oblivious of the danger of staying in a smoke-filled house, with fire underneath. Even as I dialed O for the operator and told her what was going on, then gave her the address, Mom was down on her knees hugging Bart close. "Bart, my sweetheart, if you can't accept Cindy as your sister and live happily with her, I'll send her away."

His grip loosened on the portrait as his eyes grew wider. "No you won't . . ."

"Yes, I swear I will. You are my son, born from my love for your father . . ."

"You loved my real daddy?" he asked unbelievably. "You really did love him, even if you seduced and killed him?"

I groaned, then ran to seize hold of Bart. "Come on, let's get out of here while we have the chance."

"Bart, you go with Jory," called my grandmother, "and I'll take care of my daughter."

There was the side door Bart used to sneak inside the house, and I dragged him toward that, looking back to see Mom was being pulled along by her mother. Mom seemed on the verge of fainting, so my grandmother almost had to carry her.

As I ran from the house, forcing Bart to join Dad under the tree where I'd left him, I saw Mom had sagged in her mother's arms. When she did, both women tumbled over backward, and for a moment the smoke obscured them.

"Oh, my God, is Cathy still in that house?" asked Dad, still wiping at the blood which wouldn't stop flowing from the deep gash on the side of his head.

"Momma's gonna die, I know it!" cried Bart, racing toward

the house and forcing me to run after him. I hurled myself forward and brought him down with a tackle. He fought me like a madman. "Momma, gotta save Momma! Jory, let me, please let me!"

"You don't have to. Her mother is going to save her," I said, looking over my shoulder as I held him down and prevented him from entering that house of fire again.

Suddenly Emma and Madame Marisha were in the yard, holding on to me, to Bart, hurrying us both toward Dad, who had managed to stand. Blindly, with his hands groping before him he was headed toward the house, crying out, "Cathy, where are you? Come out of that house! Cathy, I'm coming!"

That's when Momma was shoved violently through one of the French doors that opened onto the patio.

I ran forward to lift her up and carry her to Dad. "Neither one of you has to die," I said with a sob in my throat. "Your mother has saved at least one of her children."

But cries and screams were in the air. My grandmother's black clothes were on fire! I saw her as one sees a nightmare, trying to beat out the flames.

"Fall down and roll on the ground!" roared Dad, releasing my mom so quickly she fell. He ran toward his mother, seized her up and rolled her on the ground. She was gasping and choking as he slapped out the fire. One long wild look of terror she gave him before some kind of peace came over her face—and stayed there. Why did that expression just stay there? Dad cried out, then leaned to put his ear to her chest. "Momma," he sobbed, "please don't be dead before I've had the chance to say what I must . . . Momma, don't be dead . . ."

But she was dead. Even I could tell that from the glazed way her eyes kept staring up at a starry winter night sky.

"Her heart," said Dad with a dazed look. "Just like her father had . . . it seemed her heart was about to jump from her chest as I rolled her about. And now she's dead. But she died saving her daughter."

Jory

All the shadows that clouded my youthful days, all the questions and the doubts I'd been afraid to speak about, all have been cleared away now, like cobwebs from the corners.

I thought when we came back from the funeral of our grandmother that life would go on as usual and nothing much would be changed.

Some things have changed. Some weight lifted from Bart's shoulders and he became again the quiet, meek, little boy who couldn't really like himself very much. His psychiatrist said he would grow out of that gradually, with enough love given him, and enough friends his own age to play with.

Even as I write this I can look through the open window and see Bart playing with the Shetland pony our parents gave him for Christmas. At last he had his "heart's desire."

I watch him often, the way he looks at the pony, the way he stares at the St. Bernard puppy my daddy gave him too. Then he turns his head and stares over at the ruins of the mansion. He never speaks of her, the grandmother of our lost summer. We never speak the name of John Amos Jackson, nor mention Apple or Clover. We can't risk the health and happiness of one unstable little boy trying to find his way in a world that isn't always like a fairy tale.

We passed a true Arab woman on the street the other day. Bart turned around to stare after her, wistful longing in his dark-dark eyes. I know now that whatever else she was, Bart loved her—so she couldn't have been as awful as I think when I read Mom's book. She made Bart love her, even as John Amos took a vulnerable child and warped him.

And so John Amos got what he deserved, and, like my grandmother, he too lies dead in his grave, way back in Virginia, the home of his ancestors who settled in what history books call "The Lost Colony." All his plotting and scheming was for nothing. If, wherever he is, he can think, I wonder what he thinks and feels knowing what was in the will my grandmother left. Did he turn over in his grave when the lawyer told us that our grandmother had left the entire Foxworth estate to Jory Janus Marquet, Bartholomew Scott Winslow Sheffield, and surprisingly enough, Cynthia Jane Nickols too would get her share. And none of us were legally her blood kin—*legally*. All that money held in trust for us, until we reach the age of twenty-five. All held in trust, my father and mother the administrators.

We could live in splendor if we chose, or if my parents chose, but we live on in the same redwood house with the marble statues out back, and every year the garden grows more lush.

Bart keeps himself exceptionally clean now. He will not lie down to sleep at night until his room is in complete order, everything precisely placed. My parents look at each other when he insists on doing this, and I see fear in their eyes, making me wonder if Malcolm Neal Foxworth was exceptionally clean and neat.

Bart laid down the law to my mother and father one morning soon after Christmas had come and gone, and he had his pony: "If you are to keep Cindy then you can no longer live together as man and wife and contaminate my life with your sinning. You *have* to sleep in my room, Daddy, and Momma *has* to sleep alone for the rest of her life."

Neither one of my parents said anything, they just looked at him until he flushed and turned away, murmuring, "I'm sorry . . . I'm not Malcolm, am I? I'm just me, nobody much."

Bart is a true Foxworth over and over, for he will rule again, so he says, in the new Foxworth Hall that he will build. "And you can dance your head off until you are forty," he yelled at me when he was angry because I petted his new pony, "but you won't be as rich as I'll be! At forty, I'll be able to buy and sell you ten times over, for dancing legs won't matter when you grow old, and brains count more, a million times more!"

"I'll be the greatest actor the world has ever known!" he stated arrogantly, turning from meek to aggressive just because he was holding that red journal book in his hands. "And when I'm done with the stage and screen, I'll turn my talent to the business world, and everybody who didn't respect me as an actor will stand up and applaud my genius for making money."

Acting, that's all he was doing again, for he was only a little boy who seldom spoke except to himself. And yet, sometimes when I lie awake at night, thinking about all that happened before he and I were born, there must be some reason for all that went before. Out of the ruins should come the roses, right? I worry about all the women Bart would step on to get his way. Would he be as ruthless as our great-grandfather just to obtain an even greater fortune? And how many would suffer because of one eventful summer, fall, and winter in the year I was fourteen?

I'll take him by the hand tomorrow, and lead him out into the garden, and together we'll stand before the copy of Rodin's

"The Kiss" and maybe then he'll realize that God planned for men and women to love in a physical way, and it's not sinful, only natural.

I pray that someday Bart will see life my way—that love—no matter what its form, or how it comes wrapped, is worth the price, no matter how high.

Between the choice of love or money I'll take love. But first comes dancing. And when Bart is old and gray and he sits in Foxworth Hall counting his billions, I'll sit with my wife and family content with the happy memories of how it used to be when I was young, graceful, handsome, on stage with the foots in my eyes, the sound of applause in my ears, and I'll know I fulfilled my destiny.

I, Jory Janus Marquet, will carry on the family tradition.

Bart

They don't know or understand me any more than they did before. Jory looks at me with pity, like I'm different from the rest of the human race. He feels sorry that I don't like his kind of music, or any kind of music, and colors don't paint pictures in my brain or make music in the air. He thinks I will never find joy in anything. But I'll find a way to enjoy. I'll know the future that is right for me, for that was the true reason God sent my grandmother and John Amos and Malcolm to me, like the fates come to lead the way. They came to show me how to save my parents from the everlasting fires of hell.

I watch my momma and daddy night and day, and sneak into their room at night, fearing to catch them doing something wicked. But they only sleep in each other's arms, and to my relief her eyes don't move rapidly behind her closed lids. She doesn't have nightmares anymore. I see my daddy's eyes at the breakfast table, looking bluer than ever for he has let go of his stranglehold on his sister.

I have saved them.

So, Jory pities me. But one day when we're both older, wiser, and I have found the right words, I'll tell him something Malcolm wrote in his book—there has to be darkness if there is to be light.

Epilogue

I remember so much of what went on before we flew to Greenglenna to bury my mother beside her second husband. It was Bart who insisted that his grandmother had to lie in eternal sleep beside his father, his real father, Bartholomew Winslow. We cried, all of us, even Emma and Madame Marisha, and I never hoped to see the day when Madame would cry for a member of my family.

When the first clod of damp earth struck her coffin in its grave, it took me back to when I was twelve years old and Daddy was in his grave, and Momma was holding fast to my hand, and to Chris's, and each twin held on to an older brother or sister. And only when I heard the dirt hit her mahogany casket did I cry out something I'd withheld for so long—too long. It came from the depths of me, tearing away the years and making me a child again, and needing, so needing to hold on to my parents. "Momma, I forgive you! I forgive you! I still love you! Can you hear me now where you are? God, please let her know I forgive her." I sobbed then and fell into my brother's arms. I would have said more to her on her burial day, but Bart was there, glaring his dark eyes at me, commanding me to be strong, to let go of the man I loved. But how could I, when to do so would destroy him?

We still live in the house next to the ruins of the mansion where my mother died in her efforts to save my life, but it's not like it used to be before she came with her evil butler who filled Bart's head with his crazy beliefs and gave Bart that journal of Malcolm Foxworth. I love Bart, God knows I love him, but when I see those dark merciless eyes in the shadows, I cringe and wonder why I needed revenge so much when I had Chris to save me.

Last night Jory and Melodie danced an astonishingly beautiful performance of "Romeo and Juliet." I trembled to see Bart cynically smiling, as if he'd lived a century or more and he'd seen all this happen before, and it would be him who got everything he wanted in the end, as Bart has always found a way to make himself the center of attention.

He steals into our bedroom at night, having taught himself how to pick locks, and stares down at Chris and me, while I feign sleep, holding still, breathless, until he is gone, so terribly afraid that the evil that lived in Malcolm will live again in my youngest son. And sooner or later history will repeat itself.

"Today the mail brought a letter from my literary agent," I whispered to Madame M. while Jory and Melodie changed from costumes to street clothes. "She's found a publisher who's made me an offer on my book, the first one. It's not a fortune, but I'm going to accept."

Madame gave me another of those long speculative looks that had once made me feel very uneasy and vulnerable, as if she could see through me. "Yes, Catherine, you will do what you must regardless of the consequences or the protests I make, or anyone makes."

I knew who she meant, for he glared at me, telling me I should keep my secrets to myself and not let the whole world know. But Bart cannot rule my every action.

"You will be rich and famous in a different way than I expected when you were fifteen," continued Madame, who was now my dearest confidant, "for everything can come to those who have the desire, the drive, the dedication, and the determination."

I smiled uneasily, afraid to look at Bart again, but fixed my eyes on my eldest son who was the star of the evening. I knew for a certainty that when my books were published, and all the skeletons were out of the Foxworth closets, I'd lay the shade and thwart the ghost of Malcolm Neal Foxworth, and never, never would he rise up to rule over me again.

Nervously my hands fluttered up to my throat to feel for those invisible pearls that used to adorn my mother's throat, but never mine, never mine. I said again to myself that it wouldn't hurt to give it a try. Evil did thrive in the dark shadows of lies. Evil could not possibly survive in the full bright light of unstinting truth, as incredible as it may seem to some who won't believe.

Shivering, I moved a bit farther from Bart, nearer to Chris who put his arm about my shoulders, as my arm encircled his waist, and I was safe, safe. Now I could look at Bart and smile; now I could reach for Cindy's hand, and try to reach for Bart's . . .

But he drew away, refusing to join the chain I would form of our family, one for all, and all for one.

I'd like to conclude by saying I don't cry anymore at night, that I don't have nightmares in which I see my grandmother climbing the stairs to try and witness evil deeds we didn't do. I want to write that I can only be grateful that from all the thorny stems the attic flowers managed to grow and produced at least a few roses, real roses, the kind that blossom in the sun.

I'd like to conclude with that. But I can't. Nevertheless, I've grown old enough and wise enough to accept what gold coins are offered, and never, never will I turn over anything that glitters to look for the tarnish.

Seek and you shall find.

For some reason I glanced up then. Bart was sitting in a shadowy corner again, holding in his hands a red volume that appeared to be covered in leather with gold tooling. Silently he read, his lips moving as he mouthed the words of a great-grandfather he'd never seen.

I shivered. For Malcolm's journal had burned in the fire. The book Bart held was a cheap imitation of leather and every page was blank.

Not that it mattered.

Seeds of Yesterday

BOOK ONE

Foxworth Hall

And so it came to pass the summer when I was fifty-two and Chris was fifty-four that our mother's promise of riches, made long ago when I was twelve and Chris was fourteen, was at last realized.

We both stood and stared at that huge, intimidating house I'd never expected to see again. Even though it was not an exact duplicate of the original Foxworth Hall, still I quivered inside. What a price both Chris and I had paid to stand where we were now, temporary rulers over this mammoth house that should have been left in charred ruins. Once, long ago, I'd believed he and I would live in this house like a princess and prince, and between us we'd have the golden touch of King Midas, only with more control.

I no longer believed in fairy tales.

As vividly as if it had happened only yesterday, I remembered that chill summer night full of mystical moonlight and magical stars in a black velvet sky when we'd first approached this place, expecting only the best to happen. We had found only the worst.

At that time Chris and I had been so young, innocent, and trusting, believing in our mother, loving her, believing as she led us and our five-year-old twin brother and sister through the dark and somehow scary night, to that huge house called Foxworth Hall, that all our future days would be colored green for wealth and yellow for happiness.

What blind faith we'd had when we tagged along behind.

Locked away in that dim and dreary upstairs room, playing in that dusty, musty attic, we'd sustained ourselves by our belief in our mother's promises that someday Foxworth Hall and all its fabulous riches would be ours. However, despite all her promises, a cruel and heartless old grandfather with a bad but tenacious heart refused to stop beating in order to let four young and hopeful hearts live, and so we'd waited, and waited, until more than three long-long years passed, and Momma failed to keep her promise.

And not until the day *she* died—and her will was read— did Foxworth Hall fall under our control. She had left the mansion to Bart, her favorite grandson, my child by her own second husband, but until he was twenty-five, the estate was held in trust by Chris.

Foxworth Hall had been ordered reconstructed before she moved to California to find us, but it wasn't until after her death that the final touches were completed on the new Foxworth Hall.

For fifteen years the house stood empty, overseen by caretakers, legally supervised by a staff of attorneys who had either written or called Chris long distance to discuss with him the problems that arose. A waiting mansion, grieving, perhaps, waiting for the day when Bart decided he'd go there to live, as we'd always presumed one day he'd do. Now he was offering this house to us for a short while, to be our own until he arrived and took over.

There was always a catch in every lure offered, whispered my ever-suspicious mind. I felt the lure now, reaching out to ensnare us again. Had Chris and I traveled such a long road only to come full circle, back to the beginning?

What would be the catch this time?

No, no, I kept telling myself, my suspicious, ever-doubting nature was getting the better of me. We had the gold without the tarnish . . . we did! We *did* have to realize our just rewards some day. The night was over—our day had finally come, and we were now standing in the full sunlight of dreams come true.

To actually be here, planning to live in that restored home, put sudden familiar gall in my mouth. All my pleasure vanished. I was actually realizing a nightmare that wouldn't vanish when I opened my eyes.

I threw off the feeling, smiled at Chris, squeezed his fingers, and stared at the restored Foxworth Hall, risen from the ashes of the old, to confront and confound us again with its majesty, its formidable size, its sense of abiding evil, its myriad windows with their black shutters like heavy lids over stony dark eyes. It loomed high and wide, spreading over several acres in magnificent but intimidating grandeur. It was larger than most hotels, formed in the shape of a giant T, only crossed on each end to give it an enormous center section, with wings jutting off north and south, east and west.

It was constructed of rosy pink bricks. The many black shutters matched the roof of slate. Four impressive white Corinthian columns supported a gracious front portico. A sunburst of stained glass was over the black double front doors. Huge brass escutcheon plates decorated the doors and made what could have been plain rather elegant and less somber.

This might have cheered me if the sun hadn't suddenly taken a fugitive position behind a passing dark cloud. I glanced upward at a sky turned stormy and foreboding, heralding rain and wind. The trees in the surrounding forest began to sway so that birds took alarmed flight and screeched as they flew for cover. The green lawns so immaculately kept were quickly littered with broken twigs and falling leaves, and the blooming flowers in geometrically laid-out beds were lashed to the ground unmercifully.

I trembled and thought: *Tell me again, Christopher Doll, that it's going to work out fine. Tell me again, for I don't really believe now that the sun has gone and the storm is drawing nearer.*

He glanced upward, too, sensing my growing anxiety, my unwillingness to go through with this, despite my promise to Bart, my second son. Seven years ago his psychiatrists had told us their treatment was successful and that Bart was quite normal and could live out his life without needing therapy on a regular basis.

To give me comfort Chris's arm lifted to encircle my shoulders. His lips lowered to brush my cheek. "It's going to work out for all of us. I know it will. We're no longer the Dresden dolls trapped in an upstairs room, dependent on our elders to do the right thing. Now we're the adults, in control of our lives. Until Bart reaches the stated age of inheritance, you and I are the owners. Dr. and Mrs. Christopher Sheffield from Marin County, California, and no one will know us as brother and sister. They won't suspect that we are truly descendants of the Foxworths. We have left all troubles behind us. Cathy, this is our chance. Here, in this house, we can undo all the harm done to us and to our children, especially Bart. We'll rule not with steel wills and iron fists, as was Malcolm's way, but with love, compassion, and understanding."

Because Chris had his arm about me, holding me tight against his side, I gained strength enough to look at the house in a new light. It was beautiful. For Bart's sake we'd stay until his twenty-fifth birthday, and then Chris and I would take Cindy with us and fly to Hawaii, where we'd always wanted to live out our lives, near the sea and white beaches. Yes, that's the way it was supposed to be. The way it had to be. Smiling, I turned to Chris. "You're right. I am not afraid of this house, or any house." He chuckled and lowered his arm to my waist, pressuring me forward.

~   ~   ~

Soon after finishing high school, my first son Jory had flown
to New York City to join his grandmother, Madame Marisha.
There, in her ballet company, he'd soon been noticed by the
critics and was given leading roles. His childhood sweetheart,
Melodie, had flown east to join Jory.

At the age of twenty, my Jory had married Melodie, who
was only a year younger. The pair of them had struggled and
worked to reach the top. They were now the most notable ballet team in the country, a team of perfect, beautiful coordination, as if they could reach each other's mind and signal with
a flash of their eyes. For five years they'd been riding the crest
of success. Every performance brought rave reviews from the
critics and from the public. Television exposure had given
them a larger audience than they could ever have gained by
personal appearances alone.

Madame Marisha had died in her sleep two years ago,
though we could console ourselves by knowing she'd lived
to be eighty-seven and had worked up until the very day she
passed away.

Around the age of seventeen, my second son Bart had
transformed almost magically from a backward student into
the most brilliant one in his school. By that time Jory had
flown on to New York. I had thought at the time that Jory's
absence had brought Bart out of his shell and made him
interested in learning. Just two days ago, he had graduated
from Harvard Law School, the valedictorian of his class.

Chris and I had joined Melodie and Jory in Boston,
and in the huge auditorium of Harvard Law School we'd
watched Bart receive his law degree. Only Cindy, our
adopted daughter, was not there. She was at her best friend's
house in South Carolina. It had given me new pain to know
that Bart could not let go of his envy of a girl who'd done
her best to win his approval—especially when he'd done
nothing to win hers. It gave me additional pain to know that

Cindy couldn't let go of her dislike of Bart long enough to help him celebrate.

"No!" she'd shouted over the telephone, "I don't care if he did send me an invitation! It's just his way of showing off. He can put ten degrees behind his name and I still won't admire or like him—not after all he did to me. Explain to Jory and Melodie why, so their feelings won't be hurt. But you won't have to explain to Bart. He'll know."

I'd sat between Chris and Jory and stared, amazed that a son who was so reticent at home, so moody and unwilling to communicate, could rise to the top of his class and be named valedictorian. His impassioned words created a mesmerizing spell. I glanced at Chris, who looked proud enough to burst before he grinned at me.

"Wow, who would have guessed? He's terrific, Cathy. Aren't you proud? I know I am."

Yes, yes, of course, I was very proud to see Bart up there. Still, I knew the Bart behind the podium was not the Bart we all knew at home. Maybe he *was* safe now. Completely normal—his doctors had said so.

To my way of thinking, there were many small indications that Bart had not changed as dramatically as his doctors thought. He'd said just before we parted, "You must be there, Mother, when I come into my own." Not a word about Chris being there with me. "It's important to me that *you* be there."

Always he had to force himself to speak Chris's name. "We'll invite Jory and his wife down, too, and, of course, Cindy." He'd grimaced just to say her name. It was beyond me how anyone could dislike a girl as pretty and sweet as our beloved adopted daughter. I couldn't have loved Cindy more if she'd been flesh of my flesh, and blood of my Christopher Doll. In a way, since she'd come to us at the age of two, she was our child, the only one we could claim as truly belonging to both of us.

Cindy was sixteen now, and much more voluptuous than I'd been at her age. But Cindy hadn't been as deprived as I. Her vitamins had come from fresh air and sunshine, both of which had been denied four imprisoned children. Good food and exercise . . . she'd had the best. We'd had the worst.

Chris asked if we were going to stay out here all day and wait for pelting rain to drench us both before we went inside. He tugged me forward, urging me on with his cheerful confidence.

Gradually, step by slow step, as the thunder began to crash and swiftly come closer, with the swollen, heavy sky zigzagging with frightening electrical bolts, we approached the grand portico of Foxworth Hall.

I began to notice details I'd missed before. The portico floor was made of mosaic tiles in three shades of red intricately laid to form a sunburst pattern that matched the glass sunburst over the double front doors. I looked at those sunburst windows and rejoiced. They hadn't been here before. Perhaps it was just as Chris had predicted. It wouldn't be the same, just as no two snowflakes were the same.

Then I was frowning, for to all intents and purposes, who ever saw the differences in falling snowflakes?

"Stop looking for something to steal the pleasure from this day, Catherine. I see it on your face, in your eyes. I vow on my word of honor that we will leave this house as soon as Bart has his party and fly on to Hawaii. If a hurricane comes and blows a tidal wave over our home once we're there, it will be because you expect that to happen."

He made me laugh. "Don't forget the volcano," I said with a small giggle. "It could hurl hot lava at us." He grinned and playfully spanked my bottom.

"Quit! Please, please. August tenth will see us on our plane—but a hundred to one you'll worry about Jory, about Bart, and wonder what he's doing all alone in this house."

That's when I remembered something forgotten until

now. Waiting inside Foxworth Hall was the surprise Bart had promised would be there. How strangely he'd looked when he'd said that.

"Mother, it will blow your mind when you see—" He'd paused, smiled, and looked uneasy. "I've flown down there each summer just to check things over and see that the house wasn't being neglected and left to mold and decay. I gave orders to interior decorators to make it look exactly as it used to, except for my office. I want that modern, with all the electronic conveniences I'll need. But . . . if you want, you can do a few things to make it cozy."

Cozy? How could a house such as this ever be cozy? I knew what it felt like to be enclosed inside, swallowed, trapped forever. I shivered as I heard the click of my high heels beside the dull thuds of Chris's shoes as we neared the black doors with their escutcheons made decorative with heraldic shields. I wondered if Bart had looked up the Foxworth ancestry and found the titles of aristocracy and the coats of arms he desperately wanted and seemed to need. On each black door were heavy brass knockers, and in between the doors a small, almost unnoticeable button to ring a bell somewhere inside.

"I'm sure this house is full of modern gadgets that would shock genuine historical Virginia homes," whispered Chris.

No doubt Chris was right.

Bart was in love with the past, but even more infatuated with the future. Not an electronic gadget came out that he didn't buy.

Chris reached into his pocket for the door key Bart had given to me just before we flew from Boston. Chris smiled my way before he inserted the large brass key. Before he could complete the turning action, the door swung silently open.

Startled, I took a step backward.

Chris pulled me forward again, speaking politely to the old man who invitingly gestured us inside.

"Come in," he said in a weak but raspy voice as he quickly looked us over. "Your son called and told me to expect you. I'm the hired help—so to speak."

I stared at the lean old man who was bent forward so that his head projected unbecomingly, making him seem to be climbing hills even while standing on a flat surface. His hair was faded, not gray and not blond. His eyes were a watery pale blue, his cheeks gaunt, his eyes hollowed out, as if he'd suffered greatly for many, many years. There was something about him . . . something familiar.

My leaden legs didn't want to move. The fierce wind whipped my white, full-skirted summer dress high enough to show my thighs as I put one foot inside the grand entrance foyer of the Phoenix called Foxworth Hall.

Chris stayed close at my side. He released my hand to put his arm around my shoulders. "Dr. and Mrs. Christopher Sheffield," he introduced us in his kindly way, "and you?"

The wizened old man seemed reluctant to put out his right hand and shake Chris's strong, tanned one. His thin old lips wore a cynical, crooked smile that duplicated the cock of one bushy eyebrow. "My pleasure to meet you, Dr. Sheffield."

I couldn't take my eyes off that bent old man with his watery blue eyes. Something about his smile, his thinning hair with broad streaks of silver, those eyes with startling dark lashes. Daddy!

He looked as our father might have looked if he'd lived to be as old as this man before us—and had suffered through every torment known to mankind.

My daddy, my beloved handsome father who'd been the joy of my youth. How I'd prayed to see him again some day.

The stringy old hand was grasped firmly by Chris, and only then did the old man tell us who he was. "Your long-lost uncle who was, ostensibly, lost in the Swiss Alps fifty-seven years ago."

Joel Foxworth

Quickly Chris said all the right words to cover the shock that obviously showed on both our faces. "You've startled my wife," he politely explained. "You see, her maiden name was Foxworth . . . and she has believed until now that all her maternal family was dead."

Several small, crooked smiles fleeted like shadows on "Uncle Joel's" face before he pasted on the benign, pious look of the sublimely pure in heart. "I understand," said the old man in his whispery voice that sounded like a faint wind rustling unpleasantly in dead, fallen leaves.

Deep in Joel's watery cerulean eyes lingered shadows, dark, troubled shadows. I knew without speaking that Chris would tell me my imagination was working overtime again.

No shadows, no shadows, no shadows . . . but those I created myself.

To lift myself above my suspicions of this old man who claimed to be one of my mother's two older and dead brothers, I gazed with interest around the foyer that had often been used as a ballroom. I heard the wind pick up velocity as the thunderclaps drew ever closer and closer together, indicating the storm was almost directly overhead.

Oh, sigh for the day when I'd been twelve and stared out at the rain, wanting to dance in this ballroom with the man who was my mother's second husband and would later be the father of my second son, Bart.

Sigh for all that I'd been then, so young and full of faith, so hopeful that the world was a beautiful and benign place.

What had seemed to me impressive as a child should have shrunk in comparison to all I'd seen, since Chris and I had traveled all over Europe and had been to Asia, Egypt, and India. Even so, this foyer seemed to me twice as elegant and impressive as it had when I was twelve.

Oh, the pity of that, to still be overwhelmed! I gazed with reluctant awe, a strange aching beginning in my heart, making it thud louder, making my blood race fast and hot. I stared at the three chandeliers of crystal and gold that held real candles. Each was fully fifteen feet in diameter, with seven tiers of candles. How many tiers had there been before? Five? Three? I couldn't remember. I stared at the huge mirrors with gold frames that lined the foyer, reflecting the elegant Louis XIV furniture where those who didn't dance could sit and watch and converse.

It wasn't supposed to be this way! Things remembered never lived up to expectations—why was this second Foxworth Hall overwhelming me even more than the original?

Then I saw something else—something I didn't expect to see.

Those dual curving staircases, one on the right, the other on the left of the vast expanse of red and white checkered marble. Weren't they the same stairs? Refurbished, but the same? Hadn't I watched the fire that had burned Foxworth Hall until it was only red embers and smoke? All eight of the chimneys had stood; so had the marble staircases. The intricately designed banisters and rosewood railing must have burned and been replaced. I swallowed over the hard lump that lodged in my throat. I'd wanted the house to be new, all new . . . nothing left of the old.

Joel was watching me, telling me my face revealed more than Chris's. When our eyes locked, he quickly looked away before he gestured that we were to follow him. Joel showed us through all the beautiful first-floor rooms as I remained numb and speechless, and Chris asked all the questions, before at last we settled down in one of the salons and Joel began telling his own story.

Along the way he'd paused in the enormous kitchen long enough to put together a snack for our lunch. Refusing Chris's offer to help, he had carried in a tray with tea and dainty sandwiches. My appetite was small, but as was to be expected, Chris was ravenous and in a few minutes had dispatched six of the tiny sandwiches and was reaching for another as Joel poured him a second cup of tea. I ate but one of the miniature tasteless sandwiches and sipped twice from the tea, which was steaming hot and very strong, expectantly anticipating the tale Joel would tell.

His voice was frail, with those gritty undertones that made it seem he had a cold and speaking was difficult. Yet soon I forgot the unpleasant sound of his voice as he began to relate so much of what I'd always wanted to know about our grand-parents and our mother when she was a child. In no time at all it became clear that he'd hated his father very much, and only then could I begin to warm up to him.

"You called your father by his Christian name?" My first question since he'd begun his story, my voice an intimidated whisper, as if Malcolm himself might be hovering somewhere within hearing.

His thin lips moved to twist into a grotesque mockery of a smile. "Of course. My brother Mel was four years older than I, and we'd always referred to our father by his given name, but never in his presence. We didn't have that kind of nerve.

Calling him Daddy seemed ridiculous. We couldn't call him Father because he wasn't a real father. 'Dad' would have indicated a warm relationship, which we didn't have and didn't want. When we had to, we called him Father. In fact, we both tried not to be seen or heard by him. We'd disappear when he was due home. He had an office in town from which he conducted most of his business and another office here. He was always working, seated behind a massive desk that was to us a barrier. Even when he was home, he managed to keep himself remote, untouchable. He was never idle, always jumping up to take long distance calls in his office so we couldn't overhear his business transactions. He seldom talked to our mother. She didn't seem to mind. On rare occasions we'd seen him holding our baby sister on his lap, and we'd hide and watch, with strange yearnings in our chests.

"We'd talk about it afterward, wondering why we'd feel jealous of Corrine, when Corrine was often just as severely punished as we were. But always our father was sorry when he punished *her*. To make up for some humiliation, some beating, or being locked in the attic, which was one of his favorite ways to punish us, he'd bring Corrine a costly piece of jewelry, or an expensive doll or toy. She had everything any little girl could desire—but if she did one wrong thing, he took from her what she loved most and gave it to the church he patronized. She'd cry and try to win back his affection, but he could turn against her as easily as he could turn toward her.

"When Mel and I tried to win gifts of consolation from him, he'd turn his back and tell us to act like men, not children. Mel and I used to think your mother knew how to work our father very well to get what she wanted. We didn't know how to act sweet, or how to be beguiling, or demure."

Behind my eyes I could see my mother as a child, running through this beautiful but sinister home, growing accustomed to having everything lavish and expensive, so that later on when she married Daddy, who had earned a modest salary, she still didn't think about how much she paid for anything.

I sat there with wide eyes as Joel went on. "Corrine and our mother didn't like each other. As we grew up, we recognized the fact that our mother was jealous of her own daughter's beauty, and the many charms that enabled her to twist any man around her fingers. Corrine was exceptionally beautiful. Even as her brothers we could sense the power she would be able to wield one day." Joel spread his thin, pale hands on his legs. His hands were gnarled and knotted, but somehow they still maintained a remnant of elegance, perhaps because he used them gracefully, or perhaps because they were so pale. "Look around at all this grandeur and beauty—and picture a household of tormented people, all struggling to be free of the chains Malcolm put on us. Even our mother, who'd inherited a fortune from her own parents, was kept under stringent control.

"Mel escaped the banking business, which he hated and had been forced into by Malcolm, by jumping onto his motorcycle and racing away into the mountains, where he'd stay in a log cabin he and I had constructed together. We would invite our girlfriends there, and we did everything we knew our father would disapprove of deliberately, out of defiance for his absolute authority.

"One terrible summer day Mel went over a precipice; they had to dig his body out of the ravine. He was only twenty-one. I was seventeen. I felt half dead myself, so empty and alone with my brother gone. My father came to me after Mel's funeral and said I'd have to take the place of my older brother and work in one of his banks to learn about the financial world. He might as well have told me I'd have to cut off my hands and feet. I ran away that very night."

All about us the huge house seemed to wait, very quiet, too quiet. The storm outside seemed to hold its breath as well, although I could glimpse the leaden gray sky growing more and more swollen and turgid. I moved slightly closer to Chris on the elegant sofa. Across from us in a wing-back chair, Joel sat silently, as if caught in melancholy memories, and Chris and I no longer existed for him.

"Where did you go?" asked Chris, putting down his tea-cup and leaning back before he crossed his legs. His hand reached for mine. "It must have been difficult for a boy of seventeen on his own . . ."

Joel jerked back to the present, seeming startled to find himself back in his hated childhood home. "It wasn't easy. I didn't know how to do anything practical, but at music I was very talented. I caught a freight steamer and worked as a deckhand to pay my way over to France. For the first time in my life I had calluses on my hands. Once I was in France, I found a job in a nightclub and earned a few francs a week. Soon I grew tired of the long hours and moved on to Switzerland, thinking I'd see all the world and never return home. I found another job as a nightclub musician in a small Swiss inn near the Italian border and soon was joining skiing parties into the Alps. I'd spend most of my free time skiing, and in the summer, hiking or bicycling. One day good friends asked me to join them on a rather risky trip, to downhill ski from a very high peak. I was about nineteen then, and the four others ahead were laughing and yelling at each other and didn't notice when I lost control and went tumbling headlong into a deep ice crevice. I broke my leg in the fall. I lay down there a day and a half, partly in shock, when two monks travel-ing on donkeys heard my weak cries for help. They knew how to get me out—but I don't remember much about that, for I was weak with hunger and half out of my mind from pain. When I came to, I was in their monastery, and smooth, bland faces were smiling at me. Their monastery was on the Italian side of the Alps, and I didn't know a word of Italian. They taught me their Latin as my broken leg healed, and then they used my slight artistic talent to help them paint wall murals and decorate handwritten scripts with religious illustrations.

Sometimes I played their organ. By the time my leg was healed so I could walk, I found I liked their quiet life, the artwork they gave me to do, the music I played at dawn and sunset, the silent routine of their uneventful days of prayers and work and self-denial. I stayed on and eventually became one of them. In that monastery, high in the mountains, I finally found peace."

His story was over. He sat looking at Chris, then turned his pale but burning eyes on me.

Startled by his penetrating gaze, I tried not to shrink away and show the revulsion I couldn't help feeling. I didn't like him, even though he faintly resembled the father I'd loved so well, and certainly I had no reason to dislike him. I suspected it was my own anxiety and fear that he'd know that Chris was really my brother and not my husband. Had Bart told him our story? Did he see how Chris resembled the Foxworths? I couldn't really tell. He was smiling at me, using his own kind of failing charm to win me over. Already he was wise enough to know it wouldn't be Chris he had to convince . . .

"Why did you come back?" asked Chris.

Again Joel tried to smile. "One day an American journalist came to the monastery to write a feature story about what it was like to be a monk in today's modern world. Since I was the only one there who spoke English, they used me to represent all of them. I casually asked if he'd ever heard of the Foxworths of Virginia. He had, since Malcolm had made a huge fortune and was often involved in politics, and only then did I learn of his death, and that of my mother. Once the journalist had gone, I couldn't stop thinking about this house and my sister. Years can easily blend one into the other when all days are alike, and calendars weren't kept in sight. Finally came a day when I resolved that I wanted to go home again and talk to my sister and get to know her. The journalist hadn't mentioned if she had married. It wasn't until after I came to the village, almost a year ago, and settled into a motel that I heard of how the original house had burned one Christmas night and my sister had been put away in a mental rest home, and all that tremendous fortune had been left to her. It wasn't until Bart came that summer that I learned the rest—how my sister died, how he inherited."

His eyes lowered modestly. "Bart is a very remarkable young man; I enjoy his company. Before he came, I used to spend a lot of my time up here, talking to the caretaker. He told me about Bart and his many visits to talk to the builders and decorators, how he had expressed his desire to make this new house look exactly like the old one. I made it my business to be here when Bart came the next time. We met, I told him who I was, and he seemed overjoyed . . . and that's the whole of it."

Really? I stared at him hard. Had he come back thinking he'd have his share of the fortune Malcolm had left? Could he break my mother's will and take away a good portion for himself? If he could, I wondered why Bart wasn't very upset to know he was still alive.

I didn't put any of my thoughts into words, just sat on, as Joel fell into a long, moody silence. Chris stood up. "It's been a full day for us, Joel, and my wife is very tired. Could you show us to the rooms we are to use so we can rest and refresh ourselves?"

Instantly Joel was on his feet, apologizing for being a poor host, and then he was leading the way to the stairs.

"I will be happy to see Bart again. He was very generous to offer me a room in this house. However, all these rooms remind me too much of my parents. My room is over the garage, near the servants' quarters."

Just then the telephone rang. Joel handed me the telephone. "It's your older son calling from New York," he said in that stiff, gritty voice. "You can use the phone in the first salon if both of you want to talk to him."

Chris hurried to pick up another phone as I greeted Jory. His happy voice dispelled some of the gloom and depression

I was already feeling. "Mom, Dad, I've managed to cancel a few commitments, and Mel and I are free to fly down and be with you. We're both tired and need a vacation. Besides, we'd like to get a look at that house we've heard so much about. Is it really like the original?"

Oh, yes, only too much so. I was filled with joy that Jory and Melodie were coming to join us, and when Cindy and Bart arrived, too, we'd be a complete family again, all living under the same roof—something I hadn't known in a long time.

"No, of course I don't mind giving up performing for a while," he said cheerfully in answer to my question. "I'm tired. Even my bones feel weak with fatigue. We both need a good rest . . . and we have some news for you."

He'd say nothing more.

We hung up, and Chris and I smiled at each other. Joel had retreated to give us privacy, and now he reappeared, tottering uncertainly around a jutting French table with a huge marble urn filled with a dried flower arrangement, speaking of the suite of rooms Bart had planned for my use. He glanced at me, then at Chris before he added, "And for you as well, Dr. Sheffield."

Joel swiveled his watery eyes to study my expression, seeming to find something there that pleased him.

Linking my arm with Chris's, I bravely faced the stairs that would take us up, up, and back to that second floor where it had all begun, this wonderful, sinful love that Chris and I had found in the dusty, decaying attic gloom, in a dark place full of junk and old furniture, with paper flowers on the wall and broken promises at our feet.

Memories

Midway up the stairs I paused to look down, wanting to see something that might have slipped my notice before. Even as Joel had told us his story, and we'd eaten our sparse lunch, I'd stared at everything I'd seen but twice before, and never had I seen enough. From the room where we'd been, I could easily look into the foyer with its myriad mirrors and fine French furniture placed stiffly in small groupings that tried unsuccessfully to be intimate. The marble floor gleamed like glass from many polishings. I felt the overwhelming desire to dance, dance, and pirouette until I blindly fell . . .

Chris grew impatient as I lingered and tugged me upward until at last we were in the grand rotunda and again I was staring down into the ballroom-foyer.

"Cathy, are you lost in memories?" whispered Chris, somewhat crossly. "Isn't it time we both forget the past and move on? Come, I know you must be very tired."

Memories . . . they came at me fast and furious. Cory, Carrie, Bartholomew Winslow—I sensed them all around me, whispering, whispering. I glanced again at Joel, who'd told us he didn't want us to call him Uncle Joel. He was saving that distinguished title for my children.

He must look as Malcolm did, only his eyes were softer, less piercing than those we'd seen in that huge, lifesize portrait of him in the "trophy" room. I told myself that not all blue eyes were cruel and heartless. Certainly I should know that better than anyone.

Openly studying the aged face before me, I could still see the remnants of the younger man he'd once been. A man who must have had flaxen blond hair and a face very much like my father's—and his son's. Because of this I relaxed and forced myself to step forward and embrace him. "Welcome home, Joel."

His frail old body in my arms felt brittle and cold. His cheek was dry as my lips barely managed a kiss there. He shrank from me as if contaminated by my touch, or perhaps he was afraid of women. I jerked away, regretting now that I'd made an attempt to be warm and friendly. Touching was something no Foxworth was supposed to do unless there was a marriage certificate first. Nervously my eyes fled to meet Chris's. Calm down, his eyes were saying, it's going to be all right.

"My wife is very tired," reminded Chris softly. "We've had a very busy schedule what with seeing our youngest son graduate, and all the parties, and then this trip . . ."

Joel finally broke the long, stiff silence that kept us standing uncomfortably in the dim upstairs rotunda and mentioned that Bart would be hiring servants. Already he'd called an employment agency, and, in fact, had even said we could screen people for him. He mumbled so inaudibly that I didn't catch half of what he said, especially when my mind was so busy with speculations as I stared off toward the northern wing and that isolated end room where we'd been locked up. Would it still be the same? Had Bart ordered two double beds put in there, with all that clutter of dark, massive, antique furniture? I hoped and prayed not.

Suddenly from Joel came words I wasn't prepared for. "You look like your mother, Catherine."

I stared at him blankly, resenting what he must have considered a compliment.

He kept standing there, as if waiting for some silent summons, looking from me to Chris, and then back to me before he nodded and turned to lead the way to our room. The sun that had shone so brilliantly for our arrival was a forgotten memory as the rain began to pelt down with the hard, steady drive of bullets on the slate roof. The thunder rolled and crashed overhead, and lightning split the sky, crackling every few seconds, sending me into Chris's arms as I cringed back from what seemed to me the wrath of God.

Rivulets of water ran on the windowpanes, sluiced down from the roof into drains that soon would flood the gardens and erase all that was alive and beautiful. I sighed and felt miserable to be back here where I felt young and terribly vulnerable again.

"Yes, yes," Joel muttered as if to himself, "just like Corrine." His eyes scanned me critically once more, and then he was bowing his head and reflecting so long five minutes could have passed. Or five seconds.

"We have to unpack," Chris said more forcefully. "My wife is exhausted. She needs a bath, then a nap, for traveling always makes her feel tired and dirty." I wondered why he bothered to explain.

Instantly Joel pulled himself back from where he'd been. Maybe monks often just stood with bowed heads and prayed, and lost themselves in silent worship, and that was all it meant. I didn't know anything at all about monasteries and the kind of lives monks lived.

Slow, shuffling feet were at last leading us down a long hall. He made another turn, and to my distress and dismay he headed toward the southern wing where once our mother had lived in sumptuous rooms. I'd longed to sleep in her glorious swan bed, sit at her long, long dressing table, bathe in her black marble sunken tub with mirrors overhead and all around.

Joel paused before the double doors above two wide, carpeted steps that curved outward in half-moons. He smiled in a slow, peculiar way. "Your mother's wing," he said shortly.

I paused and shivered outside those too familiar double doors. Helplessly I looked back at Chris. The rain had calmed to a steady staccato drumming. Joel opened one side of the doors and stepped into the bedroom, giving Chris the chance to whisper to me, "To him we are only husband and wife, Cathy—that's all he knows."

Tears were in my eyes as I stepped into that bedroom— and then I was staring bug-eyed at what I'd thought burned in the fire. The bed! The swan bed with the fancy rosy bed curtains held back gracefully by the tips of wing feathers made into curling fingers. That graceful swan head had the same twist of its neck, the same kind of watchful but sleepy red ruby eye half open to guard the occupants of the bed.

I stared disbelievingly. Sleep in that bed? The bed where my mother had been held in the arms of Bartholomew Winslow—her second husband? The same man I'd stolen from her to father my son Bart? The man who still haunted my dreams and filled me with guilt. No! I couldn't sleep in that bed! Not ever.

Once I'd longed to sleep in that swan bed with Bartholomew Winslow. How young and foolish I'd been then, thinking material things really did bring happiness, and having him for my own would be all I'd ever want.

"Isn't that bed a marvel?" asked Joel from behind me. "Bart went to a great deal of trouble to find artisans who'd handcarve the headboard in the form of a swan. They looked at him, so he said, as if he were crazy. But he found some old men who were delighted to be doing something they found uniquely creative, and financially rewarding. It seems Bart has detailed descriptions of how the swan should have its head turned. One sleepy eye set with a ruby. Fingertip feathers to hold back filmy bed curtains. Oh, the flurry he made when they didn't do it right the first time. And then the little swan bed at the foot, he wanted that, too. For you, Catherine, for you."

Chris spoke, his voice hard. "Joel, just what has Bart told you?" He stepped beside me and encircled my shoulders with the comfort of his arm, protecting me from Joel, from everything. With him I'd live in a thatched hut, a tent, a cave. He gave me strength.

The old man's smile was faint and sardonic as he took notice of Chris's protective attitude. "Bart confided all his family history to me. You see, he's always needed an older man to talk to."

He paused meaningfully, glancing at Chris, who couldn't fail to catch the implication. Despite his control I saw him wince. Joel seemed satisfied enough to continue. "Bart told me about how his mother and her brothers and a sister were locked away for more than three years. He told me that his mother took her sister, Carrie, the twin left alive, and ran off to South Carolina, and you, Catherine, took years and years to find just the right husband to suit your needs best—and that's why you are now married to . . . Dr. Christopher Sheffield."

There were so many innuendoes in his words, so much he left unsaid. Enough to make me shiver with sudden cold.

Joel finally left the room and closed the door softly behind him. Only then could Chris give me the reassurance I had to have if I was to stay here for even one night. He kissed me, held me, stroked my back, my hair, soothed me until I could turn around and look at everything Bart had done to make this suite of rooms just as luxurious as they'd been before.

"It's only a bed, a reproduction of the original," Chris said softly, his eyes warm and understanding. "Our mother has not lain on this bed, darling. Bart read your scripts, remember that. What's here is here because you constructed the pattern for him to follow. You described that swan bed in such exquisite detail that he must have believed you wanted rooms just like our mother used to have. Maybe unconsciously you still do, and he knows that. Forgive us both for misunderstanding if I'm wrong. Think only that he wanted to please you and went to a great deal of trouble and expense to decorate this room as it used to be."

Numbly I shook my head, denying I'd ever wanted what she had. He didn't believe me. "Your wishes, Catherine! Your desire to have everything she did! I know it. Your sons know it. So don't blame any of us for being able to interpret your desires even when you cover them with clever subterfuges."

I wanted to hate him for knowing me so well. Yet my arms went around him. My face pressed against his shirtfront as I trembled and tried to hide the truth, even from myself. "Chris, don't be harsh with me," I sobbed. "It came as such a surprise to see these rooms, almost as they used to be when we came here to steal from her . . . and her husband . . ."

He held me hard against him. "What do you really feel about Joel?" I asked.

Considering thoughtfully before he answered, Chris spoke. "I like him, Cathy. He seems sincere and overjoyed that we're willing to let him stay on here."

"You told him he could stay?" I whispered.

"Sure, why not? We'll be leaving soon after Bart has that twenty-fifth birthday when he 'comes into his own.' And just think of the wonderful opportunity we'll have to learn more about the Foxworths. Joel can tell us more about our mother when she was young, and what life was like for all of them, and perhaps when we know the details, we will be able to understand how she could betray us, and why the grandfather wanted us dead. There has to be an awful truth hidden back in the past to warp Malcolm's brain so he could override our mother's natural instincts to keep her own children alive."

In my opinion Joel had said enough downstairs. I didn't want to know more. Malcolm Foxworth had been one of those strange humans born without conscience, unable to feel remorse for any wrong thing he did. There was no explaining him, and no way to understand.

Appealingly Chris gazed into my eyes, making his heart and soul vulnerable for my scorn to injure. "I'd like to hear about our mother's youth, Cathy, so I can understand what made her the way she turned out to be. She wounded us so deeply I feel neither one of us will ever recover until we do understand. I have forgiven her, but I can't forget. I want to understand so I can help *you* to forgive her . . ."

"Will that help?" I asked sarcastically. "It's too late for understanding or forgiving our mother, and, to be honest, I don't want to find understanding—for if I do, I might have to forgive her."

His arms dropped stiffly to his sides. Turning, he strode away from me. "I'm going out for our luggage now. Take a bath, and by the time you're finished I'll have everything unpacked." At the doorway he paused, not turning to look my way. "Try, really try, to use this as an opportunity to make peace with Bart. He's not beyond restoration, Cathy. You heard him behind the podium. That young man has a remarkable ability for oratory. His words make good sense. He's a leader now, Cathy, when he used to be so shy and introverted. We can count it a blessing that at last Bart has come out of his shell."

Humbly I bowed my head. "Yes, I'll do what I can. Forgive me, Chris, for being unreasonably strong-willed—again."

He smiled and left.

In "her" bath that joined a magnificent dressing room, I slowly disrobed while the black marble sunken tub filled. All about me were gold-framed mirrors to reflect back my nudity.

I was proud of my figure, still slim and firm, and my breasts that didn't sag. Stripped of everything, I lifted my arms to take out the few hairpins still left. *Déjà vu*-like, I pictured my mother as she must have stood, doing this same thing while she thought of her second and younger husband. Had she wondered where he was on the nights he spent with me? Had she known just who Bart's mistress was before my revelations at the Christmas party? Oh, I hoped she had!

An unremarkable dinner came and went.

Two hours later I was in the swan bed that had given me many daydreams, watching Chris undress. True to his word, he'd unpacked everything, hung my clothes as well as his own and stowed our underwear in the bureau. Now he looked tired, slightly unhappy. "Joel told me there will be servants coming for interviews tomorrow. I hope you feel up to that."

Startled, I sat up. "But I thought Bart would do his own hiring."

"No, he's leaving that up to you."

"Oh."

Chris hung his suit on the brass valet, again making me think of how much that valet seemed the same one Bart's father had used when he lived here—or in that other Fox-worth Hall. Haunted, that's what I was. Stark naked, Chris headed for the "his" bath. "I'll take a quick shower and join you shortly. Don't fall asleep until I'm through."

I lay in the semidarkness and stared around me, feeling strangely out of myself. In and out of my mother I flitted, sensing four children in a locked room overhead in the attic. Feeling the panic and guilt that surely must have been hers while that mean old father below lived on and on, threatening even when he was out of sight. Born bad, wicked, evil. It seemed I heard a whispery voice saying this over and over again. I closed my eyes and tried to stop this craziness. I

didn't hear any voices. I didn't hear ballet music playing, I
didn't. I couldn't smell the dry, musty scent of the attic. I
couldn't. I was fifty-two years old, not twelve, thirteen, fourteen, or fifteen.   •

All the old odors were gone. I smelled only new paint, new
wood, freshly applied wallpaper and fabric. New carpets, new
scatter rugs, new furniture. Everything new but for the fancy
antiques on the first floor. Not the real Foxworth Hall, only
an imitation. Yet, why had Joel come back if he liked being
a monk so much? Certainly he couldn't want all that money
when he'd grown accustomed to monastery austerity. There
must be some good reason he was here other than just wanting
to see what remained of his family. When the villagers must
have told him our mother was dead, still he'd stayed. Waiting his chance to meet Bart? What had he found in Bart that
kept him staying on? Even allowing Bart to put him to use
as a butler until we had a real one. Then I sighed. Why was I
making such a mystery of this when a fortune was involved.
Always it seemed money was the reason for doing anything
and everything.

Fatigue closed my eyes. I fought off sleep. I needed this
time to think of tomorrow, of this uncle come from nowhere.
Had we finally gained all that Momma had promised, only to
lose it to Joel? If he didn't try to break Momma's will, and we
managed to keep what we had, would it carry a price?

In the morning Chris and I descended the right side of the
dual staircase, feeling we had at long last come into "our own"
and we were finally in control of our lives. He caught my hand
and squeezed it, sensing from my expression that this house
no longer intimidated me.

We found Joel in the kitchen busily preparing breakfast.
He wore a long white apron and cocked on his head was a tall
chef's cap. Somehow it looked ludicrous on such a frail, tall,
old man. Only fat men should be chefs, I thought, even as I
felt grateful to have him take on a chore I'd never really liked.

"I hope you like Eggs Benedict," said Joel without glancing our way. To my surprise, his Eggs Benedict were wonderful. Chris had two servings. Then Joel was showing us rooms not yet decorated. He smiled at me crookedly. "Bart told me you like informal rooms with comfortable furniture, and he wants you to make these empty rooms cozy, in your own inimitable style."

Was he mocking me? He knew Chris and I were here only for a visit. Then I realized perhaps Bart might want me to help with the decorating and was reluctant to say so himself.

When I asked Chris if Joel could break our mother's will and take from Bart the money he felt so necessary for his self-esteem, Chris shook his head, admitting he really didn't know all the ins and outs of legal ramifications when a "dead" heir came back to life.

"Bart could give Joel enough money to see him through the few years he has left," I said, wracking my brain to remember every word of my mother's last will and testament. No mention of her older brothers, whom she'd believed dead.

When I came back from my thoughts, Joel was in the kitchen again, having found what he wanted in the pantry stocked with enough to feed a hotel. He spoke in reply to a question Chris had asked and I hadn't heard. His voice was somber. "Of course, the house isn't exactly the same, for no one uses wooden pegs for nails anymore. I put all the old furniture in my quarters. I don't *really* belong, so I'm going to stay in the servants' quarters over the garage."

"I've already said you shouldn't do that," said Chris with a frown. "It just wouldn't be right to let a family member live in such frugal style." Already we'd seen the huge garage, and the servants' quarters above could hardly be called frugal, just small.

Let him! I wanted to shout, but I said nothing.

Before I knew what was happening, Chris had Joel established on the second floor in the western wing. I sighed, somehow regretful that Joel would be under the same roof with us. But it would be all right; as soon as our curiosity was satisfied and Bart celebrated his birthday, we'd leave with Cindy for Hawaii.

In the library around two in the afternoon, Chris and I settled down to interview the man and woman who came with excellent references. There wasn't any fault I could find, except something furtive in both pairs of eyes. Uneasily I fidgeted from the way they looked so knowingly at both of us. "Sorry," said Chris, catching the slight negative gesture I made, "but we've already decided on another couple."

Husband and wife stood up to go. The woman turned in the doorway to give me a long, meaningful look. "I live in the village, *Mrs. Sheffield*," she said coldly. "Been there only five years, but we've heard a *great* deal about the Foxworths who live on the hill."

What she said made me turn my head away.

"Yes, I'm sure you have," said Chris dryly.

The woman snorted before she slammed the door behind them.

Next came a tall, aristocratic man with upright military bearing, immaculately dressed down to the slightest detail. He strode in and politely waited until Chris asked him to sit down.

"My name is Trevor Mainstream Majors," he said in his brisk British style. "I was born in Liverpool fifty-nine years ago. I was married in London when I was twenty-six, and my wife passed away three years ago, and my two sons live in North Carolina . . . so I am here hoping I can work in Virginia and visit my sons on my days off."

"Where did you work after you left the Johnstons?" asked Chris, looking down at the man's resume. "You seem to have excellent references until one year ago."

By this time Chris had invited the Englishman to seat himself. Trevor Majors shifted his long legs and adjusted his tie before he replied politely, "I worked for the Millersons, who moved away from the Hill about six months ago."

Silence. I'd heard my mother mention the Millersons many times. My heart began to beat more rapidly. "How long did you work for the Millersons?" asked Chris in a friendly way, as if he had no fears, even after having caught my look of anxiety.

"Not long, sir. They had five of their own children there, and nephews and nieces were always showing up, plus friends who stayed over for visits. I was their only servant. I did the cooking, the housework, the laundry, the chauffeuring, and it's an Englishman's pride and joy to do the gardening. What with chauffeuring the five children back and forth to school, dancing classes, sporting events, flicks, and such, I spent so much time on the road I seldom had the chance to prepare a decent meal. One day Mister Millerson complained I'd failed to mow the lawn and hadn't weeded the garden, and he hadn't eaten a good meal at home in two weeks. He snapped at me harshly because his dinner was late. Sir, that was rather much, when his wife had ordered me out on the road, kept me waiting while she shopped, sent me to pick up the children from the movies . . . and then I was supposed to have dinner on time. I told Mr. Millerson I wasn't a robot able to do everything, and all at once—and I quit. He was so angry he threatened he'd never give me a good reference. But if you wait a few days, he may cool down enough to realize I did the best I could under difficult circumstances."

I sighed, looked at Chris and made a furtive signal. This man was perfect. Chris didn't even look my way. "I think you will work out fine, Mister Majors. We'll hire you for a trial period of one month, and if at that time we find you unsatisfactory, we will terminate our employment agreement."

Chris looked at me. "That is, if my wife agrees . . ."

Silently I stood and nodded. We did need servants. I

didn't intend to spend my vacation dusting and cleaning a huge house.

"Sir, my lady, if you will, just call me Trevor. It will be my honor and pleasure to serve in this grand house." He'd jumped to his feet the moment I stood, and then, as Chris rose, he and Chris shook hands. "My pleasure indeed," he said as he smiled at us both approvingly.

In three days we hired three servants. It was easy enough when Bart was highly overpaying them.

The evening of our fifth full day here, I stood beside Chris on the balcony, staring at the mountains all around us, gazing up at that same old moon that used to look down on us as we lay on the roof of the old Foxworth Hall. That single great eye of God I'd believed when I was fifteen. Other places had given me romantic moons, beautiful moonlight to take away my fears and guilts. Here I felt the moon was a harsh investigator, ready to condemn us again, and then again and again.

"It's a beautiful night, isn't it?" asked Chris with his arm about my waist. "I like this balcony that Bart added to our suite of rooms. It doesn't distract from the outside appearance since it's on the side, and just look at the view it gives us of the mountains."

The blue-misted mountains had always represented to me a jagged fence to keep us forever trapped as prisoners of hope. Even now I saw their soft rounded tops as a barrier between me and freedom. *God, if you're up there, help me through the next few weeks.*

Near noon the next day, Chris and I, with Joel, stood on the front portico, watching the low-slung red Jaguar speeding up the steeply spiraling road that led to Foxworth Hall.

Bart drove with reckless, daredevil speed, as if challenging death to take him. I grew weak just watching the way he whipped around the dangerous curves.

"God knows he should have better sense," Chris grumbled. "He's always been accident prone—and look at the way he drives, as if he's got a hold on immortality."

"There are some who do," said Joel enigmatically.

I threw him a wondering glance, then looked again at that small red car that had cost a small fortune. Every year Bart bought a new car, never any color but red; he'd tried all the luxury cars to find which he liked best. This one was his favorite so far, he'd informed us in a brief letter.

Squealing to a stop, he burned rubber and spoiled the perfection of the curving drive with long black streaks. Waving first, Bart threw off his sunglasses, shook his head to bring his dark tumbled locks back into order, ignored the door, and jumped from his convertible, pulling off driving gloves and tossing them carelessly onto the seat. Racing up the steps, he seized me up in his strong arms and planted several kisses on my cheeks. I was stunned with the warmth of his greeting. Eagerly I responded. The moment my lips touched his cheek he put me down and shoved me away as if he tired of me very rapidly.

He stood in full sunlight, six feet three, brilliant intelligence and strength in his dark brown eyes, his shoulders broad, his well-muscled body tapering down to slim hips and long legs. He was so handsome in his casual white sports outfit. "You're looking great, Mother, just great." His dark eyes swept over me from heels to hair. "Thanks for wearing that red dress . . . it's my favorite color."

I reached for Chris's hand. "Thank you, Bart, I wore this dress just for you." Now he could say something nice to Chris, I hoped. I waited for that. Instead, Bart ignored Chris and turned to Joel.

"Hi, Uncle Joel. Isn't my mother just as beautiful as I said?"

Chris's hand clenched mine so hard it hurt. Always Bart found a way to insult the only father he could remember.

"Yes, Bart, your mother is very beautiful," said Joel in that whispery, raspy voice. "In fact, she's exactly the way I would imagine my sister Corrine looked at her age."

"Bart, say hello to your—" and here I faltered. I wanted to say *Father* but I knew Bart would deny that rudely. So I said *Chris*. Turning his dark and sometimes savage eyes briefly to stare at Chris, Bart bit out a harsh hello. "You don't ever age either, do you?" he said in an accusatory tone.

"I'm sorry about that, Bart," answered Chris evenly. "But time will do its job eventually."

"Let's hope so."

I could have slapped Bart.

Turning around, Bart ignored both Chris and me and surveyed the lawns, the house, the luxurious flower beds, the lush shrubbery, the garden paths, the birdbaths, and other statuary, and smiled with an owner's pride. "It's grand, really grand. Just as I hoped it would be. I've looked the world over and no mansion can compare with Foxworth Hall."

His dark eyes moved to clash with mine. "I know what you're thinking, Mother, I know this isn't truly the best house yet, but one day it will be. I intend to build, and add new wings, and one day this house will outshine every palace in Europe. I'm going to concentrate my energies on making Foxworth Hall truly an historic landmark."

"Who will you impress when you accomplish that?" asked Chris. "The world no longer tolerates great houses and great wealth, or respects those who gain it by inheritance."

Oh, damn it! Chris so seldom said anything tactless or rude. Why had he said what he did? Bart's face flamed beneath his deep bronze tan. "I intend to increase my fortune with my own efforts!" Bart flared, stepping closer to Chris. Because he was so lean, and Chris had put on weight, especially in the chest, he appeared to tower over Chris. I watched the man I thought of as my husband stare challengingly into my son's eyes.

"I've been doing that for you," said Chris.

To my surprise, Bart seemed pleased. "You mean as trustee you have increased my share of the inheritance?"

"Yes, it was easy enough," said Chris laconically. "Money makes money, and the investments I made for you have paid off handsomely."

"Ten to one I could have done better."

Chris smiled ironically. "I could have predicted you'd thank me like that."

From one to the other I looked, feeling sorry for both of them. Chris was a mature man who knew who and what he was, and he could ride along on that confidence with ease, while Bart was still struggling to find himself and his place in the world.

My son, my son, when will you learn humility, gratitude? Many a night I'd seen Chris working over figures, trying to decide on the best investments, as if he knew that sooner or later Bart would accuse him of poor financial judgment.

"You'll have your chance to prove yourself soon enough," Chris responded. He turned to me. "Let's take a walk, Cathy, down to the lake."

"Wait a minute," called Bart, appearing furious that we'd leave when he'd just come home. I was torn between wanting to escape with Chris and the desire to please my son. "Where's Cindy?"

"She'll be coming soon," I called back. "Right now Cindy is visiting a girlfriend's home. You might be interested to learn that Jory is going to bring Melodie here for a vacation."

Bart just stood there staring at me, perhaps appalled with the idea, and then came that strange excitement to replace all other emotions on his handsome, tanned face. "Bart," I said, resisting Chris's desire to hurry me away from a known source of trouble, "the house is truly beautiful. All that you've done to change it has been a wonderful improvement."

Again he appeared surprised. "Mother, you mean it's not exactly the same? I thought it was . . ."

"Oh, no, Bart. The balcony outside our suite of rooms wasn't there before."

Bart whirled on his great-uncle. "You told me it was!" he shouted.

Smiling sardonically, Joel stepped forward. "Bart, my son, I didn't lie. I never lie. The original Hall did have that balcony. My father's mother ordered it put there. And by using that balcony, she was able to sneak in her lover without the servants seeing. Later she ran off with that lover without waking her husband, who kept their bedroom door locked and the key hidden. Malcolm ordered the balcony torn down when he was the owner . . . but it does add a certain kind of charm to that side of the house."

Satisfied, Bart turned again to Chris and me. "See, Mother, you don't know anything at all about this house. Uncle Joel is the expert. He's described to me in great detail all the furniture, the paintings, and, in the end, I'll have not only the same, but better than the original."

Bart hadn't changed. He was still obsessed, still wanting to be a carbon copy of Malcolm Foxworth, if not in looks, in personality and in determination to be the richest man in the world, no matter what he did to gain that title.

My Second Son

Not long after Bart arrived home, he began making elaborate plans for his upcoming birthday party. Apparently, to my surprise and delight, he'd made many friends in Virginia during the summer vacations he'd spent here. It used to hurt that he spent such a few of his vacation days with us in California, where I had considered he belonged. But now it seemed he knew people we'd never heard of, and had met young men and women in college that he intended to invite down to help him celebrate.

I'd only spent a few days at Foxworth Hall and already the monotony of days with nothing to do but eat, sleep, read, look at TV, and roam the gardens and woods had me on edge and eager to escape as soon as possible. The deep silence of the mountainside gripped me in its spell of isolation and despair. The silence wore on my nerves. I wanted to hear voices, many voices, hear the telephone ring, have people drop in and say hello, and nobody did. There was a group of local society members that had known the Foxworths well, and this was the very group Chris and I had to avoid. There were old friends in New York and California that I wanted to call and invite to Bart's party, but I didn't dare without Bart's approval. Restlessly I prowled the grand rooms alone, and sometimes with Chris. He and I walked the gardens, strolled through the woods, quiet sometimes, garrulous others.

He had his old hobby of watercoloring to begin again, and that kept him busy, but I wasn't supposed to dance anymore. Nevertheless I did my ballet exercises every day of my life just to keep myself slim and supple, and willingly enough I'd pose when he asked me to do that. Joel came upon me once as I held on to a chair in our sitting room, exercising in red leotards. I heard his gasp from the open doorway and turned to find him staring at me as if I were naked. "What's wrong?" I asked worriedly. "Has something terrible happened?"

He threw his thin, long, pale hands wide, his face expressive as he scanned over my body with contempt.

"Aren't you a little old to try to be seductive?"

"Have you ever heard of exercise, Joel?" I asked impatiently. "You don't have to enter this wing. Just stay away from our rooms and your eyes won't be so scandalized."

"You are disrespectful to someone older and wiser," he said sharply.

"If I am, I apologize. But your words and your expression offend me. If there is to be peace in this house during our visit, stay away from me, Joel, while I am in my own wing. This huge house has more than enough space to give us all privacy without closing the doors."

He stiffly turned away, but not before I'd seen the indignation in his eyes. I hurried to stare after him, wondering if I could be mistaken, and he was only a harmless old man who couldn't mind his own business. But I didn't call out to apologize. Instead I took off my leotards, put on shorts and a top, and with thoughts of Jory and his wife coming soon comforting me, I went to find Chris. I hesitated outside Bart's office door and listened to him talking to the caterer, planning for a minimum of two hundred guests. Just listening to him made me feel numb inside. *Oh, Bart, you don't realize some won't come, and if they do, Lord help us all.*

As I continued to stand there, I heard him name several of his invited guests, and they were not all from this country. Many were notables from Europe that he'd met on his tours. Throughout his college days he'd been tireless in his efforts to see the world and to meet important people, people who ruled and dominated either with political power, brains, or financial wizardry. I thought his restlessness was due to his inability to be happy in one place, and he was always longing for the next greener, farther field.

"They'll all come," he said to the party on the other end of the line. "When they read my invitation, they won't be able to decline."

He hung up, then swung his chair about to face me. "Mother! Are you eavesdropping?"

"It's a habit I caught from you, my darling."

He scowled.

"Bart, why don't you just make your party a family affair? Or invite just your best friends. The villagers around here won't want to come. According to the tales my mother used to tell us, they have always disliked the Foxworths, who had too much when they had too little. The Foxworths came and went while the villagers had to stay. And please don't include the local society, even if Joel has told you they are his friends, and therefore yours and ours."

"Afraid that your sins will be found out, Mother?" he asked without mercy. I was accustomed to this, but nevertheless I recoiled inwardly. Was it so terrible that Chris and I lived together as man and wife? Weren't the newspapers full of much worse crimes than ours?

"Oh, come, Mother, don't look like that. Let's be happy for a change." His bronzed face took on a cheerful, excited look, as if nothing I said would daunt his excitement. "Mother, be excited for me, please. I'm ordering the best of everything. When the word spreads around, and it will because my caterer is the best in Virginia, and he loves to boast, no one will be able to resist coming to my party. They'll hear I'm sending to New York and to Hollywood for entertainers, and what's more, I'm sure everyone will want to see Jory and Melodie dance."

Surprise and happiness filled me. "Have you asked them?"

"No, but how can my own brother and sister-in-law refuse? You see, Mother, I'm planning to hold my party outdoors in the garden, in the moonlight. The lawns will be all lit up with golden globes. I'm having fountains put everywhere, and colored lights will play upon the sprinkling water. There'll be imported champagne by the crates, and every other liquor you can name. The food will be the best. I'm having a theater constructed in the midst of a wonderworld of fantasy where tables will be covered with beautiful cloths of every color. Color upon color. Flowers will be banked all over. I'll show the world just what a Foxworth can do."

On and on he enthused.

When I left his office and found Chris talking to one of the gardeners, I felt happy, reassured. Perhaps this was going to be the summer when Bart found himself, at last.

It would be as Chris had always predicted: Bart would not only inherit a fortune, he would inherit his sense of pride and worth and find himself . . . and pray God he found the right self.

Two days later I was in his office again, seated in one of his luxurious, deep, leather chairs, amazed to see how much he'd accomplished in his short time home. Apparently all this special extra office equipment had been ready and waiting to be installed the moment he was here to direct the placement. The small bedroom beyond the library he used for his office, where our detested grandfather had lived until he died, had been converted into a room of filing cabinets. The room where our grandfather's nurses had stayed became an office for Bart's secretary when or if he ever found one who met his stiff requirements. A computer dominated one long, curving desk, with its two printers that typed out different letters even as Bart and I conversed. It had surprised me to see him typing faster than I could. The drumming of the printers was muffled by heavy Plexiglas covers.

Proudly he showed me how he could keep in touch with the world while staying at home, just by pushing buttons and joining up with a program called "The Source." Only then did I learn that one summer he'd taken two months of computer programming. "And, Mother, I can execute my buy and sell orders and avail myself of expert technical and fundamental data just by using this computer. I'll occupy my time that way until I open my own law firm." For a moment he looked reflective, even doubtful. I still believed that he'd gone to Harvard just because his father had. Law held no real interest for him at all; he was only interested in making money, and then more money.

"Don't you have sufficient money already, Bart? What is it you can't buy?"

Something boyishly wistful and sweet visited his dark eyes. "Respect, Mother. I don't have any talent, like you, like Jory. I can't dance. I can't draw a decent representation of a flower, much less draw the human form." He was referring indirectly to Chris and his painting hobby. "When I visit an art museum, I'm baffled by everyone's awe. I don't see anything wonderful about the 'Mona Lisa.' I see only a bland-faced, rather plain-looking woman who couldn't have been exciting. I don't appreciate classical music, any kind of music . . . and I've been told I have a rather good singing voice. I used to try and sing when I was a kid. Goofy kind of kid, wasn't I? Must have given you a million laughs." He grinned appealingly, then spread his arms supplicatingly. "I have no artistic talents, and so I fall back upon the kind of figures I can readily understand, those representing dollars and cents.

I look around in museums, and the only things I see to admire are jewels."

Sparkle came to his dark eyes. "The glitter and gleam of diamonds, rubies, emeralds, pearls . . . all that I can appreciate. Gold, mountains of gold—that I can understand. I see the beauty in gold, silver, copper, and oil. Do you know I visited Washington just to watch gold minted into coins? I felt a certain kind of elation, as if one day all that gold would be mine."

Admiration faded and pity for him flooded me. "What about women, Bart? What about love? A family? Good friends? Children? Don't you hope to fall in love and marry?"

He stared at me blankly for a moment or so, drumming his strong, square-nailed fingertips on his desktop before he got up to stand before a wide wall of windows, staring out at the gardens and beyond them the blue-misted mountains. "I've experienced sex, Mother. I didn't expect to enjoy it, but I did. I felt my body betrayed my will. But I've never been in love. I can't imagine how it would be to devote myself to one woman when so many are beautiful and only too willing. I see a beautiful girl walk by, I turn and stare, only to find her turning and staring back at me. It's so easy to get them into my bed. No challenge at all." He paused and turned his head to look at me. "I use women, Mother, and sometimes I'm ashamed of myself. I take them, discard them, and even pretend I don't know them when I meet them again. They all end up hating me."

He met my wide eyes with watchful challenge. "Aren't you shocked?" he asked pleasantly. "Or am I just the churlish type you always expected?"

I swallowed, hoping this time I could say the right thing. In the past it seemed I'd never said anything right. I doubted anyone could say words that would change Bart from what he was, and what he wanted to be . . . if he even knew. "I suspect you are a product of your times," I began in a soft voice, without recriminations. "I almost pity your generation for missing out on the most beautiful aspect of falling in love. Where is the romance in your kind of taking, Bart? What do you give to the women you go to bed with? Don't you know it takes time to build a loving, lasting relationship? It doesn't happen overnight. One-night stands don't form commitments. You can look at a beautiful body and desire that body, but that's not love."

His burning eyes showed such intensity and interest I was encouraged to go on, especially when he asked, "How do you explain love?"

It was a trap he baited, knowing the loves of my life had all been ill-fated. Still I answered, hoping to save him from all the mistakes he was sure to make. "I don't explain love, Bart. I don't think anyone can. It grows from day to day from having contact with that other person who understands your needs, and you understand theirs. It starts with a faltering flutter that touches your heart and makes you vulnerable to everything beautiful. You see beauty where before you'd seen ugliness. You feel glowing inside, so happy without knowing why. You appreciate what before you'd ignored. Your eyes meet with the eyes of the one you love, and you see reflected in them your own feelings, your own hopes and desires, and you're happy just to be with that person. Even when you don't touch, you still feel the warmth of being with that one person who fills all your thoughts. Then one day you do touch. Perhaps his hand, or her hand, and it feels good. It doesn't even have to be an intimate touch. An excitement begins to grow, so you want to be with that person, not to have sex . . . just to be with them and gradually grow toward one another. You share your life in words before you share your body. Only then do you start seriously thinking about having sex with that person. You begin to dream about it. Still you put it off, waiting, waiting for the right moment. You want this love to stay, to never end. So you go slowly, slowly toward the ultimate experience of your life.

Day by day, minute by minute, second by second, and from moment to moment you anticipate that one person, knowing you won't be disappointed, knowing that person will be faithful, dependable . . . even when she's out of sight, or you're out of sight. There's trust, contentment, peace, happiness when you have genuine love. To be in love is like turning on a light in a dark room. All of a sudden everything becomes bright and visible. You're never alone because she loves you, and you love her."

I paused for breath, saw his continued interest that gave me the courage to go on. "I want that for you, Bart. More than all the billions of tons of gold in the world, more than all the jewels in vaults, I want you to find a wonderful girl to love. Forget money. You have enough. Look around, open your eyes and discover the joys of living, and forget your pursuit of money."

Musingly, he said, "So that's the way women feel about love and sex. I always wondered. It's not a man's kind of feeling, I do know that . . . still, what you said is interesting."

He turned away before he went on. "Truthfully, I don't know just what I want out of life but more money. They tell me I'll make an excellent attorney because I know how to debate. Yet I can't decide what branch of law I want. I don't want to be a criminal lawyer like my father was, for I'd often have to defend those I know were guilty. I couldn't do that. I think corporate law would be a bore. I've thought about politics, and this is the area I find most exciting, but I've got my damned psychological background to mar my record . . . so how can I go into politics?"

Rising from behind his desk, he stepped close enough to catch my hand in his. "I like what you're telling me. Tell me more about your loves, about which man you loved best. Was it Julian, your first husband? Or was it that wonderful doctor named Paul? I think I would have loved him if I could remember him. He married you to give me his name. I wish

I could see him in my memory, like Jory can, but I can't. Jory remembers him well. He even remembers seeing my father." His manner turned very intense as he leaned to lock his eyes with mine. "Tell me that you loved my father best. Say *he* was the one and only man who really seized your heart. Don't tell me you only used him for your revenge against your mother! Don't tell me that you used his love to escape from the love of your own brother."

I couldn't speak.

His brooding, morose, dark eyes studied me. "Don't you realize yet that you and your brother have always managed with your incestuous relationship to ruin and contaminate my life? I used to hope and pray someday you'd leave him, but it never happens. I've adjusted to the fact that the two of you are obsessed with one another and perhaps enjoy your relationship more because it is against the will of God."

Snared again! I rose to my feet, knowing he'd used his sweet voice to beguile me into his trap.

"Yes, I loved your father, Bart, don't you ever doubt that. I admit I wanted revenge for all that our mother had done to us, so I went after my stepfather. Then, when I had him, and I knew I loved him, and he loved me, I felt I'd trapped myself as well as him. He couldn't marry me. He loved me in one way—and my mother in another way. He was torn between us. I decided to end his indecision by becoming pregnant. Even then he was undecided. Only on the night when he believed my story of being imprisoned by his own wife did he turn against her and say he'd marry me. I thought her money would bind him to her forever, but he would have married me."

I rose to leave. Not a word did Bart say to give me a hint as to his thoughts. At the door I turned to look back at him. He was seated again in his desk chair, his elbows on the blotter, his hands cradling his bowed head. "Do you think anyone will ever love me for myself and not for my money, Mother?"

My heart skipped a beat.

"Yes, Bart. But you won't find a girl around here who doesn't know you're very wealthy. Why don't you go away? Settle in the Northeast or in the West. Then when you find a girl she won't know you are rich, especially if you work as an ordinary lawyer . . ."

He looked up then. "I've already had my surname changed legally, Mother."

Dread filled me, and I didn't really need to ask, "What is your last name now?"

"Foxworth," he said, confirming my suspicion. "After all, I can't be a Winslow when my father was not your husband. And to keep Sheffield is deceitful. Paul wasn't my father, nor was your brother, thank God."

I shivered and turned icy with apprehension. This was the first step . . . turning himself into another Malcolm, what I'd feared most. "I wish you'd chosen Winslow for your surname, Bart. That would have pleased your dead father."

"Yes, I'm sure," he said dryly. "And I did consider that seriously. But in choosing Winslow, I would forfeit my legitimate right to the Foxworth name. It's a good name, Mother, a name respected by everyone except those villagers, who don't count anyway. I feel Foxworth Hall truly belongs to me without contamination, without guilt." His eyes took on a brilliant, happy glow. "You see, and Uncle Joel agrees, not everyone hates me and thinks I am less than Jory." He paused to watch my reaction. I tried to show nothing. He seemed disappointed. "Leave, Mother. I've got a long day of work ahead of me."

I risked his anger by lingering long enough to say, "While you're shut away in this office, Bart, I want you to keep remembering your family loves you very much, and all of us want what's best for you. If more money will make you feel better about yourself, then make yourself the richest man in the world. Just find happiness, that's all we want for you. Find your niche, just where you fit, that's the most important thing."

Closing his office door behind me, I was headed for the stairs when I almost bumped into Joel. A guilty look flashed momentarily through the blue of his watery eyes. I guessed he'd been listening to Bart and me. But hadn't I done the same thing inadvertently? "I'm sorry I didn't see you in the shadows, Joel."

"I didn't mean to eavesdrop," he said with a peculiar look. "Those who expect to hear evil will not be disappointed," and away he scurried like an old church mouse, lean from lack of enough fuel to feed his appetite for making trouble. He made me feel guilty, ashamed. Suspicious, always so damned suspicious of anyone named Foxworth.

Not that I didn't have just cause.

My First Son

Six days before the party, Jory and Melodie flew into a local airport. Chris and I were there to meet them with the kind of enthusiasm you saved for those you hadn't seen for years, and we'd parted less than ten days ago. Jory was immediately chagrined because Bart hadn't come along to welcome them to his fabulous new home.

"He's busy in the gardens, Jory, Melodie, and asked us to give you his apologies" (although he hadn't). Both looked at me as if they knew differently. Quickly I went into details of how Bart was supervising hordes of workmen come to change our lawns into paradise, or something as near that as possible.

Jory smiled to hear of such an ostentatious party; he preferred small, intimate parties where everyone knew each other. He said pleasantly enough, "Nothing new under the sun. Bart's always too busy when it comes to me and my wife."

I stared up into his face so like that of my adolescent first husband, Julian, who had also been my dancing partner. The husband whose memory still hurt and filled me with that same old tormenting guilt. Guilt that I tried to erase by loving his son best. "Every time I see you you look more like your father."

We were seated side by side, as Melodie sat beside Chris, and occasionally said a few words to him. Jory laughed and put his arms about me, inclining his dark, handsome head to brush my cheek with his warm lips. "Mom . . . you say that each and every time you see me. When am I going to reach the zenith of being my father?"

Laughing, too, I released him and settled back to cross my legs and stare out at the beautiful countryside. The rolling hills, the misty mountains with the tops hidden in the clouds. Near Heaven, I kept thinking. I had to force my attention back to Jory, who had so many virtues Julian had never possessed, could never have possessed. Jory was more like Chris in personality than like Julian, although that, too, filled me with guilt, with shame, for it could have been different between Julian and I—but for Chris.

At the age of twenty-nine, Jory was a wonderfully handsome man, with long, strong, beautiful legs and firm, round buttocks that made all the women stare when he danced onto stage wearing tights. His thick hair was blue-black and curly, but not frizzy; his lips exceptionally red and sensuously shaped; his nose a perfect slope with nostrils that could flare wide with anger or passion. He had a hot temper he'd learned to control a long time ago, mostly because of all the control it took for him to tolerate Bart. Jory's inner beauty radiated from him with an electric force, a *joie de vivre*. His beauty was more than mere handsomeness; he had the added strength of a certain spiritual quality and was like Chris in his cheerful optimism, his faith that all that happened in his life had to be for the best.

Jory wore his success with grace, with touching humility and dignity, displaying none of the arrogance that had been Julian's even when he had performed poorly.

So far Melodie had said very little, as if she contained

volumes of secrets she was dying to spill out, but for some reason was holding back, awaiting her opportunity to be center stage. Customarily my daughter-in-law and I were very good friends. Countless times she twisted around in the front seat to smile back at me happily. "Stop teasing," I admonished. "What's this good news you have to tell us?"

Again came that taut look on her face as she flicked her eyes to Jory, making her appear a locked gold purse about to burst if she didn't tell us soon. "Is Cindy there yet?" she asked.

When I said no, Melodie turned again to face the windshield. Jory winked. "We're going to keep you in suspense a while longer, so everyone can enjoy our surprise to its full extent. Besides, right now Dad's so intent on seeing we reach that house safely that he couldn't give our secret the appreciation it needs."

After an hour's ride we were turning onto our private road, which spiraled up the mountain, with deep ravines or precipices always on one side, forcing Chris to drive even more carefully.

Once we were in the house and I'd shown them around downstairs, and they had exclaimed and oh'ed and ah'ed, Melodie came flying into my arms, ducking her head shyly down on my shoulder, for she was inches taller than I. "Go on, darling," encouraged Jory softly.

Quickly she released me and threw a proud smile at Jory, who smiled back at her reassuringly. Then she was spilling out the contents of that bulging gold purse.

"Cathy, I wanted to wait for Cindy and tell you all at once, but I'm so happy I'm bursting. I'm pregnant! You just don't know how thrilled I am when I've been wanting this baby ever since the first year Jory and I married. I'm a little over two months along. Our baby is due in early January."

Stunned, I could only stare at her before I glanced at Jory, who had told me many times he didn't want to begin a family until he'd had ten years at the top. Still, he stood there smiling and looking as proud as any man would at this instant, as if he were accepting this unexpected and unplanned child very well.

That was enough to make me overjoyed. "Oh, Melodie, Jory, I'm so thrilled for you both. A baby! I'm going to be a grandmother." Then I sobered. Did I want to be a grandmother? Chris was slapping Jory on the back as if he were the first man ever to impregnate his wife; then he was embracing Melodie and asking questions about how she felt and if she was experiencing morning sickness—just like the doctor he was.

Because he was seeing something I wasn't, I looked at her more closely. She had shadows beneath hollowed eyes, and was much too thin to be pregnant. However, there was nothing that could steal from Melodie her classical type of cool blond beauty. She moved with grace, appearing regal even when she just picked up a magazine and flipped through it—as she was doing now. I was baffled. "What's wrong, Melodie?"

"Nothing," she said, gone stiff for no apparent reason, telling me instead that everything was wrong.

My eyes met briefly with Jory's. He nodded, indicating he'd tell me later what was bothering Melodie.

All the way back to Foxworth Hall I'd been dreading the meeting between Bart and his older brother, fearing there would be an ugly scene to start everything out wrong. I strode to a window overlooking a side lawn and saw that Bart was on the racket ball court, playing by himself with the same kind of intensity to win, as though he had a partner to batter down to defeat. "Bart!" I called, opening a French door, "your brother and his wife are here."

"Be there in a sec," he called back, and continued to play.

"Where are all the workers?" asked Jory, looking around at the spacious gardens empty now of anyone but Bart. I explained most left about four, wanting to drive home before they were caught in the late evening traffic.

Finally Bart threw down his racket and sauntered our way, a broad, welcoming smile on his face. We all stepped onto a side terrace covered with multicolored flagstones and decorated with many live plants and pretty patio furniture with colorful umbrellas to shield us from the sun. Melodie seemed to pull in her breath and straighten her spine as she moved closer to Jory. She didn't need his protection this time. Bart's steps picked up until eventually he was running, and Jory was speeding to greet him. My heart could have burst . . . brothers, at last! Like they had been when both were very young. They pounded each other on the back, ruffled each other's hair, and then Bart was pumping Jory's hand up and down, slapping him on the shoulder again, the way men often do. He turned to look Melodie over.

All his enthusiasm died. "Hi, Melodie," he said briefly, then went on to congratulate Jory for their successes on stage and the adulation they received. "Proud of you both," he said with a strange smile.

"We've got news for you, brother," said Jory. "You are now looking at the happiest husband and wife in the world, for we're going to be parents come January."

Bart gazed at Melodie, who avoided meeting his eyes. She half turned toward Jory, with the sun behind her turning her honey-blonde hair fiery red near her scalp, making a golden haze of the outer strands, so it almost seemed she was sporting a golden halo. Madonna pure she stood in profile as if poised for flight. The grace of her long neck, the gentle slope of her small nose, the fullness of her pouting rosy lips gave her the kind of ethereal beauty that had helped to make her one of the most beautiful and admired ballerinas in America.

"Pregnancy becomes you, Melodie," Bart said softly, ignoring what Jory was telling him about canceling one year of bookings so he could be with Melodie throughout her pregnancy and help after the baby was born in all kinds of husbandly ways.

Bart stared toward the French door where Joel stood

silently watching our family reunion. I resented his being there; then, ashamed, I gestured him forward even as Bart called out, "Come, let me introduce you to my brother and his wife."

Advancing slowly, Joel shuffled along the flagstones, making each step whisper. Gravely he greeted Jory and Melodie after Bart's introduction, not extending his hand to be shaken. "I hear that you are a dancer," he said to Jory.

"Yes . . . I've worked all my life to be called that."

Joel turned and left without another word to anyone.

"Just who is that weird old man?" asked Jory. "Mom, I thought you told us that both your maternal uncles died in accidents when they were very young."

I shrugged and let Bart explain.

In no time at all, we had Jory and his wife established in a very rich-looking suite with heavy red velvet draperies, red carpet, and dark paneled walls that made the suite exceedingly masculine. Melodie took a look around, wrinkling her nose a bit in distaste. "Rich . . . nice . . . really," she said with heavy effort.

Jory laughed. "Honey, we can't always expect white walls with blue carpet, can we? I like this room, Bart. It looks like your kind of bedroom—classy."

Bart wasn't listening to Jory. He still had his eyes glued on Melodie, who glided from one piece of furniture to another, running her long, graceful fingers over the slick, polished tops before she glanced into the adjacent sitting room and then went on into the magnificent bath with an old-fashioned walnut tub lined with pewter. She laughed to see the tub. "Oh, I'm going to enjoy that. Look at the depth—water right up to your chin if you want it that way."

"Fair women look so dramatic in dark settings," said Bart almost without realizing he'd spoken. No one said a word, not even Jory, who gave him a hard look.

In that bath was also a walk-in shower and a lovely dressing table of the same walnut with a three-winged gold-framed mirror, so the occupant seated on the velvet-covered stool could see herself from every angle.

We dined early and sat outside on a terrace in the twilight hours. Joel didn't join us, and for that I was grateful. Bart had little to say, but he couldn't keep his eyes off Melodie in her frail blue dress that molded to every delicate curve of thigh, hip, waist, and bust. I felt a sinking sensation to see him studying her so closely, with desire written clearly in those dark, blistering eyes.

At the breakfast table on the terrace outside the dining room, the daisies were yellow. We had hope how. We could look at yellow and not fear we'd never see sunlight again.

Chris was laughing at something funny Jory had just reported, while Bart only smiled, still keeping his eyes on Melodie, who picked at her breakfast without appetite. "Everything I eat comes up sooner or later," she explained with a small look of embarrassment. "It's not the food, it's me. I'm supposed to eat slowly and not think about losing the meal . . . but that's all I'm thinking of." Just beyond her shoulder, in the shadows of a giant live palm planted in a huge clay pot, Joel had his gaze riveted also on Melodie, studying her profile. Then he was looking at Jory, narrowing his eyes again.

"Joel," I called, "step forward and join us for breakfast."

He advanced reluctantly, cautiously, whispering his soft-soled shoes over the flagstones, holding his arms crosswise over his chest, as if he wore an invisible coarse, brown, homespun monk's habit, and his hands were tucked neatly out of sight up the wide sleeves. He seemed a judge sent to weigh us in for Heaven's pearly gates. His voice was slight and polite as he greeted Jory and Melodie, nodding in answer to their questions that plied him for information on what it was like to live as a monk. "I couldn't bear life without women," said Jory, "without music and lots of different types of people all around. I get a little from this person, something else from another. It takes hundreds of friends to keep me happy. Already I'm missing those in our ballet company."

"It takes all kinds to make the world go round," said Joel, "and the Lord giveth before he taketh away." Then he ambled off, his head bowed low, as if he whispered prayers and fingered a rosary. "The Lord must have known what he was doing when he made each of us so different," I heard him murmur.

Jory swiveled about in his chair to stare after Joel. "So that's our great uncle, who we presumed died in a skiing accident. Mom, wouldn't it be odd if the other brother turned up as well?"

Jumping to his feet, Bart's face flamed furious. "Don't be ridiculous! Malcolm's eldest son died when his motorcycle went over a precipice, and they found his body and buried it. It's in the family cemetery that I've visited often. According to Uncle Joel, his father sent detectives looking for his lost second son, and that's one reason my uncle had to stay hidden in that monastery, until eventually he grew used to it and began to fear life on the outside." He flicked his eyes at me, as if to recognize the fact that we, too, as children, had grown accustomed to our imprisoned life, fearing the outside.

"He says when you are isolated for long periods, you begin to see people as they really are—as if distance gives you better perspective."

Chris and I met eyes. Yes, we knew about isolation. Standing, Chris gestured to Jory and offered to show him around. "Bart's planning horse stables, so he can have fox hunts like Malcolm used to have. Perhaps one day we may even want to join in that kind of sport."

"Sport?" queried Melodie, rising gracefully and hurrying to catch up with Jory. "I don't call a pack of hungry hounds chasing a cute little harmless fox a true sport—it's barbaric, that's what!"

"That's the trouble with those in the ballet—too sensitive for the real world," Bart retorted before he stalked off in a different direction.

Later on in the afternoon, I found Chris in the foyer watching Jory work out before the mirrors, using a chair for a barre. The two men shared the kind of relationship I hoped would develop one day between Chris and Bart. Father and son, both admiring and respecting the other. My arms crossed over my breasts to hug myself. I was so happy to have all my family together, or at least it would be when Cindy arrived. And the expected baby would be more cement to bind us together . . .

Jory had warmed up enough and began to dance to *The Firebird* music. Whirling so fast he was a dazzling blur, whipping his legs, leaping into the air, bounding to land as light as a feather so you didn't hear his feet hit the floor. His muscles rippled as he *jetéed* again and again, spreading his legs so his outstretched arms allowed his fingertips to touch his toes. I filled with excitement, watching him perform, knowing he was showing off for our benefit.

"Would you look at those *jetés?*" said Chris when he caught sight of me. "Why, he clears the floor by twelve feet or more. I don't believe what I'm seeing!"

"Ten feet, not twelve," corrected Jory as he whirled by, spinning, spinning, covering the immense space of the foyer in mere seconds. Then he fell breathlessly down on a quilted floor mat put there so he'd have a place to rest without his body sweat fading the delicate and fancy chair coverings.

"Damned hard floor if I fall . . . ," he gasped as he lay back and rested on his elbows.

"And the spread of his legs when he leaps, it's unbelievable he can be so supple at his age."

"Dad, I'm only twenty-nine, not thirty-nine!" protested Jory, who had a thing about growing older and losing the spotlight to a younger *danseur*. "I've got at least eleven good years ahead before I begin to slide."

I knew exactly what he was thinking as he sprawled there on the mat, looking so much like Julian. It was as if I were twenty or so again. The muscles of all male dancers approaching forty began to harden and become brittle so that their once magnificent bodies weren't as attractive to the audience any longer. Off with the old, on with the new . . . the fear of all performers, although ballerinas with their layer of fat under their skin could hold on longer. Falling on the mat beside Jory, I sat cross-legged in my pink slacks.

"Jory, you are going to last longer than most *danseurs*, so stop worrying. It's a long and glamorous road you have to travel to reach forty, and who knows, maybe you'll be fifty before you retire."

"Yeah, sure," he said, tucking his hands behind his curly head and staring up at the distant ceiling. "Fourteenth in a long line of dancers has to be the lucky number, doesn't it?"

How many times had I heard him say he couldn't live without dancing? Since he was a small boy of two, I'd put his feet on the road to where he was now.

Down the stairs Melodie glided, looking beautiful and fresh from a recent bath and shampoo, seeming a fragile spring flower in her blue leotards. "Jory, my doctor said I could keep on with light practice, and I want to dance as long as possible to keep my muscles supple and long . . . so dance with me, lover. Dance and dance, and then let's dance some more."

Instantly Jory bounded to his feet and whirled to the foot of the stairs, where he fell upon one knee in the romantic position of a prince seeing the princess of his dreams. "My pleasure, my lady . . ." and swinging her off her feet, he whirled with her in his arms before he put her down with the skilled practice and grace that made her seem to have the weight of a feather. They whirled around, always dancing for the other, as once Julian and I had danced for the pure delight of being young, alive, and able. Tears came to my eyes as I stood beside Chris and watched them.

Sensing my thoughts, Chris put his arm about my shoulder and drew me closer. "They're beautiful together, aren't they? Made for each other, I would say. If I squint my eyes and see them hazily, I see you dancing with Julian . . . only you were far prettier, Catherine, far prettier . . ."

Behind us Bart snorted.

Whipping around, I saw Joel had trailed behind Bart like a well-trained puppy and at his heel he stopped, his head low, his hands still tucked up those invisible brown homespun sleeves. "The Lord giveth, and the Lord taketh away," mumbled Joel again.

Why the devil did he keep saying that?

Uneasily I looked from Joel to Bart and found his admiring gaze again riveted on Melodie, who was in arabesque position, waiting for Jory to sweep her up in his arms. I didn't like what I saw in Bart's dark, envious look, the desire that burned hotter by the hour. The world was full of unmarried women— he didn't need Melodie, his brother's wife!

Wildly Bart applauded as their dance ended and both were gazing transfixed at each other, forgetting we were there. "You've got to dance like that at my birthday party! Jory, say that you and Melodie will."

Reluctantly Jory turned his head to smile at Bart. "Why, if you want me, of course, but not Mel. Her doctor will allow a little mild dancing and practicing, like we just did, but not that strenuous kind needed for a professional performance, and I know you'll want only the best."

"But I want Melodie, too," protested Bart. He smiled charmingly at his brother's wife. "Please, for my birthday, Melodie, just this one time . . . and you're not so far along anyone will notice your condition."

Appearing uncertain, Melodie stared at Bart. "I don't think I should," she said lamely. "I want our baby to be healthy. I can't risk losing it."

Bart tried to persuade her, and might have, but Jory put a brisk end to the debate. "Now, listen, Bart, I told our agent Mel's doctor didn't want her to perform, and if she does, he might get wind of it and we could be sued. Besides, she's very fatigued. The kind of easy fun dancing you just witnessed is not the kind we do when we're serious. A professional performance demands hours and hours of warm-ups and practice and rehearsal. Don't plead, it's embarrassing. When Cindy comes she can dance with me."

"No!" Bart snarled, frowning now and losing all his charm. "She can't dance like Melodie."

No, she couldn't. Cindy wasn't a professional, but she did well enough when she wanted to. Jory and I had trained her since she was two.

Several feet behind Bart, like a skinny dark shadow, Joel's hands came out of wide sleeves and templed beneath his bowed head. He had his eyes closed, as if again in prayer. How irritating to have him around all the time.

Deliberately I turned my thoughts from him to Cindy. I couldn't wait to see her again. Couldn't wait to hear her breathless girlish chatter that told of proms and dates and the boys she knew. All the things that brought back to me my own youth, and my own desires to have what Cindy was experiencing.

In the rosy glow of the evening sunset, I stood unobserved in the shadows of a great arch overhead and watched Jory again dancing with Melodie in the huge foyer. Again in leotards, this time violet ones, with the filmy tunic to flutter enticingly, Melodie had bound violet satin ribbons under her small, firm breasts. She appeared a princess dancing with her lover. Oh, the passion Jory and Melodie had between them stirred a wistful longing in my own loins. To be young again like them . . . to have the chance to do it all over . . . do it right the second time around . . .

Suddenly I was aware that Bart was in another alcove, as if he'd waited to spy . . . or, more generously, watch as I watched. And he was the one who didn't like ballet and didn't care for beautiful music. He leaned casually against a door frame, his arms folded over his chest. But the burning dark eyes that followed Melodie weren't casual. They were full of the desire I'd seen before. My heart skipped.

When had Bart ever not wanted what belonged to Jory?

The music soared. Jory and Melodie had forgotten they might be observed and became so involved in what they were doing that they danced on and on, wildly passionate, entranced with each other, until Melodie ran to leap into his outstretched arms. Even as she did her lips pressed down on his. Parting lips that met again and again. Hands that roamed to seek out all the secret places. I was as much caught up in their lovemaking as Bart, unable to back away. Their kisses seemed to devour one another. In the heat of kindled desire, they fell to the floor and rolled onto the mat. Even as I strode toward Bart, I heard their heavy breathing, growing louder.

"Come, Bart, it's not right to stand and watch when the dancing is over."

He jumped as if my touch on his arm burned. The yearning in his eyes both hurt and frightened me.

"They should learn to control themselves when they're guests in my home," he said in a gruff voice, not taking his eyes off the forgetful pair rolling about on the mat, arms and legs entwined, sweaty hair wet and clinging as they kissed.

I yanked Bart into the music room and softly closed the door behind us. This was not a room I favored. It had been decorated to please Bart's very masculine taste. There was a grand piano that no one ever played, although I'd seen Joel finger it once or twice, then snatch his hands away as if the ivory keys singed him with sin. But the piano lured him so often he just stood staring at it, his fingers flexing and unflexing.

Bart strode toward a cabinet that opened to reveal a lighted bar. He reached for a crystal decanter to pour himself a stiff scotch. No water or ice. In one gulp he downed it. Then he was looking at me in a guilty fashion. "Nine years of marriage. Still they aren't tired of one another. What is it that you and Chris have that Jory has captured and I haven't?"

I flushed before my head bowed low. "I didn't know you drank alone."

"There's a lot you don't know about me, dear Mother." He poured a second scotch, I heard the slow gurgle of the fluid without looking up. "Even Malcolm had a drink once in a while."

Curiosity filled me. "Do you still think about Malcolm?"

He fell into a chair, crossed his legs by placing one ankle on the opposite knee. I looked away, thinking that once my second son had the most irritating ways of putting his feet on anything available, ruining many a good chair with his muddy boots, and bedspreads suffered early deaths. Then my eyes went back to his shoes. How did he keep the soles so clean, so they appeared never to have walked on anything but velvet?

Bit by bit Bart had lost all his messy ways on the way toward manhood. "Why do you stare at my shoes, Mother?"

"They're very handsome."

"Do you really think so?" He gazed down at them indifferently. "They cost six hundred bucks, and I paid another hundred to have the soles treated so they'll never show scuff marks or dirt. It's the 'in' thing to do, you know. Wear shoes with clean soles."

I frowned. What psychological message did that impart? "The tops will wear out before the soles do."

"So what?"

I had to agree. What did money mean to any of us now? We had more than we could possibly spend.

"When the tops wear, I'll throw them out and buy a new pair."

"Then why bother to have the soles treated?"

"Mother, really," he said crossly. "I like everything to keep its new appearance until I'm ready to discard it—I'm going to hate looking at Melodie when she's bulging in the middle like some breeding cow . . ."

"I'll be happy the day she shows, then perhaps you can move your eyes away from her."

He lit a cigarette, met my eyes calmly. "I bet I could easily take her away from Jory."

"How dare you say such a thing?" I cried angrily.

"She never looks at me, have you noticed? I don't think she wants to see that I'm better-looking than Jory now, and taller, and smarter, and a hundred times richer."

Our eye contact held. I swallowed nervously, plucked invisible lint from my clothes. "Cindy's coming tomorrow."

He shut his eyes briefly, gripped the arms of his chair harder, but otherwise showed no expression. "I disapprove of that girl," he finally managed.

"I hope you won't be unkind to her while she's here. Can't you remember the way she used to tag around, adoring you? She loved you before you turned her against you. She'd still adore you if you'd stopped teasing her so unmercifully. Bart . . . aren't you sorry for all the ugly things you said and did to your sister?"

"She's *not* my sister."

"She is, Bart, she is!"

"Oh, God, Mother, I'll never think of Cindy as my sister. She's adopted, not truly one of us. I've read a few of those letters she writes to you. Can't you see what she is? Or do you only read what she says, and not what she means? How can any girl be that popular and not be giving out?"

I jumped to my feet. "What's wrong with you, Bart?" I yelled. "You deny Chris as your father, Cindy as your sister, Jory as your brother. Don't you need to have anyone but yourself—and that hateful old man who trails you about?"

"I've got a little of you, don't I, Mother?" he said, narrowing his eyes to sinister slots. "And I've got my Uncle Joel, who is a very interesting man, who is, at this moment, praying for all our souls."

A red flag waved in my face. I flamed with instant anger. "You're an idiot if you prefer that creepy old man to the only father you've ever had!" I tried to keep my emotions under control but failed, as I'd always failed when it came to Bart and control. "Have you forgotten all the many kind deeds Chris has done for you? Is still doing for you?"

Bart leaned forward, piercing me with his diamond-hard glare. "But for Chris I would have had a happy life. With you married to my real father, I could have been the perfect son! Far more perfect than Jory. Maybe I'm like *you*, Mother. Maybe I need *my* revenge more than I need anything else."

"Why do *you* need revenge?" Surprise was in my voice, a certain kind of hopelessness. "No one has done to you what was done to me."

He leaned forward, very intense as he bit out, "You think because you gave me all the necessary things, all the clothes I needed, all the food I could eat, and a house to shelter me, you made yourself believe that was enough, but it wasn't. I knew you saved the best of your love for Jory. Then, after Cindy came, you gave your second best to her. You had nothing left to give me but pity—*and I hate you for pitying me!*"

Sudden nausea almost made me gag. I was glad I had the chair beneath me. "Bart," I began, struggling not to cry and show the very kind of weakness he'd despise, "perhaps once I did pity you for being clumsy, for being unconfident. Most of all, I was sorry you hurt yourself so often. But how can I pity you now? You're very handsome, intelligent, and when you want to be, extremely charming as well. What reason do I have now for pitying you?"

"That's what bothers me," he said in a low voice. "You make me look at myself in the mirror, wondering what it is you see. I've come to the conclusion that you just don't like me. You don't trust me, don't believe in me. I see in your eyes right now that you don't believe I'm completely sane." Suddenly his eyes, which had half-closed, opened wide. He stared penetratingly into my eyes, which had always been easy to read. He laughed short and hard. "It's there, dear Mother, that suspicion, that same fear. I can read your mind, don't think I can't. You think someday I'll do something to betray you and your brother, when I've had chances enough to do exactly that and I've done nothing. I've kept your sins to myself.

"Why not be honest and say now you didn't love your mother's second husband. Say truthfully you only used him as the instrument of your revenge. You went after him, got him, conceived me, then he was dead. True to the kind of woman you are, you then headed straight back to that poor doctor in South Carolina, who no doubt believed in you and loved you beyond reason. Did he realize you married him just as a means to give your bastard child a name? Did he know you used him to escape Chris? See how much thought I've given to your motivations? And now I've come to another conclusion: You see a lot of Chris in Jory—and that's what you love! You look at me and see Malcolm, and although my face and physique may resemble that of my true father, you ignore that and see what you want to in my eyes. In my eyes you think you see the soul of Malcolm. Now tell me that I've presumed wrongly! Go on, tell me I'm not speaking the truth."

My lips parted to deny every word, but nothing came out.

I panicked inside, wanting to run to him and pull his head against my breast, as I so often comforted Jory, but I couldn't make my feet move in Bart's direction. I truthfully did fear him. As he was now, fiercely intense and cold and hard, I was afraid of him, and fear made my love turn to dislike.

He waited for me to speak, to deny his charges, and in the end, I did the worst thing possible—I ran from the room.

On my bed I threw myself down and cried. Every word he'd said was true! I hadn't known Bart could read me like an open book. Now I was terrified of what he might do some- day to destroy not only Chris and me, but Cindy, Jory, and Melodie.

Cindy

Around eleven the next day, Cindy arrived in a taxi, running into the house like a fresh, invigorating, spring breeze. She hurled herself into my arms, reeking of some exotic perfume I thought too sophisticated for a girl of sixteen, an opinion I knew I'd better keep to myself.

"Oh, Momma," she cried, kissing and hugging me repeatedly, "it's so good to see you again!" Her lavishings of affection left me quite breathless as I eagerly responded. All the while, even as we embraced, she managed to stare around at the grand rooms with all their elegant furnishings. Holding to my hand, she pulled me from one room to another, gasping and exclaiming at the beauty of everything so fine and rich.

"Where's Dad?" she asked. I explained that Chris had driven into Charlottesville to turn in his rented car for a more luxurious model.

"Darling, he hoped to be back before you reached here. Something must have slowed him down. Be patient, and in a second or two he'll stroll in the door and welcome you."

Satisfied, she again exclaimed, "Momma, wow! What a

house! You didn't tell me it would be like this. You made me think the new Foxworth Hall would be just as ugly and scary as the first."

To me, Foxworth Hall would always be ugly and scary, yet it was thrilling to watch Cindy's excitement flow over. She was taller than I, her young breasts ripe and full, her waist very slender so it emphasized the gentle swell of her beautifully formed hips with the flat belly, while her buttocks filled out the back of her jeans delightfully. Looking at her figure sideways, I had to compare her to a burgeoning flower, so tender, so frail appearing, and yet she had exceptional endurance.

Her full and heavy long golden hair was casually styled. It blew wild in the wind as we went out to watch Jory and Bart fighting it out on the new tennis courts. "Oh, gosh, Momma, you do have two beautiful sons," she whispered as she stared at their bronzed, strong bodies. "I never thought Bart would grow up to be just as handsome as Jory, not when he was such an ugly little brute."

Amazed, I stared at her. Bart had been too thin, always with scabs and scars on his legs, and his dark hair had never been tidy, but he'd been a good-looking little boy, certainly not ugly-looking—only ugly acting. And once upon a time, Cindy had worshipped Bart. A knife twisted in my heart as I realized so much of what Bart had said last night was true. I *had* put Cindy ahead of him. I had thought she was perfect and incapable of doing wrong, and still did.

"Do try to be kind and thoughtful to Bart," I whispered, seeing Joel coming our way.

"Who's that funny-looking old man?" asked Cindy, turning to stare at Joel as he bent stiffly to pull up a few weeds. "Don't tell me Bart has hired somebody like him for a gardener—why, he can hardly straighten up once he's crooked."

Before I could answer, Joel was upon us, smiling as broadly as his false teeth would allow. "Why, you must be Cindy, the one Bart talks about all the time," he said with some faint leftover charm, taking Cindy's reluctantly offered hand and putting it to his thin, crooked lips.

I could tell she wanted to yank her hand away, yet she tolerated the touch of his lips. The sun through Joel's almost white hair still streaked with Foxworth gold made it seem terribly thin. Suddenly I realized I hadn't told Cindy about Joel and hastened to introduce them. She seemed fascinated once she knew who he was. "You really mean you knew that hateful old Grandfather Malcolm? You are really *his* son? Why, you must be really ancient . . ."

"Cindy, that's not tactful . . ."

"I'm sorry, Uncle Joel. It's just when I hear my mom and dad talk of their youth, it seems a million years ago." She laughed charmingly, smiling apologetically at Joel. "You know something, you look a lot like my dad in some ways. When he's really old, no doubt he'll grow to look like you."

Joel turned his eyes toward Chris, who'd just driven up and was even now stepping out of a beautiful new blue Cadillac with his arms full of packages. He'd picked up gifts I'd had engraved for Bart's birthday. For his birthday, I'd gone all out and given him only the best, as he would expect: an attaché case of the finest leather, with combination locks, for Chris to give him. Eighteen-karat gold cufflinks with his initials in diamonds and a matching gold cigarette case, also monogrammed in diamonds—the gem Bart respected most, from me. His father had carried such a cigarette case, given to him by my mother.

Dropping the packages onto a lawn chair, Chris held his arms open. Cindy hurled herself into his welcoming embrace. She covered his face with a rain of small kisses, leaving her lip marks all over his face. Staring up into his face, she pleaded. "This is going to be the best summer of my life. Daddy, can't we stay here until school starts in the fall, so I can know what it's like to live in a real mansion, with all those beautiful rooms and fancy bathrooms? I already know which one I want, the one with all those pink and white and gold girlish things. He knows I just adore pink, really love pink, and already I adore and love this house! Just love it, love it!"

A shadow flickered through Chris's eyes as he released her and turned to look at me. "We'll have to talk that over, Cindy. As you know, your mother and I are here just to help Bart celebrate his twenty-fifth birthday."

I looked over toward where Bart smashed the tennis ball with such force it's a wonder it didn't burst. Running like a streak of white light, Jory slammed the yellow ball back to Bart, who ran just as fast to swoop and cleverly whack it back with just as much force. Both were hot and sweaty, their faces reddening from the exercise and the hot sun. "Jory, Bart," I called, "Cindy's here. Come to say hello."

Instantly Jory turned his head to smile, causing him to miss the next yellow ball that came hurtling his way. He failed to return it, and Bart whooped for joy. He jumped up and down, hurled down his expensive racket, shouting, "I win!"

"You win by default," said Jory, throwing down his racket as well. He ran our way, his face all smiles. He threw back at Bart, "Default winning doesn't count."

"It does so count!" bellowed Bart. "What the hell do we care whether or not Cindy's here? You just used that to quit before my score topped yours."

"Have it your way," answered Jory. In a moment he was swinging Cindy off her feet, whirling her around and around, making her blue skirt fly and reveal skimpy bikini panties. It amused me to see that Cindy still dressed from the skin out in one color.

Melodie rose from a marble garden seat where she'd been watching the tennis game, until now half hidden by high shrubbery. I saw her lips tighten as she observed Cindy's too affectionate greeting.

"Like mother like daughter," mumbled Bart from behind me.

Cindy approached Bart warily, with so much decorum she

didn't seem like the same girl who had kissed Jory. "Hello, brother Bart. You're looking very fit."

Bart stared at her as if he'd never seen her before. It had been two years, and at fourteen, Cindy had still worn her hair in pigtails, or ponytails, and she had braces on her teeth. Now her gleaming white teeth were perfectly spaced. Her hair was a loose-flowing mass of molten gold. There wasn't a girl in the skin magazines that had a better figure or more perfect complexion, and only too unhappily I realized that Cindy knew she looked sensational in her tight blue and white tennis dress.

Bart's dark eyes lingered on her ripe, unfettered breasts that jiggled when she walked, their peaks jutting out clearly. His eyes measured her hand-span waist before he stared at her pelvic area; then he lowered his eyes to take in very pretty long legs that ended in white sandals. Her toenails were painted bright red to match her fingernails and lipstick.

She was breathtakingly lovely in a sweet, fresh, and innocent way that strove unsuccessfully to appear sophisticated. I didn't believe for a moment that that long, intense look she gave Bart meant what apparently he took it to mean.

"You're not my type," he said scornfully, turning away. When he did, he stared long and meaningfully at Melodie. Then again he turned to Cindy. "You have a certain cheap quality, despite all your expensive clothes—you don't possess nobility."

It hurt to hear him deliberately try and squelch Cindy's youthful pride. Her radiant expression faded. Like a tender flower without the admiration of rain to nourish her faith in herself, she wilted before me as she turned into Chris's waiting arms.

"Apologize, Bart," ordered Chris. I cringed, knowing Bart would never apologize.

Bart curled his lips, his scorn so apparent, even as he acted indignant and angry. His lips parted to insult Chris as he'd done so many times, but then he glanced at Melodie, who'd turned to look at him in a detached, curious way. A deep flush heated Bart's face. "I'll apologize when she learns how to dress and act like a lady."

"Apologize *now*, Bart," ordered Chris.

"Don't make demands, *Christopher*," said Bart, looking Chris meaningfully in the eyes. "You're in a very vulnerable position. You and my mother. You're not a Sheffield, not a Foxworth—or at least you can't let it be known you're a Foxworth. So just what are you that counts? The world is full of doctors, too many doctors—and younger and more knowledgeable ones than you are."

Chris stood taller. "My ignorance about medicine has saved your life more than once, Bart. And the lives of many others. Perhaps one day you'll recognize that fact. You've never said thank you for anything I've done for you. I'm waiting for that day."

Bart paled, I suspected not so much from what Chris had just said. I thought he was embarrassed because Melodie was watching and listening. "Thank you, *Uncle* Chris," he said sarcastically.

How mocking and insincere his words and his tone of voice. I watched the two men in silent challenge, seeing Chris wince from the way Bart put stress on "Uncle." Then, for no reason at all, I glanced at Joel.

He'd moved closer to pause just behind Melodie, and on his face was the kindest, most benign smile. But in his eyes lurked something darker. I moved to stand beside Chris, just as Jory lined up with him on the other side.

My lips parted to add a long list of things Bart should thank Chris for, when suddenly Bart was striding toward Melodie, ignoring Cindy. "Have I told you the theme of my party? The dance I've chosen for you and Jory? It's going to cause a sensation."

Melodie stood up. She stared Bart straight in his eyes with

open contempt. "I'm not going to dance for your birthday guests. I think Jory has explained to you more than once that I'm doing everything I can to see I have a healthy baby—and that doesn't include dancing for your amusement and that of people I don't even know."

Her voice was cold. Dislike for Bart glared from her dark blue eyes.

She left, taking Jory with her, leaving the rest of us to follow. Joel tagged along at the very end like a tail that didn't know how to wag.

Quick to recover from all wounds, as always she'd rebounded from Bart's rebuffs, Cindy gushed happily about the expected baby that would make her an aunt. "How wonderful! I can hardly wait. It's going to be one beautiful baby, I know, when it has parents like Jory and Melodie, and grandparents like you and Dad."

Cindy's delightful presence made up for so much of Bart's hatefulness. I hugged her close and she snuggled down on the love seat in my private sitting room and began to spill out all the details of her life. I listened eagerly, fascinated by a daughter who was making up for all the excitement Carrie and I had missed out on.

Each morning Chris and I were up early to enjoy the beauty of the cool mountain mornings, with the perfume of roses and other flowers drifting to delight our nostrils. Cardinals scarlet as flames flew everywhere while bluejays shrieked and purple martins searched the grass for insects. It surprised me to see dozens of birdhouses to accommodate wrens, martins, and other species, and fabulous birdbaths and rock garden pools where the birds had a merry time taking quick, fluttery baths. We ate on one terrace or another to enjoy different views, talking often of all this that had been denied us when we were young and would have been appreciated even more than it was now. Sad, so sad to think of our little twins and how they had cried to go outside, outside, and the only playground they had was the attic garden we made for them out of paper and cardboard. And this had been there then, unused, unenjoyed, when two little five-years-olds would have been in seventh heaven to have had just a little of what we could enjoy daily now.

Cindy liked to sleep late, as did Jory and especially Melodie, who complained a great deal about nausea and fatigue. As early as seven-thirty Chris and I watched workmen and party decorators drive up. Caterers came to prepare for the party, and interior designers arrived to complete the appointments in some of the unfinished rooms, but not one neighbor dropped in to welcome us. Bart's private phone rang often, but the telephones on the other lines hardly rang at all. We sat at the top of the world, or so it seemed, all by ourselves, and in some ways it was nice, in other ways it was a little frightening.

In the distance, faint and hazy, we could faintly see two church steeples. When the nights were still and without wind, we could faintly hear them chime away the hours. I knew one had been patronized by Malcolm when he lived, and about a mile away was the cemetery where he and our grandmother were buried side by side, with elaborate headstones and guardian angels put there by our mother.

I filled my days with playing tennis with Chris, with Jory, sometimes with Bart, and that's when he really seemed to like me most. "You surprise me, Mother!" he yelled over the net, slamming that yellow ball so hard it almost went through my racket. Somehow I managed to race to hit it back, and then my troublesome knee started hurting and I had to quit. Bart complained I was using that knee as an excuse to abandon play with him.

"You find any reason to stay away from me," he yelled as if Chris's words meant nothing. "Your knee doesn't hurt . . . or you'd be limping."

I did limp as I climbed the stairs, but Bart wasn't around to notice this. I soaked in a tub of hot water for an hour to take away the pain. Chris came in to tell me I was doing it wrong again. "Ice, Catherine, ice! You only inflame your knee more when you sit in hot water. Now get out while I fill a bag with crushed ice, and keep it on your knee for twenty minutes." He kissed me to take the sting from his words. "See you later," he said, hurrying back to the tennis courts to take on Jory, while Bart left with Joel in tow. All this I could see from our bedroom balcony while I sat with that ice bag held to my knee, and soon enough the cold worked, chasing away the throbbing hot pain.

I was beginning a layette for Jory's expected baby. This demanded many shopping sprees for yarns, needles, crochet hooks, for visiting adorable baby shops. Often we drove into Charlottesville with Cindy and Chris to shop, and twice we made the longer drive to Richmond and shopped there, went to the movies, and stayed overnight. Sometimes Jory and Melodie went with us, but not as often as I would have liked. Already Foxworth Hall's charm was palling.

But if it palled for me, for Jory and Melodie, it worked its charm on Cindy, who adored her room, her fancy French furniture, her ultrafeminine bath with its pink decor enhanced with gold and mossy pale green. Hugging herself, she danced around. "So he doesn't like me," she laughed, spinning around before the many mirrors, "and yet he decorates a room exactly the way I'd want. Oh, Momma, how can either of us understand Bart?"

Who could answer that?

Preparations

As Bart's twenty-fifth birthday approached, a kind of feverish insanity descended on the Hall. Different kinds of decorators came to measure our lawns, our patios, our terraces. In groups they whispered, made lists, sketches, tried different colors for the tablecloths, talked in huddles to Bart, discussed the theme of the dance, and made their secret plans. Bart still refused to reveal the theme—at least to the members of his family. Secrets didn't sit well with anyone but Bart. The rest of us became a close-knit family that Bart didn't want to join.

Workmen with wood and paint and other construction materials began to build what appeared to be a stage and platforms for the orchestra. I heard Bart brag to one of his entourage that he was hiring opera stars, very famous ones.

Whenever I was outdoors, and I stayed outside as much as possible, I stared at the blue-misted mountains all around us and wondered if they remembered two of the attic mice shut upstairs for almost four years. I wondered if ever again they'd transform an ordinary little girl into someone full of fanciful dreams she had to make come true. And I had made a few come true, even if I'd failed more than once to keep husbands alive. I wiped away two tears and met Chris's still loving gaze and felt that old familiar sadness wash over me. How sane Bart could have been if only Chris hadn't loved me—and I hadn't loved him.

Blame the wind or stars of fate—but I still blamed my mother.

Despite our dire anticipations of what lay ahead, I couldn't help but feel happier than I'd felt in some time, just watching all the excitement in the gardens that gradually turned into something straight from a movie set. I gasped to see what Bart wanted done.

It was a biblical scene!

"Samson and Delilah," Bart said flatly when I asked, all his enthusiasm squelched because Melodie kept refusing to dance the role he wanted. "Often I've heard Jory say he loved the chance to produce his own productions, and he does love that role most of all."

Pivoting about, Melodie headed for the house without answering, her face pale with anger.

Again, I should have known. What other theme would capture Bart's fancy as much?

Cindy ran to throw her arms about Jory. "Jory, let me dance the role of Delilah, I can! I just know I can."

"I don't want your amateurish attempts!" shouted Bart.

Ignoring him, Cindy tugged pleadingly on both of Jory's hands. "Please, please, Jory. I'd love to do it. I've kept up my ballet classes, so I won't be stiff and awkward and make you look unskilled, and between now and then you can help me gain better timing. I'll rehearse morning, night, and noon!"

"There's not enough time to rehearse when the performance is two days away," complained Jory, throwing Bart a hard, angry look. "Good lord, Bart, why didn't you tell me before? Do you think just because I choreographed that par-

ticular ballet that I can remember all the difficult routines?
A role like that needs weeks of rehearsing, and you wait until
the last moment! Why?"

"Cindy's lying," said Bart, looking longingly at the door
through which Melodie had disappeared. "She was too lazy to
keep up her classes before, so why should she when Mother's
not there to force her?"

"I have! I have!" cried Cindy with great excitement and
pride, when I knew she hated violent exercises. Before the age
of six, she'd loved the pretty tutus, the cute little satin slippers, the little sparkling tiaras of fake jewels, and the fantasy
of the fanciful productions had put her in a spell of beauty I'd
once believed she'd never abandon. But Bart had ridiculed
her performances just one too many times, and she'd let him
convince her she was hopelessly inadequate. She'd been about
twelve when he stole her pleasure in the ballet. From then on
she'd never gone to classes. Therefore I was doubly amazed to
hear she'd never really given up on the dance, only on allowing Bart see her perform.

She turned to me, as if pleading for her life. "Really, I am
telling the truth! Once I was in the private girls' school, and
Bart wasn't around to ridicule me, I started again and ever
since have kept up my ballet classes, and I tap dance as well."

"Well," said Jory, apparently impressed, giving Bart
another hard look, "we can devote what time we have left to
practicing, but you were extremely unthinking to believe we
wouldn't need to practice for weeks, Bart. I don't expect to
have much difficulty myself since it's a familiar role—but
Cindy, you've not even seen that particular ballet."

Rudely interrupting, Bart asked with great excitement,
"Do you have the lenses, the white lenses? Can you really see
through them? I saw you and Melodie in New York about a
year ago, and from the orchestra you really did look blind."

Frowning at his unexpected question, Jory studied Bart
seriously. "Yes . . . I have the contacts with me," he said

slowly. "Everywhere I go someone asks me to dance the role of Samson, so I take the lenses. I didn't know you appreciated ballet so much."

Laughing, Bart slapped Jory on the back as if they'd never had a disagreement. Jory staggered from the strength of that blow. "Most ballets are stupid bores, but this particular one catches my fancy. Samson was a great hero and I admire him. And you, my brother, perform extraordinarily well as Samson. Why, you even look just as powerful. I guess that's the only ballet that has ever thrilled me."

I wasn't listening to Bart. I was staring at Joel, who leaned forward. Muscles near his thin lips worked almost spasmodically, hovering near a smirk or a laugh, I couldn't tell which. All of a sudden I didn't want Jory and Cindy to dance in that particular ballet, which included very brutal scenes. And it had been Bart's idea years and years ago . . . hadn't he been the one to suggest that the opera would provide the music for what he considered would make the most sensational ballet of all?

All through the night I thought and I thought of how to stop Bart from wanting that particular production.

He'd never been easy to stop as a boy.

As a man . . . I didn't know if I had a chance. But I was going to give it a try.

The very next morning I was up early and running out into the yard to catch Bart before he drove off. He listened to me with impatience, refusing to change the theme of his party. "I can't now, even if I wanted to. I've had the costumes designed and they are almost finished, as are the sets and flats. If I cancel anything it will be too late to plan another ballet. Besides, Jory doesn't mind, why should you?"

How could I tell him that some small, intuitive voice was warning me not to let this particular ballet be performed near the place of our confinement—with Malcolm and his wife in the ground not so far away the music wouldn't fill their dead ears.

Jory and Cindy practiced and rehearsed night and day, both catching a certain excitement as they worked together and Jory found out that Cindy was good; certainly she wouldn't perform as well as Melodie would have, but she'd dance more than adequately, and she was so lovely with her hair bound up in classical ballerina style.

The morning of Bart's birthday dawned bright and clear, heralding a perfect summer day without rain or clouds.

I was up early with Chris, strolling in the gardens before breakfast, enjoying the perfume of roses that seemed to herald a beautiful, perfect birthday for Bart. He'd always wanted birthday parties, like the ones we threw for Jory and Cindy, yet when they came around, he somehow managed to antagonize every guest so that many left early, and usually in a huff.

He was a man now, I kept telling myself, and this time it would be different. Chris was saying that to me, as if we had some sort of telepathy, both with the same thoughts.

"He's coming into his own," I said. "Isn't it odd how he's hung on to that childish expression, Chris? Will the attorneys read the will again after the party?"

Smiling and happy-looking, Chris shook his head. "No, darling, we'll all be too tired. The reading is set for the next day." A shadow came to darken his expression. "I can't remember anything in that will that would spoil Bart's birthday, can you?"

No, I couldn't, but at the time of our mother's will reading, I'd been too upset, crying, half hearing, not really caring if none of us inherited the Foxworth fortune that seemed to come with its own curse.

"There's something Bart's attorneys aren't telling me, Cathy . . . something they say indicates I must not have clearly understood at the time when our mother's will was read shortly after her death. Now they don't want to speak of it because Bart has demanded that I not be included in any legal discussions. They look at him as if he scares or intimidates them. It surprises me to see middle-aged men with years of experience yield under his pressure, as if they want to keep his good will, and mine be damned. It annoys me, and then I ask myself, what the hell do I care? Soon we'll be leaving and making a new home for ourselves, and Bart can take his fortune and rule with it . . ."

My arms went about him, angry because Bart refused to give him the credit he deserved for handling that vast fortune for so many years, and doing a darn good job of it, too, despite his medical practice that stole so much of his time.

"How many millions will he inherit?" I asked. "Twenty, fifty, more? One billion, two, three—more?"

Chris laughed. "Oh, Catherine, you never grow up. You always exaggerate. To be honest, it's difficult to calculate the net worth of all those holdings when they are scattered into so many areas of investments. However, he should be pleased when his attorneys give a rough estimate . . . it's more than enough for ten greedy young men."

In the foyer we paused to watch Jory rehearsing with Cindy, both hot and sweaty from all their efforts. Other dancers who'd be in the ballet were with them, standing around idly, either watching Jory and Cindy or staring around at what they could see of the fabulous house. Cindy was doing exceptionally well, and that truly surprised me; imagine keeping up her ballet classes and not telling me. She must have used some of her allowance meant for clothes and cosmetics and other trivial things she was always needing.

One of the older dancers strolled over to me, smiling as she spoke of seeing me dance a few times in New York. "Your son is very much like his father," she went on, glancing back at Jory, who was whipping himself up into such a passion I wondered if he'd have any energy left for tonight's performance. "Maybe I shouldn't say this, but he's ten times better. I was only about twelve when you and Julian Marquet danced in *The Sleeping Beauty,* but it was the inspiration that gave me the desire to become a dancer myself. Thank you for giving us another wonderful dancer like Jory Marquet."

What she said filled me with happiness. My marriage to Julian hadn't been a total failure when it had produced Jory. Now I had to believe Bartholomew Winslow's son would eventually fill me with just as much pride as I felt right now.

The rehearsal over, Cindy came to me, quite out of breath. "Mom, how did I do, okay?" Her eager face waited for my approval.

"You did beautifully, Cindy, really you did. Now, if you just remember to feel the music . . . keep the timing, you will turn in a remarkable performance for a novice."

She grinned at me. "Always the instructor, huh, Mom? I suspect I'm not nearly as good as you want me to believe, but I'm going to give this performance my everything, and if I fail, it won't be because I didn't try."

Jory was surrounded by admirers, while Melodie sat quietly on a love seat beside Bart. They didn't appear to be conversing, nor did they seem friendly. Yet, seeing them on that lovely small seat for two, I felt somehow uneasy. Tugging Chris forward, we moved closer to the pair on the love seat. "Happy birthday, Bart," I said cheerfully. He looked up and smiled with genuine charm.

"I told you it was going to be a great day, with sun and no rain."

"Yes, you told us."

"Can we all eat now?" he asked, standing and reaching for Melodie's hand. She ignored him and stood without assistance. "I'm starving!" Bart went on, looking only a little crestfallen from another of her rebuffs. "Those little Continental morning snacks just don't satisfy me."

We made a happy assembly at the luncheon table, all but Joel, who sat at his own small, round table on the terrace, apart from the rest of us. It was his claim that we were too rowdy and ate too much, insulting his monkish tastes, which dictated a serious attitude toward food and long prayers before and after eating. Even Bart grew annoyed with Joel when he became too pious, and especially on this day his impatience showed. "Uncle Joel, do you have to sit there all by yourself? Come, join the family group and wish me a happy birthday."

Joel shook his head. "The Lord scorns ostentatious displays of wealth and vanity. I disapprove of this party. You could show your gratitude to be alive in a better way, by contributing to charities."

"What have charities done for me? This is my time to shine, Uncle, and even if dear old dead Malcolm flips over in his grave, I'm having the time of my life tonight!"

I was flooded with delight. Quickly I leaned to kiss him. "I love to see you like this, Bart. This *is* your day . . . and the gifts we have for you are going to open your eyes wide."

"Hope so," he said, all smiles. "I see they're heaping up on the gift table. We'll open them soon after the guests are here, so we can get on to the entertainment."

Across from where I sat, Jory was staring into Melodie's eyes with concern. "Honey, are you feeling all right?"

"Yes," she whispered, "except I'd like to be dancing the role of Delilah. It feels strange watching you dance with someone else."

"After the baby comes, we'll dance together again," he said before he kissed her. Her eyes clung worshipfully to him as he got up to practice again with Cindy.

That's when Bart lost his happy expression.

Delivery men were constantly at the door bringing Bart more gifts. Many of his fraternity brothers from Harvard were coming with their girlfriends or wives. Those who couldn't make it were sending presents. Bart came and went, almost on the run, checking on every aspect of the party. Bouquets of flowers arrived by the dozens. The caterers filled the kitchen, so I felt an intruder when I wanted to prepare my own kind of mid-day snack. Then Bart had me by the arm and was pulling me through all the rooms that were overflowing with flowers. "Do you think my friends will be impressed?" he asked worriedly. "You know, I think I might have done a bit too much bragging when I was in school. They'll expect a mansion beyond compare."

I took another look around. There was something about a house ready for a party that made it especially beautiful, and Foxworth Hall was not only festive but spectacular with all its fresh flowers to give it warmth and grace, as well as beauty. All the crystal sparkled, the silver gleamed, the copper glowed . . . oh, yes, this house could rival the very best.

"Darling, stop fretting. You can't out-best everyone in the world. This is a truly beautiful house, and your decorators have done a marvelous job. Your friends will be impressed, don't you doubt that for one second. The caretakers did keep it well over the years, and gave all the gardens a chance to become well established."

He wasn't listening, just staring beyond me, frowning slightly. "You know, Mother," he said in a low voice, "I'm going to rattle around here after you and your brother go, and Melodie and Jory leave. It's a good thing I've got my Uncle Joel, who will stay on until he dies."

I heard this with a sinking heart.

Cindy's name wasn't mentioned, for obviously he'd never miss her. "Do you really like Joel that much, Bart? This morning he seemed to irk you with his monkish ways."

Clouds shadowed his already dark eyes, made grave his handsome face. "My uncle is helping me find myself, Mother, and if sometimes he annoys me, it's because I'm still so uncertain about my future. He can't help his habits formed over all those years living with monks who weren't allowed to speak, only pray out loud and sing at services. He's told me a bit about how it was, and it must have been very grim and lonely . . . yet he says he found peace there, and belief in God and everlasting life."

My arm dropped from his waist. He could have turned to Chris and found everything he needed—peace, security, and the faith that had sustained Chris throughout life. Bart had blind eyes when it came to seeing the goodness in a man who'd tried so hard to make a son out of Bart.

But my relationship with my brother condemned him, blinded Bart to anything but that.

Sadly I left Bart and climbed the stairs to find Chris on the balcony staring down at the workers in the yard. I joined him there, feeling the sun hot on my head. Silently we watched all that bustle of activity, while I prayed this house was finally going to give us something other than misery.

We napped for two hours, then ate a small dinner before all of us hurried back up to dress for the party. I went again out onto the balcony that gave Chris and me so much pleasure. Below me spread the birthday fairyland. The colors of the fading day filled the heavens with deep rose and violet, streaked it with magenta and orange, and sleepy birds flew like dark tears toward their nests. Cardinals were making their little beeping sounds, not chirps or cheeps but more like electronic, metallic bleeps. When Chris stepped up beside me, damp and fresh from his shower, we didn't speak or feel the need to; we just embraced, looking downward, before we finally turned away and went inside.

Bart, the child of my revenge, was coming into his own. I held fast to my hopes—wanting a party that turned out well and gave him the assurance he needed that he had friends and was well liked. I held off my fears and told myself over and over again that it was Bart's just due, and ours, too.

Maybe Bart would be satisfied tomorrow when the will was reread. Maybe, just maybe . . . I wanted the best for him, wanted fate to make up for so many things.

Behind me Chris moved in our dressing room, stepping into his tux trousers, stuffing in his shirttails, tying his own bow tie, then asking me to do it all over again. "Make the ends even." Gladly I retied it for him. He brushed his beautiful blond hair that was just a bit darker in back than it had been when he was forty. Each decade both darkened the blond and brought a touch more of silver in both our heads of hair. Easily I could keep mine colored, but Chris refused to do that. Fair hair had a lot to do with the way I thought about myself. My face was still pretty. I was both mature and young-looking.

Chris's reflection moved closer to my dressing table, hovering over my shoulders. His hands, so familiar to me now, moved to slip inside my bodice and cup my breasts before his lips pressed on my neck. "I love you. God knows what I would do if I didn't have you."

Why was he always saying that?

As if he expected one day I'd leave or die before he did. "Darling, you'd live, that's what. You're important to society, I'm not."

"You're the one who keeps me going," he whispered in a hoarse voice. "Without you I wouldn't know how to continue on—but without me, you'd go on and probably marry again."

I saw his eyes, his blue eyes wistfully waiting.

"I've had three husbands and one lover, and that's enough for any one woman. If I am so unlucky as to lose you first, I'll sit day by day before a window, staring out and remembering how it used to be with you."

His eyes turned softer, meeting and locking with mine as I went on. "You look so beautiful, Chris. You'll make your sons envious."

"Beautiful? Isn't that an adjective used to describe females?"

"No. there's a difference between handsome and beautiful. Some men can look handsome, but not radiate inner beauty—like you do. You, my love, are *beautiful*—inside and out."

Again his blue eyes lit up. "Thank you very much. And may I say that I find you ten times as beautiful as you find me."

"My sons will be jealous when they behold the beauty of my Christopher Doll."

"Yes, of course," he answered with a wry grin. "*Your* sons see much to envy in me."

"Chris, you know Jory loves you. Someday Bart's going to find out he loves you, too."

"Someday my ship will come . . . ," he sang lightly.

"It's his ship too, Chris. Bart is at last coming into his own. And with that fortune in his control, rather than yours, he'll relax, find himself, and turn to you as the best father he could have had."

Reflectively he smiled, a small smile of sadness. "To be honest, darling, I'll be happy when Bart has his money and I'm out of the picture. It's no easy chore handling all that money, though I could have hired a money manager to do it for me. As trustee, I guess I wanted to prove myself to Bart, that I'm more than just a doctor, since that never seemed enough for him."

What could I say? Nothing Chris did seemed to change the way Bart felt about him. Because of that one thing he couldn't change—he was my brother—Bart would never accept him as his father.

"What are you thinking, my love, that's ugly, and making you frown?"

"Nothing much," I answered, then I stood. The silky white of my clinging Grecian-styled dress felt whispery and sensuous against my bare skin. My hair had a single long curl to drape over my shoulder, the rest of it piled high on the crown of my head. Holding it in place was a diamond hair clip, the only jewelry I wore but for my wedding rings.

In the middle of the bedroom we shared, Chris and I reached for each other. There we stood, wrapped in each other's arms, holding fast to the only security we ever had that lasted: each other. All about us the house felt so quiet. We could have been lost and alone in eternity.

"All right, spill it out," said Chris after long minutes passed. "I can always tell when you're worried."

"I wish things could be different between you and Bart, that's all," I replied in an offhand way, not wanting to spoil this evening.

"I feel my relationship with Jory and Cindy more than makes up for Bart's antagonism. And, more importantly, I genuinely sense Bart *does not* hate me. There are times when I feel he wants to reach out to me, but there's that shame, that knowledge of our true relationship that holds him as if bound by chains of steel. He wants guidance but is ashamed to ask for it. He wants a father, a real father. His psychiatrists have always told us that. He looks at me, finds me sadly lacking . . . so he looks elsewhere. First it was Malcolm, his great-grandfather, already dead in his grave. Then it was John Amos, and John failed him, too. Now he turns to Joel, fearfully suspecting that he, too, may have his flaws. Yes, I can tell at times he doesn't really trust his great-uncle. And because he can think like this, Bart is not beyond saving, Cathy. We still have time to reach him—for we're alive and he's alive."

"Yes, yes! I know, I know. While there's life there's always hope. Say it again, and then again. And if you say it often enough, maybe the day will come when Bart says to you, 'Yes, I love you. Yes, you've done your best. Yes, you are the father I've been looking for all my life'—and wouldn't that be wonderful?"

His head bowed into my hair. "Don't sound so bitter. That day will come, Cathy. As surely as you and I love each other—and our three children—that day will come."

I knew I'd do anything that was necessary to see that one day Bart would speak genuine words of love to his father! I'd live forever to see the day when Bart not only accepted Chris and said he loved him and admired him and thanked him,

I'd also live to see him a real brother to Jory again . . . and a brother to Cindy.

Minutes later we were at the head of the stairs, starting to descend and join Jory and Melodie, whom we could see near the newel post at the bottom. Melodie wore a simple black gown that draped from black shoestring straps. Her only jewelry was a string of gleaming pearls.

Upon hearing the clatter of my high-heeled silver slippers on the marble, Bart stepped into view wearing his custom-tailored tux. My breath caught. He could have been his father when I'd seen him the first time.

His mustache—that small amount of fuzz first seen seven days ago—had grown thicker. He looked happy, and that was enough to make him look even more handsome. His dark eyes were full of admiration as he saw my dress, my hair, smelled my perfume. "Mother!" he cried, "you look stunning! You bought that lovely white dress especially for my party, didn't you?" Laughing, I said yes, of course, I couldn't wear anything old to a party such as this.

We all had compliments for each other, except Bart didn't say anything at all to Chris, although I saw him surreptitiously glancing at him, as if Chris's steadfast good looks kept taking him by surprise. Melodie and Jory, Chris and I, with Bart and Joel, formed a circle at the bottom of the stairs, all of us but Joel trying to talk at the same time. Then . . .

"Momma, Daddy!" called Cindy, running down the stairs toward us and holding up her long flame-red dress so she wouldn't trip. I turned to stare at her disbelievingly.

I didn't know where Cindy had found the shocking red dress she wore. It seemed the kind a hooker would wear to display her charms. I filled with such sickening dread of Bart's reaction that all my former happiness flowed like stale wine down into my slippers and disappeared through the floor. The thing she wore clung like a coat of scarlet paint, the neckline plunged almost to her waist, and obviously she wore nothing underneath. The peaks of her jutting breasts were too obvious; and when she moved she jiggled embarrassingly. The clinging satin sheath was cut on the bias, and clung . . . oh, it did cling. There wasn't a bulge or a ripple to betray an ounce of fat, only a superb young body she wanted to display.

"Cindy, go back to your room," I whispered, "and put on that blue dress you promised to wear. You're sixteen, not thirty."

"Oh, Momma, don't be so stodgy. Times have changed. Nudity is in, Momma, IN. And compared to some I could have chosen, this dress is modest, absolutely prudish."

Just one glance at Bart told me he didn't think Cindy's gown was modest. He stood as if dumbstruck until this very moment, with his face flame red, his dark eyes bulging as he stared at her mincing around, because the skirt was so tight she could hardly move her legs.

Bart stared at us, looked again at Cindy. Bart's rage was so furious he couldn't speak. In those few seconds I had to think quickly of how to appease him. "Cindy, please, run back and change into something decent."

Cindy had her eyes fixed on Bart. Obviously she was challenging him to do something to stop her. She seemed to be enjoying his reaction, his bulging eyes, his gaping lips that showed his indignation and shock. She made more of a show of herself by sashaying around like a prancing pony in heat, swishing those hips in an undulating, provocative way. Joel moved next to Bart, his watery blue eyes cold and scornful as he looked Cindy up and down, and then his eyes lifted to meet mine. *See, see what you have raised,* he said mutely.

"Cindy, do you hear your mother?" Chris bellowed. "Do as she says! Immediately!"

Appearing shocked, Cindy froze, staring at him with defiance as she flushed and stood her ground.

"Please, Cindy," I added, "do as your father says. The other dress is very pretty and appropriate. What you have on is vulgar."

"I am old enough to choose what I want to wear," she said in a quivery voice, refusing to move. "Bart likes red, so I wear red!"

Melodie stared at Cindy, glanced helplessly up at me, and tried to smile. Jory appeared amused, as if this were all a joke.

Cindy had by this time finished her burlesque performance. She looked somewhat crestfallen as she paused before Jory, staring up at him expectantly. "You look absolutely divine, Jory—and you, too, Melodie."

Obviously Jory didn't know what to say or where to look, so he looked away, then looked back. A slow blush rose from the neckline of his tucked formal shirt. "And you look like . . . Marilyn Monroe . . ."

Bart's dark head snapped around. His fiery gaze raked over Cindy again. His face flamed even redder so it seemed he might go up in smoke. He exploded, all control vanished. "You go straight back to your room and put on something decent! INSTANTLY! MOVE before you get what you deserve! I won't have anyone in my home dressing like a whore!"

"Get lost, you creep!" she snapped back.

"WHAT DID YOU SAY?" he yelled.

"I said, GET LOST, CREEP! I will wear exactly what I have on!" I saw her tremble. But for once Bart was right.

"Cindy, why? You know that dress is wrong, and everyone is right to be shocked. Now, do what's expected, go upstairs and change. Don't create more distress than you already have—for you do look like a street prostitute, and certainly you must know that. Usually you have very good taste. Why did you select that thing?"

"Momma!" she wailed, "you're making me feel bad!"

Bart stepped toward her, his expression very threatening. Instantly Melodie moved between them, spreading her slender white arms before she turned pleadingly to Bart. "Can't you see she's only doing this to annoy you? Stay calm, or else you will give Cindy exactly the satisfaction she wants."

Turning, she said to Cindy in a cool but authoritative voice, "Cindy, you have achieved the shock effects you wanted. So why don't you go back upstairs and put on that pretty blue dress you started to wear in the first place?"

Bart ignored both Chris and me as he strode to seize Cindy, but she pranced away out of his reach, turning to teasingly mock him for being slow and not as agile as she was, even hobbled as she was in that slim, straight, tight skirt. I could have slapped Cindy when I heard her say silkily, "Bart, darling, I was so sure you'd love this scarlet gown . . . since you think I'm a cheap, trashy thing, anyway, I'm just living up to your expectations—and playing the role you wrote for me."

In one flashing bound he reached her. His open palm slammed against her cheek.

The pain in his hard slap rocked Cindy backward so that she sat down very hard on the second stair step. I heard the skirt of her red gown rip down the midback seam. Moving quickly, I hurried to help her up. Tears came to Cindy's eyes.

Hurriedly standing, Cindy backed up the stairs, struggling to maintain dignity. "You are a creep, brother Bart. A weird pervert who doesn't know what the real world is about. I bet you're a virgin, or else gay!"

The rage on Bart's face sent her scurrying up the stairs in a hurry. I moved to prevent Bart from following Cindy, but he was too quick.

Ruthlessly he shoved me aside, so I, too, almost fell. Crying like a chastised child, Cindy disappeared with Bart close at her heels.

In a distant hall, I faintly heard Bart shout, "How dare you try to embarrass me? You're the trashy one I've had to protect from all the dirty stories I hear about you. I used to think they lied. Now you've proved yourself exactly what they said you were! As soon as this party is over, I don't ever want to see you again!"

"AS IF I WANT TO SEE YOU!" she screamed. "I HATE YOU, BART! HATE YOU!"

I heard her scream, the wailing cries . . . I started to head up the stairs while Chris tried to restrain me. Tugging free, I had climbed five steps when Bart appeared with a satisfied smirk on his handsome but momentarily evil face. He whispered as he passed, "I just gave her what you never did—a thorough spanking. If she can sit for a week comfortably, she's got an ass made of iron."

I glanced backward in time to see Joel scowl at the use of that word.

Ignoring Joel for a change, smiling like the perfect host, Bart arranged us into a receiving line, and soon guests began to arrive. Bart introduced all of us to people I hadn't known he knew. I was amazed at the style he showed, the poise, the ease with which he handled everyone and made them welcome. His college chums came flocking in, as if to see all that he'd told them about. If Cindy hadn't put on that horrible dress, I could have really felt proud of Bart. As it was, I was baffled, believing Bart could be anything that suited his purpose.

Right now he was set on charming everyone. And he succeeded, even more than Jory, who obviously and wisely intended to take a backseat and allow Bart to shine. Melodie stayed close at her husband's side, clinging to his hand, his arm, looking pale, unhappy. I was so absorbed in watching Bart perform that I was startled when someone tugged on my arm. It was Cindy, wearing the modest little blue silk sheath I'd chosen for her. She looked sweet-sixteen-and-never-been-kissed. I scolded, "Really, Cindy, you can't blame Bart. This time you deserved a spanking."

She choked out, "Damn him to hell! I'll show him! I'll dance ten times better than Melodie has ever danced! I'll make every man at this party want me tonight, despite this deadly mousey gown you chose."

"You don't mean that, Cindy."

Softening, she fell into my arms. "No, Momma, I don't mean that."

Bart saw Cindy with me, raked his eyes over her girlish gown, smiled sarcastically, and then came our way.

Cindy stood taller.

"Now, listen, Cindy. You'll put on your costume when the time comes and forget anything happened between us. You'll perform your part to perfection—okay?"

Playfully he pinched her cheek. So playfully his pinch left a deep red indentation on her face. She squealed and kicked out. Her high heel dug into his shin. He yelped and slapped her.

"Bart!" I hissed, "stop! Don't you hurt her again! You've done enough for one night!"

Chris yanked Bart away from Cindy. "Now, I've had enough of this idiocy," he said angrily, and Chris seldom angered. "You've invited to this party some of the most important people in Virginia—now show them you know how to behave."

Pulling roughly away from Chris, Bart glared at him, then strode away, very fast, without a comment. I smiled at Chris, and with him beside me, we headed for the gardens. Jory and Melodie took Cindy and began introducing her to some of the young people who'd come with their parents. There were many there that Bart had met through Jory and Melodie, who had hordes of friends and fans.

I could only hope for the best.

Samson and Delilah

Golden globes everywhere lit up the night, and the moon rode high in a cloudless, starry sky. Out on the lawn were dozens of buffet tables butted together to form a huge U. On these tables food was placed in large silver dishes. A fountain sprayed imported champagne into the air, then trickled it into layered pools that ran into tiny spigots. On the middle table was a huge ice sculpture of Foxworth Hall.

Besides the main tables laden with all that money could buy were dozens of small round and square individual tables covered with brilliant cloths—green over rose, turquoise over violet, yellow over orange, and other striking combinations. The tablecloths were kept from blowing by heavy garlands of flowers festooned around them.

Although Chris and I had been introduced in the receiving line, it seemed to me most of Bart's guests made it a point not to talk to us. I looked at Chris just as he looked at me. "What's going on?" he asked in a low whisper.

"The older guests are not talking to Bart, either," I answered. "Look, Chris, they've come just to drink, eat, and enjoy themselves, and they don't give a damn about Bart, or any of us. They are just here so he can dine and wine them."

"I wouldn't say that," Chris replied. "Everyone makes it a point to speak to Jory and Melodie. Some are even talking to Joel. Doesn't he look a fine and elegant gentleman tonight?"

Never would it cease to amaze me the way Chris could find something to admire in everyone.

Joel looked like a funeral director as he moved solemnly from one group to another. He didn't carry a glass like everyone else. He didn't partake of the refreshments that piled the buffet tables in such a breathtaking array. I nibbled daintily on a cracker spread with goose liver pâté and looked around for Cindy. She was in the center of five young men, very much the belle of the ball. Even her demure blue dress didn't keep her from looking very seductive—now that she'd shoved the shoulder ruffle down to bare the top half of her bosom.

"She looks like you used to," said Chris, also watching Cindy. "Except you had a more ethereal quality, as if your two feet were never firmly on the ground, and never would you stop believing miracles could happen." He paused and looked at me in that special way that kept my love for him always alive and thriving. "Yes, love," he whispered, "miracles can happen, even here."

Every wife or husband seemed to be trying to score with any member of the opposite sex besides their spouses. Only Chris and I stuck together. Jory had disappeared, and now Melodie was standing with Bart. He was saying something to her that had her eyes blazing hot. She turned to hurry away, but he seized hold of her arm and yanked her back. She snatched her arm away, only to have him seize it again, and ruthlessly he pulled her into his embrace. They began to dance, with Melodie determinedly keeping him from crushing her against him.

I started to go to them, but Chris caught my arm to restrain me. "Let Melodie handle him. You'd only make him furious."

Sighing, I watched the small conflict between Bart and his brother's wife and saw to my amazement that he won, for she relaxed and finally seemed to enjoy the dance that soon ended. Then he was leading her from group to group, as if she were his wife and not Jory's.

I'd tasted only a little of this and that when a very beautiful woman stepped forward, smiling first at Chris, then at me. "Aren't you Corrine Foxworth's daughter, the one who came to that Christmas night party and—"

Abruptly I cut her short. "If you'll excuse me, I have a few duties to perform," I said, hurrying away and keeping fast hold of Christopher. The woman ran behind us. "But Mrs. Sheffield . . ."

I was spared the need to answer by the blast of many trumpets. The entertainment began as Bart's guests seated themselves with plates of food and drinks. Bart and Melodie came to join us, while Cindy and Jory ran to warm up in practice outfits before they changed into elaborate costumes.

Soon the professional entertainers had me laughing along with everyone else.

What a wonderful party! I glanced often at Chris, at Bart and Melodie, who sat near us. The summer night was perfect. The mountains all around enclosed us in a friendly romantic ring, and I was again amazed that I could see them as anything but formidable barriers to keep freedom forever out of reach. I was happy to see Melodie laughing and, most of all, happy to see Bart really having a good time. He shifted his chair closer to mine. "Would you say my party is a success, Mother?"

"Yes, oh, indeed, yes, Bart, you've outdone anything I've ever attended. It's a marvelous party. The evening is breathtakingly beautiful, with the stars and moon overhead, and all your colored lights. When does the ballet begin?"

He smiled and put his arm lovingly about my shoulders. His voice was tender with understanding when he asked,

"Nothing for you equals the ballet, does it? And you won't be disappointed. You just wait to see if New York or London can equal my production of *Samson and Delilah*."

Jory had danced the role only three times before, but each time his performances had brought such acclaim it was no wonder Bart was fascinated with the role. The musicians in black sat down, reached for new music sheets, and started tuning their instruments.

A few yards away, Joel stood stiffly, a hateful, disapproving look on his face, as if he reflected all that his father's ghost might be feeling to see this extravagant waste of good money.

"Bart, you're twenty-five today, happy birthday! I remember clearly when a nurse laid you in my arms the first time. I had a terrible time giving birth to you, and the doctors kept coming to say I had to make a choice, your life or mine. I chose yours. But I made it, and was blessed with a second son . . . the very image of his father. You were crying, your small hands balled into fists as you flailed the air. Your feet kicked free of the blanket, but the minute you felt my body heat against yours, held close to my heart, you stopped crying. Your eyes, closed until then, parted into slits. You seemed to see me before you fell asleep."

"I'm sure you thought Jory was a prettier baby," he said with sarcasm, but his eyes were tender, as if he liked hearing of himself as a baby.

Melodie was regarding me with the strangest expression. I wished she weren't so near. "You had your own kind of beauty, Bart, your own personality, right from the start. You wanted me with you night and day. I'd put you in your crib, you'd cry. I'd pick you up, you'd stop crying."

"In other words I was a great big nuisance."

"I never thought that, Bart. I loved you from the day I conceived you. I loved you more when you smiled. Yours was such a faltering first smile, as if it hurt your face."

It seemed for a moment I'd touched him. His hand reached

for mine, and mine reached for his. But at that moment the overture to *Samson and Delilah* began, and this moment of sweetness between my second son and me was lost in the excited murmur of surprise as Bart's guests looked at the program and saw that Jory Janus Marquet was going to dance his most famous role, and his sister, Cynthia Sheffield, would play the role of Delilah. Many people looked at Melodie with curiosity, wondering why she wasn't dancing Delilah.

As always, when a ballet began, I was lost to the real world, drifting somewhere on a cloud and feeling so much it was painful, beautiful, and I was transported to another world.

The curtain lifted to show the inside of a colorful silken tent set against a backdrop representing a starry night in the desert. Stuffed but real-looking camels were there, palm trees swayed gently. On stage was Cindy, dressed in a diaphanous costume that clearly showed her slender but ripe figure. She wore a dark wig, cleverly bound around her head with jeweled bands. She began a seductive, undulating dance, enticing Samson, who lingered just off stage. When Jory came on, the birthday guests stood and gave him a resounding ovation.

He stood waiting until the applause ended, then began his dance. He wore nothing but a lion-skin loincloth held up by a strap that crossed his well-muscled broad chest. His skin, well tanned, appeared oiled. His hair was long and black and perfectly straight; muscles rippled as he whirled, *jetéed*, duplicating Delilah's steps only more violently, as if he mocked her womanly weakness and delighted in his own agile, masculine strength. The power it took to portray Samson made my spine shiver. He looked so right for the role, danced so well, I shivered again, not from cold but from the pure beauty of seeing my son up there, dancing as if God had gifted him with superhuman style and grace.

Then, as it inevitably had to be, Delilah's beguiling dance of seduction wore down his resistance, and Samson succumbed to the loveliness of Delilah, who let down her dark tresses and slowly began to undress . . . veil by veil she let fall before Samson fell upon her and bore her back onto the pile of animal skins . . . and the stage darkened just before the curtain dropped.

Applause thundered as the curtain came down. I noticed a certain look on Melodie's pale face—was that envy? Was she wishing now she'd danced Delilah?

"You would have made the best Delilah," whispered Bart softly, his lips brushing the wisps of hair that curled above her pearl-studded ear. "Cindy can't compare . . ."

"You do her an injustice, Bart," answered Melodie. "When you consider her lack of rehearsal time, she's performed beautifully. Jory told me he was surprised how good she is." Melodie leaned forward to address me. "Cathy, I'm sure Cindy has put in hours and hours of general practice, or else she wouldn't dance as well as she is."

Since the first act of the ballet had gone so well, I leaned back against Chris, who had his arm about me, and relaxed. "I feel so proud, Chris. Bart is behaving beautifully. Jory is the most accomplished *danseur* I've ever seen. I'm amazed how well Cindy is doing."

"Jory was born to dance," said Chris. "If *he'd* been raised by monks, still he would have danced. But I do remember a rebellious little girl who hated to stretch her muscles and make them hurt."

We laughed in the way long-married couples do, intimate laughter, expressing more than what we said.

The curtain rose again.

While Samson slept on the colorful couch he and Delilah had shared, she cautiously eased off, drew on a lovely garment of frail silk, then stole quietly to the opening of the tent and beckoned inside a group of six warriors previously hidden. All bore shields and swords. Already Delilah had shorn Samson's head of his long dark hair. She held it up triumphantly, giving the timid soldiers confidence.

Startled awake, Samson jumped from the bed, *jetéed* high into the air and tried to lift his weapon. What was left of his long hair was short and stubby. His sword seemed too heavy. He screamed silently on finding all his strength gone. His despair was made visual as he whirled in frustration, beating his brow with brutal fists for believing in love and Delilah; then he fell to writhe on the ground, twisting about, glaring at Delilah, who tormented him with her wild laughter. He rushed for her, but the six soldiers sprang upon Samson and brought him down. They bound him with chains and ropes as he struggled mightily to free himself.

And all the time, off stage, the most famous tenor from the Metropolitan Opera sang his pleading song of love to Delilah, asking why she had betrayed him. Tears flowed down my face to see my son lashed and whipped before he was hauled to his feet and the soldiers began their dance of torture while Delilah watched.

Even knowing all this horror was feigned, I cringed against Chris when the branding iron, heated white hot, was moved ever closer to Samson's bulging eyes. The set darkened. Only the white-hot iron lit up the stage—and the ghostly shine on Samson's near nude body. The last sound was Samson's scream of agony.

The second act curtain lowered. Again, there was wild applause, and cheers of "Bravo! Bravo!"

Between acts people chatted, got up for more drinks, to fill their plates again, but I sat beside Chris almost frozen with dread that I couldn't explain.

Beside Bart, Melodie sat as tense as I, her eyes closed and waiting.

Third act time.

Bart shifted his chair closer to Melodie. "I hate this ballet," she murmured. "It always frightens me, the brutality of it. The blood seems so real, too real. The wounds make me feel sick. Fairy tales suit me better."

"Everything will be fine," soothed Bart, putting his arm over her shoulders. Immediately Melodie jumped to her feet, and from then on she refused to sit.

The crimson curtain rose. Now we were staring at the representation of a heathen temple. Huge thick columns made of papier-mâché towered toward heaven. The vulgar squatting heathen god crouched overhead, cross-legged and center stage, with his cruel eyes gazing evilly downward. He was supported by two main columns reached by a short flight of steps.

The musical cue for the third and final act started.

Dancers represented the crowd that would watch Samson tortured before the priests of the temple danced onto stage, each doing his or her own special solo performance before settling into seats. Then dwarfs tugged on chains that dragged Samson onto the stage. Worn and weary-looking, blood streaking from many simulated wounds, Samson stumbled blindly in circles as the dwarfs meanly confused him, tripped him so he fell, only to struggle upward and be tripped again. I leaned foward anxiously. Chris's hand stayed on my shoulder, trying to calm me.

Could Jory really see through those nearly opaque lenses that made him look truly sightless? Why couldn't Bart have been satisfied with only a blindfold? But Jory had claimed Bart was right. The lenses were much more effective.

High expectancy was in the air.

Bart turned his eyes on Melodie, as inch by inch Joel was making his way closer, as if he wanted to position himself so he could watch our faces.

Samson had difficulty walking with the chains that manacled his powerful ankles together, dragging behind him a great ball of fake iron. Running and jumping beside him were the dozen dwarfs who jabbed at his strong legs with small swords, tiny lances. (The dwarfs were really children, costumed to look grotesque.) Jory hefted his fake chains, making them seem very heavy, making himself seem weary enough to drop. His wrists also wore what seemed to be iron manacles.

As he stumbled around the arena, turning in blind circles, trying to feel his way along, the lilting, heartrending music played. Stage right, in her own small blue spotlight, the opera star began to sing that most famous aria of all from *Samson and Delilah:*

"My heart at thy sweet voice . . ."

Blind and tormented from whip lashings weeping blood, Jory began a slow, mesmerizing dance of torment and loss of faith in love, his renewed credence in God restored, using the fake iron chains as part of his action. I'd never seen such a heartbreaking performance.

Blindly, agonizingly, Samson's ordeal of searching for Delilah while she dodged just out of his reach tore at my heart, as if this entire thing was real and not just a performance, so real every person in the audience forgot to eat, to drink, to whisper to a partner.

Delilah wore an even more revealing costume of green. The jewels sparkled as if they were real diamonds and emeralds, and when I peered through opera glasses, I saw to my dismay that they were part of the Foxworth legacy, glittering and shining enough to lend Delilah the appearance of wearing more than she actually did. And just a few hours ago Bart had blasted Cindy with his anger for wearing more than she did now.

Flitting around the temple, Delilah hid herself behind a fake marble column. Samson's outstretched hands pleaded for her help, even as the tenor screamed out his agony of betrayal. I quickly glanced at Bart. He was leaning forward, watching with such intensity it seemed nothing in the world interested him more than this play of agony he'd wanted between brother and sister.

Again I was filled with apprehension. The air seemed fraught with danger.

Higher and higher rose the pitch of the soprano. Samson began to shamble blindly toward his goal—the twin columns he meant to shove apart and bring down the heathen temple.

Overhead the giant obscene god grinned maliciously.

And that song of love made it a thousand times more painful.

As Samson was making his way up the shallow steps, on the temple floor Delilah writhed in apparent regret and agony to see her lover so cruelly treated. Several guards headed to capture her, and no doubt they would treat her as they had Samson. Even so, she began to crawl toward Samson, keeping her body low to the floor and just beneath the chains he lashed about so furiously. Now she grabbed his ankle, looking up at him pleadingly. It seemed he would beat her with his chains, but he hesitated, staring blindly downward before his manacled hand reached tenderly to stroke her long dark hair, to listen to words she mouthed but we couldn't hear.

With calculated thought for drama, with renewed faith in his love and his God, Jory lifted his arms, bulging his biceps, and broke his chains!

The audience gasped at the passion Jory put into the act.

He spun around wildly, lashing the separated chains that dangled from his wrist manacles, trying blindly to strike, apparently, anyone. Delilah jumped up to dodge the brutal chains that felled two guards and one dwarf. She made her attempts to get away a dance of such excitement everyone at the party was held in thrall, totally quiet as bit by bit, Delilah cleverly led her blind lover to the exact position he needed, between the two huge columns that supported the temple's god. Dodging, provoking Samson more and more with taunting, silent gestures even as the song declared her undying love for him. All meant to deceive the priests and the bloodthirsty crowd that wanted to see Samson dead.

All around the arena people were leaning forward, straining

to see the grace and beauty of one of the world's most famous *premier danseurs.*

Jory was performing astonishing *jetés,* lashing himself up into a terrible frenzy before he finally put one hand on a fake marble pillar; and then with more dramatic import, he had the other braced too.

On the floor, Delilah kissed his feet before she mocked him, tormented him with words she couldn't speak. Tricking the heathen crowd, while he knew she truly loved him and had betrayed him out of jealous spite and greed. With heaving, impressive motions Samson began to labor to bring down the entire temple by pushing against the columns! The tenor's voice called upon God to help him shove down the blasphemous god.

Again the soprano sang, tenderly seducing Samson into believing he couldn't do the impossible.

The last beseeching note died as with a mighty heave, perspiration streaming down his face, dripping onto his oiled body already streaked with red, he glistened in a ghastly way. His blind white eyes shone.

Delilah screamed.

The cue.

With a mighty and terrifying effort, Jory raised his hands again and began with greater effort to shove against the "stone" columns. My heart was in my throat as I watched those papier-mâché columns begin to bulge. As God restored Samson's strength, down would crash the temple, killing everyone!

Stagehands had cleverly arranged a large amount of cardboard backed by clanging junk to clatter down and make frightful noises. They faked thunder by rippling long rectangles of thin metal, as if God would wreak his vengeance in a personal way. Strangely enough, as the lights turned red, and the records of people screaming began to sound, Cindy was to tell me later, she thought she felt something hard brush her shoulder.

Just before the curtain lowered, I saw Jory fall from a huge false boulder that struck him on his back and head.

He sprawled face down on the floor, blood spurting from his cuts! Horrified to realize that sand didn't pour harmlessly out of the broken and tumbled columns, I jumped to my feet and began to scream. Instantly Chris was up and running toward the stage.

My knees buckled beneath me. I sank to the grass, still seeing the terrible vision of Jory flat on his face with the column smashed down on his lower back.

A second column crashed down on his legs.

The curtain was down now.

Applause thundered. I tried to rise and reach Jory, but my leg wouldn't hold me. Someone caught my elbow and half lifted me. I glanced and saw that it was Bart. Soon I was on the stage, staring down at the broken body of my first son.

I couldn't believe what I saw. Not my Jory, my dancing Jory. Not the little boy who'd asked when he was three, *"Am I dancing, Momma?"*

"Yes, Jory, you are dancing."

"Am I good, Momma?"

"No, Jory . . . you are wonderful!"

Not my Jory, who'd excelled at everything physical, beautiful, and heartfelt. Not my Jory . . . my Julian's son.

"Jory, Jory," I cried, falling upon my knees by his side, seeing Cindy through my tears, crying, too. He should be rising by this time. He lay sprawled . . . and bloody. The "fake" blood I felt was sticky, warm. It smelled like real blood. "Jory . . . you're not really hurt . . . Jory. . . ?"

Nothing. Not a sound, not a movement.

In my peripheral vision I saw Melodie as through the wrong end of a telescope, hurrying our way, her face so pale she and her black gown seemed darker than the night. "He's hurt. Really hurt." Somebody said that. Me?

"No! Don't move him. Call for an ambulance."

"Someone already has—his father, I think."

"Jory, Jory . . . you can't be hurt." Melodie's cry as she ran forward. Bart tried to hold her back. She began to scream when she saw the blood. "Jory, don't die, please don't die!" she sobbed over and over again.

I knew how she felt. As soon as the curtain was down, every dancer after "dying" on stage jumped up immediately . . . and Jory wasn't doing that.

Cries came from everywhere. The scent of blood was all around us. And I was staring at Bart, who had wanted this particular opera to be made into a ballet. Why this role for Jory? Why, Bart, why? Had he planned for the accident weeks ago?

How had Bart staged it? I picked up a handful of sand and found it wet. I glared at Bart, who stared down at Jory's sprawled body, wet from sweat, sticky from blood, gritty from sand. Bart had eyes only for Jory as two attendants from the ambulance lifted him carefully upon a stretcher and placed him in the back of the white ambulance.

Running forward, I shoved my way to where I could look inside the ambulance. "Will he live?" I asked the young doctor who was feeling Jory's pulse. Chris was nowhere in sight.

The doctor smiled. "Yes, he'll live. He's young and he's strong, but it's my calculated guess it will be a long time before he dances again."

And Jory had said ten million times that he couldn't live without dancing.

When the Party Is Over

I crowded into the ambulance beside Jory, and soon Chris was at my side, both of us crouching over Jory's still form strapped to the stretcher. He was unconscious, one side of his face very badly bruised and battered, and blood ran from many small wounds. I couldn't bear to look at his injuries, which overwhelmed me, much less concentrate on those horrible marks I'd seen on his back . . .

Closing my eyes, I turned my head to see the bright lights of Foxworth Hall like fireflies on the mountain. Later I was to hear from Cindy that at first all the guests had been appalled, not knowing what to do or how to act, but Bart had rushed in to tell them Jory was only slightly injured and would be fully recovered in a few days.

Up front, seated with the driver and an attendant, was Melodie in her black formal, glancing back from time to time and asking if Jory had come around yet. "Chris, will he live?" she asked in a voice thin with anxiety.

"Of course he'll live," said Chris, feverishly working over Jory, ruining his new tux with the blood. "He's not bleeding now, I've stopped that." He turned to the intern and asked for more dressings.

The screaming of the siren rattled my nerves, made me afraid soon all of us would be dead. How could I have deceived myself into believing Foxworth Hall would ever offer us anything but grief? I began to pray, closing my eyes and saying the same words over and over again. *Don't let Jory die, God, please don't take him. He's too young, he hasn't lived long enough. His unborn child needs him.* Only after I'd kept this up for several miles did I remember that I'd said almost the same prayers for Julian—and Julian had died.

By this time Melodie was hysterical. The intern started to inject her with some drug, but quickly I stopped him. "No! She's pregnant and that would harm her child." I leaned forward and hissed at Melodie, "Stop screaming! You're not helping Jory, or your baby." She screamed louder, turning to beat at me with small but strong fists.

"I wish we'd never come . . . I told him it was a mistake, coming to that house, the worst mistake of our lives, and now he's paying, paying, paying . . ." On and on saying that until finally her voice went, and Jory was opening his eyes and grinning at us.

"Hi," he said weakly. "Seems Samson didn't die after all."

I sobbed in relief. Chris smiled and bathed Jory's head cuts with some solution. "You're going to be fine, son, just fine. Just hold on to that."

Jory closed his eyes before he murmured in a weak way, "Was the performance good?"

"Cathy, you tell him what you think," Chris suggested in the calmest voice.

"You were incredible, darling," I said, leaning to kiss his pale face smeared with makeup.

"Tell Mel not to worry," he whispered as if he heard her crying; then he drifted into sleep from the sedative Chris injected into his arm.

~   ~   ~

We paced the hospital waiting room outside of the operating theater. Melodie was by this time a limp rag, sagging from fear, her eyes wide and staring. "Same as his father . . . same as his father," repeating the same words over so much I thought she was drilling that notion into her head—and into mine. I, too, could have screamed from the agony of believing Jory might die. More to keep her quiet than anything else, I took her into my arms and smothered her face against my breasts, soothing her with motherly words of assurance when I didn't feel confident about anything. We were, again, caught in the merciless clutches of Foxworths. How could I have been so happy earlier in the day? Where had my intuition fled? Bart had come into his own, and in so doing he had taken from Jory what belonged to him, the most valuable possession he had—his good health and his strong, agile body.

Hours later, five surgeons wearing green brought out my firstborn son from the operating theater. Jory was covered to his chin with blankets. All his summer tan had disappeared, leaving him as pale as his father had liked to keep *his* complexion. His dark curly hair seemed wet. Bruises were under his closed eyes.

"He'll be all right now, won't he?" asked Melodie, jumping up to hurry after the stretcher rolling fast toward an elevator. "He will recover and be as good as new, won't he?"

Desperation made her voice high and shrill.

No one said a word.

They lifted Jory off the stretcher by using the sheet, carefully deposited him on his bed, then chased all of us out but Chris. In the hall outside I held Melodie and waited, waited.

Melodie and I went back to Foxworth Hall toward dawn, when Jory's condition seemed stable enough for me to relax a little. Chris stayed on, sleeping in some little room used by the interns on duty.

I had wanted to stay as well, but Melodie grew ever more hysterical, hating the way Jory slept, hating the medicinal smell of the hospital corridors; hating the nurses who scurried in and out of his room with trays of instruments and bottles; hating the doctors who wouldn't give her, or me, a straight answer.

A taxi drove us both back to the Hall, where a light had been left burning near the front doors. The sun was just peeking over the horizon, flushing the sky with frail pink. Little birds woke up and fluttered tentative fledgling wings, while their parents sang or chirped their territorial rights before they flew away to find food. I supported Melodie up the stairs and into the house. She was by this time so deeply detached from reality that she staggered and seemed drunk.

Up one side of the dual staircase carefully, slowly, with my arm about her waist, thinking every second of the baby she was carrying and the effect this night might have on him or her. In the bedroom she shared with Jory she couldn't manage to undress, her hands trembled so badly. I helped, then slipped a nightgown over her head, tucked her into the bed and turned out the light. "I'll stay if you want," I said, as she lay there bleak and hopeless-looking. She wanted me to stay, wanted to talk about Jory and the doctors who wouldn't give us any encouragement. "Why do they do that?" she cried.

How could I tell her how doctors protected themselves with silence until they were sure of their facts? I covered for all Jory's doctors, telling Melodie that Jory had to be all right or they would have wanted her to stay on.

Finally she drifted into restless sleep, fretting and tossing, calling Jory's name, waking up often to jerk back to awareness and cry all over again. Her anguish was painful to see and hear, and I was left feeling as wrung out as she was.

An hour later, much to my relief, she sank into deep sleep, as if even she knew she had to escape that way.

I had a few minutes of sleep myself before Cindy barged into my room and perched anxiously on my bed, waiting for me to wake up. The very sinking of the mattress when she sat opened my eyes. I saw her face, opened my arms, and held her while she cried. "He is going to be all right, Momma?"

"Darling, your father is there with him. Jory had to have immediate surgery. He's in a private room now, asleep and resting comfortably. Chris will be there when he wakes up. I'm going to eat a quick breakfast and then drive to the city to be there too. I want you to stay here with Melodie—"

Already I'd decided that Melodie was much too hysterical to go to the hospital with me.

Instantly Cindy protested, saying she wanted to go and see Jory herself. I shook my head, insisting she stay. "Melodie is his wife, darling, and she is taking this very hard, and in her condition she shouldn't go back to the hospital until we know the truth about Jory. I've never seen a woman carry on so much about being in a hospital. She seems to think they are as bad as funeral homes. Now stay, and say anything to keep her calm, wait on her, see that she eats and drinks. Give her the peace she is seeking desperately now . . . and I'll telephone when I know something."

Melodie, when I peeked in a few minutes later, was so deeply asleep I knew I'd made the right decision. "Explain to her why I didn't wait for her to wake up, Cindy, lest she think I'm taking her place . . ."

I drove very fast toward the hospital.

Because Chris was a doctor, I'd spent a great deal of my life going to and from hospitals, letting him off, picking him up, visiting friends, meeting a few patients he particularly favored. We'd taken Jory to the best hospital in our area. The corridors were broad to allow the passing and turning of stretchers, the windows were wide, with plants hanging. Every modern diagnostic aid was there, despite the expense. But the room where Jory slept on and on was tiny, so tiny, as were all the rooms. The single window was so recessed it was difficult to look outside, and when I did, I saw nothing but the entranceway to the hospital and, farther away, another wing.

Chris was still sleeping, though a nurse told me he'd been in to check on Jory five times during the night. "He's really a devoted father, Mrs. Sheffield."

I turned to stare down at Jory, who now wore a heavy cast on his body with a window through which his incision could be viewed and treated, if necessary. I kept staring at his legs, wondering why they didn't twitch, bend, move—they weren't enclosed in the cast.

Suddenly an arm slipped around my waist and warm lips brushed the nape of my neck.

"Didn't I order you not to come back until I called?"

Relief immediately flooded me. Chris was here. "Chris, how can I stay away? I've got to know what's wrong, or I can't sleep. Tell me the truth, now that Melodie isn't here to scream and faint."

He sighed and bowed his head. Only then did I see how exhausted he looked, still wearing his rumpled and soiled tux. "It's not good news, Cathy. I'd rather not go into details until I've talked again with his physicians and surgeon."

"Don't you pull that old trick on me! I want to know! I'm not one of your patients who thinks doctors are gods on pedestals and I can't ask questions. Is Jory's back broken? Was his spinal cord injured? Will he walk again? Why doesn't he move his legs?"

First he pulled me out into the hall, in case Jory was awake but had his eyes closed. Softly he closed the door behind him and then led me into a tiny cubicle where only doctors were allowed. He sat me down, standing to tower above me, and made me realize I was about to hear very serious news. Only then did he speak. "Jory's spine was broken, Cathy. You guessed correctly. It's a lower lumbar fracture, so we can be grateful his injury wasn't higher. He will have full use of his arms and will eventually gain control over his bladder and intestinal functions, but right now they are in shock, so to speak, and tubes and bags will function until he regains the feeling of when he has to go."

He paused, but I wasn't letting him off that easily. "The spinal cord? Tell me that it wasn't crushed."

"No, not crushed, but damaged," he said reluctantly. "It is bruised severely enough to keep his legs paralyzed."

I froze. Oh, no! Not Jory! I cried out, with no more control than Melodie. "He'll never walk again?" I whispered, feeling myself go pale and weak and slightly light-headed. When next I opened my eyes, Chris was on his knees by my side, gripping both my hands hard.

"Hold on . . . he's alive, and that's what counts. He won't die—but he'll never walk again."

Sinking, I was drowning, drowning, going under again in that same old familiar pool of hopeless despair. The same little sparkling swanhead fish rushed to nibble on my brain, taking bits out of my soul. "And that means he'll never dance again . . . never walk, never dance . . . Chris, what will this do to him?"

He drew me into his embrace and bowed his head into my hair, his breath stirring it as he spoke in a choked way. "He'll survive, darling. Isn't that what all of us do when tragedy comes into our lives? We take it, grin and bear it, and make the best of what we have left. We forget what we had yesterday and concentrate on what we have today, and when we can teach Jory how to accept what has happened, we will have our son back again—disabled, but alive, intelligent, organically healthy."

I was jerking with sobs as he talked on. His hands ran up and down my back, his lips brushed over my eyes, my lips, finding ways to calm me.

"We've got to be strong for him, darling. Cry all you want now, for you can't cry when he opens his eyes and sees you.

You can't show pity. You can't be too sympathetic. When he wakes up, he's going to look into your eyes, and he's going to read your mind. Whatever fears or pity that you show on your face or in your eyes is going to determine how he looks and feels about his handicap. He's going to be devastated, we both know that. He'll want to die. He'll think about his father and how Julian escaped his plight, we have to keep that in mind as well. We'll have to talk to Cindy and Bart and explain to them the roles they'll play in his recovery. We have to form a strong family unit to see him through this ordeal, for it's going to be rough, Cathy, very rough."

I nodded, trying to control my flow of tears, feeling I was inside Jory, knowing every tormented moment he had ahead was going to tear me apart, too.

Chris went on while he kept his arms about me for support. "Jory's constructed his entire life around dancing, and he will never dance again. No, don't look at me with that hope. *NEVER AGAIN!* There is some possibility someday he'll have enough strength to get up on his feet and pull himself around on crutches . . . but he'll never walk normally. Accept that, Cathy.

"We have to convince him that his handicap doesn't matter, that he's the same person he was before. And, most importantly, we have to convince ourselves that he's just as manly, just as human . . . for many families change when a member becomes disabled. They either become too sympathetic, or they become alienated, as if the handicap changes the person they used to love and know. We have to keep to middle ground and help Jory find the strength to see this through."

I heard a little of what he said.

Crippled! My Jory was crippled. A paraplegic. I shook my head, disbelieving that fate would keep him that way. Tears fell like rain upon Chris's soiled, ruffled, dress shirt. How would Jory live when he found out he was going to spend the rest of his life confined to a wheelchair?

Cruel Fate

The sun was noon high and still Jory hadn't opened his eyes. Chris decided we both needed a hearty meal, and hospital food was always seasonless sawdust or shoe leather. "Try to nap while I'm gone, and hold on to your control. If he awakens, try not to panic, keep your cool and smile, smile, smile. He'll be fuzzy-minded and won't be fully cognizant. I'll try to hurry back . . ."

I'd never sleep; I was too busy planning on how to act when Jory eventually woke up long enough to start asking questions. Chris had no sooner closed the door behind him than Jory stirred, turned his head, and weakly smiled at me. "Hey, you been there all night? Or two nights? When was it?"

"Last night," I whispered hoarsely, hoping he wouldn't notice my throaty voice. "You've been sleeping for hours and hours."

"You look exhausted," he said weakly, touchingly showing more concern for me than for himself. "Why don't you go back to the Hall and sleep? I'm okay. I've fallen before, and, like before, in a few days I'll be whirling all over that house again. Where's my wife?"

Why wasn't he noticing the cast that bulged out his chest? Then I saw his eyes were unfocused and he hadn't fully pulled out of the sedatives given him to ease the pain. Good . . . if only he wouldn't start asking questions I wanted Chris to answer.

Sleepily he closed his eyes and dozed off, but ten minutes later he was again awake and asking questions. "Mom, I feel strange. Never felt like this before. Can't say I like the way I feel. Why this cast? Did I break something?"

"The temple papier-mâché columns fell," I weakly explained. "Knocked you out. What a way to end the ballet— too real."

"Did I bring down the house—or the sky?" he quipped, his eyes opening and brightening as the sedative I'd hoped would keep him hazy wore off. "Cindy was great, wasn't she? You know, each time I see her, she's more beautiful. And she's really a very good dancer. She's like you, Mom, improving with age."

I sat on my hands to keep them from twisting in the betraying way my mother used to use her hands. I smiled, got up to pour a glass of water. "Doctor's orders. You've got to drink a lot."

He sipped as I supported his head. It was so strange to see him helpless, when he'd never been bedridden. His colds had come and gone in a matter of days, and not once had he missed a day in school or ballet class, except in order to visit Bart in the hospital after one of his many accidents that never left him permanently damaged. Jory had sprained his ankles dozens of times, torn ligaments, fallen, gotten up, but he'd never had a serious injury until now. All dancers spent some time tending small injuries, and sometimes even larger ones, but a broken back, a damaged spinal cord—it was every dancer's most dreaded nightmare.

Again he dozed off, but before long he had his eyes open and was asking questions about himself. Perched on the side of his bed, I rattled on and on nonsensically, praying that Chris would come back. A pretty nurse came in with Jory's lunch tray, all liquids. That gave me something to do. I fiddled with a half-pint milk carton, opened yogurt, poured milk and orange juice, tucked a napkin under his chin, and began with the strawberry yogurt. Immediately he gagged and made a face. He shoved my hands away, saying he could feed himself, but he didn't have an appetite.

Once I had the tray out of the way, I hoped he'd fall asleep. Instead he lay there staring at me, his eyes lucid. "Can you tell me now why I feel so weak? Why I can't eat? Why I can't move my legs?"

"Your father has gone out to bring in food for the two of us, snack food that's not good for you, but it will be tastier than what we can eat in the cafeteria downstairs. Let him tell you. He knows all the technical terms that I don't."

"Mom, I wouldn't understand technical terms. Tell me in your own layman's words—why can't I feel or move my legs?"

His dark sapphire eyes riveted on me. "Mom, I'm not a coward. I can take whatever you have to say. Now spill it out, or else I'm going to presume my back is broken and my legs are paralyzed and I'm never going to walk again."

My heart quickened as my head lowered. He'd said all this in a jocular way, as if none of it could possibly be true . . . and he'd stated his condition exactly.

Desperation came to his eyes as I faltered, trying to find just the right words, and even the right ones would rip out his heart. Just then Chris strode in the door, carrying a paper sack with cheeseburgers. "Well," he said brightly, throwing Jory a pleased smile, "look who's awake and talking." He took out a burger and handed it to me. "Sorry, Jory, you can't have anything solid for a few days due to your operation. Cathy, eat that thing while it's still hot," he ordered, sitting down himself and immediately unwrapping his burger. I saw he'd bought two super ones for himself. He bit into it with relish before he brought out the cola drinks. "Didn't have the lime you wanted, Cathy. It's Pepsi."

"It's cold, with lots of ice, that's all I want."

Jory watched us narrowly as we ate. I forced down the cheeseburger, knowing he was suspicious. Chris did an admirable job of eating two burgers and one cardboard dish of French fries while I managed to eat only half of my burger, and didn't touch the greasy potatoes. Chris balled up his napkin and tossed it in a can, along with our other trash.

By this time Jory's lids were growing heavy. He was struggling hard to stay awake. "Dad . . . are you going to tell me now?"

"Yes, anything you want to know." Chris moved to sit on Jory's bed and placed his strong hand on top of Jory's. Jory blinked back sleep.

"Dad, I'm not feeling anything below my waist. All the time you and Mom ate, I was trying to wiggle my toes and I couldn't. If I've broken my back, and that's why I'm in this cast, I want to know the truth, all of it."

"I intend to tell you all the truth," said Chris staunchly.

"Is my spine broken?"

"Yes."

"Are my legs paralyzed?"

"Yes."

Jory blinked, looked stunned, gathered his strength for one last question. "Will I dance again?"

"No."

Jory closed his eyes, tightened his lips into a thin line and lay perfectly still.

I stepped closer to lean above him, and tenderly I brushed back the dark curls fallen over his brow. "Darling, I know you're devastated. It wasn't easy for your father to tell you the truth, but you have to know. You're not alone in this. We're all involved. We're here to see you through, to do everything we can. You'll adjust. Time will heal your body so you won't feel pain, and eventually you'll accept what can't be helped. We love you. Melodie loves you. And you'll be a father come this very January. You reached the top of your profession and have been there five years . . . that's more than most people accomplish in a lifetime."

Briefly he met my eyes. His were full of bitterness, anger, frustration, a rage so terrible I had to turn away. It was all over him, his fierce resentment at having been cheated and stolen from before he'd had enough.

When I looked again, his eyes were closed. Chris had his fingers on his pulse. "Jory, I know you're not sleeping. I'm going to give you another sedative so you can really sleep, and when you wake up, you are going to think about how important you are to a great many people. You're not going to feel sorry for yourself and allow yourself to wallow in bitterness. There are people walking the streets today who will never experience what you've already had. They haven't traveled the world over and heard the thundering applause and cries of 'bravo, bravo!' They'll never know the heights that were yours and can be yours again in some other field of artistic endeavor. Your world has not stopped, son, you've only stumbled. The road to achievement is still ahead and wide open, only you'll have to roll along that road instead of run or dance; but you'll achieve again, for it's in you to always win. You will just find another craft, another career, and with your family you will find happiness. Isn't that what life is all about when you come down to the basics? We want someone to love us, to need us, to share our lives . . . and you have all of that."

My son didn't open his eyes, didn't respond. He only lay there as still as if death had already claimed him.

Inside I was screaming, for Julian had reacted in the very same way! Jory was closing us out, locking himself in the narrow, tight cage of his mind that refused life without walking and dancing.

Silently Chris readied a hypodermic needle before he swabbed at Jory's arm, then released the fluid steadily into his arm. "Sleep, my son. When you wake up, your wife will be here. You'll have to be brave for her sake."

I thought I saw Jory shudder.

We left him deeply asleep, in the care of a private-duty nurse instructed to never leave him alone. Chris drove us back to Foxworth Hall so he could shower and shave, take a nap, put on fresh clothes before he drove back to be with Jory. We expected Melodie to return with us.

Her blue eyes went terror stricken and stark when Chris told her as kindly as possible Jory's condition.

She uttered a small cry and clutched at her abdomen. "You mean . . . never dance? Never walk?" she whispered, as if her voice were failing her. "There must be something you can do to help him."

Chris soon dashed that hope. "No, Melodie. When the spinal cord is injured, it prevents the legs from receiving the messages from the brain. Jory can will his legs to move, but they won't receive the message. You have to accept him as he is now, and do everything you can to help him survive what is probably the most traumatic event he will ever have to face."

She jumped to her feet, crying out pitifully, "But he won't be the same! You just said he's refusing to talk—I can't go there and pretend it doesn't matter when it does! What will he do? What will *I* do? Where will we go, and how will he survive without walking and dancing? What kind of father will he make now that he has to spend the rest of his life in a wheelchair?"

Standing, Chris spoke firmly. "Melodie, this is no time for you to panic and throw hysterical tantrums. You have to be strong, not weak. I realize you are suffering, too, but you have to show him a bright, smiling face that will give him the assurance that he hasn't lost the wife he loves. You don't marry just for the good times, but for the bad times as well.

You'll bathe, dress, put on your makeup, style your hair, and go to him and hold him in your arms as best you can, and kiss him and make him believe he has a future worth staying alive for."

"BUT HE DOESN'T!" she yelled. "HE DOESN'T!"

Then, breaking, she was crying bitter tears. "I didn't mean that . . . I love him, I do . . . but don't make me go and see him lying like that so still and quiet. I can't stand to see him until he's smiling and accepting, and then maybe I can face up to what he's become . . . maybe I can . . . ."

I disliked her for showing such spineless hysteria and failing Jory when he needed her most. Stepping to Chris's side, I linked my arm through his. "Melodie, do you think for one moment that you are the first wife and expectant mother to suddenly find the world crashing down on your head? You're not. I was expecting Jory when his father was in a fatal auto accident. Just be grateful Jory is alive."

She sank in a crumpled heap on a chair and bowed her head into her hands and cried for long minutes before she looked up, her eyes darker and more bleak than before. "Perhaps death is what he'd prefer—have you thought of that?"

It was the thought that tormented my hours, that Jory would do something to end his life, as Julian had done.

I wouldn't let it happen. Not again. "Then stay here and cry," I said with unintentional hardness. "But I'm not going to leave my son alone to fight this out by himself. I'm going to stay with him night and day to see that he doesn't give up hope. But you keep this in mind, Melodie: You are carrying his child, and that makes you the most important person in his life—and important in mine, too. He needs you and your support. I'm sorry if I sound harsh, but I have to think first of him . . . why can't you?"

Speechless, she stared up at me, her lovely face stricken, tears streaking her cheeks. "Tell him I'll come soon . . . tell him that," she whispered hoarsely.

We told him that.

He kept his eyes closed, his lips glued together. There were ways of telling he wasn't asleep, only shutting us out.

Jory refused to eat until tubes were put in his arms to feed him intravenously. Summer days came and went; long days that were full and mostly sad. Some hours gave me faint pleasures when I was with Chris and Cindy, but few gave me hope.

If only, if only were the words that started off my mornings, as they finished off my nights. If only I could live my life all over again, then, perhaps, I could save Jory, Chris, Cindy, Melodie, myself—and even Bart. If only.

If only he hadn't danced that role—

I tried everything, as Chris and Cindy did, to pull Jory back from that terribly lonely place where he'd taken himself. For the first time in my life I couldn't reach him, couldn't ease his sorrow.

He'd lost what mattered most to him, the use of his dancing legs. With his legs he'd soon lose his wonderfully powerful and skilled body. I couldn't look at those beautifully shaped strong legs lying so still beneath the sheet, so damned useless.

Had the grandmother been right when she said we were cursed, born for failure and pain? Had she programmed us for tragedy to steal the fruit of our successes?

Had Chris and I achieved anything of real value when our son lay as if dead, and our second son refused to visit Jory but once?

Bart had stood and stared down at Jory lying helpless and still with his eyes closed, his arms straight down at his sides. "Oh, my God," he'd whispered before he hurried from the tiny room.

Never could I convince him to visit again. "Mother, he doesn't know I'm there, so what's the good? I can't bear to see him like that. I'm sorry, really sorry . . . but I can't help."

I stared at him, wondering if I had wanted to help *him* so much I'd risked the life of my beloved Jory.

That's when I began to tell myself that I wasn't going to believe he'd never walk, never dance again. This was a nightmare to be endured, but eventually we'd awaken and Jory would be whole again, just as he'd been.

I told Chris my plan to convince Jory he could and he would walk again, even if he never danced.

"Cathy, you can't give him false hope," warned Chris, looking terribly distressed. "All you can do now is help him accept what can't be changed. Give him your kind of strength. Help him—but don't lead him down false trails that will bring him only disappointment. I know it will be difficult. I'm in hell, too, just as much as you are. But remember, our hell is nothing compared to his. We can sympathize and feel dreadfully sorry, but we're not inside his skin. We're not suffering his loss—he's all alone in that. Facing up to agony you and I can't even begin to understand. All we can do is be here when he decides to pull out of his protective shell. Be here to give him the confidence he needs to go on . . . for damned if Melodie is giving him anything!"

That was something almost as awful as Jory's injury . . . that his own wife would shun him now as if he were a leper. Both Chris and I pleaded with her to come with us, even if she said nothing but hello, I love you, *she had to come.*

"What can I say that you haven't already said?" she screamed. "He doesn't want me to come and see him like that! I know him better than either of you do. If he wanted to see me, he'd say he did. Besides, I'm afraid to go, afraid I'll cry and say all the wrong things, and even if I stay quiet, he might open his eyes and see something on my face that would make him feel worse, and I don't want to be responsible for what might happen then. Stop insisting! Wait until he wants me to visit . . . and then, maybe, I can find the courage I need."

She flew away from Chris and me as if we carried with us some plague that might contaminate *her* dream that this nightmare would end happily.

Standing in the hall outside our rooms was Bart, staring after Melodie with his heart in his eyes. He turned to glare at me.

"Why *don't* you leave her alone? I've been to see him, and it tore me all apart. Certainly in her condition she needs to find some security, even if it's only in her dreams. She sleeps a great deal, you know. While you stay with him, she cries, walks as if in a dream, with her eyes unfocused. She half eats. I have to plead with her to swallow, to drink. She stares at me, and obeys like a child. Sometimes I have to spoon the food into her mouth, hold the glass for her to sip. Mother, Melodie is in shock—and all you think about is your precious Jory, not caring what you do to her!"

Sorry now, I hurried to her side and held her in my arms. "It's all right. I understand now. Bart has explained how you can't accept this yet . . . but try, Melodie, please try. Even if he doesn't open his eyes and speak, he's aware of what's going on, and who comes to see him and who doesn't."

Her head was on my shoulder. "Cathy . . . I am trying. Just give me time."

The next morning Cindy came into our bedroom without knocking, causing Chris to frown. She should have known better. But I had to forgive her after seeing her pale face and frightened expression. "Momma . . . Daddy, I've just got to tell you something, and yet I don't know if I should. Or if it really means anything."

I was distracted from her words by the outfit she wore: a white bikini so brief it was barely there. The swimming pool Bart had ordered was now complete and this was the first day it was ready. Jory's tragic accident was not going to inhibit Bart's style of living.

"Cindy, I wish you would wear those beach coverups at the poolside. And that suit is much too skimpy."

She appeared startled, crestfallen and hurt because I criticized her suit. Glancing down at herself briefly, she shrugged indifferently. "Holy Christ, Momma! Some friends of mine wear string bikinis—you should see those if you think this one is immodest. Some of my friends wear nothing at all . . ." Her large blue eyes studied mine seriously.

Chris tossed her a towel, which she wrapped around herself. "Momma, I've got to say I don't like the way you make me feel, somehow dirty, like Bart makes me feel—when I came to tell you something I overheard Bart talking about."

"Go on, Cindy," urged Chris.

"Bart was on the telephone. He'd left his door ajar. I heard him talking to an insurance agency." She paused, sat down on our unmade bed and lowered her head before she spoke again. Her soft, silky hair hid her expression. "Mom, Dad, it seems Bart took out some kind of special 'party' insurance in case any of his guests were injured."

"Why, that's not at all unusual," said Chris. "The house is covered by homeowner's insurance . . . but with two hundred guests, he needed plenty of extra insurance that night."

Cindy's head jerked upward. She stared at her father, then at me. A sigh escaped her lips. "I guess it's okay then. I just thought maybe . . . maybe . . ."

"Maybe what?" I asked sharply.

"Momma, you picked up a handful of that sand that spilled from the columns when they broke. Wasn't the sand supposed to be dry? It wasn't dry. Someone made it wet—and that made it heavier. The sand didn't come pouring out like it was supposed to. It made those columns stand upright—and the sand clumped down on Jory like cement. Otherwise Jory wouldn't have been hurt so severely."

"I knew about the insurance," said Chris dully, refusing to meet my eyes. "I didn't know about the wet sand."

Neither Chris nor I could find words to defend Bart. Still, surely, surely he wouldn't want to injure Jory—or kill him? At some point in our lives, we had to believe in Bart, give him the benefit of doubt.

Chris paced our bedroom, his brow deeply wrinkled as he explained one of the stage crew could have put water on the sand, hoping to make the columns steadier. It didn't have to be Bart's order he was following.

All three of us descended the stairs solemnly, finding Bart outside on the morning terrace with Melodie. With the mountains in the distance, the woods before them, the gardens lush with blooming flowers, the setting was beautifully romantic. Sunlight filtered through the lacy leaves of the fruit trees, slipped under the brightly striped umbrella that was supposed to shield the occupants seated at the white wrought-iron table.

Melodie, to my surprise, was smiling as her eyes lingered on the strong lines of Bart's face. "Bart, your parents don't understand why I can't bring myself to go and see Jory in the hospital. I see your mother looking at me resentfully. I'm disappointing her, disappointing myself. I'm a coward about illnesses. Always have been. But I know what's going on. I know Jory lies on that bed, staring up at the ceiling, refusing to talk. I know what he's thinking. He's lost not only the use of his legs, but all the goals he's set for himself. He's thinking of his father and the way he died. He's trying to withdraw from the world by making himself into a nothing thing that we won't miss when one day he kills himself just like his father did."

Bart quickly looked at her disapprovingly. "Melodie, you don't know my brother. Jory would never kill himself. Maybe he does feel lost now, but he'll come around."

"How can he?" she wailed. "He's lost the most important thing in his life. Our marriage was based not only on our love for each other, but on our mutual careers. Each day I tell myself that I can go to him, and smile, and give him what he needs. Then I pause, flounder, and wonder what can I say. I'm not good with words like your mother. I can't smile and be optimistic like his father—"

"Chris is not Jory's father," stated Bart flatly.

"Oh, to Jory Chris is his father. At least the one who counts most. He loves Chris, Bart, respects and admires him, and forgives him for what you call his sins." She went on while we three hung back, waiting to hear more of why she was acting as she was.

And all we heard was a concluding statement. "I'm ashamed to say it, but I can't go and see him like he is."

"Then what are you going to do?" asked Bart in a cynical way. He sipped his coffee while staring directly into her eyes. If he'd turn his head just a little, he'd see the three of us watching and listening, and learning so much.

Her answer was an anguished wail. "I don't know! I'm coming apart inside! I hate waking up and knowing that Jory will never be a real husband to me again. If you don't mind, I'm going to move into the room across the hall that doesn't hold so many painful memories of what we used to share. Your mother doesn't realize that I'm just as lost as he is, and I'm having his baby!"

Her sobs started then. Bowing her head, she put it down on the arms she folded on the table. "Someone has to think of me, help *me* . . . someone . . ."

"I'll help," said Bart softly, laying his tanned hand on her shoulder. His right hand set the coffee aside and lightly he brushed that hand over her spill of flowing hair. "Whenever you need me, if only for a shoulder to cry on, I'll be there, anytime."

If I'd heard Bart speak as compassionately before to anyone but Melodie, my heart would have jumped for joy. As it was, it plunged. Jory needed his wife—not Bart!

I stepped forward into the sunlight and took my place at the breakfast table. Bart snatched his hands away from Melodie, staring at me as if I'd interrupted something that was very important to him. Then Chris and Cindy joined us. Silence came that I had to break.

"Melodie, I want to have a long talk with you as soon as we finish breakfast. You're not going to run away this time, or turn deaf ears, and shut out my voice with your blank stare."

"Mother!" flared Bart. "Can't you see her viewpoint? Maybe someday Jory will be able to drag himself around on crutches, if he wears a heavy back brace and a harness . . . can you imagine Jory like that? I can't. Even I don't want to see him like that."

Melodie let out a shrieking cry, jumping to her feet. Bart followed suit, to hold her protectively in his arms.

"Don't cry, Melodie," he soothed in a tender, caring voice. Melodie uttered another small cry of distress, then fled the terrace. The three of us sat quietly staring after her. When she was out of sight, our eyes fixed on Bart, who sat down to finish his breakfast as if we weren't there.

"Bart," said Chris in this opportune moment before Joel joined us, "what do you know about the wet sand in the papier-mâché columns?"

"I don't understand," said Bart smoothly, appearing very distracted as he stared at the door through which Melodie had disappeared.

"Then I'll explain more carefully," went on Chris. "It was understood the sand would be dry so it would spill out easily and not harm anyone. Who wet the sand?"

Narrowing his eyes first, Bart answered sharply, "So now I'm going to be accused of causing Jory's accident—and deliberately ruining the best time I've had until he was hurt. Why, it's just like it used to be when I was nine and ten. My fault, everything was always my fault. When Clover died, you both presumed I was the one to wrap the wire about his neck, never giving me the benefit of a doubt. When Apple was killed, again you thought it was me, when you knew I loved both Clover and Apple. I've never killed anything. Even when you found out later it was John Amos, you put me through hell before you said you were sorry. Well, say you're sorry now, for damned if I'll take the blame for Jory's broken back!"

I wanted to believe him so much tears came to my eyes. "But who wet the sand, Bart?" I asked, leaning forward and reaching for his hand. "Somebody did."

His dark eyes went bleak. "Several of the workhands disliked me for being too bossy . . . but I don't really think they would do anything to hurt Jory. After all, it wasn't me up there."

For some reason I believed him. He didn't know anything about the wet sand, and when I met Chris's eyes, I knew he was convinced as well. But in asking, we'd alienated Bart . . . again.

He sat silently now, not smiling as he finished his meal. In the garden I glimpsed Joel in the shadows of dense shrubbery as if he'd been eavesdropping on our conversation while pretending to admire the flowers in bloom.

"Forgive us if we hurt you, Bart. Please, do what you can to help us find out who did wet the sand. But for that, Jory would have the use of his legs."

Wisely Cindy had kept very quiet during all of this.

Bart started to reply, but at that moment Trevor stepped from the house and began serving us. Quickly I swallowed a light breakfast, then rose to go. I had to do something to bring back Melodie's sense of responsibility. "Excuse me, Chris, Cindy. Take your time and finish your breakfast. I'll join you later."

Joel slipped out of the shadows of the dense shrubbery and seated himself beside Bart. As I turned to glance back over my shoulder, I saw Joel lean toward Bart, whispering something I couldn't make out.

Feeling heavy of heart, I headed for the room that Melodie now used.

Face down on the bed she and Jory had shared, Melodie was crying. I perched on the side of her bed, thinking about all the right words to say—but where were the right words?

"He's alive, Melodie, and that counts, doesn't it? He's still with us. With you. You can reach out and touch him, talk to him, say all the things I wish I'd said to his father. Go to the hospital. Every day you stay away, he dies a bit more. If you don't go, if you just stay here and feel sorry for yourself, you'll live to regret it. Jory can still hear you, Melodie. Don't leave him now. He needs you now more than he's ever needed you before."

Wild and hysterical, she turned to beat at me with small fists. I caught her wrists to keep from being injured.

"But I can't face him, Cathy! I've known he lies there, silent and alone where I can't reach him. He doesn't answer when *you* speak, so why would he respond to me? If I kissed him and he said or did nothing, I'd die inside. Besides, you don't really know him, not like I do. You're his mother, not his wife. You don't realize just how important his sexual life is to him. Now he won't have any. Do you have any idea of what that one thing is doing to him? To say nothing of losing the use of his legs, and giving up his career. He so wanted to prove himself for his father's sake—his real father's sake. And you kid yourself to think he's alive. He isn't. He's already left you, Cathy. Left me, too. He doesn't have to die. He's already dead while he's still alive."

How her impassioned words stung me. Maybe because they were all too true.

I panicked inside, realizing that Jory could very well do as Julian had done—find a way to end his life. I tried to console myself. Jory was not like his father, he was like Chris. Eventually Jory would come around and make the best of what he had left.

I sat on that bed, staring at my daughter-in-law, and realized I didn't know her. Didn't know the girl I'd seen off and on since she was eleven. I'd seen the facade of a pretty, graceful girl who'd always seemed to adore Jory. "What kind of woman are you, Melodie? Just what kind?"

She flipped over on her back and glared angrily at me.

"Not your kind, Cathy!" she almost screamed. "You're made of special rugged stuff. I'm not. I was spoiled like you spoil your dear little Cindy. I was an only child and was given everything I wanted. I found out when I was small that life isn't all pretty picture book fables. And I didn't want it that way. When I was old enough, I ran to hide in the ballet. I told myself only in the world of fantasy could I find happiness. When I met Jory he seemed the prince I needed. Princes don't fall and injure their spinal cords, Cathy. They are never crippled. How can I live with Jory when I don't see him as a prince anymore? How, Cathy? Tell me how I can blind my eyes, and numb my senses, so I won't feel revulsion when he touches me."

I stood up.

I stared down at her reddened eyes, her face made puffy from so much crying and felt all my admiration for her fade away. Weak, that's what she was. What a fool to believe that Jory wasn't made of the same flesh and blood as any other man. "Suppose the injury had been yours, Melodie. Would you want Jory to desert you?"

She met my eyes squarely. "Yes, I would."

I left Melodie still crying on her bed.

Chris was waiting for me downstairs. "I thought if you went this morning, I'd visit him this afternoon, and Melodie can go to him tonight with Cindy. I'm sure you convinced her to go."

"Yes, she'll go, but not today," I said without meeting his eyes. "She wants to wait until he opens his eyes and speaks—so that's my plan, to somehow reach him and make him respond."

"If anyone can do that, it will be you," Chris murmured in my hair.

~   ~   ~

Jory lay supine on his hospital bed. The fracture was so low on his back that one fine day in the far future he might even gain back his potency. There were certain exercises he could do later on.

I'd bought two huge long boxes of mixed bouquets that I'd put into tall vases.

"Good morning, darling," I said brightly as I entered his small, sterile room.

Jory didn't turn his head to look my way. He lay as I'd seen him last, staring straight up at the ceiling. Kissing his faintly chilled face, I began to arrange the flowers.

"You'll be happy to know Melodie is no longer suffering from morning sickness. But she's tired most of the time. I remember I was tired, too, when I was pregnant with you."

I bit down on my tongue, for I'd lost Julian not long after I knew I was with child. "It's a strange kind of summer, Jory. I can't say I really care for Joel. He seems very fond of Bart, but he does nothing but criticize Cindy. She can do nothing right in Joel's eyes, or in Bart's. I'm thinking it would be a good idea to send Cindy off to a summer camp until school starts in the fall. You don't think Cindy is misbehaving, do you?"

No answer.

I tried not to sigh, or look at him with impatience. I drew a chair close to Jory's bed and caught hold of his limp hand. No response. It was like holding a dead fish. "Jory, they're going to keep on feeding you intravenously," I warned. "And if you still refuse to eat, they will put tubes in other veins, and use other methods to keep you alive, even if we have to eventually put you on every machine that will keep you going until you stop acting stubborn and come back to us."

He didn't blink, or speak.

"All right, Jory. I've been easy on you up until now—but I've had enough!" My tone turned harsh. "I love you too much to see you lie there and will yourself to die. So you don't care about anything anymore, do you?

"So you're crippled and you'll have to sit in a wheelchair until you can manage crutches, if you ever have that much ambition. So you're feeling sorry for yourself, and wondering how you can go on. Others have done it. Others have made lives for themselves, and been in worse condition than you are. So you tell yourself what others do doesn't count when it's your body, and your life—and maybe you're right. It doesn't matter what others do, if you want to think selfishly.

"Tell me that the future holds nothing for you now. I thought that, too, at first. I don't like to see you lying there so still, Jory. It breaks my heart, your father's heart, and Cindy is beside herself with worry. Bart is so concerned he can't bear to come and see you lying there so withdrawn. And what do you think you're doing to Melodie? She's carrying your child, Jory. She's crying all day long. She's changing into a different person because she hears us talking about your lack of response and your stubborn inability to accept what can't be changed. We're sorry, terribly sorry you've lost the use of your legs—but what can any of us do but make the best out of a miserable situation? Jory, come back to us. We need you with us. We're not willing to stand back and watch you kill yourself. We love you. We don't give a damn if you can't dance and can't walk, we just want you alive, where we can see you, talk to you. Speak to us, Jory. Say something, anything. Speak to Melodie when she comes. Respond when she touches you . . . or you'll lose Melodie and your child. She loves you, you know that. But no woman can live on love when the object of her love turns away and rejects her. She doesn't come because she can't face the rejection that she knows you give us."

During this long, impassioned speech, I'd kept my eyes on his face, hoping for some slight change of expression. I was rewarded by seeing a muscle near his tight lips twitch.

Encouraged, I went on. "Melodie's parents have called and suggested that she return to them to have the baby. Do you want Melodie to go, thinking she can't do anything more for you? Jory, please, please, don't do this to all of us, to yourself. You have so much you can give the world. You're more than just a dancer, don't you know that? When you have talent it's only one branch on a tree full of many limbs. Why, you've never begun to explore the other branches. Who knows just what you might discover? Remember, I, too, made dancing my life, and when I couldn't dance, I didn't know what to do with myself. I'd hear the music playing, and you'd be dancing with Melodie in our family room. I'd stiffen inside and try to shut out the music that made my legs want to dance. My soul went soaring . . . and then I'd crash to earth and cry. But when I started writing, I stopped thinking about dancing. Jory, you'll find something of interest to replace dancing, I know you will."

For the first time since he'd known he would never walk or dance again, Jory turned his head. That alone filled me with breathless joy.

He met my eyes briefly. I saw the tears there, unshed but shining. "Mel is thinking about going to her parents?" he asked in a hoarse voice.

Hope struggled to survive within me. I didn't know what Melodie would do now, even if he did come back to being himself. Yet I had to say everything right, and so seldom was I adequate. I'd failed with Julian, failed with Carrie. *Please, God, don't let me fail with Jory.*

"She'd never leave you if you'd come back to her. She needs you, wants you. You turn away from us, proving to her that you'll turn from her as well. Your prolonged silence and unwillingness to eat say so much, Jory, so much to keep Melodie afraid. She's not like me. She doesn't bounce back, spring forth, and kick and yell. She cries all the time. She only half eats . . . and she's pregnant, Jory. Pregnant with your baby. You think about how you felt when you heard what your father did and consider the effects your death will have on your child. Think long and hard about that before you continue with what you've got your mind set on. Think about yourself, and how much you wanted to have your own natural father. Jory, don't be like your father and leave a fatherless child behind you. Don't destroy us, when you destroy yourself!"

"But, Mom!" he cried in great distress. "What am I going to do? I don't want to sit in a wheelchair the rest of my life! I'm angry, so damned angry I want to strike out and hurt everyone! What have I done to deserve this kind of punishment? I've been a good son, a faithful husband. But I can't be a husband now. There's no excitement down there anymore. I feel nothing below my waist. I'd be better off dead than like this!"

My head lowered to press my cheek against his inert hand. "Maybe you would be, Jory. So go on and starve yourself, and will yourself to die, and never sit in a wheelchair— and don't think about any of us. Forget the grief you'll bring into our lives when you're gone. Forget about all those Chris and I have lost before. We can adjust, we're used to losing those we love most. We'll just add you to our long list of those to feel guilty about . . . for we will feel guilty. We'll search and search until we find something we failed to do right, and we'll enlarge that and make it grow, until it shuts out the sun and all happiness, and we'll go into our graves blaming ourselves for yet another life gone."

"Mom! Stop! I can't stand to hear you talk like that!"

"I can't stand what you're doing to us! Jory! Don't give up. It's not like you to even think of surrendering. Fight back. Tell yourself you're going to lick this and turn out a better, stronger person because you've faced up to adversities others can't even imagine."

He was listening. "I don't know if I want to fight back. I've lain here since that night and thought about what I could do. Don't tell me I don't have to do anything because you're rich, and I've got money, too. Life is nothing without a goal, you know that."

"Your child . . . make your child your goal. Making Melodie happy, another goal. Stay, Jory, stay . . . I can't bear to lose another, I can't, can't . . . "And then I was crying.

And I'd determined not to show weakness and cry. I sobbed brokenly without looking at him. "After your father died, I made my baby the most important thing in my life. Maybe I did that to ease a guilty conscience, I don't know. But when you came along on Valentine's night and they laid you on my stomach so I could see you, my heart almost burst with pride. You were so strong-looking, and your blue eyes were so bright. You grasped my finger and didn't want to let go. Paul was there, and Chris, too. They both adored you right from the beginning. You were such a happy, well-behaved baby. I think we all spoiled you, and you never had to cry to get what you wanted. Jory, now I know you are incapable of being spoiled. You've got an inner strength that will see you through. Eventually you'll be glad you hung on to see that child of yours. I know you'll be glad."

During all of this, I'd sobbed my words almost incoherently. I think Jory felt sorry for me. His hand moved so he could wipe away my tears with the edge of his white sheet.

"Got any ideas about what I could do in a wheelchair?" he asked in a small, mocking voice.

"A thousand ideas, Jory. Why, this day isn't long enough to list them. You can learn to play the piano, study art, learn to write. Or you can become a ballet instructor. You don't have to strut around to do that—all you need is a good vocabulary and an untiring tongue. Or you can do something more mundane, like become a CPA, study law and give Bart some competition. In fact, there is very little you can't do. We're all handicapped in one way or another. You should know that. Bart's got his invisible handicap, worse than any you'll ever have. Think back to all his problems while you were dancing and having the time of your life. He was tormented by psychiatrists probing painfully into his deepest self."

His eyes were brighter now, filling with vague hope that tried to find a mooring.

"And think about the swimming pool Bart put in the yard. Your doctors say your arms are very strong, and after some physical therapy you can swim again."

"What do *you* want me to do, Mom?" His voice was soft, gentle as his hand moved over my hair, and his gaze was tender.

"Live, Jory, that's all."

His eyes were soft now, full of tears that didn't fall. "What about you, Dad, and Cindy? Weren't you planning to move to Hawaii?"

For weeks I hadn't thought of Hawaii. I stared blankly before me. How could we leave now that Jory was injured and Melodie was in such distress? We couldn't leave.

Foxworth Hall had trapped us again.

BOOK TWO

The Reluctant Wife

Regretfully Chris and I neglected Cindy as we spent most of our time in the hospital with Jory. Cindy grew restless and bored in a hostile house with Joel, who gave her only disapproval, with Bart, who gave her only scorn, with Melodie, who had nothing to give to anyone.

"Momma," she wailed. "I'm not having a good time! It's been a terrible summer, the worst. I'm sorry Jory's in the hospital and he won't ever walk or dance again, and I want to do what I can for him, but what about me? They only allow him to have two visitors at a time and you and Daddy are always with him. Even when I do see him, half the time I don't know what to say, or what to do. And I don't know what to do with myself when I'm here, either. This house is so isolated from the rest of the world it's like living on the moon—boring, boring. You tell me not to go into the village, not to have dates unless you know about them, and you're never here to ask when someone invites me. You tell me not to swim when Bart and Joel are around. You tell me not to do so many things . . . what is it that I *can* do?"

"Tell me what you want to do," I said with sympathy. She was sixteen and had expected this vacation to give her great pleasure. Now the mansion she'd admired so much in the beginning was proving, in some ways, to be as much a prison for her as the old one had been for us.

She came to sit cross-legged on the floor near my feet. "I don't want to hurt Jory's feelings by leaving, but I'm going crazy here. Melodie stays in her room all the time with her door locked and refuses to let me in. Joel dries me up with his mean old eyes. Bart pretends he doesn't see me. Today a letter came from my friend Bary Boswell, and she's going to this marvelous summer camp just a few miles north of Boston, where there is a summer stock theater nearby. And there's swimming in the lake nearby, and sailing, and dances every Saturday, plus they teach all kinds of crafts. I like being with girls my own age, and I think that's just the kind of camp I'd enjoy. You can check into it and see that it has a good reputation, but let me go, please, before I go batty."

I'd so wanted all of us to have a close getting-to-know-you-all-over-again kind of summer, and here she was, wanting to leave, and I hadn't spent nearly enough time with her. Still, I easily understood. "I'll talk to your father about it tonight," I promised. "We want you to be happy, Cindy, you know that. I'm sorry if we've neglected you while we care for Jory. Let's talk now about you. What about boys you met at Bart's party, Cindy? What's going on between you and them?"

"Bart and Joel hide the keys to the cars so I can't drive off. And that's exactly what I would do, permission or not. I want to slip out a window, but they're all so high above the ground, and I'm afraid to jump and fall and hurt myself. But I think about boys all the time, that's what. I miss being with them, having dates and going to dances. I know what you're thinking, because Joel is always muttering about me being without morals . . . I'm trying hard to hang on to them, really I am. Yet I don't know how long I can keep myself a virgin. I tell myself that I'm going to be old-fashioned and hold out until I'm married, but I plan not to marry until I'm at least thirty. Then, when I'm out with a boy I really like, and he begins to apply pressure, I want to surrender. I like the sensations I feel leaping up and making my heart beat faster. My body wants it to happen. Momma, why can't I find the kind of strength you have? How do I find the real me? I'm caught in a world that doesn't really know what it wants, you tell me that all the time. So if the world doesn't know, how can I? I want to be what you want me to be, sweet and pure, while *I* want to be sexy. The two contradict each other. I want you and Daddy to always love me, so I try to be as sweet as you think I am—but I'm not that innocent, Momma. I want all the good-looking boys to be in love with me—but someday I'm not going to be able to hold back."

I smiled to see her troubled expression, her fearful glance to see if I'd be shocked. I guessed, too, that she was afraid she'd just ruined her chances to escape this house. My arms went around her. "Hang on to morality, Cindy. You're much too talented and too beautiful to give yourself away like a bit of worthless trash. Think highly of yourself, and others will as well."

"But Momma—how do I say no, and still keep the boys liking me?"

"There are a lot of boys who won't expect you to 'give out,' Cindy, and that's the kind you want. Those who demand sex for one reason or another are more than likely to dump you quickly after they get what they want. There's something about men that makes them want to conquer every woman, especially an exceptional beauty like you. Remember, too, they talk amongst themselves and report on the most intimate details when they don't really love you."

"Momma! You make me feel that being a woman is a trap! I don't want them to trap *me*—I want to trap them! But I have to confess, I'm not good about resisting. Bart's made me feel so insecure about myself that I keep wanting the boys to convince me differently. But every time from this day forward, when some jerk gets me on the backseat and says he'll fall ill if I don't satisfy his lust, I won't feel sorry for him. I'll just think of you and Daddy and bash in his head—or give him the knee where it hurts worse."

She made me laugh, when I hadn't laughed in weeks. "All right, darling, I know in the end you'll do the right thing. So let's talk more about that summer camp so I can give your father all the details."

"You mean I haven't spoiled my chances?" she asked in a delighted way.

"Of course not. I think Chris will agree that you need a break from all this tragedy here."

Chris did agree, thinking as I did that a sixteen-year-old girl needed this special summer for fun. The moment Cindy knew, she had to visit Jory and spill it all out to him. "Now, just because I'm leaving doesn't mean I don't care, but I'm so damned bored, Jory. I'm going to write often and send you little gifts." She embraced him, kissed him, her tears falling to put beads on his clean-shaven face. "Nothing can take away what you are, Jory—that wonderful thing that makes you so special, and it doesn't live in your legs. I'd want you for my own if you weren't my brother."

"Sure you would," he said with some irony. "But thanks anyway."

Chris and I left Jory alone with his nurse long enough to drive Cindy to the nearest airport, where we kissed her goodbye and he handed her some "pin" money. She was delighted with the amount and had to kiss him again and again before she backed off, waving vigorously. "I'll write real letters," she promised, "not just postcards, and I'll send pictures. Thanks for everything, and don't forget to write often and tell me what's going on. In a way, living in Foxworth Hall is like being caught up in some deep, dark, mysterious novel, only it's too frightening when you're actually living the story."

On the way to the hospital to stay with Jory again, Chris told me of his plans. We couldn't move to Hawaii now and abandon Jory to the frail mercies of Bart and Joel, and Melodie wasn't able to care for herself, much less a husband in a back cast, even if she did hire a nurse. And neither Jory nor Melodie would be in any condition to make the long plane trip to Hawaii for many months.

"I won't know what to do with myself when Jory goes back to the Hall and has his own attendants, any more than Cindy knew how to keep herself occupied and happy. Jory won't need me every hour. I'm going to feel useless unless I do something meaningful, Cathy. I'm not an old man. I still have many good years ahead of me."

Sadly I turned my head to watch him as he kept his eyes on the traffic. He went on without turning to meet my eyes. "Medicine has always played a very important part in my life. That doesn't mean I'm breaking my promise to share more time with you and my family than I do professionally. Just remember what losing a career means to Jory . . ."

Sliding closer on the seat, I lowered my head to his shoulder, telling him in a choked voice to go ahead and do what he felt was right. ". . . but keep in mind a physician has to have an impeccable record, and someday there may be gossip about us."

He nodded, saying he'd already considered that fact. This time he was going into the research side of medicine. He wouldn't be meeting the public, who might recognize him as a Foxworth. He'd already thought enough on the subject. Already he was bored with staying home and contributing nothing. He had to do something important or lose the identity he felt he needed. I put on a bright smile even if my heart was sinking, for his dream of living in Hawaii had also been my dream.

With arms about each other, we entered the huge house that waited with its gaping jaws wide.

Melodie had sequestered herself in her room, Joel was in that little room without furniture, down on his knees praying while a single candle burned in the gloom. "Where is Bart?" asked Chris, looking around as if astonished that anyone would want to spend so many hours in such a dismal place.

Joel frowned, then faintly smiled, as if he had to remember to appear friendly. "Bart is off in some bar drinking himself under the table, as he put it."

I'd never known Bart to do such a thing. Regret for setting up the performance that ruined his brother's legs, and cost him his career? Regret for driving Cindy away? Did Bart know how to feel regret? I didn't know. I stared blankly at Joel as he paced the floor, seeming terribly upset, when what difference did Bart's behavior make to him?

The old man followed us as usually he followed Bart. "He should know better," muttered Joel. "Whores and harlots hang out in bars, though I've warned him about them."

His words intrigued me. "What's the difference between a whore and a harlot, Joel?"

His smeary eyes turned my way. As if light blinded him, he shaded those eyes with his gnarled hand.

"Are you mocking me, niece? The Bible mentions both nouns, so there must be some difference."

"Perhaps a whore is worse than a harlot, or vice versa? Is that what you mean?"

He glared at me, telling me with his glittering, faded eyes that I was tormenting him with my silly questions.

"Then's there's a strumpet, Joel, and today we have hookers, call girls, and prostitutes—do they come between harlots and whores, or are they the same?"

His eyes hardened to rivet on me with the piercing glare of a virgin saint. "You don't like me, Catherine. Why don't you like me? What have I done to make you distrust me? I stay to save Bart from the worst in himself, or I'd leave today because of your attitude, and I am more Foxworth than you are." Then his expression changed, and his lips quirked. "No, I take that back. You are *twice* the Foxworth I am."

How I hated him for reminding me! Still, he did manage to make me feel ashamed, as if I'd misconstrued the silent messages he sent out. I didn't defend myself, or protest to convince him otherwise. Nor did Chris say a word to prevent this confrontation he'd already sensed would come sooner or later.

"I don't know why I distrust you, Joel," I said in a kinder voice than I customarily used with him. "Perhaps you protest too much about your father, making me doubt you are one whit better or different."

Without another word, but with a sad look that I think he feigned, he turned and shuffled off, his hands again tucked up those invisible brown monk sleeves.

That very evening, when Melodie insisted on dining in her room alone again, I made up my mind. Even if she didn't want to go, and fought against me, I was driving Melodie to see Jory!

I stalked into her room and removed her almost untouched dinner tray without saying a word. She wore the same shabby robe that she'd worn for days. I pulled her best-looking summer outfit from her closet and tossed it on the bed. "Shower, Melodie, and shampoo your hair. Then get dressed—you are going to visit Jory tonight, whether or not you want to."

Instantly she jumped up and protested, acting hysterical as she said she couldn't go yet, wasn't ready yet, and I couldn't make her do anything she didn't want to do. I overrode everything she said, shouting back it seemed she'd never be ready, and I didn't care what excuses she offered, she was going.

"You can't make me do one damned thing!" she yelled, very pale as she backed away. Then, sobbing, she pleaded for me to give her more time to become adjusted to the idea of Jory being crippled. I said she'd had enough time. I'd adjusted, Chris had, Cindy had . . . and she could pretend; after all, she was supposed to be a professional used to playing roles.

I had to literally drag Melodie to the shower and shove her inside when she wanted the tub. But I knew about Melodie in a bathtub. There she'd sit until her skin puckered, and visiting hours would be over. Waiting outside the shower door, I urged her to hurry. She stepped out, swathed in a towel, still sobbing as her blue eyes pleaded for mercy.

"Stop crying!" I ordered, shoving her down on the dressing room stool. "I'm going to blow-dry your hair while you put on your makeup—and do a good job of concealing that red puffiness around your eyes, for Jory will be very perceptive. You've got to convince him that your love for him hasn't changed."

On and on I talked to convince her that she would find the right words to say, the right expressions to wear, as I dried her pretty honey-blond hair.

Her hair had marvelous sheen, more depth to the color than mine had. No red in mine at all. The texture was stronger, than my frail, fine hair of flaxen color. When I had Melodie dressed, I sprayed her lightly with the perfume Jory loved most, as she stood as if in a trance of not knowing what to do next. I hugged her before I pulled her to the door.

"Come now, Melodie, it's not going to be that bad. He loves and needs you. Once you're there and he looks at you, you'll forget his legs are paralyzed. You'll instinctively do and say the right things. I know you will because you love him."

Pale beneath the makeup, her large eyes stared at me bleakly, as if she had her doubts and knew better than to bring them up again.

By this time Bart had come home from whatever bar had served him enough to make his legs limp and his eyes unfocused. He slouched in a deep chair, legs sprawled forward, and behind him in the shadows, Joel sagged limp as a dying palm. "Where yuh goin'?" Bart asked in a slurred voice, as I tried to slip Melodie down the hall to the garage without him noticing us.

"To the hospital," I said, pulling Melodie toward the huge garage. "And I think it's time you went to visit your brother again, Bart. Not tonight, but tomorrow. Buy him a gift that will entertain him . . . he's going mad in there from doing nothing."

"Melodie, you don't have to go if you don't want to," Bart said, rising unsteadily to his feet. "Don't let my dominating mother push you around."

She was trembling, hanging back to plead mutely with him. Ruthlessly I pulled her on and forced her into the car.

Bart came staggering into the garage, calling out to Melodie that he would save her . . . and then he lost his drunken balance and fell to the floor. I pushed the electric button to open one of the huge garage doors and backed out of the garage.

All the way into Charlottesville, until I was parking in the hospital lot, Melodie trembled, sobbed, and tried to convince me she'd harm Jory more than she'd help him. And all the way, I'd tried to give her confidence that she could handle the situation.

"Please, Melodie, walk into that room with a smile. Put on your nobility, that regal princess air that you used to wear all the time. Then when you're near his bed, take him in your arms and kiss him."

Numbly she nodded, as a terrified child would.

I shoved the roses I'd purchased into her arms, and other gifts I'd wrapped prettily, one she'd chosen to give him after Bart's party. "Now, tell him you haven't been before because you've been feeling weak, sleepy, and sick. Tell him all your other concerns if you want to. But don't you dare even hint that you can't feel toward him like a wife anymore."

Like a blind, automated robot she nodded stiffly, forcing herself to keep pace with me.

We ran into Chris coming down the hall as we left the elevator on the sixth floor. He beamed happily to see Melodie with me. "How wonderful, Melodie," he said, giving her a quick hug before he turned to me. "I went out and bought Jory his dinner, and enough for me as well. He's in a fairly good mood. He drank all his milk and ate two bites of the pecan pie. And usually he adores pecan pie. Melodie, if you can, try to see that he eats more of that pie. He's losing weight rapidly, and I'd like to see him gain some back."

Still speechless, her eyes wide and blank, Melodie nodded, looking toward the door numbered 606 as if she faced the electric chair. Chris gave her a friendly, understanding pat on her back, kissed me, then strode off. "I'm going to talk to his doctors. I will join you later on and follow you home in my car."

For the life of me I couldn't feel confident as I ushered Melodie toward Jory's closed door. He had a privacy fetish about keeping his door closed at all times so no one could see a former *premier danseur* lying helpless on his bed. I rapped once, then twice, our signal. "Jory, it's only I, your mother."

"Come in, Mom," he called with more welcome than he'd used before. "Dad told me you'd be showing up any second. I hope you brought me a good book to read. I've finished—"

He broke off and stared as I shoved Melodie into his room first.

Because I'd called Chris to tell him my plans, Chris had helped Jory out of his hospital garment, and he was now wearing a blue silk pajama top. His hair was neatly brushed, his face was clean shaven and he'd had his first haircut since his accident. He looked better than he had since that horrible night.

He tried to smile. Hope flared in his eyes, so glad to see her again.

She stood where I'd pushed her and didn't take another step toward his bed. This caused his tentative smile to freeze on his face as he tried to hide his hunger . . . his faltering flame of hope as his eyes tried to meet with hers. She refused to meet his eyes. Quickly the smile vanished as the flame in his eyes sputtered, flickered, then went out. Dead eyes now. He turned his face toward the wall.

Instantly I stepped up behind Melodie, pushing her toward his bed, before I moved to see what she was revealing on her face. She stood there with her arms full of red roses and gifts, rooted to the floor and trembling like an aspen tree in a high wind. I gave her a sharp nudge. "Say something," I whispered.

"Hi, Jory," she said in a quivery, small voice, her eyes desperate. I shoved her closer to him. "I've brought you roses . . . ," she added.

Still he kept his face to the wall.

Again I nudged her, thinking I should get out and leave them alone; yet I feared the minute I did she'd whirl about and run.

"I'm sorry I haven't visited before," she said in a stumbling way, inching bit by bit closer to his bed. "I've also brought you gifts . . . a few things your mother said you needed."

He whipped his head about, his dark blue eyes full of smoldering rage and resentment. "And my mother forced you to come, right? Well, you don't have to stay. You've delivered your roses and your gifts—now GET OUT!"

Melodie broke, dropping the roses onto his bed, her gifts to the floor. She cried out as she tried to take his hand, a hand he quickly snatched away. "I love you, Jory . . . and I'm sorry, so sorry . . ."

"I don't doubt for a minute you are sorry!" he shouted. "So sorry to see all the glamour disappear in a flashing moment, and now you're stuck with a crippled husband! Well, you're not stuck, Melodie! You can file for divorce tomorrow and leave!"

Back toward the door, I was filled with pity for him—and for her. Gently I eased out but left the door ajar just enough to hear and see what went on. I was so afraid Melodie would take this chance to leave, or else she'd do something to kill his desire to live . . . and if I could, I would do anything to stop her.

One by one Melodie picked up the fallen roses. She threw old, dying flowers into the trash basket, filled the vase with water in the small adjacent bath, then carefully arranged the red roses, so carefully, taking so long, as if just by doing something she could hold off destroying him. When she'd done that, she turned again to the bed and picked up the three gifts. "Don't you want to open them?" she asked weakly.

"I don't need anything," he said flatly, again staring at the wall so she saw only the back of his curly head.

From somewhere she drew courage. "I think you'll like what's inside. I've heard you say many a time what you wanted . . ."

"All I ever wanted was to dance until I was forty," he choked out. "Now that is over, and I don't need a wife or a dance partner, I don't need or want anything."

She put the gifts on the bed and stood there wringing her pale, thin hands, her silent tears beginning to fall. "I love you, Jory," she choked. "I want to do everything right, but I'm not brave like your mother and father, and that's why I didn't visit before. Your mother wanted me to say I was sick, unable to come, but I could have come. I stayed in that house and cried, hoping I could find the strength I needed to smile when I did eventually come. I'm coming apart with shame for being weak, for not doing all I should for you when you need me . . . and the longer I stayed away, the harder it became for me to show up. I feared you wouldn't talk to me, wouldn't look at me, and I'd do something stupid to make you hate me. I don't want a divorce, Jory. I'm still your wife. Chris took me to an obstetrician yesterday, and our baby is progressing normally."

Pausing, she tentatively reached to touch his arm. He jerked spasmodically, as if her hand burned, but he didn't snatch his arm away—she snatched hers.

From where I stood in the hallway, I could see enough of Jory's face to know he was crying and trying hard not to let Melodie know that. Tears were in my eyes, too, as I cringed there, feeling a sneaky intruder who had no right to watch and listen. Even so I couldn't move away, when I'd moved from Julian's side only to find him dead the next time I looked. Like father, like son, like father like son beat the unhappy tattoo of the drums of fear in my head.

Again she reached to touch him, this time his hair. "Don't turn your face away, Jory. Look at me. Let me see that you don't hate me for failing you when you needed me most. Shout at me, hit me, but don't stop communicating. I'm tied up in knots. I can't sleep at night, feeling I should have done something to keep you from dancing that role. I've always hated that particular ballet and didn't want to tell you when you choreographed it and made it your signature." She wiped at her tears, then sank to her knees by his bed and bowed her head onto his hand, which she'd managed to seize.

Her low voice barely reached my ears. "We can make a life together. You can teach me how. Wherever you lead, Jory, I'll follow . . . just tell me that you want me to stay."

Maybe because she was hiding her face now, with her tears wetting his hand beneath her cheek, he turned his head and looked at her with such tormented, tragic eyes. He cleared his throat before he spoke and dried his tears with the edge of the sheet.

"I don't want you to stay if living with me is going to be a burden. You can always go back to New York and dance with other partners. Because I'm crippled doesn't mean you have to be crippled too. You have your career, and all those years of dedicated work. So go, Mel, with my blessings . . . I don't need you now."

My heart cried out, knowing differently.

She looked up, her makeup ruined from so many tears. "How could I live with myself, Jory? I'll stay. I'll do my best to make you a good wife." She paused while I thought her timing was so wrong, so damned wrong. She gave him time to think that he didn't need a wife, only a nurse and companion, and a substitute mother for his child.

I closed my eyes and began to pray. *God, let her find the right words.* Why isn't she telling him the ballet meant nothing without him? Why didn't she say his happiness counted more than anything else? Melodie, Melodie, say something to make him believe his handicap doesn't matter, it's the man he'll always be that you love. But she said nothing like this.

She only opened his gifts for him, showed them to him, while he studied her face with bleaker and bleaker eyes.

He thanked her for the bestselling novel she'd brought (chosen by me); thanked her for the traveling shaving kit with the sterling silver razors—straight edged, electric, and a third kind, dual edged—with a silver-handled lathering brush and a round mirror that could be attached to anything with a suction cup guaranteed to work. There was also a fancy silver mug with soap, cologne, and aftershave lotion. Then finally she was opening the best gift, a huge mahogany box full of watercolors, a hobby that Chris enjoyed. He planned to teach Jory the technique of using watercolors as soon as he came home. Jory stared at the paintbox for the longest time without interest before he looked away. "You have good taste, Mel."

Bowing her head, she nodded. "Is there anything else you need?"

"No. Just leave. I'm sleepy. It's nice to see you again, but I'm tired."

She backed off hesitatingly, while my heart cried for them both. So much in love before his accident, and all that passion had been washed away in the deluge of her shock and his humiliation.

I stepped into the room.

"I hope I'm not interrupting anything, but I think Jory is tired, Melodie." I smiled at both brightly. "You just wait until you see what we're planning for your return home. If painting doesn't interest you now, it will later on. At home we've got other treasures waiting for you. You're going to be thrilled, but I can't tell you anything. It's all supposed to be a huge welcome-back surprise." I hurried to embrace him, which wasn't easy to do when his body was so bulky and hard with the cast. I kissed his cheek, ruffled his hair, and squeezed his fingers. "It's going to be all right, darling," I whispered. "She has to learn to accept just like you do. She's trying hard, and if she doesn't say the words you want to hear, it's because she's too much in shock to think straight."

Ironically he smiled. "Sure, Mom, sure. She loves me just as much as she did when I could walk and dance. Nothing has changed. Nothing important."

Melodie was already out of his room and standing in the hall waiting, so she didn't hear any of this. Over and over again she repeated on our way home, with Chris following in his car, "Oh, my God, my God . . . oh, my God . . . what are we going to do?"

"You did fine, Melodie, just fine. The next time you'll do even better," said I, brightly.

A week passed and Melodie did do better on her second visit, and even better on her third. Now she didn't resist when I told her where she had to go. She knew it wouldn't do her any good to resist.

Another day I sat in my dressing room before the long mirror, carefully applying mascara. Chris stepped into view with a look of pleasure on his face.

"I've got something great to tell you," he started. "Last week I went to visit the university scientific staff and filled out an application for their cancer research team. They realize there, of course, that I've only been an amateur biochemist in my spare time. Nevertheless, for some reason, some of my answers seemed to please them, and they have asked me to join their staff of scientists. Cathy, I'm thrilled to have something to do. Bart has agreed to allow us to stay on here as long as we like, or until he marries. I've talked to Jory, and he wants to be near us. His apartment in New York is so small. Here he'll have wide halls and large rooms that will accommodate his wheelchair. Right now he says he'll never use one, but he will change his mind when that cast comes off."

Chris's enthusiasm for the new job was contagious. I wanted to see him happy, with something to do to take his mind off Jory's problems. I stood to head for the closet, but he pulled me down on his lap to polish off his story. Some of what he said I didn't understand, for every so often he'd forgetfully slip into medical jargon, which was still Greek to me.

"Will you be happy, Chris? It's important for you to do what you want with your life. Jory's happiness is important as well, but I don't want you staying on here if Bart is going to be insufferable. Be honest . . . can you tolerate Bart just to give Jory a wonderful place to live?"

"Catherine, my love, as long as you are here, then of course I'll be happy. As for Bart, I've put up with him all these years, and I can take it for as long as need be. I know who is seeing Jory through this traumatic period. I may help a little, but it's you who brings more sunshine with your gossipy chatter, your lilting manner, your armloads of gifts, and your consistent reassurances that Melodie will change. He considers every word you say as if it comes straight from God."

"But you'll be coming and going, and we won't see much of you," I moaned.

"Hey, take that look off your face. I'll drive home every night and try to reach here before dark." He went on to explain that he didn't have to reach the university lab until ten, and that would give us plenty of time to breakfast together. There wouldn't be emergency calls to take him away at night; he'd have every weekend off, a month off with pay, not that money mattered to us. We'd take trips to conventions where I'd meet people with innovative ideas, the kind of creative people I enjoyed best.

On and on he extolled the virtues of his new enterprise, making me accept something he seemed to want very much. Still, I slept in his arms that night, fretting, wishing we'd never come to this house that held so many terrible memories and had caused so many tragedies.

Around midnight, unable to sleep, I got up to sit in our private sitting room that adjoined our bedroom, knitting what was supposed to end up a fluffy white baby bonnet. I almost felt like my mother as I furiously knitted on and on with such intensity I couldn't put it down. Like her I could never let anything alone until it was finished.

A soft rapping sounded on the door, soon followed by Melodie's request to come in. Delighted to have her visit, I answered, "Of course, come in. I'm glad you saw the light under my door. I was thinking about you and Jory while I knitted, and darn if I know how to stop once I start a project."

Falteringly she came to perch on the love seat next to me; her very uncertainty immediately put me on guard. She glance at my knitting, looked away. "I need someone to talk to, Cathy, someone wise, like you."

How pitiful and young she sounded, even younger than Cindy. I put down my knitting to turn and embrace her. "Cry, Melodie, go on. You have enough to cry about. I've been harsh with you, and I know that."

Her head bowed down on my shoulder as she let go and sobbed with abandon.

"Help me, Cathy, please help me. I don't know what to do. I keep thinking of Jory and how terrible he must feel. I think about me and how inadequate *I* feel. I'm glad you made me go to see him, thought I hated you for doing that at the time. Today when I went alone, he smiled as if that proved something to him. I know I've been childish and weak. Yet each time I have to force myself to enter his room. I hate seeing him lying so still on that bed, moving nothing but his arms and head. I kiss him, hold his hand, but once I start to talk about important things, he turns his head toward the wall and refuses to respond. Cathy . . . you may think he's learning to accept his disability, but I think he's willing himself to die— and it's my fault, my fault!"

Astonishment widened my eyes. "Your fault? It was an accident, you can't blame yourself."

In a breathless gush her words spilled forth. "You don't understand why I feel as I do! It's been troubling me so much I feel haunted with guilt. It's because we're here, in this cursed house! Jory didn't want to have a baby until years from now. He made me promise before we married that until we'd been on the top for at least ten years, we wouldn't start a family— but I deliberately broke my word and stopped taking the pill. I wanted to have my first baby before I was thirty. I reasoned that after the baby was conceived he wouldn't want me to have an abortion. When I told him he blew! He stormed at me— and *demanded* I have an abortion."

"Oh, no . . ." I was shocked, thinking I didn't know Jory nearly as well as I'd thought.

"Don't blame him; it was my own doing. Dancing was his world," Melodie continued in a gasping way, as if she'd been running uphill for weeks. "I shouldn't have done what I did. I told him I'd just forgotten. I knew on our wedding day that dancing came first with him, and I was second. He never lied or told me differently, though he loved me. Then, because I was pregnant, we abandoned our tour, came here . . . and look what happened! It's not fair, Cathy, not fair! On this very day we'd be in London but for the baby. He'd be on stage, bowing, accepting the applause, the bouquets, doing what he was born for. I tricked him, and in so doing, I brought about his accident, and what's he going to do now? How can I make up for what I've stolen from him?"

She trembled all over as I held her. What could I say? I bit down on my lip, hurting for her, for Jory. We were so much alike in some ways, for I'd caused Julian's death by deserting him, leaving him in Spain—and that had led to his end. Never deliberately harming, just coincidentally doing what I felt was right, as Melodie did what she considered right.

Who ever counted the flowers that died when we pulled up the weeds? I shook my head, pulling myself out of the abyss of yesterdays and turned my full concentration on the moment.

"Melodie, Jory's just as scared as you are, much more so, and with good reason. You aren't to blame for anything. He's happy about the baby now that it's on its way. Many men protest when wives want babies, but when they see the child they helped create, they're won over. He lies there on his bed, as you lie on yours, wondering how his marriage is going to work out now that he can't dance. He's the one who is crippled. He's the one who has to face up to everyday life, knowing he'll be unable to sit when he wants to; knowing he can't sit in a regular chair and get up and down when he feels like it; nor can he walk in the rain, or run on the grass, or even go to the bathroom in a normal way.

"All the simple normal everyday things he took for granted will now be very difficult for him. And think of what he was. This is a terrible blow to his pride. He wasn't even going to try and cope for fear he'd burden you too much. But listen to this. This afternoon when I was with him, he said he was going to make a big effort to cheer up and lift himself out of his depression. And he will. He'll make it, and a lot of it will be because you've helped by just visiting and sitting there with him. Each time you go you convince him you still love him."

Why did she draw from my arms and turn her face away? I watched her brush the tears from her face impatiently; then she blew her nose and tried to stop crying.

With effort she spoke again. "I don't know what it is, but I keep having scary dreams. I wake up frightened, thinking something even more dreadful is going to happen. There's something weird about this house. Something strange and frightening. When everyone is gone, and Bart is in his office, and Joel is praying in that ugly, bare room, I lie on my bed and seem to hear the house whispering. It seems to call to me. I hear the wind blow as if it's trying to tell me something. I hear the floor squeak outside my door so I jump up and race to throw open the door—and no one is there, no one is ever there. I suspect it's only my imagination, but I hear, as you've said you do sometimes, so much of what isn't real. Am I losing my mind, Cathy? Am I?"

"Oh, Melodie," I murmured, trying to draw her close again, but she put me off by moving to the far end of the sofa.

"Cathy, why is this house different?"

"Different from what?" I asked uneasily.

"From all other houses." She glanced fearfully toward the door to the hall. "Don't you feel it? Can't you hear it? Do you sense this house is breathing, like it has a life of its own?"

My eyes widened as a chill stole the comfort from my pretty sitting room. In the bedroom I could faintly hear Chris's regular, heavy breathing.

Melodie, usually too reticent to talk, gushed onward breathlessly. "This house wants to use the people inside as a way to keep it living on forever. It's like a vampire, sucking our lifeblood from all of us. I wish it hadn't been restored. It's not a new house. It's been here for centuries. Only the wall-paper and the paint and the furniture are new, but those stairs in the foyer I never climb up or descend without seeing the ghosts of others . . ."

A kind of paralyzing numbness gripped me.

Every word she said was only too frighteningly true. I *could* hear it breathe! I tried to pull myself back to reality. "Listen, Melodie. Bart was only a little boy when my mother ordered it reconstructed on the foundations of the old manor home. Before she died it was up, but not completely finished inside.

When her will was read, and she left this house to Bart, with Chris as trustee to manage until he came of age, we decided it was a waste not to have it completed. Chris and our attorney contacted the architects and contractors, and the job went forward until it was finished, only the inside needed furbishing. That had to wait until Bart came here in his college days and ordered the interior decorators to style it as it had been in the old days. And you're right. I, too, wish this house had been left in ashes . . ."

"Maybe your mother knew this house was what Bart would want most to give him confidence. It's so imposing. Haven't you noticed how much he's changed? He's not like the little boy who used to hide away in the shadows and lurk behind trees. He's the master here, like a baron overseeing his domain. Or maybe I should say king of the mountain, for he's so rich, so terribly rich . . ."

Not yet . . . not yet, I kept thinking. Nevertheless, her frail, whispering voice disturbed me. I didn't want to think Bart was as overbearing as a medieval lord. But she went on. "Bart's happy, Cathy, extraordinarily happy. He tells me he's sorry about Jory. Then he telephones those attorneys and wants to know why they keep postponing the rereading of his grandmother's will. They've told him they can't read it unless everyone mentioned in the will is here to hear the reading, and so they put it off until the day when Jory comes home from the hospital. They will read the will in Bart's office."

"How do you know so much about Bart's business?" I asked sharply, suddenly very suspicious of all that time when she was alone in this house with my second son . . . and an old man who spent most of his time in that tiny, naked room he used as a chapel. Joel would quite happily see Jory destroyed if that would satisfy Bart. In Joel's eyes a dancing man was no better than the worst sinner, displaying his body. Leaping and bounding in front of women, wearing nothing but a loincloth . . . I stared again at Melodie.

"Do you and Bart spend much time together?"

Quickly she stood. "I'm tired now, Cathy. I've said enough to make you think I'm crazy. Do all expectant mothers have such fearful dreams—did you? I'm afraid, too, that my baby won't be normal since I've grieved so much for Jory."

I gave her what comfort I could when I felt sick inside, and later that night while I lay beside Chris I began to toss and turn, to flit in and out of nightmares, until he wakened and pleaded with me to let him get some sleep. Turning, I wrapped my arms about him, clinging to him as if to some unsinkable raft—as I'd always clung to the only straw that kept me from drowning in the cruel sea of Foxworth Hall.

Homecoming

Finally the decorators I'd hired to do over Jory's suite of rooms were finished. Now everything there was planned for his entertainment and comfort and convenience. With Melodie beside me, we stood and surveyed all that had been done to make the room bright and cheerful.

"Jory likes color and lots of light, unlike some who want only darkness because it's richer appearing," explained Melodie with a strange look haunting her eyes. Of course I knew she meant Bart. I gave her a quizzical look, wondering again how much time she spent with Bart, and what they talked about, and if he'd tried anything. Certainly all that wistful yearning I'd seen in his eyes would force him to make advances. And what better time than while Jory was away and Melodie was desperately needing? Then my safety valve turned on . . . Melodie despised Bart. She might need him to talk to, but that was all.

"Tell me what else I can do to help," I said, wanting her to do most of it so she'd feel needed, useful. In response she smiled for the first time with some show of happiness. "You can help me make the bed with the pretty new sheets I ordered." She ripped open the plastic wrappings, the movement making her fuller breasts jiggle. Her jeans were just beginning to show a slight bulge.

I was almost as worried about her as I was about Jory. An expectant mother needed to eat more, drink milk, take vitamins, and then there was this unexpected reversal of her former heavy depression. She was now completely accepting of Jory's unhappy situation. It was what I had wanted, yet it had come about too quickly, and that gave me the feeling it was false.

Then came an explanation of her newfound security. "Cathy, Jory's going to get well and dance again. I dreamed last night he was, and my dreams always come true."

Now I knew she was going to do what I'd done in the beginning, convince herself that Jory would recover someday, and on that kind of fantasy she was going to construct her life—and his.

I started to speak, to say what Chris had to me, but Bart stepped into the hallway outside, his large feet clumping heavily down the long, dim hall. He glowered at the once dark paneling that was now painted off white so that painting of the sea and shore would show up beautifully. Easy enough to see he was displeased with our changes.

"We did it to please Jory," I said before he could object, while Melodie stood silent and stared at him with the wide-eyed, helpless look of a child caught in a sticky situation. "I know you want your brother to be happy, and no one loves the sea, the surf, the sand, and seabirds more than Jory. So, into this room we're putting a bit of the sea and shore—giving him the knowledge that all the important things in life will still exist for him. The sky above, the earth below, and the sea in between. He's not going to lack for anything, Bart. He's going to have what it takes to keep him alive and happy, and I know you want to do your part."

He was staring at Melodie, not half listening to me. His eyes riveted to those larger breasts, moving to study the curve of the baby swelling her belly. "Melodie, you could have come to me and asked before you did anything, since I'm the one who'll pay the bills." I was completely ignored, as if I weren't there at all.

"Oh, no," denied Melodie. "Jory and I have money. We can pay for the changes we've made in here . . . and I didn't think you would mind since you seem so concerned about him."

"You don't have to pay for anything," said Bart with surprising warmth. "The day Jory comes home, attorneys will be coming in the afternoon to read the will again, and this time I'll know exactly my full worth. I'm damned sick and tired of having that day postponed."

"Bart," I said, stepping so I was between him and Melodie, "you know why they haven't reread the will. They want Jory to be here and fully cognizant of what's going on."

He walked around me to deliberately lock his eyes with the huge, sad ones of Melodie. He spoke to her and her alone. "*You* just tell me what you need, and I'll deliver it yesterday. You and Jory can stay as long as you like."

They stood staring at each other across twenty feet of sea-blue velvet carpeting. Bart's dark eyes probed into her blue ones before he said softly, winningly, "Don't worry so much, Melodie. You and Jory have a home here forever if you want. I don't really give a damn what you do with these rooms. I do want Jory to be as comfortable and happy as possible."

Were they formula words to satisfy me—or calculated words to seduce her? Why did Melodie blush and gaze down at her feet?

Cindy's tale resounded like distant church bells in my memory. Insurance for all the guests . . . in case of accidents. Wet sand that should have been dry sand. Sand that clumped into cement and didn't instantly pour out to make the papier-mâché columns safe.

Into my thoughts flitted memories of Bart when he was seven, eight, nine, and ten . . .

*Wish I had legs as pretty as Jory's. Wish I could
run and dance like Jory. Gonna grow taller, gonna
grow much bigger, gonna be more powerful than
Jory. Someday. Someday.*

Bart's mumbling boyhood wishes, said so many times I'd
grown indifferent to them. Then when he was older . . .

*Who is gonna love me, like Melodie loves Jory?
Nobody. Nobody.*

I shook my head to rid myself of unwelcome memories of
a little boy wanting to equal the stature of his older and more
talented brother.

But why was he looking now at Melodie with such sig-
nificance? Her blue eyes lifted to meet his briefly; then she
looked away, blushing again, positioning her hands in the ballet position all dancers used to keep from drawing attention
away from the main performer—her feet toed out. On stage,
Melodie was on stage, playing a role.

Bart strode off, his legs confident and sure, as they'd never
been when he was a young boy. I felt sad and sorry he had to
wait until he was out of Jory's shadow before he could find
even the ability to use his body coordination with skill. Sighing, I decided to think of the present and all that had been
done to give Jory's convalescence the perfect environment.

A large color TV was at the foot of his bed, and he had a
remote control unit to change channels and turn it off and
on from his bed. An electrician had arranged a way for Jory
to open and close his draperies when he chose. A stereo was
within his reach. Books lined the back of his adjustable bed,
which would sit him up and turn him into almost any position he wanted. Melodie and I, with Chris's help, had wracked
our brains to come up with every modern convenience that
would enable him to do what he could for himself. Now all we

had to do was to see he stayed busy with some occupation of real interest, enough to absorb his energies and challenge his innate talents.

A long time ago I'd started reading books on psychology, my poor attempt to try and help Bart. Now I could help Jory with his "racehorse" personality that had to compete and win. He couldn't endure boredom, lying about doing nothing. There was already a barre along the wall without windows, put there recently, to give him the promise that one day he'd stand up, even if he would have to wear a back brace connected to leg braces. I sighed to think of my beautiful, graceful son stumbling along like a horse in a harness; then tears were streaking my face. Tears I quickly blinked away so Melodie wouldn't see them.

Soon Melodie was tired and left to lie down and rest. I finished up in the room, then hurried to oversee the ramps being constructed to take Jory down to the terraces and the gardens. No effort was being spared to see he would not be confined to his room. There was also a newly installed elevator put where once there had been a butler's pantry.

At last came the wonderful day when Jory was allowed to leave the hospital and come home. The cast was still on his back, but he was eating and drinking normally and had gained back his color and a little of the weight he'd lost. My heart ached with pity to see him flat on a stretcher, being rolled to the elevator, when once he'd taken the stairs three at a time. I saw him turn his head to stare at the stairs as if he'd sell his soul to use them again.

But, smiling, he looked around the grand suite of rooms all refurbished and his eyes sparkled. "It's great, what you've done, really great. My favorite color combination, white and blue. You've given me the seashore—why, I can almost smell the surf, hear the seagulls. It's wonderful, truly wonderful what paint and pictures, green plants and planning can do."

His wife stood at the foot of the narrow bed he'd have to use until the cast came off, but she took pains not to meet his eyes. "Thanks for liking what we've done. Your mother and I, and Chris, too, really tried to please you."

His blue eyes turned navy as he stared at her, sensing something I, too, felt. He looked toward the windows, his full lips thinning, before he drew back into his shell.

Immediately I stepped forward to hand him a huge box, saved for this kind of uncomfortable moment. "Jory, something meaningful for you to do while you're still confined to the bed. Don't want you staring at that boob tube all the time."

Seeming relieved not to have to trouble his wife with words she didn't want to hear, he feigned childish eagerness by shaking the huge box. "A compressed elephant? An unsinkable surfboard?" he guessed, looking only at me. I ruffled his curly hair, leaned to hug and kiss him and ordered him to hurry and open that box. I was dying to hear what he thought of my gift that had traveled all the way from New England.

Soon he had the ribbons and pretty wrapping off and was staring down at the long box containing what appeared to be neat bundles of super-long matchsticks. Tiny bottles of paint, larger bottles of glue, with spools of thin cording, carefully packaged cloth. "A kit to make a clipper ship," he said with both wonder and dismay. "Mom, there are ten pages of instructions! This thing is so complicated it will take me the better part of my life to complete. And when it's done—if ever—what will I have?"

"What will you have? My son, you will have when you are finished an heirloom that will be priceless, to leave to your son or daughter." All said so proudly, so sure he could follow the difficult directions. "You have steady hands, a good eye for details, a ready understanding of the written word, and such determination. Besides, take a look at that empty mantel that demands a ship smack in the middle."

Laughing, he laid his head back on the pillow, already exhausted. He closed his eyes. "Okay, you've convinced me. I'll give it a go—but I've not had much experience with any craft since I was a kid gluing airplane parts together."

Oh, yes, I remembered clearly. They'd dangled down from his ceiling, infuriating Bart, who couldn't glue anything together properly at that time.

"Mom . . . I'm tired. Give me a chance to nap before the lawyers come to read that will. I don't know if I'm up to all the excitement of Bart's 'coming into his own'—at last."

It was at this moment that Bart stepped into the room. Jory sensed him there and opened his eyes. The dark brown and dark blue brotherly eyes met, locked, challenging the other for a dreadfully long time. The silence grew and grew until I became aware of my own heart throbs; the clock behind me ticked too loud, and Melodie was breathing heavily. I heard the birds outside twittering before Melodie began to rearrange another vase of flowers just for something to do.

On and on they clashed eyes, wills, when Bart should speak and welcome home the brother he'd visited only once. Still he just stood there, as if he'd keep his eyes locked on Jory until Jory broke the spell and lost the silent battle of wills.

I had my lips parted to stop this contest when Jory smiled and said warmly, without lowering his eyes or breaking the bind, "Hi, brother. I know how much you hate hospitals, so it was doubly nice for you to visit me. Since I'm here, in your home . . . isn't it easier to say hello? I'm glad my accident didn't spoil your birthday party. I heard from Cindy that my fall only momentarily lulled the hilarity, and the party went on as if nothing had happened."

Still Bart stood there saying nothing. Melodie put the last rose in the vase and lifted her head. A few tendrils of her fair hair had escaped the tight confinement of her ballerina bun to make her look charmingly casual and antiquely fragile. There was an air of weariness about her as if she'd surrendered to life and all its vicissitudes. Was I imagining that she sent some silent warning to Bart—and he understood? Suddenly he was smiling, even if it was stiff.

"I'm glad you're back. Welcome home, Jory." He strode forward to clasp his brother's hand. "If there's anything I can do, just let me know." Then he left the room, and I was staring after him, wondering . . .

At four exactly, that very afternoon, shortly after Jory woke up and Chris and Bart lifted him onto a stretcher, three attorneys came to take over Bart's grand home office. We sat in fine milk-chocolate-colored leather chairs, all but Jory, who lay on a rolling stretcher very still and quiet. His tired eyes were half opened, showing his interest was small. Cindy had flown home to be here, as was required, for she, too, was mentioned in the will. She perched on the arm of my chair, swinging her shapely leg back and forth, treating all of this as a joke while Joel glared to see that blue high-heeled shoe moving constantly and calling attention to those remarkably lovely legs. We all sat as if at a funeral, as papers were shuffled, spectacles were put on, and whisperings between the lawyers made us all uneasy.

Bart was particularly nervous, exalted-looking, but suspicious of the way the attorneys kept glancing at him. The eldest of the three acted as spokesman as word by careful word the main portion of my mother's will was read once again. We'd heard it all before.

". . . when my grandson, Bartholomew Winslow Scott Sheffield, who will eventually claim his rightful surname of Foxworth, reaches the age of twenty-five," read the man in his late sixties with the glasses perched low on his nose, "he will be given the annual sum of five hundred thousand dollars, until he reaches the age of thirty-five. At this stated age, the remainder of my estate, hereafter called The Corrine Foxworth Winslow Trust, will be turned over in entirety to my grandson, Bartholomew Winslow Scott Sheffield Foxworth. My firstborn son, Christopher Garland Sheffield Foxworth, will remain in his position as trustee until the aforesaid time. If he, the trustee, should not survive until the time when my grandson Bartholomew Winslow Scott Sheffield Foxworth reaches the age of thirty-five, then my daughter, Catherine Sheffield Foxworth, shall be named as replacement trustee until my aforesaid grandson reaches his thirty-fifth birthday."

There was more, much more, but I didn't hear anything else. I filled with shock and glanced at Chris, who seemed dumbfounded. Then my eyes rested on Bart.

His face was pale, registering a kaleidoscope of changing expressions. His color waxed and waned. He raked his long, strong fingers through his perfect hairstyle and left it rumpled. Helplessly he looked at Joel as if for guidance, but Joel only shrugged and crooked his lips as if to say, "I told you so."

Next Bart was glaring at Cindy as if her presence had magically changed his grandmother's will. His eyes flitted to Jory, who was lying sleepily on the stretcher, appearing disinterested in everything going on but Melodie, who stared at Bart with her pale, woebegone face flickering like a weak candle flame in the strong wind of Bart's disappointment.

Quickly Bart jerked his sizzling gaze away when her head lowered to Jory's chest. Almost silently she was crying.

An eternity seemed to pass before that elderly lawyer folded the long will, replaced it in a blue folder, then put that on Bart's desk. He stood with folded arms to wait for Bart's questions.

"What the hell is going on?" shouted Bart.

He jumped to his feet, stalked to his desk, and seized up the will, which he thumbed through quickly with the eye of an expert. Finished, he hurled down the will. "Damn her to hell! She promised me everything, everything! Now I have to wait ten more years . . . why wasn't that part read before? I was there. I was ten years old, but I remember her will stating I'd come into my own when I was twenty-five. I'm twenty-five and one month old—where is my reward?"

Chris stood. "Bart," he said calmly, "you have five hundred thousand dollars a year—that kind of money isn't to be shrugged off. And didn't you hear that all your living expenses, and the cost of running this house and maintaining it, will be taken care of by the bulk of monies still in trust? All your taxes will be prepaid. And five hundred thousand a year for ten years is more money than ninety-nine point nine percent of the world will ever know in an entire lifetime. How much can you spend on supporting your own lifestyle after all other expenses are taken care of? Besides, those ten years will fly by, and then everything will be yours to do with as you want."

"How much more is there in toto?" Bart fired, his dark eyes rapacious and so intense they seemed to burn. His face was magenta-colored from his rage.

"Five million paid to me over a period of ten years, but what will be left? Ten million more? Twenty, fifty, a billion—how much?"

"I really don't know," replied Chris coolly as the lawyers stared at Bart. "But I'd say, with honesty, that day when you finally do come into your own, all of it, you will be, beyond a doubt, one of the richest men in the world."

"But until then—you are!" screamed Bart. "YOU! Of all people, you! The very one who's sinned the most! It isn't fair, not fair at all! I've been misled, tricked!" His eyes glared at all of us first as he slammed out of his office, only to stick his head in a second later.

"You'll be sorry, Chris," he blazed fiercely. "You must have talked her into having that codicil added—and instructed the attorneys not to read it aloud the day I heard it first, when I was ten. *It's your fault I haven't come into everything due me!*"

As always it had been Chris's fault—or mine.

Brotherly Love

Most of the miserably hot month of August had come and gone while Jory stayed in the hospital, and September arrived with its cooler nights, only too soon starting the colorful process of autumn. Chris and I raked leaves after the gardeners had come and gone, thinking they carelessly overlooked so many. The leaves never stopped falling, and it was something we both liked to do.

We heaped them in deep ravines, dropped down a match and crouched close together on the grass to watch the fire blaze high and warm enough to heat our cold hands and faces. The fire down below was so safe we could enjoy just watching and turning often to gaze at one another and the way the glow lit up our eyes and turned our skins a lovely shade of scarlet. Chris had a lover's way of looking at me, of reaching to caress my cheek with the back of his hand, brushing my hair with his fingertips, kissing my neck, and in all ways touching me deeply with his abiding love. In the firelight of those leaves burning at night, we found each other in new ways, in mature ways that were even better than what we'd had before, and that had always been overwhelmingly sweet.

And behind us, staying forever locked within her room in that horrible house, Melodie's baby swelled her out more and more.

The month of October came to us in a stunning blaze of colors that stole my breath away, filling me with awe as only the works of nature could. These were the same trees whose tops we'd only glimpsed in our hideaway attic schoolroom. I could almost see the four of us staring out when I glanced up at the attic dormer windows, the twins only five, pining away to large-eyed gnomes, all our small, pale faces pasted wistfully to the smudgy glass, staring out, yearning to be free to do what now I took as only natural and our due.

Ghosts up there, our ghosts up there.

Color all our days gray, was the way I'd used to think. Color all Jory's day gray now, for he wouldn't let himself see the beauty of autumn in the mountains when he couldn't stroll the woodsy paths, or dance over the browning grass, or lean to sniff the fall flowers, or jog alongside Melodie.

The tennis courts stayed empty as Bart abandoned them for lack of a partner. Chris would have loved a Saturday or Sunday tennis game with Bart, but Bart still ignored Chris.

The large swimming pool that had been Cindy's special delight was drained, cleaned, covered over. The screens came down, the glass was cleaned before the storm windows went up. The cords of wood stacked out of sight behind the garage grew by the dozens, and trucks delivered coal to use when or if our oil furnaces failed, or our electricity went off. We had an auxiliary unit to light our rooms and keep our electric appliances working, and yet somehow I feared this winter as I'd never feared any winter but those in the attic.

Freezing cold it had been in the attic, like the Arctic zone. Now we were going to have the chance to experience what it had been like downstairs, while Momma enjoyed life with her parents and friends, and the lover she found, while four unwanted children froze and starved and suffered upstairs.

Sunday mornings were the best. Chris and I gloried in our time together. We ate breakfast in Jory's room so he wouldn't feel so separate from his family, and only a few times could I persuade Bart and Melodie to join us.

"Go on," urged Jory, when he saw me glance often at the window, "go walking. Don't think I'm going to begrudge you and Dad your legs because mine don't work anymore. I'm not a baby, or that selfish."

We had to go or he'd think he was inhibiting our style of living. And so we went, hoping Melodie would join him.

One day we woke up so early the frost was still thick upon the ground and pumpkins were ripening under the stacked corn stalks where farmers eked out a poor living. The frost looked sweet, liked powdered sugar that would soon melt when the sun came out fully.

On our walk we stopped to stare up at the sky as Canadian geese flew south, telling us that winter would come earlier than usual this year. We heard the distant melancholy honking of those untiring birds fade as they disappeared in the morning clouds. Flying toward South Carolina—where once we had fled just before winter's sharp bite.

In mid-October the orthopedist came to use huge electric shears to split Jory's cast halfway through; then he used handheld shears to gently cut through what remained. Jory said he felt now like a turtle without its shell. His strong body had wasted inside that cast. "A few weeks of exercising your arms and shoulder muscles will see your chest as developed as ever," encouraged Chris. "You're going to need strong arms, so keep on using that trapeze, and we'll have parallel bars put in your sitting room so you can eventually pull yourself up into a standing position. Don't think life is over for you, that all challenges are behind you and nothing matters now, for you have miles and miles to go before you're done with life, don't you ever forget that."

"Yeah," murmured Jory bleakly, staring empty-eyed toward the door, which Melodie seldom passed through. "Miles and miles to travel before I can find another body that works like it should. I guess I'll start believing in reincarnation."

The quickly chilling days turned bitterly cold, with autumn nights that took us quickly toward freezing. The migrating birds stopped flying overhead now that the wind was whistling through the treetops, howling around the house, stealing inside our rooms. The moon was again a raiding Viking longboat sailing high, flooding our bed with moonlight, giving us kindling for a new kind of romance. Clean, cool, bright love that lit up our spirits, and told us we weren't really sinners of the worst kind. Not when our love could last as it had, while other marriages broke up after a few months or years. We couldn't be sinning and feel as we did toward one another. Who were we hurting? No one, not really. Bart was hurting himself, we reasoned.

Still, why was I haunted by nightmares that said differently? I'd become an expert at turning off disturbing thoughts by thinking of all the trivial details in my life. There was nothing as diverting as the startling beauty of nature. I wanted nature to heal my wounds, and Jory's—and perhaps even Bart's.

With a keen eye I studied all the signs as a farmer might and reported them back to Jory. The rabbits grew suddenly fatter. The squirrels seemed to be storing more nuts. Woolly caterpillars looked like tiny train cars of fur inching toward safety—wherever that was.

Soon I was pulling out winter coats that I'd intended to give to charities; heavy sweaters and wool skirts I'd never expected to wear in Hawaii. In September Cindy had flown back to her high school in South Carolina. This was her last year in a very expensive private school that she "absolutely adored." Her letters poured in like unseasonable warm rain, wanting more money for this or that.

On and on flowed Cindy's sprawling girlish script, needing everything, despite all the gifts I was constantly bombarding her with. She had dozens of boyfriends, a new one each time she wrote. She needed casual clothes for the boy who liked to hunt and fish. She needed dressy clothes for the boy who liked operas and concerts. She needed jeans and warm tops for herself, and luxury underwear and nightclothes, for she just couldn't sleep in anything inexpensive.

Her letters emphasized all that I'd missed when I was sixteen. I remembered Clairmont and my days in Dr. Paul's house, with Henny in the kitchen teaching me how to cook by example, not with words. I'd bought a cookbook on how to win your man and hold him by cooking all the right dishes. What a child I'd been. I sighed. Perhaps I'd had it just as good as Cindy, after all—in a different way—after we escaped Foxworth Hall. I sniffed Cindy's pink, perfumed stationery before I put down her letter, then turned my attention to the present and all the problems in this Foxworth Hall, without the paper flowers in the attic.

Day after day of closely observing Bart when he was with Melodie was convincing me that they saw a great deal of one another, while Jory saw very little of his wife. I tried to believe that Melodie was trying to console Bart for not inheriting as much as he'd believed . . . but despite myself, I presumed there was more to it than pity.

Like a faithful puppy with only one friend, Joel followed Bart everywhere, except into his office or bedroom. He prayed in that tiny room before breakfast, lunch, and dinner. He prayed before he went to bed, and prayed as he walked about, muttering to himself the appropriate quotes from the Bible to suit whatever occasion provoked him into pious mumbles.

In his own way, Chris was in Heaven, enjoying the best years of his life, or so he said. "I love my new job. The men I work with are bright, humorous, and have unending tales to tell and take away the monotony of doing a lot of drudgery. We go into the lab each day, don our white coats, check our petri dishes, expecting miracles, and grin and bear it when miracles just don't happen."

Bart was neither friend nor foe to Jory, just someone who stuck his head in the door and said a few words before he hurried on to something he considered more important than wasting time with a crippled brother. I often wondered what he did with his time besides study the financial markets and buy and sell stocks and bonds. I suspected he was risking much of his five hundred thousand in order to prove to all of us he was smarter than Chris and craftier than the foxiest of all Foxworths, Malcolm.

Soon after Chris drove off on a Tuesday morning in late October, I hurried back up the stairs to check on Jory and see that he was properly taken care of. Chris had hired a male nurse to tend to Jory, but he was only here every other day.

Jory seldom complained about being housebound, although his head was often turned toward the windows to stare out at the brilliance of autumn.

"The summer's gone," he said flatly, lifelessly, as the wind tossed colorful leaves playfully about, "and it's taken my legs with it."

"Autumn will bring you reasons for being happy, Jory. Winter will make you a father. Life still has many happy surprises in store for you, whether or not you want to believe that. I believe like Chris, that the best is still to come. Now . . . let's see what we can do to give you substitute legs. Now that you're strong enough to sit up, there's no reason why you can't move into that wheelchair your father brought home. Jory, please. I hate seeing you in bed all the time. Try the chair, maybe it won't be as obnoxious as you think."

Stubbornly he shook his head.

I ignored that and went on with my persuasions. "Easily

we can take you outside. We can stroll through the woods as soon as Bart has workmen clear the paths that might hinder your progress, and right now you could sit on a terrace in the sunshine and gain back some of your color. Soon it will be too cold to go outside. And when the time comes, I can push you through the gardens and the woods."

He threw the chair, kept where he could see it every day, a hard, scornful look. "That thing would turn over."

"We'll buy you one of those electric chairs that's so heavy and well balanced it can't turn over."

"I don't think so, Mom. I've always loved autumn, but this one makes me feel so sad. I feel I've lost everything that was truly important. I'm like a broken compass, spinning without direction. Nothing seems worthwhile. I've been cheated, and I resent it. I hate the days. But the nights are worse. I want to hold fast to summer and what I used to have, and the falling leaves are the tears I shed inside, and the wind whistling at night are my howls of anguish, and the birds flying south are all telling me that the summer of my life has come and gone and never, never again will I feel as happy, or as special. I'm nobody now, Mom, nobody."

He was breaking my heart.

Only when he turned to look at me did he see this. Shame flushed his face. Guilt turned his head. "I'm sorry, Mom. You're the only one I can talk to like this. With Dad, who is wonderful, I have to act manly. Once I spill out to you all I feel, it doesn't eat at me inside so much. Forgive me for laying all my heavy feelings on you."

"It's all right. Never stop telling me just how you feel. If you do, then I won't know how to help. That's what I'm here for, Jory. That's why you have parents. Don't feel that your father won't understand, for he will. Talk to him like you talk to me. Say anything you need to say, don't hold back. Ask for anything within reason, and Chris and I give all we can—but don't ask for the impossible."

Silently he nodded, then forced a weak smile. "Okay. Maybe, after all, I can stand to sit in an electric wheelchair someday."

Before him, spread on the table with casters that fitted over his bed, were the many parts of the clipper ship he was tediously gluing together. He seldom turned on the stereo, as if beautiful music was an abomination to his ears now that he couldn't dance. He ignored the television as a waste of time, reading when he wasn't working on the model ship. A tiny part of the wood was held by tweezers as he applied a bit of glue; then, squinting his eye, he looked at the directions and completed the hull.

Casually he asked without meeting my eyes, "Where's my wife? She seldom comes to visit before five. What the hell does she do all day?"

It seemed a casual enough question for Jory to ask as Jory's nurse came in again to say he was off for classes. He waved a cheerful good-bye and left. During his absence either Melodie or I were supposed to do what we could to make Jory comfortable, as well as keep him entertained. Keeping him occupied was the most difficult part. His life had been a physical one, and now he had to be content with mental activities. The nearest thing he had that even approached a physical life was putting the ship together.

At least I'd presumed Melodie came in to do what she could for him.

I very seldom saw Melodie. The house was so large it was easy to avoid those whom you didn't want to see. Lately she'd taken to eating not only breakfast but lunch as well in her bedroom across the hall from Jory's suite.

Chris brought home the custom-made electric wheelchair with its joystick for driving. Immediately the nurse began to teach Jory the methods he'd use to swing his body out of the bed and into a chair he'd have locked beside his bed, with the arm nearest the bed pulled out.

Jory had been crippled for more than three and a half long, long miserable months. For him they were more like years. He'd been forced to change into another kind of person, the kind of person I could tell he really didn't like.

Another day came without a visit from Melodie, and Jory was asking again where she was, and what she did with her time. "Mom, did you hear my question? Please tell me what my wife does all day." His usually pleasant voice held a sharp edge. "She doesn't spend it with me, I know that."

Bitterness was in his eyes as he nailed me with his penetrating dark blue eyes. "Right this minute I want you to go to Melodie and tell her I want to see her—NOW! Not later, when she feels like it—for it seems she never feels like it!"

"I'll get her," I said with determination. "She's no doubt in her room listening to ballet music."

With trepidation I left Jory still working on the model ship. Even as I looked back at him, I saw the wind was picking up and beginning to hurl the falling leaves toward the house. Golden and scarlet and russet leaves that he refused to see— and once he'd heard the music of colors.

Look, now, Jory, look now. This is beauty you won't see again, perhaps. Don't ignore it—take it and seize the day, as you used to do.

But had I, back then . . . ? Had I?

As I stood and looked at him, trying to bring him back to himself, the sky suddenly darkened and all the bright falling leaves went limp in the cold, drenching rain that plastered them against the glass. "Daddy used to do all the chores when we lived in Gladstone. Momma used to complain the storm windows gave her twice as many to clean . . ."

"I want my wife, Mom, NOW!"

I was reluctant to go in search of Melodie for no reason I could name. In the dreary gloom Jory was forced to turn on a lamp at ten in the morning.

"Would you like a cheerful wood fire burning?"

"I only want my wife. Do I have to repeat this ten

times? Once she's here, *she* can start the fire."

I left him alone, realizing my presence irritated him when he wanted her—the only one who could bring him back to himself.

Melodie was not in her room as I'd expected her to be.

The halls I trod seemed the same halls I'd walked before when I was younger. The closed doors I passed seemed the same heavy, solid doors I'd stealthily opened when I'd been fourteen, fifteen. Behind me I sensed the omniscient presence of Malcolm, the malice of the hostile grandmother.

I turned to the western wing. Bart's wing.

Almost automatically my feet took me there as my mind stayed blank. Intuition had ruled most of my life and, it seemed, would rule my future as well. Why was I going this way? Why didn't I look elsewhere for Melodie? What instinct was guiding me to my second son's rooms, where he never wanted me to go?

Before Bart's wide double doors that were heavily padded with luxurious black leather, gold-tooled with his monogram and the family crest, I called softly, "Bart, are you in there?"

I heard nothing. However, all the doors were made of solid oak, heavily paneled beneath the ostentatious padding. Very soundproof doors and thick walls that knew how to hold secrets, so no wonder we four had been so easily hidden away. I turned the doorlatch, expecting to find it locked. It wasn't.

Almost stealthily I stepped inside Bart's sitting room, which was kept immaculate, not one book or magazine out of place. On his walls hung his sporting equipment: tennis rackets and fishing rods, a golf bag in a corner, a rowing machine inside a closet with the door partially open. I stared at the photographs of his favorite sports stars. I often thought Bart made a pretense of admiring football and baseball athletes just so he'd have something in common with the rest of his sex. To my way of thinking he'd have been more honest to plaster his walls with pictures of those who'd earned fortunes in the stock market, or wheeling and dealing in industry, or politics.

His rooms were all black and white with red accents; dramatic, but somehow cold. I sat down on his white leather sofa fully twelve feet long, my feet on his red carpet, with black velvet and satin pillows behind my back. In one corner was a marvelous bar sparkling with crystal decanters and various stemmed glasses, and every kind of liquor he kept there for his private use, along with snack foods. There was also a small fridge and a micro oven for melting cheese, or doing whatever light cooking he wanted.

Every photograph was matted in black or red and framed in gold. Three walls were of white moire fabric. One wall was covered with padded and quilted black leather. A deceiving wall. One of those leather buttons concealed the large safe in which he kept his stock and bond certificates, for he'd proudly shown me his suite just once, soon after it was completely decorated. He'd operated the secret buttons, happy to display the complexity of all he controlled. The safe in his office downstairs was used for less permanent and important papers.

I turned my head to stare at the door to his bedroom, covered with black leather too. Beautiful doors to a magnificent bedroom with the same decor as this room. I thought I heard something. The soft rumble of male laughter—the softer giggle of a woman. Could I be wrong? Did Bart have the ability to make Melodie laugh when none of the rest of us could?

My imagination worked overtime, picturing what they had to be doing, and I felt sick at heart, thinking of Jory in his room, hopefully waiting for a wife who never came to him. Sick because Bart would do this to him, his own brother, whom he'd loved and admired very much for a short while, such a pitifully short while . . .

Just then the door opened and Bart came striding out, wearing not one stitch of clothing. He moved swiftly, his long legs a fast blur. Embarrassed to see him naked, I shrank back into the soft cushions, hoping he wouldn't see me. He'd never forgive me. I shouldn't be here.

Due to the sudden storm, the gloom in his sitting room was so dense there was some hope he wouldn't notice me sitting on his white sofa. Straight to the fully equipped bar he stalked, and with quick, skilled hands mixed some drink using crystal decanters. He sliced lemon, filled two cocktail glasses, put those half-filled glasses on a silver tray and headed back for his bedroom. The door behind him was kicked closed.

Cocktails in the morning, before twelve . . . ?

What would Joel think of that?

I sat on, hardly breathing.

Thunder rolled and lightning cracked, the rain beat on the windowpanes. Lightning zagged and lit up the gloom every few seconds.

Moving to a more secluded spot in his room, I made myself part of the shadows behind a huge plant, then waited.

It seemed an eternity passed before that door opened again, and I knew Jory was waiting anxiously, perhaps even angrily, for Melodie to show up. *Two* glasses, *two*. She was here. She had to be here.

In the dimness I finally saw Melodie step out of Bart's bedroom wearing a filmy peignoir that clearly showed she wore nothing beneath. A flash of lightning briefly illuminated her, showing the bulge of the baby that was due early in January.

Oh, Melodie, how can you do this to Jory?

"Come back," called Bart in a slurred, satisfied voice. "It's raining. The fire in here makes it cozier—and we have nothing better to do . . ."

"I've got to bathe and dress and visit Jory," she said, hesitating in the doorway, looking at him with apparent longing. "I want to stay, really I do, but Jory needs me once in a while."

"Can he give you what I've just given you?"

"Please, Bart. He needs me. You don't know what it's like to be needed."

"No, I don't know. Only the weak depend on others for sustenance."

"You've never been in love, Bart," she answered hoarsely, "so you can't understand. You take me, use me, tell me I'm wonderful, but you don't love me, or truly need me. Someone else would serve your purpose just as well. It feels good to be needed, to know someone wants you more than he wants anyone else."

"Leave, then," he said, his happy tone turning quickly icy as he stayed hidden from my sight. "Of course I don't need you. I don't need anyone. I don't know if what I feel for you is love or just desire. Even pregnant, you're very beautiful, and if your body does give me pleasure now, it might not tomorrow."

I could tell from her profile that she was hurt. She cried out pitifully, "Then why do you want me to come every day, every night? Why do your eyes follow wherever I go? You *do* need me, Bart! You *do* love me! You're just ashamed to admit it. Please don't talk so cruelly to me. It hurts. You seduced me when I was weak and afraid, and Jory was still in the hospital. You took me when I needed *him*, and told me my need was *you*! You knew I was terrified Jory might die . . . and I needed someone."

"And that's all I am?" he roared. "A need? I thought you loved me, really loved me!"

"I do, I do!"

"No, you don't! How can you love me and still talk of him? So go to him. See what he can give you now!"

She left, her frail garment fluttering behind her, reminding me of a ghost frantically fleeing to try and find life.

The door slammed behind her.

Stiffly I rose from my chair, feeling my knee throbbing with pain, like it always ached when it rained. I limped a little as I neared the closed door of Bart's bedroom. I didn't even hesitate as I threw it open. Before he could protest I'd reached inside to throw the switch and bring his cozy, firelit room into electric brightness.

Immediately he bolted up in the middle of his king-sized bed. "Mother! What the hell are you doing in my bedroom? Get out, *out!*"

I strode forward, covering the large space between the door and the bed in a second.

"What the hell are you doing sleeping with your brother's wife? Your injured brother's wife?"

"Get out of here!" he bellowed, taking care to keep his privates well covered, while the mat of dark hair on his chest seemed to bristle with indignity. "How dare you spy on me?"

"Don't you yell at me, Bart Foxworth! I'm your mother, and you are not thirty-five years old yet, so you can't order me out of this house. I'll go when I'm ready, and that time hasn't arrived. You owe me so much, Bart, so much."

"I owe you, Mother?" he asked sarcastically, bitterly. "Pray tell me why I owe you anything. Should I thank you for my father, whom you helped to kill? Should I say thank you for all those miserable days when I was young and neglected, and unsure of myself? Should I thank you now for putting me on such unstable ground that I don't feel I'm a normal man, capable of inspiring love?"

His voice broke as his head bowed. "Don't stand there and accuse me with those cursed Foxworth blue eyes. You don't have to do one damned thing to make me feel guilty. I was born feeling that way. I took Melodie when she was crying and needing someone to hold her and give her confidence and love. And I found for the first time the kind of love I've been hearing and reading about all my life, from the noble type of woman who's only had *one* man. Do you realize how rare they are? Melodie is the first woman who has made me feel truly human. With her I can relax, put down my guard, and she doesn't try to wound me. She loves me, Mother. I don't think I've ever been happier."

"How can you say that when I just overheard the words the two of you exchanged?"

He sobbed and fell back to roll on his side away from me, the sheet just barely covering enough. "I'm on the defensive, and so is she. She feels she's betraying Jory by loving me. I feel much the same way. Sometimes we can let go of guilt and shame, and it's wonderful then. When Jory was in the hospital, and you and Chris were gone all the time, she didn't need a great deal of seducing. She fell with only a little reluctance into my arms, glad to have someone who cared enough to understand her feelings. Our fights all grow from the mire of guilt. Without Jory in the way, eagerly she'd run to me, be my wife."

"BART! You can't take Jory's wife from him. He needs her as he has never needed her before! You were wrong to take her when she was weak from desperation and loneliness. Give her up. Stop making love to her. Be loyal to Jory, as he's been loyal to you. Through everything, Jory has stood behind you—remember that."

He flipped over, clutching the black sheet modestly. Something fragile broke behind his eyes and made him seem vulnerable, a pathetic child again. A wounded, small child who didn't like himself. His voice was hoarse when he said, "Yes, I love Melodie. I love her enough to marry her. I love her with every bone, muscle, ounce of my flesh. She's awakened me from a deep sleep. You see, she's the first woman I've loved. I have never been touched or moved by a woman as I've been touched and moved by Melodie. She slipped into my heart and now I can't push her out. She steals into my room wearing her delicate clothes, with her beautiful long and shining hair down, fresh from her bath and smelling sweet, and she just stands there, pleading with her eyes, and I feel my heart begin to beat faster, and when I dream, I dream of her. She's become the most wonderful thing in my life.

"Don't you see why I can't give her up? She's the one

who has really awakened this burning desire for love and
sex that I didn't even know I had. I thought that sex was a
sin, and never did I pull away from a woman without feeling dirty, even dirtier than I thought I left her. When I made
love to other women, I was always left feeling guilty, as if
two naked bodies meeting in passion was evil—now I know
differently. She's made me realize how beautiful loving can
be, and now I don't know how to carry on without her. Jory
can't be a real lover anymore. Let me be the husband she
needs and wants. Help me to build a normal life for her and
for myself . . . or else . . . I don't know . . . I just don't know
what will happen . . ." His dark eyes turned my way, pleading for my understanding.

Oh, to hear him say all of that, when all his life I'd longed
to have his confidence, and now that I had it, what could I do?
I loved Bart, as I loved Jory. I stood there wringing my hands,
twisting my conscience, and tormenting myself with guilt,
for somehow I must have brought this about. I had neglected
Bart, favored Jory, Cindy . . .

Now I, and Jory, had to pay the price . . . again.

He spoke, his voice lower and cracked, making him seem
even younger and more vulnerable as he lay there, trying to
lock his happiness away in a safe place I couldn't reach, and
in this way forever shield it from killing exposure.

"Mother, for once in your life, see something from my
side. I'm not bad, not wicked, or the beast you sometimes
make me feel I am. I'm only a man who has never felt good
about himself. Help me, Mother. Help Melodie have the kind
of husband she needs now that Jory can't be a real man anymore."

The rain beat a frantic tattoo on the window glass. It
matched the rhythm of my heart. The wind whistled and
shrieked around the house, while frenzied bat wings threw
themselves against the inside of my skull. I couldn't split
Melodie into two equal halves and give to Jory and Bart each

their share. I had to stick with what I knew was right. Bart's love for Melodie was wrong. Jory needed her most.

Still I stood there, riveted to the carpet . . . and felt overwhelmed with my second son's desperate need to be loved. So many times in the past I'd believed him capable of evil, and he'd been proven innocent. Did my own guilt for bringing him into being curse me with eyes that refused to see the good in Bart?

"Are you sure, Bart? Do you truly love Melodie—or do you just want her because she belongs to Jory?"

Turning on his back, his dark eyes met mine with more honesty than he'd ever shown. How those dark eyes pleaded for understanding. "In the beginning I wanted Melodie only because she belonged to Jory. I honestly admit that. I wanted to take from him what he treasured most. Because he'd taken from me what I wanted most—YOU!"

I cringed as he went on. "She rejected my advances so many times that I began to respect her, to see her as different from other women who were easy to get. The more she shoved me away, the higher burned my desire, until I had to have her or die. I love her! Yes, she's made me vulnerable . . . and now I don't know how to live without her!"

I threw my hands wide before I sank to the side of his king-sized bed. "Oh, Bart . . . what a pity it couldn't have been another woman. Any woman but Melodie. I'm glad you've experienced love—and know it isn't dirty or sinful. Would God have made men and women the way he did if he hadn't meant for them to join together? He planned it that way. We recreate ourselves through love. But, Bart, you have to promise not to see her alone again. Wait until Melodie has her baby before you and she decide anything."

His eyes filled with hope, with gratitude. "You'll help me?" Disbelief flooded his eyes. "I never thought you would . . ."

"Wait, please wait. Let Melodie have her child, then go to her, and then to Jory, and face up to him, Bart. Tell him how you feel about her. Don't steal his wife without giving him a chance to have his say."

"What can he say, Mother, that will make any difference? He's already lost. He can't dance. He can't even walk. He can't perform physically."

Seconds ticked away before I found more useless words to speak. "But does she honestly love *you*? I was in your sitting room. I heard her. She hasn't had her say in this matter. From what I can tell, she's torn between loving Jory and needing you. Don't take advantage of her weakness, or Jory's disabilities. Give him time to recover—then do what you must. It isn't fair to steal from Jory when he can't fight back. Give her time to adjust to Jory's condition. Then, if she still wants you, take her, for she'd only harm him more. But what would you do with Jory's child? Will you take that child from Jory, as well as take his wife? Are you planning to leave him nothing?"

Staring up at me, his eyes glittered suspiciously. Bart jerked his eyes away to stare up at the ceiling. "I don't know yet about the baby. I haven't thought it out to that extent. I try not to think of the baby—and you don't have to go running to Chris or Jory with this. For once in your life, give me a chance to have something of my very own."

"Bart—"

"Go now, please. Leave me alone to think. I'm tired. You can weaken a man, Mother, with your demands, with your judgments. Just give me a fair chance this time to prove to you that I'm not as bad as you think, or as crazy as I once believed myself to be."

He didn't ask me again not to tell Jory, or Chris. As if he knew I wouldn't. Standing and turning about, I left his room.

On the way back to my room I thought about confronting Melodie, but I was too upset to face her without giving it more thought. She was already distraught enough, and I had to consider the health of her child.

Alone in my rooms, I sat before a guttering log fire and contemplated what to do. Jory's needs came first. In three months Jory's strong legs had begun to wither into thin sticks, reminding me of Bart's legs when he was very young. Short, thin legs covered with scratches, cuts, and bruises, always falling, always breaking his bones. Punishing himself for being born and not living up to the standards Jory had set. That alone stood me up and headed me toward Jory's bedroom.

I stood in his doorway, my face washed clean of tear streaks, my eyes cooled by ice packs so they weren't red, and I smiled brightly at my firstborn. "Melodie is napping, Jory. But she'll see you before dinner. I think it would be nice for the two of you to dine alone before the fireplace. The rain outside will make it very cozy in here. I've asked Trevor and Henry to carry up logs and a special small table for dining. I've planned a menu with everything you like. Now, what can I do to help you dress and look your best?"

He shrugged indifferently. Before the accident he'd always loved clothes, had always groomed himself to perfection. "What difference now, Mom, what difference? I see you didn't bring her back with you, and why did it take you so long to come back and say she's napping?"

"The telephone rang . . . and Jory, I have to do a few things for myself once in a while. So now, what suit do you favor most?"

"Pajamas and a robe will do," he said distantly.

"Listen to me, Jory. Tonight you are going to sit in that electric wheelchair, wearing one of your father's suits, since you didn't bring a winter suit with you." Immediately he objected, while I insisted.

Already we'd sent to New York for all of Jory's clothes, but Melodie had requested we leave hers where they were—and that had made me heat with anger inside, although I'd said nothing.

"When you look good, you feel good, and that's half the battle. You've stopped caring about your appearance. I'm going to shave your face even if you do want to grow a beard. You're much too handsome to hide behind bristly hair. You've got the most beautiful mouth, and a strong chin. Only weak-chinned men should hide behind beards."

Eventually he gave up and smiled sardonically, agreeing to all I wanted to do to make him look more like himself. "Mom, you're something else. You care so damned much—but I won't ask why. I'm just grateful somebody cares enough."

About that time Chris drove home from Charlottesville, and he was eager to help. He shaved Jory's handsome face with a straight-edge razor, claiming that kind of shave did more for a man than anything else.

I sat on the bed to watch Chris finish the shaving before he splashed on lotion and cologne. All the time Jory looked so tolerant. I couldn't help but wonder what Bart was doing, and how I was going to approach Melodie and tell her that I knew what was going on between her and my second son.

Already Jory's arms were strong enough to swing his upper body into the chair. Chris and I stood back and watched, not offering to help, knowing he had to do this for himself. He seemed somewhat humiliated, and also somewhat proud that he did it easily the first time. Once he was in the chair, Jory looked pleased despite himself. "Not so bad," he said as he studied his face in the mirror I held up. He activated the chair and buzzed around the room for a trial spin. He grinned at us both. "It is better than the bed. What a fool you must think me—now it will be easier to finish the ship before Christmas, and maybe, with pampering like this, I'll struggle through."

"As if we ever believed anything else," said Chris happily.

"Now, contain yourself, Jory . . . I'm going for Melodie," I said, delighted with the way he looked, and the glow of happiness in his eyes, and his excitement to be mobile again, even if he had wheels instead of legs. "Melodie is probably dressed and ready for dinner downstairs. As you know, our formerly sloppy Bart is now a stickler for all the niceties of living elegantly."

"Tell her to hurry," called Jory behind me, sounding more like his old self. "I'm famished. And the sight of that fire burning makes me want her very badly."

With many trepidations I headed for Melodie's room, knowing I was going to face her down with what I'd found out—and when I was finished, I might very well have driven her straight into Bart's ready arms. That was the chance I took.

One brother would win.

The other would lose.

And I wanted them both to win.

Melodie's Betrayal

Softly I rapped on Melodie's door. I could hear faintly through the heavy wood the music from *Swan Lake*. She must have had it playing very loud, or else I wouldn't be hearing it at all. I knocked again. She didn't respond. This time when she didn't answer I opened her door and stepped inside, quietly closing the door behind me. Her room was messy with clothes dropped on the floor; cosmetics littered the dressing room table. "Melodie, where are you?"

Her bathroom was empty. Oh, damn! She'd gone to Bart. In a flash I was off and running back to Bart's wing. On his door I banged furiously. "Bart, Melodie . . . you can't do this to Jory."

They weren't there.

I flew down the back stairs, heading for the dining room, half expecting they'd start dinner without Chris and me. Trevor was setting the table for two, measuring with his eye the distance of the plate from the edge of the table with such precision it was as if he used a ruler. I slowed down to walk into the dining room. "Trevor, have you seen my second son?"

"Oh, yes, my lady," he said in his polite British way,

beginning to lay out the silver flatware. "Mr. Foxworth and Mrs. Marquet just left to eat in a restaurant. Mr. Foxworth requested that I tell you he'd be back . . . soon."

"What did he really say, Trevor?" I asked, feeling sick at heart.

"My lady, Mr. Foxworth was just a wee bit drunk. Not too drunk, so don't worry about the rain and accidents. I'm sure he can control the car, and Mrs. Marquet will be just fine. It's a lovely night for driving if you like rain."

I hurried on toward the garage, hoping to be in time to stop them. Too late! And it was just as I'd feared. Bart had taken Melodie in his small, fast, sports car, the red Jaguar.

My steps were snail-like as I headed back up the stairs. Jory was glowing from the champagne he'd sipped as he waited. Chris had gone on to our room to change for dinner.

"Where is my wife?" asked Jory, seated at the small table Henry and Trevor had carried up. Fresh flowers from our greenhouse centered the table, and with the champagne cooling in a silver ice bucket the atmosphere was festive and seductive, especially with the log fire burning to chase away the damp chill. Jory looked very much like himself with his legs hidden, and the chair he'd hated was hardly noticeable.

Should I make up a lie this time, as I had before?

All the brightness in his eyes faded. "So she's not coming," he said in a flat way. "She never comes here anymore—at least not inside the room. She lingers in the doorway and speaks to me from a distance." His husky voice cracked, then broke entirely and he was crying.

"I'm trying, Mom, really trying to accept this and not be bitter. But when I see what's happening between me and my wife, I come apart inside. I know what she's thinking even when she says nothing. I'm not a real man anymore, and she doesn't know how to cope with that."

I fell upon my knees at his side and took him into my arms. "She'll learn, Jory, she'll learn. We all have to learn how to cope with what can't be helped. Give her time. Wait until after the baby comes. She'll change. I promise she'll change. You will have given her your child. There's nothing like a baby of your own to hold in your arms to put joy in your heart. The sweetness of a baby, the thrill of having one small, tiny bit of humanity entirely dependent on you to shape and mold. Jory, just you wait and see how Melodie changes."

His tears had stopped, but the anguish in his eyes stayed.

"I don't know if I can wait," he whispered hoarsely. "When there are others around to see, I smile and act content. But I'm thinking all the time about putting an end to this and setting Melodie free of all obligations. It's not fair to expect her to stay on. I'm going to tell her tonight that she can go if she wants, or she can stay until after the baby is born and then leave, and file for divorce. I won't contest."

"No, Jory!" I flared. "Say nothing to upset her more—just give her time. Let her adjust. The baby will help her adjust."

"But, Mom, I don't know if I can live through to the end now. I think all the time about suicide. I think of my father and wish I had the courage to do what he did."

"No, darling, hang on. You'll never be alone."

Chris and I sat down at the small table to keep him company. He didn't speak a dozen words during the meal.

At bedtime, I stealthily put away all the razors and everything with which he could harm himself. I slept on the couch in his room that night, fearful he was so despondent he might try to end his life just to give Melodie freedom to leave without guilt. His moans reached me even as I dreamed.

"Mel . . . my legs ache!" he cried out in his sleep. I got up to comfort him. He wakened and stared at me in a disoriented way. "Every night my back and my legs ache," he answered sleepily in reply to my questions. "I don't need sympathy for my phantom pains. I just want a full night's rest."

All through the night he writhed in agony. The legs that he couldn't feel during the day by night tormented him with constant pain. The lower part of his back stabbed him with repeated jabs.

"Why do I feel pain at night, when I feel nothing during the day?" he cried out, sweat pouring down his face, sticking his pajama jacket to his chest. "I still wish I had the nerve my father did—that would solve all our problems!"

No, no, no. I clung to him, covering his face with kisses, promising him everything and anything to make him cling to life. "It will work out, Jory, it will! Hang in there. Don't give up and lose the greatest challenge of your life. You have me and you have Chris and sooner or later Melodie will come around and be your wife again."

Bleakly he stared at me, as if I spoke of pipe dreams made of nothing but smoke.

"Go sleep in your own room, Mom. You make me feel more like a child by staying here. I promise not to do anything to make you cry again."

"Darling, be sure and ring for your father or me if you need anything. Neither one of us minds getting up. Don't call for Melodie, for she might trip and fall in the dark now that she's kind of unsteady on her feet. I've always been a light sleeper, and it's easy for me to fall asleep again. Are you listening, Jory?"

"Sure, I'm listening," he said with his eyes blank and remote. "If there's one thing I'm good at now, it's listening."

"And soon the physical therapist will come to start you on the road to recovery."

"Recovery, Mom?" His eyes looked tired, very shadowed and dark. "You mean that back brace I'll be fitted for? Indeed, I am looking forward to using that thing. The leg braces are going to be a real joy to wear. Isn't it fortunate I won't feel them? And I'm not even going to mention that harness contraption that will make me think of myself as a horse. I'll just think it will keep me from falling . . ." He paused, covered his face with his hands briefly, threw back his head, and sighed.

"Lord, give me strength to endure—are you punishing me for having too much pride in my legs and body? You've done a damned good job of bringing me low."

His hands came down. Tears shone in his eyes, streaked his cheeks. In a moment he was apologizing. "Sorry about that, Mom. Tears of self-pity aren't very manly, are they? Can't be brave and strong all the time. Got my moments of weakness just like everyone else. Go back to your room. I'm not going to do anything to cause you and Dad more grief. I'll see this thing through to the end. Good night. Say good night to Melodie for me when she comes in."

I cried in Chris's arms, causing him to ask a thousand questions that I refused to answer. Frustrated and more than a bit angry, he flipped away. "You can't fool me, Catherine. You're holding something back, thinking it will add another burden, when not to know what's going on is the heaviest of all burdens!"

He waited for me to reply. When I didn't, he quickly fell asleep on his side. He had the most irritating habit of being able to sleep when I couldn't. I wanted him awake, forcing me to answer the questions I'd just avoided. But he slept on and on, turning to embrace me in his sleep, burying his face in my hair.

Every hour I was up and checking to see if Bart had brought Melodie home, checking to see if Jory was all right. Jory lay on his bed with his eyes wide open, apparently waiting, as I did, for Melodie to come home.

"Has the phantom pain eased up?"

"Yes, go back to bed. I'm fine."

I met Joel in the hallway outside Bart's room. He flushed to see me in my lacy white negligee. "Joel," I said, "I thought you changed your mind about living under this roof and went back to that small cell over the garage . . ."

"Used to, Catherine, used to," he muttered. "Bart ordered me into the house, saying a Foxworth shouldn't be treated like a servant." His watery eyes reproached me for not objecting when he'd informed us he liked the garage cell better than the nice room in Bart's wing of the house.

"You don't know what it's like to be old and lonely, niece. I've suffered from insomnia for years and years, troubled by bad dreams, with vague aches and pains that kept me from ever reaching that deep sleep I yearn for. So I get up to tire myself, I roam about . . ."

Roam about? Spying, that's what he did! Then, looking at him more closely, I felt ashamed. Standing there in the gloom of the hall, he appeared so frail, so sickly and thin—was I being unfair to Joel? Did I dislike him only because he was Malcolm's son?—and had that detestable habit of muttering to himself incessant quotes from the Bible to take me back in time to our grandmother, and her insistence that we learn a quote each day from the holy book.

"Good night, Joel," I said with more kindness than usual. Still, as he continued to stand there, as if to win me to his side, I thought of Bart, who had said many a painful thing to me when he was a boy, but not since he'd been an adult. Now he, too, was reading the Bible, using the words written in there to prove some moot point. Had Joel helped bring life back to what I thought was dormant? I stared at the old man, who edged away from me almost fearfully.

"Why do you look like that?" I asked sharply.

"Like what, Catherine?"

"Like you're afraid of me."

His smile was thin, pitiful. "You are a fearsome woman, Catherine. Despite all your blond prettiness, you can sometimes act as hard as my mother."

I started, stunned that he could think that. I could not possibly be like that mean old woman.

"You also remind me of your mother," he whispered in his thin, brittle voice, drawing his old bathrobe more tightly about his skinny frame. "And you seem far too young to be in

your fifties. My father used to say the wicked always managed
to stay young and healthy longer than those who had a place
waiting for them in Heaven."

"If your father went on to Heaven, Joel, then I will gladly
go in the opposite direction."

He eyed me as if I were a pitiful object who just didn't
understand before he ambled away.

Once I was back beside Chris, he woke up long enough for
me to spill out the scene between Joel and me. Chris glared
at me in the dimness. "Catherine, how rude of you to talk to
an old man like that. Of course you can't drive him out. In a
way he has more right here than all of us, and it is Bart's home
legally, even if we do have lifetime residency privileges."

Anger filled me. "Can't you recognize that Joel has
become the father figure Bart has been looking for all his
life?" And there I'd gone and hurt him. He stiffened and
turned away from me.

"Good night, Catherine. Perhaps you should stay in bed
and mind your own business for a rare change. Joel is a
lonely old man who is grateful to have a champion like Bart
and a place where he can live out the rest of his life. Stop
imagining you see Malcolm in every old man you meet,
for eventually, if I live long enough, I'll be another old
man."

"If you look and act like Joel, I'll be glad to see the end
of you as well."

Oh, how could I say that to the man I loved? He shifted
farther away, then refused to respond to my touch on his arm.
"Chris, I'm sorry. I didn't mean that." My hand caressed his
arm, then moved to slip inside his pajama jacket.

"I think it best if you keep your hands to yourself. I'm
not in the mood now. Good night, Catherine, and remember,
when you look for trouble, you usually find it."

~   ~   ~

I heard a distant door close. My illuminated wristwatch read three-thirty. Drawing on a robe, I slipped into Melodie's room and sat down to wait. It was four before she managed the long trip from the garage to her bedroom. Did she and Bart stop to embrace and kiss? Did they whisper love words they couldn't save for tomorrow? What else could be talking her so long? Faint hints of dawn approaching showed over the rimming mountains. I paced the floor of her room, growing terribly impatient. Finally I heard her coming. Stumbling in the door of her room, Melodie held her high-heeled silver slippers in one hand, and in her other hand she held a small silver clutch.

She was six months pregnant, but in her loose-fitting black dress it was hardly noticeable. She jerked when she saw me rise from a chair, then choked as she backed away. "Well, Melodie," I said cynically, "don't you look pretty."

"Cathy, is Jory all right?"

"Do you really care?"

"You sound so angry with me. You look at me so hard—what have I done, Cathy?"

"As if you don't know," I said to her with angry emphasis, forgetting the tact I'd intended to use. "You slip out on a rainy night with my second son, and you come home hours later with red strawberry marks on your neck, with your lipstick smeared and your hair unbound, and still you ask, *what . . . have . . . you . . . done*. Why don't you tell me . . . *what* you have done."

She stared at me with huge eyes of disbelief, half-blended with guilt, with shame, but there was some element of hope there as well. "You've been like my mother, Cathy," she cried, her eyes tearing as they pleaded for my understanding. "Please don't fail me now—now when I need a mother more than I ever have before."

"But you forget, I am Jory's mother first and foremost. I am also Bart's mother. When you betray Jory, you betray me."

Melodie cried out again, pleading with me to listen to her.

"Don't turn away from me now, Cathy. I have no one but you who will understand. Certainly you of all people have to understand! I love Jory, I'll always love him—"

"And so you go to bed with Bart? What a fine way to show your love," I interrupted. My voice sounded cold and hard.

Her face lowered into my lap as her arms wrapped around my waist. She clung to me. "Cathy, please. Wait until you hear my side." Her face lifted, already stained with tears, black tears because of her mascara. Somehow this served only to make her look more pitifully vulnerable. "I'm part of the ballet world, Cathy, and you know what that means. We are the dancers who take music into our bodies and souls and make it visible for all to see, and for that we pay a price, a heavy price. You know the price. We dance with our souls bared for all to view and criticize if they will, and when the dance ends, and we hear the applause, and we accept the roses, and take the bows and the curtain calls, and hear the calls of *bravo! bravo!* finally we end up backstage to take off the makeup, to put on everyday mundane clothes, and then we know the best of what we are isn't real, only fantasy. We float on wings of sensuality so powerful nobody can realize as we do the pain of all that's so insensitive and cruel and brutal in reality."

She hesitated to gain the strength to go on, while I sat stunned with her acuteness, for I knew the truth when I heard it—who would know better than I?

"Out there in the audience they think most of us are gay. They don't realize we're borne on the music, sustained by the music, made bigger than life by the sets, the applause, the adulation, and least of all do they realize that lovemaking is all that keeps us really nourished. Jory and I used to fall passionately into each other's arms the minute we were alone and only then could we find the release we needed to wind down enough to fall asleep. Now I have no release, nor does he. He won't listen to the music, and I can't turn it off."

"But you have a lover," I said weakly, fully understanding

every word she'd said. Once I, too, had flown on the joyous wings of music, and drifted downward, sick because there was no one to love me and lend reality to the fantasy world I loved best of all.

"Listen, Cathy, please. Give me a chance to explain. You know how boring it is in this house, with no one ever visiting, and the only time the phone rings it's Bart they want. You and Chris and Cindy were always in the hospital with Jory, while I was a coward and hung back, scared, so scared he'd see my fright. I tried to read, tried to entertain myself with knitting like you do, but I couldn't do it. I gave up and waited for the telephone to ring. Nobody from New York ever calls me. I took walks, pulled weeds from the garden. Cried in the woods, stared at the sky, watched the butterflies, and cried some more.

"Several nights after we found out that Jory would never walk or dance again, Bart came to my room. He closed the door behind him and just stood there looking at me. I was on the bed, crying as usual. I had ballet music playing, trying to recreate the feeling of how it had been with Jory, and Bart was there, staring at me with those dark, mesmerizing eyes. He stood waiting, just looking at me, until I stopped crying and he came closer to wipe the tears from my face. His eyes turned soft with love when I sat up and just stared at him. I'd never seen his eyes so kind, so full of tenderness and compassion. He touched me. My cheek, my hair, my lips. Shivers began to race up and down my spine. He put his hands in my hair, stared into my eyes, and slowly, ever so slowly he inclined his head until his lips brushed over mine. I'd never guessed he could be so gentle. I'd always presumed he'd take a woman by brutal force. Maybe if he had touched me with rough, uncaring hands I would have turned away. But his gentleness was my undoing. He reminded me of Jory."

Oh, I didn't want to hear any more. I had to stop her before I felt pity and sympathy for her, for Bart.

"I don't want to hear any more, Melodie," I said coldly, jerking my head so I didn't have to look at the love marks that Jory might notice if she went to him now. "So now when Jory needs you most, you intend to fail him and turn to Bart," I said bitterly. "What a wonderful wife you are, Melodie."

She sobbed louder, covering her face with her hands.

"I remember your wedding day when you stood before the altar and made your vows of fidelity, for better or for worse— and the first worse that turns up, you find a new lover."

While she sniffled and tried to find better words to win me to her side, I thought of how lonely this mountainside home was, how isolated. And we'd left Melodie here thinking she was too upset to want to drive anywhere. Thoughtless about what she and Bart could be doing, never suspecting she'd turn to him—the very one she'd seemed to dislike so much.

Still sniffling and crying, Melodie fiddled with her strap, while her washed-out eyes took on a certain wariness. "How can you condemn me, Cathy, when you have done even worse?"

Stung, I rose to leave, feeling that my legs had turned to lead along with my heart. She was right. I wasn't any better. I, too, had failed, and more than once, to do the right thing. "Will you forget Bart and stay away from him, and convince Jory you still love him?"

"I do still love Jory, Cathy. It may sound strange, but I love Bart in a different way, a strange way that has nothing at all to do with the way I feel about Jory. Jory was my childhood sweetheart and my best friend. His younger brother was someone I never really liked, but he's changed, Cathy, he has, really. No man who really hates women can make love as he does . . ."

My lips tightened. I stood in the open doorway condemning her, as once my grandmother had condemned me with her pitiless steel-gray eyes alone telling me I was the worst kind of sinner.

"Don't go before I make you understand!" she cried, putting forth her arms and beseeching me. I closed the door, thinking of Joel, and backed against it. "All right. I'll stay, but I won't understand."

"Bart loves me, Cathy, really loves me. When he says it, I can't help but believe him. He wants me to divorce Jory. Bart has said he will marry me." Her tearful voice diminished to a husky whisper. "I don't truthfully know if I can live out my life with a husband confined to a wheelchair."

Sobbing more than before, she broke and from her kneeling position fell in a crumpled heap on the floor. "I'm not strong like you are, Cathy. I can't give Jory the support he needs now. I don't know what to say, or what to do for him. I want to turn back the clock and bring back the Jory I used to have, for I don't know this one. I don't even think I want to know him . . . and I'm ashamed, so ashamed! Now all I want to do is vanish."

My voice took on the steely edge of a razor. "You're not going to escape your responsibilities that easily, Melodie. I'm here to see that you live up to your marriage vows. First, you will cut Bart out of your life. You will never allow him to touch you again. You will say no every time he tries anything. I am going to confront him again. Yes, I've already faced him down, but I'm going to be tougher. If I have to, I will go to Chris and tell him what's going on. As you know, Chris is a very patient, understanding man with a great deal of control, but he won't condone what you're doing with Bart."

"Please," she cried. "I love Chris like a father! I want him to keep on respecting me."

"*Then leave Bart alone!* Think of your child, which should come first. You shouldn't be having sex now anyway, it's sometimes not safe."

Her huge eyes closed, squeezed back the tears; then she was nodding and promising never to make love with Bart again. Even as she vowed, I didn't believe her. I didn't believe Bart either when I spoke to him before I went to bed.

~   ~   ~

Morning came and I hadn't slept at all. I rose tired and listless, putting on a false smile for Jory before I tapped on his door, announcing myself. He invited me to come in. He appeared happier than he had last night for some reason, as if overnight thought had calmed him down. "I'm glad Melodie has you to lean on," said Jory as I helped him to turn over.

Each day Chris, the nurse, and I took turns moving his legs and massaging them when the therapist wasn't there to do it for him. This way his muscles wouldn't atrophy. His legs, due to the massaging, had regained a little of their former shape.

I took that as a huge step forward. Hope . . . in this house of dark misery we were always clinging to hope we colored yellow—like the sun we'd seldom seen.

"I was expecting Melodie to come in this morning," Jory said with a bit of wistfulness, "since she failed to even stop by and say good night last night."

Days passed. Melodie disappeared often, as did Bart. My faith in Melodie had eroded. No longer could I meet her eyes and smile. I stopped trying to talk to Bart and turned to Jory for companionship. We watched TV together. We played games together. We competed in silly jigsaw competitions to see who could find the right pieces faster. We sipped wine in the afternoon, grew sleepy by nine and pretended, pretended that everything would work out fine.

There was something about being in bed most of the time that made him exceptionally fatigued. "It's the lack of proper exercise," he said, pulling on the trapeze fastened to his head-board. "At least I'm keeping my arms strong—where did you say Melodie was?"

I put down the bootee I'd just finished and picked up the yarn to make another. In between games I knitted and watched TV. When I wasn't with Jory, I was in my room typing the journal I was keeping of our lives. My last book, I told myself. What more did I have to say? What else could happen to us?

"Mom! Don't you ever listen to me? I asked if you knew where Melodie was, and what she's doing."

"She's in the kitchen, Jory," I said quickly. "Busy preparing just the kind of dinner you like most."

A look of relief brightened his face. "I'm worried about my wife, Mom. She comes in and does small things for me, but her heart doesn't seem in it." A shadow fleeted through his eyes, quick to disappear when he saw my piercing look. "I say to you all the things I need to say to her. It hurts to watch her pulling away from me bit by bit. I want to speak out and say I'm still the same man inside, but I don't think she wants to know that. I believe she wants to think that I'm different because I can no longer dance or walk, and that makes it easier for her to break away and release all the ties that bind us. She never talks to me about the future. She hasn't even discussed names for our child. I've been looking in books for just the right names for our son or daughter. I tell myself, like you said, that she's pregnant, and I've been reading up on that subject, too. Just to make up for my former lack of interest . . ."

On and on he talked, convincing himself with his own words that it was her pregnancy that was responsible for all the changes in his wife.

I cleared my throat and used my chance. "Jory, I've been giving this serious thought. Your doctor said once you'd be better off in the hospital than staying here and having someone come to help with your rehabilitation. You and Melodie can rent a small apartment near the hospital, and she can drive you each day to rehab. It's almost winter, Jory. You don't know about winters in this western mountainous part of Virginia. They're freezing. The wind never stops blowing. It snows often. The roads leading here from the village are often blocked. The state keeps the highways and expressways open, but the small

private roads to this estate are often closed. I'm thinking of the
days when your nurse won't be able to come, or your physical
therapist, and you need daily exercise. If you live near the hospital, all your physical needs can easily be met."

He stared at me in hurt surprise. "You mean you want to
get rid of me?"

"Of course not. You've got to confess you don't like this
house."

His eyes darted to the windows where the rain was coming
down hard, driving dead leaves and late-blooming roses into
the earth. All the summer birds had flown away.

The wind whipped around the house, finding its way
through small crevices, shrieking and howling in this replica
just as much as it had in the old, old original.

Jory said from behind me, as I just continued staring out,
"I like what you and Mel did to these rooms. You've given me
a haven safe from the scorn of the world, and right now, I don't
want to leave and face those who used to admire my grace and
skill. I don't want to be separated from you and Dad. I feel
we've grown closer than we've ever been, and the holidays are
coming up.

"And if the roads from here to there might be closed for
my nurse and my therapist, they'll also be closed for you and
Dad. Don't put me out, Mom, when I most want to stay. I need
you. I need Dad. I even need this chance to grow closer to my
brother. I've been thinking a lot about Bart recently. Sometimes he comes and sits nearby, and we talk. I think, at last,
we're beginning to be the kind of friends we were before your
mother moved into that house next door, way back when he was
nine . . ."

Uneasily I fidgeted, thinking of Bart's dual face, coming
in to be his brother's friend and seducing his wife behind his
back.

"If it's what you want, Jory, stay. But give it more thought.
Chris and I could move to the city just to be with you and

Melodie, and we can make things as comfortable for you there as they are here."

"But you can't give me another brother at this late date, can you, Mom? Bart's the only brother I'm going to have. Before I die, or he does, I want him to know I care what happens to him. I want to see him happy. I want him to have the kind of married life I share with Mel. Someday he's got to wake up to the fact that money can't buy everything, and most certainly, it can't buy love. Not the kind of love Mel and I have."

He looked thoughtful, as I inwardly cried for him and his "love"; then a blush rose up from the neck of his sports shirt covered with a red sweater that put color in his wan cheeks. "At least, I should add, the kind of marriage we used to have. It's not much of a marriage now, I'm sorry to admit. But that's not her fault."

A week later I was alone in my room, furiously writing in the journal, when I heard the pounding of Chris's footfalls as he ran and burst in on me. "Cathy," he said excitedly, throwing off his topcoat, hurling it to a chair, "I've got wonderful news! You know that experiment I was assisting with? There's been a breakthrough." He pulled me up from my desk, shoved me into a chair before the roaring fire. He explained in minute detail all that he and other scientists were trying to accomplish. "It means I'll be away from home five nights a week, now that winter's come. The snow isn't cleared until around noon, and that gives me so little time in the lab. But don't look sad, I'll be here on weekends. But if you object, tell me honestly. My first duty is to you and our family."

His excitement over this new project was so evident I couldn't dash his enthusiasm with my fears. He'd given so much to me, to Jory and Bart, and received so little appreciation. My arms went automatically around his neck. I scanned over his dear, familiar face. I saw faint etchings around his blue eyes that I hadn't noticed before. My fingers in his hair found silver that was coarser in texture than the gold. There were a few gray hairs in his eyebrows.

"If this is going to make you unhappy, I can always quit and forget about research, and devote all my time to my family. But I'll be very grateful if you give me this opportunity. I thought when I gave up my practice in California that I would never find anything to interest me more, but I was wrong. Perhaps this was meant to be—but, if necessary, I *can* give it up and stay here with my family."

Give up medicine entirely? He'd centered the major portion of his life on the study of medicine. To feel useful gave added zest to his life. To keep him here just to please myself, doing nothing that would contribute to mankind at this crucial point when he felt vulnerable by being middle-aged, would destroy him.

"Cathy," Chris said, interrupting my thoughts as he pulled on his heavy woolen coat again, "are you all right? Why do you look so strange? So sad? I'll be back every Friday evening and won't leave until Monday morning. Explain to Jory everything I've told you. No, on second thought, I'll stop by his room and explain myself."

"If it's what you want, then it's what you have to do. But we're going to miss you. I don't know how I can sleep without you beside me. You see, I talked to Jory, and he doesn't want to move to Charlottesville. I think he's grown to like his rooms very much. He's almost finished that clipper ship. And it would be a pity to deprive him of all the comforts he has here. And Christmas isn't too far away. Cindy will be coming home for Thanksgiving to stay until the New Year. Chris, promise to make real efforts to come home every Friday. Jory needs your strength as well as mine since Melodie fails him entirely."

Oh, I'd said too much.

His eyes narrowed. "What's going on that you're not telling me?" He pulled off the heavy coat and carefully hung it up. Swallowing first, I started to speak, faltered, tried to pull my eyes from the strong hold of his . . . but those blue eyes forced me to say, "Chris, would you think it terrible if you knew that Bart has fallen in love with Melodie?"

His lips twitched. "Oh, that. I know Bart's been infatuated with her since the day she came here. I've seen him watching her. One day I found the two of them in the back salon, seated on the sofa. He had her dress open and was kissing her breasts. I walked away. Cathy, if Melodie didn't want him, she'd slap his face and make him stop. You may think their affair is stealing Jory's wife when he needs her most, but he doesn't need a woman who doesn't love him anymore. Let him have her—what good can she do Jory now?"

I glared at him with total disbelief. "You're defending Bart! Do you think it's fair what he's done?"

"No, I don't think it is fair. When is life fair, Cathy? Was it fair when Jory's back was broken, and now he can't walk? No, it's *not* fair. I've been in medicine too long not to know justice isn't doled out equally. The good often die before the bad. Children die before grandparents, and who is to say that's right? But what can we do about it? Life is a gift, and perhaps death is another kind of gift. Who am I, or you, to say? Accept what has happened between Bart and Melodie, and stay close to Jory. Keep him happy until the day comes when he can find another wife."

Reeling from his words, I felt hazy and unreal. "And the baby, what of the baby?"

Now his voice turned hard. "The baby is another matter. He or she will belong to Jory, no matter which brother Melodie chooses. That child will help see Jory through—for he may never be able to sire another."

"Chris, please. Go to Bart and tell him to let Melodie go. I cannot stand the thought of Jory losing his wife at this point in his life."

He shook his head, telling me that Bart had never listened

to him, and it wasn't likely he would now. And already he'd spoken without my knowledge to Melodie.

"Darling, face up to the facts. In her heart Melodie doesn't want Jory now. She won't come out and say that, but behind every word she doesn't say, behind all her excuses, is the plain fact that she just does not want to stay married to a man who can't walk. In my way of thinking it would be cruel to force her to stay, and even harder on Jory in the long run. If we do try to force her to stay, sooner or later she'd strike back at him for not being the man he was and I want to spare him that. Better to let her go before she hurts him even worse than by just having an affair with Bart."

"Chris!" I cried, shocked that he would think as he did. "We can't let her do this to Jory!"

"Cathy, who are we to judge this matter? Right or wrong, should we, who are considered sinners by Bart, sit in judgment on him?"

In the morning Chris drove away after telling me he'd be back Friday evening around six. I watched from my bedroom window until his car was out of sight.

How empty the days when Chris was away, how bleak the nights without his arms to hold me and his whispers to assure me everything would work out fine. I smiled and laughed for Jory, not wanting him to know that I was suffering from the lack of having Chris in my bed every night. Jory slept alone, I told myself, and I could manage if he could. I knew that Melodie and Bart were still lovers; however, they were discreet enough to try and hide that from me. But I knew from the way Joel glared at Jory's wife that he considered her a bitch. Strange that he didn't glare at Bart, when he was just as guilty. But then men had a way of thinking what was right for the gander was wrong for the goose, even pious religious ones like Joel.

We were two weeks into November, and our plans for Thanksgiving were complete. Our weather turned more severe and hurled blustery winds and snow our way, stacking snow around our doors, freezing it overnight to ice so we couldn't leave the garage in one of our many cars. One by one our servants deserted until there was only Trevor to prepare the meals with my off-and-on help.

Cindy flew home and helped cheer our hours with her easy laughter, her winning ways that charmed everyone but Bart and Joel. Even Melodie seemed a bit happier. Then she took to her bed, to stay there all day long, trying to keep warm now that our electricity went off so often, and that meant our furnaces controlled by electric thermostats refused to give out heat. We then had to resort to our coal furnace auxiliary.

Freely Bart carried in the wood he wanted to burn in his office fireplace and forgot the rest of us would enjoy a fire.

Bart was secreted away with Joel, whispering of the Christmas ball he planned, so I had to carry in enough logs to build a fire in Jory's room, where Cindy was playing a game with him. He sat in his chair, wrapped with an afghan, his shoulders covered with a jacket, and smiled at my futile attempts to set the kindling ablaze. "Open the damper, Mom, that always helps a little."

How had I forgotten that?

Soon I had a fire going. The bright glow cheered up the room, which seemed so right in summer but not so right in winter, just as Bart had predicted. Now the dark paneling would have made Jory feel cozier.

"Mom," Jory said, suddenly looking very cheerful, "I've been thinking about something for days. I'm a fool to act as I am. You're right—been right all along. I'm not going to feel sorry for myself the minute I'm alone and no one can see, as I've been doing since the accident. I am going to accept what can't be helped and make the most of a difficult situation. Just like you and Dad did when you were locked away, I'm going to turn my idle moments into creative moments. I'll have plenty of time to read all the books I've never had time to read before, and I'm going to say yes to Dad the next time he offers to teach me how to paint with watercolors. I'll go outdoors and try landscapes. Perhaps I'll even venture into oils, other mediums. I want to thank you both for giving me the incentive to go on. I'm a lucky guy to have parents like you and Dad."

Feeling proud enough to cry myself, I embraced him, congratulating him for coming back to being his natural, enthusiastic self.

Cindy had set a bridge table for two, but Jory soon turned back to the clipper ship he was determined to finish before Christmas. He was stringing the threadlike cords to the rigging, which was the last step before a little touch-up painting here and there.

"I'm going to give this to someone very special, Mom," he informed me. "On Christmas day, one person in this house is going to have my first difficult piece of handicraft."

"I bought it for you, Jory, to become an heirloom to pass down to your children . . ." I blanched when I heard myself say "children."

"It's all right, Mom, for with this gift I am going to win back the younger brother who loved me before that old man came and changed him. He wants it badly; I see it in his eyes every time he comes in and checks to see my progress. Besides, I can always put together another one for my child. Right now I want to do something for Bart. He thinks none of us need him or like him. I've never seen a man as uncertain about himself . . . and that's such a pity."

Holiday Joys

Thanksgiving Day came, and with it arrived Chris early in the morning. Jory's nurse ate Thanksgiving dinner with us, keeping his lovesick eyes glued on Cindy as if she had him under a spell. She couldn't have behaved more like a lady, making me tremendously proud of her. The next day she eagerly accepted our invitation to go shopping in Richmond. Melodie shook her head. "Sorry, I just don't feel up to it."

Chris, Cindy, and I drove off with a clear conscience, knowing Bart had flown to New York and wouldn't be with Melodie. Jory's nurse had promised to stay with Jory until we returned.

Our three-day holiday in Richmond refreshed our minds and souls, gave me the sense of being still beautiful and very much in love, and Cindy had the time of her life spending, and spending, and spending some more. "You see," she said proudly, "I don't waste all the allowance you send me on myself. I save to buy wonderful gifts for my family . . . and Momma, Daddy, you just wait until you see what I bought for you both. And I certainly hope Jory likes his gift. As for

Bart, he can take what I give and like it or not."

"What about your Uncle Joel?" I asked with curiosity.

Laughing, she hugged me. "Wait until you see."

Hours later Chris turned onto the private road that would wend its crooked way up to Foxworth Hall. In one of the boxes that filled our trunk and rear seat of the car, I had an expensive dress to wear to the Christmas ball I'd overheard Bart arranging with the same caterers who'd taken care of his birthday party. In her own huge box, Cindy had chosen a spectacular dress, daring but at the same time wonderfully appropriate. "Thank you, Momma, for not objecting," she'd whispered before she kissed me.

Nothing unusual had occurred during our absence, except Jory had finally completed the clipper ship. It stood proud and exquisitely finished down to the last detail, its tiny brass helm gleaming, its sails full and bulging with invisible and unfelt high winds. "Sugar stiffening," revealed Jory with a small laugh, "and it worked. I took the sails and shaped them around a bottle like the instructions read, and now our maiden voyage is well under way." He was proud of his work, smiling as Chris stepped over to admire his meticulous craftsmanship more closely. Then we had to help him lift the ship into a styrofoam form-fitting mold that would hold it securely until it reached the hands of the new owner.

His beautiful eyes turned to me. "Thanks for giving me something to do during all these long, boring hours, Mom. When I first saw it I was overwhelmed, thinking I'd never be able to do something that appeared so difficult. But I took one step at a time, and now I feel I won over those hideously complicated directions."

"That's the way all life's battles are won, Jory," said Chris as I hugged Jory close. "You don't look at the overall picture. You take one step, then another, and another . . . until you arrive at your destination. And I must say, you did a magnificent job on this ship. It's as professionally made as any I've seen. If Bart doesn't appreciate all the effort you put into this, he'll really disappoint me."

Standing, Chris beamed at Jory. "You're looking healthier, stronger. And don't give up on the watercolors. It is a difficult medium, but I thought you would enjoy it more than oils. I think one day you are going to be a fine artist."

Downstairs, Bart was on the phone directing a bank official to take over a failing business. Then he was talking to someone else about the Christmas party he was planning, a ball to make up for the tragedy of his birthday party. I stood in his open doorway thinking it was a good thing that all he ordered did not come from his personal fund but from the Corrine Foxworth Winslow Trust, which left Bart his annual five hundred thousand as "pin" money to spend only on himself. It more than irked Bart to be forced to confer with Chris each time he spent over the named figure of ten thousand.

Bart slammed down the receiver, glared at me. "Mother, do you have to stand in the doorway and eavesdrop? Haven't I told you before to stay away from me when I'm busy?"

"When do I see you if I don't do this?"

"Why do you need to see me?"

"Why does any mother need to see her son?"

His dark eyes softened. "You've got Jory—and he always seemed more than sufficient."

"No, you're wrong there. If I had never had you, Jory would have been sufficient. But I *did* have you, and that makes you a vital part of my life."

Uncertain-looking, he stood up and strode to a window, keeping his back toward me. His voice came to me deep and gruff, with a melancholy sadness. "Remember when I used to keep Malcolm's journal stuffed inside my shirt? Malcolm wrote so much about his mother, and how much he loved her until she ran off with her lover and left him alone with a father he didn't like. Some of Malcolm's hate for her rubbed off on me, I'm afraid. Each time I see you and Chris head up those stairs together, I feel the need to cleanse myself from the shame I feel and you two don't. So don't you start lecturing to me about Melodie, for what I do with her is far less sinful than what you do with Chris."

He was no doubt right, and that's what hurt worse than anything.

More or less I grew unhappily accustomed to seeing Chris only on the weekends, although my heart ached and my bed felt huge and lonely without him, and all my mornings alone were wistful, wishing I could hear him whistling as he shaved and showered, missing his cheerfulness, his optimism. When the weather kept him away on the weekends, even then, I grew used to that. How adaptable we humans were, how willing to suffer through any horror, any adjustment, any deprivations just to gain those few minutes of priceless joy.

To stand at the window and watch Chris drive up filled me with surprising youthful excitement so overwhelming it was as if I were waiting for Bart's father to steal away from Foxworth Hall and meet me in the cottage. Certainly I didn't act as placidly accepting as when I'd seen him every night, every morning. The weekends were something to be anticipated and dreamed about. However, Chris was both more and less to me—more a lover and less a husband. I missed the brother who'd been my other half, and loved the lover-husband who didn't remind me as much of the brother I'd known.

There was no way and there were no words that could separate the two of us now that I'd accepted him and taken him as my husband, defying all scorn and society's moral rules.

Still, my unconscious was trying peculiar tricks to give my conscious relief. With determination I was separating Chris the man from Chris the boy who'd been my brother. An unconscious, unplanned game we both began to play with some finesse. We didn't discuss it, we didn't have to. No longer did Chris call me "my lady Cath-er-ine." No more did he say teasingly, "Don't let the bedbugs bite." All the charms and enchantments of those yesterdays when we were locked up, meant to keep away evil spirits, we let go, at last, in the middle years of our contentment.

He came home late one Friday night in December, stomping his feet in the foyer as I lingered in the shadows of the rotunda watching him take off his topcoat and hang it neatly in the guest closet before he raced up the stairs two at a time, calling my name. I stepped out of the shadows and threw myself into his eager arms. "You're late again!" I cried. "Who do you see in your lab that sends shivers up and down your spine?"

No one! No one! his passionate kisses assured.

The weekends were so short, so dreadfully short.

I was spilling out all that troubled me, about Joel and his weird ways of roaming about the house, scowling his disap-proval at everything I did. I told him about Melodie and Bart, and Jory, who was depressed and yearning for Melodie, hating her indifference, loving her even so, while I was trying constantly to remind Melodie of her responsibilities, which hurt him even more grievously than the loss of the use of his legs.

Chris lay beside me and listened to my long tirade with quiet impatience before he said sleepily and a bit out of patience, "Catherine, sometimes you make me dread coming home." He rolled on his side away from me. "You spoil everything wonderful and sweet we have between us with your incessant, unpleasant, suspicious tales. And most of all that troubles you is in your imagination. Haven't you always had too much of it? Grow up, Catherine. You are contaminating Jory with your suspicions as well. Once you learn to expect only good from people, then perhaps that's all you'll get."

"I've heard your philosophy before, *Christopher*," I said with a flash of bitterness that shot through my brain like a laser beam, bringing to mind his faith in our mother, and the good he'd expected from her by his devotion. *Chris, Chris, don't YOU ever learn?* But I didn't say it, didn't dare to say it.

There he was, middle-aged, even if he didn't look it, presenting me with his same old rosy-glow boyish optimism. Though I could ridicule him verbally for this, inside I longed for his kind of redeeming faith . . . for it gave him peace, while I lived day in and day out, juggling from one foot to another on a hot frying pan.

Bart sat before the roaring fire, trying to concentrate on *The Wall Street Journal* as Jory and I wrapped Christmas gifts on a long table we'd cleared of all accessories. All of a sudden it occurred to me as I tied fancy bows and cut foil paper to size, that since Cindy had arrived, she'd drifted dream-like throughout the house, lost in her own world, so that she seemed almost not there. Because of the peace this brought, I had more or less forgotten her needs as I attended to Jory's. I hadn't been surprised when she wanted to go with Chris into Charlottesville to finish up her shopping and see a movie before she came back with him on Friday. Chris had a one-bedroom apartment and planned to sleep Cindy on his sofa bed.

"Really, Momma, my special Christmas surprise will please you." Only when she was gone did I wonder what put that secret smile of pleasure on her pretty face.

As Jory and I topped off all his presents with huge satin bows and name tags, I heard the banging of car doors, the stomping feet on the portico, and then the sound of Chris calling out. It was only about two in the afternoon as he strolled into our favorite salon with Cindy at his side—and, to my amazement, a strikingly handsome boy about eighteen was with them. I already knew Cindy considered any boy less than two years older too young for her. The older and more experienced the better was the way she liked to tease me.

"Mom," said Cindy happily, her face radiant, "here is the surprise you said I could bring home."

Startled, I still managed a smile. Cindy had not once said her "secret" surprise was a guest she'd invited without asking anyone's permission. I stood so Chris could introduce the boyfriend Cindy had met in South Carolina as Lance Spalding. The young man had considerable poise as he shook hands with me, with Jory, with Bart, who glowered.

Chris kissed my cheek and briefly embraced Jory before he hurried toward the door. "Cathy, forgive me for leaving so soon, but I'll be back tomorrow early. Cindy couldn't wait until tomorrow to bring her houseguest home. I've got a few things to wrap up at the university. And I haven't finished my shopping." He flashed me a brilliant smile full of charm. "Darling, I've got two weeks off for the holidays. So take it easy and keep your imagination under lock and key." He turned to Lance. "Enjoy your holiday, Lance."

Cindy, very full of herself, pulled her boyfriend closer to the very one who was least likely to be hospitable to her guest. "Bart, I knew you wouldn't mind if I invited Lance. His father is president of the chain of Chemical Banks of Virginia."

Magic words. I smiled at Cindy's cleverness. Instantly Bart's hostile attitude changed into interest. It was embarrassing to see the way he tried to milk every bit of information he could from the young man, who was obviously very much infatuated with Cindy.

Cindy was lovelier than ever, glowing like a winter rose in her tight white sweater banded with stripes of rose to match her tight knit pants. She had a wonderful figure she was determined to display.

Laughing and full of joy, she caught hold of Lance's hand and tugged him away from Bart. "Lance, you just wait until you see all of this house. We have authentic suits of armor— two of them—and they would be too small for me to wear. Momma, maybe, but not me. And just think, knights were supposed to be big, powerful men, and they weren't big. The music room is larger than this room, and my room is the prettiest room of all. The suite my parents share is incredible. I've not been invited to view Bart's rooms, but I'm sure they must be fabulous." Here she half turned to toss Bart a wicked, teasing smile. His scowl deepened.

"Stay out of my rooms!" he ordered harshly. "Don't go near my office. And Lance, while you are here, you will remember you are under my roof and I expect you to treat Cindy with honor."

The boy's face turned red before he meekly said, "Of course. I understand."

The second the two of them were out of sight, though we could still hear Cindy singing the praises of Foxworth Hall, Bart hurled at me his opinion of Cindy's boyfriend. "I don't like them. He's too old for her and too slick. She or you should have told me. You know I don't want unexpected guests just dropping in."

"Bart, I agree with you entirely. Cindy should have warned us, but perhaps she was fearful that if she did, you would say no. And he seems a very nice young man to me. Remember how sweet Cindy has been since Thanksgiving. She hasn't given you one second of trouble. She's growing up."

"Let's hope she continues to behave herself," he grumbled before he smiled faintly. "Did you see him looking at her? She's got that poor kid snowed under."

Relieved, I settled back to smile at Bart, then at Jory, who was fiddling with the Christmas lights before he began to quietly arrange his gifts beneath the tree.

"The Foxworths had a tradition for always throwing a Christmas ball on Christmas night," said Bart in a pleasant tone, "and Uncle Joel himself drove to mail my invitations two weeks ago. I'm expecting at least two hundred if the weather remains fairly decent. Even if a blizzard blows in, I still think half will manage to get here. After all, they can't afford to slight me when I give them so much business. Bankers, attorneys, brokers, doctors, businessmen and their wives and girlfriends, as well as the best of the local society. And a few of my fraternity brothers will be showing up. So for once, Mother, you shouldn't complain that our lives are lonely in this isolated area."

Jory went back to reading his book, seemingly determined not to let anything Bart said or did upset him. In the firelight his profile was classically perfect. His dark hair curled softly around his face, turning up at the collar of his knit sports shirt. Bart lounged in a business suit, as if at any moment he'd be up and away to attend a corporation meeting. That's when Melodie drifted in wearing a shapeless gray garment that hung from her shoulders and bulged out as if she had a watermelon beneath. Her eyes went immediately to Bart, who jumped up, turned his eyes away, and hastily left the room, leaving behind him an uncomfortable silence.

"I met Cindy upstairs," said Melodie huskily, her forlorn eyes avoiding contact with Jory's. She sat down near the fire and stretched forth her hands to warm them. "Her boyfriend seems very pleasant and well bred, and also very handsome." She kept her eyes on the fire while Jory diligently tried to force her to look at him. His heart was in his eyes as he wistfully gave up and turned back to his book. "It seems Cindy likes dark-haired men who look like her brothers," she went on in a vague, distant way, as if nothing mattered and she was only making an effort, for a change.

Angrily Jory jerked his eyes up. "Mel, can't you even say hello to me?" he asked hoarsely. "I'm here, I'm alive. I'm doing my best to survive. Can't you say or do something to tell me you remember that I'm your husband?"

Reluctantly turning her head his way, Melodie gave him a vague smile of recognition. Something in her eyes said she didn't see him anymore as the husband she'd so passionately loved and admired. She saw only a crippled man in a wheelchair and as he was now, he made her uneasy and embarrassed.

"Hello, Jory," she said dutifully.

Why didn't she get up and kiss him? Why didn't she see the pleading in his eyes? Why couldn't she make an effort, even if she didn't love him anymore? Slowly Jory's wan face reddened before he bowed his head and stared down at all the gifts he'd so beautifully wrapped.

I was about to say something cruel to Melodie when Cindy and Lance came strolling back, both with starry eyes and flushed faces. Bart wasn't long in following them in. He raked the room with his eyes, saw that Melodie was still there, and turned to leave again. Instantly Melodie rose and quickly disappeared. Bart must have seen her leave, for shortly he returned and sat down and crossed his legs, looking relieved now that Melodie was gone.

The boyfriend spoke up, looking at Bart and smiling widely. "I hear all this belongs to you, Mr. Foxworth."

"Call him Bart," ordered Cindy.

Bart frowned.

"Bart . . . ," began Lance hesitatingly, "truly this is a remarkable house. Thank you for inviting me." I glanced at Cindy, who stood her ground as Bart threw her an angry look, even as Lance went on innocently, "Cindy didn't show me your suite of rooms, or your office, but I hope you will do that. Someday I hope to own something like this . . . and I have a passion for electronic gadgets, as Cindy tells me you have."

Instantly Bart was on his feet, seemingly proud to show off his electronic equipment. "Sure, if you want to see my rooms, and my office, I'll be delighted to show you. But I'd rather Cindy didn't accompany us."

After a sumptuous dinner, which Trevor served, we conversed in the music room with Jory and Bart. Melodie was upstairs, already in bed. Soon Bart said he had to rise early and *he* was going to bed. Instantly the conversation dwindled to nothing as we all stood and headed for the stairs. I showed Lance into a lovely room with its own connecting bath. It was in the eastern wing, not so far from Bart's own rooms, while Cindy's was near my own. Cindy smiled sweetly and kissed the cheek of Lance Spalding. "Good night, sweet prince," she whispered. "Parting is such sweet-sweet sorrow."

His arms folded over his chest, as Joel folded his, Bart stood back and watched this tender scene with scorn. "Let it be a true parting," he said meaningfully, looking directly at Lance, then at Cindy, before he stalked off toward his rooms.

First I saw Cindy to her room and we exchanged a few words and our regular good night kisses. Then I paused outside Melodie's door, wondering if I should rap and go in and try to reason with her. I sighed, knowing it wouldn't do any good, not when I'd tried so many times before. Next I was crossing over to Jory's room.

He lay on his bed, staring up at the ceiling. His dark blue eyes rolled my way, shiny with unshed tears. "It's been so long since Melodie came in to kiss me good night. You and Cindy always find the time to do that, but my wife ignores me as if I don't exist for her. There's no real reason now why I couldn't sleep in a larger bed, and she could sleep beside me, but she wouldn't even if I asked. Now I've finished the clipper ship, and I don't know what to begin next to occupy my time. I really don't want to start another ship for our child. I feel so unfulfilled, so at odds with life, with myself, and most of all, with my wife. I want to turn to my wife, but she turns from me. Mom . . . without you, Dad, and Cindy, I wouldn't know how to live through the days."

I held him in my arms, ran my fingers through his hair as I had when he was a little boy. I said all the things that should have come from Melodie. I pitied her, disliked her for being weak, hated her for not loving enough, for not knowing how to give even when it hurt.

"Good night, *my* sweet prince," I said from Jory's doorway. "Hold tight to your dreams, don't abandon them now, for life offers many chances at happiness, Jory. It's not all over for you."

He smiled, said good night, and I headed for the southern-wing suite I shared with Chris.

All of a sudden Joel was in front of me, blocking my passage. He wore a shabby old bathrobe of some faded color that seemed more gray than anything else. His thin, pale hair stood up in small peaks like horns, while the long end of his corded sash trailed behind him like a limp tail.

"Catherine," he said sharply, "do you realize what that girl is doing this very minute?"

"*That* girl? What girl?" I answered just as sharply.

"You know who I mean, that daughter of yours. Right now, at this moment, she is entertaining that young man she brought home with her."

"Entertaining? What do you mean?"

His smile came crooked and mean. "Why, if anyone should know, it should be you. She's got that boy in her bed."

"I don't believe you!"

"Then go and see for yourself!" he answered quickly, with some delight. "You never believe anything I say. I was in the back hall and just happened to see this boy stealing down the halls, and I followed. Before he reached Cindy's door, she had it open and was welcoming him inside."

"I don't believe you," I said again, more weakly this time.

"Are you afraid to check and find out I might be telling the truth? Would that convince you then that I am not the enemy you presume me to be?"

I didn't know what to say or think. Cindy had promised to behave herself. She was innocent, I knew she was. She'd been so perfect, helping with Jory, resisting her natural tendency to argue with Bart. Joel had to be lying. Spinning about, I headed toward Cindy's room with Joel close at my heels.

"You are lying about her, Joel, and I intend to prove that to you," I said as I almost ran.

Just outside her door I paused and listened, hearing nothing at all. I lifted my hand to knock. "No!" hissed Joel. "Don't give them any warning if you want to know the full truth. Just throw open the door and step inside the room and see for yourself."

I paused, not wanting to even think he could possibly be right. And I didn't want Joel to tell me what to do. I glared at him before I knocked sharply just once, waited a few seconds, then threw open Cindy's bedroom door and stepped inside her room, which was lit by moonlight flooding in through her windows.

Two totally naked bodies were entwined on Cindy's virgin bed!

I stared, shocked, feeling a scream in my throat that just stayed there. Before my amazed eyes Lance Spalding sprawled over my sixteen-year-old daughter, jerking spasmodically. Cindy's hands clutched at his buttocks, her long red fingernails digging in, her head rolling from side to side as she moaned with pleasure, telling me this was not their first time.

What should I do now? Close the door and say nothing? Fly into a towering rage and drive Lance out of our home? Helplessly caught in a web of indecision I stood there as only seconds must have passed, until I heard a faint noise behind me.

Another gasped. I whirled around to see Bart, who was staring at Cindy, who'd rolled on top of Lance and was lustily riding him, crying out four-letter word vulgarities in between her moans of ecstasy, entirely unaware of anything but what she was doing and what was being done to her.

Bart had no indecision.

He strode directly to the bed and caught hold of Cindy around the waist. With a mighty heave he tore her off the boy, who seemed helpless in his nakedness and the bliss of what had been going on. Bart ruthlessly hurled Cindy to the floor. She screamed as she fell face downward on the carpet.

Bart didn't hear.

He was too busy handling the youth. Again and again his fists slammed into Lance's handsome face. I heard the crack of his nose as blood spurted everywhere. "NOT UNDER MY ROOF!" he roared, repeatedly battering Lance's face. "NO SINNING UNDER MY ROOF!"

A moment ago I felt like doing the same thing. Now I ran to save the boy. "Bart, STOP! YOU'LL KILL HIM!"

Cindy kept screaming hysterically even as she tried to cover her nudity with the clothes she'd dropped on the floor. They were all mixed up with Lance's discarded garments. Joel was now in the room, raking his eyes scornfully over Cindy; then he was turning to smile at me with gloating satisfaction that said over and over again: *See, I told you so. Like mother, like daughter.*

"See what you've raised with your pampering?" Joel intoned, as if behind a pulpit. "It was evident from the first time I saw her that that girl was nothing but a harlot under the roof of my father's house."

"You fool!" I stormed. "Who are you to condemn anyone?"

"You are the fool, Catherine. Just like your mother, in more than one way. She, too, wanted every man she saw, even her own half uncle. She was like this naked girl crawling lewdly around on the floor—ready to bed down with anything in pants."

Unexpectedly Bart dropped Lance on the bed and hurled himself at Joel. "Stop it! Don't you dare tell my mother she's like her mother! She isn't, she isn't!"

"You'll see it my way eventually, Bart," said Joel in his softest, most sanctimonious tone. "Corrine got what she deserved. Just as your mother will get hers one day. And if justice and right still rule in this world, and God is in his Heaven, that indecent, naked girl on the floor trying to cover herself will meet her end in fiery flames, as she deserves."

"Don't you say anything like that again!" bellowed Bart, so furious with Joel he forgot all about Cindy and Lance, who were both hastily pulling on the night clothes they'd abandoned. He hesitated, as if shocked to find himself defending the girl he incessantly denied was his sister. "This is my life, Uncle," he said sternly, "and my family more than it is yours. I will deal out what justice is demanded, and not you."

Seemingly very distressed and shaken, shuffling lamely like an older man, Joel ambled off down the hall, bent over almost double.

The moment Joel was out of sight, Bart turned his furious temper on me. "YOU SEE!" he roared. "Cindy has just proven what I suspected she was all along! She's no good, Mother! NO GOOD! All the time she played the game of being sweet, she was planning how she'd enjoy herself when Lance came. I want her out of this house and out of my life forever!"

"Bart, you can't send Cindy away—she's my daughter! If you have to punish someone more than you have, send Lance away. You're right, of course, Cindy shouldn't have done what she did, nor should Lance have taken advantage of our hospitality."

Somewhat mollified, he managed to simmer down a little. "All right, Cindy can stay since you insist on loving her no matter what. But that boy is going tonight!" He yelled at Lance, "Hurry and pack your things—for in five minutes I'm driving you to the airport. If you ever dare touch Cindy again, I'll break the rest of your bones! And don't think I won't know. I have friends in South Carolina, too!"

Lance Spalding was very pale as he hurried to throw his clothes back into suitcases he'd just emptied. He couldn't even look at me as he hurried by and whispered huskily, "I'm sorry and so ashamed, Mrs. Sheffield . . ." and then he was gone, with Bart right behind him, shoving him on faster from time to time.

Now I turned to Cindy, who had donned a very modest granny gown and was huddled under the covers of her bed, staring at me wide-eyed and scared-looking. "I hope you are satisfied, Cindy," I said coldly. "You have truly disappointed me. I expected more from you . . . you promised me. Don't your promises mean anything at all?"

"Momma, please," she sobbed. "I love him, and I wanted him, and I think I waited long enough. It was my Christmas gift to him—and to myself."

"Don't lie to me, Cynthia! Tonight wasn't your first time with him. I'm not as stupid as you presume I am. You and Lance have been lovers before."

She wailed loudly, "Momma, aren't you going to love me anymore? You can't just turn it off, 'cause if you do, then I'll want to die! I don't have any parents but you and Daddy . . . and I swear it won't happen again. Please forgive me, please!"

"I'll think about it," I said coldly as I closed her door.

The next morning as I dressed, Cindy came running into my room, crying out hysterically, "Momma, please don't let Bart force me to leave too. I've never had a happy Christmas when Bart was around. I hate him! Really hate him! He's ruined Lance's face, ruined it."

More than likely she was right. I had to teach Bart how to hold back his rage. How terrible for such a good-looking boy to have his beautiful nose broken, to say nothing of his black eyes and many cuts and bruises.

However, after Lance was gone, something peculiar laid a ghostly hand on Bart and turned him very quiet. Lines I hadn't seen before etched from his nose to his beautifully shaped lips, and he was too young for face lines. He refused to look or talk to Cindy. He treated me as if I weren't there, either. He sat sullen and quiet, staring at me, then rested his dark eyes fleetingly on Cindy, who was weeping, and I couldn't remember another time when Cindy had allowed any of us to see her cry.

Through my mind flitted all kinds of dreary thoughts. The place where owls and foxes resided, remembering the Bible we used to have to study every day. Where could understanding be found? There was a time for planting, a time for reaping, a time to gather in . . . where was our time for joy?

Hadn't we waited long enough?

Later that morning I had a talk with Cindy. "Cindy, I am shocked at your behavior. Bart had every right to be enraged, even though I disapprove of the way he was so rough on that boy. I can understand *his* actions, but not yours. Any young man would have entered your room when you willingly opened your door and invited him in. Cindy, you have to promise not to do anything like that again. Once you are eighteen, you become your own boss—but until that day, and while you are under this roof, you will not play sex games with anyone here or anywhere else. Do you understand?"

Her blue eyes widened, took on the shine of forthcoming tears. "Momma, I don't live in the eighteenth century! All the girls are *doing it*! I held out much longer than most do, and from all I've heard about you . . . you went after men too."

"Cindy!" I snapped sharply. "Don't you ever throw my past or present in my face! You don't know what I had to endure—while you have had nothing but happy days full of everything that was denied me."

"Happy days?" she asked bitterly. "Have you forgotten all the nasty, mean things Bart did to me? Maybe I wasn't locked up, starved, or beaten, but I've had my problems, and don't think I haven't. Bart makes me feel so unsure about my femininity that I have to test all the boys I meet . . . I just can't help it."

We were at that time in her bedroom, while Bart was downstairs.

I stepped forward to take Cindy into my arms. "Don't cry, darling. I do understand how you must feel. But you must try to understand how parents feel about their daughters. Your father and I want only the best for you. We don't want you to be hurt. Let this experience with Lance teach you a lesson, and hold back until you are eighteen and able to reason with more maturity. Hold out longer than that if you can. When you grab at sex too soon, it has a way of biting back and giving you exactly what you don't want. It did that to me, and I've heard you say a thousand times you want a stage and film career, and husbands and babies have to wait. Many a girl has been thwarted by a baby that started because of uncontrollable passion. Be careful before committing yourself to anyone. Don't fall in love too soon, for when you do you make yourself vulnerable to so many unforeseen events. Give romance a try without sex, Cindy, and save yourself all the pain of giving too much too soon."

Her arms were tight about me, her eyes turned soft and told me we were again mother and daughter.

Later Cindy and I stood side by side downstairs, watching everything whiten with snow, grow misty with distance, cruelly isolating us even more from the rest of the world. "Now all roads from Charlottesville will be blocked," I said tonelessly to Cindy. "What's more, Melodie is acting so strangely she makes me fear for the good health of her child. Jory's staying in his room as if he doesn't want to encounter her, or any of us. Bart saunters around like he owns all of us as well as the house. Oh, I wish Chris were here. I hate it when he's gone."

I turned to find Cindy staring at me with a kind of wonderment. She flushed when she met my eyes. When I asked why, she murmured, "I just wonder sometimes how the two of you hang on to what you have, when I fall in and out of love so often. Momma, someday you've got to tell me how to make a man really love me, and not just my body. I wish boys would look first into my eyes like Daddy looks into yours; I wish they'd look at my face at least once in a while, for it's not an ugly face, but they all stare at my boobs. I wish their eyes would follow me around like Jory's follow Melodie . . ."

Cindy put her arm around me and buried her face against my shoulder. "I'm so sorry, Momma, really so sorry I caused all that trouble last night. Thank you for not scolding me more than you did. I've been thinking about what you said, and you're right. Lance has paid a heavy price, and I should have known better." Pleadingly she gazed into my eyes. "Momma, I was serious, all the girls at school started way back when they were eleven, twelve, and thirteen, and I love Lance. And I held back, although all the boys chased after me more than they did the others. The girls thought I was doing it when I wasn't. I pretended to be really with it, but then one day I heard some boys comparing notes and they were all saying they hadn't scored all the way with me. They talked as if I were some kind of freak— or maybe a lesbian. That's when I decided I'd let Lance have his way this Christmas. The special gift I had for him."

I stared at her hard, wondering if she told all the truth, as she went on to tell me she was the only girl in her group to hold out until sixteen, and that was really old for a girl in today's world. "Please don't be ashamed, for if you are, then I'll be. I've wanted to do it since I was twelve but held back because of what you said. But you've got to understand that what I did with Lance wasn't casual. I love him. And for a while, before you and Bart came in . . . it felt . . . felt . . . so good."

What could I say now ?

I had my own willful youth clearly tucked in a memory closet, ready to jump forward and put the vision of Paul before me . . . and the way I'd wanted him to teach me all the ways of love, especially when my first experience with sex had been so devastating, filling me with the kind of guilt that even now I could cry to look up at the moon that had seen Chris's sin, and mine.

About six Chris called to say he'd been trying to reach me all day but the lines had been down. "You'll be seeing me

Christmas Eve," he said cheerfully. "I've hired a snowplow to precede me to the Hall, and I'll be right behind. How are things going?"

"Fine, just fine," I lied, telling him Lance's father had fallen down the stairs and he had to fly home immediately. Then I rattled on and on, saying we were all set for Christmas, gifts wrapped, tree up, but Melodie was, as usual, clinging to her rooms as if they offered her the only sanctuary in the world.

"Cathy," said Chris in a tight voice, "how nice it would be if you'd only level with me on occasion. Lance didn't fly home. All the planes are grounded. Lance is, at this moment, not ten feet away from this very phone booth. He came to me and confessed everything. I took care of his broken nose, his other wounds, and cursed Bart all the time. That boy is a mess."

Early the next morning, we heard on the radio that all roads to the village and the nearest city were snowed under. Travelers were warned to stay home. We kept the radio on all day, listening to the weathermen who seemed to control our lives. "Never before has there been a winter more dramatic than this one," went the singsong male voice, extolling the virtues of weather. "Records are being broken . . ."

Hour by miserable hour Cindy and I stood at the windows, with Jory often joining us to stare as we did at the snow coming down with relentless determination to isolate us.

Behind my eyes I saw the four of us, locked in that room, whispering about Santa Claus and telling the twins that surely he would find us. Chris had written him a letter. Oh, the pity of those little twins waking up on Christmas morning, not even remembering the good times that had gone on before.

Hearing Jory cough brought me back to the present. Every few minutes Jory suffered through paroxysms of racking coughs. I glanced at him fearfully.

Soon he was heading his chair for his room, saying he could put himself back into bed. I wanted to go with him but knew he wanted to do all he could for himself.

"I'm beginning to hate this place," grumbled Cindy. "Now Jory's got a cold. That's why I brought Lance home with me, knowing it would be this. I was hoping every night we'd have a party, and being slightly drunk would take away the pall of living under the shadows of Bart and that creepy old Joel. I was expecting Lance to keep me happy while I was here. Now I've got no one but you, Momma. Jory seems so aloof and alone, and he thinks I'm too young to understand his problems. Melodie never says anything to me, or anybody. Bart stalks around like the grim reaper—and that old man sends shivers up my spine. We don't have any friends. No one ever calls unexpectedly. We're all alone, getting on each other's nerves. And it's Christmas. I'm looking forward to that ball Bart says he's throwing. At least that would give me the chance to meet some people and brush off the moss I feel creeping up my legs."

Suddenly Bart was there, yelling at Cindy. "You don't have to stay. You're just the bastard my mother had to have."

Cindy blushed deeply red. "Are you trying to hurt me again, jerk? You can't hurt me *now*! I'm through with that!"

"Don't you ever call me jerk again, bastard!"

"CREEP, JERK, CREEP, JERK!" she taunted, backing up and dodging behind chairs and tables, deliberately baiting him to give chase, and in this way, give her dull day a bit of excitement.

"Cindy!" I stormed, furious now. "How dare you talk to Bart that way? Now, say you're sorry . . . say it!"

"No, I won't say it, for I'm not sorry!" she yelled not at me but at Bart. "He's a brute, a maniac, a crazy, and he's trying to drive us all as batty as he is!"

"STOP!" I yelled, seeing Bart's face go very pale. Then he lunged forward and caught her by her hair. She tried to run, but he had her held too securely. I rushed forward to prevent him from striking her by clinging onto his free arm. Above her he towered. "If you ever so much as speak to me again, little girl, you'll rue the day. You're very proud of your body, of your hair, of your face. One more insult and you'll hide in closets and break all the mirrors."

His deadly tone of voice said he was serious. I moved to help Cindy stand. "Bart, you don't mean that. All your life you've tormented Cindy. Can you blame her for wanting her revenge?"

"You take her side, after what she said to me?"

"Say you're sorry, Cindy," I pleaded, turning to her. Then I turned appealing eyes on Bart. "You say it, too, please."

Indecision flashed in Bart's fiery dark eyes as he saw how upset I was, but it vanished the moment Cindy screamed out, "NO! I'm *not* sorry! And I'm not afraid of him! You're just as creepy and senile as that old jerk who wanders around muttering to himself. Boy, do you have a thing for old men! Maybe that's your hang-up, *brother!*"

"Cindy!" I whispered, very much shocked, "apologize to Bart."

"Never, never, NEVER!—not after what he did to Lance!"

The anger on Bart's face frightened me.

Just then Joel ambled into the room. He stood with his long arms crossed over his chest and met Bart's fiery eyes. "Son . . . let it go. The Lord sees and hears all and, in time, wreaks his own justice. She's a child like a bird chirping in the trees, led by instincts that know nothing of morality. She acts, speaks, moves, all without thinking. She's nothing compared to you, Bart. Nothing but a hank of hair, a bone, and a rag— you are born to lead."

As if transfixed, Bart's anger simmered down. He followed Joel from the room without looking our way. To see Bart follow that old man so obediently and without question filled my head with fresh fears. How had Joel gained such control?

Cindy fell into my arms and began to cry. "Momma, what's wrong with me, with Bart? Why do I say such hateful things to hurt him? Why does he say them to me? I want to hurt Bart. I want to pay him back for every ugly thing he's done to hurt me."

In my arms she sobbed out her anxieties until she was limp.

In many ways Cindy reminded me of myself, so eager to love and be loved, to live a full, exciting life even before she was mature enough to accept the emotional responsibilities.

I sighed and held her closer. Someday, somehow, all family problems would be resolved. I held to that belief, praying that Chris would come home soon.

Christmas

As it had in the past, Christmas Eve arrived with its charm and festive peace to reign over troubled spirits and gave even Foxworth Hall its own beauty. The snow still fell, but it was not so wild and wind driven. In our favorite room for getting together, Bart and Cindy, with Jory directing, were decorating the gigantic Christmas tree. Cindy was up on a ladder on one side, Bart was on the second ladder, as Jory sat in his wheelchair, fiddling with strings of lights meant for our door wreaths. Decorators were working in other rooms to make them festive enough for the hundreds of guests Bart expected to entertain at the ball. He was terribly excited. To see him happy and laughing added joy to my heart, especially when Chris came in the door loaded down with all he'd purchased at the last moment, as was his customary procrastinating way.

I ran to greet him with hungry arms and eager kisses that Bart couldn't see from his position behind the tree. "Whatever took you so long?" I asked, and he laughed, indicating the beautifully wrapped gifts.

"Out in the car I've got more," he said with a happy smile.

"I know what you're thinking, that I should do my shopping earlier, but I never seem to find the time. Then all of a sudden it's Christmas Eve, and I end up paying twice as much, but you're going to be very pleased—and if you're not, don't tell me."

Melodie was crouched down on a low stool near the fireplace in the salon just off the foyer, looking miserable. In fact, when I studied her more closely she appeared to be in pain. "Are you all right, Melodie?" I asked. She nodded to say she was fine, and I foolishly took her word for that. When Chris questioned her, she stood and denied anything was wrong. She threw Bart an imploring glance he didn't see, and then she was heading for the back stairs. In her shapeless, dull-colored garment, she seemed a drab thing that had aged ten years since July. Jory, who always kept a close eye on Melodie, turned to watch her drift away, a terrible haunted sadness in his eyes that stole his pleasure from the happy occupation at hand. The string of lights slid from his lap to entangle the wheels of his chair. He didn't notice, only sat with clenched fists, as if he'd like to smash Fate in the face for taking away the use of his marvelous body, and in so doing stealing from him the woman he loved.

On the way to the stairs, Chris stopped to clap Jory heartily on the back. "You're looking fit and healthy. And don't worry about Melodie. It's normal for a woman in the last trimester to become irritable and moody. So would you if you were carrying around all that extra weight."

"She could at least speak to me occasionally," complained Jory, "or look at me. She doesn't even cozy up to Bart anymore."

I looked at him with alarm. Could he know that only a short while ago Bart and Melodie had been lovers? I didn't believe they were anymore, and that was the true explanation of Melodie's miserable state. I tried to read his eyes, but he lowered his lids and pretended to be interested in decorating the tree again.

Long ago Chris and I had established a tradition of opening at least one gift on Christmas Eve. When night came, Chris and I sat alone in the best of our downstairs salons, toasting one another with champagne. We lifted our glasses high. "To all our tomorrows together," he said with his warm eyes full of love and happiness. I repeated the same words before Chris handed me my "special" gift. I opened the small jewelry box to find a two-carat pear-shaped diamond suspended on a fine gold chain.

"Now, don't object and say you don't like jewelry," Chris said hastily when I just stared at the object that glittered and refracted rainbow colors. "Our mother never wore anything like this. I really wanted to buy you opera-length pearls like the ones she used to wear, because I think they are both elegant and understated. But knowing you, I forgot the pearls and settled for this beautiful diamond. It's tear-shaped, Cathy—for all the tears I would have cried inside if you had never let me love you."

The way he said that put tears in my eyes and swelled my heart with the guilty sadness of being us, the special joy of being us; the complications of being us sometimes were just too overwhelming. Silently I handed him my "special" gift—a fine star-sapphire ring to fit his forefinger. He laughed, saying it was ostentatious but beautiful.

No sooner were those words out of his mouth than Jory, Melodie, and Bart joined us. Jory smiled to see the glow in our eyes. Bart frowned. Melodie sank into a deep-cushioned chair and seemed to disappear in the depths. Cindy came running in with bells that she shook merrily, her pants and sweater bright red. Finally Joel slunk into the room to stand in a corner with his arms folded over his chest, casting his own pall, like a somber judge overseeing wicked and dangerous children.

It was Jory who first responded to Cindy's charm by raising his glass of champagne high and toasting. "Hail to the joys of Christmas Eve! May my mother and father always look at one another as they do this night, with love and tenderness, with compassion and understanding. May I find that kind of love in the eyes of my wife again . . . soon."

He was directly challenging Melodie and in front of all of us. Sadly, his timing was bad for this kind of confrontation. She drew herself into a tighter knot and refused to meet his eyes; instead, she leaned forward to stare more intensely into the fire. The hope in Jory's eyes faded. His shoulders sagged before he swiveled his chair so that he couldn't see her. He put down his champagne and fixed his eyes on the fire just as intensely as his wife, as if to read what symbolism she was seeing. In a distant dim corner, Joel smiled.

Cindy tried to force gaiety. Bart, by attrition, gave in to the corroding gloominess that Melodie emitted like a gray fog. Truly our little family get-together in a gloriously festive room was a flop. Bart refused even to look at Melodie now that she was so grossly out of shape.

Soon he was pacing the room restlessly, glancing at all the gifts under the "family" tree. His eyes accidentally found Melodie staring at him hopefully, and only too quickly he looked away, as if embarrassed by her too overt pleading. In a few minutes Melodie excused herself, saying in a low voice that she didn't feel well.

"Anything I can do?" Chris asked immediately, jumping up to assist her up the stairs. She plodded along heavily, flat footed. "I'm all right," she snapped near one newel post. "I don't need your help—or anyone's!"

"And a merry Christmas was had by all," intoned Bart, much in the manner of Joel, who still stood in the shadows, watching, always watching.

The moment Melodie was gone from the room, Jory slumped forward in his chair before he stated, too, that he was tired and not feeling too well. His next prolonged bout of coughing revealed that. "I've got just the medicine you need," said Chris, jumping up and heading for the stairs. "You can't go to bed yet, Jory. Stay a while longer. We have to celebrate. Before I dose you with something that might not be appropriate, I need to listen to your lungs."

Bart leaned casually against the mantel, watching this caring scene between Jory and Chris as if jealous of their relationship. Chris came to me. "Perhaps it is better if we retire now, so we can be up at dawn to eat breakfast, open our presents, and then have naps before we start getting ready for the ball tomorrow night."

"Oh, glory hallelujah!" cried Cindy, whirling around the room in a small dance. "People, hordes of people, all dressed in their best—I can hardly wait for tomorrow night! Laughter, how I long to hear it. Jokes and small talk, how my ears crave that. I'm so tired of being serious, looking at grim faces that don't know how to smile, hearing sad talk. I hope all those old fuddy-duds bring along their college-aged sons—or any son as long as he's over twelve. I'm that desperate!"

Bart wasn't the only one of us to throw her disapproving looks, which Cindy ignored. "I'm gonna dance all night, I'm gonna dance all night," she sang, whirling around by herself, pretending to have a partner, refusing to let her anticipations be diminished by anything any one of us could say. "And then I'll dance some more . . ."

Despite themselves, Chris and Jory were charmed with her actions, her bright, happy song. Chris smiled before he said, "There should be at least twenty young men here tomorrow night. Just try to contain yourself. Now, since Jory looks so beat, let's head for bed. Tomorrow will be a long day."

It seemed a good idea.

All of a sudden, falling into a chair, Cindy sagged as limp as Melodie had, looking sad and near tears. "I wish Lance could have stayed. I'd rather have him than any other."

Bart threw her a furious look. "That particular young man will never enter this house again." He turned to me next. "We don't need Melodie at the party," he went on with determination and continued anger, "not when she's acting so miserable and sick. Let her sulk in her room tomorrow morning so we can enjoy opening our gifts. I think afternoon naps are a good idea, so tomorrow night we'll look fresh from plenty of rest and bright and happy for my party."

Jory had gone on ahead, entering the elevator by himself, as if to prove his independence. The rest of us seemed reluctant to part. As I sat there hearing the Christmas carols that Bart had put on the stereo to play, I thought of all his newly acquired fastidious habits.

As a boy he'd loved being not just dirty, but filthy. Now he took several showers a day, kept himself immaculately groomed. He couldn't retire until he'd checked over "his house" from top to bottom, seeing that the doors were locked, the windows, too, and that the new kitten Trevor had as his pet hadn't stained a carpet. (Trevor had been fired a dozen times by Bart, but still he stayed on, and Bart didn't insist that he go.)

Even as I watched, Bart got up to fluff the throw pillows, smoothed wrinkles out of downy sofa cushions, picked up magazines and arranged them in neat piles. All the things the servants forgot to do, he did. Then he'd jump on Trevor in the morning and order the maids to do better—or out they'd go without severance pay. No wonder we couldn't keep servants. Only Trevor remained loyal, ignoring the rudeness of Bart, whom he looked at with pity, although Bart didn't know that.

All this was on my mind as I took note of Bart's growing enthusiasm for tomorrow night's party. I glanced toward the windows and saw the snow was still falling, and already two feet of snow were on the ground. "Bart . . . the roads are going to be icy tomorrow night, perhaps closed, and many of your guests might not be able to make it here for the traditional Foxworth ball."

"Nonsense! I'll fly them in if they call to cancel. A helicopter could land on the lawn."

I sighed, for some reason made uneasy by the strangely malicious look of Joel, who chose that time to leave the room.

"Your mother is right, Bart," said Chris kindly, "so don't feel disappointed if only a few are able to show up. I had a devil of a time reaching here a few hours ago, and it's snowing harder now."

It was as if Chris hadn't said a word. Bart bade me good night, then strode toward the stairs. Shortly afterward, Chris, Cindy, and I ascended the stairs.

While Chris went in to say a few words to Jory, I waited for Cindy to come from her bath. Another shower (at least two a day with shampoos) brought her fresh and bright from the bath, wearing the briefest little red nightie. "Momma, don't you lecture me again. I just can't take any more. When I first came to this house, I thought it like a fairy tale palace. Now I think of it as a gloomy fortress to keep us all prisoners. As soon as this ball is over, I'm leaving—and to hell with Bart! I love you and Daddy and Jory, but Melodie has turned into a boring pain in the neck and Bart will never change. He'll always hate me, so I'm going to stop even trying to be nice to him."

She slipped between the sheets, pulled the covers high, turned on her side away from me. "Good night, Momma. Please turn out the light when you leave. Don't ask me to behave myself tomorrow night, for I intend to be the model of ladylike decorum. Wake me three hours before the ball begins."

"In other words, you don't even want to share Christmas morning with us?"

"Oh," she said indifferently, "I guess I can wake up long enough to open my gifts . . . and watch the rest of you open yours. Then back to bed so I can be the belle of the ball tomorrow night."

"I love you, Cindy," I said as I switched off her lamp, and then bent to lift her hair and kiss the warm nape of her neck.

Flipping over, her slim young arms tightened around my neck as she sobbed, "Oh, Momma, you're the best! I promise to be good from now on. I won't let any boy so much as hold my hand. But let me escape this house and fly to New York and attend that New Year's party my best friend is throwing in a grand hotel ballroom."

Silently I nodded. "All right. If you want to enjoy yourself at the home of your friend, that's fine, but please do your best not to rile Bart tomorrow. You know his problem, and he has worked hard to overcome all those disturbing ideas planted in his head when he was very young. Help him, Cindy. Let him realize he has a family backing him up."

"I will, Momma, I promise I will."

I closed the door and was soon saying good night to Jory. He was unusually quiet. "It's going to be all right, darling. Just as soon as the baby is here, Melodie will see you again."

"Will she?" he asked bitterly. "I doubt it. She'll have the baby then to occupy her time and thoughts. She'll need me even less than she does now."

Half an hour later, Chris opened his arms to me, and eagerly I surrendered to the only love in my life that had lasted long enough to let me know I had a firm grip on happiness . . . despite everything that could have ruined what we had cultivated and grown in the shade.

The morning light crept eerily into my room, bringing me out of sleep even before the alarm sounded. Quickly I was up and staring out the windows. The snow had stopped. Thank God for that; Bart would be pleased. I hurried back to the bed to kiss Chris awake. "Merry Christmas, darling Doctor Christopher Sheffield," I whispered in his ear.

"I'd rather you call me just darling," he mumbled as he came awake and looked around in a disoriented way.

Determined that this day was going to be successful, I

tugged him out of bed, and soon we were both dressed and heading for the breakfast room.

For two days men and women had been coming to the house, repeating what had been done in the summer, only this time the entire downstairs had been transformed into a Christmas fantasy.

I watched with a certain indifference as the workers from the caterer Bart had hired finally finished making our home look like a wonderland. Cindy stood at my side watching all they did to turn the rooms into extraordinarily festive rooms, full of color, candles, wreaths, garlands, a towering Christmas tree that outdid our family tree by ten feet.

All she saw soon had Cindy convinced she didn't want to spend the better part of her day in bed. She forgot Lance and loneliness, for Christmas Day worked better magic than Christmas Eve.

"Look at that pie, Momma! It's huge. Four and twenty blackbirds baked in a pie," she sang, all of a sudden glowing with life. "Sorry I've acted ugly. I've been thinking, there'll be boys here tonight, and lots of handsome rich men. Oh, maybe this house can give more than misery after all."

"Of course it can," Bart said as he came in to stand between us, his eyes shining as he surveyed all that had been done. He seemed thrilled by his expectations. "You just be sure and wear a decent dress, and don't do anything outrageous." Then he was following the workmen and giving directions, laughing often, even including Jory, Cindy, Melodie, and me, as if all were forgiven now that it was Christmas.

Day after day, like some dark, gloomy shadow, Joel had trailed behind Bart, his old voice cracking as he intoned words from the Bible. He said again this morning, fully dressed at six-thirty, "It is easier for a camel to go through the eye of a needle than for a rich man to enter the kingdom of God . . ."

"What the hell are you trying to say, old man?" shouted Bart.

Momentarily Joel's watery eyes flared with anger, like a spark ready to ignite from a brisk, unexpected wind.

"You're throwing away thousands of dollars hoping to impress someone—and no one will be impressed, for the others have money, too. Some live in finer homes. Foxworth Hall was the best of its kind in its day, but its day has come and gone."

Bart turned on him with fury. "SHUT UP! You're trying to spoil whatever happiness I reach for. Everything I do is a sin! You're an old man and have done your share; now you try to spoil mine. This is my time to be young and fully enjoy my life. Keep your religious quotes to yourself!"

"Pride goeth before a fall."

"Pride goeth before destruction," corrected Bart, glaring at his great-uncle and giving me delicious satisfaction.

At last, at last, Bart was seeing Joel as a threat and not as the respectable father he'd sought all his life.

"Pride is the never-failing vice of fools," extolled Joel, looking with disgust at all that had been done. "You have wasted money that would be better off given to charities."

"Get out! Go to your room and polish your pride, Uncle! For obviously you have nothing in your heart but jealousy!"

Joel stumbled from the room, muttering to himself, "He'll find out. Nothing is forgotten or forgiven here in the hills. I know. Who would know better than I? Bitter, bitter are the days of the Foxworths despite all their wealth."

I stepped forward to hug Bart. "Don't listen to him, Bart. You'll have a wonderful party. Everyone will come now that the sun is shining and melting the snow. God is on your side this day, so rejoice and have the time of your life."

The look in his eyes when I said that, oh, that grateful look. He stared at me, trying to say something—but the words couldn't form. Finally he could do nothing but briefly embrace me; then he was striding away as if embarrassed. Such a wonderful-looking man, so wasted, I was thinking. There had to be someplace where Bart fitted.

Rooms that had been closed off since winter began were opened, the dustcovers removed and freshened so that no one would know we ever made an effort to conserve heat or money. Bathrooms and powder rooms were given special attention to make them both immaculate and attractive. Expensive soaps and lavish guest towels were put out. Every toiletry item that a guest might need was displayed. Special Christmas china and crystal were taken from the party cabinets, along with seasonal decorations too expensive for the caterer to supply.

We gathered around the Christmas tree about eleven o'clock. Bart was freshly shaven, splendidly well groomed, as was Jory. Only Melodie looked stale in her worn maternity dress that she wore day in and week out. Trying as always to ease tensions, I picked up the Christ child from the realistic manger and held the baby in my arms. "Bart, I haven't seen this before. Did you buy this? If so, I've never seen a more beautifully carved set of Biblical figures."

"It just arrived yesterday, and only today I unpacked it," Bart answered. "I bought it in Italy last winter and had them ship it over."

I gushed on, happy to see him so animated. "This Christ child looks like a real baby, when most don't, and the virgin Mary is absolutely beautiful. Joseph looks so kind and under-standing."

"He'd have to be, wouldn't he?" asked Jory, who was lean-ing forward to put more of his gifts under our family tree. "After all, it must have seemed a bit incredible for him to believe a virgin could be impregnated by an invisible, abstract God."

"You're not supposed to question," answered Bart, his eyes lovingly caressing the almost life-sized figures he'd pur-chased. "You just blindly accept what is written."

"Then why did you argue with Joel?"

"Jory . . . don't push me too far. Joel is helping me find myself. He's an old man who lived in sin when he was young and is redeeming himself in his old age through good deeds. I am a young man who wants to sin, feeling my traumatic child-hood has already redeemed me."

"I suggest a few orgies in some big city will have you run-ning back here, as old and hypocritical acting as your great-uncle Joel," answered Jory fearlessly. "I don't like him. And you'd be wise to drive him out, Bart. Give him a few hundred thousand and say good-bye."

Something yearning struggled in Bart's eyes, as if he'd like to do exactly this. He leaned forward to stare into Jory's eyes. "Why don't you like him?"

"I can't really say, Bart," said Jory, who'd always forgiven easily. "He looks around your home like it should be his. I've caught him glaring at you when you aren't paying attention. I don't believe he's your friend, only your enemy."

Deeply distressed and disturbed-looking, Bart left the room, tossing back his cynical remark. "When have I ever had anything but enemies?"

In a few moments Bart was back, bearing his own heavy stack of gifts. It took him three trips from his office to put all he'd bought under the family tree.

Then it was Chris. Carefully arranging all his presents, and that took some doing. The gifts were stacked up three feet high and spreading to fill most of one corner.

Melodie crept dismally into the cheerful room like a dark shadow and settled down near the fireplace, close enough to feel the warmth, crumpled like a rag in her chair, still ever-lastingly finding more fascination in the dancing flames than in anything else. She appeared sullen, moody, withdrawn, and determined to be there in physical appearance only as her spirit roamed free. Her abdomen was tremendously swol-len, and she still had a few weeks to go. Her eyes were darkly shadowed.

Soon all of us were making an effort to be a loving family as Cindy played Santa Claus. Christmas, as I'd learned a long time ago, had its own gifts to give. Grudges could be forgotten, enemies forgiven as we all united around the tree, even Joel, and one by one shook our packages, made our guesses, then tore into our packages, laughing and drowning out the carols I'd put on the stereo. Soon glittering paper and shining ribbons littered the floor.

Cindy at last handed Joel the gift she had for him. He accepted it tentatively as he'd taken all our gifts, as if we were heathen fools who didn't know the real meaning of a Christmas that didn't need gifts. Then his eyes were bulging at the white nightshirt and the peaked sleeping cap Cindy must have really hunted to find. Definitely he would look like Scrooge wearing those things. Included was an ebony walking stick, which he hurled to the floor along with the nightshirt and cap. "Are you mocking me, girl?"

"I only wanted you to have warm sleeping garments, Uncle," she said demurely, her sparkling eyes downcast, "and the walking stick would hurry your steps."

"Away from you? Is that what you mean?" He stooped painfully to pick up the stick and brandished it wildly in the air. "Maybe I will keep this thing after all; great weapon in case I'm attacked one night when I stroll the gardens . . . and long corridors."

Silent for a moment, not one of us could speak. Then Cindy laughed. "Uncle, I thought of that in advance. I knew one day you'd feel threatened."

He left the room then.

Only too soon all the gifts were unwrapped, and Jory was staring worriedly at the litter on the floor, then scanning all around the room. "I didn't forget you, Bart," he said with concern. "Cindy and Dad helped me wrap it once, but then I undid the wrapping, touched up again, wrapped it myself the last time after Cindy helped me lift it in." He kept looking through the rubble of discarded foil and ribbons. "Early this morning, before the rest of you were up, I came down here and I put it under the tree. Where the hell did it go, I wonder? It's a huge box, wrapped in red foil, tied with silver ribbons—and by far the largest box under the tree."

Bart didn't say a word, as if he'd grown accustomed to disappointments and the lack of Jory's gift was of no importance.

Of course I knew Jory had worked for months and months to finish the clipper ship that had ended up three feet in length and just as tall, with all its fragile riggings exactly right. He'd even sent for special copper fittings and a solid brass wheel for the helm. Desperately Jory looked around. "Has anyone seen the big box wrapped in red foil, with Bart's name on the tag?" he asked.

Immediately I was on my feet and scrambling through the piles of boxes, papers, ribbons, tissues, with Chris soon joining me in the search. Cindy began her own search on the other side of the room. "Oh," she cried out. "Here it is, behind this red sofa." She carried it to Bart and put it on the floor near his feet, bowing in mocking obeisance. "For our lord, our master," she said sweetly, backing away. "I think Jory's a fool to give it to you after all the hard work he put into this thing, but maybe you'll be appreciative, for once."

Suddenly I noticed Joel had slipped back into the room to observe Bart. How strange his expression, how strange.

Bart dropped his sophistication like an unwanted garment and became childishly eager to open this particular gift. Already he was tearing into the package Jory had so beautifully and carefully wrapped. He glanced up at Jory, his smile warm, wide, and happy, his dark eyes lit with boyish anticipation. "Ten to one it's that clipper ship you made, Jory. You really should keep that yourself . . . but thanks, thanks a heap—" He paused, then sucked in his breath.

He stared down into the box, paling before he looked upward, his happiness vanished. Now his eyes were full of bitterness. "It's broken," he said in a dull tone. "Smashed to small pieces. There's nothing in this box but broken matchsticks and tangled rigging."

His voice cracked as he stood up and dropped the box to the floor. Violently he kicked it aside before he threw a hard look at Melodie, who hadn't said a word even when she opened her gifts, only thanked us with nods and weak smiles. "I should have known you would find the perfect way to repay me for sleeping with your wife."

Stunned silence rumbled louder than thunder. Melodie sat on, bleakly staring, seeming an empty shell, even as she mumbled on and on about how much she hated this house. Jory's eyes went starkly blank.

Had he guessed all along? All of Jory's color vanished before finally he could force his eyes to look at Melodie. "I don't believe you, Bart. You've always had a nasty, hateful way of kicking where it hurts most."

"I'm not lying," lashed out Bart, disregarding the pain he was inflicting on Jory, on me and Chris. "While you lay on your hospital bed, inside your cast, your wife and I shared one bed, and eagerly enough she spread her legs for me."

Chris jumped to his feet, his face angrier than I'd ever seen it. "Bart, how dare you say such things to your brother? Apologize to Jory and Melodie, immediately! How can you hurt him like this, when already he's hurt enough? Do you hear me? You tell him every word you just said is a lie! A damned lie!"

"It's not a lie," raged Bart. "If you never believe anything I say again, believe me when I say that Melodie was a very cooperative bed companion."

Cindy squealed, then jumped up to slap Melodie's stricken white face. "How dare you do that to Jory?" she screamed. "You know how much he loves you!"

Then Bart was laughing, hysterically laughing. Chris thundered, "*STOP THAT!* Face up to this situation, Bart—the loss of the clipper ship is not a good excuse for trying to destroy your brother's marriage. Where is your honor, your integrity?"

Almost instantly Bart's laughter faded. His eyes turned

crystal hard and cold as they surveyed Chris from head to toe. "Don't *you* talk to me about honor and integrity. Where was yours when it came to your sister? Where is it now when you continue to sleep with her? Don't you realize yet that your relationship with her has warped me so that I don't care about anything but seeing the two of you separated? I want my mother to finish out her life as a decent, respectable woman . . . and it's you who keeps her from that! *You*, Christopher, *you!*"

His face full of disgust and no remorse, Bart spun on his heel and left the room.

Left us all in the shambles of our Christmas joy.

Eager to do the same, Melodie rose awkwardly, stood trembling with her head bowed, before Cindy yelled, "Did you sleep with Bart? Did you? It isn't fair for you to just say nothing when Jory's heart is breaking."

Melodie's darkly shadowed eyes seemed to sink deeper into her skull even as they grew larger and larger, her pupils dilating as if with fear. "Why can't you leave me alone?" she cried pitifully. "I'm not made of the same iron as the rest of you! I can't take one tragedy after another. Jory lay stricken in the hospital, unable to ever walk or dance again, and Bart was here. I needed someone. He held me, comforted me. I closed my eyes and pretended he was Jory."

Jory fell forward in his chair. I ran to hold him, only to find him gasping so rackingly he couldn't even control his shaking hands. I held him in my arms as Chris tried to stop Melodie from running up the stairs. "Be careful!" he called. "You could fall and lose your baby!"

"I don't care," came back her pitiful wail before she disappeared from sight.

By this time Jory had gained enough control to wipe away his tears and find a weak smile. "Well, now I know," he said in a cracked voice. "I guessed a long time ago that she and Bart had something going on, but I hoped it was only my suspicions working overtime. But I should have known better. Mel can't live without a man beside her, especially in bed . . . and I can hardly blame her, can I?"

Stricken to the bone, I began to pick up the wrappings that had been so carefully applied and so ruthlessly ripped off. Like life, and how carefully we tried to maintain our illusions when things were seldom what they had appeared to be.

Soon Jory excused himself, saying he needed to be alone.

"Who could have smashed that wonderful ship?" I whispered. "Cindy helped Jory wrap that gift the last time he touched up the paint, and I was there watching. The ship was carefully put in a special plastic foam shell to hold it upright. It shouldn't have had one crack, one thing broken."

"How can I ever explain what goes on in this house?" answered Chris in a throaty voice full of pain. He looked up to see Bart standing in the doorway, his long legs spread wide, his fists on his hips as he glared at me. In a louder tone Chris addressed Bart. "What's done is done, and I'm sure it's not Jory's fault the clipper ship was broken. He meant well. All along he told us he was putting that ship together for your office mantel."

"I'm sure Jory did mean well," said Bart evenly, his control regained. "But there is my dear little adopted sister who hates me and no doubt wants to punish me for giving her boyfriend what he deserved. Next time it will be *her* I punish."

"Maybe Jory dropped the box," said Joel in a saintly way. I stared at that old man with his glittering weak eyes and waited my opportunity to say what I had to when no one else was around.

"No," denied Bart. "It had to be Cindy. I have to admit my brother has always given me fair treatment, even when I didn't deserve it."

And all the while he said this, I was staring at Joel with his smirky face, his glittery, satisfied eyes.

Just before retiring, I had my chance. We were in a back second-floor hallway. "Joel, Cindy wouldn't have destroyed all Jory's work and ruined Bart's gift. But you like to drive wedges between members of our family. I believe it was *you* who smashed the ship, then rewrapped it."

He said nothing, only put more hatred in his unrelenting stare.

"Why did you come back, Joel?" I shouted. "You claim you hated your father and were happy in your Italian monastery. Why didn't you stay there? Certainly in all those years you made a few friends. You must have known you wouldn't find any here. My mother told me you always hated this house. Now you walk through it as if you owned it."

Still he said nothing.

I followed him into his room and looked around for the first time. Biblical illustrations on his walls. Quotes from the Bible put in cheap frames.

He moved so that he was behind me. I felt his wheezy warm breath on my neck, smelling old and faintly sick. I sensed when he moved his arms he meant to choke me. Startled, I whirled about to find him inches away.

How silently and quickly he could move. "My father's mother was named Corrine," he said in the sweetest possible voice, enough to make me doubt my reasoning. "My sister had the same name, given to her as a form of punishment, a constant reminder to my father of his unfaithful mother, proving to him again and again that no beautiful woman could be trusted—how right he was."

He was an old man, in his eighties, yet I slapped him, slapped him hard. He staggered backward, then lost his balance and fell to the floor.

"You'll regret that slap, Catherine," he cried with more anger than he'd as yet shown. "Just as much as Corrine regretted all her sins. You, too, will live long enough to regret yours!"

I fled his room, fearing what he said was only too true.

The Traditional Foxworth Ball

On Christmas night our dinner was served around five in order to give the family plenty of time to prepare for the big event that would begin at nine-thirty. Bart wore a glow of happiness. His warm hand reached to cover mine, sending a shock of pleasure through me, for so seldom did he show affection by touching. "If I can't have all my wealth right away, then I should have at least all the prestige due the owner of this house."

I smiled and covered the hand that held mine with my free hand. "Yes, I understand, and we'll do everything possible to see that your party is a huge success."

Joel sat nearby, sending out invisible vibes. He was smiling cynically. "Lord help those fools who deceive themselves," he muttered half under his breath. Bart closed his ears and pretended not to hear, but I was worried. Someone had broken Jory's clipper ship, which had been meant as a reconciliation gift to Bart. It had to be Joel who had heartlessly ruined that ship that Jory had slaved over for months and months. What else would he do?

My eyes met Joel's. I couldn't quite put my finger on how

Joel looked at this moment, except sanctimonious. He daintily picked at his food, cutting his fruitcake into tiny morsels
that he picked up with his long fingers. These he chewed with
intense concentration, using only his front teeth, much as a
rabbit ate a carrot.

"I'm going to bed now," announced Joel. "I don't approve
of tonight's party, Bart, you might as well know that. Remember what happened at your birthday party, and you should
have known better. Again I say it's a waste of good money
entertaining people you don't know well enough. I also disapprove of people who drink, who cavort and act wild on a day
meant for worship. This day belongs to the Lord and his son.
We should all go down on our knees and stay there from dawn
until midnight, like we did in my monastery, as we gave silent
thanks for just being alive."

Since not one of us said a word, Joel went on. "I know
drunken men and women will eventually try to fornicate with
someone other than whom they came with. I remember your
birthday party and what went on. Sinful modern life makes
me realize how pure the world was when I was young. Nothing
is the same as it used to be. People knew how to act decently
in public then, no matter what they did behind closed doors.
Now nobody cares who sees them do what. Women didn't bare
their bosoms when I was a boy, nor pull up their skirts for
every man who wanted them."

He riveted his cold blue eyes on me, and then on Cindy.
"Those who sin, and sin again, always pay dearly, as some here
should already know." Next he was staring at Jory meaningfully.

"The old son of a bitch," murmured Cindy, watching him
slip out of the room with the same stealth as he had entered.

"Cindy, don't you ever let me hear you say anything like
that again!" fired Bart. "Nobody uses obscenities under *my*
roof."

"Well, I'll be damned!" flared Cindy. "Just the other day I

overheard you calling Joel the same thing. And what's more, Bart Foxworth, I'll call a spade a spade—even under your roof!"

"Go to your room and stay there!" bellowed Bart.

"Everybody continue having fun," said Jory, guiding his chair toward the elevator. "As for me, damned if I don't want to turn in my Christian membership."

"You've never been a Christian to begin with," called Bart. "Nobody here goes to church. But there will come a day in the near future when *everyone* here will attend church."

Chris stood up and precisely put down his napkin, fixing Bart and Cindy with commanding eyes. "I've had enough of this childish quibbling. I'm surprised that all of you who think you are adults can revert to children in a wink of the eye."

But Jory was not to be stopped this time. He wheeled his chair about abruptly, rage flaming his usually controlled face, flaring wide his nostrils. "Dad, I'm sorry, but I've got to have my say." He turned toward Bart, who had risen to his feet. "Now, you listen to me, *little* brother." His strong hands released the joystick to clench into fists. "I believe in God . . . but I don't believe in religion. Religion is used to manipulate and punish. Used in a thousand ways for profit, for even in the church, money is still the *real* God."

"Bart," I implored, so afraid he'd harm Jory again, "it's time we all headed upstairs."

Bart had paled. "No wonder you sit there in that chair if you believe what you just said. You are being punished by God, just as Joel says."

"Joel," sneered Jory. "Who the hell cares what an old fool like Joel says? I'm punished because some stupid idiot wet the sand! God didn't pour down rain to do that. A garden hose took God's place, and that's why I'm in this chair and not where I belong. As soon as possible, I'm leaving here, Bart! I'm forgetting you're my brother, whom I've always tried to love and help. I'm not going to try again."

"Hooray for you, Jory!" cried Cindy, jumping to her feet and applauding.

"STOP!" I yelled, seizing Cindy by the arm while Chris grabbed her other arm and we dragged her away from Bart. Still she twisted and fought to free herself. "You damned freaky hypocrite!" she yelled back at Bart. "I heard at your birthday party that you do your share of using the local brothel . . ."

Thank God the elevator door closed behind us and we were on our way up before Bart could reach Cindy.

"Learn to keep your mouth shut," said Jory. "You only make him worse, Cindy—and I regret what I just said. Did you see his face? I don't think he's pretending about religion. He's deadly serious. He seems to truly believe. If Joel is a hypocrite, Bart is not."

Chris fixed his strong regard on both before he stepped out of the elevator. "Jory, Cindy, you listen to me carefully. I want you both to do your best tonight to see that Bart's party is successful. Forget your enmity, at least for one night. He was a troubled little boy, and he has grown into a more troubled man. He needs help, and badly. Not from more sessions with psychiatrists, but help from those who love him most—and despite everything, I know you both love him. Just as his mother and I love him and care what happens to him. As for Melodie, I visited her before dinner, and she's not feeling well enough to attend the party. She wouldn't let me examine her, though I tried to insist, and she says she feels too big, too clumsy and won't be coming out where guests can stare at her enormous size. I think that might be the best solution for her. But if you would, look in on her and say a few kind words of encouragement, for that poor girl is coming apart from worry . . ."

Jory steered his chair down the hall, turning directly into his room, ignoring Melodie's closed door. I sighed, as did Chris.

Dutifully Cindy tried to say a few consoling words to Melodie outside of her locked door before she came prancing back to join Chris and I. "I'm not going to let Melodie spoil my fun. I think she's acting like a damned selfish fool. As for me, I intend to have the time of my life tonight," said Cindy in parting. "I don't give a damn about Bart and his party except what pleasure it gives me."

"I'm concerned about Cindy," said Chris when we were lying on our wide bed, trying to catch a short nap. "I have the feeling Cindy is not stingy with her favors."

"Chris, don't you dare say that! Just because we caught her with that boy Lance doesn't mean she is loose. She's looking, looking all the time at each young man she meets, hoping he's the one. If one says he loves her, she believes because she needs to believe. Don't you realize Bart has stolen her confidence? She's afraid she is exactly what Bart thinks she is. She's torn between being as wicked as he thinks and being as nice as we want her to be. Cindy's a beautiful young woman . . . and Bart treats her like filth."

It had been a long day for Chris. He closed his eyes and turned on his side to embrace me. "Eventually Bart will straighten out," he murmured. "For the first time I'm seeing in his eyes the need to find a compromise. He has the desperate desire to find someone or something to believe in. Someday he will find what he needs, and when he does, he'll be set free to be the fine man he is under that hateful exterior."

Sleep and dream of impossible things, like harmony in the family, like brothers and a sister who found love for each other. Dream on, dreamer . . .

I heard the grandfather clock down the hall chiming the hour of seven when we were supposed to rise from our naps to bathe and dress. I shook Chris awake and told him to hurry and dress. He stretched, yawned, lazily got up to shower while I took a quick tub bath; then he was shaving before donning his custom-tailored tux. Chris stared at himself in a pier glass. "Cathy, am I gaining weight?" he asked with concern.

"No, darling. You look terrif—as Cindy would say."

"What do *you* say?"

"You grow more handsome with each passing year." I stepped closer to encircle his waist with my arms as my cheek rested against his back. "I love you more each year . . . and even when you are as old as Joel, I will see you as you are now . . . standing twelve feet tall, in your shining suit of armor, soon to ride your white unicorn. In your hand you'll carry a twelve-foot spear with a green dragon's head perched upon its point."

In the mirror I saw his reflection; tears had come to glisten in his eyes. "After all this time, you remember," he whispered hoarsely. "After all these many years . . ."

"As if I could forget . . ."

"But it's been so long ago."

"And today the moon shone at noon," I murmured, moving to face him and slide my arms up around his neck, "and a blizzard blew in your unicorn . . . and I saw to my own delight that you've always had my respect. You didn't need to earn it."

Those two tears trickled slowly down his cheeks. I kissed them away. "So you forgive me, Catherine? Say now, while we have the chance, that you forgive me for putting you through so much hell. For Bart would have turned out differently if I had stayed only his uncle and found another wife."

I was careful not to smudge his jacket with my makeup as I rested my cheek over his heart, which I heard thumpity-thump-thumping. Just as I'd heard it the first time our love changed and became more than it should have been. "If I blink my eyes just once, I'm twelve years old again, and you're fourteen. I can see you as you were then . . . but I can't see me. Chris, why can't I see me?"

His crooked smile was bittersweet. "Because I've stolen all the memories of what you were and stored them in my heart. But you haven't said you forgive me."

"Would I be here, where I am, if I didn't want to be?"

"I hope and pray not," and I was held, held so tightly in his arms my ribs ached.

Outside the snow began to fall again. Inside my Christopher Doll had turned back the clock, and if there was no magic for Melodie in this house, and Lance's departure had stolen romance from Cindy, there was more than enough magic for me when Chris was there to cast his spell.

At nine-thirty we sat, all ready to stand when Trevor hurried to open the door. He stood anxiously looking at his watch, glancing at us with great pride. Bart, Chris, Jory, and myself in our elegant expensive formal clothes faced the front windows with their splendid draperies. The towering Christmas tree in the foyer sparkled with a thousand tiny white lights. It had taken five people hours to decorate that tree.

As I sat there like some middle-aged Cinderella who had already found her prince and married him and was caught in the spell of the happy-ever-after, which wasn't all that perfect, something pulled my eyes upward. In the shadows of the rotunda where two knights in full armor stood on pedestals opposite each other, I saw a dark shadow move. Even in the shade of that smaller closer knight, I thought I knew who it was. Joel, who was supposed to be in bed asleep, or on his knees praying for all our sinning un-Christian souls.

"Bart," I whispered to my second son, who moved to stand beside my chair, "wasn't this supposed to be the special party to reintroduce Joel to all his old friends?"

"Yes," he whispered back, putting his arm over my shoulders. "But that was just my excuse. I knew he wouldn't want to come. The truth of the matter is, few of his old friends are still alive, although many of my grandmother's school chums are still around." His strong fingers bit down into my shoulder's tender flesh. "You look lovely—like an angel."

Was that a compliment, or a suggestion?

He smiled at me cynically, then snatched his arm away as if it had betrayed him.

I laughed nervously. "Oh, someday when I'm as old as Joel I suppose I'll take on a dowager's hump and shuffle my feet along, and when my sinning is over, I'll put on the halo I lost way back when I was in puberty . . ."

Both Bart and Chris scowled to hear me talk that way, but I felt good when I saw the shadow of Joel slink away.

Liveried servants readied the buffet tables as Bart got up to pace the floor, looking exceptionally handsome in his black tux with the pleated formal shirt.

I reached for Jory's hand, squeezed it. "You're looking just as handsome as Bart," I whispered.

"Mom, have you given him a compliment? He looks great, really great, the very man his father must have been."

Blushing, I felt ashamed. "No, I haven't said a word because he seems so devilishly pleased with himself that I think he'd burst with any praise he might hear from me."

"Mom, you're wrong. Go on, say to him what you say to me. You may think I need it more, but I think he does."

Standing, I strode over to where Bart was peering out onto the drive, which curved gradually downward. "Can't see a single headlight," he gruffly complained. "It's not snowing now. The roads have been cleared. Ours is sprinkled over with gravel; where the hell are they?"

"I've never seen you look more handsome than you do tonight, Bart."

He turned to stare into my eyes, then he glanced at Jory. "More handsome than Jory?"

"Equally as handsome."

Scowling, he turned back to the window. Out there he saw something to take his mind off of himself.

"Hey—look, here they come!"

I watched the string of headlights in the distance, heading up the hill. "Get ready, everybody," called Bart, giving Trevor an excited gesture to be ready to swing wide the doors.

Chris strolled beside Jory's chair, which he guided

expertly, as I caught hold of Bart's arm and went to form a receiving line. Trevor hurried up to give us all a bright smile.

"I just love parties, I always have, I always will. Makes the heart beat faster. Makes old bones feel young again. I can tell it's going to be a jolly smashing one tonight."

Two or three times Trevor said that—with less conviction each time, as still not one pair of those headlights climbed high enough to reach our drive. No one rang our bell, banged our door knocker.

The musicians were in position under the rotunda, on a dais that had been constructed especially for them, centered directly between the curving dual stairways. They tuned their instruments over and over again as my feet in their high-heeled fancy slippers began to ache. I sat again on an elegant chair and wiggled my shoes off under the folds of my gown, which was growing heavier and more uncomfortable by the minute. Eventually Chris sat beside me, and Bart took the righthand chair, all of us very silent, almost holding our breaths. Jory had his own special chair that could buzz him around tirelessly. From window to window he drove, looking out and reporting.

I knew that Cindy was upstairs, all dressed and ready, waiting to be "fashionably" late and impress everyone when finally she drifted down the stairs. She had to be growing very impatient.

"They must be coming soon—" Jory said when the hour reached ten-thirty. "There's lots of banked snow on the side roads to confuse them . . ."

Bart's lips were tight and grim, his eyes stony cold.

No one said anything. I was afraid to even speculate on why no one had arrived. Trevor looked very anxious when he thought we weren't noticing.

To give myself something pleasant to think about, I fixed my eyes on the buffet tables, which reminded me so much of that first ball I'd seen in the original Foxworth Hall.

Very much like what I was staring at.

Red linen tablecloths, silver dishes and bowls. A fountain spraying champagne. Huge, gleaming, chafing dishes emitting delicious odors. Heaps and heaps of food on fancy tiered plates of crystal, porcelain, gold, and silver. At last I could resist no longer and got up to taste of this and that while Bart frowned and complained I was ruining the beautiful designs. I wrinkled my nose his way and handed Chris a plate full of everything I knew he'd like best. Soon Jory was helping himself.

Red beeswax bayberry candles burned lower and lower. Towering gelatin masterpieces began to sag. Melted cheeses began to toughen, and the heating sauces thickened. Crepe batter waited to be poured on turned over thin pans, while chefs eyed each other curiously. I had to look away from all that was going bad.

Fires cheered all our main rooms, making them cozy, exceptionally lovely. Extra servants grew restless and anxious-looking as they fidgeted and began to mill about, whispering amongst themselves, not knowing what to do.

Down the stairs drifted Cindy in a crimson hooped-skirted gown, so elaborate it put my delicately beaded gown to shame. Hers had a tight bodice, with a flounce of fluted ruffles to cover a little of her upper arms, displaying her shoulders to advantage and creating a magnificent frame for her creamy, swelling breasts. The red gown was cut very low. The skirt was a masterpiece of ruffles, caught with white silk flowers rain-dropped with iridescent crystals, A few of these white silk blossoms were tucked in her upswept hair, duplicating something Scarlett O'Hara might have liked.

"Where's everybody?" she asked, looking around, her radiant expression fading. "I waited and waited to hear the music playing, then sort of dozed off, thinking when I woke that I was missing out on all the fun."

She paused and glanced around before a look of dismay flooded her expression. "Don't tell me nobody's going to come!

I just can't stand another disappointment!" Dramatically she threw her hands about.

"No one has as yet arrived, Miss," said Trevor tactfully. "They must have lost their way, and I must say you look a dream of loveliness, as does your mother."

"Thank you," she said, floating his way and brushing his cheek with a daughterly kiss. "You look very distinguished yourself." She dashed past Bart's look of astonishment and ran to the piano. "Please, may I?" she asked a young, good-looking musician who seemed delighted to have something happening, at last.

Cindy sat down beside him, put her hands on the keys, threw back her head, and began to sing: "Oh, holy night, Oh, night when stars are shining."

I stared, as did all of us, at the girl we thought we knew so well. It wasn't an easy song to sing, but she did it so well, with so much emotion even Bart stopped pacing the floor to turn and stare at her in amazement.

Tears were in my eyes. Oh, Cindy, how could you keep that voice a secret for so long? Her piano playing was only adequate, but that voice, the feeling she put into her phrasing. All the musicians then joined in to drown out her piano playing, if not her voice.

I sat, stunned, hardly believing that my Cindy could sing so beautifully. When she'd finished, we all applauded enthusiastically. As Jory called out, "Sensational! Fantastic! Absolutely wonderful, Cindy! You sneak—you never told us you continued with your voice lessons."

"I haven't. It's just me expressing the way I feel."

She cast her eyes down, then took a sly, hooded look at Bart's astonished expression, which showed not only his surprise but some pleasure as well. For the first time he had found something to admire about Cindy. Her small smile of satisfaction fleeted quickly by, kind of a sad smile, as if she wished Bart could like her for other reasons as well.

"I love Christmas carols and religious songs, they do something for me. Once in school I sang 'Swing Low, Sweet Chariot,' and the teacher said I had the kind of emotional feeling to make a great singer. But I still want most to be an actress."

Laughing and happy again, she asked us to join in and we'd make this a real party, even if no one showed up. She began to bang out a tune resembling "Joy to the World." Then "Jingle Bells."

This time Bart was not moved.

He strode again to the windows to stare out, his back straight. "They can't ignore my invitations, not when they responded," he mumbled to himself.

I couldn't understand how his business friends could dare to offend him when he had to be their most important client, and everyone loved a party, especially the kind of party they had to know would be sensational.

Somehow or other, Bart was accomplishing miracles with that five hundred thousand a year, making it grow in ways that Chris would have found too risky. Bart risked everything . . . calculated gambles that paid off handsomely. Only then did I realize that perhaps my mother had meant it to be this way. If she had given Bart all the fortune in one grand huge sum, he wouldn't have worked as hard to build his own fortune, which would, if he kept it up, far exceed what Malcolm had left him. And in this way Bart would find his own worth.

Yet what did money matter when he was so disappointed he couldn't eat a thing that was lavishly displayed? However, disillusionment drove him to the liquor, and in a short while he'd managed to swallow half a dozen strong drinks as he paced the floors, growing angrier by the second.

I could hardly bear to watch his disappointment, and soon, despite myself, tears were silently wetting my face.

Chris whispered, "We can't go to bed and leave him here alone. Cathy, he's suffering. Look at him pacing back and forth. With every step he takes his anger grows. Somebody is going to pay for this slight."

Eleven-thirty came and went.

By this time Cindy was the only one having a good time. The musicians and servants seemed to adore her. Eagerly they played and she sang. When she wasn't singing, she was dancing with every man there, even Trevor and other male servants. She gestured to the maids, inviting them to dance, and happily they joined in the festivity she created around her as they took turns to see that she, at least, was entertained.

"Let's all eat, drink, and be merry!" Cindy cried, smiling at Bart. "It's not the end of the world, brother Bart. What do you care? We're too rich to be well liked. We're also too rich to feel sorry for ourselves. And look, we have at least twenty guests . . . let's dance, drink, eat, have a ball!"

Bart stopped pacing to stare at her. Cindy held high her glass of champagne. "My toast to you, brother Bart. For every ugly thing you've said to me, I give you back blessings of good will, good health, long life, and much love." She touched his highball glass with her champagne glass and then sipped, smiling into his eyes charmingly before she offered another toast. "I think you look absolutely terrif, and the girls who don't show up tonight are missing the chance of their lifetimes. So here it is, another toast to the most eligible bachelor in the world. I wish you joy, I wish you happiness, I wish you love. I would wish you success, but you don't need that."

He couldn't move his eyes away. "Why don't I need success?" he asked in a low tone.

"Because what more could you want? You have success when you have millions, and soon enough you'll have more money than you know what to do with."

Bart's dark head bowed. "I don't feel successful. Not when no one will even come to my party." His voice cracked as he turned his back.

I got up to go to him. "Will you dance with me, Bart?"

"No!" he snapped, hurrying to a distant window where he could stand and stare again.

Cindy had a wonderful time with the musicians and the men and women who'd come to serve Bart's guests. However, I was deeply downcast, feeling sorry for Bart, who had counted so much on this. Out of sympathy for him, all of us but Cindy and the hired help moved into the front parlor, and there we sat in our fabulous expensive clothes and waited for guests who obviously had accepted, only to trick Bart later on—and in this way tell us what they thought of the Foxworths on the hill.

The grandfather clock began to toll the hour of twelve. Bart left the windows and fell upon the sofa before the guttering log fire. "I should have known it would turn out this way." He glanced bitterly at Jory. "Perhaps they came to my birthday party only to see you dance, and now, when you can't—to hell with me! They've snubbed me—and they're going to pay for it," he said in a hard, cold voice, louder and stronger than Joel's but with the same kind of zealot's fury. "Before I'm through, there won't be a house in a twenty-mile radius that doesn't belong to me. I'll ruin them. All of them. With the power of the Foxworth trust behind me I can borrow millions, and then I'll buy out the banks and demand they pay off their mortgages. I'll buy out the village stores, close them down. I'll hire other attorneys, fire the ones I have now and see that they're disbarred. I'll find new stockbrokers, hire new real estate agents, see that real estate property values are undermined, and when they sell cheap, I'll buy. By the time I'm through, there won't be one old aristocratic Virginia family left this side of Charlottesville! And not one of my business colleagues will be left with anything but debts to pay off!"

"Then will you feel satisfied?" asked Chris.

"NO!" flared Bart, his eyes hard, glaring. "I won't be satisfied until justice has ruled! I have done nothing to deserve this night! Nothing but try to give them what our ancestors did—

and they have rejected me! They'll pay, and pay, and then pay some more."

He sounded like me! To hear my very own words coming from the mouth of the child I'd carried when I'd said them made all my blood drain into my feet. Shivering, I tried to appear normal. "I'm sorry, Bart. But it wasn't a total loss, was it? We're all together under one roof, a united family for once. And Cindy's music and singing made this a festive occasion after all."

He wasn't listening.

He was staring at all the food that had yet to be eaten. All the champagne with the bubbles gone flat. All the wine and liquor that could have loosened many a tongue and given him information he wanted to use. He glared at the maids in their pretty black and white uniforms, drunken and stagger-ing around, some still dancing as the music played on and on. He glowered at the few waiters who still held trays of drinks gone warm. Some stood and looked at him and waited for his signal to say the night was over. The impressive centerpiece of an ice crystal manger, with the three shepherds, the wise men and all the animals, had melted into a puddle and spilled over to darken the red cloth.

"How lucky you were when you danced in *The Nutcracker*, Jory," said Bart as he headed fast for the stairs. "You were the ugly nutcracker that turned into the handsome prince. You dominated every male role—and won the prettiest ballerina every time. In *Cinderella*, in *Romeo and Juliet*. In *The Sleeping Beauty*, *Giselle*, *Swan Lake*—every time but the last time. And it's the last time that counts, isn't it?"

How cruel! How very cruel! I watched Jory wince, and for once he allowed his pain to show, making my heart ache for him.

"Merry Christmas," Bart called as he disappeared up the stairs. "We'll never again celebrate this holiday, or any other in this house as long as I run it. Joel was right. He warned me not to try and conform and be like others. He said I shouldn't try to make people like or respect me. From now on, I'll be like Malcolm. I'll gain respect by inflicting my will on others, with fists of iron, and with ruthless determination. All who have alienated me tonight will feel my might."

I turned to Chris when he was out of sight. "He sounds crazy!"

"No, darling, he's not crazy—he's just Bart, young and vulnerable again and very, very hurt. He used to break his bones when he was a child to punish himself because he failed socially and in school. Now he's going to break the lives of others. Isn't it a pity, Cathy, that nothing works out for him?"

I stood at the newel post looking upward to where an old man hid in the shadows, seeming to shake from his silent laughter.

"Chris, you go on up, and I'll follow in a few seconds." Chris wanted to know what I was planning, so I lied and said I was going to have a few words with our housekeeper about cleaning up the mess. But I had something far different in mind.

As soon as everyone was out of sight, I ducked into Bart's huge office, closed the door and was soon rifling through his desk to find the R.S.V.P. cards that had dutifully arrived weeks ago.

They must have been fingered many a time from the ink smudges on the envelopes. Two hundred and fifty cards had accepted. My teeth bit down on my lower lip. Not one rejection, not even one. People didn't do things like this, even to someone they disliked. If they hadn't wanted to come, they would have tossed the invitations into the trash along with the return card, or sent back the card declining.

Carefully I replaced the cards and then headed up the back stairs to Joel's room.

Without even a preliminary knock I opened his door to find him sitting on the edge of his narrow bed, doubled over in what appeared to be a terrible stomach cramp, or that hateful

silent laughter. He was in quiet convulsion, quivering, jerking, hugging himself with skinny arms.

Quietly I waited until his hysteria was over, and only then
did he see the long shadow I cast. Gasping, his mouth sunken
because his teeth were in a cup by the bed, he stared up at
me. "Why are you here, niece?" he asked in that whiny but
raspy voice, his thin hair rumpled into devil horns that stood
straight up.

"Downstairs, a while ago, I looked up and saw you in the
rotunda shadows, laughing. Why were you laughing, Joel?
You must have seen that Bart was suffering."

"I don't know," he mumbled, half turning to replace the
teeth in his mouth. When he had them in, he ran a hand over
his spikey hair, smoothing it down. Only his cowlick refused
to behave. Now he could meet my eyes. "Your daughter made
so much racket down there I couldn't sleep. I guess the sight
of all of you in your fancy clothes waiting for guests that didn't
come tickled my sense of humor."

"You have a very cruel sense of humor, Joel. I thought you
cared for Bart."

"I do love that boy."

"Do you?" I asked sharply. "I don't think so, or else you
would have sympathized." I glanced around his sparsely fur-
nished room, thinking back. "Weren't you the one who mailed
off the party invitations?"

"I don't remember," he said calmly. "Time doesn't mean
much to an old man like me when it's growing so short. What
happened years ago seems clearer than what happened a
month ago."

"My memory is much better than yours, Joel."

I sat down in the one chair he had in his room. "Bart had
an important appointment, and, as I recall, he turned over
that stack of invitations to you. Did you mail them, Joel?"

"Of course I mailed them!" he snapped angrily.

"But you just said you couldn't remember."

"I remember *that* day. It took so long, dropping them in the slot one by one."

All the time I'd closely watched his eyes. "You're lying, Joel," I said, taking a wild shot in the dark. "You didn't mail those invitations. You brought them up here, and in the privacy of this room, you opened each one, filled in the blank places for "Yes, we will be happy to attend," and then mailed those in the provided envelope back to Bart. You see, I found them in Bart's office. I never saw such a strange assortment of crooked handwriting, all in various shades of blue, violet, green, black, and brown ink. Joel, you changed pens to make it seem those cards were signed by different guests, when it was you who signed them all!"

Slowly Joel stood. He gathered about him the handwoven invisible brown habit of a saintly monk, thrusting his gnarled hands up those imaginary sleeves. "I think you have lost your mind, woman," he said coldly. "If you wish, go to your son and tell him your barbaric suspicions, and see if he believes you."

Jumping up, I headed for the door. "I intend to do just that!" I slammed the door hard behind me and hurried off.

In his study Bart was seated behind his desk, now wearing pajamas covered by a black woolen robe piped in red. Drunkenly he was tossing the R.S.V.P. cards one by one into the roaring fire. I saw to my dismay the last of the pile go up in flames as I watched Bart pour another drink.

"What do you want?" he asked in a slurred way, narrowing his eyes and seeming surprised to see me.

"Bart, I've got to say this, and you have to listen. I don't think Joel mailed your invitations, and that is why your guests didn't show up."

He tried to focus his eyes and his intellect, which must have reeled under the influences of all he'd drunk. "Of course he did. Joel always does as I order." He leaned back in his swivel chair with its back that lowered automatically from the pressure he applied and closed his eyes. "Tired now. Go away.

Don't stand and stare at me with eyes of pity. And they did accept . . . didn't I just burn their replies?"

"Bart, listen to me. Don't fall asleep before I finish. Didn't you notice now strangely they were signed? All the different colored ink? The crooked, awkward handwriting? Joel did not mail your invitations, but instead took them to his room, opened them, extracted the R.S.V.P. cards and envelopes, and since you had put stamps on all of them, all he had to do was drive to the post office and mail them back to you a few each day."

His closed eyes slotted. "Mother, I think you should go to bed. My great-uncle is the best friend I've ever had. He'd never do anything to hurt me."

"Bart, please. Don't put too much faith in Joel."

"GET OUT!" he roared. "It's your fault they didn't come! Yours and that man you sleep with!"

I stumbled as I turned away, feeling defeated and so afraid this could very well be true—and Joel was just what Bart and Chris believed him to be, a harmless old man who wanted to live out his days in this house, near the one person who respected and loved him.

Unto Us Is Born . . .

Christmas Day was over. I was in bed curled up beside Chris, who could always fall easily into deep sleep, leaving me to fret and stew and flip and turn. Behind me the great one-eyed swan kept its ruby eye alert, causing me to look around often at what it could be seeing. I heard the deep, mellow tones of the grandfather clock at the end of our hall strike three o'clock. A few minutes ago I'd gotten up to watch Bart's red car speed down the drive, heading toward the local tavern where no doubt he'd drown his sorrows in additional liquor and end up in some whore's bed. More than once he'd come home reeking of liquor and cheap perfume.

Hour after hour passed as I waited for Bart to come home. I pictured all sorts of calamities. On a night like this the drunks were out, deadlier than arsenic.

Why lie here doing nothing? I slipped out of the bed, arranged the covers neatly over Chris's sleeping bulk, kissed his cheek, then arranged his heavy arms around a pillow that I presumed he'd think was me, and he did from the way he snuggled it close. It was my intention to wait for Bart in his room.

It was almost five on a cold, blustery, winter morning before I heard his car approaching. I was huddled in a deep pile robe of red-rose, curled up on one of his white sofas with his black and red pillows behind my back.

I dozed, then heard him climbing the stairs, heard him moving drunkenly from room to room, bumping into furniture as he had when he was a child. He was dedicated to checking each room to see if it had been neatly tidied before the servants retired. And to my dismay, from the length of time it was taking him to appear in his own rooms, he was doing that now. No newspapers could be left in sight. No magazines not neatly stacked in their respective piles. No articles of clothing left on the floor, or coats on doorknobs or draped on chair backs.

Minutes later Bart was in his room, flicking the switch to light the lamps. He swayed to and fro before he stared at me sitting in the dimness of his room, where I'd started a fire that crackled cheerfully in the darkness. Shadows danced on the white walls, turning them orange and rosy, the black leather of another wall catching red highlights, creating a kind of fake inferno.

"Mother, what the hell is going on? Didn't I tell you to stay out of my wing?" Yet, in his drunken state, he looked glad to see me.

He wove his way uncertainly to a chair, took careful aim and fell down, closing his darkly shadowed eyes. I got up to massage the back of his neck while he drooped his head forward and held it as if it pained him dreadfully. His hands cupped his face as my hands took away the pain. Then he sighed, leaned back, and stared fuzzily up into my eyes. "I should know better than to drink," he murmured in a slurred way, sighing as I stepped back and sat before him. "It always makes me do crazy things, and then I feel sick. Stupid to keep it up when liquor has never done anything for me but add to my problems. Mother, what's wrong with me? I can't even drink myself into a forgetful stupor. I'm always too sensitive. I overheard Jory tell you one day he was building that wonderful clipper ship to give to me, and I was secretly thrilled. No one has ever spent months and months making me a gift—and then it's broken. He did such a great job, taking so many pains to see that everything was exactly right. Now all that work is in the trash pile."

He sounded childlike, vulnerable, easy to reach and I was going to try, try to give him every ounce of love I had. Not mean when he was drunk, not silly but loveable, touching in his humanity. "Darling, Jory will gladly make you another," I volunteered, not sure he would be glad to do all that tedious work a second time.

"No, Mother, I don't want it now. Something would happen to that one, too. That's the way my life goes. Life has a cruel way of taking from me what I want most. There's no happiness or love waiting for me around the bend of tomorrow. No gaining what I want—my heart's desire, as I used to call the impossible dreams of my youth. Wasn't that childish and silly? No wonder you pitied me—I wanted so much. Too much. I was never satisfied. You and that man you love gave me everything I ever said I wanted, and many things I didn't even mention, and still you never gave me happiness. So I've decided not to care about anything anymore. The Christmas ball wouldn't have given me pleasure even if the guests had showed up. I still would have failed to impress them. Inside, all along, I knew my party would prove just another failure, like all the other parties you used to give me. Still I went ahead and hypnotized myself into believing that if tonight was successful it would set a precedent, so to speak, and all my life would then change for the better."

My second son was talking to me as he'd never done before. Liquor was loosening his tongue.

"Stupid, aren't I?" he went on. "Cindy's right when she calls me a jerk and a creep. I look in my mirrors and see a handsome man, very much like my father, whom you say you loved more than any other man. But I don't feel I am handsome inside. I'm uglier than sin inside. Then I wake up, feel the fresh morning mountain air, see the dew sparkling on the roses, see the winter sun shining on the snow, and that tells me maybe life is going to offer me my chance after all. I have hopes of one day finding the real me—the one I can like, and that's why, months ago, I decided to make this the happiest Christmas of all our lives, not only for Jory, who deserves it, but for you and for myself. You think I don't love Jory, but I do."

He bowed his head into his waiting hands and sighed heavily. "Confession time, Mother. I hate Jory too, I don't deny that. But I hold no love at all for Cindy. She's done nothing but steal from me—and she isn't even one of us. Jory's always had the largest portion of your love, the part you've got left over after giving your brother the best. I've never had the major portion of anyone's love. I thought that Melodie had given me that. Now I know she'd have taken any man just to replace Jory. Any man at all who was available and willing, and that's why I hate her now, just as much as I hate Cindy."

His hands came down to show how bitterly his dark eyes glowed; the reflection from the fire made them like red-hot coals. Those drinks had made his breath reek. My heart almost stopped beating. What would he want? I stood up, moved behind his chair and slid my arms around his neck before my head lowered to rest on top of his disheveled hair. "Bart, you drove away tonight and left me sleepless and waiting for you to come home. Tell me what can I do to help. Nobody here hates you like you think. Not even Cindy. Often you make us angry because you disappoint us, not because we want to reject you."

"Send Chris away," he said tonelessly as if he said this without hope of ever seeing Chris gone from my life. "That will tell me you love me. Only when you break with him can I feel good about myself, and you."

Pain stabbed me. "He'd die without me, Bart," I whispered. "I know you can't understand the way it is between us, and I myself can't explain why he needs me, and why I need him, except we were young and alone and in a terrifying situation, and we had only each other. We created a fantasy dreamlike world when we were locked away and trapped ourselves in so doing, and now that we're both middle-aged we still live in that fantasy. We can't survive without it. To lose him now would destroy not only him, but me as well."

"But Mother!" he cried out passionately, turning to hold me, to press his face between my breasts, "you'd still have me!" He gazed up into my face, his arms around my waist. "I want you to purify your soul before it's too late. What you do with Chris is against the rules of God and society. Let him go, Mother. *Please let him go*—before someone does something terrible, let go of your brother's love."

I drew away, brushed back a fallen wisp of my hair. Feeling defeated and hopeless, for it was so impossible, what he asked. "Would you hurt me, Bart?"

He bit down on his lip, a childish habit that came back when he was disturbed. "I don't know. Sometimes I want to. More than I want to hurt him. You smile at me with such sweetness, and my heart reaches out, wanting you never to change. Then I go to bed and hear whispers in my head that tell me you are evil and deserve to die. When I think of you dead and in the ground, tears fill my eyes and my heart feels empty and broken, heavier than lead—and I'm undone. I feel so cold, so alone and scared. Mother, am I crazy? Why is it I can't fall in love with confidence that it will last? Why can't I forget about what you do?

"I thought for a while that Melodie and I had it made. She seemed to me so perfect, and then she began to turn fat and ugly. She whined and nagged, and complained about my home. Even Cindy was more appreciative. I took her to the best restaurants, to plays and movies, and tried to take her mind off Jory, but she wouldn't let it go. She kept talking of the ballet and how much it means to her, and that's when I found out I was only a substitute for Jory and she never loved me, never loved me at all. She used me as a way to forget her loss for a while. Now she doesn't even look like the girl I fell in love with. She wants pity and sympathy, not love. She took my love and turned it around, so now I can't stand to look at her."

Sighing, he lowered his eyes and said in such a low voice I could hardly hear him, "I see that kid, Cindy, and realize she must look the way you used to, and a little bit of me knows why Chris fell in love with you. That makes me hate her worse. She teases me, you know. Cindy would like to creep under my skin and make me do something as wicked as what Chris does with you. She strolls around in her bedroom wearing nothing but bikini bra and bottoms. And she knows I check her rooms before I retire. Tonight she had on a nightgown so transparent I could see right through it. She just stood there and let me stare. Joel tells me she's nothing but a whore."

"Then don't go to her bedroom," I said with control. "Lord knows we don't have to see anyone who lives here if we don't want to—and Joel is a bigoted, narrow-minded fool. All Cindy's generation wears next-to-nothing undergarments. But you're right, she shouldn't parade around in them. I'll speak to her about that in the morning. You're sure she displayed herself deliberately?"

"You must have done the same thing," he said, dully accusing. "All those years locked up with Chris—did you show him your body—deliberately?"

How could I tell him how it had been and make him understand? He'd never understand. "We all tried to be decent, Bart. It's so long ago and I don't like to remember. I try to forget. I want to think that Chris is my husband and not my brother. We can't have children, never could. Doesn't that make it better—a little better?"

Shaking his head, his eyes darkened. "Go away. You just

give me excuses, and you bring it all back, the sickness I used to feel when I found out about you and him. I was just a kid wanting to feel clean and wholesome. I still want to feel that way. That's why I keep showering, shaving, picking up, ordering the servants to scrub, vacuum, dust and dust, and do it every day. I'm trying to eliminate the dirt you and Chris put in my life—and *I can't do it!*"

There was no comfort in Chris's arms as I tried to sleep. I drifted into an uneasy dream. Then I bolted awake to hear distant screams. Leaving my bed for the second time in the same night, I raced toward the screams.

Disoriented, I stared down at Melodie on the floor of the long corridor. She seemed to be wearing a white nightgown with ragged red stripes. She crawled along, moaning, causing me to think I was still dreaming. Her long hair was in damp disarray, her brow dripped sweat—and behind her was a trail of blood!

Blindly she stared up at me, imploring. "Cathy, my baby is coming . . ." She screamed, then slowly, slowly, her pleading eyes went blank before she keeled over in a dead faint.

I ran for Chris, shaking him awake. "It's Melodie!" I cried as he sat up and rubbed at his tired eyes. "She's in labor. Right now she's fainted, lying facedown in the hall with a trail of blood behind her . . ."

"Take it easy," he soothed, leaping out of bed and pulling on his bathrobe. "First babies are notoriously slow in arriving." Nevertheless there was a look of anxiety in his eyes, as if he were mentally calculating just how long Melodie had been in labor. "I've got everything I'll need in my bag," he said as he rushed about gathering up blankets, clean sheets, towels. He still had the same black doctor's bag they'd given him when he graduated from medical school, as if that bag were sacred to him. "No time to get her to the hospital if she's hemorrhaging like you say. Now all *you* have to do is rush down to the kitchen and put on all that hot water all doctors in the movies seem to need."

I yelled impatiently, thinking he just wanted me out of his way. "We're not in the movies, Chris!"

We were in the hall now, and he was bending over Melodie. "I know that—it would help if you did something except run beside me and act hysterical. Now move aside, Catherine," he barked as he leaned to pick Melodie up. In his arms she seemed to weigh no more than a feather, while her middle seemed a mountain high.

In her room he stuffed pillows under her hips, asked for more white towels, sheets, newspapers, even as he glared at me. "Move, Catherine, move! From the position of the baby, its head is down and is already well on its way. RUN! I do have to sterilize a few instruments. Damn her for not speaking up and telling me she'd started her contractions early. While we were opening our gifts, she just sat there and said nothing. What the hell is wrong with everybody in this house? All she had to do was speak up and say something!"

Even before he finished muttering all this, as if to himself more than to me, I fled down the long dim halls, dashed recklessly down the back stairs closest to the kitchen. I drew hot water from the tap, put the kettle on to boil. Anxiously I waited, thinking Melodie enjoyed pity and wanted to punish us, and perhaps even wanted her baby to die so she could go back to New York unencumbered by a crippled husband and a fatherless child.

A watched pot takes so long to boil. A thousand thoughts went through my mind, ugly thoughts as I peered into the water to see the slightest roll. What was Chris doing? Should I waken Jory and tell him what was going on? Why had Melodie done this? Was she in some ways like Bart—inflicting punishment on herself for her sins? Finally, after what seemed an hour, the water began to bubble, then roll furiously. With steam pouring from the spout, I sprinted up the stairs and down more endless halls until I came to Melodie's bedroom.

Chris had arranged Melodie so she was sitting up, backed with many pillows. Her knees were shoved upward and held spread wide apart by pillows he used to support them. She was naked from the waist down, and I could see blood still trickling from her body. Feeling peculiar to see something like this, I fixed my eyes on the pads of towels and sheets he'd spread over newspapers to catch the blood. "I can't stop the bleeding," he said in a worried way. "Scares me to think the baby might swallow some." He threw me a glance. "Cathy, put on that extra pair of rubber gloves and use the calipers you see in my bag to dip each instrument I've laid out into that boiling water. I expect you to hand me what I need when I ask for it."

I nodded, terribly afraid I wouldn't remember the instrument names, when it had been so long ago, before he'd even graduated from medical school.

"Wake up, Melodie," he said over and over. "I need your help." Lightly he slapped her face. "Cathy, wet a washcloth in cold water. Wipe her face with that to bring her around so she can bear down and help push the baby out."

The cold cloth on her head brought Melodie back to reality filled with pain. Right away she began to scream, to try and shove Chris away, to pull the covers over herself. "Don't fight me," said Chris in a fatherly way. "Your baby is almost here, Melodie, but you have to bear down and take deep breaths, and I can't see what I'm doing if you cover yourself."

Still screaming in a jerky, spasmodic way, she tried to obey Chris's orders as the sweat streamed off her face and wet her hair and chest. Her gown, which was shoved up to her waist, was soon sopping. "Help her, Cathy," ordered Chris, fiddling with what I thought were forceps. I put my hands where he told me and bore down.

"Please, darling," I whispered when she stopped yelling long enough to hear me, "you have to help. Right now your baby is struggling to survive and get out."

Her wild eyes fraught with pain and fear struggled to focus on reality. "I'm dying!" she yelled before she squinched her eyes shut, pulled in a deep breath and then, with my hands assisting the shove, bore down with more determination.

"You're doing fine, Melodie," encouraged Chris. "Now another hard shove and I should be able to see the top of your baby's head." Sweating, holding on to my hands and squinting her eyes even tighter, Melodie gave one last mighty effort.

"Fine . . . you're doing fine! I can see the top of the baby's head," said Chris in a happier tone, throwing me a look of pride. At that moment Melodie's head fell to the side and her eyes closed.

She'd fainted again. "It's all right," said Chris, glancing at her face. "She's done a good job, and I can do my part now. She's through the worst part and can rest. I was thinking I'd have to use forceps, but it won't be necessary."

With confident, kind hands, he carefully slid his hand inside the birth canal and somehow drew out a very small baby and handed it to me. I held the tiny, slimy, red baby and stared down in awe at Jory's son. Oh, how perfect this miniature little boy who flailed the air with his tiny fists and kicked with incredibly small feet, and screwed his apple-sized face into a knot as he prepared to let go with a howl as Chris tied off and severed the umbilical cord. Thrills that felt cold made my spine shiver. Out of the joining of my son with his wife came this perfect little grandson who had already seized my heart even before he cried. With tears in my eyes, my heart beating joyously for Jory, who would be so happy, I glanced up to see Chris working over Melodie and drawing from her what must be the afterbirth.

Again, I stared down at the crying, doll-sized, slimy infant that seemed to weigh less than four pounds. A child born from the passion and beauty of the ballet world . . . born on the music that must have played when he was conceived. I hugged the child to my heart, thinking this was God's finest miracle, more beautiful than a tree, more lasting than a rose, a human born in His likeness. Tears flowed down my cheeks, for, like God's son, this child was born almost on Christmas day. My grandson! "Chris, he's so little. Will he live?"

"Absolutely," he said in an absorbed, abstracted tone as he continued to work over Melodie, frowning with some perplexity. "How about using the mail scales and weighing him in. Then, if you would, give him a nice bath in tepid water. He'll begin to feel much better. Use the solution I mixed and put in a blue bowl to wash out his eyes, and use the solution in the pink bowl to clean his mouth and ears. There should be diapers and receiving blankets around here somewhere. He needs to be kept very warm."

"In her suitcase," I called out as I hurried into the adjacent bath and held the little boy in the cradle of my arm and began filling a pink plastic basin. "For weeks she's had baby things packed and ready."

I was excited, feeling exalted, wishing now I'd gone to Jory and given him the chance to see his child born. I sighed then, thinking this would be his one and only child. The chances were very slim that he could father another. How lucky he was to be blessed with this little boy.

The baby I held was so frail, with just a fuzz of blond making the top of his small head softly hazy. Miniature hands and incredibly small feet flailed the chilly air. His rosebud mouth worked in sucking motions even as he tried to open eyes that seemed glued together. Despite all the slime of childbirth smeared on his red skin, my heart went out to him.

Beautiful little baby. Dear, sweet little boy to make my Jory happy. I wanted to see the color of his eyes, but he kept them tightly closed.

I was nervous, as if I'd never had a newborn of my own,

and in a way, I hadn't. This baby was so small, so delicate-looking. My two had been full term and had been cared for by experienced nurses immediately after their birth.

"Wrap him up tight," reminded Chris from the other room. "Be sure to run your finger around in his mouth to take out any blood clots or mucous you'll find. Newborns can choke on what's in their mouths."

The baby's cries were distraught over the loss of the warm, familiar fluid of the womb, but as soon as I gently eased him into the warm water, he stopped crying and seemed to fall asleep. This little babe was so new, so raw-looking that he seemed pitiful as I did what I had to. Even asleep his tiny, doll-like hands reached to find his mother and her breasts. His tiny penis stood straight up as I poured warm water over his genitals. Then, to my astonishment, I heard another baby cry!

Quickly wrapping my clean little grandson in a thick white towel, I hurried into the bedroom to see Chris staring down at a second child.

Chris looked up with the strangest expression. "A girl," he said softly. "Blond hair, blue eyes. I talked to her obstetrician myself, and he didn't mention anything about hearing two heartbeats. Sometimes that happens because one child is behind the other . . . but how odd that not once—" He broke off before he changed the subject and continued. "Twins are usually smaller than other babies, and their small size, plus the weight of the second bearing down, helps the first come quicker than a single birth—usually. Melodie was lucky this time . . ."

"Ohhh," I breathed, taking the small girl into my free arm and gazing down at her. I knew immediately who they were. Carrie and Cory born all over again!

"Chris, how fantastically marvelous!" I laughed, then saddened as I thought of my beloved twin brother and sister, now dead for so long. Still I could see them behind my eyes, racing through the backyard garden in Gladstone; running through the pitiful attic garden of paper flora and fauna. "The same twins. Doppelgangers."

Chris looked up, his rubber-gloved hands quite bloody. "No, Cathy," he stated firmly, "not doppelgangers. These are not the same twins born again. Remember that. Carrie came first then; this time the boy was first. This is not an unlucky, doomed set of children. These two will have only the best. Now, would you please stop staring and get busy? She needs a bath, too. And diaper that boy before he sprays everything."

Handling such slippery tiny babies wasn't at all easy. Still, I managed, feeling overwhelmingly happy. Despite what Chris had said, I knew who these twins were—Cory and Carrie, reborn to live the kind of wonderful lives that were their due, the happy lives stolen from them by greed and selfishness.

"Don't you worry," I whispered as I kissed each small red cheek and then their sweet tiny hands and feet. "Your grandmother will see that you're happy. No matter what I have to do, you two are going to have everything that Carrie and Cory didn't."

I glanced toward the bedroom where Melodie lay spent, just pulling out of her faint.

Chris called in to say he thought Melodie could use a nice sponge bath now, before he strode into the bathroom to take both babies from me. He sent me out to tend to the new mother while he gave the newborn twins a more complete inspection.

As I bathed Melodie and then slipped a fresh pink gown over her head, she awakened to stare at me with blank, disinterested eyes. "Is it over?" she asked in a weak, weary way. I picked up her hairbrush and went to work to unsnarl her damp, stringy hair.

"Yes, darling, it's over. You have delivered."

"What is it? A boy?" There was hope in her eyes, the first I'd seen in many a day.

"Yes, darling, a boy . . . and a girl. You have just given birth to beautiful, perfect twins."

Her eyes grew huge, dark, full of anxieties so numerous she seemed about to faint again.

"They are perfect, with everything where it's supposed to be."

She stared at me until I hurried to show her the twins. She stared with the look of utmost amazement before she smiled faintly. "Oh, they're cute . . . but I thought they'd be dark like Jory."

I placed the two babies in her arms. She gazed down at them as if all this was totally unreal. "Two," she whispered weakly again and again, "two!" Her eyes fixed somewhere in space. "*Two.* I used to tell Jory we'd stop having children when we had two. I wanted a boy and a girl . . . but not twins. Now I have to be both mother and father to two! Twins! It's not fair, not fair!"

Gently I smoothed back her hair. "Darling, this is God's way of blessing both you and Jory. He has delivered to you the complete family you wanted, and you won't have to go through this again. And you're not alone in this; we'll do all we can to help you. We'll hire nurses, maids, the best. Neither you nor they will lack for anything."

Hope came to her eyes before she closed them. "I'm tired, Cathy, so tired. I guess it is nice to have both a boy and a girl, now that Jory can't make more. I just hope this will make up for a little that he's lost . . . and he'll be pleased."

With those words she fell into deep sleep, even as I finished brushing her hair. Once her hair had been so lovely; now it was dull, lifeless. I'd have to shampoo it before Jory saw her. When next Jory saw his wife, he'd see again the lovely girl he'd married.

For I was going to reunite this pair if it was the last thing I did.

Chris stepped up beside me and took the twins from her arms. "Leave now, Cathy. She's exhausted and needs a long rest. Time to shampoo tomorrow."

"Did I say that aloud? I was only thinking about it."

He laughed. "You did only think it, but you were also fingering her hair, and in your eyes your thoughts shone clearly. I know how you feel about clean hair—the remedy for all depressions."

Kissing him first and hugging him tight, I left him with Melodie, then went to shake Jory awake. He came back from dreams, rubbing at his eyes, squinting at me. "What's up now? More trouble?"

"No trouble this time, darling." I stood and grinned at him until he must have thought I'd lost my mind. He looked so perplexed as he shoved himself up on his elbows. "I have belated Christmas gifts for you, Jory, my love." He shook his head in a bewildered way.

"Mom, couldn't that gift have waited until morning?"

"No, not this one. You're a father, Jory!" I laughed and hugged him again. "Oh, Jory, God is kind. Remember when you and Melodie planned your family, you said you wanted two children, first a boy, then a girl? Well, as a special gift, sent straight from Heaven, you have twins! A boy, a girl!"

Tears flooded his eyes. He choked out his first concern. "How is Mel?"

"Chris is in there now, taking care of her. You see, ever since the wee hours of yesterday, Melodie was in labor and she didn't say a word."

"Why?" he bemoaned, his hands covering his face. "Why, when Dad was here all the time and he could have helped?"

"I don't know, son, but let's not think about that. She'll be fine, just fine. He says she won't even need to go to the hospital, although he does want to drive the twins in for a checkup just to be safe. Such tiny babies need more care than full-term ones. And he also said it wouldn't hurt if Melodie had the attention of an obstetrician. He had to cut her, an episiotomy he called it. Without the surgery she would have torn. He sewed her up nicely, but it hurts, Jory, until the stitches come out. No doubt he'll bring them and her back the same day."

"God *is* good, Mom," he whispered hoarsely, swiping at the tears as he tried to smile. "I can't wait to see them. It will take me too much time to get up and go to them—will you bring them here to me?"

First he had to sit up to be ready to receive the twins into his arms. I turned to look at him from the doorway, thinking I'd never seen a happier-looking man.

During my absence, Chris had fashioned cribs out of two drawers pulled open and lined with soft blankets. He immediately wanted to know how Jory took my news and smiled when he heard of Jory's delight. Tenderly he put both babies in my arms. "Walk carefully, my love," he whispered before he kissed me. Then I was hurrying back to my eldest son with his firstborn. He received them as tender gifts to cherish forever, staring down with pride and love at the children he'd created.

"They look so much like Cory and Carrie did," I said softly in the warm glow of his dimly lit room. "So beautiful, even if they are very small. Have you thought about names?"

He flushed and continued to admire the babies in his arms. "Sure, I've got names all ready, although Mel failed to tell me there was a chance of twins. This makes up for so much." He looked up, his eyes shining with hope. "Mom, all the time you've been saying Mel would change after the baby came. I can't wait to see her, to hold her in my arms again."

That's when he paused and blushed. "Well, at least we can sleep together, if nothing more."

"Jory, you'll find ways . . ."

He went on as if he hadn't heard. "We constructed our lives around a plan, thinking we'd dance until I was forty, and then we'd both go into teaching or choreography. We didn't include the chance of accidents, or sudden tragedies, no more than your parents did, and on the whole, I think my wife has held up rather well."

He was being kind, overly generous! Melodie had been his brother's lover, but perhaps he didn't want to believe that.

Or, more likely, he understood her need and had already forgiven not only Melodie but Bart as well. Reluctantly Jory allowed me to take the twins away.

In Melodie's room, Chris said, "I'm taking Melodie and the twins to the hospital. I'll be back as soon as possible. I'd like another doctor to check Melodie over, and, of course, the twins need to be put in incubators until they weigh five pounds. The boy weighs three pounds thirteen ounces and the girl three pounds seven ounces . . . but nice healthy babies, even so.

"In your heart you'll fit the new twins and love them just as much as you did Cory and Carrie." How did he know each time I looked at those small babies, visions of "our" twins came to haunt me?

Glowing, Jory was at the breakfast table seated beside Bart when I entered our sunny room saved for special mornings. The plates were bright red on a white tablecloth, and a bowl of fresh holly was the centerpiece. Poinsettias were everywhere, both red and white.

"Good morning, Mom," said Jory as he met my eyes. "I'm a very happy man today . . . and I saved my news to tell Bart until you and Cindy and Dad arrived."

Small happy smiles played about Jory's mouth. His bright eyes pleaded with me not to hold anger, as once Cindy stumbled in, all sleepy and tousled-looking, Jory proudly announced that he was now the father of twins, both a girl and boy whom he and Melodie had decided to name Darren and Deirdre. "Once there were C-named twins. We're following precedent a little, but traveling further through the alphabet."

The frown on Bart's face was envious, scornful, too. "Twins, twice the trouble as one. Poor Melodie, no wonder she grew so huge. What a pain—as if she didn't have enough problems."

Cindy let out a squeal of delight. "Twins? Really? How wonderful! Can I see them now? Can I hold them?"

But Jory was still bristling from Bart's cruel remark. "Don't count me out, Bart, just because I'm down. Mel and I have no problems we can't overcome—once we're gone from this place."

Bart got up and left his breakfast uneaten.

Jory and Melodie were going to leave and take the twins with them? My heart sank. My hands on my lap worked nervously.

I didn't see the hand that took mine and pressured my fingers. "Mom, don't look so sad. We'd never cut you or Dad out of our lives. Where you go, we'll go—only we can't stay on here if Bart doesn't start acting differently. When you need to see your grandchildren, all you have to do is yell—or whisper."

Around ten Chris drove home with Melodie, who was put immediately to bed. "She's fine now, Jory. We would have liked to keep her in the hospital for a few days, but she made such a fuss that I brought her back. We left the twins in the nursery, put in separate incubators until they gain weight."

Chris leaned to kiss my cheek, then beamed brightly. "See, Cathy. I told you everything would work out fine. And I do like those names you and Melodie chose, Jory. Really fine names."

Soon I carried a tray up to Melodie, who was out of bed and staring out of a window to see snow. She began to speak immediately.

"I'm thinking of when I was a child and how much I wanted to see snow," she said dreamily, as if babies out of sight were also out of mind. "I always wanted a white Christmas away from New York. Now I have a white Christmas, and nothing has changed. No magic to give Jory back the use of his legs."

She went on in that strange, dreamlike way that frightened me. "How am I going to manage with two babies? How? One at a time was the way I planned it. And Jory won't be any help . . ."

"Didn't I say we'd help?" I said with some irritation, for it seemed Melodie was determined to feel sorry for herself no matter what. Then I understood, for Bart stood in the open doorway.

His unsmiling face showed no expression. "Congratulations, Melodie," he said calmly. "Cindy made me drive her to the hospital to see your twins. They're very . . . very . . ." He hesitated and finished—"small."

He left.

Melodie stared vacantly at the place where he'd stood.

Later Chris drove Jory, Cindy, and me to the hospital to again look at the twins. Melodie was left in her bed, deeply asleep and looking very worn. Cindy took another look at the tiny babies in their little glassed-in cages. "Oh, aren't they adorable? Jory, how proud you must feel. I'm going to make the best aunt, you just wait and see. I can't wait to hold them in my arms." She was behind his chair, leaning over to hug him. "You've been such a special brother . . . thank you for that."

Soon we were home again, and Melodie was asking weakly about her children, then falling asleep as soon as she knew they were fine. The day wore on without guests who dropped in, without the telephone ringing with friends to congratulate Jory on becoming a father. How lonely it was on this mountainside.

Shadows Fade Away

Miserable winter days slipped by, filled with myriad trivial details. We'd gone to a party on New Year's Eve, taking Cindy and Jory with us. Cindy finally had her chance to meet all the young men in the area. She'd been an overwhelming hit. Bart had failed to join us, thinking he'd have a better time in an exclusive men's club he'd joined.

"It's not a club for only men," whispered Cindy, who thought she had all the answers. "He's going to some cat-house."

"Don't you ever say anything like that again!" I repri-manded. "What Bart does is his own business. Where do you hear such gossip?"

At that New Year's Eve party a few of the guests that Bart had invited to his party had showed up, and soon enough I was tactfully finding out if they'd received Bart's invitation. No, everyone said, though they stared at Chris and me, then at Jory in his chair, as if they had many secret thoughts they'd never speak.

"Mother, I don't believe you," said Bart coldly when I told

him the guests I'd met hadn't received his invitations. "You hate Joel, you see only Malcolm in him, and therefore you want to undermine my faith in a good and pious old man. He's sworn to me he did mail off the invitations, and I believe him."

"And you don't believe me?"

He shrugged. "People are tricky. Maybe those you talked to only wanted to appear polite."

Cindy left for school the second of January, eager to escape the boredom of what she considered Hell on earth. She'd finish high school this spring and had no intentions of going on to college as Chris had tried to persuade her.

"Even an actress needs culture." But it hadn't worked. Our Cindy was just as stubborn in her own way as Carrie had been in hers.

Melodie was quiet, moody, and melancholy, and so tediously boring to be around that everyone avoided her. She resented caring for the small babies I had thought would give her pleasure and something meaningful to do. Soon we had to hire a nurse. Melodie also did very little to help with Jory, so I did for him what he couldn't do for himself.

Chris had his work that kept him happy and away until Fridays around four when he'd come in the door, much as Daddy had once returned to us on Fridays. Time repeating itself. Chris was in his own busy would, we on the mountainside stayed put in ours. Chris came and went, looking fresh, breezy, confident, and overjoyed to be with us on the weekends. He brushed aside problems as if they were lint not worth noticing.

We in Foxworth Hall stayed, never going anywhere now that Jory didn't want to leave the security of his wonderful rooms.

Soon it would be Jory's thirtieth birthday. We'd have to do something special. Then it came to me. I'd invite all the members of his New York ballet company to come to his party. First, of course, I'd have to discuss this with Bart.

He swiveled his office desk chair away from the computer. "No! I don't want a group of dancers in my house! I'm not ever going to throw another party and waste my good money on people I don't even want to know. Do something else for him—but don't invite them."

"But, Bart, once I heard you say you'd like to have his ballet company entertain at your parties."

"Not now. I've changed. Besides, I've never really approved of dancers. Never have, never will. This is the Lord's house . . . and in the spring a temple of worship will be raised to celebrate his rule over all of us."

"What do you mean, a temple will be raised?"

He grinned before he turned his attention back to the computer. "A chapel so near you can't avoid it, Mother. Won't that be nice? Every Sunday we'll rise early to attend services. *All* of us."

"And who will be on the podium delivering those sermons? You?"

"No, Mother, not me. As yet I am not washed clean of my sins. My uncle will be the minister. He is a very saintly, righteous man."

"Chris enjoys sleeping late on Sunday mornings, and so do I," I said despite my will to always keep him placated. "We like to eat breakfast in bed, and in the summers, the bedroom balcony is the perfect place to start off a happy day. As for Jory and Melodie, you should discuss the subject with them."

"I already have. They will do as I say."

"Bart . . . Jory's birthday is the fourteenth. Remember, he was born on Valentine's Day."

Again he looked at me. "Isn't it weird and meaningful that babies come often to our family on holidays—or very near them? Uncle Joel says it means something—something significant."

"No doubt!" I flared. "Dear Joel thinks everything is significant—and offensive in the eyes of *his* God. It's as if he not only owns God but controls him as well!" I whirled to confront Joel, who was never more than ten feet away from Bart. I shouted because for some reason he made me afraid. "Stop filling my son's head with crazy notions, Joel!"

"I don't have to fill his head with those kind of notions, dear niece. You established his brain patterns long before he was born. Out of hatred came the child. And out of need comes the angel of salvation. Think of that before you condemn me."

One morning the headlines of the local paper told of a family who'd gone bankrupt. A notable family that my mother had often mentioned. I read the details, folded the newspaper and stared thoughtfully before me. Had Bart had anything to do with that man's fortune suddenly disappearing? He'd been one of the guests who hadn't shown up.

Another day the newspaper told of a father who killed his wife and two children because he'd put the main part of his savings into the commodity market, and wheat had dropped drastically in price. There went another of Bart's enemies— once an invited guest to that unhappy Christmas ball. But if so, how was Bart manipulating the markets, the bankruptcy?

"I know nothing about any of that!" flared Bart when I questioned. "Those people dig their own graves with their greed. Who do you think I am, God? I said a lot of things Christmas night, but I'm not quite as crazy as you think. I have no intention of putting my soul in jeopardy. Fools always manage to trip themselves."

We celebrated Jory's birthday with a family party; Cindy flew home to stay two days, happy to celebrate with Jory. Her suitcases were full of gifts meant to keep him busy. "When I

meet a man like you, Jory, I'm going to grab him so quickly!
I'm just waiting to see if any other man is half as wonderful. So far Lance Spalding hasn't proved to be half the man
you are."

"And how would you know?" joked Jory, who had not
heard the details of Lance's sudden departure. He flashed his
wife a hard look as she held Darren and I held Deirdre. We
were both supporting nursing bottles as we sat before the cozy
log fire. The babies gave all of us reasons for feeling the future
held great promise. I think even Bart was fascinated with how
swiftly they grew, how sweet and cuddly they felt when on
a few occasions he held them for several uncomfortable seconds. He'd looked at me with a certain pride.

Melodie put Darren in the large cradle Chris had found
in an antique shop and had refinished so it looked almost
new. With one foot she rocked the baby as she glared hard
at Bart before once again gazing pensively into the roaring
fire. Seldom did she speak, and she showed no real interest in
her children. Only negligently did she pick them up, as if for
show, as she showed no interest in any one of us, or anything
we did.

Jory shopped by mail for gifts that were delivered almost
daily to surprise her. She'd open each box, faintly smile and
say a weak thank you, and sometimes she even put the package down unopened, thanking Jory without even looking his
way. It pained me to see him wince, or bow his head to hide his
expression. He was trying—why couldn't she try?

Each passing day saw Melodie withdrawing not only from
her husband but, much to my amazement, also from her children. Hers was an indecisive love, without strong commit-
ment, like the frail flutterings of moth wings beating at the
candle flame of motherly love. I was the one who got up in
the middle of the night to feed them. I was the one who paced
the floor and tried to change two diapers at once, and it was I
who raced down to the kitchen to mix their formula and held

them on my shoulder for burping, I who took the time and trouble to rock them to sleep as I sang soft lullabies while their huge blue eyes stared up at me with fascination until they grew sleepy and with great reluctance closed their eyes. Often I could tell they were still listening from their small, pleased smiles. It filled me with joy to see them growing more and more like Cory and Carrie.

If we lived isolated from society, we did not live isolated from the malicious rumors that the servants brought home with them from the local stores. Often I overheard their whispers as they chopped onions, green peppers, and made the pies and cakes and other desserts we all loved to eat. I knew our maids lingered too long in back halls and deliberately made our beds when we were still upstairs. Thinking we were alone, we'd let out many secrets for them to feed their gossip.

Much of what they speculated on I speculated on as well. Bart was so seldom home, and sometimes I was grateful for that. With him out of the house, there was no one to create arguments; Joel stayed in his room and prayed, or so I presumed.

It came to me one morning that maybe I should try the servants' tricks and hang out near the kitchen . . . and when I did, our cook and maids filled my ears with knowledge gained from those in the village. Bart, according to them, was having many affairs with the prettiest and richest society ladies, both married and unmarried. Already he'd ruined one marriage that just happened to be one of the couples that had been on his Christmas guest list. Also, according to what I overheard, Bart often visited a brothel ten miles away, not within any city's limits.

I had evidence that some of those tales might be true. Often I saw him come home drunk and in mild, happy moods that made me wish, regretfully, that he'd stay drunk. Only then could he smile and laugh easily.

One day I had to ask. "What are you doing all those nights you stay out so late?"

He giggled easily when he drank too much; he giggled now. "Uncle Joel says the best evangelists have been the worst sinners; he says you have to roll in the gutter filth to know what it's like to be clean, and saved."

"And that's what you're doing all those nights, rolling in the gutter filth?"

"Yes, Mother darling—for damned if I know what it's like to feel clean, or saved."

Spring approached cautiously like a timid bluebird. Blustery cold winds softened to warm southern breezes. The sky turned that certain shade of blue that made me feel young and hopeful. I was often out in the gardens raking leaves and pulling up weeds that the gardeners overlooked.

I couldn't wait to see the crocus peek from the ground in the woods, couldn't wait to see the tulips and daffodils and watch pink and white dogwood blossoms spring forth. Couldn't wait for the azaleas everywhere to make my life a fairyland of many delights, for the twins, for all of us. I'd look up and admire the wonder of the trees that never seemed depressed or lonely. Nature—how much we could learn if only we would.

I took Jory with me as far as he could easily guide his sturdy electric chair with the huge balloon wheels that climbed most gradual grades. "We've got to find a better way to get you deeper into the woods," I said thoughtfully. "Now, if we laid flagstones everywhere, they'd be very lovely, but if they freeze in the winter they'd poke up and could possibly snag your chair and tip you over. As much as I hate cement, we'll have to use that or blacktop. Somehow I like blacktop better, what about you?"

He laughed at my silliness. "Red bricks, Mom. Brick

walks are so colorful, and besides, this chair of mine is a real marvel." He looked around, smiling with pleasure, then tilted his face so the sun could warm it. "I only wish Mel would accept what's happened to me and show more interest in the twins."

What could I say to that, when already I'd had it out with Melodie more than a dozen times, and the more I said the more resentful she grew. "This is MY life, Cathy!" she'd shouted. "MY LIFE—not yours!" Screaming at me, her face a red mask of fury.

Jory's physical therapist showed Jory how to lower himself to the ground without so much effort, and then he taught Jory how to get back into his chair without assistance. And all so Jory could help me plant more rose bushes. His strong hands used the trowel much better than mine.

The gardeners eagerly taught Jory how to prune our shrubbery, when to fertilize, how to mulch and with what. He and I made gardening not just a hobby but a lifestyle to save us both from going crazy. The greenhouse was enlarged so we could grow exotic flowers, and in there we had a world of our own to control, full of its own kind of quiet excitement. But it wasn't enough for Jory, who decided he had to stay in the arts in one form or another.

"Dad is not the only one in this family who can paint a hazy sky and make you feel the humidity, or put a dewdrop on a painted rose so real you can smell it," he said to me with a broad smile. "I'm growing as an artist, Mom."

Even with Melodie in the same house, Jory was making a life without her. He fashioned slings to his chair that fitted over his shoulder so he could carry his twins with him. His delight to see them smile when they saw him coming touched my heart, just as it drove Melodie from the nursery. "They love me now, Mom! It's in their eyes!"

They knew Jory better than they knew their mother. They gave her void and somehow pitifully hopeful smiles, perhaps because her expression was so blank and thoughtful when she stared at them.

Yes, the twins not only loved and knew who was their father, they also trusted him fully. When he reached to pick them up, they didn't flinch or fear he'd drop them. They laughed as if they knew he'd never, never drop them.

I found Melodie sulking in her room, really thin now, her once beautiful hair dull and stringy. "It takes time, Melodie, to develop motherly instincts," I said as I sat down unasked and, apparently, unwanted. "You allow me and the maids to wait upon them too much. They don't recognize you as their mother when you stay away. The day you see their small faces light up when you come in, and they smile from the happiness they feel to see you, their mother, you'll find the love you're searching for. Your heart will melt. Their needs will give you something nothing else can, and never again will you feel anything but an all-encompassing love for your children, when they love you, and you love them."

Her faint smile flashed bittersweet and was quickly gone. "When do you give me the chance to mother my children, Cathy? When I get up in the night, you are already there. When I rise early, you've already bathed and dressed them. They don't need a mother when they have a grandmother like you."

I was stunned by her unfair attack. Often I lay on my bed and heard the twins cry and cry before I got up to tend to their needs. In torment while I waited and waited for Melodie to go to them. What was I supposed to do, ignore their cries? I gave her time enough. Her room was across the hall from theirs, and mine was in another wing.

She apparently saw my thoughts, for her voice came almost like the hiss of a venomous snake. "You always come out on top, don't you, mother-in-law? You always manage to get what you want, but there's one thing you will never get, and that's Bart's love and respect. When he loved me—*and once he did love me*—he told me he hated you, really despised you. I felt sorry for him then, and sorrier for you. Now I understand why he feels as he does. For with a mother like you, Jory doesn't need a wife like me."

The next day was Thursday. I felt heavy-hearted to think of all the ugly words Melodie had screamed and hissed at me yesterday. I sighed, sat up, and swung my legs off the bed, slipping my feet into satin mules. A busy day ahead since this was the day all our servants but Trevor had off. On Thursdays I was like Momma had been, preparing myself for Friday, coming fully alive only when the man I loved strolled through the door.

Jory was quietly sobbing when I entered his room with the freshly bathed and diapered twins held one in each of my arms. In his hands he loosely held a creamy long sheet of stationery.

"Read this," he choked, putting the paper on the table beside his chair before he reached for his children. When he had them both in his arms, he bowed his face into the soft hair of his son, then his daughter's hair.

I picked up the creamy sheets; always bad news on cream-colored paper came from Foxworth Hall.

> *My dearest darling Jory,*
>
> *I'm a coward. I've always known that, and hoped you'd never find out. You were always the one with all the strength. I love you, and no doubt will always love you, but I can't live with a man who can never make love to me again.*
>
> *I look at you in that horrible chair that you've grown to accept, when I cannot accept it, or your handicap. Your parents came to my room and confronted me and urged me to face up to you and say everything I feel. I'm unable to do that, for if I do,*

you might say or do something that would change my mind, and I've got to leave, or lose my mind.

You see, my love, I already feel half insane from being in this house, this horrible, hateful house with all its deceiving beauty. I lie on my lonely bed and dream of the ballet. I hear the music playing even when it isn't. I've got to go back to where I can hear it play, and if that is ugly and selfish, as I know it is, forgive me, if you can.

Say kind things about me to our children when they are old enough to ask questions about their mother. Say those nice words even if they aren't true, for I know I've failed you just as much as I've failed them. I've given you every reason to hate me, but please don't remember me with hate. Remember me as I used to be when we were younger, and very much in control of our lives.

Don't blame yourself for anything, or blame anyone else for what I have to do. Everything is my own fault. You see, I'm not real, I never was, and I never will be. I can't face up to the kind of cruel reality that destroys lives and leaves behind broken dreams. Then, too, remember this: I'm the fantasy you helped create out of your desire and my own.

So farewell, my love, my first and sweetest love, and sadly perhaps my only true love. Find someone rare like your mother who can take my place. She's the one who gave you the ability to cope with reality, no matter how harsh.

God would have been kind if he had given me your kind of mother.

Yours regretfully,
Mel

The note fell from my hand, fluttering its pathetic certain way to the carpet. Both Jory and I stared at it lying there, so sad—and so final.

"It's over, Mom," he said tonelessly, his voice deep and gruff. "What began when I was twelve and she was eleven, all over. I built my life around her, thinking she'd last until we were old. I gave her the best I had to offer, and still it wasn't enough once the glamour was gone."

How could I tell him that Melodie wouldn't have lasted even if he was still on stage dancing. Something in her resented his strength, his innate ability to cope with situations beyond her ability to comprehend.

I shook my head. No, I was being unfair. "I'm sorry, Jory, so terribly sorry." I didn't say, *perhaps you'll be better off without her.*

"I'm sorry, too," he whispered, refusing to meet my eyes. "What woman will want me now?"

Perhaps he would never perform sexually again in the normal way, and I knew he needed someone in the bed with him during all those long, lonely nights. I could tell from his morning face that the nights were the worst part of his life, leaving him feeling isolated, vulnerable emotionally, as well as physically helpless. He was like me, needing arms to hold me safe during the darkness, wanting kisses on my face to put me to sleep, to wake me up, to put over me a safe parasol of love.

"Last night I heard the wind blowing," he confided to me as the twins sat in their highchairs and smeared their faces with warm, mushy cereal. "I woke up. I thought I heard Mel breathing beside me, but there was nothing. I saw the birds happily building their nests, heard them chirping to greet the new day, and then I saw her note. I knew without reading what was inside, and I went on thinking about the birds, and all their love songs suddenly turned into only territorial rights." His voice broke again as he lowered his head to hide his face. "I've heard that geese, once mated, never mate again, and I keep seeing Melodie as the swan, loyal forever, no matter what the circumstances."

"Darling, I know, I know," I soothed, stroking his dark curls. "But love can come again, you hold on to that—and you're not alone."

He nodded, saying, "Thanks for always being here when I need you. Thank Dad for me, too . . ."

Brusquely, fearing I'd cry as well, I put my arms about him. "Jory, Melodie is gone, but she's left you with a son and a daughter, be grateful for that. Because she did leave you, that makes them all yours now. She walked out not only on you, but also on her own children. You can divorce her and use your strength to help your children develop your own kind of courage and determination. You'll manage without her, Jory, and as long as you need us, you have your parents' willing help."

And all the time I was thinking that Melodie had deliberately withdrawn from her own children in order to make the break easier; she hadn't allowed herself to love them, or them to love her. Her parting gift of love to her childhood sweetheart was his own children.

Jory brushed the tears from his eyes and tried to grin. When he did it was full of irony.

BOOK THREE

The Summer of Cindy

All of a sudden Bart was taking business trips, flying off to return in a few days, never staying away more than two or three days, as if afraid that during his absence as he wheeled and dealed we would run away with his fortune. As he put it, "I have to keep on top of things. Can't trust anyone more than I trust myself."

He had just happened to be gone the day that Melodie slipped out of Foxworth Hall and left that pitiful note for Jory to find on his night table. Bart's expression didn't change when he came home and found Melodie's chair at the dining table empty. "Upstairs moping again?" he asked indifferently, indicating her chair, which was a constant reminder of her absence.

"No, Bart," I answered when Jory refused to look his way or even answer. "Melodie decided she wanted to resume her career, and she left, leaving Jory a note."

His left eyebrow quirked upward cynically; then he flashed Jory a glance, but not one word to say he was sorry to find her gone, or one word of condolence to his brother.

Later, when Jory was upstairs and I was changing diapers, Bart came in and stood at my side. "Too bad I was in New York at the time. I would have enjoyed seeing Jory's expression when he read her note. By the way, where is it? I'd like to read what she had to say."

I turned to stare at him. For the first time it occurred to me that Melodie might have arranged to meet him in New York. "No, Bart, you will never read that note . . . and I hope to God you had nothing to do with her decision to go."

Angry, his face reddened. "I went on a business trip! I haven't said two words to Melodie since Christmas. And as far as I'm concerned, it's good riddance."

In some ways it was better without Melodie always sitting around moodily, shadowing the rooms with her dreary depression. I made it a practice to visit Jory just before bedtime, tucking him in, opening his window, dimming the lights, and seeing he had water where he could reach it. My kiss on his cheek tried to substitute for a wife's kiss.

Now that Melodie was gone, I soon found out that she had helped a little just by getting up early once in a while to change and feed the babies. She'd even bothered to diaper them several times a day.

Often Bart drifted into the nursery, as if irresistibly drawn, and stared down at the tiny twins, who had learned how to smile and had found out to their delight that those waving shadowy things were their own feet and their own small hands. They reached for the mobiles of pretty colorful birds, struggled to pull them down and put them in their mouths.

"They are kind of cute," Bart commented in a musing way that pleased me, even doing a little to help by handing me the baby oil and talcum. Unfortunately, just when the twins almost had him won over, Joel strode into the nursery and scowled down at the beautiful babies, and all the kindness and sympathy growing in Bart vanished completely, leaving him standing beside me looking guilty.

Joel gave the twins one hard, quick glance before he turned away his offended eyes. "Just like the first twins, the evil ones," muttered Joel. "Same blond hair and blue eyes . . . no good will come of this pair either."

"What do you mean by that?" I raged. "Cory and Carrie never harmed anyone! They were the ones who were harmed. They suffered what was inflicted on them by your own sister, mother, and father, Joel. Don't you ever dare to forget that."

With silence Joel answered before he left the room, taking Bart with him.

In mid-June, Cindy flew home to stay the summer. She made determined efforts to keep her rooms neater, hanging up her own clothes, which she used to drop on the floor. She helped me by changing the twins and holding their bottles as she rocked them to sleep. It was sweet to see her sitting in the rocker, a baby in the crook of each arm, struggling to hold two bottles at the same time while she wore baby doll pajamas, her lovely long legs bare and tucked under her. She seemed very much a child herself. She bathed and showered so often I thought she'd shrivel into a dried prune.

One evening she came from her luxurious bath and dressing room looking radiantly fresh and alive, smelling like an exotic flower garden. "I love twilight," she gushed, twirling around and around. "Just adore strolling the woods when the moon is on the rise."

By this time we were all seated on our favorite terrace, sipping drinks. Bart pricked up his ears and glared at her. "Who's waiting for you in the woods?"

"Not who, dear brother, but what." She turned her head to smile at him in an innocent, charming way. "I'm going to be nice to you, Bart, no matter how nasty you are to me. I've decided I cannot win friends by tossing out rude and nasty remarks."

He glared suspiciously. "I still think you're meeting some boy in the woods."

"Thank you, brother Bart, for only thinking of punishing me with nasty suspicions. I expected more—and worse. There's a boy in South Carolina that I've fallen madly for, and he's a nature lover. He's taught me how to appreciate all that money can't buy. I adore sunrises and sunsets. When rabbits run, I follow. Together we catch rare butterflies and he mounts them. We picnic in the woods, swim in the lakes. Since I'm not allowed to have a boyfriend here, I'm going to stand alone at the top of a hill and try just strolling down. It's fun to challenge gravity and try not to run all breathless and out of control."

"By what name do you call gravity? Bill, John, Mark, or Lance?"

"I'm not going to let you annoy me this time," she said arrogantly. "I like to stare up at the sky, count the stars, find the constellations, watch the moon play hide-and-seek. Sometimes the man in the moon winks at me, and I wink back. Dennis has taught me how to stand perfectly still and absorb the feel of the night. Why, I'm seeing wonders I didn't even know existed because I'm in love—madly, passionately, ridiculously, insanely in love!"

Envy flashed through his dark eyes before he growled, "What about Lance Spalding? I thought you felt that way about him. Or did I ruin his pretty face permanently so you can't bear to look at him?"

Cindy paled. "Unlike you, Bart Foxworth, Lance is beautiful inside and out, like Daddy, and I do still love him, and Dennis, too."

Bart's frown deepened. "I know all about your nature loving! You want to sprawl on your back and spread your legs for some village idiot—and I won't have it!"

"What's going on here?" asked Chris, appearing dumb-founded to come back from the telephone and find all the peace gone.

Cindy jumped to her feet, took her stance, and put her hands on her hips. She glared down into Bart's face, struggling to hold fast to that adult control she was determined to have with him. "Why do you always presume the worst about me? I just want to walk in the moonlight, and the village is ten miles away. What a pity you don't understand what it's like to be human."

Her answer and her glare seemed to infuriate him more. "You're not my sister, just a smart-ass little bitch in heat—the same as your mother!"

This time it was Chris who jumped up from the table and slapped Bart hard. Bart drew back and raised his fists, as if ready to punch Chris in the jaw—when *I* jumped to my feet and placed myself in front of Chris. "No, don't you dare ever hit the man who's tried to be the best father possible! If you do, Bart, you and I are through forever!" That was enough for him to turn his dark, fiery eyes on me, so furious his look could have started a blaze.

"Why can't you see that little whore for what she is? You both see everything wrong about me, but you close your eyes to the sins of your favorites! She's nothing but a tramp, a goddamned tramp." He froze, his eyes wide and startled.

He'd taken the Lord's name in vain. He looked around to see Joel, who for once was out of sight and hearing. "You see, Mother, what she does to me? She corrupts—and in my own home, too."

Looking at Bart disapprovingly, Chris sat down again. Cindy disappeared into the house. I stared forlornly after her, as Chris spoke harshly, confronting Bart. "Can't you see that Cindy is doing her best to please you? She's been trying since she came home to do her utmost to appease you, but you won't let her. How can you take a stroll in these lonely woods as anything but innocent? From now on, I want you to treat her with respect—for if you don't you may well drive her into doing something rash. Losing Melodie is quite enough for one summer."

It was just as if Chris had no voice and Bart had no ears, from all the effect those words had. Chris ended by giving Bart an even harder look and more reprimanding words before Chris stood and disappeared inside the house. I suspected he would follow Cindy upstairs and do what he could to comfort her.

Alone with my second son, I tried to rationalize, as I always did. "Bart, why do you talk so ugly to Cindy?" I began. "She's at a very vulnerable age and is a decent human being who needs to be appreciated. She's not a tramp, a whore, or a bitch. She's a lovely young girl who is very thrilled to be pretty and attracting so much attention from the boys. That doesn't mean she's giving in to every one. She has scruples, honor. That one episode with Lance Spalding has not corrupted her."

"Mother, she was corrupted long ago, only you don't want to believe that. Lance Spalding wasn't the first."

"How dare you say that?" I asked, really enraged. "What kind of man are you, anyway? You sleep with whom you please, do what you please, but she's supposed to be an angel with a halo and wings on her back. Now you go upstairs and apologize to Cindy!"

"An apology is something she'll never get from me." He sat down to finish his meal. "The servants talk about Cindy. You don't hear them, for you're too busy with those two babies you can't leave alone. But I hear them as they clean and dust. Your Cindy is a red-hot number. The trouble is you think she's an angel. You think that just because she looks like one."

I sank down to lean my elbows heavily on the glass-topped wrought-iron white table, feeling overwhelmingly tired, just as Jory did, and he hadn't said one word for or against Cindy. To be for any length of time around Bart was so exhausting; the tension of saying one wrong thing kept you wired tight.

My eyes fixed on the crimson roses that were this evening's centerpiece. "Bart, has it ever occurred to you that Cindy may feel she's been contaminated, so that now she doesn't care? And certainly you don't give her any reason to value her self-esteem."

"She's a wanton, loose slut." Said with absolute conviction.

My voice turned as uncompromising as his. "Apparently from what I overhear when the servants whisper, you are drawn to the very type of woman you condemn."

Standing, he threw down his napkin and stalked purposefully into the house. "I'll fire every damn one who gossips about me!"

I sighed. Soon we wouldn't be able to hire any servants if he kept hiring and firing.

"Mom, I'm going to hit the sack," said Jory. "This pleasant evening meal on the terrace has turned out just as I could have predicted."

That very evening Bart fired every servant but Trevor, who seldom said anything except to me or Chris. If Trevor had left every time Bart fired him, he'd have been gone long ago. Trevor had an understanding way of knowing just when to believe Bart was serious. Never, never did he rebuke Bart, nor did he meet Bart's eyes squarely. Perhaps because of this, Bart thought he had Trevor cowed. I thought Trevor forgave Bart, because he understood and pitied him.

I headed for Cindy's room, meeting Chris as he came down. "She's very upset. Try to calm her down, Cathy. She's talking about leaving here and never coming back."

Cindy was facedown on her bed. Small grunts and groans came from her throat. "He ruins everything," she wailed. "I never knew my own father and mother—and Bart wants to chase me away from you and Daddy," she sobbed as I perched on the side of her bed. "Now he's determined to spoil my summer, drive me away like he did Melodie."

I held her slight body in my arms and comforted her as

best I could, thinking I'd have to send her away to keep her safe from being hurt again by Bart. Where could I send Cindy and not injure her feelings, which didn't need another cruel blow? I went to bed thinking about that, as Cindy escaped the house to meet a boy from the village.

I was to hear about this later.

As Bart had predicted, Cindy's nature-loving experience did have a name. Victor Wade. And while I lay on my bed, and Chris slept beside me, pondering what to do with Cindy, and still keep her love, how to keep Bart from being his worst self, our Cindy sneaked out of the house and went with Victor Wade to Charlottesville.

In Charlottesville Cindy had a glorious time, dancing with Victor Wade until she wore holes in the thin soles of her fragile, sparkling sandals with the four-inch glass heels (really only Lucite and not as heavy as glass). Then Victor, true to his word, drove back toward Foxworth Hall. Near one of the roads leading to our hill, he parked and drew Cindy into his arms.

"I've fallen in love," he whispered huskily, raining kisses expertly on her face, behind her ears, traveling down her neck to end up on her breast that he bared. "I've never met a girl who was half the fun you are. And you were right. They don't grow 'em better in Texas . . ."

Half drunk on too much wine, intoxicated, too, with the expertise of his foreplay, Cindy's efforts to resist his lovemaking were weak, ineffectual. Soon her own passionate nature was responding, and eagerly she helped him to undress as he unzipped her dress and soon had it off, along with everything else. He fell upon her—and that's when Bart showed up.

Bellowing like an enraged bull, Bart rushed the parked car, catching Cindy and Victor in the very act of copulating.

Seeing their naked bodies with arms and legs entwined

on the backseat confirmed all his suspicions and enraged him more. Bart threw open the door and yanked Victor out by the ankles, forcefully dragging him off the top of Cindy so he fell face downward upon the rough gravel of the roadside.

Not giving the body a chance to recover, Bart attacked, using his fists brutally.

Screaming her anger, disregarding her nudity, Cindy hurled her dress directly into Bart's face, blinding him momentarily. This gave Victor the chance to jump to his feet and deliver his own blow that momentarily gave Bart pause, but already Victor's nose was bleeding and he had a black eye.

In the moonlight his nakedness seemed blue in Cindy's eyes. "And Bart was so ruthless, Momma! So awful! He seemed like a madman—especially when Victor managed to smash a good right hook into his jaw. Then he tried to kick Bart in the groin. It did hit him there, but not hard enough. Bart doubled up, cried out, then rushed Victor with so much fierce anger that I was scared he'd kill him! He came out of that pain so fast, Momma, so fast—and I'd always heard that stopped a man cold." Cindy sobbed with her head on my lap.

"He was like the Devil straight from hell, screaming abuse at Victor, using all the obscene words he never wants me to use. He knocked Victor down, then beat him into unconsciousness. Then he came at me! I was terrified he'd batter my face and break my nose and make me ugly, like he's always threatened to do. Somehow I'd managed to pull on that dress, but the zipper was wide open down the back. He grabbed me by the shoulders, shook me so hard the dress fell to my ankles and I was naked—but he didn't look to see anything. He kept his eyes on my face as he slapped one cheek and then the other and my head was rocked from side to side, until I felt dizzy and faint. My head was reeling before he picked me up like a sack of grain, threw me over his shoulder, and took off through the woods, leaving Victor lying on the ground.

"It was awful, Momma, so humiliating! To be carried like

that, as if I were cattle! I cried all the way, pleading with Bart to call an ambulance in case Victor was seriously hurt . . . but he wouldn't listen. I begged him to put me down and let me cover myself, but he ordered me to shut up or else he'd do something terrible. Then he took me to—"

She cut off her words abruptly, staring before her as if mesmerized by fear.

"Where did he take you, Cindy?" I asked, feeling sick, as if her humiliation was mine, and so furious with Bart, feeling sorry for her shocking plight. At the same time I was so angry that she'd brought this upon herself by disobeying and disregarding everything I'd tried to teach her.

In a small, weak voice, with her head lowered so her long hair fell to hide her face, she finished, "Just home, Mom . . . just home."

There was more to it, but she refused to tell me anything else. I wanted to scold her, to chastise her, remind her again that she knew all about Bart and his fierce temper, but she was too traumatized to hear more.

I got up to leave her room. "I'm taking away all your privileges, Cindy. I'll send up a servant to take out your telephone so you can't call one of your boyfriends to help you escape. I've heard your side of the story now, and Bart just this morning told me his side. I don't agree with his method of punishing you or that boy. He was much too brutal, and for that, I apologize. However, it seems you are very free with your sexual favors. You can't deny that any longer, for I've seen you with my own eyes when that boy Lance was here. It hurts to know that you've heeded so little of what I've tried to teach you. I realize it's hard to be young and different from your peers, but still I was hoping you'd wait until you knew how to handle intimate relationships. I couldn't bear for an unknown man to lay a finger on me—much less take me totally—and you just met that boy, Cindy! A complete stranger who might have hurt you!"

Her pitiful pretty face lifted. "Momma, help me!"

"Haven't I done my best to help you all your life? Listen to me, Cindy, for once really listen. The best part of loving comes with learning to know a man, by allowing him to know you as a person before you begin to think about sex—you don't pick up the first man you meet!"

Bitterly she railed back. "Momma, all the books write about sex. They don't mention love. Most psychiatrists say there is no such thing as love. You've never explained to me exactly what love is. I don't even know if it really exists. I think that sex is as necessary at my age as water and food, and love is nothing but excitement; it's your blood heating up; your pulse racing, your heart pounding, your breath coming faster, heavier, and in the end it's only a natural need no worse than wanting to sleep. So despite you and your old-fashioned ideas, I give in when a boy I like wants to make out. Victor Wade wanted me . . . and I wanted him. Now, don't blaze your eyes at me that way! He didn't force me. Didn't rape me—I just let him! I wanted him to do what he did!"

Her blue eyes defied me as she jumped up and stared me in the eyes. "Now go on and call me a sinner like Bart did! Yell and scream and say I'll go to hell, but I don't believe you any more than I believe him! If so, ninety-nine percent of the world's population are sinners—including you and your brother!"

Stunned, deeply hurt, I turned and left.

The beautiful summer days dragged by while Cindy sulked in her room, angry at Bart, at me, even at Chris. She refused to eat at the table if Bart or Joel were there. She stopped showering two and three times a day and allowed her hair to become just as stringy and dull as Melodie's, as if proving to us she was now on her way to abandoning us as Melodie had, and it was Melodie's manner she tried to duplicate as much as possible. However, even in sullenness her eyes still sparked with fire, and she managed to look pretty even when she looked messy.

"You're not accomplishing anything but making yourself miserable," I said when I saw her quickly turn off the TV set she had in her bedroom, as if she wanted me to believe she didn't have a single pleasure left to enjoy when her room contained every luxury but the telephone, which I'd removed so she couldn't arrange secret dates with Victor Wade or anyone else.

She sat on the bed, staring at me resentfully. "You just let me go, Momma. You go and tell Bart to let me go and I'll never bother him again. I'll never come back to this house again! NEVER!"

"Where will you go and what will you do, Cindy?" I asked with concern, afraid she'd slip out one night and we'd never hear from her again. And I knew she didn't have enough money saved to see her through longer than two weeks.

"I'LL DO WHAT I HAVE TO!" she screamed, tears of self-pity streaking her pale face, which was already losing its rosy tan. "You and Daddy gave to me generously, so I won't have to sell my body if that's what you're thinking. Unless I just want to. Right this moment I feel like being everything Bart doesn't want me to be, and that would show him, really show him."

"Then you stay in this room until you feel like being everything *I* want you to be. When you can speak to me with respect, without yelling, and express to me some mature decisions on what you intend to do with your life, I'll help you escape this house."

"Momma!" she wailed. "Don't hate me! I can't help it if I like the boys and they like me! I'd like to save myself for that special Mister Right, but I've never met anyone that special. When I refuse to let them, they go straight from me to some other girl who doesn't refuse. How did you manage it,

Momma? What did you do to keep all those men loving you, and only you?"

All those men? I didn't know how to answer.

Instead, like other parents put on the spot, I avoided giving the straight answer I didn't have anyway. "Cindy, your father and I love you very much, you should know that. Jory loves you. And the twins smile just to see you come near them. Before you decide to do something rash, let's sit down with your father, with Jory, and then you have your say, and let us know what you want for yourself. And if it is at all reasonable, we will do what we can to see that you obtain your goals."

"You won't let Bart in on any of this?" she asked suspiciously.

"No, darling. Bart has proven he doesn't reason when it comes to you. Ever since the day you joined our family he's resented you, and at this late date there doesn't seem to be much any of us can do about that. As for Joel, I don't like him, either, and he has no place in our family discussion about your future."

Suddenly she flung her arms about my neck. "Oh, Momma, I'm so ashamed I said so many ugly things. I wanted to hurt you the other day because Bart had shamed me so much. Save me from Bart, Momma. Find a way, please, please."

After Chris, Jory, Cindy, and I talked, we found a way to save Cindy not only from Bart but from herself. I tried to calm Bart, who wanted to punish her more drastically.

"She's only adding fuel to the fire already burning in the village," he shouted when I entered his office. "I try to lead a decent, God-fearing life—now don't you yell at me and say you've heard differently. I'll admit I was rolling in filth for a while, but things have changed. I didn't enjoy those women. Melodie was the only one who gave me anything that approached love."

I tried to keep the frown from my face. How easily he had turned away from her once he knew he had her loving him . . .

Looking around at all the valuables in his office, I wondered again if Bart didn't love things more than he loved people; I stared at the luxurious antique Orientals that he'd purchase at auctions, costing hundreds of thousands. His furniture put that in the White House to shame. He *would* be the wealthiest man in the world if he kept doubling his five hundred thousand a year every few months, the way he was somehow managing to do now. Even before he came fully "into his own" he'd have made his billion or so. He was clever, quick, brilliant. What a pity he couldn't be more to mankind than just another greedy, selfish millionaire.

"Leave now, Mother. You waste my time." He swiveled his chair around and stared out at the beautiful gardens now in full bloom. "Send Cindy away—anywhere. Just get her out of my hair."

"Cindy told us last night she'd like to spend the remainder of the summer in a New England drama school. She had the name and address of the one she preferred. Chris called to check them out, and they seem reliable and have a good reputation. So she's leaving in three days."

"Good riddance to rubbish," he said indifferently.

Standing, I threw him a look of pity. "Before you condemn Cindy so harshly, Bart, think about yourself. Has she done any worse than you have?"

He began to use his computer without replying.

I slammed the door behind me.

Three days later I was helping Cindy finish her packing. We'd been shopping, so she had more than enough casual clothes, six pairs of new shoes, and two new swimsuits. She kissed Jory good-bye, then lingered with the twins cuddled in her arms. "Dear little babies," she crooned, "I'll be back. I'll sneak in and out and won't let Bart even see me. Jory, you should get away from here, too. Momma, you and Daddy go with him." Reluctantly she put the twins back in their play pen and came to hug and kiss me. I was already crying. I was losing my daughter. I knew from the way she looked at me that nothing between us would ever be quite the same again.

Still she came to me and hugged me. "Daddy's going to drive me to the airport," she said as she bowed her head on my shoulder. "You can come too, if you don't cry and feel sorry for me, because I'm happier than any lark to be free of this damned house. And take me seriously for once—get Jory and yourselves free of this house. It's an evil house, and now I hate its spirit just as much as once I loved its beauty."

We drove to the airport without Cindy bidding Bart or Joel farewell.

Without another word to me, her remote expression told me everything. She was warmer with Chris, kissing him good-bye. She only waved to me as she raced toward her departure gate. "Don't hang around and wait for my plane to take off. I'm boarding it gladly."

"You will write?" Chris asked.

"Naturally, when I can find time."

"Cindy," I called despite myself, wanting to protect her again, "write at least once a week. We care about what happens to you. We'll be here to do what we can when you need us. And sooner or later, Bart will find what he's looking for. He'll change. I'll see to it that he changes. I'll do anything I have to so we can be a family again."

"He won't find his soul, Momma," she called back coolly, backing away even farther. "He was born without one."

Before her plane left the ground, my tears stopped flowing and my determination hardened into concrete. *Indeed, before I died, I was going to see my family united,* made whole and healthy—if it took the rest of my life.

Chris made attempts to pull me out of my depression as he drove me back to what had to be called "home." "How's the nurse making out?"

My concern for Cindy had kept me so involved that I'd paid little attention to the beautiful, dark-haired nurse Chris had recently hired to live in and help with the twins and Jory. She'd been in the house a few days and I'd hardly said more than six words to her.

"What does Jory think of Toni?" he asked. "I took considerable pains looking for just the right one. In my opinion, she's a real find."

"I don't think he's even looked at her, Chris. He stays so busy with his painting and the babies. They're just beginning to crawl without so much effort. Why, yesterday I saw Cory— I mean Darren—pick up a bug from the grass and try to put it in his mouth. It was Toni who ran to prevent that. I don't recall Jory even looking at her."

"He will, sooner or later. And Cathy, you've got to stop thinking of his twins as Cory and Carrie. If Jory hears you call them Cory or Carrie he'll be angry. They are not *our* twins— they are Jory's."

Chris said nothing more during the long drive back to Foxworth Hall, not even when he turned into our long drive and then drove slowly into the garage.

"What's going on in this crazy house?" Jory asked as soon as I stepped onto the terrace, where he was seated on an athletic mat put on the flagstones. The twins were with him, playing happily in the sunshine. "Shortly after you left to drive Cindy to the airport, a crew of construction workers arrived and knocked and banged away in that downstairs room Joel likes to pray in. I didn't see Bart, and I didn't want to talk to Joel. And then there's something else—"

"I don't understand . . ."

"It's that damned nurse you and Dad hired, Mom. She's gorgeous and she's good at her job—when I can get hold of her. I've been calling for ten minutes and she hasn't responded.

The twins are dripping wet, and she didn't bring out enough diapers so I can change them again. I can't go in the house and get more without leaving them alone. They scream now when I try to put them in the slings. They want to be on their own. Especially Deirdre."

I diapered the twins myself and put them down for naps, then went in search of the newest member in our household.

To my astonishment I found her in the new swimming pool with Bart, both of them laughing, splashing water at one another.

"Hi, Mother!" called Bart, looking tan and healthy, and happier than I'd seen him since the days when he had believed himself in love with Melodie. "Toni plays a super game of tennis. It's great having her here. We were both so hot after all that exercise that we decided to cool off in the pool."

The look in my eyes was read clearly by Antonia Winters. Immediately she clambered out of the pool and began to dry off. She toweled her dark curly hair dry, then wrapped her red bikini with the same white towel. "Bart has asked me to call him by his first name. You won't mind if I do that, will you, Mrs. Sheffield?"

I looked her over appraisingly, wondering if she was truly responsible enough to take care of Jory and the twins. I liked her dark hair that sprang immediately into soft waves and curls to frame her face becomingly without makeup. She was about five eight and had as many voluptuous curves as Cindy, curves that Bart had despised on his sister. But from the way he was looking at the nurse, he approved of her figure very much.

"Toni," I began with control, "Jory, who I hired you to help, tried to call you to bring more diapers for the twins. He was out on the terrace with his children, and you should have been with *him,* not Bart. We hired you expecting you'd see that neither Jory or his children would be neglected."

Embarrassment heated her face. "I'm sorry, but Bart . . ."

and here she hesitated, seeming flustered as she glanced at him.

"It's all right, Toni. I accept the blame," said Bart. "I told her Jory was fine and able to take care of himself and the twins. It seems to me he has made a big point of being independent."

"See that this doesn't happen again, Toni," I said, disregarding Bart.

That damned man was going to drive all of us batty! Then I had a brilliant idea. "Bart, you and Toni would have done Jory a great favor if you had included him in your swimming party. He has full use of his arms. In fact, he has very powerful arms. And you should remember, Bart, that it's rather dangerous to have a pool like this without a fence, when two small children are around. So, Toni, with Jory's help, I'd like you both to begin teaching the twins how to swim . . . just in case."

Thoughtfully Bart stared at me, seeming to read my mind. He glanced again at Antonia, who was striding toward the house. "So you're going to stay on—why?"

"Don't you want us to stay?"

His smile radiated his dead father's charm. "Why, yes, of course, I do. Now that Toni has come to brighten up my lonely hours."

"You leave her alone, Bart!"

He grinned at me wickedly and began to backpaddle in the pool, performing a backward flip that brought him up near my feet to grasp my ankles so hard it hurt. For a moment I feared he'd pull me in the pool and ruin the silk dress I wore.

I stared down and met his dark, suddenly menacing, eyes, not flinching. "Let go of my ankles. I've already had my morning swim."

"Why not swim with me sometimes?"

What did he see that made the threat leave and sadness come, a look so wistful he leaned to kiss my toes with the pink nails that peeked through the sandals? Then *he* was breaking my heart. Speaking with the exact tones of his dead father: "I think that I shall never see, anyone quite as lovely as thee . . ." He looked up. "See, Mother, I've got a bit of artistic talent, too."

This was my moment. He was vulnerable, touched by something he saw on my face. "Yes, of course you do, but Bart, don't you feel just a little sorry that Cindy is gone?"

His dark eyes grew hard, remote. "No, not sorry. I'm glad she's gone. Did I prove to you what she really was?"

"You proved just how hateful you can be."

His eyes darkened more. A fiercely determined look came to frighten me. He glanced toward the house on hearing some slight shuffling noise. I looked that way. Joel had come out onto the grassy area that enclosed our long oval pool.

Silently Joel condemned us with his pale blue eyes, his long-fingered bony hands steepled beneath his chin. He tilted back his head and stared heavenwise. His weak, sweet voice came to us falteringly. "You keep the Lord waiting, Bart, while you waste your time."

Helplessly I watched Bart's eyes flood with guilt before he scampered from the pool. For a moment he stood in all his youthful male glory, his long, strong legs deeply bronze, his belly hard and flat, his shoulders wide, his muscles firm, rippling beneath his skin, the hair on his chest curling, and for a flashing second I thought he was flexing his strong muscles, preparing them for a lion's charge that would lunge him straight at Joel's throat. I tensed, wondering if he would even consider striking his uncle.

A cloud drifted over the sun. Somehow it caused shadows from the unlit poolside lamps to form a cross on the ground. Bart stared downward.

"You see, Bart," said Joel in a compelling voice I'd never heard before, "you neglect your duties and the sun disappears. God gives you his sign of the cross. He's always watching. He hears. He knows you. For you have been chosen."

Chosen for what?

Almost as if Joel had him hypnotized, Bart followed his great-uncle into the house, leaving me standing alone beside the pool. I hurried to tell Chris about Joel. "What can he mean, Chris—by saying that Bart has been chosen?"

Chris had just come in from visiting Jory and the twins. He forced me to sit, to relax. He even handed me my favorite mixed drink before he sat beside me on our small balcony overlooking the gardens and the mountains all around. "I had a few words with Joel minutes ago. It seems Bart hired workers to construct a small chapel in that small, empty room he favors for his prayers."

"A chapel?" I asked with bewilderment. "Why do we need a chapel?"

"I don't think it is meant for us, it's for Bart and Joel. A place where they can worship without going into the village and facing up to all the villagers who despise Foxworths. And if it's what Bart thinks will help him to find himself, for God's sake, don't say a word to condemn what he's doing with Joel. Cathy, I don't think Joel is an evil man. I think, more than anything he's trying to make himself a candidate for sainthood."

"A saint? Why, that would be like putting a halo above the head of Malcolm!"

Chris grew impatient with me. "Let Bart do what he wants. I've decided it's time we left here, anyway. I can't talk to you in this house and expect a sane answer. We'll move to Charlottesville and take Jory, the twins, and Toni with us, just as soon as I can find a house that's suitable."

Unknown to me, Jory had rolled himself into our suite of rooms, and he startled me when he spoke up. "Mom, Dad may be right. Joel could be the kind, benign saint he often appears. Sometimes I think we are both overly suspicious, and then again, you are so often right. I study Joel when he isn't watching. I think in many ways he's trying not to be what we most fear—a duplicate of the grandfather you both hated."

"I think all of this is ridiculous! Of course Joel isn't like his father, or else he wouldn't have hated him so much," Chris flared with sudden and unusual anger, his expression hard and totally out of patience not only with me but with Jory. "All this talk about souls being born again in later generations is absolute nonsense. We don't need to add complications to our lives when they're complicated enough already."

The next Monday Chris drove off again, heading back to the job he now loved just as much as he'd loved being a practicing physician. I stood staring after his car, feeling my rival was his blossoming love affair with biochemistry.

The dinner table seemed lonely without Chris or Cindy there, and Toni was upstairs putting the twins to bed, a fact that annoyed Bart greatly. He said several things to Jory about Toni, meant to imply she was already madly in love with him. This information didn't affect Jory one way or another; he was too deep in his own thoughts. He didn't say two words during the entire meal, even when eventually Toni did join us.

Another Friday evening came, and with it Chris returned, as once Daddy had come home every Friday. Somehow or other I was disturbed by the similarities of our lives compared to our parents' lives. Saturday we spent most of the day in the pool with Jory and the twins, with Toni and I supporting the babies as Chris helped Jory, who really didn't need much help. He took off across the water, expertly swimming, his strong arms more than making up for his legs that trailed limply behind. In the pool, with his legs under the water, he appeared so much himself that it showed on his happy face.

"Hey, this is great! Let's not move away from here yet. There aren't many houses in Charlottesville with pools like this. And I need the wide hallways and the elevator. And I've grown accustomed to Bart, and even to Joel."

"I might not be coming next weekend." Chris didn't meet

my eyes as he gave out this startling information at our Sunday breakfast table. He went on, steadfastly refusing to look my way or meet anyone's eyes. "There's a convention of biochemists in Chicago and I'd like to fly there. I'll be gone two weeks. If you want to join me, Cathy, I'd be grateful."

Bart keened his ears my way, digging his spoon into his ripe melon. His dark eyes held a quiet, waiting look, as if his entire life depended upon my answer. I wanted to go with Chris. In the worst way I wanted to escape this house, its problems, and to be alone with the man I loved. I wanted to be near him, but I had to deny him and make this last-ditch effort to save Bart. "I'd like very much to go with you, Chris. But Jory is embarrassed to ask Toni to do some intimate things for him. He needs me here."

"For Christ's sake! That's why we hired her! She's a nurse!"

"Chris, not under my roof do you take the Lord's name in vain."

Glaring at Bart for saying this, Chris rose to his feet. "I've suddenly lost my appetite. I'll eat breakfast in town, if I can regain an appetite for anything again."

He glared at me accusingly, flashed angry eyes at Bart, put his hand briefly on Jory's shoulder, and then he was off.

It was a good thing I'd asked him to find a nurse before this happened. Now he'd more than likely close his ears to what I wanted to do for my two sons who were, in one way or another, driving a wedge between us. Yet I couldn't leave Jory when I wasn't really sure Toni would take good care of him, not yet.

Toni joined us at our luncheon table wearing a fresh white uniform. The three of us at the table talked of the weather and of other mundane things while she sat with her eyes fixed on Bart. Beautiful soft, luminous, gray eyes filled with awe—and infatuation. It was so obvious I wanted to warn her to look at Jory, to see him and not the man who was most likely to destroy her.

Sensing her admiration, Bart turned on his charm, laughing and telling her some silly stories that mocked the little boy he'd been. Each word he said entranced her more, as Jory sat unnoticed in his detested chair, pretending to read the morning newspaper.

Day by day I could see Toni's infatuation with Bart growing, even as she kindly tended to the twins and patiently did what she could for Jory. My firstborn son stayed in a sullen mood, waiting constantly for telephone calls from Melodie, waiting for letters that didn't come, waiting for someone to help with things he used to do for himself and no longer could. I sensed his impatience when it took the servants so long to make up his bed, to tidy his rooms, to get out of his way and leave him alone.

He drove himself relentlessly, hired an art instructor to come three times a week and teach him different techniques. Work, work, work . . . he was driving himself to become the best artist possible, as once he'd dedicated himself to practicing his ballet exercises morning, night, and noon.

The four *D*s of the ballet world never died in some of us. Drive, Dedication, Desire, Determination.

"Do you think Toni is an adequate nursemaid for the twins?" I asked one evening as she took off down the road, pushing the twins in a double stroller. They loved being outdoors. Just to see the stroller brought squeals of pleasure and excitement. No sooner were the words out of my mouth than both Jory and I saw Bart racing to catch up with the nurse. Then the two of them were pushing Jory's children.

Uneasily I waited for Jory to speak. He said nothing. I glanced to see his bitter expression as he stared after Bart, now taking charge of his children, and the nurse I'd hired for him. It was as if I could read his thoughts. He didn't stand a chance with any woman now that he was in that chair. Now that his legs didn't dance, or even walk. Yet his doctors had told Chris and me that many handicapped men married and lived more or less normal lives. The percentages for marriage were much higher for disabled men than for handicapped women. "Women have more compassion than men. Most normal men think more of their own needs. It takes an exceptionally compassionate and understanding man to marry a woman who isn't physically normal."

"Jory, do you still miss Melodie?"

He stared gloomily before him, deliberately turning his eyes away from Toni and Bart, who'd paused to sit on a tree stump, apparently talking.

"I try not to do much thinking at all. It's a good way to keep from worrying about the years ahead, and how I'm going to manage. Eventually I will be alone, and I fear that day, fearing it's more than I can handle."

"Chris and I will always be with you, as long as you need us, and as long as we live; but long before either of us die, you will have found someone else. I know that will happen."

"How do you know that? I'm not sure I even want anyone. I'd be embarrassed now to have a wife. I'm trying to find something to do to fill the empty place that dancing left, and so far I haven't. The best thing in my life now are my twins and my parents."

I glanced again at the pair on the tree stump, just in time to see Bart jump up to lift the twins out of their double stroller, and then he was playing with them on the roadside grass. They liked everyone and even tried to charm Joel, who never touched them, never spoke to them as we did. Faintly we could hear the laughter of the little boy and girl who grew prettier and prettier each day. Bart looked and acted happy. I told myself that Bart needed someone too, just as desperately as Jory did. In a way, he needed someone even more than Jory. Inevitably Jory would find his way, with or without a wife.

We sat on and on, watching the pair who played with the twins. A full moon rose, appearing exceedingly large and golden in the twilight. A bird over the lake not so far away made its lonely cry. "What's that?" I asked, sitting up straighter. "I never heard a bird like that before down here."

"It's a loon," said Jory, looking in the direction of the lake. "Sometimes a storm blows them down this way. Mel and I used to rent a cottage on Mount Desert Isle, and we'd hear the cries of the loons and think them romantic. I wonder why we thought that. Now that cry just sounds forlorn, even eerie."

Out of the dark near the shrubbery, Joel spoke up. "There are some who say that lost souls inhabit the bodies of loons."

His benign voice said softly, "Those who can't find peace in their graves, Catherine. Those who hesitate between Heaven and Hell, looking back to their time on earth to see what they left unfinished. By looking back, they are trapped forever, or at least until their life's work is done."

I shivered as if a cold wind blew from the cemetery.

"Don't try to digest that, Mom," said Jory impatiently. "I wish I could use some of the descriptive adjectives that Cindy's age group can throw out with so much ease and not feel crass. Funny," he added more thoughtfully as Joel disappeared again in the darkness, "when I was in New York and I was disgusted, impatient, or angry, I used gutter language, too. Now, even when I think about saying those words, something keeps me from doing it."

He didn't have to explain. I knew exactly what he meant. It was all around us, in the atmosphere, the clarity of the mountain air, the closeness of the stars . . . the presence of a strict and demanding God. Everywhere.

The New Lovers

They met in the shadows. They kissed in the halls. They haunted the sunny, spacious gardens, roamed there in the moonlight, too. They swam together, played tennis together, strolled hand in hand by the lakeshores; they walked and jogged in the woods, had picnics by the pool, by the lake, in the woods; went dancing, to restaurants, then the theater, the movies.

They lived in their own world while we were apparently invisible, not seen or heard by them, not when they could look at each other across the dining table with dazzled eyes, as if they had the world by its tail and would never let it go. I was caught up in their romance, despite myself, thrilled to be around such glowing, beautiful young lovers, a matched pair with their dark hair almost the same color. I was happy and I was unhappy, delighted, yet so sad that it was not Jory who had found another woman to love. I wanted to warn Toni she was on treacherous ground, that Bart was not to be trusted, but then I'd look at Bart's radiant face, free of guilt or shame. This time he wasn't stealing anything that belonged to his brother. My critical words would fade away unspoken. Who was I to tell him whom he could love? I, of all people, had to stay quiet and let him have his chance. This was different than it had been with Melodie; Toni didn't belong to Jory.

Bart showed his happiness by becoming more confident, and with the security in his newfound love he forgot all his peculiar habits and his obsessive concern for neatness and allowed himself to relax in sports clothes. In the past, a thousand-dollar suit worn with expensive silk shirts and ties had given him his status symbols; now he didn't care, for Toni had given him his sense of worth. I could tell that for the first time in his life he seemed to have found stable ground to stand on.

He smiled and kissed me several times on the cheek. "I know what you wanted to happen, I do! I do! But it's me she loves, Mother! *Me!* Toni sees something wonderful and noble in *me!* Do you realize how that makes me feel? Melodie used to say she saw these qualities in me too, but I didn't feel noble or wonderful when I knew what harm I was doing to Jory. Now it's different. Toni's never been married, never had a lover before, although she's had lots of boyfriends. Mother, think of that! I am her first lover! It makes me feel so special to be the one she waited for. Mother, we have something wonderfully special. In me she sees the same things that *you see* in Jory."

"I think that's wonderful, Bart. I am happy for you both."

"Are you really?" His dark eyes turned serious as they sought to delve the truth of my statement. Before I could reply, Joel spoke from the open doorway of Bart's study.

"You stupid fool! You think that nurse really wants *you*? That woman sees the nobility of your money! It's your bank accounts she's after, Bart Foxworth! Have you observed the way she strolls through this house, her eyes half closed, obviously pretending that she's the mistress here! She doesn't love you. She is using you to get what every woman wants—money, control, power, and then more money—and once you marry her, she'll be set for life, even if you divorce her later on."

"Shut up!" barked Bart, turning to glare furiously at the old man. "You're jealous because I have no time left to spend with you. This is the cleanest, purest love of my life—and I'm not going to allow you to spoil it!"

Joel bowed his head meekly, appearing crestfallen as he templed his palms together under his chin before he slipped down the hall, obviously headed for that special small room that Bart had converted into a family chapel, although only Joel and Bart ever prayed there. I'd never even bothered to look inside.

I stood on my toes to kiss Bart's cheek, to hug him and wish him good luck. "I'm happy for you, Bart. Sincerely happy. I truthfully admit I had hopes that Toni might fall in love with Jory and make up for his loss of Melodie. I wanted the twins to have a mother while they are still babies. She would have the chance to learn to love them like her own, and they wouldn't remember any mother but her. But since it hasn't happened that way, seeing your happiness and hers makes me feel warm and good inside."

Delving, delving, those dark eyes that tried to read my soul. I had to ask: "Will you marry her?"

His hands rested lightly on my shoulders. "Yes, I'll ask her soon, after I make sure she isn't deceiving me. I have a method all planned to test her."

"Bart that's not fair. When you love you have to trust."

"To have blind faith in anyone but God is idiotic."

Only too well I remembered what Chris was always telling me. *Seek and you shall find.* I knew that well enough. I'd always been suspicious of the best that life gave me, and soon enough the best had disappeared.

"Mother . . . ," he began with surprising candor, "if Jory had kept his dancing legs, I know now that Melodie would never have let me touch her. She loved him, not me. She may have even pretended I was him, for sometimes I see a certain resemblance between us. I also think Melodie saw what she wanted to see, and she turned to me because he couldn't satisfy her physical needs any longer. I was a substitute lover for my brother, just as I've always come in second to Jory. Only with Toni have I come first."

"You're right this time, Bart. Jory is here and Toni isn't seeing him. She sees you, only you."

His lips took on an ironic twist. "Yeah . . . but you're not mentioning that I'm up on my legs and he's down. I've got the most money, and he's got a pittance in comparison. And he's already burdened with two children that won't be hers. Three strikes against Jory . . . so I win."

Now I was wanting him to win; he needed Toni ten times more than Jory did. My Jory was strong even when he was down, and Bart was so vulnerable and uncertain while he was perfectly healthy. "Bart, if you can't love yourself for what you are, how do you expect anyone else to? You've got to start believing that even without money Toni would still love you."

"We will soon find out," he said tonelessly, a certain something in his eyes that reminded me of Joel. He turned to dismiss me. "I've got work to do, Mother. See you later . . ." and he was smiling at me with more love than he'd shown since he was nine.

Contrary, complex, perplexing, challenging, the man my little troubled Bart had grown into . . .

Cindy had written to tell us how fabulous her summer days in the New England drama class were going. "We act in real productions, Momma, in real barns that are temporarily converted into theaters. I love it, really love every aspect of show biz."

Often I missed Cindy as the summer days passed. We all swam in the lake or pool, introducing the rapidly growing twins to all the wonders of nature. They had small teeth now and were both fast crawlers to wherever they wanted to go, and that was everywhere. Nothing was safe from their small, grasping hands that considered every object a food item. Flaxen blond hair turned into ringlets on their heads, pink lips turned rosy from the sun, and their cheeks stayed flushed with color, while their wide, innocent, blue eyes devoured all faces, swallowed down all first impressions.

We swept the glorious hot summer days away like iridescent dust settling into photograph albums that would never let the days and happy moments truly disappear. Snap snap snap went three different kinds of cameras, as Chris, Jory, and I took picture after picture of our wonderful twins. They adored being outdoors, sniffing the flowers, feeling the tree bark, watching the birds, squirrels, rabbits, raccoons, the ducks and geese that often invaded our swimming pool, only to be chased off quickly by the adults.

Before I knew it, summer was gone and autumn was upon us again. This year Jory could enjoy this glorious season of splendor in the mountains. The trees foresting the mountainside flamed into spectacular colors.

"A year ago I was in Hell," said Jory, staring at the trees and mountains and glancing down at his left hand, which no longer wore a wedding band of gold. "My final divorce papers came, and you know, I didn't feel anything but numb. I lost my wife the day I lost the use of my legs, and still I'm surviving and finding that life does go on and it can be good, even when experienced from a chair."

My arms went around him. "Because you have strength, Jory, and determination. You have your children, so your marriage was not without its rewards. You still have celebrity status, don't forget that, and you can, if you want, start teaching ballet classes."

"Nope, I can't neglect my son and daughter, not when they don't have a mother." Then he tilted his head back to smile at me. "Not that you don't make a super mother figure, but I want you and Dad to live your own lives, not be burdened down with small children who might hamper your lifestyle."

Laughing, I tousled his dark curls. "What lifestyle, Jory? Chris and I are happy where we are, with our sons and grand-children."

The bright fall days slowly chilled, bringing the acrid scent of woodfires burning. I was drawn outside early each day, taking Jory and the twins with me. The twins were pulling themselves up to stand by holding on to hands or furniture. Deirdre had even taken a few faltering, wide-legged steps, her bottom fat with diapers and plastic panties, covered by other pretty panties that she seemed to adore. Darren seemed more than content with his fast crawl that took him speedily wherever he wanted to go—which was everywhere. I'd even caught him crawling backward down those high front stairs, with Deirdre close behind him.

On this fine early October day, Deirdre rode on Jory's lap, happily jabbering to herself, as I carried a more subdued Darren, using the new dirt trails that Bart had considerately ordered leveled so Jory could drive his chair through the woods. Tree roots that might have tripped up his chair had been removed at considerable cost. Now that Bart had a love of his own, he treated his brother with much more consider-ation and respect.

"Mother, Bart and Toni are lovers, aren't they?" Jory shot out unexpectedly.

"Yes," I admitted with reluctance.

He said something then that startled me. "Isn't it odd how we're born into families and have to accept what we're given? We don't ask for each other, yet we're glued all our lives to those whom we'd never speak to twice if they weren't blood related."

"Jory, you don't really dislike Bart that much, do you?"

"I'm not speaking of Bart, Mom. He's been rather decent lately. It's that old man who says he's your uncle that I dislike. The more I see of him the more I detest him. At first when he showed up, I pitied him. Now I look at Joel and see something evil beneath those faded blue eyes. Somehow or other he reminds me of John Amos Jackson. I believe he's using us, Mom. Not just for practical reasons of having a home and food to eat . . . he has something else in mind. Just today, I happened to hear Joel whispering to Bart in the back hall. I think from what I overheard, Bart is going to tell Toni the complete truth about his past—his psychological problems—and the fact that if he's ever committed to an institution he'll lose his entire inheritance. He's being urged to do this by Joel. Mom, he shouldn't tell her! If Toni truly loves him, she'll accept the fact he's had his problems. From all I can see, he's normal now, and very brilliant at making money grow."

My head bowed. "Yes, Jory. Bart told me himself, but he keeps putting off that revelation, as if he himself believes it's his money she's after."

Jory nodded, holding fast to Deirdre, who was trying to climb down from his lap and explore by herself. Just seeing his sister do that made Darren anxious to be free as well.

"Has Joel ever said anything to indicate he might try to break his sister's will and take the money that Bart expects to inherit the day he's thirty-five?"

Jory's laugh was short, dry. "Mom, that old man never says anything that isn't a *double entendre*. He doesn't like me and avoids me as much as possible. He disapproves of the fact that once I was a dancer and wore skimpy costumes. He disapproves of you. I see him watching you with narrowed eyes, and he mutters to himself, 'Just like her mother . . . only worse, far worse.' I'm sorry to tell you that, but he's scary, Mom, really a sinister old man. He looks at Dad with hatred. And he prowls the house at night. Since I've been disabled, my ears have become very sharp. I hear the floorboards in the hall outside my door squeak, and sometimes my door is opened ever so slightly. It's Joel, I know it's him."

"But why would he be peeking in on you?"

"I don't know."

I bit down on my lower lip, imitating Bart's nervous habit. "Now you are frightening me, Jory. I have reasons to think he means harm for all of us, too. I believe it was Joel who smashed the ship you made for Bart, and I truly believe Joel never mailed off those Christmas invitations. He wanted Bart to be hurt, so he took them up to his room, removed the R.S.V.P. cards, signed them as if the invitations were accepted, and then mailed them back to Bart. It's the only explanation of why no one showed up."

"Mom . . . why didn't you tell me this before?"

How could I tell him of all my suspicions about Joel without his reacting much like Chris had? Chris had completely rejected my story of how Joel might have planned to hurt Bart. And sometimes even I thought I was much too imaginative and gave Joel credit for being more evil than he actually was.

"And what's more, Jory, I think it was Joel who overheard the servants in the kitchen talking about Cindy meeting that boy, Victor Wade, and he quickly passed that information along to Bart. How else would Bart have known? Servants are to Bart like designs on the wallpaper, not worthy of his notice—it's Joel who does the eavesdropping so he can report what they say to Bart."

"Mom . . . I think you could very well be right about the ship, the invitations, and Cindy, too. Joel has something in mind for all of us, and I'm afraid it's not for our good."

Deep in thought, Jory had to tell me twice that I should put his son on his lap, to ride on his other leg, and we'd make better progress through the woods. Even one twin was a load to carry for a long distance, and more than willingly I lowered Darren to his father's lap. Deirdre squealed her delight and hugged her small brother. "Mom, I believe if Toni really loves Bart enough, she'll stay, no matter what his background—or how much he inherits."

"Jory . . . that's exactly what he's trying to prove."

~   ~   ~

Around midnight, when I was almost asleep, a soft tapping sounded on my door. It was Toni.

She came in wearing a pretty rosy peignoir, her long dark hair loose and flowing, her long legs appearing as she neared my bed. "I hope you don't mind, Mrs. Sheffield . . . I waited for a night when your husband wasn't with you."

"Call me Cathy," I said as I sat up and reached for my own robe. "I'm not sleeping. Just lying here thinking, and I appreciate another woman to talk to."

She began to pace the floor of my large bedroom. "I've got to speak to a woman, someone who can understand more readily than a man, so that's why I'm here."

"Sit down. I'm ready to listen." Tentatively she perched on a love seat, twisting a tress of her dark hair over and over, sometimes pulling it in between her lips.

"I'm terribly upset . . . Cathy. Bart's told me some very disturbing facts today. He mentioned that you already know about us, that he loves me and I love him. I think you have caught us a few times in one room or another in rather intimate moments. And I thank you for pretending not to notice, so I wouldn't feel embarrassed. I've got all kinds of notions that most people think are obsolete."

She gave me a nervous smile, seeking my understanding. "The moment I looked at Bart I fell in love. There's something so magnetic about his dark eyes, so mystical and compelling. And then tonight he took me into his office, sat down behind his desk and like a cold and distant stranger told me a long story about himself, as if he were talking about someone else, someone he didn't like. I felt like a business client whose every reaction was being judged. I didn't know just what he thought I'd reveal. It occurred to me he expected me to appear shocked or disgusted, and at the same time his eyes were so beseeching.

"He loves you, Cathy . . . loves you almost to the point of

718   Seeds of Yesterday

obsession," she said, making me sit up straighter, stunned with her crazy notion. "I don't even think he realizes how much he adores you. He thinks he hates you because of your relationship with your brother." She flushed and lowered her eyes. "I'm sorry I have to even mention this, but I'm trying to be open."

"Go on," I urged.

"Because Bart feels he should hate you for that, he tries to. Still, something in you, in him, keeps him from ever really deciding which emotion will reign, love or hatred. He wants a woman like you, only he doesn't know that." She paused, looked up to meet my wide and interested eyes. "Cathy, I told him what I honestly thought, that he was looking for a woman like his mother. He went pale, almost dead white. He appeared totally shocked at the idea."

She paused to watch my reaction. "Toni, you have to be wrong. Bart doesn't want a woman like me, but the exact opposite."

"Cathy, I've studied psychology, and Bart does protest too much about you, so while I listened, I tried to keep an open mind. Bart impounded also the fact that he's never been mentally stable, and that any day he could lose his mind and, with it, his inheritance. Why, it's as if he wants me to hate him, to cut all ties and run away . . . so I am going to run," she sobbed, her hands covering her face so that her tears trickled between her long, elegant fingers. "As much as I love him and I thought he loved me, I can't continue to love and sleep with a man who has so little faith in my integrity—and worse than that, in his own."

Quickly I was on my feet and striding to comfort her. "Don't go, please, Toni, stay. Give Bart another chance. Give him time to think this through. Bart has always been inclined to act on impulse. He also has that old great-uncle who whispers in his ears, telling him you love him for his money alone. It's not Bart who is crazy, but Joel, who tells Bart what he should look for in a future wife."

Hopefully she stared at me, trying to check her flow of
tears. I went on, determined to help Bart escape the childhood sense of being unworthy and the adult influence of Joel.
"Toni, the twins adore you, and there's only so much I can
do. Stay to help with Jory and help me keep him entertained.
He needs professional help to maintain physical progress,
too. And keep in mind that Bart is unpredictable, sometimes
unreasonable, but he loves you. He's told me several times
how much he loves and admires you. He's testing your love
for him by telling you what is the truth. He *was* unstable mentally when he was a child, but there were good reasons that
caused his mental disturbance. Hold fast to your belief in him
and you can save him from himself and his great-uncle."

Toni stayed.

Life went on as usual.

Deirdre, before her first birthday, was walking anywhere she chose to go, or we'd allow. Small and dainty, her
golden curls bobbing, she charmed us all with her incessant
babbling, which soon turned into simple words, leading the
way for Darren to follow. Once she heard herself speak, she
couldn't stop. Although Darren was slower to walk, he was
not slower to investigate dark, dim places that scared his twin
sister. He was the incessant explorer, the one who had to pick
everything up and examine it, so I was forced to put expensive
and delicate objets d'art on shelves he couldn't reach.

A letter came from Cindy stating that she was homesick
for her family and wanted to come home and spend Thanksgiving through Christmas, but she was invited to a fabulous
New Year's Eve party and would fly back to attend that.

I gave the letter to Jory to read. Smiling, he looked
up. "Have you told her about Bart and his love affair with
Toni?"

"No," I said, for I was going to let her see and find out
for herself. Of course, before she'd left last summer, Toni
had been with us only two days, but at that time Cindy had

been so discontented she hadn't paid attention to what she thought was just more hired help.

The day came when we were expecting Cindy home for the holidays, a bitterly cold day. Chris and I were at the airport when she came through the gate, dressed in bright crimson, looking so beautiful all the people in the airport turned to stare her way. "Mom! Dad!" she cried happily, flinging herself first into my arms and then into Chris's. "I'm so happy to see you. And before you warn me, I promise to do and say nothing that will upset the applecart named Bart. This Christmas I'm going to be the perfect sweet little angel he wants me to be . . . and no doubt even then he'll find something to criticize, but I won't care." Then she was asking about Jory, about the twins, and had we heard from Melodie? And how was the new nurse working out? And was our chef the same? Was Trevor still as sweet as ever?

Somehow or other, Cindy gave me the feeling we were, after all, a real family . . . and that was enough to make me very happy. Once she was in the grand foyer, Toni and Bart, with Jory holding the twins on his lap, were all waiting to sing out greetings. Only Joel hung back and refused to welcome out daughter home. Bart shook her hand in a warm fashion, and that gave me such relief and pleasure. Cindy laughed. "Someday, brother Bart, you are going to be really overjoyed to see me, and maybe then you can allow your chaste lips to kiss my unholy cheek."

He flushed and glanced uneasily at Toni. "I've got a confession, Toni. In the past, Cindy and I haven't always gotten along."

"To say the least," said Cindy. "But rest easy, Bart, I'm not here to make trouble. I didn't bring a boyfriend. I'm going to behave myself. I've come because I love my family and can't stand being away during the holidays."

The holidays that year couldn't have been better, unless we could have turned back the clock and made Jory whole again, and restored Melodie to him.

In a matter of a few days, Cindy and Toni became close friends. Toni went shopping with us as Jory took care of the twins with the help of a maid. Time flew as it never did when Cindy wasn't around. The four years' difference between her age and Toni's didn't matter. Generously Cindy loaned Toni one of her prettiest dresses for that Christmas Eve trip into Charlottesville where she could dance with one of the doctor's sons she'd met the year before. Jory went as well but sat looking unhappy while Bart danced with Toni.

"Mom," whispered Cindy when she came back to our table, "I think Bart has changed. He's a much warmer person now. Why, I'm even beginning to think he's human."

Smiling, I nodded, but still I couldn't help thinking of Joel and the way he and Bart spent so much time in that small room they'd converted into a chapel. Why? There were churches all around.

New Year's Eve came and Bart and Toni decided to fly to New York with Cindy and celebrate there. Leaving Chris, Jory, and I to do the best we could without them. We used this opportunity to invite a few of Chris's colleagues to our home, along with their spouses, knowing that Joel would report this to Bart when he came back. Still I didn't care.

I bumped into Joel that night as I left the nursery. Smiling, I met his eyes. "Well, Joel, it seems my son won't be as dependent on you once he marries Toni."

"He'll never marry her," said Joel in his harsh, forecasting way. "He's like all young men in love, a fool who can't see the truth. She wants his money, not him, and he'll soon find that out."

"Joel," I said softly, pityingly, "Bart is a very handsome young man, and a passionate one, and even if he were a ditch digger, the girls would fall for him. When he lets go of his determination to show the world how brilliant he is, he's a very likeable young man. Leave him alone. Stop trying to mold him into something that will please you but might not suit him. Let him find his own way . . . for that will be what's the right thing for him, even if it's not what you have in mind."

Scornfully he looked me over. "What do you know about what's right and wrong, niece? Haven't you already proved you have no perception of morality? Bart will never find himself without my guidance. Hasn't he been searching all his life and failed? Did you help him then—do you help him now? God will provide for Bart, Catherine, while you continue to plague Bart with your sins."

He turned from me and shuffled off down the hall.

While Bart was in New York with Toni and Cindy, Jory completed his most impressive watercolor depicting Foxworth Hall. He'd darkened the rosy bricks to a dusty and dreary old ash rose, made the immaculate gardens overgrown with weeds; the cemetery was moved in closer so that tombstones showed off to the left, casting long shadows that snared the Hall in their web. Foxworth Hall looked two thousand years old and full of specters.

"Put that thing away, Jory, and try a happier subject," I said, feeling strange. I think that was the only watercolor Jory painted that didn't please me.

Bart and Toni flew home from New York, and immediately I noticed the difference. They didn't look or speak to each other but went quietly to their rooms without spilling out happy tales of the fun they'd had. When I tried to broach the subject, both refused to give me details. "Leave me alone!" stormed Bart. "She's just another woman after all."

"I can't tell you, Cathy," cried Toni. "He doesn't love me, that's all!"

January fled by, and then came the February when we celebrated Jory's thirty-first birthday. We had a huge cake baked for him in the shape of a heart covered with red frosting to represent the Valentine gift he'd been, with his name in white icing, trimmed with white roses. The twins were delighted, squealing when they saw him blow out the candles. Both were

seated in highchairs, one on each side of him, and before Jory
could slice down into the cake, Deirdre and Darren reached
simultaneously and grabbed great handfuls of the soft fresh
cake. We all stared at the mess they'd made of a work of art,
while they jammed the cake into their mouths and smeared
their faces with red.

"What's left is still edible," said Jory with a laugh.

Silently Toni got up to wash the hands and faces of two
very messy little one-year-olds. Bart followed her every movement with sad, wistful eyes.

We were trapped, all of us, in the winter blizzards, caught
in frozen time, making do with each other when others would
have been welcomed, even as some of us kept on loving the
wrong person.

The day came when the snow stopped and Chris could
drive back to his cancer research team, which worked on and
on without ever reaching any conclusions that were absolute.

Another blizzard kept Chris in Charlottesville, and two
weeks dragged slowly by, although we talked every day when
the lines weren't down—but they weren't comfortable conversations. Always I had the sensation that someone was listening in on another telephone.

Chris called on the next Thursday to say he'd be home,
have the home fires burning, the steak charcoaled, the salad
fresh, ". . . and wear that new white nightgown I gave you for
Christmas."

Eagerly I waited at an upstairs window to spot Chris's
blue car coming around the drive, and when I did, I raced
down the stairs to the garage to be there when he left his car.
We came together like long separated lovers who might never
have the chance to kiss and hug again. But it wasn't until we
were in the sanctuary of our rooms with the doors closed that
my arms slipped around his neck again. "You still feel cold.
So, just to warm you up, you are going to hear all the dull
things that go on here—and in exquisite detail. Last night

I overheard Joel telling Bart again that Toni is only after his money."

"Is she?" he asked, nibbling on my ear.

"I don't think so, Chris. I think she sincerely loves him, but I'm not sure how long her love will last, or his. It seems when they went with Cindy to New York for New Year's Eve, Bart scolded Cindy ruthlessly again, humiliating her in a nightclub, and Cindy's letter said he later on jumped on Toni for dancing with another man. He so shocked Toni with his brutal accusations that she hasn't been the same since. I think she's afraid of his jealousy."

His eyebrows shot up quizzically, though he said nothing to remind me he was "my Bart." "And Jory, how is he?"

"He's adjusting marvelously, but he's lonely and melancholy, wanting Melodie to write. He wakes up in the night and calls her name. Sometimes he inadvertently calls me Mel. I found a small article about Melodie in *Variety*. Melodie has rejoined their old ballet company and has a new partner. I showed that to Jory just today, feeling he should know. His eyes went blank. He put away his watercolors just when he'd washed in the most beautiful winter sky and refused to finish the painting. Anyway, I put the painting in a safe place, thinking he can finish it later."

"Yes . . . everything will work out." And with that we surrendered to each other, forgetting our problems in the ecstasy we knew so well how to create.

Time flew by, wasted by small, trivial things. Daily arguments between Bart and Toni concerning his attitude toward Cindy, whom Toni really liked, as well as his suspicions of her loyalty to him and only him. "You shouldn't have danced with that man you just met!" and on and on. There were also daily fights between them about the twins and how they should be handled, and soon enough the narrow gulf between them widened into an ocean.

We wore on each other's nerves. The sight, the sound, the closeness of living so tightly knit had its toll.

I contributed nothing to help and nothing to harm as Bart and Toni fought it out. I felt they had to solve their differences between themselves, and I would only have added complications. Once again Bart started visiting the local bars, often staying out all night. I suspected he spent many a night in brothels, or else he'd found someone else in the city. Toni spent more time with the twins, and since Jory was trying to teach them to dance and speak more clearly, naturally she spent more time with him as well.

March finally arrived with its fierce rains and winds, but also with welcome faint heralding signs of spring. I watched Toni carefully for signs of taking notice of Jory as a man and not as a patient. His eyes followed wherever she went. There were a few weeks that year when I was under the weather with a severe cold, and she took over all duties, including washing Jory's back, massaging his long legs that were bit by bit losing their fine shape. I hated seeing his beautiful legs turn into thin sticks. I suggested to Toni that she massage them several times a day. "He was always very proud of his legs, Toni. They served him so well and looked so great in tights. So, even if they don't walk or dance, or even move, do what you can to see they don't lose all their shape. Then he can retain a bit of his pride."

"Cathy, his legs are still beautiful; thin, but well shaped. He's a wonderful man, so kind and understanding and naturally cheerful. And you know, for the longest time I didn't see anyone but Bart."

"Do you think of Bart as beautiful?"

Her expression changed and grew hard. "I used to. Now I'm seeing that he's very handsome, but not beautiful in the way that Jory is. Once I thought he was perfect, but during our stay in New York, he showed so much ugliness toward me and Cindy that I began to see him differently. He was nasty and cruel to both of us. Before I knew what was happening, he embarrassed me in a nightclub by jumping on me about my dress, when it was a perfectly nice dress. Maybe it was cut a little low, but all the girls wear dresses like that. I came home from that trip a little afraid of him. Every day my fear of him grows; he seems too harsh about harmless events and believes that everyone is wicked. I think he corrupts himself with his thoughts and forgets that beauty comes from the soul. Just last night he accused me of trying to arouse his brother sexually. He couldn't talk like that to me if he really loved me. Cathy, he'll never love me as I want and need to be loved. I woke up this morning feeling a huge emptiness in my heart, realizing that what I felt for Bart is over. He's ruined what we had by letting me know what I'm in for if I marry him," she went on brokenly. "He's got an invisible model of the perfect woman, and I'm not perfect. He thinks your one flaw is your love for Chris . . . and if he ever found a woman he believed is perfect in the beginning, I'm sure he'll keep looking until he finds something he can hate about her. So I've given up on Bart."

I felt embarrassed to ask what I did, but still I had to know. "But . . . are you and Bart still lovers, despite your disagreements?"

Furiously she shook her head. "NO! Of course not! He's changing every day into someone I really can't even like. He's found religion, Cathy, and according to the way he tells it, religion is going to be his salvation. Every day he tells me I should pray more, go to church . . . and stay away from Jory. If he keeps it up I think I may well end up hating him, and I don't want that to happen. We had something so beautiful between us in the beginning. I want to keep that special time like a flower I can press between the pages of my memory."

She stood up to go, smearing her tears with her balled handkerchief, tugging down her tight white skirt and trying to smile. "If you want me to quit so you can hire a new nurse for Jory and his children, I'll do that."

"No, Toni, stay on," I answered quickly, afraid she'd go anyway. I didn't want her to leave now that I knew without a doubt that she didn't love Bart anymore, and Jory had finally given up hope of Melodie returning to him. And with the final hope dead, Jory had at last turned his eyes on the woman he believed was his brother's mistress.

As soon as possible I was going to inform him differently. But . . . even as Toni left the room, I sat on and on, thinking of Bart and how sad it was that he couldn't hold on to love once he had it. Did he deliberately destroy love, afraid it would enslave him as he often accused me of having enslaved Chris, my own brother?

The endless days crept by. No longer did Toni's eyes follow Bart with wistful yearning, pleading mutely with him to love her again as he had in the beginning. I began to admire the way she could keep her poise regardless of some of the insulting innuendoes Bart made during meal times. He took her former love for him and turned it against her, making it seem she was loose, depraved, immoral, and he'd been wrongfully seduced.

Dinner after dinner, sitting there and watching the two drift further and further apart, driven there by all the ugly words Bart found so easy to say.

Toni took my place and played the games I used to entertain Jory with . . . only she could do so much more to light up his eyes and make him feel a man again.

Bit by bit the days began to mellow, the brown grass showed spikes of fresh green, the crocus came up in the woods, the daffodils blossomed, the tulips fired into flame, and the Grecian windflowers that Jory and I had planted everywhere the grass didn't grow turned the hills into paint-smeared palettes. Chris and I stood again on the balcony watching the geese return north as we stared up at our old friend and sometimes enemy, the moon. I couldn't take my eyes from the winged skein as they disappeared beyond the hills.

Life grew better with the coming of summer, when the snow couldn't keep Chris away during the weekends. Tensions eased now that we had the great outdoors to escape to.

In June the twins were one year and six months old and able to run freely anywhere we would permit. We had swings from which they couldn't fall hung from tree limbs, and how happy they were to be swung high . . . or what they considered high enough to be dangerous. They pulled the blossoms off the best of my flowers, but I didn't care—we had thousands blooming, enough to fill all the rooms with daily fresh bouquets.

Now Bart was insisting that not only the twins should attend church services but Chris and I and Jory and Toni as well. It seemed a small enough thing to do. Each Sunday we sat in our front-row pews and stared up at the beautiful stained-glass window behind the pulpit. The twins always sat between Jory and me. Joel would don a black robe as he preached fire-and-brimstone sermons. Bart sat beside me, holding my hand in such a tight grip I had to listen or have my bones broken. Next to Toni, deliberately separated from me by my second son, was Chris. I knew those sermons were meant for us, to save us from eternal hellfires. The twins were restless, like all children their age, and didn't like the pew, the confinement, the dullness of the overlong services. Only when we stood up to sing hymns did they stare up at us and seem enchanted.

"Sing, sing," encouraged Bart, leaning to pinch tiny arms or tug on golden locks.

"Take your hands off my children!" snapped Jory. "They will sing or not sing, as is their choice."

It was on again, the war between brothers.

Autumn again, then Halloween when Chris and I took the twins by their small hands and led them to the one neighbor we considered "safe" enough not to recriminate us or our children. Our little goblins timidly accepted their first Halloween trick-or-treat candy, then screamed all the way home with the thrill of having two Hershey bars and two packs of chewing gum of their very own.

Winter came, and Christmas and the New Year started without anything special happening, for this year Cindy didn't fly home. She was too busy with her budding career to do more than call long distance or write short but informative letters.

Bart and Toni now moved in different universes.

Perhaps I was not the only one who guessed that Jory had fallen deeply in love with Toni, now that all attempts at restoring a brotherly relationship with Bart had failed. I couldn't blame Jory, not when Bart had taken Melodie and driven her away and was even now trying to hold fast to Toni just because he could detect Jory's growing interest. To keep Jory from having her, he was turning again toward Toni . . .

Loving Toni gave Jory new reasons for living. It was written in his eyes, written on his new zeal for getting up early and beginning all those difficult exercises, standing for the first time, using parallel bars we'd had put in his room. As soon as the water was warm enough, he swam the length of our large swimming pool three times in early mornings and late evenings.

Maybe Toni was still waiting for Bart to make her his wife, though she often denied this. "No, Cathy, I don't love him now. I only pity him for not knowing who or what he is and, more importantly, what he wants for himself but money and more money." It occurred to me that, inexplicably, Toni was as rooted here as any one of us.

The Sunday church services made me nervous and tired. The strong words shouted from the weak lungs of an old man brought back terrifying memories of another old man I'd seen but once. *Devil's issue. Devil's spawn.* Evil seed planted in the wrong soil. Even wicked thoughts were judged the same as wicked deeds—and what wasn't sinful to Joel? Nothing. Nothing at all.

"We're not going to attend anymore," I stated firmly to Chris, "and we were fools to even try to please Bart. I don't like the kind of ideas Joel is planting in the twins' impressionable young heads." True to Chris's agreement, he and I refused to attend "church" services or allow the twins to hear all that shouting about Hell and its punishments.

Joel came to the play area in the gardens, under the trees where there were a sandbox, swings, a slide, and a spin-a-round that the twins loved to play on. It was a fine sunny day in July, and he looked rather touching and sweet as he sat between the twins and began to teach them how to do cat cradles, twining the string and intriguing the curious twins. They abandoned the sandpile with the pretty awning overhead and sat beside him, looking up at him in bright anticipation of making a new friend out of an old enemy.

"An old man knows many little skills to entertain small children. Do you know I can make airplanes and boats out of paper? And the boats will sail on the water."

Their round eyes of amazement didn't please me. I frowned. Anyone could do that.

"Save your energies for writing new sermons, Joel," I said, meeting his meek, watery eyes. "I grew tired of the old ones. Where is the New Testament in your sermons? Teach Bart about that. Christ *was* born. He did deliver his Sermon on the Mount. Deliver to him *that* particular sermon, *Uncle*. Speak to us of forgiveness, of doing unto others as you would have done unto you. Tell us of the bread cast upon the waters of forgiveness returning to us tenfold."

"Forgive me if I have been neglectful of our Lord's one truly begotten son," he said humbly.

"Come, Cory, Carrie," I called, getting up to leave. "Let's go see what Daddy is doing."

Joel's lowered head jerked upright. His faded blue eyes took on heaven's deeper blue. I bit down on my tongue to observe the twisted smile that Joel displayed. He nodded sagely. "Yes, I know. To you they are the 'other twins'—those born of evil seed planted in the wrong soil."

"How dare you say that to me!" I flared.

I didn't realize then that by occasionally calling Jory's twins by the names of my beloved dead twins I was only adding fuel to the fire—a fire that was already, unknown to me, sending up small red sparks of brimstone.

Comes a Morning Dark

A storm threatened a perfectly lovely summer day with dark ominous clouds, forcing me to hurry outdoors to cut my morning flowers while they were still fresh with dew. I drew up short when I saw Toni snipping yellow and white daisies that she brought to Jory in a small milkglass vase. She put them near the table where Jory was working on another watercolor showing a lovely dark-haired woman very much like Toni picking flowers. I was hidden by the dense shrubbery and could take a peek now and then without either one seeing me. For some strange reason, my intuitiveness warned me to stay quiet and say nothing.

Jory thanked Toni politely, gave her a brief smile, swished his brush in clean water, dipped it in his blue mixture and added a few touches here and there. "Never can seem to mix the exact color of the sky," he murmured as if to himself. "The sky is always changing . . . oh, what I could give to have Turner for my teacher . . ."

She stood watching the sun play on Jory's waving blue-black hair. He hadn't shaved, and that made him look twice as virile, although not as fresh. Suddenly he looked up and noticed her overlong stare. "I apologize for the way I look, Toni," he said as if embarrassed. "I was very anxious to be up and busy this morning before the rain sets in and spoils another day for me. I hate the days when I can't stay outside."

Still she said nothing, only stood there, the peekaboo sun glorifying her beautifully tanned skin. His eyes drifted over her clean, fresh face even before he briefly dropped his eyes and took in the rest of her. "Thank you for the daisies. They're not supposed to tell. What is the secret?"

Swooping down, she picked up a few sketches he'd tossed at the wastebasket and missed. Before she could drop them in the can, she gave the subjects her attention, and then her lovely face flushed. "You've been sketching me," she said in a low tone.

"Throw them away!" he said sharply. "They're no good. I can paint flowers and hills and make fairly good landscapes, but portraits are so damned difficult. I can never capture the essence of you."

"I think these are very good," she objected, studying them again. "You shouldn't throw away your sketches. May I keep them?"

Carefully she tried to flatten out the wrinkles, and then she was placing them on a table and stacking heavy books upon them. "I was hired to take care of you and the twins. But you never ask me to do anything for you. And your mother likes to play with the twins in the mornings, so that gives me extra time, time enough to do many things for you. What can I do for you?"

The brush dripping with gray colored the bottoms of clouds before he paused and turned his chair so he could look at her. A wry smile moved his lips. "Once I could have thought of something. Now I suggest you leave me alone. Crippled men don't play very exciting games, I'm sorry to say."

Appearing weary with defeat, she crumpled down on a long, comfortable chaise. "Now you're saying to me what Bart does all the time—'Go away,' he shouts, 'Leave me alone,' he yells. I didn't think you'd be the same."

"Why not?" he asked with his own bitterness. "We're brothers, half brothers. We both have our hateful moments—and it's better to leave us alone then."

"I thought he was the most wonderful man alive," she said sadly. "But I guess I can't trust my own judgment anymore. I believed Bart wanted to marry me—now he yells and orders me out of sight. Then he calls me back and begs forgiveness. I want to leave this house and never come back—but something holds me here, keeps whispering that it's not time for me to go . . ."

"Yes," said Jory, beginning to paint again with careful strokes, tipping the board to make his washes run and create "accidental" blendings that sometimes worked out beautifully. "That's Foxworth Hall. Once you enter its portals, you seldom are seen again."

"Your wife escaped."

"So she did; more credit to her than I believed when it happened."

"You sound so bitter."

"I'm not bitter, I'm sour, like a pickle. I enjoy my life. I am caught between Heaven and Hell in a kind of purgatory where ghosts of the past roam the hallways at night. I can hear the clank and clonk of their restraining chains, and I can only be grateful they never appear, or perhaps the silent tread of my rubber-rimmed wheels scares them off."

"Why do you stay if you feel that way?"

Jory shoved away from his painting table, then riveted his dark eyes on her. "What the hell are you doing here with me? Go to your lover. Apparently you like the way he treats you, or easily enough *you* could escape. You aren't chained here with memories, with hopes or dreams that don't come true. You aren't a Foxworth, nor a Sheffield. This Hall holds no chains to blind you."

"Why do you hate him?"

"Why *don't* you hate him?"

"I do sometimes."

"Trust your sometime judgment and get out. Get out before you are made, by osmosis, into one of us."

"And what are you?"

Jory drove his chair to the rim of the flagstones, where the flowerbeds began, and stared off toward the mountains. "Once I was a dancer, and I never thought beyond that. Now that I can't dance, I have to presume that I am nothing of importance to anyone. So I stay, thinking I belong here more than I belong anywhere else."

"How can you say what you just did? Don't you believe you're important to your parents, your sister, and most of all to your children?"

"They don't really need me, do they? And my parents have each other. My children have them. Bart has you. Cindy has her career. That leaves me the odd man out."

Toni stood, stepped behind his chair and began to massage his neck with skillful fingers. "Does your back still bother you at night?"

"No," he said in a hoarse voice. But it did, I knew it did, I knew it did. Hidden behind the shrubs, I went right on snipping roses, sensing they didn't know I was there.

"If ever your back aches again, buzz for me and I'll give you a massage to take away the pain."

Whirling his chair around in a full about-face, Jory confronted her fiercely. She had to jump back out of the way or be knocked down. "So, it seems if you can't get one brother, you'll settle for the other—the crippled one who can't possibly resist your many charms? Thanks, but no thanks. My mother will massage my aching back."

Slowly she drifted away, turning twice to look back at

him. She didn't know that she left him staring after her with his heart in his eyes. She closed a French door behind her quietly. I stopped cutting roses for the breakfast table and sat on the grass. Behind me the twins were playing "church."

Following Chris's instructions, we were doing what we could to increase their vocabulary daily, and our instructions seemed to be working wonders.

"And the Lord said to Eve, go forth from this place." Darren's childish voice was full of giggles.

I turned to look.

Both children had removed their brief sunsuits and taken off small white sandals. Deirdre stuck a leaf on her brother's small male organ, then stared down at her own private place. She frowned. "Dare . . . what's sinning?"

"Like running," answered her brother. "Bad when you're barefoot."

They both giggled and jumped up to run toward me. I caught them in my arms and held their soft, warm, nude bodies close, raining kisses on their faces. "Have you eaten your breakfast?"

"Yes, Granny. Toni fed us grapefruit, which we hate. We ate everything but the eggs. Don't like eggs."

That was Deirdre who did most of the talking for Darren, just as Carrie had been Cory's voice most of the time.

"Mom—how long have you been there?" called Jory. He sounded annoyed, a bit embarrassed.

Rising, I held the naked twins in my arms, and headed for Jory. "I found Toni in the pool teaching the twins how to swim, so I took over and asked her to look in on you. They're doing very nicely in the water now, paddling all around with confidence. Why didn't you join us this morning?"

"Why did you keep yourself hidden?"

"Just snipping my morning roses, Jory. You know I do that every day. It's the one thing that makes this house cozy, the cut flowers I put in every room the first thing in the mornings."

Playfully I stuck a red rose behind his ear. Quickly he snatched it away and stuffed it in with the daisies Toni had brought him.

"Jory, when I am outdoors in August knowing September isn't far away, I just grab each moment and value it for what it is. The rose scent is in my nostrils, making me think I am in Heaven, or in Paul's garden. He had the most beautiful gardens. All kinds. He divided sections into those that held English gardens, Japanese, Italian—"

"I've heard all that before!" he said impatiently. "I asked if you heard us?"

"Yes, as a matter of fact, I did hear every fascinating thing, and when I had the chance, I peeked above the roses to watch the two of you."

He scowled very much like Bart as I moved to put the twins on their feet, then gave their bare bottoms small spanks, telling them to find Toni, who would help them dress. They scuttled away, little naked dolls.

I sat down to smile at Jory, who glowered at me accusingly. He seemed even more like Bart when he looked angry. "Really, Jory, I didn't mean to eavesdrop. I was there before either of you came out." I paused and looked at his frowning face. "You love Toni, don't you?"

"I *don't* love her! She's Bart's! Damned if I want to take Bart's leavings again."

"Again?"

"Come off it, Mom. You know as well as I do the real reason why Mel left this house. He made it plain enough, and so did she that Christmas morning when the clipper ship was mysteriously broken. She'd have stayed on here forever if Bart had kept his position as replacement for me. I think she fell in love with him inadvertently, while trying to satisfy her need for me and the sex we shared. I used to hear her crying in the night. I'd lie on my bed, wanting to go to her but unable to move, feeling sorry for her, sorrier for myself. It was hell then. It's hell now. A different kind of hell."

"Jory—what can I do to help?"

He leaned forward, meeting my eyes with such intensity I was reminded of Julian and the many ways in which I had thwarted him.

"Mom, despite all this house represents to you, it's grown to feel like home to me. The halls and doorways are wide. There's the elevator to take me up and down. There're the swimming pool, the terraces, the gardens, and the woods. Actually, a kind of paradise on earth—but for a few flaws. I used to think I couldn't wait to get away. Now I don't want to go, and I don't really want to worry you any more than you already are, yet I must speak."

I waited with dread to hear about those few "flaws."

"When I was a child, I believed the world was full of many wonders, and miracles could still happen, and blind men would one day see, and the lame would one day walk, and so forth. Thinking like that made all the unfairness I saw all around, all the ugliness, much better. I think the ballet kept me from fully growing up, so I maintained the idea that miracles could truly happen if you believed in them enough— like that song 'When you wish upon a star, your dreams come true.' And in the ballet miracles do happen all the time, so I stayed childlike even after I became an adult. I still believed that in the outside world, the real world, everything would work out fine in the long run if I believed enough. Mel and I had that in common. There's something about ballet that keeps you virginal, so to speak. You see no evil, hear no evil, though I won't mention speak no evil. You know what I mean, I'm sure, for it was your world too." He paused and glanced up at the threatening sky.

"In that world I had a wife who loved me. In the outside world, the real world, she quickly found a replacement lover. I hated Bart for taking her when I needed her most. Then I'd hate Mel for allowing him to use her as just another way to get back at me. He's still doing it, Mom. And I wouldn't trouble you with what's going on if I wasn't sometimes afraid for my life. Afraid for my children."

I listened to him, trying not to show shock as he spoke of all he'd never hinted at before.

"Remember the parallel bars I exercise on, in order to use the back and leg braces? Well, somebody scraped the metal so that when I slip my hands along the rails I get metal splinters in both hands. Dad dug them out for me and made me promise not to tell you."

I shivered, shrank inside. "What else, Jory? That's not all, I can tell from the way you look."

"Nothing much, Mom. Just little things to make my life miserable, like insects in my coffee, tea, and milk. My sugar bowl filled with salt, and my salt cellar full of sugar . . . dumb tricks, childish pranks that could be dangerous. Tacks appear in my bed, in the seat of my chair . . . oh, it's Halloween time all the time in this house for me. At times I want to laugh, it's so silly. But when I slip on a shoe and there's a nail in the toe that I can't feel, and it gives me an infection because my leg circulation isn't top-notch, it's not a laughing matter. It could cost me a leg. I waste so much time looking everything over before I use it, like my razor with new blades that are suddenly rusty."

He looked around as if to see if Joel or Bart were in earshot, and even though he saw nothing, for I looked, too, still his voice lowered to a whisper. "Yesterday was very warm, remember? You yourself opened three of my windows so I'd have fresh, cool breezes—then the wind shifted and blew from the north, and it turned dramatically cold. You came on the run to close my windows, to cover me with another blanket. I fell back to sleep. Half an hour later I woke up from a dream of being at the North Pole. The windows—all six of them—were wide open. Rain blew in and wet my bed. But that wasn't the worst of it. My blankets had been removed. I turned to ring for someone to come to my assistance. My buzzer was gone. I sat up and reached for my chair. It wasn't where I usually put it, right beside my bed. For a moment I panicked. Then, because I'm much stronger now in my arms, I lowered myself to the floor, used my arms to pull myself over to a regular chair that I could shove near the windows. Once I was on the chair seat, I could have easily pulled the windows down. But the first one refused to budge. I moved the chair to another window, and that wouldn't close any more than the first one would. Stuck with the fresh coat of paint applied a few weeks ago. I knew then it was useless to try the other four and brave that fiercely cold wet rain and wind, for my leverage wasn't right, even if my arms are strong. Yet, foolhardy as you often say I am, I persisted. No luck. That's when I put myself on the floor again and made my way to the door. It was locked. I dragged myself along by pulling on furniture legs until I was in the closet, and there I pulled down a winter coat, covered myself and fell asleep."

What had happened to my face? It felt so numb that I couldn't move my lips and speak, nor could I manage to show shock. Jory stared at me hard.

"Mom, are you listening? Are you thinking? Now . . . don't try to comment until I complete this story. As I just said, I fell asleep in the closet, on the floor, soaking wet. When I woke up, I was back on my bed. A *dry* bed, the sheet and blankets covered me, and I was wearing a fresh pair of pajamas." He paused dramatically and met my horrified eyes.

"Mom . . . if someone in this house wanted me to catch pneumonia and die, would that someone have put me back in bed and covered me up? Dad wasn't home to pick me up and carry me, and certainly you don't have the strength to do that."

"But," I whispered, "Bart doesn't hate you that much. He doesn't hate you at all . . ."

"Perhaps it was Trevor who found me, and not Bart. But somehow I don't think Trevor is young and strong enough to lift me. Still, somebody here hates me," Jory stated firmly. "Somebody who would like to see me gone. I've thought about this considerably and come to the conclusion that it had to have been Bart who found me in the closet and put me back to bed. Has this occurred to you: If you, Dad, I, and the twins were out of the way, Bart would have our money as well as his own?"

"But he's already filthy rich! He doesn't need more!"

Jory spun his chair so that it faced east, staring at the faded sun. "I've never really been afraid of Bart before. I have always pitied him and wanted to help him. I think about taking the twins and leaving with you and Dad . . . but that's a coward's way. If Bart did open those windows to let in the rain and wind, he later changed his mind and came back to rescue me. I think about the clipper ship and how it was broken, and certainly Bart couldn't have been responsible for that, not when he wanted it so much. And I think about Joel, whom you think was responsible—and again I think about who influences Bart more than anyone here. Someone is taking Bart and twisting him and turning back the clock, so he's again like that tormented ten-year-old kid who wanted you and his grandmother to die in fire and be redeemed . . ."

"Please, Jory, you said you'd never mention that period in our lives again."

Silence came, stretched out interminably before he went on. "The fish in my aquarium died last night. Their air filter was turned off. The temperature control smashed." Once again he paused, watching my face closely. "Do you believe any of what I've just told you?"

I fixed my eyes on the blue-misted mountains with their soft, rounded tops to remind me of ancient, gigantic, dead virgins laid out in jagged rows, their upthrust, moss-covered bosoms all that remained. My eyes lifted to the sky, deeply blue, and the feather-brushed storm clouds with wisps of shimmering gold clouds behind them, heralding a better day.

Under such skies as this, surrounded by the same mountains, Chris, Cory, Carrie, and I had faced terrors while God watched. My fingers nervously wiped away those invisible cobwebs, trying to find the right words to say.

"Mom, as much as I hate to say this, I think we have to give up on Bart. We can't trust his now-and-then love for us. He needs professional help again. Truthfully, I've always believed he had a great deal of love within him that he didn't know how to release or express. And here I am, now thinking he's beyond saving. We can't drive him out of his own home—unless we want him declared insane and put in an institution. I don't want that to happen, and I know you don't. So, all we can do is leave. And isn't it funny—now I don't want to go, even when my life is threatened. I've grown accustomed to this house; I love it here, so I risk my life, the lives of all of us. The intrigue of what might happen today keeps me from ever being bored. Mom, the worst thing in my life is boredom."

I wasn't half listening to Jory.

My eyes widened as I saw Deirdre and Darren following Joel and Bart to the small chapel, which had its own outside door that could be reached from the gardens. They disappeared inside, and the door closed.

I forgot my basket of cut roses and jumped to my feet. Where was Toni? Why wasn't she protecting the twins from Bart, from Joel? Then I felt foolish, for why should she feel that Bart or Joel was a threat to two such small, innocent children? Still I said a hasty good-bye to Jory, told him not to worry, I'd be back in a few minutes with Darren and Deirdre so we could all eat lunch together. "Jory, you will be all right if I leave you alone for a few moments?"

"Sure, Mom. Go after my kids. I spoke to Trevor this morning, and he gave me a battery-operated two-way intercom. Trevor can be fully trusted."

Believing wholeheartedly in our butler's loyalty, I sped after the foursome already in the chapel.

~   ~   ~

Minutes later I sneaked through the small downstairs inside door to enter the chapel that Joel had told Bart was truly necessary if he were to redeem his soul from sin. It was a small room that tried to duplicate what many old castles and palaces contained for family worship. There was Bart kneeling behind the first pew, with Darren on one side and Deirdre on the other. Joel stood behind the pulpit, his gray head bowed as he began to pray. Stealthily I inched myself closer to hide in the shadow of an arch strut.

"We don't like it here," complained Deirdre in a loud whisper to Bart.

"Be quiet. This is God's place," Bart warned.

"I hear my kitty crying," said Darren weakly, cringing away from Bart.

"You cannot possibly hear your cat, or any cat crying from such a distance. Besides, it's not your kitty. It's Trevor's kitten, which he only allows you to play with."

Both the twins began to sniffle, trying to hold back cries of distress. They both adored kittens, puppies, birds, anything that was little and cute. "SILENCE!" roared Bart. "I don't hear anything from the outside, but if you listen carefully, God will speak and tell you how to survive."

"What's survive?"

"Darren, why do you let your sister ask all the questions?"

"She likes questions better."

"Why is it so dark in here, Uncle Bart?"

"Deirdre, like all females, you talk too much."

She began to wail louder. "I do not! Gramma likes my talk . . ."

"Your gramma likes anyone's talk as long as it isn't mine," answered Bart bitterly, pinching Deirdre's small arm to make her stay quiet.

Dozens of candles burned on the podium where Joel lifted his head. The architects had arranged for ceiling spots to converge on whoever was behind the pulpit, placing Joel squarely in the center of a mystical, artificial, light cross.

In a clear and loud voice he said, "We will stand and we will sing the praises of the Lord before today's sermon begins." His voice was resonant, assured, and authoritative.

I had eased myself by this time to a position behind a supporting pillar from which I could spy and not be seen. Like two small robots, the twins, who'd obviously been here many times before without their father, Chris, me, or Toni, were well trained and intimidated. They stood obediently, one on each side of Bart, who kept his hands restrainingly on their small shoulders and they began, with him, to sing hymns. Their voices were frail, faltering, unable to carry the tune well. Yet they made mighty efforts to keep up with Bart, who stunned me with his surprisingly good baritone singing voice.

Why hadn't Bart sung out like that when we attended the chapel services? Did Chris and I, with Jory, so intimidate Bart that he held back what had to be a God-given natural gift? When we'd praised Cindy for her singing voice, he had just frowned and said nothing to indicate that he had a wonderful voice as well. Oh, the complexity of Bart was likely to drive me crazy.

Under other, less sinister circumstances I would have been thrilled to hear Bart's voice lifted so joyously, his whole heart in it. Some filtering sunlight fell through the stained glass windows to glorify his face with colors of purple, rose, and green. How beautiful he appeared as he sang, with his eyes lit up, as if he truly had the power of the Holy Ghost.

I was touched by his faith in God. Tears came to my eyes as a sense of relief washed over me and made me feel clean.

Oh, Bart, you can't be all evil if you can sing like that, and look like that. It isn't too late to save you, it can't be.

No wonder Melodie had loved him. No wonder Toni was unable to turn her back and leave such a man.

"Oh, sing this song . . . this song of love to thee,
In God we trust, in God we trust . . ."

His voice soared, overwhelming the thin voices of the
twins. I was lifted up and out of myself, willing to believe
in the powers of God. I sank down on my knees, bowing my
head.

"Thank you, God," I whispered. "Thank you for saving
my son."

Then I was staring at him again, catching the Holy Spirit
and willing to believe in anything he did. Words came out of
the past. Bart had been with us at the time. "We've got to be
careful with Jory," warned Chris. "His immune system has
been impaired. We can't allow him to catch a cold that might
fill his lungs with fluid . . ."

Still I knelt on, transfixed. Now I could not believe Bart
was anything but a very troubled young man trying desperately to find what was right for himself.

Bart's powerful singing voice drew to the end of the hymn.
Oh, if only Cindy could have heard him. If only they could
both sing together, the two of them friends at last, joined by
their equal talents. There was no one to applaud when his
song ended. There was only silence and the thud of my beating heart.

The twins stared up at Bart with wide, innocent, blue
eyes. "Sing again, Uncle Bart," pleaded Deirdre. "Sing about
the rock . . ."

Now I knew why they came to this chapel—to hear their
uncle sing, to feel what I was feeling, an unseen presence that
was warm and comforting.

Without any accompaniment, Bart sang "Rock of Ages."
I was by this time a limp rag of emotions. With a voice like
that he could have the world at his feet, and he locked away
his talent in an office.

"That's enough, nephew," said Joel when the second song

was over. "Everyone will sit, and we will begin today's sermon."

Obediently, Bart sat and pulled the twins down beside him. He kept his arm about each in such a protective way that I was again moved to tears. Did he love Jory's twins? Had he, all this time, only pretended to dislike them because they resembled the *evil* twins of yesterday?

"Let us bow our heads and pray," instructed Joel.

My head bowed as well.

I listened to his prayer with incredulity. He sounded so professional, so concerned for those who had never experienced the joy of being "saved" and belonging entirely to Christ.

"When you open your heart and let Christ enter, he fills you with love. When you love the Lord, love his son who died for you, and you believe in the righteous ways of God and his son crucified so cruelly on that cross, you will find the peace of fulfillment that's always eluded you before. Lay down your sins, your swords, your shields, your thirsts for power and money. Put away your earthly lusts that crave the pleasures of flesh. Lay down all your earthly appetites that can never be satisfied and believe, believe! Follow in the footsteps of Christ. Follow where he led, believe in his teachings, and you will be saved. Saved from the evils of this world of sin and lust for sex and power. Save yourselves before it is too late!"

His zealot's fire was frightening. Why couldn't I believe in his fiery sermon as I believed in Bart's beautiful singing voice? Why were visions of wind and rain pouring in on Jory washing me clean of Joel's evangelistic oratory? I felt I'd betrayed Jory by my moment's belief that even Joel was what he seemed to be at this moment.

There was more to his sermon. I was startled at the casual, conversational tone he now assumed, as if he were talking directly to Bart. "The voices in the village are momentarily lulled because we have constructed in this great mountain mansion a small temple dedicated to the worship of God. The

workmen who constructed this divine house of worship and
created the elaborate embellishments have told them what we
have done, and others spread the word that the Foxworths are
trying to salvage their souls. They no longer speak of revenge
upon the Foxworths, who have ruled over them for more
than two hundred years. They bear deep in their hearts many
grudges for deeds done to them in the past by our self-serving,
self-centered ancestors. They have not forgotten or forgiven
the sins of Corrine Foxworth, who married her half uncle,
nor have they forgotten the sins of thy mother, Bart, and the
brother she loves. Under your very roof she still gives him the
pleasure of enjoying her body, as she takes her pleasure with
him . . . and under God's own heavenly blue sky, those two lie
naked in the sun before they blend one with the other. They
are addicted to one another, as surely as if they were addicted
to one of the many drugs that abound in today's immoral,
headstrong, selfish, heedless society.

"He, the doctor, her very own brother, redeems himself
somewhat in his efforts to serve mankind, dedicating his
professional life to medicine and science. So he can be more
easily forgiven than the sinful woman, thy mother, who gives
nothing to the world but a perverted daughter who will turn
out perhaps even worse, and a firstborn son who danced inde-
cently for money! For glorifying his body! And for that sin he
has paid, and dearly paid, by losing the use of his legs, and in
losing his legs, he lost his body, and in losing his body, he lost
his wife. Fate has infinite wisdom when it comes to deciding
whom to punish and whom to assist." Again he paused, as if
for dramatic effect, before he fixed his piercing zealot's eyes
on Bart, as if to burn his will into the brain of my son by pure
force. "Now, my son, I know you love your mother and you
would at times forgive her anything . . . wrong, wrong—for
will God? No, I don't think so. Save her, for how can God forgive *her* when she is responsible for luring her brother into
her arms?"

He paused, his pale eyes lit with religious zeal, waiting for Bart to respond.

"I'm hungry!" wailed Deirdre suddenly.

"Me too," cried Darren.

"You'll stay, and you will do what you have to do, or suffer the consequences!" shouted Joel from the pulpit.

Immediately the twins shrank into small, tight shells, staring at Joel with immense eyes of fear. What had Joel done to put that fear there? Oh, God, had I given Joel or Bart an opportunity to hurt them in some way?

Long minutes passed, as if Joel were deliberately testing them. I wanted to jump up and cry out to stop Joel from implanting foul ideas in the heads of innocent babes. But there sat Bart, as if not hearing Joel's words at all. He had his dark eyes riveted on the magnificent stained-glass window directly behind the pulpit. Stained glass that showed Jesus with the little children at his feet, leaning against his knees, staring up into his face with adoration. That same adoration was on Bart's face. He wasn't listening to his great-uncle. He was filling himself with the presence even I could feel in this place.

God did exist, had always been there even when I wanted to deny him.

The words of Christ did have meaning in today's world— and somehow his teachings had reached out and found a place in Bart's maze of troubled brain waves.

"Bart, your niece and nephew are falling asleep!" roared Joel angrily. "You neglect your duty! Wake them up! Immediately!"

"Suffer the little children, Uncle Joel," said Bart. "Your sermons last too long and they become bored and restless. They are not evil or contaminated. They were born within the holy vows of marriage. They are not the first twins, the blood-related twins, Uncle—not the *evil* twins . . ."

Even as I saw Bart lifting Darren and Deirdre up into his arms, holding them in a protective way, I felt fear confused with hope. Bart was proving himself to be just as fine and noble as his father. No sooner did I think that when I heard words that chilled my blood. I froze in the shadows.

Bart had risen with the twins in his arms. "Put them down," ordered Joel, his sermon over and his strong voice diminished to his habitual thin whisper. Had he drained his supply of energy so that now he was ineffective? I prayed so.

"Now, children who have not learned how to control physical demands, repeat the lessons I have tried to teach you. Speak, and tell me, Darren, Deirdre! Speak the words you are supposed to keep forever in your minds and hearts. Speak, and let God hear."

They had such babyishly small voices that seldom said more than a few words at a time. They sometimes used the wrong syntax . . . but this time they intoned as correctly and as seriously as adults.

Bart listened carefully, as if he'd helped coach them.

"We are children born of evil seed. We are the Devil's issue, the Devil's spawn. We have inherited all the evil genes that lead to inces—ncestuous relationships."

Pleased with themselves, they grinned at each other for having said it right, not understanding in the least the meaning of the words. Then both the twins turned serious blue eyes on that forbidding old man behind the pulpit.

"Tomorrow we will continue with our lessons." So said, Joel closed his huge black Bible.

Bart picked up the twins, kissed their cheeks, and told them that now they could put on clean, dry pants, eat lunch, take baths, and have nice naps before they attended chapel services again.

That's when I stood up and stepped into full view. "Bart, what are you trying to do to Jory's children?"

My son stared at me, his sun-bronzed skin going very pale. "Mother, you aren't supposed to come here except on Sundays . . ."

"Why? Do you hope to keep me away so you can mold the twins into warped human beings you can punish later on? Is that your purpose?"

"Who warped you into what you are?" asked Joel coldly, his eyes small and hard.

In a wild fury of rage, I spun to confront him. "Your parents!" I screamed. "Your sister, Joel, locked us up and kept us there, living on promises year after year, while Chris and I were turning into adults with no one to love but each other. So place the blame on those who made Chris and I what we are. But before you say one more word, I'm having my say.

"I love Chris, and *I am not ashamed*. You think I have given nothing of importance to the world, yet there stands your great-nephew, holding my grandchildren, and on the terrace is another of my sons. And they are not contaminated! They are not Devil's issue, or Devil's spawn—and don't you ever, as long as you live, dare to say those words again to anyone who belongs to me, or I will see that you are put away and declared senile!"

Color came to Bart's face as what color he had left departed from Joel's pasty skin. His desperate, faded, blue eyes sought to meet Bart's, but Bart was staring at me as if he'd never seen me before. "Mother," he said weakly, and would have said more, but the twins tore from his arms and ran to me.

"Hungry, Gramma, hungry . . ."

My eyes locked with Bart's. "You have the most beautiful singing voice I have ever heard," I said, backing away and taking the twins with me. "Be your own man, Bart. You don't need Joel. You have found your talent, now use it."

He stood there frozen, as if he had volumes to say, but Joel was tugging on his arm, imploring, just as the twins were crying for lunch.

Heaven Can't Wait

Jory fell very ill a few days later with a cold that just wouldn't go away. The cold, wet rain and winds had done their work. He lay on his bed with his temperature soaring, his brow glistening with beads of perspiration, writhing and turning his head incessantly from side to side, as he moaned, groaned, and called repeatedly for Melodie. I saw Toni wince each time he did that, even as she did her best to nurse him.

As I watched her with him, I saw that she truly did care for Jory; it was clear in every caring thing she did, in her soft, compassionate eyes and her lips that brushed his face whenever she thought I wasn't looking.

She turned to give me a brave smile. "Try not to worry so much, Cathy," she pleaded, bathing Jory's bare chest with cool water. "Most people don't realize that a fever is usually very helpful in burning up viruses. As a doctor's wife I'm sure you already know this and are just worried that he will go into pneumonia. He won't. I'm sure he won't."

"Let's pray he won't . . ."

I still worried; she was only a nurse without the medical

expertise of Chris. I called him every hour, trying to find him in that huge university lab. Why wasn't Chris responding to my urgent calls? I began to feel not only worried but angry that Chris couldn't be reached. Hadn't he promised to always be here when he was needed?

Two days had passed since Joel preached his sermon, and Chris had not called home.

The sweltering, humid weather and intermittent rain and electrical storms did nothing but create more misery and havoc in my mind. Thunder crashed overhead. Lightning flashed, momentarily lighting up dark, forbidding skies. Near my feet the twins were playing and whispering about it being time for lessons in the chapel. "Please, Gramma. Uncle Joel says we must come."

"Deirdre, Darren, I want you to listen to me and forget what your Uncle Joel and Uncle Bart tell you. Your father wants you to stay with me and Toni, near him. You know your daddy is sick, and the last thing he'd want is for his son and daughter to be visiting that chapel where . . . where . . ." and here I stumbled. For what could I say about Joel that wouldn't somehow rebound later? He was teaching what he believed was right. If only he had not taught them those phrases . . . Devil's issue. Devil's spawn.

Instantly the two of them wailed, as if of one mind. "Will Daddy die?" they cried out simultaneously.

"No, of course he won't die. What do you two know about death, anyway?" I went on to explain that their grandfather was a wonderful doctor and he'd be coming home any second.

They stared at me without comprehension before I realized they often mouthed words they'd learned by rote and had no understanding of what they said. Death—what could they know about that?

Toni turned to give me a strange look. "You know something? As I help those two on and off with their clothes and give them baths, they keep up a constant chatter. They're really very remarkable and bright children. I guess being around adults so much has taught them more swiftly than playing with other children would have. Most of what they say while playing alone is silly gibberish. Then out of this silly gibberty-junk come serious words, adult words. Their eyes widen. They speak in whispers. They look around and seem afraid. It's as if they are expecting to see someone, or something, and in low tones they suddenly warn each other of God and his wrath. It alarms me." She looked from me and the twins back to Jory.

"Toni, listen carefully. Never allow the twins out of your sight. Keep them with you at all times during the day, unless you know positively they are with me or Jory, or my husband. When you're caring for Jory and are too preoccupied to keep an eye on them, call me and I'll take them over. Above all, don't let them go off with Joel," and as much as I hated to, I had to add Bart's name.

She threw me another worried look. "Cathy, I think it was not only that thing that happened in New York with Cindy, and with me, but also what Joel had to say when we came back that made Bart start looking at me as if I were the worst kind of sinner. It hurts to have the man you think you love hurl such ugly accusations."

Again she was bathing Jory's arms and chest. "Jory would never say such ugly things, no matter what I did. Sometimes he looks fierce, but even then he's thoughtful enough to say nothing to damage my ego. I never knew a man so thoughtful and compassionate."

"Are you saying now that you love Jory?" I asked, wanting to believe she did but afraid her disappointment was rebounding and making Jory only a substitute love.

She blushed and bowed her head. "I've been in this house almost two years, and I've seen and heard a great many things. In this house I found sexual satisfaction with Bart, but it wasn't romantic or sweet, just exciting. Only now am

I beginning to feel the romance of a man who tries to understand me and give me what I need. His eyes never condemn. Never do his lips shout out terrible things, when I haven't done anything I think is terrible. My love for Bart was a burning hot fire, kindled to a blaze the first day we met, while my feet stayed in quicksand, never knowing what he wanted, or what he needed, except he wanted someone like you . . ."

"I wish you'd stop saying that, Toni," I objected with discomfort. Bart still disliked himself so much he feared a woman turning away from him first, and to keep that from happening, he discarded Melodie before she had the chance to turn against him. Later, he turned his self-loathing against Toni before she could hate him and leave him. Again I sighed.

Toni agreed never to discuss Bart with me again, and then she began with my help to slip a clean pajama jacket onto Jory. We worked together as a team while the twins played on the floor, shoving little cars and trucks along just like Cory and Carrie had done.

"Just be sure which brother it is you love before you hurt both of them. I'm going to talk to my husband and Jory again, and I'm doing my damnedest to see that we move out of this house just as soon as Jory recovers. You can go with us if that is your choice."

Her pretty gray eyes widened. She looked from me back to Jory, who had rolled on his side and was murmuring incoherently in his delirium. "Mel . . . is that our cue?" I think he was saying.

"No, it's Toni, your nurse," she said softly, caressing his hair and brushing it back from his beaded brow. "You have a very bad cold . . . but soon you'll feel just fine."

Jory stared up at her in a disoriented way, as if trying to distinguish this woman from the one he dreamed about every night. During the day he had eyes only for Toni, but in the night, Melodie came back to haunt him. What was there about the human condition that made us hold on to tragedy with such tenacity and easily forgo the happiness we could reach readily?

He began to cough violently, choking and pulling up huge wads of phlegm. Tenderly Toni held his head, then threw away the soiled tissues.

Everything she did for him she did with tenderness, fluffing his pillows, massaging his back, moving his legs to keep them supple even if he couldn't control them. I couldn't help but be impressed with all that she did to make him comfortable.

I backed off toward the door, feeling I was an intruder during a very important private moment as Jory's eyes came into focus enough for him to pick up her hand and meet her eyes. Even as sick as he was, something in his eyes spoke to her. Quietly I caught hold of Darren's hand, and then Deirdre's. "Got to go now," I whispered even as I watched Toni tremble before her head bowed.

To my surprise, just before I closed the door, she put his hand to her lips and kissed each of his fingers. "I'm taking advantage of you," she whispered, "at a time when you can't fight back, but I need to tell you what a fool I've been. You were here all the time, and I never saw you. Never saw you at all when Bart stood in the way."

Weakly Jory answered, his eyes warm as they drank in the sincerity of her words and most of all, her loving, warm expression. "I guess it's easy to overlook a man in a wheelchair, and perhaps that alone was enough to make you blind. But I've been here, waiting, hoping . . ."

"Oh, Jory, don't hold it against me because I let Bart dazzle me with his charm. I was overwhelmed and sort of flabbergasted that he found me so desirable. He swept me off my feet. I think every woman secretly wants a man who refuses to take no for an answer, and pursues her relentlessly until she has to give in. Forgive me for being a fool, and an easy conquest."

"It's all right, all right," he whispered, then closed his

eyes. "Just don't let what you feel for me be pity—or I'll know."

"You're what I wanted Bart to be!" she cried out as her lips neared his.

This time I did close the door.

Back in my own rooms, I sat down near the telephone waiting for Chris to call in response to my many urgent messages. On the verge of sleep, with the twins tucked neatly in my bed for their naps, the phone rang. I snatched up the receiver, said hello. A deep, gruff voice asked for Mrs. Sheffield, and I identified myself.

"We don't want you and your kind here," said that frightening, deep voice. "We know what's going on up there. That little chapel you built don't fool us none. It's a sham to hide behind while you flaunt God's rules of decency. Get out—before we take God's will into our own hands and drive every last one of you away from *our* mountains."

Unable to find a clever reply, I sat stunned and very shaky before he hung up. For long moments I just sat there with the receiver in my hand. The sun broke through the clouds and warmed my face . . . only then did I hang up. I looked around me at the rooms I myself had decorated to please my own taste, and found, much to my surprise, that these rooms no longer reminded me of my mother and her second husband. In here were only remnants of the past that I wanted to remember.

Cory and Carrie's baby pictures in silver frames on my dresser, placed next to those of Darren and Deirdre. They were look-alike twins, but when you knew them well, you could see they weren't the same. My eyes moved to the next silver frame, and there was Paul smiling at me, and Henny was in another. Julian sulked, in a way he used to think sexy, from a gold frame, and I also had a few snapshots of his mother, Madame Marisha, framed to keep near her son. But nowhere did I have a photograph of Bartholomew Winslow. I stared at the picture of my own father, who'd died when I was twelve. So much like Chris, only now Chris looked older.

Turn around, and the boy you knew so well was a man. The years flew by so swiftly; once a day had seemed longer than a year did now.

Again I looked at the two sets of twins. It would take only someone very familiar with both sets to recognize the slight differences. There was a hint of Melodie in Jory's children, a vague resemblance. I stared at another picture, with Chris and myself, taken when we still lived in Gladstone, Pennsylvania. I'd been ten, he'd just turned thirteen. We stood in three feet of snow beside the snowman we'd just finished, smiling at Daddy as he took yet another picture. A photograph turning brown, one that our mother had put in her blue album. Our blue album now.

Little snippets of our lives were caught in all those little squares and oblongs of slick paper. Frozen forever in time, that Catherine Doll who sat on an attic windowsill, wearing a flimsy nightgown as Chris in the shadows took a time-lapse photo. How had I managed to sit so still, and hold that expression—how? Through the nightgown I could see the tender form of young breasts—and in that girlish profile all the wistful sadness I'd felt back then.

How lovely she was—I'd been. I stared at her hard and long. That frail, slender girl had long ago disappeared in the middle-aged woman I was now. I sighed for the loss of her, that special girl with her head full of dreams. I tried to tear my gaze away; instead, I got up to pick up the picture that Chris had carried with him to college, to medical school. When he was an intern, still he had this photograph with him. Was it this paper in my hand that had kept his love for me so strong? This attic face of a girl of fifteen, sitting in the moonlight? Longing, always longing for love that would last forever? I no longer looked like this girl I held in my hand. I looked like my mother the night she burned down the original Foxworth Hall.

Shrill telephone rings startled me back to the here and now. "I've had a flat tire," said Chris on hearing my small voice. "I had driven to another lab and spent a few hours there, so when I came back I saw all those messages from you about Jory. Jory can't be worse, can he?"

"No, darling, he's no worse."

"Cathy, what's wrong?"

"I'll tell you when you get here."

Chris reached home an hour later and rushed in to embrace me before he hurried to Jory. "How's my son?" he asked even as he sat on Jory's bed and reached to feel his pulse. "I hear from your mother that someone opened all your windows and the rain soaked you."

"Oh!" cried Toni. "Who could have done such an awful thing? I'm so sorry, Doctor Sheffield. It's my habit to check on Jory, I mean Mister Marquet, two or three times during the night, even if he doesn't call for me."

Jory grinned at her in a happy way. "I think you can stop calling me Mister Marquet now, Toni." His voice was very weak and hoarse. "And this happened on your day off."

"Oh," she said, "that must have been the morning I drove into the city to visit my girlfriend."

"It's just a cold, Jory," said Chris, checking his lungs again. "There's no hint of fluid in your lungs, and from your symptoms you don't have the flu. So swallow your medicine, drink the fluids Toni brings you, and stop fretting about Melodie."

Later, sprawled in his favorite chair in our sitting room, Chris listened to everything I had to say. "Did you recognize the voice?"

"Chris, I don't know any of the villagers well enough. I do my damnedest to stay away from them."

"How do you know it was a villager?"

That thought had never occurred to me. I'd just presumed. Nevertheless, as soon as Jory was well enough, we both determined to leave this house.

"If it's what you want," said Chris, looking around with some regret. "I like it here, I must admit. I like all the space around us, the gardens, the servants who wait on us, and I'll be sorry to leave. But let's not flee too far. I don't want to leave my work in the university."

"Chris, don't worry. I won't take that away from you. When we leave here, we will go to Charlottesville and pray to God nobody there will know that I'm your sister."

"Cathy, my dearest, sweetest wife, I don't think even if they knew, they'd give a damn. And besides, you look more like my daughter than my wife."

Wonderfully sweet as he was, he could say that with honesty in his eyes. I knew then he was blind when he looked at me. He saw what he wanted to see, and that was the girl I used to be.

He laughed at my doubting expression. "I love the woman you've become. So don't you go looking for the tarnish when I deliver to you eighteen-karat-gold honesty. I'd say twenty-four karat, but you'd then say it was too soft and therefore useless functionally. So I give to you the best there is: my eighteen-karat love that truly believes you are beautiful inside, outside, and in between."

Cindy flew in for one of her whirlwind visits, breathlessly gushing out every detail of her life in exquisite minute detail since last she'd seen us. It seemed incredible that so much could happen to one girl of nineteen.

The instant we were inside the grand foyer, she raced up the stairs, hurling herself into Jory's arms with such abandon I thought she might tip over his chair. "Really," he laughed, "you weigh more than a feather, Cindy." He kissed her, looked her over, then laughed. "Wow! What kind of outfit is that, anyway?"

"The kind that is going to fill the eyes of a certain brother named Bart with horror. I picked this out just to annoy him and dear Uncle Joel."

Jory turned solemn. "Cindy, if I were you, I'd stop deliberately baiting Bart. He's not a little boy anymore."

Unknown to Cindy, Toni had stepped into the room and stood patiently waiting to take Jory's temperature.

"Oh," said Cindy, turning to see Toni. "I thought after that terrible scene Bart made in New York that you'd see him for what he really is and leave this place." The look in Toni's eyes made Cindy glance again at Jory, then back to Toni again, and she laughed. "Well, *now* you've got good sense! I can read your eyes, Toni, Jory. You're in love! Hooray!" She rushed to hug and kiss Toni before she settled down near Jory's chair and stared up at him with adoration. "I met Melodie in New York. She cried a lot when I told her how pretty the twins are . . . but the day after your divorce went through, she married another dancer. Jory, he looks a lot like you, only not nearly as handsome, and he doesn't dance as well, either."

Jory kept his small smile, as if Melodie had been put on the shelf and there she'd stay. He turned his head to grin at Toni. "Well, there goes my alimony payment. At least she could have let me know."

Again Cindy was staring at Toni. "What about Bart?"

"What about me?" asked a baritone voice from the open doorway.

Only then did we all notice that Bart was in the doorway, lounging insolently against the frame, taking in all we said and did as if we were specimens in his special zoo of family oddities.

"Well," he drawled, "as I live and breathe, our breathless little imitation Marilyn Monroe has come to thrill us all with her stagey presence."

"That's not how I'd describe my feelings on seeing you again," Cindy said with her eyes flashing. "I'm chilled, not thrilled."

Bart looked her over, taking in her skin-tight gold leather pants, her striped cotton knit sweater of white and gold. The horizontal stripes emphasized her breasts, which jiggled freely each time she moved, and knee-high gold boots decorated her feet and legs.

"When are you leaving?" asked Bart while he stared at Toni sitting on Jory's bed and holding his hand. Chris sat next to me on a love seat, trying to catch up on some mail that had been delivered to the house and not to his office.

"Dear brother, say what you will, I don't care. I've come to see my parents and the rest of my family. I'll be leaving soon enough. Chains of steel couldn't keep me here longer than necessary." She laughed and stepped closer and looked up into his face. "You don't have to like me, or approve of me. And even if you open your mouth and say something insulting I'll just laugh again. I've found a man to love me that makes you look like something drug up from the Dismal Swamp!"

"Cindy!" said Chris sharply, putting down his unopened mail. "While you are here, you will dress appropriately, and you will treat Bart with respect, as he will treat you. I'm sick of these childish arguments about nothing."

Cindy looked at him with hurt eyes, making me say apologetically, "Darling, it is Bart's home. And sometimes I would like to see you in clothes that aren't too small."

Her blue eyes changed from those of a woman to those of a child. She wailed, "You're both taking his side—when you know he's nothing but a crazy creep out to make us all unhappy!"

Toni sat uncomfortably until Jory leaned to whisper something in her ear, and then she was smiling. "It doesn't mean anything," I heard him say in an undertone. "I believe Bart and Cindy enjoy tormenting one another."

Unfortunately Bart's attention was drawn from Cindy to take notice of Jory with his arm about Toni's shoulders. He scowled, then beckoned to Toni. "Come with me. I want to show you the inside of the chapel with all its new additions."

"A chapel? Why do we need a chapel?" asked Cindy, who had not been informed of the newest room transformed.

"Cindy, Bart wanted a chapel added to this house."

"Well, Mom, if anybody ever needed a chapel close at hand, it's the creep of the hill and the Hall."

My second son didn't say a word.

Toni refused to go with him. She gave him the excuse of needing to bathe the twins. Anger lit up Bart's eyes before it died, leaving him standing there, strangely desolate-looking. I got up to take his hand. "Darling, I'd love to see what new additions you've made in the chapel."

"Some other time," he said.

I watched him covertly at the dinner table as Cindy taunted Bart in rather ridiculous ways that might have made the rest of us laugh if he could only see the humor she displayed. However, Bart had never been able to laugh at himself, more the pity. He took everything so seriously. Her grin was triumphant. "You see, Bart," she teased, "I can put away my childish foibles, even physical ones. But you can't put away anything that sours your guts and chews away on your brain. You're like a sewer, ready to hold all that's sinking and rotten and never give it up."

Still he said nothing.

"Cindy," spoke up Chris, who'd remained quiet during our evening meal, "apologize to Bart."

"No."

"Then get up and leave the table, and eat in your room until you can learn to speak pleasantly."

Her eyes flashed balefully again, this time at Chris. "ALL RIGHT! I'll go to my room—but tomorrow I'm leaving this house and I'm never coming back! NOT EVER!"

Finally Bart had something to say. "The best news I've heard in years."

Cindy was in tears before she reached the dining room archway. I didn't jump up to follow her this time. I sat on, pretending nothing was amiss. Always in the past I'd shielded Cindy, chastised Bart, but I was seeing him with new eyes. The son I'd never known had facets that weren't all dark and dangerous.

"Why don't you go to Cindy, as you always have in the past, Mother?" asked Bart, as if challenging me.

"I haven't finished my dinner, Bart. And Cindy has to learn to respect the opinions of others."

He sat staring at me as if completely taken off guard.

Early the next morning, Cindy stormed into our room without knocking, catching me wrapped in a towel, fresh from my bath, and Chris was still shaving. "Mom, Dad, I'm leaving," she said stiffly. "I won't enjoy myself here. I'm wondering why I even bothered to come back. It's clear you've decided to take Bart's side on every issue, and if that's the case, then I'm finished. I'll be twenty next April, and that's old enough not to need a family."

Her eyes smeared with the tears that came unbidden. Her voice turned small and broken. "I want to say thanks to both of you for being wonderful parents when I was little and needed someone like both of you. I'm going to miss you and Daddy, and Jory and Darren and Deirdre, but every time I come here, I leave feeling sick. If ever you decide to live somewhere far from Bart, maybe you'll see me again . . . maybe."

"Oh, Cindy!" I cried, rushing to embrace her. "don't leave!"

"No, Momma," she said staunchly. "I'm going back to New York. My friends there will throw me a party, the best kind. They do everything better in New York."

But her tears were coming faster, harder. Chris wiped his face free of shaving lather and came to hug her close. "I can understand how you feel, Cindy. Bart can be irritating, but you did go too far last night. In a way you were very funny, but sadly, he can't see that. You have to judge whom you can tease, and whom you cannot. You've outgrown Bart, Cindy. And we won't object if you want to leave so soon. But, before you go, we want you to know your mother and I are taking Jory and his children, and Toni, too, and moving to Charlottesville. We'll find a large house there and settle down in the midst of people, so when you come again, you won't be lonely, and Bart will still be here, high on this hill and far from you."

Sobbing, she clutched Chris. "I'm sorry, Daddy. I was nasty to him, but he always says such mean things to me, and I have to hit back or feel like a doormat. I don't like for him to wipe his feet on me—and he is like a sewer, *he is*."

"Someday I hope you'll see him differently," said Chris softly, tilting up her pretty tear-stained face and kissing her lightly. "So kiss your mother, say good-bye to Jory, Toni, Darren, and Deirdre . . . but don't say you won't come back to see us again. That would make us both very unhappy. You give us a great deal of joy, and nothing should spoil that."

I helped Cindy pack the clothes she'd just unpacked. And even as we did this together, I saw that she was undecided and wanted to stay on if only I'd plead. Unfortunately we'd left her door open, and I looked around to see Joel standing in the doorway watching us.

Joel turned pale eyes on Cindy. "Why are you red-eyed, little girl?"

"I'm not a little girl!" she screamed. She turned wrathful eyes on him. "You're in league with him, aren't you? You help make him what he is. You stand there and gloat because I'm packing my bags, don't you? Glad I'm leaving—but before I go, I'm telling you off, too, old man. And I don't care if my parents scold me for not showing respect for old age." She stepped closer, her posture dominating his cringing form. "I hate you, old man! Hate you for preventing my brother from being normal, and he could have been without you! I HATE YOU!"

Hearing this, Chris, who'd been seated near the window, became furious. "Cindy, why? You could have gone and said nothing." Joel had disappeared by this time, leaving Cindy staring at Chris, bleak-eyed. "Cindy," Chris said softly, reaching out to caress her hair. "Joel is an old man dying of cancer. He won't be around much longer."

"What do you mean?" she asked. "He looks healthier than when he came."

"Perhaps he's had a remission. He refuses to see a doctor and won't let me check him over. He says he's resigned to dying soon. So, I take him at his word."

"I expect now you want me to apologize to him—well, I won't! I meant every word! That time in New York, when Bart was so happy with Toni, and they seemed so much in love, we were at a party, when suddenly an old man appeared that looked like Joel—and instantly Bart changed. He turned mean, hateful, like a spell had been cast, he began to criticize my clothes, Toni's pretty dress that he said was shameless . . . and only a few minutes before, he'd complimented the way she looked in that very same dress. So don't tell me that Joel doesn't have a great deal to do with Bart's nutty behavior."

Instantly I was with Cindy. "You see, Chris. Cindy believes just as I do. If Joel weren't here using his influence, Bart would straighten out. Drive Joel out, Chris, before it's too late."

"Yes, Daddy, make that old man leave. Pay him off, get rid of him."

"And what do I say to Bart?" asked Chris, looking from one to the other of us. "Don't you realize he has to be the one who sees Joel for what he is? We can't tell him Joel's not a healthy influence. Bart has to discover that for himself."

Soon after this we drove to Richmond to see that Cindy caught a plane back to New York. In another week she was moving to

Hollywood to try and begin a film career. "I won't be coming to Foxworth Hall again, Momma," she repeated. "I love you, and I love Dad, even if he is angry with me for speaking my mind. Tell Jory again that I love him and his children. But hate and ugly thoughts come into my mind the minute I step inside that house. Leave there, Momma. Daddy. Leave before it's too late."

Numbly I nodded.

"Momma, remember the night when Bart beat up Victor Wade? He carried me home naked—and he took me up to Joel's room. He held me so Joel could look me over, and that old man spat on me, cursed me. I couldn't tell you then. The two of them scare me when they get together. Alone, Bart might straighten out. With Joel there to influence him, he could be dangerous."

She was soon on the plane and we were on the ground watching her fly away again.

She flew toward morning. We drove home toward night.

This couldn't go on any longer. To save Jory, Chris, the twins, and myself, we had to leave, even if it meant we'd never see Bart again.

Garden in the Sky

Poor Cindy, I was thinking, how would she fare in Hollywood? I sighed, then began to look around for the twins. They sat solemnly in their sandbox with the rainbowed canopy overhead, although in early September the weather was steadily cooling off. They sat without shoveling sand into pretty buckets, not building sand castles. Not doing anything. "Just listening to the wind blow," said Deirdre.

"Don't like the wind," added Darren.

Before I could speak, Chris was striding toward us, and soon I was telling him, "Cindy just called from Hollywood. She says she has lots of friends there already. I don't know if she does or not. But she does have plenty of money. Already I've called one of my friends who will check on her."

"It's better so," he said with a troubled sigh. "It seems nothing can work out for Cindy here. She can't get along with Bart, and now she's started on Joel as well. In fact, she seems to think Joel is worse than Bart."

"He is, Chris! Don't you know that by now?"

He grew impatient with me, just when I thought I had

him convinced. "You're prejudiced because he is Malcolm's son, and that's all it is. For a while when Cindy was berating him, too, the two of you almost convinced me, but Joel is not doing one thing to influence Bart. Bart, from all I hear, is a full-blooded young stud, having the time of his life, only you don't know that. And Joel can't have much longer to live. That cancer is devouring him day by day, even if he does maintain his weight. He can't possibly hold on more than a month or two more."

I wasn't distressed. I didn't even feel guilty or ashamed at that moment, I told myself with sincerity, that Joel was getting out of life exactly what he deserved. "How do you know he's ill with cancer?" I asked.

"He told me that's why he came back to die on home ground, so to speak. He wants to be buried in the family cemetery."

"Chris, like Cindy said, he does look better now than when he came."

"Because he's well fed and well housed. He lived in poverty at that monastery. You see him in one way, I see him another. He confides in me, Catherine, and tells me how hard he's tried to win you to his side. Tears come into his eyes. 'And she's so much like her dear mother, my dear sister' he'll say over and over again."

Not for one minute, after witnessing Joel in that chapel, would I ever believe in that evil old man. Even when I told Chris about the chapel incident in great detail, he didn't think it so terrible until I mentioned what had been taught to the twins.

"You heard that? Actually heard those babies say they were Devil's issue?" Disbelief was clear in his blue eyes.

"Does it ring a familiar bell? Do you see Cory and Carrie on their knees by their beds, praying for God to forgive them for being born Devil's spawn? Even when they didn't know what that meant? Does anyone know more than you and I what harm can be done from ideas like that planted in such young minds? Chris, we have to leave soon! Not after Joel dies, but soon as possible!"

He said exactly what I'd feared he would. We had to think of Jory, who needed special quarters, special equipment. "He'll have to have an elevator. Doors will have to be enlarged. The halls must be wide. And there is another consideration— Jory may marry Toni. He asked me what I thought about it, wanting to know if I believed he had a chance of making Toni happy. I said yes, of course he could. I can see the love between them growing day by day. I like the way she treats him, as if she doesn't see the wheelchair, or what he can't do—only what he can.

"And Cathy, it wasn't love between Toni and Bart. It was infatuation, glands calling to glands—or call it whatever you will, but it wasn't love. Not our kind of everlasting love."

"No . . . ," I breathed, "not the kind that lasts forever . . ."

Two days later Chris called from Charlottesville, telling me he'd found a house.

"Exactly how many rooms?"

"Eleven. It's going to seem small after Foxworth Hall. But the rooms are large, airy, cheerful. It has four baths and a powder room, five bedrooms, a guest room and another bath over the garage, and also on the second floor is a huge room we can convert into a studio for Jory, and one of the extra bedrooms can be my home office. You're going to love this house."

I doubted that, he'd found it too quickly, even though that's what I'd asked him to do. He sounded so happy, and that gave me happy expectations. He laughed, then explained more. "It's beautiful, Cathy, really just the kind of house I've always heard you say you wanted. Not too big, not too small, with plenty of privacy. Three acres with flowerbeds everywhere."

It was settled.

As soon as we could pack our bags and many personal possessions accumulated over the years we'd lived in Foxworth Hall, we would move out.

I felt sad in some ways as I sauntered through the grand rooms that I'd gradually made cozy with my own decorating ideas. Bart had complained more than once that I was changing what should never change. But even he, once he'd seen the improvements that made this a home rather than a museum, had finally agreed to let me have my way.

Chris came to me Friday evening, looking at me with soft eyes. "So, my beautiful, hold on for just a few more days and let me drive back to Charlottesville and check out that house more thoroughly before we sign the contract bid. I've found a nice apartment we can rent until we can close on the house. Also, I have a few things to clear up at the lab, so I can take off several days and help get us settled. As I was telling you on the phone, I think two weeks of work, after the closing, and our new home will be ready for all of us—ramps, elevator, and all."

He graciously didn't mention all the years he'd lived with Bart, knowing it was like living with an explosive hidden somewhere, bound to go off sooner or later. Never a word to reproach me for giving him a defiant, disrespectful son who refused to care how much love was given him.

Oh, how much agony he'd suffered because of Bart, and still he didn't say a word to condemn me for going with deliberate intentions after my mother's second husband. I put my hands to my head, feeling that deep ache beginning again.

My Christopher drove away in the early morning, leaving me to fret through yet another anxiety-ridden day. Over the years I'd grown more and more dependent on him, when once I'd prided myself for being independent, able to go my own way and not need anyone nearly as badly as they needed me. How selfishly I'd looked at life when I was younger. My needs had come first. Now it was the needs of others that came first.

Restlessly I roamed about, checking on all those I loved, staring at Bart when he came home, dying to throw all kinds of accusations his way, yet somehow feeling so much pity for him. He sat behind his desk, looking absolutely the perfect young executive. No guilt. No shame as he bargained, manipulated, negotiated, making more and more money just by talking over the telephone, or communicating with his computer. He looked up at me and smiled. A genuine smile of welcome.

"When Joel told me Cindy had decided to leave, it cheered my whole day, and I still feel that way." Yet what was that oddness behind the darkness of his eyes? Why did he look at me as if soon he'd cry?

"Bart, if ever you want to confide in me—"

"I have nothing to confide, Mother."

His voice was soft. Too soft, as if he spoke to someone that would soon be gone—forever gone.

"You may not know this, Bart, but the man you so hate, my brother and your uncle, has done the best he could to be a good father replacement."

Shaking his head, he denied this. "To do this best would have been abandoning his relationship with you, his sister, and he hasn't done that. I could have loved him if he'd only stayed my uncle. You should have known better than to try to deceive me. You should know by now all children grow up to ask questions and remember well scenes you think they'll soon forget, but those children don't forget. They take those memories and bury them deep in their brains, to bring them out later when they can understand. And all that I can remember tells me that the two of you are bound in ways that seem unbreakable, except by death."

My heart quickened. On the roof of Foxworth Hall, under the sun and stars, Chris and I had sworn certain vows to see us through eternity. How young and foolish to create our own traps . . .

Tears could so easily flood my eyes lately. "Bart—how could *I* live without *him?*"

"Oh, Mother, you could! You know you could. *Let him go, Mother.* Give to me the kind of decent, God-fearing mother I've always needed to keep my sanity."

"And if I can't say good-bye to Chris—what then, Bart?"

His dark head bowed. "God help you, Mother. I won't be able to. God help me, too. Even so, I do have to think of my own eternal soul."

I went away.

All through the night I dreamed of fire, of such terrible things I woke up, not clearly remembering anything but the fire, yet there had been something else, some dreadful remembered thing I kept shoving to the back of my mind. What? What? Unable to overcome the inexplicable fatigue I felt, I drifted back to sleep and fell again immediately into a continuing nightmare where I saw Jory's twins as Cory and Carrie, carried off to be devoured. For the second time I forced myself awake. Forced myself to get up, although my head ached badly.

I felt woozy-headed, half drunk as I set about my daily chores. At my heels the twins tagged behind, asking a thousand and one questions, in particular Deirdre. She reminded me so much of Carrie with her why? where? and whose is it? And how did it come to be his or hers or its? Jibberty-jabber, chitter-chat, on and on as Darren poked into closets, pulled open drawers, investigated envelopes, leafed through magazines and in the process ruined them for reading, making me say, "Cory, put those down! They belong to your grandfather and he likes to read the writing even if you don't like anything but the pictures. Carrie, would you please be quiet for just five minutes? Just five?" That, of course, drew another question that wanted to know who was Cory and who was Carrie, and why was I always calling them those funny names?

Finally Toni came to relieve me of the too inquisitive children. "Sorry, Cathy, but Jory wanted me to model for him in the garden today before all the roses die . . ."

Before all the roses die? I stared at her, then shook my head, thinking I was reading too much into ordinary words. The roses would live until a heavy freeze came, and winter was months away.

Around two in the afternoon, the telephone in my room rang. I'd just laid down to rest. It was Chris. "Darling, I can't stop worrying about what might happen. I think your fears are getting to me. Have patience. I'll be seeing you in an hour. Are you all right?"

"Why wouldn't I be all right?"

"Just checking. I've had a bad feeling. I love you."

"I love you, too."

The twins were restless, not wanting to play in the sandbox, not wanting to do one thing I suggested.

"Dee-dee don't like jump rope," said Deirdre, who couldn't pronounce her name correctly and didn't really want to. The more we tried to teach her the correct way, the more she lisped. She had Carrie's stubbornness. Just as Darren was more than willing to follow where she led, and he'd lisp when she did. And what difference did it make if a little boy his age played house?

I put the twins down for their naps. They noisily objected and didn't stop until Toni came in and read to them a story she'd promised she'd read—when I'd just read the same blasted story three times! Soon they were asleep in their pretty room with the draperies drawn. How sweet they looked, turned on their sides to face one another, just as Cory and Carrie had done.

In my own room, after checking on Jory, who was busy

reading a book on how to strengthen certain lower sexual muscles, I turned to my neglected manuscript and brought it up to date. When I grew tired, distracted by the absolute silence in the house, I went to waken the twins.

They were not in their small beds!

Jory and Toni were on the terrace, both lying on their sides on the quilted exercise mat. They were embracing, kissing long and passionately. "Sorry to interrupt," I said, feeling ashamed I had to intrude on their privacy and ruin what had to be a wonderful experience for Jory—and for her. "Where are the twins?"

"We thought they were with you," said Jory, winking at me before he turned back to Toni. "Run find them, Mom . . . I'm busy with today's lesson."

I used the quickest way to reach the chapel. Through all the gardens I hurried, glancing uneasily at the woods that hid the cemetery. Tree shadows on the ground were beginning to stretch out and cross one another as I neared the chapel door. A strange scent was wafted on the warm summer breezes. Incense. I ran on, reaching the chapel quite out of breath, with my heart pounding. An organ had been installed since I was here last. I stole as quietly as possible into the chapel.

Joel was seated at the organ playing beautifully, showing that once he had been truly a professional musician with remarkable ability. Bart stood up to sing. I relaxed when I saw the twins in the front pew, looking content as they stared up at their uncle, who sang so well it almost stole my fear and gave me peace.

The hymn ended. Automatically the twins went down on their knees and placed their small palms beneath their chins. They seemed cherubs—or lambs for the slaughter.

Why was I thinking that? This was a holy place.

"And lo, though we walk through the valley of the shadow of death, we will fear no evil . . . ," spoke Bart, now on his knees. "Repeat after me, Darren, Deirdre."

"And lo, though we walk through the valley of the shadow of death, we will fear no evil," obeyed Deirdre, her high-pitched, small voice leading the way for Darren to follow.

"For thou art with me . . . ," instructed Bart.

"For thou art with me . . ."

"Thy rod and thy staff shall comfort me."

"Thy rod and thy staff shall comfort me."

I stepped forward. "Bart, what the devil are you doing? This is not Sunday, nor has anyone died."

His bowed head raised. His dark eyes met mine and held such sorrow. "Leave, Mother, please."

I ran to the children, who jumped up. I gathered them into my arms. "We don't like it here," whispered Deirdre. "Hate here."

Joel had risen to his feet. He stood tall and lean in the shadows, with color from the stained glass falling on his long, gaunt face. He said not a word, just looked me up and down—scathingly.

"Go back to your rooms, Mother, please, please."

"You have no right to teach these children fear of God. When you teach religion, Bart, you speak of God's love, not his wrath."

"*They* have no fear of God, Mother. You speak of your own fear."

I began to back away, pulling the twins with me. "Someday you are going to understand about love, Bart. You are going to find out it doesn't come because you want it, or need it. It's yours only when you earn it. It comes to you when you least expect it, walks in the door and closes it quietly and when it's right, it stays. You don't plot to find it. Or seduce to try and make it happen. You have to deserve it, or you'll never have anyone who will stay long enough."

His dark eyes looked bleak. He stood, towering up there; then he advanced, taking the three steps down.

"We are all leaving, Bart. That should delight you. None

of us will come back to bother you again. Jory and Toni will go with us. You will have *come into your own*. Every room of this mammoth lonely Foxworth Hall will be all yours. If you wish, Chris will turn over the trusteeship to Joel until you are thirty-five."

For a moment, a brief illuminating moment, fear lit up Bart's face, just as jubilance lit up Joel's watery eyes.

"Have Chris turn the trusteeship over to my attorney," Bart said quickly.

"Yes, if that's what you want." I smiled at Joel, whose face then turned. He shot Bart a hard look of disappointment, confirming my suspicions—he was angry because Bart would take what might have been his . . .

"By morning we will be gone, all of us," I whispered hoarsely.

"Yes, Mother. I wish you godspeed and good luck."

I stared at my second son, who stood three feet from me. Where had I heard that said last? Oh, oh . . . so very long ago. The tall conductor on the night train that brought us here as children. He'd stood on the steps of the sleeper train and called that back to us, and the train had sounded a mournful good-bye whistle.

It came to me as I met Bart's brooding gaze that I should speak my parting words now, in this chapel of his building, and forget about saying anything tomorrow when I was likely to cry.

He spoke first. "Mothers always seem to run and leave the sons to suffer. *Why are you deserting me?*"

The tone of his throaty voice, full of pain, filled me with suffering. Still I said what I had to say. "Because you deserted me years ago," I answered brokenly. "I love you, Bart. I've always loved you, though you don't want to believe that. Chris loves you. But you don't want his love. You tell yourself each day you live that your own natural father would have been a better father—but you don't know that he would have been.

He wasn't faithful to his wife, my mother—and I wasn't his first dalliance. I don't want to speak disrespectfully of a man whom I loved very much at the time, but he wasn't the same kind of man Chris is. He wouldn't have given you so much of himself."

The sun through the windows turned Bart's face fire-red. His head moved from side to side. Tormented again. At his sides his hands clenched into tight fists. "Don't say one word more!" he shouted. "He's the father I want, have always wanted! Chris has given me nothing but shame and embarrassment. Get out! I'm glad you're leaving. Take your filth with you and forget I exist!"

Hours passed, and still Chris didn't show. I called the university lab. His secretary said he'd left three hours ago. "He should have been there, Mrs. Sheffield."

Immediately thoughts of my own father came to torment me. An accident on the highway. Were we duplicating our mother's act in reverse, running away from, not to, Foxworth Hall? Tick-tock went the clocks. Thumpity-thump-thump went my heartbeats. Nursery rhymes I had to read so the twins would sleep and stop asking questions. Little Tommy Tucker, sing for your supper ... When you wish upon a star ... dancing in the dark ... all our lives, dancing in the dark ...

"Mother, please stop pacing the floor," ordered Jory. "You rub my nerves raw. Why this grand rush to leave? Tell me why, please say something."

Joel and Bart strolled in to join us.

"You weren't at the dinner table, Mother. I'll tell the chef to prepare a tray." He glanced at Toni. "YOU can stay."

"No, thank you, Bart. Jory has asked me to marry him." Her chin lifted defiantly. "He loves me in a way you never can."

Bart turned betrayed, hurt eyes on his brother. "You can't marry. What kind of husband can you make now?"

"The very kind I want!" cried Toni, striding to stand beside Jory's chair and putting her hand lightly on his shoulder.

"If you want money, he doesn't have one percent of what I have."

"I wouldn't care if he had nothing," she answered proudly, meeting squarely his dark, forbidding gaze. "I love him as I've never loved anyone before."

"You pity him," stated Bart matter-of-factly.

Jory winced but said nothing. He seemed to know Toni needed to have it out with Bart.

"Once I did pity him," she confessed honestly. "I thought it a terrible shame such a wonderful man with so much talent had to be handicapped. Now I don't see him as handicapped. You see, Bart, all of us are handicapped in one way or another. Jory's is in the open, very visible. Yours is hidden—and sick. You are so sick, and it's pity I feel now—FOR YOU."

Seething emotions contorted Bart's face. I glanced at Joel for some reason and saw him staring at Bart, as if commanding him to stay silent.

Twisting about, Bart barked at me, "Why are you all gathered in this room? Why don't you go to bed? It's late."

"We are waiting for Chris to come home."

"There was an accident on the highway," spoke up Joel. "I heard the news on the radio. A man killed." He seemed delighted to give me this news.

My heart seemed to drop a mile—another Foxworth downed by an accident?

Not Chris, not my Christopher Doll. No, not yet, not yet.

From far away I faintly heard the kitchen door open and close. The chef leaving for his apartment over the garage I thought—or maybe Chris. Hopefully I turned toward the garage. No bright blue eyes, no ready smile and arms outstretched to hold me. No one came through the door.

Minutes passed as we all stared at each other uncomfortably. My heart began to throb painfully; it was time he was home. Time enough.

Joel was staring at me, his lips cocked in a peculiarly hateful way, as if he knew more than he'd said. I turned to Jory, knelt beside his chair, and allowed him to hold me close. "I'm scared, Jory," I sobbed. "He should be home by now. It couldn't take him three hours even in the winter with icy roads."

No one said anything, Not Jory, who held me tight. Not Toni. Not Bart or even Joel. The very show of all of us being together, waiting, waiting brought back only too vividly the scene of my father's thirty-sixth birthday party and the two state policemen who'd come to say he'd been killed.

I felt a scream in my throat ready to sound when I saw a white car heading up our private road, a red light spinning on the top.

Time turned backward.

NO! NO! NO! Over and over again, my brain screamed even as they spilled out the facts about the accident, the doctor who'd jumped out of his car to help the injured and dying victims laid on the roadside and as he ran to cross the highway, he'd been struck by a hit-and-run driver.

They carefully, respectfully put his things on a table, just as they'd dumped my father's possessions on another table in Gladstone. This time I was staring at all the items that Chris usually carried in his pockets. All this was unreal, just another nightmare to wake up from—not my photograph in his wallet, not my Chris's wristwatch and the sapphire ring I'd given him for Christmas. Not my Christopher Doll, no, no, no.

Objects grew hazy, dim. Twilight gloom pervaded my entire being, leaving me nowhere, nowhere. The policemen shrank in size. Jory and Bart seemed so far away. Toni loomed up huge as she came to lift me to my feet. "Cathy, I'm so sorry . . . so terribly sorry . . ."

I think she said more. But I tore from her grip and ran,

ran as if all the nightmares I'd ever dreamed in my life were catching up with me. *Seek the tarnish and you shall find.*

On and on running, trying to escape the truth, running until I reached the chapel where I threw myself down in front of the pulpit and began to pray as I'd never prayed before.

"Please, God, you can't do this to me, or to Chris! There's not a better man alive than Chris . . . you must know that . . ." And then I was sobbing. For my father had been a wonderful man, and that hadn't mattered. Fate didn't choose the unloved, the derelicts, the unneeded or unwanted. Fate was a bodiless form with a cruel hand that reached out randomly, carelessly, and seized up with ruthlessness.

They buried the body of my Christopher Doll, not in the Foxworth family plot, but in the cemetery where Paul, my mother, Bart's father, and Julian all lay under the earth. Not so far away was the small grave of Carrie.

Already I'd given the order to have the body of my father moved from that cold, hard, lonely ground in Gladstone, Pennsylvania so he, too, could lie with the rest of us. I thought he would like that, if he knew.

I was the last of the four Dresden dolls. Only me . . . and I didn't want to be here.

The sun was hot and bright. A day for fishing, for swimming, for playing tennis and having fun, and they put my Christopher in the ground.

I tried not see him down there with his blue eyes closed forever. I stared at Bart, who spoke the eulogy with tears in his eyes. I heard his voice as if from a far-far distance, saying all the words he should have said when Chris was alive and he could have appreciated hearing those kind, loving words.

"It is said in the Bible," began Bart in that beautiful, persuasive voice he could use when he wanted, "that it is never too late to ask for forgiveness. I hope and pray this is true, for

I will ask of this man who lies before me that his soul will look down from Heaven and forgive me for not being the loving, understanding son I could and should have been. This father, that I never accepted as my father, saved my life many times, and I stand here, shafted to my heart with all the guilt and shame of a wasted childhood and youth that could have made his life happier."

His dark head bowed so the sun made his hair and his falling tears gleam. "I love you, Christopher Sheffield Foxworth. I hope you hear me. I hope and pray you forgive me for being blind to what you were." Tears flowed down his cheeks. His voice turned hoarse. People started to cry.

Only I had dry eyes, a dry heart.

"Doctor Christopher Sheffield denied his surname of Foxworth," he went on when he found his voice again. "I know now he had to. He was a physician right up to his last moment, dedicated to doing what he could to relieve human suffering, while I, as his son, would deny him the right to be my substitute father. In humiliation, in remorse, and in shame, I bow my head and say this prayer . . ."

On and on he went while I closed my ears and turned away my eyes, gone numb from grief.

"Wasn't it a wonderful tribute, Mom?" asked Jory one dark day. "I cried, couldn't help it. Bart humbled himself, Mom, and in front of that huge crowd. I've never seen him humble before. You have to give him credit for doing that."

His dark blue eyes pleaded with me.

"Mom, you've got to cry, too. It's not right for you to just sit and stare into space. It's been two weeks now. You're not alone. You have us. Joel has flown back to that monastery to die there with that cancer he says he has. We'll never see him again. He wrote his last words, saying he didn't want to be buried on Foxworth ground. You have me, you have Toni,

Bart, Cindy, and your grandchildren. We love you and need you. The twins are wondering why you don't play with them. Don't shut us out. You've always bounced back after every tragedy. Come back this time. Come back to all of us—but come back mostly for Bart's sake, for if you allow yourself to grieve to death, you will destroy him."

For Bart's sake I stayed on in Foxworth Hall, trying to fit myself into a world that didn't really need me anymore.

Nine lonely months passed. In every blue sky I saw Chris's blue eyes. In everything golden I saw the color of his hair. I paused on the streets to stare at young boys who looked as Chris had at their ages; I stared at young men who reminded me of him when he was their age; I gazed longingly at the backs of tall, strong-looking men with blond hair going gray, wistfully hoping they'd turn and I'd see Chris smile at me again. They did turn sometimes, as if they felt the yearning hot blaze of my eyes, and I'd turn away my eyes, for they weren't him, not ever him.

I roamed the woods, the hills, feeling him beside me, just out of reach, but still beside me.

As I walked on and on alone, but for Chris's spirit, it came to me that there was a pattern in our lives, and nothing that had happened was coincidental.

In all ways possible Bart did what he could to bring me back to myself, and I smiled, forced myself to laugh, and in so doing I gave him peace and the confidence he'd always needed to give him a feeling of value.

Yet, yet, who and what was I now that Bart had found himself? That feeling of knowing the pattern grew and grew as I sat often alone in the grand elegance of Foxworth Hall.

Out of all the darkness, the anguish, the apparently hapless tragedies, and pathetic events of our lives, I finally understood. Why hadn't all of Bart's psychiatrists realized when he was young that he was testing, seeking, trying to find the role that suited him best? Through all that childhood agony, throughout his youth, he'd chiseled at his flaws ruthlessly, backing off the ugliness he believed marred his soul, steadfastly holding on to his credence that good eventually won over evil. And in his eyes, Chris and I had been evil.

Finally, at long last, Bart found his niche in the scheme of what had to be. All I had to do was turn on the TV on any Sunday morning and sometimes during midweek and I could see and hear my second son singing, preaching, acknowledged as the most mesmerizing evangelist in the world. Rapier-sharp, his words stabbed into the conscience of everyone, causing money to pour into his coffers by the millions. He used the money to spread his ministry.

Then came the surprise one Sunday morning of seeing Cindy rise and join Bart on the podium. Standing beside him, she linked her arm through his. Bart smiled proudly before he announced, "My sister and I dedicate this song to our mother. Mother, if you are watching, you'll know exactly how much this song means not only to both of us, but to you, as well."

Together, as brother and sister, they sang my favorite hymn . . . and a long time ago I'd given up on religion, thinking it wasn't for me when so many were bigoted, narrow-minded, and cruel.

Yet, tears streaked my face . . . and I was crying. After all the months since Chris had been struck down on that highway, I was crying dry that bottomless well of tears.

Bart had hacked off the last rotten bit of Malcolm's genes and had left only the good. To create him, the paper flowers had bloomed in the dusty attic.

To create him, fires had burned houses, our mother had died, our father, too . . . just to create the leader who would turn mankind away from the road to destruction.

I switched off the TV when Bart's program was over. His was the only one I watched. Not so far away, they were building a huge memorial honoring my Christopher.

THE CHRISTOPHER SHEFFIELD MEMORIAL CANCER RESEARCH CENTER, it was to be called.

In Greenglenna, South Carolina, Bart was also the founder of a grant for struggling young lawyers, and this was called THE BARTHOLOMEW WINSLOW LEGAL GRANT.

I knew Bart was trying to return good for the evil he'd done by denying the man who'd tried his best to be his father. A hundred times I reassured him that Chris would be pleased, very pleased.

Toni had married Jory. The twins adored her. Cindy had a film contract and was a fast-rising star. It seemed strange, after living a lifetime of giving, first to my mother's twins, then to my husbands, and my children and grandchildren, not to be needed, not to have a place of my own. Now I was the odd one out.

"Mom!" Jory told me one day, "Toni is pregnant! You don't know what that does for me. If we have a boy, he will be called Christopher. If we have a girl, she will be Catherine. Now, don't you say we can't do that, for we will anyway."

I prayed they'd have a boy like my Christopher, or my Jory, and one day in the future, I prayed Bart would find the right woman to make him happy. And only then did I realize that Toni had been right, he was looking for a woman like me, without my weaknesses, wanting her to have only my strengths, and perhaps with me as a living model—he'd never find her.

"And Mom," Jory had gone on during that same conversation, "I won my first prize, in the watercolor division . . . so I'm on my way to another successful career."

"Just as your father predicted," I answered.

~   ~   ~

All of this was in my mind, making me vaguely happy for Jory and Toni, happy for Bart and Cindy, as I turned toward the dual winding staircase that would take me up, up.

I had heard the wind from the mountains calling me last night, telling me it was my time to go, and I woke up, knowing what to do.

Once I was in that cold dim room, without furniture or carpet or rugs, only a dollhouse that wasn't as wonderful as the original, I opened the tall and narrow closet door and began my ascent up the steep and narrow stairs.

On my way to the attic.

On my way to where I'd find my Christopher, again . . .

Epilogue

It was Trevor who found my mother up there, sitting in the windowsill of what could have been the window of the schoolroom that she'd mentioned so often in the stories of her imprisoned life in Foxworth Hall. Her beautiful long hair was loose and flowing over her shoulders. Her eyes were open and staring glassily up at the sky.

He called to tell me the details, heavy sorrow in his voice, as I beckoned Toni closer so she could listen too. Too bad that Bart was away on a tour around the world. For he would have flown home in a minute if he'd even guessed she needed him.

Trevor went on. "She hadn't been feeling well for days, I could tell. She was so reflective, as if she were trying to make sense out of her life. There was that terrible sadness in her eyes, that pathetic yearning that made my heart ache to see her. I went searching to find her, and eventually I used the second set of narrow, steep stairs to the attic. I looked around. It surprised me when I saw that she must have, for some time, been decorating the attic with paper flowers . . ."

He paused as I choked up with tears, with regrets that

I hadn't done more to make her feel needed and necessary. Trevor went on, a strange note in his heavy voice. "I must tell you something strange. Your mother, sitting there in the windowsill, looked so young, so slender and frail—and her face even in death held an expression of great joy, and happiness."

Trevor gave me other details. As if she knew she was soon to die, my mother had glued paper flowers on the attic walls, including, too, a strange-looking orange snail and a purple worm. She had written a note that was found in her hand, clutched tight in her death grip.

> *There's a garden in the sky, waiting there for me. It's a garden that Chris and I imagined years ago, while we lay on a hard black slate roof and stared up at the sun and the stars.*
>
> *He's up there, whispering in the winds to tell me that's where the purple grass grows. They're all up there waiting for me.*
>
> *So, forgive me for being tired, too tired to stay. I have lived long enough, and can say my life was full of happiness as well as sadness. Though some might not see it that way.*
>
> *I love all of you, each equally. I love Darren and Deirdre and wish them good luck throughout their lives, as I wish the same for your child-to-be, Jory.*
>
> *The Dollanganger Saga is over.*
>
> *You'll find my last manuscript in my private vault. Do with it what you will.*
>
> *It was meant to be this way. I have no place to go but there. No one needs me more than Chris does.*
>
> *But please don't ever say I failed in reaching my most important goal. I may not have been*

the prima ballerina I set out to be. Nor was I the perfect wife or mother—but I did manage to convince one person, at last, that he did have the right father.

And it wasn't too late, Bart.

It's never too late.

**Before terror flowered in the attic, there was
a young girl. An innocent, hopeful girl . . .**

Garden of Shadows

When I was a little girl, my father bought me a priceless
handcrafted dollhouse. It was a magical miniature world,
with beautiful tiny porcelain dolls, furniture, even paintings
and chandeliers and rugs all made to scale. But the house
was enclosed in a glass case and I was never allowed to touch
the family inside—indeed, I was not even permitted to touch
the glass case, for fear of leaving smudges. Dainty things had
always been at peril in my large hands, and the dollhouse was
for me to admire but never to touch.

I kept it on an oak table under the sash of stained-glass
windows in my bedroom. The sun coming through the tinted
windows always spread a soft, rainbow-colored sky over the
tiny universe and put the light of happiness into the faces of
the miniature family. Even the servants in the kitchen, the
butler dressed in white livery who stood near the entrance
door, and the nanny in the nursery all wore looks of contentment.

That was as it should be, as it should always be—as I
fervently hoped and prayed it would be for me someday. That

miniature world was without shadows; for, even on overcast days, when clouds hung their gloom outside, the tinted-glass windows magically turned the gray light into rainbows.

The real world, my own world, seemed always to be gray, without rainbows. Gray for my eyes, which I had always been told were too stern, gray for my hopes, gray for the old maid no one wanted in the deck of cards. At twenty-four, I was an old maid, already a spinster. It seemed I intimidated eligible young men with my height and intelligence. It seemed that the rainbow world of love and marriage and babies would always be as closed off to me as that dollhouse I so admired. For it was only in make-believe that my hopes took wing.

In my fantasies I was pretty, lighthearted, charming, like the other young women I had met but never befriended. Mine was a lonely life, filled mostly with books and dreams. And though I did not talk about it, I clung to the small hope my dear mother had given me just before she died.

"Life is very much like a garden, Olivia. And people are like tiny seeds, nurtured by love and friendship and caring. And if enough time and care are spent, they bloom into gorgeous flowers. And sometimes, even an old, neglected plant left in a yard gone to seed will unexpectedly burst into blossom. These are the most precious, the most cherished blossoms of all. You will be that sort of flower, Olivia. It may take time, but your flowering will come."

How I missed my optimistic mother. I was sixteen when she died—just when I most needed to have those woman-to-woman talks with her that would tell me how to win a man's heart, how to be like her: respectable, competent, yet a woman in every way. My mother was forever involved in one thing or another, and in everything she was competent and in charge. She threaded her way through each crisis, and when one ended, there was always another to replace it. My father seemed content that she was busy. It mattered not with what.

He often said that just because women weren't involved in serious business, that didn't mean they should be idle. They had their "womanly" things to do.

Yet, when it came to me, he encouraged me to go to business school. It seemed right and proper that I would become his private accountant, that he would give me a place in his den, a manly room with one wall covered with firearms and another with pictures from his hunting and fishing expeditions, a room that always had the odor of cigar smoke and whiskey, its dark brown rug the most worn-looking of any rug in the house. He set aside a portion of his large black oakwood desk for me to work meticulously on his accounts, his business expenses, his employees' wages, and even his household expenses. Working with my father, I often felt more like the son he had always longed for—but never got—than the daughter I was. Oh, I did want to please, but it seemed I would never be just what anyone wanted.

He used to say I would be a great help to any husband, and I used to believe that was why he was so determined I would get a business education and have that experience. He didn't come out and say it in so many words, but I could hear them anyway—a woman six feet tall needed something more to capture a man's love.

Yes, I was six feet tall; I had shot up as a teenager, much to my dismay, to giant proportions. I was the beanstalk in Jack's garden. I was the giant. There was nothing dainty or fragile about me.

I had my mother's auburn hair, but my shoulders were too wide and my bosom large. I often stood before my mirror and wished my arms shorter. My gray eyes were too long and catlike and my nose was too sharp. My lips were thin, my complexion pale and gray. Gray, gray, gray. How I longed to be pretty and bright. But when I sat before my vanilla marble vanity table trying to blush and to flutter my eyelashes—look flirtatious—I managed only to look a fool. I didn't want to look empty-headed and silly, yet I couldn't help but sit before the glass-encased dollhouse and study the pretty, delicate porcelain face of the tiny wife. How I wished it were my face. Maybe then this would be my world.

But it was not.

And so I left my hope encased with the porcelain figures and went about my way.

If my father had really expected to make me more attractive to a man by providing me with an education and practical business experience, he must have been sorely disappointed in the result. Gentlemen came and went, all coming because of his manipulations, I discovered; and still I was yet to be courted and loved. I was always afraid that my money, my father's money, money I would inherit, would bring a man to the door pretending to be in love with me. I think my father feared the same thing, because he came to me one day and said, "I have written into my will that whatever money you receive shall be only yours and yours to do with what you like. No husband will ever expect to take control of your fortune simply by marrying you."

He made his announcement and left before I could even respond. Then he screened any candidates for my romance carefully, exposing me only to the highest class of gentleman, men of some fortune themselves. I had yet to meet one I didn't tower over, or one who wouldn't scowl at the things I said. It seemed I'd die a spinster.

But my father wouldn't have it so.

"There's a young man coming to dinner tonight," he began one Friday morning late in April, "who I must say is one of the most impressive I've met. I want you to wear that blue dress you had made for yourself last Easter."

"Oh, Father." It was on the tip of my tongue to say, "Why bother," but he anticipated my reaction.

"Don't argue about it, and for heaven's sake don't start in on the woman suffrage movement when we're at the table."

My eyes flamed. He knew how I hated to be bridled like one of his horses.

"A man no sooner shows some interest in you than you challenge the most treasured of manly privileges. It never fails. The blue dress," he repeated, and pivoted and left before I could offer an argument.

It seemed pointless to me to go through the rituals at my vanity table. I shampooed my hair vigorously and then sat down to brush it a hundred times, softening it and pinning it back neatly but not too harshly with the ivory combs my father had given me for Christmas the previous year.

My father didn't know or even seem to recognize that I had commissioned the "blue dress" because I wanted a dress that looked like the dresses women wore in fashion photographs. The bodice was low enough to expose some of the fullness of my bosom, and the tight waist gave me a suggestion of an "hourglass" figure. It was made of silk, and the material was exceptionally soft and had a sheen to it like nothing else I owned. The sleeves were cut just above the elbow. I thought that made my arms look shorter.

I put on my mother's blue sapphire pendant, which I thought made my neck look slimmer. There was a blush in my cheeks but I couldn't say if it was there because of my healthy body or because of my nervousness. I was nervous. I'd been through enough of those evenings before—watching the man's face fall as he rose to greet me and I towered over him.

I was merely rehearsing for another failure.

By the time I went downstairs, my father's guest had arrived. They were together in the den. I heard my father's loud laugher, and then I heard the gentleman's voice, low but deeply resonant, the voice of a man with some confidence. I pressed my palms against my hips to dry off the wetness and proceeded to the doorway of the den.

The moment I appeared, Malcolm Neal Foxworth stood up and my heart skipped a beat. He was at least six foot two and easily the most handsome young man who had ever come to our house.

"Malcolm," my father said, "I'm proud to present my lovely daughter."

He took my hand and said, "Charmed, Miss Winfield."

I was looking directly into his sky-blue eyes. And he was gazing just as forthrightly into mine. I'd never believed in schoolgirl romantic notions such as love at first sight, but I felt his gaze slide right over my heart and lodge in the pit of my stomach.

He had flaxen blonde hair, a little longer in the back than most men wore, but the strands were brushed neatly and looked heavenly light. He had a strong Roman nose and a thin straight mouth. Broad shouldered, slim-hipped, he had an almost athletic air about him. And I could tell by the way he was gazing at me, with almost a wry smile of amusement, that he was quite accustomed to women falling into a flutter about him. Well, I thought, I mustn't give him something more to be amused at Olivia Winfield. Of course, such a man would hardly give me the time of day, and I would have to get through another evening of Father's doomed matchmaking. I shook his hand firmly, smiled back, and quickly looked away.

After we were introduced, my father explained that Malcolm had come to New London from Yale, where he had attended a class reunion. He was interested in investing in the shipbuilding industry because he believed that with the Great War over, the markets for exporting would develop. From what I learned of his background that night, I understood that he already owned a number of cloth factories, had commanding interest in a few banks, and owned some lumber mills in Virginia. He was in business with his father, but his father, even though he was only fifty-five, was distracted. I didn't learn until later what that meant.

At dinner I tried to be the polite, quiet observer that my father wanted me to be, the way my mother used to be.

Margaret and Philip, our servants, served an elegant dinner of beef Wellington, a menu my father had chosen himself. He did so only on special occasions. I thought my father was being quite obvious when he said, "Olivia's a college graduate, you know. She has a business degree and handles a major portion of my bookkeeping."

"Really?" Malcolm seemed genuinely impressed. His cerulean blue eyes brightened even more with interest and I felt he was taking a second, more serious look at me. "Do you enjoy the work, Miss Winfield?"

I shot a glance at my father, who sat back in his high-backed light-maple chair and nodded as if prompting my responses. I did so want this Malcolm Foxworth to like me, but I was determined to be who I was.

"It's better to fill your time with sensible and productive things," I said. "Even for a woman."

My father's smile faded, but Malcolm's widened. "I totally agree," he said. He didn't turn back to my father. "I find most so-called beautiful women vapid and rather silly. It's as if their good looks are enough to see them through life. I prefer intelligent women who know how to think for themselves, women who can be real assets to their husbands."

My father cleared his throat. "Yes, yes," he said, and turned the conversation back to the shipping industry. He had it from good sources that the merchant marine fleet, built for the war effort, would soon be offered to private owners. His topic took Malcolm's attention for most of the dinner, but nevertheless, I felt Malcolm's eyes on me and at times, when I looked up at him, he was smiling at me.

Never had I sat with one of my father's guests and been so enraptured. Never had I felt as welcome at the table. Malcolm was polite to my father, but it was clear to me that he wanted to talk more to me.

To me!

The handsomest man ever to come to our house was

interested in me? But he could have a hundred beautiful girls to adore him forever. Why should he be interested in a Plain Jane such as I? But oh how I wanted to believe I wasn't imagining all those side glances, those times he asked me to pass him things he could have easily gotten himself, the way he tried to bring me into the conversation. Perhaps, just for a few hours I could allow my slight bud of hope to blossom. Just for tonight! Tomorrow I'd let it gray again.

After dinner Malcolm and my father adjourned to the den to smoke their cigars and talk more about the investments Malcolm wanted to make. With them my hopes, so briefly flowered, so quickly withered. Of course Malcolm wasn't interested in me—he was interested in business with my father. They would be in there for the rest of the evening. I might as well retire to my room to read that new novel that was attracting attention, Edith Wharton's *Age of Innocence*. But I decided instead to bring the book down to the sitting room and read by the Tiffany lamp, happy to see Malcolm just to say good-bye.

It was very quiet on our street that time of evening, but I looked up to see a couple walking arm in arm. It was the way the husband and wife in my glass-encased doll world would walk if they could escape their imprisonment, I thought. I watched them until they disappeared around the corner. How I wished I could someday walk with a man like that—a man like Malcolm. But it was not to be. It seemed God was deaf to my hopes and prayers for love. I sighed. As I turned back to my book, I realized all I could know of love and life would be from books.

Then I spied Malcolm in the doorway. Why, he had been watching me! He stood so straight and still, his shoulders drawn back, his head high. There was a calculating look in his eyes, as if he were sizing me up unawares, but I didn't know what to make of it.

"Oh!" My surprise brought heat to my cheeks. My heart

began to thump so loudly, I thought he might even hear it across the room.

"It is a lovely evening," he said. "Could I interest you in a walk?"

For a moment I just stared. He wanted to take me out walking!

"Yes," I said. I could see he liked the way I came to a quick decision. I didn't try to flutter my eyelashes or act uncertain to tease him with my answer. I wanted to go for a walk and I wanted very much to go for a walk with *him*. If I had a hope that what appeared to be his interest in me would flower, I was going to be just who I was. "I'll just run up and get my coat." I was glad for a reason to go off and catch my breath.

Malcolm was waiting at the front door when I returned. Philip had gotten him his overcoat and stood beside him waiting to open the door. I wondered where my father was and if this was something he might have arranged. But even though I knew Malcolm only a short while, I believed he was not a man to do something he didn't want to do.

When Philip opened the front door, I caught a look of satisfaction in his eyes. He approved of this gentleman.

Malcolm took my arm and escorted me down the six front steps. Both of us were quiet as we proceeded down the walkway until we reached the front gate. Malcolm opened the gate and stepped back to permit me to pass through first. It was a cool April evening, with just a hint of spring in the air. The trees by the gate still reached into the sky with bare gray arms, but their arms were softened by hundreds of tiny buds about to spring to life. Yet winter's chill still hung in the air, still hung in me. For a crazy moment I wished to turn to Malcolm and bury myself in his arms, something I'd certainly never done with a man, not even my father. I determinedly walked ahead and pointed toward the river.

"If we go to the end of the street here," I said, "and turn right, we have a beautiful view of the Thames River."

"Fine," he said.

It was always a fantasy of mine to walk along the banks of the river on a spring evening with a man who was falling in love with me. I was a blur of emotion—so many hopes and fears, confusion, frightening feelings moving through my body, I felt dizzy. But I couldn't let Malcolm see my agitation, so I kept my bearing straight, my head high as we walked. The lights of the ships moved up and down with their cargo. On a night as dark as that one was, the lights on the water in the distance looked like fireflies caught in cobwebs.

"Rather beautiful view," he said.

"Yes."

"How is it," he said, "that your father hasn't married you off yet? I won't insult your intelligence and tell you that you're beautiful; but you are extremely attractive and it's quite apparent that you have an extraordinary mind. How is it no man has captured you yet?"

"How is it you haven't taken a wife?" I responded.

He laughed. "Answer a question with a question. Well, Miss Winfield," he said, "if you must know, I find most women today tedious with their effort to be beguiling. A man who is serious about his life, who is determined to build something significant of himself and his family, must, it seems to me, avoid this type."

"And this is the only kind of woman you've known?" I asked. I couldn't see precisely, of course, but I felt he blushed. "Haven't you searched for others?"

"No. I've been too occupied with my business."

We paused, and he looked out at the ships.

"If I may be a little forward," he went on, "I feel you and I share some things in common. From what your father tells me and from what I can observe, you are a serious-minded person, pragmatic and diligent. You appreciate the business world already, and therefore you are already head and shoulders above most women in this country today."

"Because of the way most men have treated them," I said quickly. I nearly bit my lip. I wasn't going to express my controversial opinions, but the words just seemed to form on my lips by themselves.

"I don't know. Maybe," he said quickly. "The point is, it's true. And you know," he said, taking my elbow gently and turning me so we would walk on, "we have other things in common as well. We both lost our mothers at an early age. Your father explained your circumstances," he added quickly, "so I hope you don't feel I'm intruding."

"No. You lost your mother at an early age?"

"Five." His voice grew somber and faraway.

"Oh, how hard it must have been."

"Sometimes," he said, "the harder things are, the better we become. Or should I say, the tougher." Indeed, he did sound tough when he said that, so cold that I feared to ask him more.

We walked on that night. I listened to him talk about his various enterprises. We had a little discussion about the upcoming presidential elections and he was surprised at how informed I was about the candidates vying for the Republican and Democratic nominations.

I was sorry when we reached my house so soon, but then I thought, at least I had my walk with a handsome young man. I thought it would be left at that.

But at the doorway he asked if he could call again.

"I feel as if I have dominated the evening with my conversation," he said. "I'd like to be more of a listener next time."

Was I hearing right? A man wanted to hear *me* talk, wanted to know *my* thoughts?

"You could call tomorrow," I said. I suppose I sounded as eager as a schoolgirl. He didn't smile or laugh.

"Fine," he said. "There's a good seafood restaurant where I am staying. Perhaps we could have dinner."

Dinner? An actual date. Of course, I agreed. I wanted to

watch him get into his car and drive off, but I couldn't do anything so obvious. When I reentered the house, my father was standing in the den doorway.

"Interesting young man," he said. "Something of a business genius, I'd say. And good-looking, too, eh?"

"Yes, Father," I said.

He chuckled.

"He's coming to call tomorrow and we're going to dinner."

His smile faded. His face took on that look of serious hope I had seen before.

"Really? Well, what do you know? What do you know?"

"I don't know what to tell you, Father."

I couldn't contain myself anymore. I had to excuse myself and go upstairs. For a while I simply sat in my room staring at myself in the mirror. What had I done differently? My hair was the same.

I pulled my shoulders back. I had a tendency to turn them in because they were so wide. I knew it was bad posture and Malcolm had such good posture, such confident posture. He didn't seem to see my inadequacies and imperfections, and it was so good not having to look down at a man.

And he had told me I was very attractive, implied that I was desirable to men. Maybe I had underestimated myself all those years. Maybe I had unnecessarily accepted a dreadful fate?

Of course, I tried chastising myself, warning myself. A man who's been to dinner has asked you out. It doesn't have to mean he has romantic inclinations. Maybe he's just lonely here.

No, I thought, we'll have dinner, talk some more, and he will be gone. Perhaps, some distant day, on some occasion, like Christmas, I'll receive a card from him, on which he will write, "Belated thanks for your fine conversation. Happiest of holidays. Malcolm."

My heart fluttered in fear. I went out to the glass-enclosed dollhouse and looked for the hope I left encased there. Then I went to sleep dreaming about the porcelain figures. I was one of them. I was the happy wife—and Malcolm, he was the handsome husband.

Our dinner date was elegant. I tried not to overdress, but everything I picked out to wear looked so plain. It was my own fault for not caring enough about my wardrobe. In the end I chose the gown I had worn to a wedding reception last year. Perhaps it would bring me good luck, I thought.

Malcolm said I looked nice, but the conversation at dinner quickly turned to more mundane things. He wanted to know all about the work I did for my father and he made me elaborate in detail. I was afraid the conversation would prove boring, but he showed such interest that I went on and on. Apparently, he was quite impressed with my knowledge of my father's affairs.

"Tell me," he asked when we returned to my house, "what do you do to entertain yourself?" At last the conversation was to be more personal; at last there was interest in me.

"I read a great deal. I listen to music. I take walks. My one sport is horseback riding."

"Oh, really. I own a number of horses, and Foxworth Hall, my home, is situated on grounds that would fascinate any explorer of nature."

"It sounds wonderful," I said.

He saw me to the door and, once again, I thought this would be the end. But he surprised me.

"I suppose you know I will be joining you and your father to attend church tomorrow."

"No," I said. "I didn't know."

"Well, I look forward to it," he added. "I must thank you for a most enjoyable evening."

"I enjoyed it too," I said, and waited. Was this the moment when the man was supposed to kiss the woman? How I regretted not having a close girlfriend in whom I could confide and with whom I could discuss the affairs between men and women, but all the girls I had known in school were married and gone.

Was I supposed to do something to encourage him? Lean toward him, pause dramatically, smile in some way? I felt so lost, standing before the door, waiting.

"Until the morning, then," he said, tipped his hat, and went down the steps to his car.

I opened the door and rushed into the house, feeling both excited and disappointed. My father was in the sitting room, reading the paper, pretending to be interested in other things; but I knew he was waiting to hear about my date. I made up my mind I would not give him a review. It made me feel more like someone auditioning and I didn't like all these expectations.

What could I tell him anyway? Malcolm took me out to dinner. We talked a great deal. Rather, I talked a great deal and he listened. Maybe he thought I was a chatterbox after all, even though my conversation was about things in which he showed some interest. I'm sure I talked so much because I was so nervous. In a way I was grateful for his questions about business. That was a subject on which I could expand.

I could have talked about books, of course, or horses, but it wasn't until just now that I learned he had any interests in anything other than making money.

So what would I tell my father? The dinner was wonderful. I tried not to eat too much, even though I could have eaten more. I tried to look dainty and feminine and even refused to order dessert. It was he who insisted.

"Did you have a good time?" my father asked quickly. He saw I would just go right up to my room.

"Yes, but why didn't you tell me you had invited him to join us for church?"

"Oh, didn't I?"

"Father, despite your expertise in business, you're not a good liar," I said. He roared. I even laughed a bit myself.

Why should I be mad anyway? I thought. I knew what he was doing and I wanted him to do it.

"I'm going to sleep," I said, thinking about how early I would get up the next morning. I had to take extra pains with my appearance for church.

Before I fell asleep that night, I reviewed every moment of my date with Malcolm, condemning myself for this, congratulating myself for that. And when I recalled our moments at the door, I imagined that he did kiss me.

Never was I as nervous about going to church as I was that morning. I couldn't eat a thing at breakfast. I rushed about, not quite confident about my dress, not sure about my hair. When the time finally came to leave and Malcolm had arrived, my heart was beating so rapidly, I thought I would go into a faint and collapse on the stairway.

"Good morning, Olivia," he said, and looked quite satisfied with my appearance. I didn't even realize until we were all in the car and on the way to church that he called me "Olivia" and not "Miss Winfield."

It was a lovely, warm spring day, really the first warm Sunday of the year. All the young ladies were dressed in their new spring dresses with veiled hats and parasols. And the families all looked so fresh, with the children scampering about in the sun, waiting to go in to the service. As we stepped from the car, it seemed all those gathered turned to look at me. Me, Olivia Winfield, arriving at church on a fine Sunday morning with my father and a strikingly handsome young man. Yes, I wanted to scream, yes, it's me! See? But of course I would never stoop to such guttersnipe behavior. I stood straighter, taller, and held my chin high as we walked directly from the car and into the dark, musky church. Most had stayed outdoors to enjoy the sun, so we had our choice of pews, and Malcolm led us directly to the very front seats. We sat silently as we waited for the sermon to begin. Never had I had such difficulty following the sermon; never did I feel so self-conscious about the sound of my voice when we stood to sing the hymns. Yet Malcolm sang out clearly and loudly, and recited the Lord's Prayer at the end in a deep, strong voice. Then he turned to me and took my arm to escort me out. How proud I felt walking down the aisle with him.

Of course, I saw the way other members of the congregation were watching us and wondering who was the handsome young man accompanying the Winfields and standing beside Olivia Winfield?

We left a stream of chatter behind us and I knew that Malcolm's appearance would be the subject of parlor talk all day.

That afternoon we went horseback riding. It was the first time I had gone horseback riding alone with a man and I found his company invigorating. He rode like an experienced English huntsman. He seemed to enjoy the way I could keep up with him.

He came to Sunday dinner and we took another walk along the river. For the first part of the walk I found him more quiet than ever and I anticipated the announcement of his departure. Perhaps he would promise to write. Actually, I was hoping for that promise, even if he didn't hold to it. At least I would have something to look forward to. I would cherish every one of his letters, should there be more than one.

"Look here, Miss Winfield," he suddenly began. I didn't like his reverting back to calling me Miss Winfield. I thought that was a dark omen. But it wasn't. "I don't see the point in two people who have so much in common, two sensible people, that is, delaying and unnecessarily prolonging a relationship just to arrive at the point they both agree would be best."

"Point?"

"I'm speaking of marriage," he said. "One of the most holy sacraments, something that must never be taken lightly.

Marriage is more than the logical result of a romance; it's a contractual union, teamwork. A man has to know that his wife is part of the effort, someone on whom he can depend. Contrary to what some men think, my father included, a man must have a woman who has strength. I'm impressed with you, Miss Winfield. I would like your permission to ask your father for your hand in marriage."

For a moment I could not speak. Malcolm Neal Foxworth, six feet two inches tall, as handsome a man as there could be, a man of intelligence, wealth, and looks, wanted to marry me? And we were standing on the bank of the river with the stars above us more brilliant than ever. Had I wandered into one of my own dreams?

"Well . . . ," I said. I brought my hand to my throat and looked at him. I was at a loss for words. I didn't know how to phrase my response.

"I realize this seems rather sudden, but I'm a man with a destiny who has the good fortune to realize almost immediately what is valuable and what is not. My instincts have always proven reliable. I am confident that this proposal will be a good one for both of us. If you can place your trust in that . . ."

"Yes, Malcolm. I can," I said quickly, perhaps too quickly.

"Good. Thank you," he said.

I waited. This was surely the moment for us to kiss. We should consummate our faith in each other under the stars. But maybe I was being childishly romantic. Malcolm was the kind to do things properly, correctly. I had to have faith in that too.

"Then, if you will, let us return to your home so that I can speak to your father," he said. He did take my arm and draw me closer to him. As we walked back to my father's house, I thought about the couple I had seen strolling on the street that first night he came to dinner. My dream had come true. For the first time in my life, I felt truly happy.

My father waited in his den as if he had anticipated the news. Things were moving so quickly. On more than one occasion, I had brought myself to the double doors that separated my father's den from the sitting room and listened in on conversations. I resented being left out of some of the conversations anyway. They had to do with family affairs or business affairs that could affect me.

Nothing would affect me more than the conversation that was about to ensue. I stood quietly to the side and listened, eager to hear Malcolm express his love for me.

"As I told you the first night, Mr. Winfield," he began, "I am quite taken with your daughter. It is rare to find a woman with her poise and dignity, a woman who can appreciate the pursuit of economic success and grow gracefully with it."

"I am proud of Olivia's achievements," my father said. "She is as brilliant an accountant and bookkeeper as any man I know," he added. My father's compliments always had a way of making me feel less desirable.

"Yes. She's a woman with a steady, strong temperament. I have always wanted a wife who would let me pursue my life as I will, and would not cling to me helplessly like a choking vine. I want to be confident that when I come home, she won't be sulky or moody, or even vindictive as so many flimsy women can be. I like the fact that she is not concerned with superficial things, that she doesn't dote on her own coiffure, that she doesn't giggle and flirt. In short, I like her maturity. I compliment you, sir. You have brought up a fine, responsible woman."

"Well, I—"

"And I can think of no other way to express that compliment better than to ask for your permission to marry her."

"Does Olivia . . . ?"

"Know that I have come in here to make this proposal? She has given me permission to do so. Knowing she is a woman of strong mind, I thought it best to ask her first. I hope you understand."

"Oh, I understand that." My father cleared his throat. "Well, Mr. Foxworth," he said. He felt it necessary to refer to him as Mr. Foxworth during this conversation. "I'm sure you understand as well that my daughter will come into a sizable fortune. I want you to know beforehand that her money will be her own. It is specifically stated in my will that no one but she will have access to those funds."

There was what I thought to be a long silence.

"That's as it should be," Malcolm finally said. "I don't know what your plans might be for a wedding," he added quickly, "but I would favor a small church ceremony as quickly as possible. I need to return soon to Virginia."

"If Olivia wants that," my father said. He knew that I would.

"Fine. Then I have your permission, sir?"

"You understand what I have said about her money?"

"Yes, sir, I do."

"You have my permission," my father said. "And we'll shake on it."

I released the air that I held in my lungs and stepped quickly away from the double doors.

A man, most handsome and elegant, had come calling and then had asked for my hand in marriage. I had heard it all and it had all happened so quickly, I had to catch my breath and keep telling myself it wasn't a dream.

I hurried upstairs and sat before the dollhouse. I would live in a big house with servants and there would be people coming and going. We would entertain with elaborate dinner parties and I would be an asset to my husband who was, as my father had said, something of a business genius. In time we would be envied by all.

"Just like I have envied you," I said to the porcelain family within the glass.

I looked about me.

Good-bye to lonely nights. Good-bye to this world of fantasy and dreams.

Good-bye to my father's face of pity and to my own forlorn look in the mirror. There was a new face to know—and so much to learn about Malcolm Neal Foxworth—and a lifetime to learn it in. I was to become Olivia Foxworth, Mrs. Malcolm Neal Foxworth. All my mother had predicted had come true.

I was blooming. I felt myself opening out toward Malcolm like a tightly closed bud bursting into blossom. And when his blue, blue eyes looked into my gray ones, I knew the sun had come and melted the fog away. My life would no longer be colored gray. No, from now on it would be blue—blue as the sun-filled skies of a cloudless day. Blue as Malcolm's eyes. In the flush of being swept away by love, like any foolish schoolgirl I forgot all I knew about caution and looking beyond appearances to see the truth. I forgot that never once when Malcolm proposed to me and then made his proposal to my father had he mentioned the word "love." Like a foolish schoolgirl I believed I would lie beneath the blue sky of Malcolm's eyes, and my tiny little blossom would grow into a sturdy, long-lasting bloom. Like any woman stupidly believing in love, I never realized that the blue sky I saw was not the warm, soft, nurturing sky of spring, but the cold, chilling, lonely sky of winter.

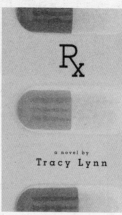

Girls searching for answers . . .
and finding themselves.

Terra Elan McVoy — *Pure*

Eileen Cook — *What Would Emma Do?*

Bil Wright — *when the black girl sings*

Blake Nelson — *GIRL*

From Simon Pulse | Published by Simon & Schuster

Which will be *your* first?